The Skylark of Space

Brilliant scientist Richard Seaton discovers a remarkable faster-than-light fuel that will power his interstellar spaceship, the *Skylark*. His ruthless rival, Marc DuQuesne, and the sinister World Steel Corporation will do anything to get their hands on the fuel. When they kidnap Seaton's fiancée and friends, they unleash a furious pursuit that will propel the *Skylark* across the galaxy and back.

Skylark Three

Genius inventor Richard Seaton has developed a 'Zone of Force' to protect his ship, the *Skylark* – but with the Zone up and running, he can no longer control his vessel. Can this new invention help them prevail against the Fenachronians, with their advanced technology and their determination to conquer the galaxy … and destroy the Earth?

Skylark of Valeron

As the mighty spaceship *Skylark* roamed the intergalactic spaceways, Richard Seaton and his companions found a world of disembodied intelligences. A world of four dimensions where time was insanely distorted and matter obeyed no Terrestrial laws – where three-dimensional human intellects had to fight hard to thwart malevolent invisible mentalities …

Skylark DuQuesne

Richard Seaton and Marc DuQuesne were the deadliest enemies in the galaxy. Their feud had blazed among the stars and challenged the history of a thousand planets. But now a threat from outside the galaxy drives them into a desperate alliance. Seaton and DuQuesne must fight side by side to fend off the invasion – as Seaton keeps constant, perilous watch for DuQuesne's inevitable double-cross.

Also by E.E. 'Doc' Smith

Skylark

1. The Skylark of Space (1928)
2. Skylark Three (1948)
3. Skylark of Valeron (1949)
4. Skylark DuQuesne (1966)

Lensman

1. Triplanetary (1934)*
2. First Lensman (1950)*
3. Galactic Patrol (1950)*
4. Gray Lensman (1951)*
5. Second Stage Lensmen (1953)*
6. Children of the Lens (1954)*
7. The Vortex Blaster (aka Masters of the Vortex) (1960)*

Subspace

1. Subspace Explorers (1965)
2. Subspace Encounter (1983)

Family D'Alembert (with Stephen Goldin)

1. Imperial Stars (1976)
2. Stranglers' Moon (1976)
3. The Clockwork Traitor (1976)
4. Getaway World (1977)
5. Appointment at Bloodstar (aka The Bloodstar Conspiracy) (1978)
6. The Purity Plot (1978)
7. Planet of Treachery (1981)
8. Eclipsing Binaries (1983)
9. The Omicron Invasion (1984)
10. Revolt of the Galaxy (1985)

Lord Tedric (with Gordon Eklund)

1. Lord Tedric (1978)
2. The Space Pirates (1979)
3. Black Knight of the Iron Sphere (1979)
4. Alien Realms (1980)

Non-series novels and collections

1. Spacehounds of IPC (1947)
2. The Galaxy Primes (1965)
3. Masters of Space (1976) (with E. Everett Evans)

* Not available as an SF Gateway eBook

E.E. 'Doc' Smith
SF GATEWAY OMNIBUS

THE SKYLARK OF SPACE
SKYLARK THREE
SKYLARK OF VALERON
SKYLARK DUQUESNE

GOLLANCZ

LONDON

First published in Great Britain in 2013 by
Gollancz
An imprint of the Orion Publishing Group
Orion House, 5 Upper St Martin's Lane,
London WC2H 9EA

An Hachette UK Company

A CIP catalogue record for this book is
available from the British Library

ISBN 978 0 575 12266 6

1 3 5 7 9 10 8 6 4 2

Typeset by Jouve (UK), Milton Keynes

Printed and bounded by CPI Group (UK) Ltd, Croydon, CR0 4YY

The Orion Publishing Group's policy is to use papers
that are natural, renewable and recyclable products and
made from wood grown in sustainable forests. The logging
and manufacturing processes are expected to conform to
the environmental regulations of the country of origin.

www.orionbooks.co.uk
www.gollancz.co.uk

CONTENTS

ENTER THE SF GATEWAY . . .

Towards the end of 2011, in conjunction with the celebration of fifty years of coherent, continuous science fiction and fantasy publishing, Gollancz launched the SF Gateway.

Over a decade after launching the landmark SF Masterworks series, we realised that the realities of commercial publishing are such that even the Masterworks could only ever scratch the surface of an author's career. Vast troves of classic SF & Fantasy were almost certainly destined never again to see print. Until very recently, this meant that anyone interested in reading any of those books would have been confined to scouring second-hand bookshops. The advent of digital publishing changed that paradigm for ever.

Embracing the future even as we honour the past, Gollancz launched the SF Gateway with a view to utilising the technology that now exists to make available, for the first time, the entire backlists of an incredibly wide range of classic and modern SF and fantasy authors. Our plan, at its simplest, was – and still is! – to use this technology to build on the success of the SF and Fantasy Masterworks series and to go even further.

The SF Gateway was designed to be the new home of classic Science Fiction & Fantasy – the most comprehensive electronic library of classic SFF titles ever assembled. The programme has been extremely well received and we've been very happy with the results. So happy, in fact, that we've decided to complete the circle and return a selection of our titles to print, in these omnibus editions.

We hope you enjoy this selection. And we hope that you'll want to explore more of the classic SF and fantasy we have available. These are wonderful books you're holding in your hand, but you'll find much, much more … through the SF Gateway.

www.sfgateway.com

INTRODUCTION

from The Encyclopedia of Science Fiction

Edward Elmer 'Doc' Smith (1890–1965) was a US food chemist (he special-ised in doughnut mixes), and author, often called the 'Father of Space Opera'; because Hugo Gernsback had appended 'PhD' to Smith's name for his con-tributions to *Amazing* from 1928, he also became known as 'Doc' Smith. Greatly influential in US pulp-magazine sf between 1928 and about 1945, he found his reputation fading somewhat after the end of World War Two, when it seemed that the dream-like simplicities of his world-view could no longer attract the modern reader of Genre SF. But more than one of the speciality houses that became active after 1945 were founded in the awareness that his vast pre-War space-opera sagas, published only in magazines, had never achieved book publications; and his central corpus was soon made available to new readers. Towards the end of his life, after he retired around 1960, he began producing space operas again, and the work of his prime began to appear in mass-market paperbacks; his popularity soared, and though his reputa-tion has faded to a degree in recent decades, he is by no means forgotten.

Smith's work is strongly identified with the beginnings of US pulp sf as a separate marketing genre, and did much to define its essential territory: galactic space dominated by Galactic Empires, these usually being run by humans, though Aliens appear frequently, not only as villains; Space Opera plots, featuring heroes and their inventions, are the norm; wars rage across the parsecs. But although Smith's protagonists fit comfortably into this uni-verse, it is the case that his most developed (and numerous) protagonists, the Lensmen at the heart of the Lensmen epic, are also soldiers: willing employ-ees in a higher cause. his later heroes – like Kim Kinnison himself – advance through promotion, and rule their universes as dictators in all but name, for the cause of Good.

When in 1915 Smith began to write the first novel of his Skylark series with Mrs Lee Hawkins Garby (1892–1953), a neighbour seconded to help with feminine matters such as dialogue, no prior models existed in popular fiction to source the combined exuberance and scale that *The Skylark of Space* (see below) demonstrated when the magazine version finally began to appear in *Amazing Stories* in 1928 (the book form only appeared in 1946); its two imme-diate sequels – *Skylark Three, Skylark of Valeron* (see below for both) – add to the exuberance. (*Skylark DuQuesne* was published posthumously in 1966.)

But it was not until he began to unveil the architectural structure of his second and career-climaxing series that Smith was able to demonstrate the thoroughness of his thinking about Space Opera, though perhaps losing some of the spontaneity of Skylark. It is with the Lensman series – or *The History of Civilization*, the over-title for the 1953–1955 limited-edition boxed reprint of the original books – that his name is most strongly associated. In order of internal chronology, the sequence comprises *Triplanetary*, *First Lensman*, *Galactic Patrol*, *Gray Lensman*, *Second-Stage Lensmen* and *Children of the Lens*. *The Vortex Blaster*, assembling stories published during World War Two, and only put in book form after Smith's death, is also set in the Lensman Universe, probably some time before *Children of the Lens*; but does not deal with the central progress of the main series, the working out of which was Smith's most brilliant auctorial coup. As resorted and augmented in book form, the first two novels, one of them written much later, likewise stand outside the main action; it is the central four volumes that constitute the heart of Smith's accomplishment. Conceived as one 400,000-word novel, and divided into separate titles for publication between 1937 and 1948 in *Astounding*, this central Lensman tale is constructed around the gradual revelation, paced by moments that for many readers caught the essence of the Sense Of Wonder, of the hierarchical nature of the Universe: a sense that the universe was both infinitely surprising but, in the end, *controlled* by Arisians.

That gradual revelation is eschewed in the full series as published in book form. Here, we learn immediately that two vastly advanced and radically opposed Forerunner races, the good Arisians and the evil Eddorians, each dominating a separate galaxy, have been in essential opposition for billions of years. The Arisians understand that the only hope of defeating the absolute Evil represented by the Eddorians is to nurture the growth over aeons of a countervailing Civilization developed from their own 'spores' via special breeding lines on selected planets, of which Earth (Tellus) is one. Guided by their Arisian Secret Masters, these breeding lines develop heroes capable of enduring the enormous stress of inevitable conflict with the escalating galactic conspiracy of evil known collectively as Boskone, a force inimical to Civilization and secretly commanded through a nest of hierarchies by the invisible Eddorians.

As the conflict deepens, the Arisians (always in disguise) make available to their unknowing scions a Psionic pseudo-gem known as the Lens which – when attached physically to advanced specimens of the breeding programme, who have already formed a Galactic Patrol responsible for defending Civilization – awards them certain telepathic and other Psi Powers, operating both as a weapon and a communication device. The central figure of the series is the human Kim Kinnison, who with his wife represents the penultimate stage in the Arisian breeding programme, and whose children will finally defeat the Eddorians. As the central sequence progresses, we climb with Kinnison, link by link, through a vast chain of command, evil empire after evil empire, until he defeats Boskone and becomes, in essence, the ruler of the civilized universe. But Kinnison is destined only slowly to understand that the empire of Boskone, which he has destroyed through the use of weapons of unparalleled immensity, is not the final enemy, whose name he never learns, no more than he ever discovers the full truth about his own Arisian mentors, whose civilized precepts he enacts. Though his powers are vast, he remains ignorant of the true scale and nature of the Universe, which is greater, and requires greater powers to comprehend and confront, than even a hero with superpowers is capable of grasping. Perhaps the deepest attraction of the Lensman series lies in the fact that Kinnison, as ultimate commander of the organization of Lensmen (itself hierarchical), is *licensed*; but that only we (and his children) know who issued the licence.

After completing his central series, Smith wrote some rather less popular out-of-series books, none having anything like the force of his major effort. A decade after his death, books he had begun or completed in manuscript, or had merely inspired or authorized, began to appear in response to his great posthumous popularity. The best known of these is the Family d'Alembert series, published as by Smith 'with Stephen Goldin', derived some material from posthumous manuscripts; the first volume, *The Imperial Stars* (1976), was based on published material, but subsequent volumes were essentially the work of Goldin.

Smith was posthumously inducted into the Science Fiction Hall Of Fame in 2004.Today, while he must be read by anyone interested in understanding the deep appeal of American Genre SF in the days before World War Two, any revisit to his work should be made in the loving awareness that he is a creature of the dawn.

The novels of the Skylark of Space sequence – *The Skylark of Space, Skylark Three, Skylark of Valeron* and *Skylark DuQuesne* – are here reprinted in one volume. The magazine publication of the first volume – which appeared in the same issue of *Amazing* that also featured Philip Nowlan's 'Armageddon – 2419 AD', the story which introduced Buck Rogers to the world – marked the coming of age of early American sf. Even then, Smith was more fun. Elements of his dawn-age exuberance may have been discernible in some of the Edisonades which proliferated in America from about 1890; and a certain cosmogonic high-handedness can be traced to the works of H. G. Wells and his UK contemporaries. But it was Smith who combined the two.

The Skylark of Space brings the Edisonade to its first full maturity, creating a proper galactic forum for the exploits of the inventor/scientist/action-hero who keeps the world (or the Universe) safe for American values, despite the efforts of a foreign-hued villain (Marc 'Blackie' DuQuesne) to subvert those values. At the heart of the action lies a highly personalized conflict between hero-inventor Richard Seaton, who always triumphs through luck, gumption, vast intellect, and athletic prowess, and villain-inventor DuQuesne, who develops from the stage histrionics of the first novel into a dominating antihero, and who is perhaps Smith's most vivid creation. As their conflict escalates, the scale of everything – the potency of the weapons, the power, size and speed of the spaceships, the number of planets overawed or annihilated – also escalates by leaps and bounds. Earth is soon left behind. The galaxy beckons! The galaxy is ours! We read the Skylark of Space in a kind of exhilarated daze. When we finish, we awaken from a marvellous dream.

For a more detailed version of the above, see E.E. 'Doc' Smith's author entry in *The Encyclopedia of Science Fiction*: http://sf-encyclopedia.com/entry/ smith_e_e

Some terms above are capitalised when they would not normally be so rendered; this indicates that the terms represent discrete entries in *The Encyclopedia of Science Fiction*.

THE SKYLARK OF SPACE

I

Petrified with astonishment, Richard Seaton stared after the copper steam-bath upon which, a moment before, he had been electrolyzing his solution of 'X,' the unknown metal. As soon as he had removed the beaker with its precious contents the heavy bath had jumped endwise from under his hand as though it were alive. It had flown with terrific speed over the table, smashing a dozen reagent-bottles on its way, and straight on out through the open window. Hastily setting the beaker down, he seized his binoculars and focused them upon the flying bath, which now, to the unaided vision, was merely a speck in the distance. Through the glass he saw that it did not fall to the ground, but continued on in a straight line, its rapidly diminishing size alone showing the enormous velocity at which it was moving. It grew smaller and smaller. In a few seconds it disappeared.

Slowly lowering the binoculars to his side, Seaton turned like a man in a trance. He stared dazedly, first at the litter of broken bottles covering the table, and then at the empty space under the hood where the bath had stood for so many years.

Aroused by the entrance of his laboratory helper, he silently motioned him to clean up the wreckage.

'What happened, doctor?'

'Search me, Dan ... wish I knew, myself,' Seaton replied, absently, lost in wonder at what he had just seen.

Ferdinand Scott, a chemist from an adjoining laboratory, entered breezily.

'Hello, Dicky, thought I heard a rack— Good Lord! What you been celebrating? Had an explosion?'

'Uh-uh.' Seaton shook his head. 'Something *funny* – *darned* funny. I can tell you what happened, but that's all.'

He did so, and while he talked he prowled about the big room, examining minutely every instrument, dial, meter, gauge, and indicator in the place.

Scott's face showed in turn interest, surprise, and pitying alarm. 'Dick, boy, I don't know why you wrecked the joint, and I don't know whether that yarn came out of a bottle or a needle, but believe me, it stinks. It's an honest-to-God, bottled-in-bond stinkeroo if I ever heard one. You'd better lay off the stuff, whatever it is.'

Seeing that Seaton was paying no attention to him, Scott left the room, shaking his head.

Seaton walked slowly to his desk, picked up his blackened and battered briar pipe, and sat down. What could *possibly* have happened, to result in such shattering of all the natural laws he knew? An inert mass of metal *couldn't* fly off into space without the application of a force – in this case an enormous, a really tremendous force – a force probably of the order of magnitude of atomic energy. But it hadn't been atomic energy. That was out. Definitely. No hard radiation … His instruments would have indicated and recorded a hundredth of a millimicrocurie, and every one of them had sat placidly on dead-center zero through the whole show. *What was that force?*

And where? In the cell? The solution? The bath? Those three places were … all the places there were.

Concentrating all the power of his mind – deaf, dumb, and blind to every external thing – he sat motionless, with his forgotten pipe clenched between his teeth.

He sat there while most of his fellow chemists finished the day's work and went home; sat there while the room slowly darkened with the coming of night.

Finally he stood up and turned on the lights. Tapping the stem of his pipe against his palm, he spoke aloud. 'Absolutely the only unusual incidents in this whole job were a slight slopping over of the solution onto the copper and the short-circuiting of the wires when I grabbed the beaker … wonder if it will repeat …'

He took a piece of copper wire and dipped it into the solution of the mysterious metal. Upon withdrawing it he saw that the wire had changed its appearance, the X having apparently replaced a layer of the original metal. Standing well clear of the table, he touched the wire with the conductors. There was a slight spark, a snap, and it disappeared. Simultaneously there was a sharp sound, like that made by the impact of a rifle bullet, and Seaton saw with amazement a small round hole where the wire had gone completely through the heavy brick wall. There was power – and how! – but whatever it was, it was a fact. A demonstrable fact.

Suddenly he realized that he was hungry; and, glancing at his watch, saw that it was ten o'clock. And he had had a date for dinner at seven with his fiancée at her home, their first dinner since their engagement! Cursing himself for an idiot, he hastily left the laboratory. Going down the corridor, he saw that Marc DuQuesne, a fellow research man, was also working late. He left the building, mounted his motor-cycle, and was soon tearing up Connecticut Avenue toward his sweetheart's home.

On the way, an idea struck him like a blow of a fist. He forgot even his motorcycle, and only the instinct of the trained rider saved him from disaster during the next few blocks. As he drew near his destination, however, he made a determined effort to pull himself together.

'What a stunt!' he muttered ruefully to himself as he considered what he had done. 'What a stupid jerk! If she doesn't give me the bum's rush for this I'll never do it again if I live to be a million years old!'

II

As evening came on and the fireflies began flashing over the grounds of her luxurious Chevy Chase home, Dorothy Vaneman went upstairs to dress. Mrs Vaneman's eyes followed her daughter's tall, trim figure more than a little apprehensively. She was wondering about this engagement. True, Richard was a fine chap and might make a name for himself, but at present he was a nobody and, socially, he would always be a nobody ... and men of wealth, of distinction, of impeccable social status, had paid court ... but Dorothy – no, 'stubborn' was not too strong a term – when Dorothy made up her mind ...

Unaware of her mother's look, Dorothy went happily up the stairs. She glanced at the clock, saw that it was only a little after six, and sat down at her dressing table, upon which there stood a picture of Richard. A strong, not unhandsome face, with keen, wide-set gray eyes; the wide brow of the thinker, surmounted by thick, unruly, dark hair; the firm, square jaw of the born fighter – such was the man whose vivid personality, fierce impetuosity, and indomitable perseverance had set him apart from all other men ever since their first meeting, and who had rapidly cleared the field of all other aspirants for her favor. Her breath came faster and her cheeks showed a lovelier color as she sat there, the lights playing in her heavy auburn hair and a tender smile upon her lips.

Dorothy dressed with unusual care, the last touches deftly made, went downstairs and out upon the porch to wait for her guest.

Half an hour passed. Mrs Vaneman came to the door and said anxiously, 'I wonder if anything could have happened to him?'

'Of course there hasn't,' Dorothy tried to keep all concern out of her voice. 'Traffic jams – or perhaps he has been picked up again for speeding. Can Alice keep dinner a little longer?'

'To be sure,' her mother answered, and disappeared.

But when another half hour had passed Dorothy went in, holding her head somewhat higher than usual and wearing a say-something-if-you-dare expression.

The meal was eaten in polite disregard of the unused plate. The family left the table. For Dorothy the evening was endless; but at the usual time it was ten o'clock, and then ten-thirty, and then Seaton appeared.

Dorothy opened the door, but Seaton did not come in. He stood close to her, but did not touch her. His eyes searched her face anxiously. Upon his face was a look of indecision, almost of fright – a look so foreign to his usual expression that the girl smiled in spite of herself.

'I'm awfully sorry, sweetheart, but I couldn't help it. You've got a right to be sore and I ought to be kicked from here to there, but are you too sore to let me talk to you for a couple of minutes?'

'I was never so mad at anybody in my life, until I started getting scared witless. I simply couldn't and can't believe you'd do anything like that on purpose. Come in.'

He came. She closed the door. He half-extended his arms, then paused, irresolute, like a puppy hoping for a pat but expecting a kick. She grinned then, and came into his arms.

'But what *happened*, Dick?' she asked later. 'Something terrible, to make you act like this. I've never seen you act so – so funny.'

'Not terrible, Dotty, just extraordinary. So outrageously extraordinary that before I begin I wish you'd look me in the eye and tell me if you have any doubts about my sanity.' She led him into the living room, held his face up to the light, and made a pretense of studying his eyes.

'Richard Ballinger Seaton, I certify that you are entirely sane – quite the sanest man I ever knew. Now tell me the worst. Did you blow up the Bureau with a C-bomb?'

'Nothing like that,' he laughed. 'Just a thing I can't understand. You know I've been reworking the platinum wastes that have been accumulating for the last ten or fifteen years.'

'Yes, you told me you'd recovered a small fortune in platinum and some of those other metals. You thought you'd found a brand-new one. Did you?'

'I sure did. After I'd separated out everything I could identify, there was quite a lot of something left – something that didn't respond to any tests I knew or could find in the literature.

'That brings us up to today. As a last resort, because there wasn't anything else left, I started testing for trans-uranics, and there it was. A stable – almost stable, I mean – isotope; up where no almost-stable isotopes are supposed to exist. Up where I would've bet my last shirt no such isotope could *possibly* exist.

'Well, I was trying to electrolyze it out when the fireworks started. The solution started to fizz over, so I grabbed the beaker – fast. The wires dropped onto the steam-bath and the whole outfit, except the beaker, took off out of the window at six or eight times the speed of sound and in a straight line, without dropping a foot in as far as I could keep it in sight with a pair of *good* binoculars. And my hunch is that it's still going. That's what happened. It's enough to knock any physicist into an outside loop, and with my one-cylinder brain I got to thinking about it and simply didn't come to until after ten o'clock. All I can say is, I'm sorry and I love you. As much as I ever did or could. More, if possible. And I always will. Can you let it go – this time?'

'Dick ... oh, Dick!'

There was more – much more – but eventually Seaton mounted his motor-cycle and Dorothy walked beside him down to the street. A final kiss and the man drove away.

After the last faint glimmer of red tail-light had disappeared in the darkness Dorothy made her way to her room, breathing a long and slightly tremulous, but supremely happy sigh.

III

Seaton's childhood had been spent in the mountains of northern Idaho, a region not much out of the pioneer stage and offering few inducements to intellectual effort. He could only dimly remember his mother, a sweet, gentle woman with a great love for books; but his father, 'Big Fred' Seaton, a man of but one love, almost filled the vacant place. Fred owned a quarter-section of virgin white-pine timber, and in that splendid grove he established a home for himself and his motherless boy.

In front of the cabin lay a level strip of meadow, beyond which rose a magnificent, snow-covered peak that caught the earliest rays of the sun.

This mountain, dominating the entire countryside, was to the boy a challenge, a question, and a secret. He accepted the challenge, scaling its steep sides, hunting its forests, and fishing its streams. He toughened his sturdy young body by days and nights upon its slopes. He puzzled over the question of its origin as he lay upon the needles under some monster pine. He put staggering questions to his father; and when in books he found some partial answers his joy was complete. He discovered some of the mountain's secrets then – some of the laws that govern the world of matter, some of the beginnings man's mind has made toward understanding the hidden mechanism of Nature's great simplicity.

Each taste of knowledge whetted his appetite for more. Books! Books! More and more he devoured them; finding in them meat for the hunger that filled him, answers to the questions that haunted him.

After Big Fred lost his life in the forest fire that destroyed his property, Seaton turned his back upon the woods forever. He worked his way through high school and won a scholarship at college. Study was a pleasure to his keen mind; and he had ample time for athletics, for which his backwoods life had fitted him outstandingly. He went out for everything, and excelled in football and tennis.

In spite of the fact that he had to work his way he was popular with his college mates, and his popularity was not lessened by an almost professional knowledge of sleight-of-hand.

His long, strong fingers could move faster than the eye could follow, and many a lively college party watched in vain to see how he did what he did.

After graduating with highest honors as a physical chemist, he was appointed research fellow in a great university, where he won his Ph.D. by brilliant research upon rare metals – his dissertation having the lively title of 'Some Observations upon Certain Properties of Certain Metals, Including Certain Trans-Uranic Elements.' Soon afterward he had his own room in the Rare Metals Laboratory, in Washington, D.C.

He was a striking figure – well over six feet in height, broad-shouldered, narrow-waisted, a man of tremendous physical strength. He did not let himself grow soft in his laboratory job, but kept in hard, fine condition. He spent most of his spare time playing tennis, swimming and motor-cycling.

As a tennis-player he quickly became well known in Washington sporting and social circles. During the District Tournament he met M. Reynolds Crane – known to only a very few intimates as 'Martin' – the multi-millionaire explorer-archaeologist-sportsman who was then District singles champion. Seaton had cleared the lower half of the list and played Crane in the final round. Crane succeeded in retaining his title, but only after five of the most grueling, most bitterly contested sets ever seen in Washington.

Impressed by Seaton's powerful, slashing game, Crane suggested that they train together as a doubles team. Seaton accepted instantly, and the combination was highly effective.

Practicing together almost daily, each came to know the other as a man of his own kind, and a real friendship grew up between them. When the Crane–Seaton team had won the District Championship and had gone to the semi-finals of the National before losing, the two were upon a footing which most brothers could have envied. Their friendship was such that neither Crane's immense wealth and high social standing nor Seaton's comparative poverty and lack of standing offered any obstacle whatever. Their comradeship was the same, whether they were in Seaton's modest room or in Crane's palatial yacht.

Crane had never known the lack of anything that money could buy. He had inherited his fortune and had little or nothing to do with its management, preferring to delegate that job to financial specialists. However, he was in no sense an idle rich man with no purpose in life. As well as being an explorer and an archaeologist and a sportsman, he was also an engineer – a good one – and a rocket-instrument man second to none in the world.

The old Crane estate in Chevy Chase was now, of course, Martin's, and he had left it pretty much as it was. He had, however, altered one room, the library, and it was now peculiarly typical of the man. It was a large room, very long, with many windows. At one end was a huge fireplace, before which Crane often sat with his long legs outstretched, studying one or several books from the cases close at hand. The essential furnishings were of a rigid simplicity, but the treasures he had gathered transformed the room into a veritable museum.

He played no instrument, but in a corner stood a magnificent piano, bare of any ornament; and a Stradivarius reposed in a special cabinet. Few people were asked to play either of those instruments; but to those few Crane listened in silence, and his brief words of thanks showed his real appreciation of music.

He made few friends, not because he hoarded his friendship, but because, even more than most rich men, he had been forced to erect around his real self an almost impenetrable screen.

As for women, Crane frankly avoided them, partly because his greatest interests in life were things in which women had neither interest nor place, but mostly because he had for years been the prime target of the man-hunting debutantes and the matchmaking mothers of three continents.

Dorothy Vaneman, with whom he had become acquainted through his friendship with Seaton, had been admitted to his friendship. Her frank comradeship was a continuing revelation, and it was she who had last played for him.

She and Seaton had been caught near his home by a sudden shower and had dashed in for shelter. While the rain beat outside, Crane had suggested that she pass the time by playing his 'fiddle.' Dorothy, a doctor of music and an accomplished violinist, realized with the first sweep of the bow that she was playing an instrument such as she had known only in her dreams, and promptly forgot everything else. She forgot the rain, the listeners, the time and the place; she simply poured into that wonderful violin everything she had of beauty, of tenderness, of artistry.

Sure, true, and full, the tones filled the big room, and in Crane's vision there rose a home filled with happy work, with laughter and comradeship. Sensing the girl's dreams as the music filled his ears, he realized as never before in his busy and purposeful life what a home with the right woman could be like. No thought of love for Dorothy entered his mind – he knew that the love existing between her and Dick was of the sort that only death could alter – but he knew that she had unwittingly given him a great gift. Often thereafter in his lonely hours he saw that dream home, and knew that nothing less than its realization would ever satisfy him.

IV

Returning to his boarding house, Seaton undressed and went to bed, but not to sleep. He knew that he had seen what could very well become a workable space-drive that afternoon ... After an hour of trying to force himself to Sleep he gave up, went to his desk, and started to study. The more he studied, the more strongly convinced he became that his first thought was right – the thing *could* become a space-drive.

By breakfast time he had the beginnings of a tentative theory roughed out, and also had gained some idea of the nature and magnitude of the obstacles to overcome.

Arriving at the Laboratory, he found that Scott had spread the news of his adventure, and his room was soon the center of interest. He described what he had seen and done to the impromptu assembly of scientists, and was starting in on the explanation he had deduced when he was interrupted by Ferdinand Scott.

'Quick, Dr Watson, the needle!' he exclaimed. Seizing a huge pipette from a rack, he went through the motions of injecting its contents into Seaton's arm.

'It *does* sound like a combination of science-fiction and Sherlock Holmes,' one of the visitors remarked.

' "Nobody Holme," you mean,' Scott said, and a general chorus of friendly but skeptical jibes followed.

'Wait a minute, you hidebound dopes, and I'll *show* you!' Seaton snapped. He dipped a short piece of copper wire into his solution.

It did not turn brown; and when he touched it with his conductors, nothing happened. The group melted away. As they left, some of the men maintained a pitying silence, but Seaton heard one half-smothered chuckle and several remarks about 'cracking under the strain.'

Bitterly humiliated at the failure of his demonstration, Seaton scowled morosely at the offending wire. Why should the thing work twice yesterday and not even once today? He reviewed his theory and could find no flaw in it. There must have been something going last night that wasn't going now ... something capable of affecting ultra-fine structure ... It had to be either in the room or very close by ... and no ordinary generator or X-ray machine could possibly have had any effect ...

There was one possibility – only one. The machine in DuQuesne's room next to his own, the machine he himself had, every once in a while, helped rebuild.

It was not a cyclotron, not a betatron. In fact, it had as yet no official name. Unofficially, it was the 'whatsitron,' or the 'maybetron,' or the 'itaintsotron' or any one of many less descriptive and more profane titles which he, DuQuesne, and the other researchers used among themselves. It did not take up much room. It did not weigh ten thousand tons. It did not require a million kilowatts of power. Nevertheless it was – theoretically– capable of affecting super-fine structure.

But in the next room? Seaton doubted it.

However, there was nothing else, and it *had* been running the night before – its glare was unique and unmistakable. Knowing that DuQuesne would turn his machine on very shortly, Seaton sat in suspense, staring at the wire. Suddenly the subdued reflection of the familiar glare appeared on the wall outside his door – and simultaneously the treated wire turned brown.

Heaving a profound sigh of relief, Seaton again touched the bit of metal with the wires from the Redeker cell. It disappeared simultaneously with a high whining sound.

Seaton started for the door, to call his neighbors in for another demonstration, but in mid-stride changed his mind. He wouldn't tell anybody anything until he knew something about the thing himself. He had to find out what it was, what it did, how and why it did it, and how – or if – it could be controlled. That meant time, apparatus and, above all, money. Money meant Crane; and Mart would be interested, anyway.

Seaton made out a leave slip for the rest of the day, and was soon piloting his motorcycle out Connecticut Avenue and into Crane's private drive. Swinging under the imposing porte-cochère he jammed on his brakes and stopped in a shower of gravel, a perilous two inches from granite. He dashed up the steps and held his finger firmly against the bell button. The door was opened hastily by Crane's Japanese servant, whose face lit up on seeing the visitor.

'Hello, Shiro. Is the honorable son of Heaven up yet?' 'Yes, sir, but he is at present in his bath.'

'Tell him to snap it up, please. Tell him I've got a thing on the fire that'll break him right off at the ankles.'

Bowing the guest to a chair in the library, Shiro hurried away. Returning shortly, he placed before Seaton the *Post,* the *Herald,* and a jar of Seaton's favorite brand of tobacco, and said, with his unfailing bow, 'Mr Crane will appear in less than one moment, sir.'

Seaton filled and lit his briar and paced up and down the room, smoking furiously. In a short time Crane came in.

'Good morning, Dick.' The men shook hands cordially. 'Your message was slightly garbled in transmission. Something about a fire and ankles is all that came through. What fire? And whose ankles were – or are about to be – broken?'

Seaton repeated.

'Ah, yes, I thought it must have been something like that. While I have breakfast, will you have lunch?'

'Thanks, Mart, guess I will. I was too excited to eat much of anything this morning.' A table appeared and the two men sat down at it. 'I'll just spring it on you cold, I guess. Just what would you think of working with me on a widget to liberate and control the entire constituent energy of metallic copper? Not in little dribbles and drabbles, like fission or fusion, but one hundred point zero zero zero zero per cent conversion? No radiation, no residue, no by-products – which means no shielding or protection would be necessary – just pure and total conversion of matter to controllable energy?'

Crane, who had a cup of coffee halfway to his mouth, stopped it in mid-air, and stared at Seaton eye to eye. This, in Crane the Imperturbable, betrayed more excitement than Seaton had ever seen him show. He finished lifting the cup, sipped, and replaced the cup studiously, meticulously, in the exact center of its saucer.

'That would undoubtedly constitute the greatest technological advance the world has ever seen,' he said, finally. 'But, if you will excuse the question, how much of that is fact, and how much fancy? That is, what portion have you actually done, and what portion is more or less justified projection into the future?'

'About one to ninety-nine – maybe less,' Seaton admitted. 'I've hardly started. I don't blame you for gagging on it a bit – everybody down at the lab thinks I'm nuttier than a fruitcake. Here's what actually happened,' and he described the accident in full detail. 'And here's the theory I've worked out, so far, to cover it.' He went on to explain.

'That's the works,' Seaton concluded, tensely, 'as clearly as I can put it. What do you think of it?'

'An extraordinary story, Dick ... really extraordinary. I understand why the men at the Laboratory thought as they did, especially after your demonstration failed. I would like to see it work, myself, before discussing further actions or procedures.'

'Fine! That suits me down to the ground – get into your clothes and I'll take you down to the lab on my bike. If I don't show you enough to make your eyes stick out a foot I'll eat that motorsickle, clear down to the tires!'

As soon as they arrived at the Laboratory, Seaton assured himself that the 'whatsitron' was still running, and arranged his demonstration. Crane remained silent, but watched closely every movement Seaton made.

'I take a piece of ordinary copper wire, so,' Seaton began. 'I dip it into this beaker of solution, thus. Note the marked change in its appearance. I place the wire upon this bench – so – with the treated end pointed out of the window ...'

'No. Toward the wall. I want to see the hole made.'

'Very well – with the treated end pointing toward that brick wall. This is an ordinary eight-watt Redeker cell. When I touch these lead-wires to the treated wire, watch closely. The speed is supersonic, but you'll hear it, whether you see what happens or not. Ready?'

'Ready.' Crane riveted his gaze upon the wire.

Seaton touched the wire with the Redeker leads, and it promptly and enthusiastically disappeared. Turning to Crane, who was staring alternately at the new hole in the wall and at the spot where the wire had been, he cried exultantly, 'Well, Doubting Thomas, how do you like *them* potatoes? Did that wire travel, or did it not? Was there some kick to it, or was there not?'

Crane walked to the wall and examined the hole minutely. He explored it with his forefinger; then, bending over, looked through it.

'Hm-m-m ... well ...' he said, straightening up. 'That hole is as real as the bricks of the wall ... and you certainly did not make it by sleight-of-hand ... if you can control that power ... put it into a hull ... harness it to the wheels of industry ... You are offering me a partnership?'

'Yes. I can't even afford to quit the Service, to say nothing of setting up what we'll have to have for this job. Besides, working this out is going to be a lot more than a one-man job. It'll take all the brains both of us have got, and probably a nickel's worth beside, to lick it.'

'Check. I accept – and thanks a lot for letting me in.' The two shook hands vigorously. Crane said, 'The first thing to do, and it must be done with all possible speed, is to get unassailably clear title to that solution, which is, of course, government property. How do you propose going about that?'

'It's government property – technically– yes; but it was worthless after I had recovered the values and ordinarily it would have been poured down the sink. I saved it just to satisfy my own curiosity as to what was in it. I'll just stick it in a paper bag and walk out with it, and if anybody asks any questions later, it simply went down the drain, as it was supposed to:

'Not good enough. We must have clear title, signed, sealed, and delivered. Can it be done?'

'I think so ... pretty sure of it. There'll be an auction in about an hour – they have one every Friday – and I can get this bottle of waste condemned easy enough. I can't imagine anybody bidding on it but us. I'll fly at it.'

'One other thing first. Will there be any difficulty about your resignation?'

'Not a chance.' Seaton grinned mirthlessly. 'They all think I'm screwy – they'll be glad to get rid of me so easy.'

'All right. Go ahead – the solution first.'

'Check,' Seaton said; and very shortly the bottle, sealed by the chief clerk and labeled *Item QX47R769BC: one bottle containing waste solution,* was on its way to the auction room.

13

Nor was there any more difficulty about his resignation from the Rare Metals Laboratory. Gossip spreads rapidly.

When the auctioneer reached the one-bottle lot, he looked at it in disgust. Why auction one bottle, when he had been selling barrels of them? But it had an official number; auctioned it must be.

'One bottle full of waste,' he droned, tonelessly. 'Any bidders? If not, I'll throw it—'

Seaton jumped forward and opened his mouth to yell, but was quelled by a sharp dig in the ribs.

'Five cents.' He heard Crane's calm voice.

'Five cents bid. Any more? Going – going –'

Seaton gulped to steady his voice. 'Ten cents.'

'Ten cents. Any more? Going – going– gone,' and Item QX47R769BC became the officially-recorded personal property of Richard B. Seaton.

Just as the transfer was completed Scott caught sight of Seaton.

'Hello, Nobody Holme!' he called gaily. 'Was that the famous solution of zero? Wish we'd known it – we'd've had fun bidding you up.'

'Not too much, Ferdy.' Seaton was calm enough, now that the precious solution was definitely his own. 'This is a cash sale, you know, so it wouldn't have cost us much, anyway.'

'That's true, too,' Scott admitted, nonchalantly enough. 'This poor government clerk is broke, as usual. But who's the "we"?'

'Mr Scott, meet my friend M. Reynolds Crane,' and, as Scott's eyes opened in astonishment, he added, 'He doesn't think I'm ready for St. Elizabeth's yet.'

'It's the bunk, Mr Crane,' Scott said, twirling his right forefinger near his right ear. 'Dick used to be a good old wagon, but he done broke down.'

'That's what you think!' Seaton took a half step forward, but checked himself even before Crane touched his elbow. 'Wait a few weeks, Scotty, and see.'

The two took a cab back to Crane's house – the bottle being far too valuable to risk on any motorcycle – where Crane poured out a little of the solution into a small vial, which he placed in his safe. He then put the large bottle, carefully packed, into his massive underground vault, remarking, 'We'll take no chances at all with that.'

'Right,' Seaton agreed. 'Well, let's get busy. The first thing to do is to hunt up a small laboratory that's for rent.'

'Wrong. The organization of our company comes first – suppose I should die before we solve the problem? I suggest something like this. Neither of us want to handle the company as such, so it will be a stock company, capitalized at one million dollars, with ten thousand shares of stock. McQueen, who is handling my affairs at the bank, can be president; Winters, his attorney, and Robinson, his C.P.A., secretary and treasurer; you and I will be superintendent and general manager. To make up seven directors, we could elect Mr

Vaneman and Shiro. As for the capital, I will put in half a million; you will put in your idea and your solution, at a preliminary, tentative valuation of half a million—'

'But, Mart—'

'Hold on, Dick. Let me finish. They are worth much more than that, of course, and will be revalued later, but that will do for a start ...'

'Hold on yourself for a minute. Why tie up all that cash when a few thousand bucks is all we'll need?'

'A few thousand? Think a minute, Dick. How much testing equipment will you need? How about salaries and wages? How much of a spaceship can you build for a million dollars? And power plants run from a hundred million up. Convinced?'

'Well, maybe ... except, right at first, I thought ...'

'You will see that this is a very small start, the way it is. Now to call the meeting.'

He called McQueen, the president of the great trust company in whose care the bulk of his fortune was. Seaton, listening to the brief conversation, realized as never before what power was wielded by his friend.

In a surprisingly short time the men were assembled in Crane's library. Crane called the meeting to order; outlined the nature and scope of the proposed corporation; and The Seaton-Crane Company, Engineers, began to come into being.

After the visitors had gone, Seaton asked, 'Do you know what kind of a rental agent to call to get hold of a laboratory?'

'For a while at least, the best place for you to work is right here.'

'Here! You don't want stuff like *that* loose around here, do you?'

'Yes. The reasons are: first, privacy; second, convenience. We have much of the material and equipment you will need already on hand, out in the hangar and the shops, and plenty of room to install anything new you may need. Third, no curiosity. The Cranes have been inventors, tinkerers, and mechanics so long, that no planning board has ever been able to zone our shops out; and our nearest neighbors – and none are very near, as you know, since I own over forty acres here – are so used to peculiar happenings that they no longer pay any attention to anything that goes on here.'

'Fine! If that's the way you want it, it suits me down to the ground. Let's get busy!'

V

Dr Marc C. DuQuesne was a tall, powerful man, built very much like Richard Seaton. His thick, slightly wavy hair was intensely black. His eyes, only a trifle lighter in shade, were surmounted by thick black eyebrows, which grew together above his aquiline, finely-chiseled nose. His face, although not pale, appeared so because of the heavy black beard always showing through, even after the closest possible shave. In his early thirties, he was widely known as one of the best men in his field.

Scott came into his laboratory immediately after the auction, finding him leaning over the console of the whatsitron, his forbidding but handsome face strangely illuminated by the greenish-yellowish-blue glare of the machine.

'Hello, Blackie,' Scott said. 'What d'you think of Seaton? Think he's quite right in the head?'

'Speaking off-hand,' DuQuesne replied, without looking up, 'I'd say he's been putting in too many hours working and not enough sleeping. I don't think he's insane – I'd swear in court that he's the sanest crazy man I ever heard of.'

'I think he's a plain nut, myself – that was a lulu he pulled yesterday. He seems to believe it himself, though. He got them to put that junk solution into the auction this noon and he and M. Reynolds Crane bid it in for ten cents.'

'M. Reynolds Crane?' DuQuesne managed to conceal his start of surprise. 'Where does he come in on this?'

'Oh, he and Seaton have been buddy-buddy for a long time, you know. Probably humoring him. After they got the solution they called a cab and somebody said the address they gave the hackie was Crane's, the other side of Chevy Chase, but … oh, that's my call – so long.'

As Scott left, DuQuesne strode over to his desk, a new expression, half of chagrin, half of admiration, on his face. He picked up his telephone and dialed a number.

'Brookings? DuQuesne speaking. I've got to see you as fast as I can get there. Can't talk on the phone … Yes, I'll be right out.'

He left the Laboratory building and was soon in the private office of the head of the Washington, or 'diplomatic,' branch of the immense World Steel Corporation.

'How do you do, Dr DuQuesne,' Brookings said, as he seated his visitor. 'You seem excited.'

'Not excited, but in a hurry. The biggest thing in history is just breaking and we've got to work fast if we want to land it. But before I start – have you any sneaking doubts that I know what I'm talking about?'

'Why, no, doctor, not the slightest. You are widely known; you have helped us in various de— in various matters.'

'Say it, Brookings, "Deals" is right. This is going to be the biggest ever. It should be easy – one simple killing and an equally simple burglary – and won't mean wholesale murder, like that tungsten job.'

'Oh, no, doctor, not murder. Accidents.'

'I call things by their right names. I'm not squeamish. But what I'm here about is that Seaton, of our division, has discovered, more or less accidentally, total conversion atomic energy.'

'And that means?'

'To break it down to where you can understand it, it means a billion kilowatts per plant at a total amortized cost of approximately one one-hundredth of a mil per KW hour.'

'Huh?' A look of scornful disbelief settled on Brookings' face.

'Sneer if you like. Your ignorance doesn't change the facts and doesn't hurt my feelings a bit. Call Chambers in and ask him what would happen if a man should liberate the total energy of a hundred pounds of copper in, say, ten microseconds.'

'Pardon me, doctor. I didn't mean to insult you. I'll call him in.'

Brookings called, and a man in white appeared. In response to the question he thought for a moment, then smiled.

'At a rough guess, it would blow the whole world into vapor and might blow it clear out of its orbit. However, you needn't worry about anything like that happening, Mr Brookings. It won't. It can't.'

'Why not?'

'Because only two nuclear reactions yield energy – fission and fusion. Very heavy elements fission; very light elements fuse; intermediate ones, such as copper, do neither. Any possible operation on the copper atom, such as splitting, must necessarily absorb vastly more energy than it produces. Is that all?'

'That's all. Thanks.'

'You see?' Brookings said, when they were again alone. 'Chambers is a good man, too, and he says it's impossible.'

'As far as he knows, he's right. I'd have said the same thing this morning. However, it has just been done.'

'How?'

DuQuesne repeated certain parts of Seaton's story.

'But suppose the man *is* crazy? He could be, couldn't he?'

'Yeah, he's crazy – like a fox. If it were only Seaton, I might buy that; but nobody ever thought M. Reynolds Crane had any loose screws. With *him* backing Seaton you can bet your last dollar that Seaton showed him plenty of real stuff.' As a look of conviction appeared upon Brookings' face DuQuesne went on. 'Don't you understand? The solution was government property and he had to do something to make everybody think it was worthless, so he could get title to it. It was a bold move – it would have been foolhardy in anyone else. The reason he got away with it is that he's always been an open-faced talker, always telling everything he knows. He fooled me completely, and I'm not usually asleep out of bed.'

'What is your idea? Where do we come in?'

'You come in by getting that solution away from Seaton and Crane, and furnishing the money to develop the stuff and to build, under my direction, such a power plant as the world never saw before.'

'Why is it necessary to get that particular solution? Why not refine some more platinum wastes?'

'Not a chance. Chemists have been recovering platinum for a hundred years, and nothing like that was ever found before. The stuff, whatever it is, must have been present in some particular lot of platinum. They haven't got all of it there is in the world, of course, but the chance of finding any without knowing exactly what to look for is extremely slight. Besides, we *must* have a monopoly on it – Crane would be satisfied with ten per cent net profit. No, we've got to get every milliliter of that solution and we've got to kill Seaton – he knows too much. I want to take a couple of your goons and attend to it tonight.'

Brookings thought for a moment, his face blandly empty of expression. Then he spoke.

'I'm sorry, doctor, but we can't do it. It's too flagrant, too risky. Besides, we can afford to buy it from Seaton if, as, and when he proves it is worth anything.'

'Bah!' DuQuesne snorted. 'Who do you think you're kidding? Do you think I told you enough so that you can sidetrack me out of the deal? Get that idea out of your head – fast. There are only two men in the world who can handle it – R. B. Seaton and M. C. DuQuesne. Take your pick. Put anybody else on it – *anybody* else – and he'll blow himself and his whole neighborhood out beyond the orbit of Mars.'

Brookings, caught flat-footed and half convinced of the truth of DuQuesne's statements, still temporized.

'You're very modest, DuQuesne.'

'Modesty gets a man praise, but I prefer cash. However, you ought to know by this time that what I say is true. And I'm in a hurry. The difficulty of getting hold of that solution is growing greater every minute and my price is rising every minute.'

'What is your price at the present minute?'

'Ten thousand dollars a month during development, five million cash when the first plant goes onto the line, and ten per cent of the net – on all plants – thereafter.'

'Oh, come, doctor, let's be sensible. You don't mean that.'

'I don't say anything I don't mean. I've done a lot of dirty work for you people and never got much of anything out of it – I couldn't force you without exposing myself. But this time I've got you where the hair's short and I'm going to collect. And you still can't kill me – I'm not Ainsworth. Not only because you'll have to have me, but because it'd still send all you big shots clear down to Perkins, to the chair, or up the river for life.'

'Please, DuQuesne, *please* don't use such language!'

'Why not?' DuQuesne's voice was cold and level. 'What do a few lives amount to, as long as they're not yours or mine? I can trust you, more or less, and you can trust me the same, because you know I can't send you up without going with you. If that's the way you want it, I'll let you try it without me – you won't get far. So decide, right now, whether you want me now, or later. If it's later, the first two of those figures I gave you will be doubled.'

'We can't do business on any such terms.' Brookings shook his head. 'We can buy the power rights from Seaton for less.'

'You want it the hard way, eh?' DuQuesne sneered as he came to his feet. 'Go ahead. Steal the solution. But don't give your man much of it, not more than half a teaspoonful – I want as much as possible of it left. Set up the laboratory a hundred miles from anywhere – not that I give a damn how many people you kill, but I don't want to go along – and caution whoever does the work to use *very* small quantities of copper. Goodbye.'

As the door closed behind the cynical scientist, Brookings took a small instrument, very like a watch, from his pocket, touched a button, raised it to his lips, and spoke. 'Perkins.'

'Yes, sir.'

'M. Reynolds Crane has in or around his house somewhere a small bottle of solution.'

'Yes, sir. Can you describe it?'

'Not exactly.' Brookings went on to tell his minion all he knew about the matter. 'If the bottle were only partly emptied and filled up with water, I don't believe anybody would notice the difference.'

'Probably not, sir. Goodbye.'

Brookings then took his personal typewriter out of a drawer and typed busily for a few minutes. Among other things, he wrote:

'... and do not work on too much copper at once. I gather that an ounce or two should be enough ...'

VI

From daylight until late in the evening Seaton worked in the shop, sometimes supervising expert mechanics, sometimes working alone. Every night when Crane went to bed he saw Seaton in his room in a cloud of smoke, poring over blueprints or seated at the computer, making interminable calculations. Deaf to Crane's remonstrances, he was driving himself at an inhuman rate, completely absorbed in his project. While he did not forget Dorothy, he had a terrific lot to do and none of it was getting done. He was going to see her just as soon as he was over this hump, he insisted; but every hump was followed by another, higher and worse. And day after day went by.

Meanwhile, Dorothy was feeling considerably glum. Here was her engagement only a week old – and *what* an engagement! Before that enchanted evening he had been an almost daily visitor. They had ridden and talked and played together, and he had forced his impetuous way into all her plans. Now, after she had promised to marry him, he had called once – at eleven o'clock – with his mind completely out of this world, and she hadn't even heard from him for six long days. A queer happening at the laboratory seemed scant excuse for such long-continued neglect, and she knew no other.

Puzzled and hurt, her mother's solicitous looks unbearable, she left the house for a long, aimless walk. She paid no attention to the spring beauty around her. She did not even notice footsteps following her, and was too deeply engrossed in her own somber thoughts to be more than mildly surprised when Martin Crane spoke to her. For a while she tried to rouse herself into animation, but her usual ease had deserted her and her false gaiety did not deceive the keen-minded Crane. Soon they were walking along together in silence, a silence finally broken by the man.

'I have just left Seaton,' he said. Paying no attention to her startled glance, he went on, 'Did you ever see anyone else with his singleness of purpose? Of course, though, that is one of the traits that make him what he is ... He is working himself into a breakdown. Has he told you about leaving the Rare Metals Laboratory?'

'No, I haven't seen him since the night the accident, or discovery, or whatever it was, happened. He tried to explain it to me then, but what little I could understand of what he said sounded simply preposterous.'

'I can't explain the thing to you – Dick himself can't explain it to me – but I can give you an idea of what we both think it may come to.'

'I wish you would. I'll be mighty glad to hear it.'

'Dick discovered something that converts copper into pure energy. That water-bath took off in a straight line—'

'That *still* sounds preposterous, Martin,' the girl interrupted, 'even when you say it.'

'Careful, Dorothy,' he cautioned her. 'Nothing that actually happens is or can be preposterous. But as I said, this copper bath left Washington in a straight line for scenes unknown. We intend to follow it in a suitable vehicle.'

He paused, looking at his companion's face. She did not speak, and he went on in his matter-of-fact tone.

'Building the spaceship is where I come in. As you know, I have almost as much money as Dick has brains; and some day, before the summer is over, we expect to go somewhere … some place a considerable distance from this earth.'

Then, after enjoining strict secrecy, he told her what he had seen in the laboratory and described the present state of affairs.

'But if he thought of all that … was brilliant enough to work out such a theory and to actually plan such an unheard-of thing as space-travel … all on such a slight foundation of fact … why couldn't he have *told* me?'

'He fully intended to. He still intends to. Don't believe for a moment that his absorption implies any lack of love for you. I was coming to visit you about that when I saw you out here. He's driving himself unmercifully. He eats hardly anything and doesn't seem to sleep at all. He has to take it easy or break down, but nothing I can say has had any effect. Can you think of anything you, or you and I together, can do?'

Dorothy still walked along, but it was a different Dorothy. She was erect and springy, her eyes sparkled, all her charm and vitality were back in force.

'I'll say I can!' she breathed. 'I'll stuff him to the ears and put him to sleep right after dinner, the big dope!'

This time it was Crane who was surprised, so surprised that he stopped, practically in mid-stride. 'How?' he demanded. 'You talk about something being preposterous – how?'

'Maybe you hadn't better know the gory details.' She grinned impishly. 'You lack quite a bit, Marty, of being the world's best actor, and Dick mustn't be warned. Just run along home, and be *sure* you're there when I get there. I've got to do some phoning … I'll be there at six o'clock, and tell Shiro not to make you two any dinner.'

She was there at six o'clock.

'Where is he, Marty? Out in the shop?'

'Yes.'

In the shop, she strode purposefully toward Seaton's oblivious back. 'Hi, Dick. How's it coming?'

'Huh?' He started violently, almost jumping off his stool – then did jump off it as the knowledge filtered through that it was really Dorothy who was standing at his back. He swept her off her feet in the intensity of his embrace; she pressed her every inch tighter and tighter against his rock-hard body. Their lips met and clung.

Dorothy finally released herself enough to look into his eyes. 'I was so mad, Dick. I simply didn't know whether to kiss you or kill you, but I decided to kiss you – this time.'

'I know, sweetheart. I've been trying my level best to get a couple of hours to come over and see you, but everything's been going so slow – my head's so thick it takes a thousand years for an idea to percolate—'

'Hush! I've been doing a lot of thinking this last week, especially today. I love you as you are. I can either do that or give you up. I can't even imagine giving you up, because I know I'd cold-bloodedly strangle with her own hair any woman who ever cocked an eye at you … Come on, Dick, no more work tonight. I'm taking you and Martin home for dinner.' Then, as his eyes strayed involuntarily back toward the computer, she said, more forcefully, 'I – said– no – more – work – tonight. Do you want to fight about it?'

'Uh-uh! I'll say I don't – I wasn't even *thinking* of working!' Seaton was panic-stricken. 'No fights, Dottie. Not with you. Ever. About anything. Believe me.'

'I do, lover,' and, arms around each other, they strolled unhurriedly up to and into the house.

Crane accepted enthusiastically – for him – the invitation to dinner, and was going to dress, but Dorothy would not have it. 'Strictly informal,' she insisted. 'Just as you are.' 'I'll wash up, then, and be with you in a sec,' Seaton said, and left the room. Dorothy turned to Crane.

'I've got a tremendous favor to ask of you, Martin. I drove the Cad – it's air-conditioned, you know – could you possibly bring your Stradivarius along? My best violin would do, I'm sure, but I'd rather have the heaviest artillery I can get.'

'I see – at last.' Crane's face lit up. 'Certainly. Play it outdoors in the rain, if necessary. Masterful strategy, Dorothy – masterful.'

'Well, one does what one can,' Dorothy murmured in mock modesty. Then, as Seaton appeared, she said, 'Let's go, boys. Dinner is served at seven-thirty sharp, and we're going to be there right on the chime.'

As they sat down at the table Dorothy studied again the changes that six days had made in Seaton. His face was pale and thin, almost haggard. Lines had appeared at the corners of his eyes and around his mouth, and faint but unmistakable blue rings encircled his eyes.

'You've been going altogether too hard, Dick. You've got to cut down.'

'Oh no, I'm all right. I never felt better. I could whip a rattlesnake and give him the first bite!'

She laughed, but the look of concern did not leave her face.

During the meal no mention was made of the project, the conversation being deftly held to tennis, swimming, and other sports; and Seaton, whose plate was unobtrusively kept full, ate such a dinner as he had not eaten for weeks. After dessert they all went into the living room and ensconced themselves in comfortable chairs. The men smoked; all five continued their conversation.

After a time three left the room, Vaneman took Crane into his study to show him a rare folio; Mrs Vaneman went upstairs, remarking plaintively that she *had* to finish writing that article, and if she put it off much longer she'd *never* get it done.

Dorothy said, 'I skipped practice today, Dick, on account of traipsing out there after you two geniuses. Could you stand it to have me play at you for half an hour?'

'Don't fish, Dottie Dimple. You know there's nothing I'd like better. But if you want me to beg you I'd be glad to. Please – PUH-LEEZE – oh fair and musicianly damsel, fill ye circumambient atmosphere with thy tuneful notes.'

'Wilco. Roger,' she snickered. 'Over and out.'

She took up a violin – Crane's violin – and played. First his favorites; crashing selections from operas and solos by the great masters, abounding in harmonies on two strings. Then she slowly changed her playing to softer, simpler melodies, then to old, old songs. Seaton, listening with profound enjoyment, relaxed more and more. Pipe finished and hands at rest, his eyes closed of themselves and he lay back at ease. The music changed again, gradually, to reveries; each one softer, slower, dreamier than the last. Then to sheer, crooning lullabies; and it was in these that magnificent instrument and consummate artist combined to show their true qualities at their very best.

Dorothy diminuendoed the final note into silence and stood there, bow poised, ready to resume; but there was no need. Freed from the tyranny of the brain that had been driving it so unmercifully, Seaton's body had begun to make up for many hours of lost sleep.

Assured that he was really asleep, Dorothy tiptoed to the door of the study and whispered, 'He's asleep in his chair.'

'I believe that,' her father smiled. 'That last one was like a bottle of veronal – it was all Crane and I could do to keep each other awake. You're a smart girl.'

'She is a musician,' Crane said. 'What a musician!'

'Partly me, of course, but – *what* a violin! But what'll we do with him? Let him sleep there?'

'No, he'd be more comfortable on the couch. I'll get a couple of blankets,' Vaneman said.

He did so and the three went into the living room together. Seaton lay motionless, only the lifting and falling of his powerful chest showing that he was alive.

'You take his …'

'Sh … Sh!' Dorothy whispered, intensely. 'You'll wake him up, dad.'

'Bosh! You couldn't wake him up now with a club. You take his head and shoulders, Crane – heave-ho!'

With Dorothy anxiously watching the proceedings and trying to help, the two men picked Seaton up out of the chair and carried him across the room to the couch. They removed his outer clothing; the girl arranged pillows and tucked blankets around him; then touched her lips lightly to his. 'Goodnight, sweetheart,' she whispered.

His lips responded faintly to her caress, and, '… dnigh …' he murmured in his sleep.

It was three o'clock in the afternoon when Seaton, looking vastly better, came into the shop. When Crane saw him and called out a greeting, he returned it with a sheepish grin.

'Don't say a word, Martin; I'm thinking it all, and then some. I never felt so cheap in my life as when I woke up on the Vanemans' couch this noon – where you helped put me, no doubt.'

'No doubt at all,' Crane agreed, cheerfully, 'and listen to this. More of the same, or worse, if you keep on going as you were.'

'Don't rub it in – can't you see I'm flat on my back with all four paws in the air? I'll be good. I'm going to bed at eleven every night and I'm going to see Dottie every other evening and all day Sunday.'

'Very fine, if true – and it had better be true.'

'It will, so help me. Well, while I was eating breakfast this morning – this afternoon, rather – I saw that missing factor in the theory. And don't tell me it was because I was rested up and fresh, either – I know it.'

'I was refraining heroically from mentioning the fact.'

'Thanks so much. Well, the knotty point, you remember, was what could be the possible effect of a small electric current in liberating the power. I think I've got it. It must shift the epsilon-gamma-zeta plane – and if it does, the rate of liberation must be zero when the angle theta is zero, and approach infinity as theta approaches pi over two.'

'It does not,' Crane contradicted, flatly. 'It can't. The orientation of that plane is fixed by temperature – by nothing except temperature.'

'That's so, usually, but that's where the X comes in. Here's the proof …'

On and on the argument raged. Reference works littered the table and overflowed onto the floor, scratch-paper grew into piles, both computers ran almost continuously.

Since the mathematical details of the Seaton-Crane Effect are of little or no interest here, it will suffice to mention a few of the conclusions at which the two men arrived. The power could be controlled. It could drive – or pull – a spaceship. It could be used as an explosive, in violences ranging from that of a twenty-millimeter shell up to any upper limit desired, however fantastic when expressed in megatons of T.N.T. There were many other possibilities inherent in their final equations, possibilities which the men did not at that time explore.

VII

'Say, Blackie,' Scott called from the door of DuQuesne's laboratory, 'did you get the news flash that just came over on KSKM-TV? It was right down your alley.'

'No. What about it?'

'Somebody piled up a million tons of tetryl, T.N.T., picric acid, nitroglycerine, and so forth up in the hills and touched it off. Blooie! Whole town of Bankerville, West Virginia – population two hundred – gone. No survivors. No debris, even, the man said. Just a hole in the ground a couple of miles in diameter and God only knows how deep.'

'Baloney!' DuQuesne snapped. 'What would anybody be doing with an atomic bomb up there?'

'That's the funny part of it – it *wasn't* an atomic bomb No radioactivity anywhere, not even a trace. Just skillions and whillions of tons of high explosive and nobody can figure it. "All scientists baffled," the flash said. How about you Blackie? You baffled, too?'

'I would be, if I believed any part of it.' DuQuesne turned back to his work.

'Well, don't blame *me* for it, I'm just telling you what Fritz Habelmann just said.'

Since DuQuesne showed no interest at all in his news, Scott wandered away.

'The fool did it. That will cure him of sucking eggs – I hope,' he muttered, and picked up his telephone.

'Operator? DuQuesne speaking. I am expecting a call here this afternoon. Please have the party call me at my home, Lincoln six four six two oh … Thank you.'

He left the building and got his car out of the parking lot. In less than half an hour he reached his house on Park Road, overlooking beautiful Rock Creek Park, in which he lived alone save for an elderly colored couple who were his servants.

*

In the busiest part of the afternoon Chambers rushed unannounced into Brookings' private office, his face white, a newspaper in his hand.

'Read that, Mr Brookings!' he gasped.

Brookings read, his face turning gray. 'Ours, of course.'

'Ours,' Chambers agreed, dully.

'The fool! Didn't you tell him to work with very small quantities?'

'I did. He said not to worry, he was taking no chances he wouldn't have more than one gram of copper on hand at once in the whole laboratory.'

'Well … I'll … be … jiggered!' Turning slowly to the telephone, Brookings called a number and asked for Dr DuQuesne, then he called another.

'Brookings. I would like to see you as soon as possible … I'll be there in about an hour … Goodbye.'

Brookings arrived and was shown into DuQuesne's study. The two shook hands perfunctorily and sat down. The scientist waited for the other to speak.

'You were right, doctor,' Brookings said. 'Our man couldn't handle it. I have contracts here …'

'At twenty and ten?' DuQuesne's lips smiled, a cold, hard smile.

'Twenty and ten. The Company expects to pay for its mistakes. Here they are.'

DuQuesne glanced over the documents and thrust them into a pocket. 'I'll go over them with my attorney tonight and mail one copy back to you if he says to. In the meantime we may as well get started.'

'What do you suggest?'

'First, the solution. You stole it, I—'

'Don't use such language, doctor!'

'Why not? I'm for direct action, first, last, and all the time. This thing is too important to mince words. Have you got it with you?'

'Yes. Here it is.'

'Where's the rest of it?'

'All that we found is here, except for half a teaspoonful our expert had in his laboratory. We didn't get it all; only half of it. The rest was diluted with water, so it wouldn't be missed. We can get the rest of it later. That will cause a disturbance, but it may become …'

'Half of it! You haven't a twentieth of it here. Seaton had about four hundred milliliters – almost a pint – of it. I wonder … who's holding out on – or double-crossing – whom?

'No, not you,' he went on, as Brookings protested innocence. 'That wouldn't make sense. Your thief turned in only this much. Could he be holding out on us … no, that doesn't make sense, either.'

'No. You know Perkins.'

'His crook missed the main bottle, then. That's where your methods give me an acute bellyache. When I want anything done I do it myself. But it isn't too late yet. I'll take a couple of your goons tonight and go out there.'

'And do exactly what?'

'Shoot Seaton, open the safe, take their solution, plans, and notes. Loose cash, too, of course – I'll give that to the goons.'

'No, no, doctor. That's too crude altogether. I could permit that only as the last possible resort.'

'I say do it first. I'm afraid of pussyfooting and gumshoeing around Seaton and Crane. Seaton has developed a lot of late, and Crane never was anybody's fool. They're a hard combination to beat, and we've done plenty worse and got away with it.'

'Why not work it out from the solution we have, and then get the rest of it? Then, if Seaton had an accident, we could prove that we discovered the stuff long ago.'

'Because development work on that stuff is risky, as you found out. Also, it'd take too much time. Why should we go to all that trouble and expense when they've got the worst of it done? The police may stir around for a few days, but they won't know anything or find out anything. Nobody will suspect anything except Crane – if he is still alive – and he won't be able to do anything.'

So the argument raged. Brookings agreed with DuQuesne in aim, but would not sanction his means, holding out for quieter, more devious, less actionable methods. Finally he ended the discussion with a flat refusal and called Perkins. He told him of the larger bottle of solution; instructing him to secure it and bring back all plans, notes, and other material pertaining to the matter in hand. Then, after giving DuQuesne an instrument like the one he himself carried, Brookings took his leave.

Late in the afternoon of the day of the explosion, Seaton came up to Crane with a mass of notes in his hand.

'I've got some of it, Mart. The power is what we figured – anything you want short of infinity. I've got the three answers you wanted most. First, the transformation is complete. No loss, no residue, no radiation or other waste. Thus, no danger and no shielding or other protection is necessary. Second, X acts only as a catalyst and is not itself consumed. Hence, an infinitesimally thin coating is all that's necessary. Third, the power is exerted as a pull along the axis of the X figure, whatever that figure is, focused at infinity.

'I also investigated those two border-line conditions. In one it generates an attractive force focused on the nearest object in line with its axis of X. In the second it's an all-out repulsion.'

'Splendid, Dick.' Crane thought for a minute or two. 'Data enough, I think, to go ahead on. I particularly like that first border-line case. You could call it an object-compass. Focus one on the Earth and we could always find our way back here, no matter how far away we get.'

'Say, that's right – I never thought of anything like that. But what I came over here for was to tell you that I've got a model built that will handle me like small change. It's got more oof than a ramjet, small as it is – ten G's at least. Want to see it in action?'

'I certainly do.'

As they were walking out toward the field Shiro called to them and they turned back toward the house, learning that Dorothy and her father had just arrived.

'Hello, boys.' Dorothy smiled radiantly, her dimples very much in evidence. 'Dad and I came out to see how – and what – you're doing.'

'You came at exactly the right time,' Crane said. 'Dick has built a model and was just going to demonstrate it. Come and watch.'

On the field, Seaton buckled on a heavy harness, which carried numerous handles, switches, boxes, and other pieces of apparatus. He snapped the switch of the whatsitron. He then moved a slider on a flashlight-like tube which was attached to the harness by an adjustable steel cable and which he was gripping with both hands.

There was a creak of straining leather and he shot into the air for a couple of hundred feet, where he stopped and remained motionless for several seconds. Then he darted off; going forward and backward, up and down, describing zigzags and loops and circles and figures-of-eight. After a few minutes of this display he came down in a power dive, slowing up spectacularly to a perfect landing.

'There, O beauteous damsel and esteemed sirs –' he began, with a low bow and a sweeping flourish, then there was a sharp snap and he was jerked sideways off his feet. In the flourish his thumb had moved the slider a fraction of an inch and the power-tube had torn itself out of his grasp. It was now out at the full length of the cable, dragging him helplessly after it, straight toward a high stone wall.

But Seaton was helpless only for a second. Throwing his body sideways and reaching out along the taut cable, he succeeded in swinging the thing around so that he was galloping back toward the party and the field. Dorothy and her father were standing motionless, staring; Crane was running toward the shop.

'Don't touch that switch?' Seaton yelled. 'I'll handle the bloody thing myself!'

At this evidence that Seaton thought himself master of the situation Crane began to laugh, but held one finger lightly on the whatsitron switch; and Dorothy, relieved of her fear, burst into a fit of the giggles. The bar was straight out in front of him, going somewhat faster than a man could normally run, swinging now right, now left as his weight was thrown from one side to the other. Seaton, dragged along like a boy holding a runaway calf by the tail, was covering the ground in prodigious leaps, at the same time pulling himself up hand over hand toward the tube. He reached it, grabbed it in both hands, again darted into the air, and came down lightly near the others, who were rocking with laughter.

'I said it would be undignified,' said Seaton, somewhat short of breath, but laughing, too, 'but I didn't think it would end up like this.'

Dorothy seized his hand. 'Are you hurt anywhere, Dick?'

'Uh-uh. Not a bit.'

'I was scared green until you told Martin to lay off, but it *was* funny then. How about doing it again and I'll shoot it in full color?'

'Dorothy!' her father chided. 'Next time it might not be funny at all.'

'There'll be no next time for this rig,' Seaton declared. 'From here we ought to be able to go to a full-scale ship.'

Dorothy and Seaton set out toward the house and Vaneman turned to Crane.

'What are you going to do with it commercially? Dick, of course, hasn't thought of anything except his spaceship. Equally of course, you have.'

Crane frowned. 'Yes. I've had a crew of designers working for weeks. In units of half-million to a million kilowatts we could sell power for a small fraction of a mil. However, the deeper we go into it the more likely it appears that it will make all big central power plants obsolete.'

'How could that be?'

'Individual units on individual spots – but it will be some time yet before we have enough data for the machines to work on.'

The evening passed rapidly. As the guests were getting ready to leave, Dorothy asked, 'What are you going to call it? You both have called it forty different things this evening, and none of them were right.'

'Why, "spaceship," of course,' Seaton said.

'Oh, I didn't mean the class, I meant this particular one. There's only one possible name for her: the *Skylark*.'

'Exactly right, Dorothy,' Crane said.

'Perfect!' Seaton applauded. 'And you'll christen it, Dottie, with a fifty-liter flask full of hard vacuum. "I christen thee the *Skylark – bang!*"'

As an afterthought, Vaneman pulled a newspaper out of his pocket.

'Oh yes, I bought a *Clarion* on our way out here. It tells about an extraordinary explosion – at least, the story is extraordinary. It may not be true, but it may make interesting reading for you two scientific sharps. Goodnight.'

Seaton walked Dorothy to the car. When he came back Crane handed him the paper without a word. Seaton read.

'It's X, all right. Not even a *Clarion* reporter could dream that up. Some poor devil tried it without my rabbit's foot in his pocket.'

'But think, Dick! Something is very seriously wrong. Two people did *not* discover X at the same time. Someone stole your idea, but the idea is worthless without the metal. Where did he get it?'

'That's right. The stuff is extremely rare. In fact, it isn't supposed even to exist. I'd bet my case buck that we had every microgram of it known to science.'

'Well, then,' said the practical Crane, 'We'd better find out if we have all we started with.'

The storage bottle was still almost full, its seal unbroken; the vial was apparently exactly as Seaton had left it. 'It seems to be all here,' Crane said.

'It can't be,' Seaton declared. 'It's too rare – coincidence *can't* go that far … I can tell by taking the densities.'

He did so, finding that the solution in the vial was only half as strong as that in the reserve bottle.

'That's it, Mart. Somebody stole half of this vial. But he's gone where the … say, do you suppose …?'

'I do indeed. Just that.'

'And the difficulty will lie in finding out which one, among the dozens of outfits who would want the stuff, is the one that actually got it?'

'Check. The idea was – must have been – taken from your demonstration. Or, rather, one man knew, from the wreckage of your laboratory, that your demonstration would not have failed had all the factors then operative been present. Who was there?'

'Oh, a lot of people came around at one time or another, but your specifications narrow the field to five men – Scott, Smith, Penfield, DuQuesne, and Roberts. Hmmm, let's see – if Scott's brain was solid cyclonite, the detonation wouldn't crack his skull; Smith is a pure theoretician; Penfield wouldn't dare quote an authority without asking permission; DuQuesne *is* … umm … that is, DuQuesne isn't … I mean, Du—'

'DuQuesne, then, is suspect number one.'

'But wait a minute! I didn't say …'

'Exactly. That makes him suspect number one. How about the fifth man, Roberts?'

'Not the type – definitely. He's a career man. If he got blasted out of the Civil Service all the clocks in the city would stop.

Crane picked up his telephone and dialed.

'This is Crane. Please give me a complete report on Dr Marc C. DuQuesne of the Rare Metals Laboratory as soon as possible … Yes, full coverage … no limit … and please send two or three guards out here right now, men you can trust … Thanks.'

VIII

Seaton and Crane spent some time in developing the 'object-compass'. They made several of them, mounted in gymbals on super-shock-proof jeweled bearings. Strictly according to Seaton's Theory, the instruments were of extreme sensitivity; the one set on the smallest object at the greatest distance – a tiny glass bead at three thousand miles – registering a true line in less than one second.

Having solved the problem of navigation, they made up graduated series of 'X-plosive' bullets, each one matching perfectly its standard .45-caliber counterpart. They placed their blueprints and working notes in the safe as usual, taking with them only those dealing with the object-compass and the X-plosive bullet, on which they were still working. They cautioned Shiro and the three guards to watch everything closely until they got back. Then they set out in the helicopter, to try out the new weapon in a place where the explosions could do no damage.

It came fully up to expectations. A Mark One charge, fired by Crane at a stump over a hundred yards from the flat-topped knoll that had afforded them a landing-place, tore it bodily from the ground and reduced it to splinters. The force of the explosion made the two men stagger.

'Wow!' Seaton exclaimed. 'Wonder what a Mark Five will do?'

'Careful, Dick. What are you going to shoot at?'

'That rock across the valley. Range-finder says nine hundred yards. Bet me a buck I can't hit it?'

'The pistol champion of the District? Hardly!'

The pistol cracked, and when the bullet reached its destination the boulder was obliterated in a vast ball of … of *something*. It was not exactly – nor all – flame. It had none of the searing, killing, unbearable radiance of an atomic bomb. It did not look much, if any, hotter than the sphere of primary action of a massive charge of high explosive. It did not look, even remotely, like anything either man had ever seen before.

Their observations were interrupted by the arrival of the shock wave. They were hurled violently backward, stumbling and falling flat. When they could again keep their feet, both stared silently at the tremendous mushroom-shaped cloud which was hurling itself upward at an appalling pace and spreading itself outward almost as fast.

Crane examined Geiger and scintillometer, reporting that both had continued to register only background radiation throughout the test. Seaton made observations and used his slide rule.

'Can't do much from here, right under it, but the probable minimum is ninety-seven thousand feet and it's still boiling upward. I … will … be … tee … totally … jiggered.'

Both men stood for minutes awed into silence by the incredible forces they had loosed. Then Seaton made the understatement of his long life.

'I don't think I'll shoot a Mark Ten around here.'

'Haven't you done anything yet?' Brookings demanded.

'I can't help it, Mr Brookings,' Perkins replied. 'Prescott's men are hard to do business with.'

'I know that, but surely *one* of them can be reached.'

'Not at ten, and that was your limit. Twenty-five or no dice.'

Brookings drummed fingers on desk. 'Well … if we have to …' and wrote out an order on the cashier for twenty-five thousand dollars in small-to-medium bills. 'I'll see you at the cafe, tomorrow at four o'clock.'

The place referred to was the Perkins Café, a restaurant on Pennsylvania Avenue. It was the favorite eating-place of the diplomatic, political, financial, and social élite of Washington, none of whom even suspected that it had been designed and was being maintained by the world-girdling World Steel Corporation as the hub and center of its world-girdling nefarious activities.

At four o'clock on the following day Brookings was ushered into Perkins' private office.

'Blast it, Perkins, can't you do *anything*?' he demanded.

'It just couldn't be helped,' Perkins replied doggedly. 'Everything was figured to the second, but the Jap smelled a rat or something and jumped us. I managed to get away, but he laid Tony out cold. But don't worry – I sent Silk Humphrey and a couple of the boys out to get him. Told him to report at four oh eight. Any second now.'

In less than a minute Perkins' communicator buzzed.

'This is the dick, not Silk,' it said, in its tiny, tinny voice. 'He's dead. So are the two goons. That Jap, he's chain lightning on greased wheels, got all three of them. Anything else I can do for you?'

'No. Your job's done.' Perkins closed the switch, fusing the spy's communicator into a blob of metal; and Brookings called DuQuesne.

'Can you come to my office, or are you bugged?'

'Yes, to both. Bugged from stem to gudgeon, Prescott men in front, back, on the sides, and up in the trees. I'll be right over.'

'But wait …!'

'Relax. D'you think they can outsmart *me*? I know more about bugging – and de-bugging – than Prescott and his dicks ever will learn.'

In Brookings' office DuQuesne told, with saturnine amusement, of the devices he had rigged to misinform the private eyes. He listened to Brookings' recital of failure.

Then he said, 'I knew you'd louse it up, so I've been making some plans of my own. One thing, though, I want limpidly clear. From now on I give the orders. Right?

'Get me a helicopter just like Crane's. Get a hophead six feet tall that weighs about a hundred and sixty pounds. Give him a three-hour jolt. Have them at the field two hours from now.'

'Can do.'

DuQuesne was at the field on time. So were the flying machine and the unconscious man. Both were exactly what he had ordered. He took off, climbed swiftly, made a wide circle to the west and north.

Shiro and the two guards, hearing the roar of engines, looked up and saw what they supposed to be Crane's helicopter coming down in a vertical drop. Slowing at the last possible second, it taxied up the field toward them. A man, recognizable as Seaton by his suit and physique, stood up, shouted hoarsely, pointed to the lean, still form beside him, beckoned frantically with both arms, then slumped down, completely inert.

All three rushed up to help.

There were three silenced reports and three men dropped.

DuQuesne leaped lightly out of the 'copter and scanned the three bodies. The two guards were dead, but Shiro, to his chagrin, showed faint signs of life. But very faint – he wouldn't live long.

He put on gloves, went into the house, blew the safe and rifled it. He found the vial of solution, but could find neither the larger bottle nor any reference to it. He then searched the house, from attic to basement. He found the vault, carefully concealed though its steel door was; but even he could do nothing about that. Nor was there any need, he decided, as he stood staring at it, the only change in his expression being a slight narrowing of the eyes in concentrated thought. The bulk of that solution was probably in the heaviest, deepest, safest vault in the country.

He returned to the helicopter. In a short time he was back in his own room, poring over blueprints and notebooks.

Coming in in the dusk, Crane and Seaton both began to worry when they saw that their landing lights were not burning. They made a bumpy landing and hurried toward the house. They heard a faint moan and turned, Seaton whipping out his flashlight with one hand his automatic with the other. He hastily replaced the weapon and bent over Shiro, a touch having assured him that the other two were beyond help. They picked Shiro up and carried him into his own room. While Seaton applied first-aid treatment to the ghastly wound in Shiro's head, Crane called a surgeon, the coroner, the police, and finally Prescott, with whom he held a long conversation.

Having done all they could for the injured man, they stood by his bedside, their anger all the more deadly for being silent. Seaton stood with every muscle tense. His right hand, white-knuckled, gripped the butt of his pistol, while under his left the heavy brass rail of the bed began slowly to bend. Crane stood impassive, but his face white and every feature hard as marble. Seaton was the first to speak.

'Mart,' he gritted, husky with fury, 'a man who could leave another man dying like that ain't a man at all – he's a thing. I'll shoot him with the biggest charge we've got … No, I won't, either, I'll take him apart with my bare hands.'

'We'll find him, Dick.' Crane's voice was low, level, deadly. 'That is one thing money can do.'

The tension was relieved by the arrival of the surgeon and nurses, who set to work with the deftness and precision of their highly-specialized crafts. After a time the doctor turned to Crane.

'Merely a scalp wound, Mr Crane. He should be up in a few days.'

The police, Prescott, and the coroner arrived in that order. There was a great deal of bustling, stirring about, and investigating, some of which was profitable. There were many guesses and a few sound deductions.

And Crane offered a reward of one million tax-paid dollars for information leading to the arrest and conviction of the murderer.

IX

Prescott, after a sleepless night, joined Crane and Seaton at breakfast.

'What do you make of it?' Crane asked.

'Very little, at present. Whoever did it had exactly detailed knowledge of your movements.'

'Check. And you know what that means. The third guard, the one that escaped.'

'Yes.' The great detective's face grew grim. 'The trouble will be proving it on him.'

'Second, he was your size and build, Seaton; close enough to fool Shiro, and that would have to be ungodly close.'

'DuQuesne. For all the tea in China, it was DuQuesne.'

'Third, he was an expert safecracker, and that alone lets DuQuesne out. That's just as much of a specialty as yours is, and he did a beautiful job on that safe – really beautiful.'

'I *still* won't buy it,' Seaton insisted. 'Don't forget that DuQuesne's a living encyclopedia and as much smarter than any yegg as I am than that tomcat over there. He could study safe-blowing fifteen minutes and be top man in the field; and he's got guts enough to supply a regiment.'

'Fourth, it *couldn't* have been DuQuesne. Everything out there is bugged and we've had him under continuous observation. I know exactly where he has been, every minute.'

'You *think* you do,' Seaton corrected. 'He knows more about electricity than the guy who invented it. I'm going to ask you a question. Have you ever got a man into his house?'

'Well … no, not exactly … but that isn't necessary, these days.'

'It might be, in this case. But don't try it. Unless I'm wronger than wrong, you won't.'

'I'm afraid so,' Prescott agreed. 'But you're softening me up for something, Seaton. What is it?'

'This.' Seaton placed an object-compass on the table. 'I set this on him late last night, and he didn't leave his house all night – which may or may not mean a thing. That end of that needle will point at him from now on, wherever he goes and whatever comes between, and as far as I know – and I bashfully admit that I know all that's known about the thing – it can't be debugged. If you want to *really* know where DuQuesne is, take this and watch it. Top secret, of course.'

'Of course. I'll be glad to … but how on Earth can a thing like that work?'

After an explanation that left the common-sense-minded detective as much in the dark as before, Prescott left.

Late that evening, he joined his men at DuQuesne's house. Everything was quiet. The scientist was in his study; the speakers registered the usual faint sounds of a man absorbed in work. But after a time, and while a speaker emitted the noise of rustling papers, the needle began to move slowly – downward. Simultaneously, the shadow of his unmistakable profile was thrown upon the window shade as he apparently crossed the room.

'Can't you hear him walk?' Prescott demanded.

'No. Heavy rugs – and for such a big man, he walks very lightly.'

Prescott watched the needle in amazement as it dipped deeper and deeper; straight down and then behind him; as though DuQuesne had actually walked right under him! He did not quite know whether to believe it or not, nevertheless, he followed the pointing needle. It led him beside Park Road, down the hill, straight toward the long bridge which forms one entrance to Rock Creek Park. Prescott left the road and hid behind a clump of shrubbery.

The bridge trembled under the passage of a high-speed automobile, which slowed down abruptly. DuQuesne, carrying a roll of papers, scrambled up from beneath the bridge and boarded it, whereupon it resumed speed. It was of a popular make and color; and its license plates were so smeared with dirt that not even their color could be seen. The needle now pointed steadily at the distant car.

Prescott ran back to his men.

'Get your car,' he told one of them. 'I'll tell you where to drive as we go.'

In the automobile, Prescott issued instructions by means of surreptitious glances at the compass concealed in his hand. The destination proved to be the residence of Brookings, the general manager of World Steel. Prescott told his operative to park the car somewhere and stand by; he himself settled down on watch.

After four hours a small car bearing a license number of a distant state – which was found later to be unknown to the authorities of that state – drove up; and the hidden watchers saw DuQuesne, without the papers, step into it. Knowing now what to expect, the detectives drove at high speed to the Park Road bridge and concealed themselves.

The car came up to the bridge and stopped. DuQuesne got out of it – it was too dark to recognize him by eye, but the needle pointed straight at him – and half-walked, half-slid down the embankment. He stood, a dark outline against the gray abutment. He lifted one hand above his head; a black rectangle engulfed his outline; the abutment became again a solid gray.

With his flashlight Prescott traced the almost imperceptible crack of the hidden door, and found the concealed button which DuQuesne had pressed. He did not press the button, but, deep in thought, went home to get a few hours of sleep before reporting to Crane next morning.

Both men were waiting when he appeared. Shiro, with a heavily-bandaged head, had insisted that he was perfectly able to work, and was ceremoniously ordering out of the kitchen the man who had been hired to take his place.

'Well, gentlemen, your compass did the trick,' and Prescott reported in full.

'I'd like to beat him to death with a club,' Seaton said, savagely. 'The chair's too good for him.'

'Not that he is in much danger of the chair.' Crane's expression was wry.

'Why, we know he did it! Surely we can prove it?'

'Knowing a thing and proving it to a jury are two entirely different breeds of cats. We haven't a shred of evidence. If we asked for an indictment we'd be laughed out of court. Check, Mr Crane?'

'Check.'

'I've bucked Steel before. They account for half my business, and for ninety-nine percent of my failures. The same thing goes for all the other agencies in town. The cops have hit them time after time with everything they've got, and simply bounced. So has the F.B.I. All any of us has been able to get is an occasional small fish.'

'You think it's hopeless, then?'

'Not exactly. I'll keep on working, on my own. I owe them something for killing my men, as well as for other favors they've done me in the past. But I don't believe in holding out false hopes.'

'Optimistic cuss, ain't he?' Seaton remarked as Prescott went out.

'He has cause to be, Dick. Report has it that they use murder, arson, and anything else useful in getting what they want; but they have not been caught yet.'

'Well, now that we know, we're in the clear. They can't possibly get a monopoly—'

'No? You aren't getting the point. If we should both happen to die – accidentally, of course – then what?'

'They couldn't get away with it, Mart; you're too big. I'm small fry, but you are M. Reynolds Crane.'

'No good, Dick; no good at all. Jets still crash; and so, occasionally, do egg-beaters. Worse – it does not seem to have occurred to you that World Steel is making the heavy forgings and plates for the *Skylark*.'

'Hades' – brazen – bells!' Seaton was dumbfounded. 'And what – if anything – can we do about *that?*'

'Very little, until after the parts get here, beyond investigating independent sources of supply.'

DuQuesne and Brookings met in the Perkins Café.

'How did your independent engineers like the power plant?'

'The report was very favorable, doctor. The stuff is all you said it was. But until we get the rest of the solution – by the way, how is the search for more X progressing?'

'Just as I told you it would – flat zero. X *can't* exist naturally on any planet having any significant amount of copper. Either the copper will go or the planet will, or both. Seaton's X was meteoric. It was all in one lot of platinum; and probably that one X meteor was all there ever was. However, the boys are still looking, just in case.'

'Well, we'd have to get Seaton's, some day, anyway. Have you decided how to get it?'

'No. That solution is in the safest safe-deposit vault in the world, probably in Crane's name, and both keys to that box are in another one, and so on, *ad infinitum*. He's got to get it *himself*, and *willingly*. Not that it'd be any easier to force Seaton; but can you imagine anything strong enough to make M. Reynolds cave in now?'

'I can't say that I can … no. But you remarked once that your forte is direct action. How about talking with Perkins … no, he flopped on three tries.'

'Yes, call him in. It's on execution he's weak, not planning. I'm not.'

Perkins was called in, and studied the problem for many minutes. Finally he said, 'There's only one way. We'll have to get a handle …'

'Don't be a fool!' DuQuesne snapped. 'You can't get a thing on either of them – not even a frame!'

'You misunderstand, doctor. You can get a handle on any man living, if you know enough about him. Not necessarily in his past; present or future is oftentimes better. Money … power … position … fame … women – have you considered women in this case?'

'Women, bah!' DuQuesne snorted. 'Crane's been chased so long he's woman-proof, and Seaton is worse. He's engaged to Dorothy Vaneman, so he's stone blind.'

'Better and better. There's your perfect handle, gentlemen; not only to the solution, but to everything else you want after Seaton and Crane have been taken out of circulation.'

Brookings and DuQuesne looked at each other in perplexity. Then DuQuesne said, 'All right, Perkins, after the way I popped off I'm perfectly willing to let you have a triumph. Draw us a sketch.'

'Build a spaceship from Seaton's own plans and carry her off in it. Take her up out of sight – of course you'll have to have plenty of witnesses that it was a spaceship and that it did go straight up out of sight – then hide her in one of our places – say with the Spencer girl – then tell Seaton and Crane she's on Mars and will stay there till she rots if they don't come across. They'll wilt – and they wouldn't dare take a story like that to the cops. Any holes in that?'

'Not that I can see at the moment …' Brookings drummed his fingers abstractedly on the desk. 'Would it make any difference if they chased us in their ship – in the condition it will be in?'

'Not a bit,' DuQuesne declared. 'All the better – they'll be gone, and in a wreck that will be so self-explanatory that nobody would think of making a metallurgical post-mortem.'

'That's true. Who's going to drive the ship?'

'I am,' DuQuesne said. 'I'll need help, though. One man from the inner circle. You or Perkins. Perkins, I'd say.'

'Is it safe?' Perkins asked.

'Absolutely. It's worked out to the queen's taste.'

'I'll go along, then. Is that all?'

No,' Brookings replied. 'You mentioned Spencer. Haven't you got that stuff away from her yet?'

'No, she's stubborn as a mule.'

'Time's running out. Take her along, and don't bring her back. We'll get the stuff back some other way.'

Perkins left the room; and after a long discussion of details, DuQuesne and Brookings left the restaurant, each by a different route.

X

The great steel forgings which were to form the framework of the *Skylark* arrived and were hauled into the testing room, where ralium-capsule X-raying revealed flaws in every member. Seaton, after mapping the imperfections by orthometric projection, spent an hour with calipers and slide rule.

'Strong enough to stand shipment and fabrication, and maybe a little to spare – perhaps one G of acceleration while we're in the air. Any real shot of power, though, or any sudden turn, and *pop*! She collapses like a soap bubble. Want to recheck my figures?'

'No. I told you not to bother about analysis. We want sound metal, not junk.'

'Ship 'em back, then – with an inspector?'

'No.' At Seaton's look of surprise, Crane went on. 'I've been thinking about this possibility for a long time. If we reject these forgings, they will – immediately – try to kill us some other way; and they may well succeed. On the other hand, if we go ahead all unsuspectingly and use them, they will let us alone until the *Skylark* is done. That will give us months of free, undisturbed time. Expensive time, I grant; but worth every dollar.'

'Maybe so. As the money man, you're the judge of that. But we *can't* fly a heap of scrap, Mart!'

'No, but while we are going ahead with this just as though we meant it, we can build another one, about four times its size, in complete secrecy.'

'Mart! You're talking like a man with a paper nose! How d'you figure on keeping stuff *that* size secret from Steel?'

'It can be done. I know a chap who owns a steel mill – so insignificant, relatively speaking, that he has not been bought out or frozen out by Steel. I have helped him out from time to time, and he assures me that he will be glad to cooperate. We will not be able to oversee much of the work ourselves, which is a drawback. However, we can get MacDougall to do it for us.'

'MacDougall? The man who built Intercontinental? He wouldn't touch a little job like this with a pole!'

'On the contrary, he is keen on doing it. It means building the first spaceship, you know.'

'He's too big to disappear, I'd think. Wouldn't Steel follow him up?'

'They never have, a few times when he and I have been out of touch with civilization for three months at a time.'

'Well, it would cost more than our whole capital.'

'No more talk of money, Dick. Your contribution to the firm is worth more than everything I have.'

'Hokay – if that's the way you want it, it tickles me like I'd swallowed an ostrich feather … and I can't think of any more objections. Four times the size – wheeeeekity-wheek! A two-hundred-pound bar – k-z-r-e-e-p-t-POWIE!

'And why don't we built an attractor – a thing like an object-compass except with a ten-pound bar instead of a needle, so if anything chases us in space we can reach out and shake the whey out of it – or machine guns shooting Mark Ones-to-Tens through pressure gaskets in the walls? I just bodaciously do NOT relish the prospect of fleeing from a gaggle of semi-intelligent alien monstrosities merely because I got nothing bigger than a rifle to fight back with.'

'All you have to do is design them, Dick; and that shouldn't be too hard. But, speaking of emergencies, the power plant should really have a very large factor of safety. Four hundred pounds, say, and everything in duplicate, from power-bars to push-buttons?'

'I'll buy that.'

Work was soon begun on the huge steel shell in the independent steel plant under the direct supervision of MacDougall by men who had been in his employ for years. While it was being built, Seaton and Crane went ahead with the construction of the original spaceship. Practically all of their time, however, was spent in perfecting the many essential things that were to go into the real *Skylark*.

Thus they did not know that to the flawed members there were being attached faulty plates by imperfect welding. Nor could they have detected the poor workmanship by any ordinary inspection, for it was being done by a picked crew of experts, picked by Perkins. To make things even, Steel did not know that the many peculiar instruments installed by Seaton and Crane were not exactly what they should have been.

In due course 'The Cripple'– a name which Seaton soon shortened to 'Old Crip'– was finished. The foreman overheard a conversation between Crane and Seaton in which it was decided not to start for a couple of weeks, as they *had* to work out some kind of a book of navigation tables. Prescott reported that Steel was still sitting on its hands, waiting for the first flight. Word came from MacDougall that the *Skylark* was ready. Crane and Seaton went somewhere in the helicopter 'to make a few final tests.'

A few nights later a huge ball landed on Crane Field. It moved lightly, easily, betraying its thousands of tons of weight only by the hole it made in the hard-beaten ground. Seaton and Crane sprang out.

Dorothy and her father were waiting. Seaton caught her up and kissed her vigorously. Then, a look of sheerest triumph on his face, he extended a hand to Vaneman.

'She flies! *How* she flies! We've been around the moon!'

'*What?*' Dorothy was shocked. 'Without even *telling me*? Why, I'd've been scared pea-green if I'd known!'

'That was why,' Seaton assured her. 'Now you won't have to worry next time we take off.'

'I will so,' she protested; but Seaton was listening to Vaneman.

'... it take?'

'Not quite an hour. We could have done it in much less time.' Crane's voice was calm, his face quiet; but to those who knew him so well, every feature showed emotion.

Both inventors were at the summit, moved more than either could have told by their achievement, by the success of the flyer upon which they had worked so long.

Shiro broke the tension by bowing until his head almost touched the floor. 'Sirs and lady, I impel myself to state this to be wonder extreme. If permitting, I shall delightful luxuriate in preparation suitable refreshment.'

Permission granted, he trotted away and the engineers invited the visitors to inspect their new craft.

Although Dorothy knew what to expect, from plans and drawings and from her own knowledge of 'Old Crip,' she caught her breath as she looked about the brilliantly lighted interior of the great sky-rover.

It was a spherical shell of hardened steel of great thickness, some forty feet in diameter. Its true shape was not readily apparent from inside, as it was divided into levels and compartments by decks and walls. In its center was a spherical structure of girders and beams. Inside this structure was a similar one which, on smooth but immensely strong universal bearings, was free to revolve in any direction. This inner sphere was filled with machinery surrounding a shining copper cylinder.

Six tremendous fabricated columns radiated outward; branching in maximum-strength design out into the hull. The floor was heavily upholstered and was not solid; the same was true of the dozen or more seats built in various places. There were two instrument boards, upon which tiny lights flashed and plate glass, plastic and metal gleamed.

Both Vanemans began to ask questions and Seaton showed them the principal features of the novel vessel. Crane accompanied them in silence, enjoying their pleasure, glorying in the mighty ship of space.

Seaton called attention to the great size and strength of one of the lateral supporting columns, then led them over to the vertical column that pierced the floor. Enormous as the lateral was, it appeared puny beside this monster of fabricated steel. Seaton explained that the two verticals had to be much stronger than the four laterals, as the center of gravity of the ship had been placed lower than its geometrical center, so that the apparent motion of the vessel would always be upward. Resting one hand caressingly upon the huge member, he explained exultantly that it was the ultimately last word in strength made of the strongest known high-tensile, heat-treated, special-alloy steel.

'But why go to such an extreme?' the lawyer asked. 'It looks as though it could support a bridge.'

'It could. It'll have to, if we ever really cut loose with the power. Have you got any idea of how fast this thing can fly?'

'I have heard you talk of approaching the velocity of light, but that's a little overdrawn, isn't it?'

'Not a bit. If it wasn't for Einstein and his famous theory we could develop an acceleration twice as great as one light-velocity. As it is, we're going to see how close we can crowd it – and it'll be close, believe me. Out in space, that is. In air we'll be limited to three or four times sound, in spite of all we could do in the line of heat-exchangers and refrigeration.'

'But, from what I read about jets, ten gravities for ten minutes can be fatal.'

'That's right. But these floors are special, and those seats are infinitely more so. That was one of our hardest jobs; designing supporting surfaces to hold a man safe through forces that would ordinarily flatten him out into a thin layer of goo.'

'I see. How are you going to steer? And how about stable reference planes to steer by? Or are you merely going to head for Mars or Venus or Neptune or Aldebaran as the case may be?'

'That wouldn't be so good. We thought for a while we'd have to, but Mart licked it. The power plant is entirely separate from the ship, inside that inner sphere, about which the outer sphere and the ship itself are free to revolve. Even if the ship rolls or pitches, the bar stays right where it is pointed. Those six big jackets cover gyroscopes, which keep the outer sphere in exactly the same position—'

'Relative to what?' Vaneman asked. 'It seems to have moved since we came in … Yes, if you look closely, you can see it move.'

'Naturally. Um … m. Never thought of it from that angle – just that its orientation isn't affected by either the ship or the power plant. If you want to pin me down, though, it's oriented solidly to the three dimensions of the steel plant at the time MacDougall got the gyroscopes up to holding speed. Since that doesn't mean much here and now, I'd say, as an approximation, that it is locked to the fixed stars. Or, rather, to the effective mass of the galaxy as a whole …'

'*Please*, Dick,' Dorothy interrupted. 'Enough of the jargon. Show us the important things – kitchen, bedrooms, bath.'

Seaton did so, explaining in detail some of the many differences between living on Earth and in a small, necessarily self-sufficient worldlet out in airless, lightless, heatless space.

'Oh, I'm just wild to go out with you, Dick. When will you take me?'

'Very soon, Dottie. Just as soon as we're sure we've got all the bugs ironed out. You'll be our first passenger, so help me.'

'How do you see out? How about air and water? How do you keep warm, or cool, as the case may be?' Vaneman fired the questions as though he were cross-examining a witness. 'No, excuse me; you've already mentioned the heaters and refrigerators.'

'The pilots see outside, the whole sphere of vision, by means of special instruments, something like periscopes but vastly different – electronic. Passengers can see out by uncovering windows – they're made of fused quartz. We carry air – oxygen, nitrogen, helium and argon – in tanks, although we won't need much new air because of our purifiers and recovery units. We also have oxygen-generating apparatus aboard, for emergencies.'

'We carry water enough to last us three months – or indefinitely if necessary, as we can recover all waste water as chemically pure H_2O. Anything else?'

'You'd better give up, dad,' Dorothy advised, laughing. 'It's perfectly safe for me to go along!'

'It seems to be. But it's getting pretty well along toward morning, Dorothy, and if any of us are to get any sleep at all tonight you and I should go home.'

'That's so, and I'm the one who has been screaming at Dick about going to bed every night at eleven. I'll go powder my nose – I'll be right back.'

Vaneman said, after Dorothy had gone. 'You mentioned "bugs" only in a very light and passing way.'

'And you didn't mention them at all,' Seaton countered.

'Naturally not,' with a jerk of his head in the direction his daughter had taken. 'How did it *really* go, boys?'

'Wonderful, really—' Dick began to enthuse.

'*You* tell me, Martin.'

'In the main, very well. Of course this was a very short flight, but we found nothing wrong with the engines or their controls; we are fairly certain that no major alterations will be necessary. The optical system needs some more work; the attractors and repellors are not at all what they should be in either accuracy or delicacy. The rifles work perfectly. The air-purifiers do not remove all odors, but the air after purification is safe to breathe and physiologically adequate. The water-recovery system does not work at all – it delivers sewage.'

'Well, that's not too serious, with all the water you carry.'

'No, but it malfunctions so grossly that some mistake was made – obviously. It should be easy to find and to fix. For a thing so new, we both are very well satisfied with its performance.'

'You're ready for Steel, then? I don't know what they'll do when they find out that you don't intend to do anything with "Old Crip," but they'll do something.'

'I hope they blow their stacks,' Seaton said, grimly. 'We're ready for 'em, with a lot of stuff they never heard of and won't like a little bit. Give us four or five days to straighten out the bugs Mart told you about – then let 'em do anything they want to.'

XI

The afternoon following the home-coming of the *Skylark,* Seaton and Dorothy returned from a long horseback ride in the park. After Seaton had mounted his motorcycle, Dorothy turned toward a bench in the shade of an old elm to watch a game of tennis on the court next door. Scarcely had she seated herself when a great copper-plated ball landed directly in front of her. A heavy steel door snapped open and a powerful figure clad in leather leapt out. The man's face and eyes were covered by his helmet flaps and amber goggles.

Dorothy leaped to her feet with a shriek – Seaton had just left her and this spaceship was far too small to be the *Skylark* – it was the counterpart of 'Old Crip,' which, she knew, could never fly. As these thoughts raced through her she screamed again and turned in flight; but the stranger caught her in three strides and she found herself helpless in a pair of arms as strong as Seaton's.

Picking her up lightly, DuQuesne carried her over the lawn to his spaceship. Dorothy screamed wildly as she found that her fiercest struggles made no impression on her captor. Her clawing nails glanced harmlessly off the glass and leather of his helmet; her teeth were equally ineffective against his leather coat.

With the girl in his arms, DuQuesne stepped into the vessel. The door clanged shut behind them. Dorothy caught a glimpse of another woman, tied tightly into one of the side seats.

'Tie her feet, Perkins,' DuQuesne ordered, holding her around the body so that her feet extended straight out in front of him. 'She's a fighting wildcat.'

As Perkins threw one end of a small rope around her ankles Dorothy doubled up her knees, drawing her feet as far away from him as she could. He stepped up carelessly and reached out to grasp her ankles. She straightened out, viciously driving her riding-boots into the pit of his stomach with all her strength.

It was a true solar-plexus blow; and, completely knocked out, Perkins staggered backward against the instrument board. His outflung arm pushed the power lever out to its last notch, throwing full current through the bar, which was pointed straight up as it had been when they made their landing.

There was the creak of fabricated steel stressed almost to its limit as the vessel shot upward with a tremendous velocity, and only the ultra-protective and super-resilient properties of the floor saved their lives as they were thrown flat upon it by the awful force of their acceleration.

The maddened space-ship tore through the thin layer of the Earth's atmosphere in instants – it was through it and into the almost-perfect vacuum of interplanetary space before the thick steel hull was even warmed through.

Dorothy lay flat upon her back, just as she had fallen, unable even to move her arms, gaining each breath by a terrible effort. Perkins was a huddled heap under the instrument board. The other captive, Brookings' ex-secretary, was in somewhat better case, as her bonds had snapped and she was lying in optimum position in one of the seats – forced into that position and held there, as the designer of those seats had intended. She, like Dorothy, was gasping for breath, her straining muscles barely able to force air into her lungs because of the paralyzing weight of her chest.

DuQuesne alone was able to move, and it required all of his Herculean strength to creep and crawl, snakelike, toward the instrument board. Finally, attaining his goal, he summoned all his strength to grasp, not the controlling lever, which he knew was beyond his reach, but a cutout switch only a couple of feet above his head. With a series of convulsive movements he fought his way up, first until he was crouching on elbows and knees, then into a squatting position. Then, placing his left hand under his right, he made a last supreme effort. Perspiration streamed from his face; his muscles stood out in ridges visible even under the heavy leather of his coat; his lips parted in a snarl over his locked teeth as he threw every ounce of his powerful body into an effort to force his right hand up to that switch. His hand approached it slowly – closed over it – pulled it out.

The result was startling. With the terrific power instantly cut off, and with not even the ordinary force of gravity to counteract the force DuQuesne was exerting, his own muscular effort hurled him upward, toward the center of the ship and against the instrument board. The switch, still in his grasp, was again closed. His shoulder crashed against the knobs which controlled the direction of the power-bar, swinging it through a wide arc. As the ship darted off in a new direction with all its former acceleration he was hurled back against the board, tearing one end loose from its supports, and falling unconscious to the floor on the other side. After what seemed like an eternity, Dorothy and the other girl felt their senses slowly leave them.

With its four unconscious passengers the ship hurtled through empty space, its already inconceivable velocity being augmented every second by a quantity almost equal to the velocity of light – driven furiously onward by the prodigious power of the disintegrating copper bar.

*

Seaton had gone only a short distance from his sweetheart's home when, over the purring of his engine, he thought he heard Dorothy scream. He did not wait to make sure, but whirled his machine around and its purring changed to a bellowing roar as he opened the throttle. Gravel flew under skidding wheels as he made the turn into the Vaneman grounds at suicidal speed. He arrived at the scene just in time to see the door of the spaceship close. Before he could reach it the vessel disappeared, with nothing to mark its departure except a violent whirl of grass and sod, uprooted and carried high into the air by the vacuum of its wake. To the excited tennis players and the screaming mother of the abducted girl it seemed as though the great metal ball had vanished utterly. Only Seaton traced the line of debris in the air and saw, for a fraction of an instant, an infinitesimal black dot in the sky before it disappeared.

Interrupting the clamor of the young people, each of whom was trying to tell him what had happened, he spoke to Mrs Vaneman rapidly but gently. 'Mother, Dottie's all right. Steel's got her, but they won't keep her long. Don't worry, we'll get her. It may be a week or it may take a year; but we'll bring her back!'

He leaped upon his motorcycle and shattered all speed laws on the way to Crane's house.

'Mart!' he yelled. 'They've got Dottie, in a ship made from our plans. Let's go!'

'Slow down – don't go off half-cocked. What do you plan?'

'Plan! Just chase 'em and kill 'em!'

'Which way did they go, and when?'

'Straight up. Full power. Twenty minutes ago.'

'Too long ago. Straight up has moved five degrees. They may have covered a million miles, or they may have come down only a few miles away. Sit down and think – use your brain.'

Seaton sat down and pulled out his pipe, fighting for self-possession. Then he jumped up and ran into his room, coming back with an object compass whose needle pointed upward.

'DuQuesne did it!' he cried, exultantly. 'This is still looking right at him. Now let's go, and snap it up!'

'Not yet. How far away are they?'

Seaton touched the stud that set the needle swinging and snapped on the millisecond timer. Both men watched in strained attention as second after second went by and the needle continued to oscillate. It finally came to rest and Crane punched keys on the computer.

'Three hundred and fifty million miles. Halfway out of the solar system. That means a constant acceleration of about one light.'

'Nothing *can* go that fast, Mart. E equals M C square.'

'Einstein's Theory is still a theory. This distance is an observed fact.'

'And theories are modified to fit facts. Hokay. He's out of control – something went haywire.'

'Undoubtedly.'

'We don't know how big a bar he's got, so we can't figure how long it'll take us to catch him. For Pete's sake, Mart, let's get at it!'

They hurried out to the *Skylark* and made a quick check. Seaton was closing the lock when Crane stopped him with a gesture toward the power plant.

'We have only four bars, Dick – two for each engine. It will take at least one to overtake them, and at least one to stop. If we expect to get back within our lifetime it will take the other two to get us back. Even with no allowance at all for the unexpected, we are short on power.'

Seaton, though furiously eager to be off, was stopped cold. 'Check. We'd better get a couple more – maybe four. We'd better load up on grub and X-plosive ammunition, too.'

'And water,' Crane added. 'Especially water.'

Seaton called the brass foundry. The manager took his order, but blandly informed him that there was not that much copper in the city, that it would be ten days or two weeks before such an order could be filled. Seaton suggested that they melt up some finished goods – bus bars and the like – price no object; but the manager was obdurate. He could not violate the priority rule.

Seaton then called other places, every place he could think of or find in the yellow pages, trying to buy anything made of copper. Bar – sheet – shapes – trolley wire – cable – house wire – *anything*. There was nothing available in any quantity large enough to be of any use.

After an hour of fruitless telephoning he reported, in fulminating language, to Crane.

'I'm not too surprised. Steel might not want us to have too much copper.'

Sparks almost shot from Seaton's eyes. 'I'm going to see Brookings. He'll give me some copper or a few of the atoms of his carcass will land in Andromeda.' He started for the door.

'No, Dick, *no!*' Crane seized Seaton by the arm. 'That wouldn't – couldn't – get us anything except indefinite delay.'

'What else, then? How?'

'We can be at Wilson's in five minutes. He has some copper on hand, and can get more. The *Skylark* is ready to travel.'

In a few minutes they were in the office of the plant in which their vessel had been built. When they had made their wants known the ironmaster shook his head.

'I'm sorry, but I don't think I've got over a hundred pounds of copper in the place, and no non-ferrous equipment …

Seaton started to explode, but Crane silenced him and told Wilson the whole story.

Wilson slammed his fist down onto his desk and roared, 'I'll get copper if I have to tear the roof off the church!' Then, more quietly, 'We'll have to cobble up a furnace and crucible … and hand-make patterns and molds … and borrow a big lathe … but you'll get your bars just as fast as I can possibly get them out.'

Two days passed before the gleaming copper cylinders were ready. During this time Crane added to their equipment every article for which he could conceive any possible use, while Seaton raged up and down in a black fury of impatience. While the bars were being loaded they made another reading on the object compass. Their faces grew tense and their hearts turned sick as minute followed minute and the needle still would not settle down. Finally, however, it came to rest. Seaton's voice almost failed him as he said, 'About two hundred and thirty-five light-years. Couldn't nail the exact end-point, but that's fairly close. They're lost like nobody was ever lost before. So long, guy.' He held out his hand. 'It's been mighty nice knowing you. Tell Vaneman if I come back I'll bring her with me.'

Crane refused the hand. 'Since when am I not going along, Dick?'

'As of just now. No sense in it. If Dottie's gone I'm going too; but M. Reynolds Crane very positively is not.'

'Nonsense. This is somewhat further than we had planned for the first trip, but there is no real difference. It is just as safe to go a thousand light-years as one, and we have ample supplies. In any event, I am going.'

'Who do you think you're kidding? … Thanks, ace.' This time, hands met in a crushing grip. 'You're worth three of me.'

'I'll call Vaneman,' Crane said, hastily.

He did not tell the lawyer the truth, or any close approximation of it – merely that the chase would probably be longer than had been supposed, that communication could very well be impossible, that they would in all probability be gone a long time, and that he could not even guess at how long that time would be.

They closed the locks and took off. Seaton crowded on power until Crane, reading the prometers, warned him to cut back – the skin was getting too hot.

Free of atmosphere, Seaton again advanced the lever, notch by notch, until he could no longer support the weight of his hand, but had to resort to the arm-support designed for that emergency. He pushed the lever a few notches farther, and was forced violently down into his seat, which had automatically moved upward so that his hand still controlled the ratchet handle. Still he kept the ratchet clicking, until he knew that he could not endure much more.

'How … you … coming?' he wheezed into his microphone. He could not really talk.

'Paas … s … sing … ou … u … t.' Crane's reply was barely audible. 'If …

f … y … y … o … uu … c … c … ss … t … a … n … g … g … o … a … h …
e … d … d …

Seaton cut back a few notches. 'How about this?'

'I can take this much, I think. I was right on the edge.'

'I'll let her ride here, then. How long?'

'Four or five hours. Then we had better eat and take another reading.'

'All right. Talking's too much work, so if it gets too much for you, yell while you still can. I'm sure glad we're on our way at last.'

XII

For forty-eight hours the uncontrolled engine dragged DuQuesne's vessel through the empty reaches of space with an awful and constantly-increasing velocity. Then, when only a few traces of copper remained, the acceleration began to decrease. Floor and seats began to return to their normal positions. When the last particle of copper was gone, the ship's speed became constant. Apparently motionless to those inside her, she was in reality moving with a velocity thousands of times greater than that of light.

DuQuesne was the first to gain control of himself. His first effort to get up lifted him from the floor and he floated lightly upward to the ceiling, striking it with a gentle bump and remaining, motionless and unsupported, in the air. The others, none of whom had attempted to move, stared at him in amazement.

DuQuesne reached out, clutched a hand-grip, and drew himself down to the floor. With great caution he removed his suit, transferring two automatic pistols as he did so. By feeling gingerly of his body he found that no bones were broken. Only then did he look around to see how his companions were faring.

They were all sitting up and holding onto something. The girls were resting quietly; Perkins was removing his leather costume.

'Good morning, Dr DuQuesne. Something must have happened when I kicked your friend.'

'Good morning, Miss Vaneman.' DuQuesne smiled, more than half in relief. 'Several things happened. He fell into the controls, turning on all the juice, and we left considerably faster than I intended to. I tried to get control, but couldn't. Then we all went to sleep and just woke up.'

'Have you any idea where we are?'

No … but I can make a fair estimate.' He glanced at the empty chamber where the copper cylinder had been; took out notebook, pencil, and slide rule; and figured for minutes.

He then drew himself to one of the windows and stared out, then went to another window, and another. He seated himself at the crazily-tilted control board and studied it. He worked the computer for a few moments.

'I don't know exactly what to make of this,' he told Dorothy, quietly. 'Since the power was on exactly forty-eight hours, we should not be more than two light-days away from our sun. However, we certainly are. I could recognize at least some of the fixed stars and constellations from anywhere within a light-year or so of Sol, and I can't find even one familiar thing. Therefore we must have been accelerating all the time. We must be somewhere in the neighbor-hood of two hundred thirty-seven light-years away from home. For you two who don't know what a light-year is, about six quadrillion – six thousand million million – miles.'

Dorothy's face turned white; Margaret Spencer fainted; Perkins merely gog-gled, his face working convulsively. 'Then we'll never get back?' Dorothy asked.

'I wouldn't say that—'

'You got us into this!' Perkins screamed, and leaped at Dorothy, murder-ous fury in his glare, his fingers curved into talons. Instead of reaching her, however, he merely sprawled grotesquely in the air. DuQuesne, bracing one foot against the wall and seizing a hand-grip with his left hand, knocked Perkins clear across the room with one blow of his right.

'None of that, louse,' DuQuesne said, evenly. 'One more wrong move out of you and I'll throw you out. It isn't her fault we're here, it's our own. And mostly yours – if you'd had three brain cells working she couldn't have kicked you. But that's past. The only thing of interest now is getting back.'

'But we can't get back.' Perkins whimpered. 'The power's gone, the controls are wrecked, and you just said you're lost.'

'I did not.' DuQuesne's voice was icy. 'What I said was that I don't know where we are – a different statement entirely.'

'Isn't that a distinction without a difference?' Dorothy asked acidly.

'By no means, Miss Vaneman. I can repair the control board. I have two extra power-bars. One of them, with direction exactly reversed, will stop us, relative to the Earth. I'll burn half of the last one, then coast until, by recog-nizing fixed stars and triangulating them, I can fix our position. I will then know where our solar system is and will go there. In the meantime, I suggest that we have something to eat.'

'A beautiful and timely thought!' Dorothy exclaimed. 'I'm famished. Where's your refrigerator? But something else comes first. I'm a mess, and she must be, too. Where's our room … that is, we *have a* room?'

'Yes. That one, and there's the galley, over there. We're cramped, but you'll be able to make out. Let me say, Miss Vaneman, that I really admire your nerve. I didn't expect that lunk to disintegrate the way he did, but I thought you girls might. Miss Spencer will, yet, unless you …

'I'll try to. I'm scared, of course, but falling apart won't help … and we've simply *got* to get back.'

'We will. Two of us, at least.'

Dorothy nudged the other girl, who had not paid any attention to anything around her, and led her along a hand-rail. As she went, she could not help but think – with more than a touch of admiration – of the man who had abducted her. Calm, cool, master of himself and the situation, disregarding completely the terrible bruises that disfigured half his face and doubtless half his body as well – she admitted to herself that it was only his example which had enabled her to maintain her self-control.

As she crawled over Perkins' suit she remembered that he had not taken any weapons from it, and a glance assured her that Perkins was not watching her. She searched it quickly, finding two automatics. She noted with relief that they were standard .45's and stuck them into her pockets.

In the room, Dorothy took one look at the other girl, then went to the galley and back.

'Here, swallow this,' she ordered.

The girl did so. She shuddered uncontrollably, but did begin to come to life.

'That's better. Now, snap out of it,' Dorothy said, sharply. 'We aren't dead and we aren't going to be.'

'I am,' came the wooden reply. 'You don't know that beast Perkins.'

'I do so. And better yet, I know things that neither DuQuesne nor that Perkins even guess. Two of the smartest men that ever lived are on our tail, and when they catch up with us … well, I wouldn't be in their *shoes* for *anything*.'

'What?' Dorothy's confident words and bearing, as much as the potent pill, were taking effect. The strange girl was coming back rapidly to sanity and normality. 'Not *really*?'

'Really. We've got a lot to do, and we've got to clean up first. And with no weight … does it make you sick?'

'It did, dreadfully, but I've got nothing left to be sick with. Doesn't it you?'

'Not very much. I don't like it, but I'm getting used to it. And I don't suppose you know anything about it.'

'No. All I can feel is that I'm falling, and it's almost unbearable.'

'It isn't pleasant. I've studied it a lot – in theory – and the boys say all you've got to do is forget that falling sensation. Not that I've been able to do it but I'm still trying. The first thing's a bath, and then –'

'A bath! *Here? How?*'

'Sponge-bath. I'll show you. Then … they brought along quite a lot of clothes to fit me, and you're just about my size ... and you'll look nice in green ...'

After they had put themselves to rights, Dorothy said, 'That's a *lot* better.' Each girl looked at the other, and each liked what she saw.

The stranger was about twenty-two, with heavy, wavy black hair. Her eyes were a rich, deep brown; her skin clear, smooth ivory. Normally a beautiful girl, thought Dorothy, even though she was now thin, haggard and worn.

'Let's get acquainted before we do anything else,' she said. 'I'm Margaret Spencer, formerly private secretary to His High Mightiness, Brookings of Steel. They swindled my father out of an invention worth millions and then killed him. I got the job to see if I could prove it, but I didn't get much evidence before they caught me. So, after two months of things you wouldn't believe, here I am. Talking never would have done me any good, and I'm certain it won't now. Perkins will kill me ... or maybe, if what you say is true, I should add "if he can." This is the first time I've had that much hope.'

'But how about Dr DuQuesne? Surely he wouldn't let him:'

'I've never met DuQuesne before, but from what I heard around the office, he's worse than Perkins – in a different way, of course. He's absolutely cold and utterly hard – a perfect fiend.'

'Oh, come, you're too hard on him. Didn't you see him knock Perkins down when he came after me?'

'No – or perhaps I did, in a dim sort of way. But that doesn't mean anything. He probably wants you left alive – of course that's it, since he went to all the trouble of kidnapping you. Otherwise he would have let Perkins do anything he wanted to with you, without lifting a finger.'

'I can't believe that.' Nevertheless, a chill struck at Dorothy's heart as she remembered the inhuman crimes attributed to the man. 'He has treated us with every consideration so far – let's hope for the best. Anyway, I'm sure we'll get back safely.'

'You keep saying that. What makes you so sure?'

'Well, I'm Dorothy Vaneman, and I'm engaged to Dick Seaton, the man who invented this spaceship, and I'm as sure as can be that he is chasing us right now.'

'But that's just what they want!' Margaret exclaimed. 'I heard some Top Secret stuff about that. Your name and Seaton's brings it back to me. Their ship is rigged, some way or other, so it will blow up or something the first time they go anywhere!'

'That's what *they* think.' Dorothy's voice dripped scorn. 'Dick and his partner – you've heard of Martin Crane, of course?'

'I heard the name mentioned with Seaton's, but that's all.'

'Well, he's quite a wonderful inventor, and almost as smart as Dick is. Together they found out about that sabotage and built another ship that

Steel doesn't know anything about. Bigger and better and faster than this one.'

'That makes me feel better,' Margaret really brightened for the first time. 'No matter how rough this trip will be, it'll be a vacation for me now. If I only had a gun ...'

'Here,' and as Margaret stared at the proffered weapon, 'I've got another. I got them out of Perkins' suit.'

'Glory be!' Margaret fairly beamed. 'There is balm in Gilead, after all! Just watch, next time Perkins threatens to cut my heart out with his knife ... and we'd better go make those sandwiches, don't you think? And call me Peggy, please.'

'Will do, Peggy my dear – we're going to be great friends. And I'm Dot or Dottie to you.'

In the galley the girls set about making dainty sandwiches, but the going was very hard indeed. Margaret was particularly inept. Slices of bread went one way, bits of butter another, ham and sausage in several others. She seized two trays and tried to trap the escaping food between them – but in the attempt she released her hold and floated helplessly into the air.

'Oh, Dot, what'll we *do*, anyway?' she wailed. 'Everything wants to fly all over the place!'

'I don't quite know – I wish we had a bird-cage, so we could reach in and grab anything before it could escape. We'd better tie everything down, I guess, and let everybody come in and cut off a chunk of anything they want. But what I'm wondering about is drinking. I'm simply dying of thirst and I'm afraid to open this bottle.' She had a bottle of ginger ale clutched in her left hand, an opener in her right; one leg was hooked around a vertical rail. 'I'm afraid it'll go into a million drops and Dick says if you breathe them in you're apt to choke to death.'

'Seaton was right – as usual.' Dorothy whirled around. DuQuesne was surveying the room, a glint of amusement in his one sound eye. 'I wouldn't recommend playing with charged drinks while weightless. Just a minute – I'll get the net.'

He got it; and while he was deftly clearing the air of floating items of food he went on. 'Charged stuff could be murderous unless you're wearing a mask. Plain liquids you can drink through a straw, after you learn how. Your swallowing has got to be conscious and all muscular with no gravity. But what I came here for was to tell you I'm ready to put on one G of acceleration so we'll have normal gravity. I'll put it on easy, but watch it.'

'What a *heavenly* relief!' Margaret cried, when everything again stayed put. 'I never thought I'd ever be grateful for just being able to stand still in one place, did you?'

Preparing the meal was now of course simple enough. As the four ate,

Dorothy noticed that DuQuesne's left arm was almost useless and that he ate with difficulty because of his terribly bruised face. After the meal was done she went to the medicine chest and selected containers, swabs, and gauze.

'Come over here, doctor. First aid is indicated.'

'I'm all right ...' he began, but at her imperious gesture he got up carefully and came toward her.

'Your arm is lame. Where's the damage?'

'The shoulder is the worst. I rammed it through the board.'

'Take off your shirt and lie down here.'

He did so and Dorothy gasped at the extent and severity of the man's injuries.

'Will you get me some towels and hot water, please, Peggy?' She worked busily for minutes, bathing away clotted blood, applying antiseptics, and bandaging. 'Now for those bruises – I *never* saw anything like them before. I'm not really a nurse. What would you use? Tripidiagen or ...

'Amylophene. Massage it in as I move the arm.'

He did not wince and his expression did not change; but he began to sweat and his face turned white. She paused.

'Keep it up, nurse,' he directed, coolly. 'That stuff's murder in the first degree, but it does the job and it's fast.'

When she had finished and he was putting his shirt back on: 'Thanks, Miss Vaneman – thanks a lot. It feels a hundred per cent better already. But why did you do it? I'd think you'd want to bash me with that basin instead.'

'Efficiency.' She smiled. 'As our chief engineer it won't do to have you laid up.'

'Logical enough, in a way ... but ... I wonder ...'

She did not reply, but turned to Perkins.

'How are you, Mr Perkins? Do you require medical attention?'

'No,' Perkins growled. 'Keep away from me or I'll cut your heart out.'

'Shut up!' DuQuesne snapped.

'I haven't done anything!'

'Maybe it didn't quite constitute making a break, so I'll broaden the definition. If you can't talk like a man, keep still.'

'Lay off Miss Vaneman – thoughts, words, and actions. I'm in charge of her and I will have no interference whatever. This is your last warning.'

'How about Spencer, then?'

'She's your responsibility, not mine.'

An evil light appeared in Perkins' eyes. He took out a wicked-looking knife and began to strop it carefully on the leather of the seat, glaring at his victim the while.

Dorothy started to protest, but was silenced by a gesture from Margaret, who calmly took the pistol out of her pocket. She jerked the slide and held the weapon up on one finger. 'Don't worry about his knife. He's been sharpening it for my benefit for the last month. It doesn't mean a thing. But you shouldn't play with it so much, Perkins, you might be tempted to try to throw it. So drop it on the floor and kick it over here to me. Before I count three. One.' The heavy pistol steadied into line with his chest and her finger tightened on the trigger. 'Two.' Perkins obeyed and Margaret picked up the knife. 'Doctor!' Perkins appealed to DuQuesne, who had watched the scene unmoved, a faint smile upon his saturnine face. 'Why don't you shoot her? You won't sit there and *see me* murdered!'

'Won't I? It makes no difference to me which of you kills the other, or if you both do, or neither. You brought this on yourself. Anyone with any fraction of a brain doesn't leave guns lying around loose. You should have seen Miss Vaneman take them – I did.'

'You saw her take them and didn't warn me?' Perkins croaked.

'Certainly. If you can't take care of yourself I'm not going to take care of you. Especially after the way you bungled the job. I could have recovered the stuff she stole from that ass Brookings inside an hour.'

'How?' Perkins sneered. 'If you're so good, why did you have to come to me about Seaton and Crane?'

'Because my methods wouldn't work and yours would. It isn't on planning that you're weak, as I told Brookings – it's on execution.'

'Well, what are you going to *do* about her? Are you going to sit there and lecture all day?'

'I am going to do nothing whatever. Fight your own battles.'

Dorothy broke the silence that followed. 'You *did* see me take the guns, doctor?'

'I did. You have one in your right breeches pocket now.'

'Then why didn't you, or don't you, try to take it away from me?' she asked, wonderingly.

'"Try" is the wrong word. If I had not wanted you to take them you wouldn't have. If I didn't want you to have a gun now I would take it away from you,' and his black eyes stared into her violet ones with such calm certainty that she felt her heart sink.

'Has Perkins got any more knives or guns or things in his room?' Dorothy demanded.

'I don't know,' indifferently. Then, as both girls started for Perkins' room DuQuesne rapped out, 'Sit down, Miss Vaneman. Let them fight it out. Perkins has his orders about you; I'm giving you orders about him. If he oversteps, shoot him. Otherwise, hands off completely – in every respect.'

Dorothy threw up her head in defiance; but, meeting his cold stare, she paused irresolutely and sat down, while the other girl went on.

'That's better,' DuQuesne said. 'Besides, it would be my guess that she doesn't need any help.'

Margaret returned from the search and thrust her pistol back into her pocket. 'That ends that,' she declared. 'Are you going to behave yourself or do I chain you by the neck to a post?'

'I suppose I'll have to, if the doc's gone back on me,' Perkins snarled. 'But I'll get you when we get back, you—'

'Stop it!' Margaret snapped. 'Now listen. Call me names any more and I'll start shooting. One name, one shot; two names, two shots; and so on. Each shot in a carefully selected place. Go ahead.'

DuQuesne broke the silence that followed. 'Well, now that the battle's over and we're fed and rested, I'll put on some power. Everybody into seats.'

For sixty hours he drove through space, reducing the acceleration only at mealtimes, when they ate and exercised their stiffened, tormented bodies. The power was not cut down for sleep; everyone slept as best he could.

Dorothy and Margaret were together constantly and a real intimacy grew up between them. Perkins was for the most part sullenly quiet. DuQuesne worked steadily during all his waking hours, except at mealtimes when he talked easily and well. There was no animosity in his bearing or in his words; but his discipline was strict and his reproofs merciless.

When the power-bar was exhausted DuQuesne lifted the sole remaining cylinder into the engine, remarking:

'Well, we should be approximately stationary, relative to Earth. Now we'll start back.'

He advanced the lever, and for many hours the regular routine of the ship went on. Then DuQuesne, on waking, saw that the engine was no longer perpendicular to the floor, but was inclined slightly. He read the angle of inclination on the great circles, then scanned a sector of space. He reduced the current, whereupon all four felt a lurch as the angle was increased many degrees. He read the new angle hastily and restored touring power. He then sat down at the computer and figured – with that much power on, a tremendous and unnerving job.

'What's the matter, doctor?' Dorothy asked.

'We're being deflected a little from our course.'

'Is that bad?'

'Ordinarily, no. Every time we pass a star its gravity pulls us a little out of line. But the effects are slight, do not last long, and tend to cancel each other out. This is too big and has lasted altogether too long. If it keeps on, we could miss the solar system altogether; and I can't find anything to account for it.'

He watched the bar anxiously, expecting to see it swing back into the vertical, but the angle grew steadily larger. He again reduced the current and searched the heavens for the troublesome body.

'Do you see it yet?' Dorothy asked, apprehensively.

'No ... but this optical system could be improved. I could do better with night-glasses, I think.'

He brought out a pair of grotesque-looking binoculars and stared through them out of an upper window for perhaps five minutes.

'Good God!' he exclaimed. 'It's a dead star and we're almost onto it!'

Springing to the board, he whirled the bar into and through the vertical, then measured the apparent diameter of the strange object. Then, after cautioning the others, he put on more power than he had been using. After exactly fifteen minutes he slackened off and made another reading. Seeing his expression, Dorothy was about to speak, but he forestalled her.

'We lost more ground. It must be a lot bigger than anything known to our astronomers. And I'm not trying to pull away from it; just to make an orbit around it. We'll have to put on full power – take seats!'

He left full power on until the bar was nearly gone and made another series of observations. 'Not enough,' he said, quietly.

Perkins screamed and flung himself upon the floor; Margaret clutched at her heart with both hands; Dorothy, though her eyes looked like black holes in her white face, looked at him steadily and asked, 'This is the end, then?'

'Not yet.' His voice was calm and level. 'It'll take two days, more or less, to fall that far, and we have a little copper left for one last shot. I'm going to figure the angle to make that last shot as effective as possible.'

'Won't the repulsive outer coating do any good?'

'No; it'll be gone long before we hit. I'd strip it and feed it to the engine if I could think of a way of getting it off.'

He lit a cigarette and sat at ease at the computer. He sat there, smoking and computing, for over an hour. He then changed, very slightly, the angle of the engine.

'Now we look for copper,' he said. 'There isn't any in the ship itself – everything electrical is silver, down to our flashlights and the bases of the lamps. But examine the furnishings and all your personal stuff – *anything* with copper or brass in it. That includes metallic money – pennies, nickels, and silver.'

They found a few items, but very few. DuQuesne added his watch, his heavy signet ring, his keys, his tie-clasp, and the cartridges from his pistol. He made sure that Perkins did not hold anything out. The girls gave up not only their money and cartridges but the jewelry, including Dorothy's engagement ring.

'I'd like to keep it, but ...' She said, as she added it to the collection.

'Everything goes that has any copper in it; and I'm glad Seaton's too much of a scientist to buy platinum jewelry. But, if we get away, I doubt very much if you'll be able to see any difference in your ring. Very little copper in it – but we need every milligram we can get.'

He threw all the metal into the power chamber and advanced the level. It was soon spent; and after the final observation, while the others waited in suspense, he made his curt announcement.

'Not quite enough.'

Perkins, his mind already weakened, went completely insane.

With a wild howl he threw himself at the unmoved scientist, who struck him on the head with the butt of his pistol as he leaped. The force of the blow crushed Perkins' head and drove his body to the other side of the ship. Margaret looked as though she were about to faint. Dorothy and DuQuesne looked at each other. To the girl's amazement the man was as calm as though he were in his own room at home on Earth. She made an effort to hold her voice steady. 'What next, doctor?'

'I don't exactly know. I still haven't been able to work out a method of recovering that plating … It's so thin that there isn't much copper, even on a sphere as big as this one.'

'Even if you could get it, and it were enough, we'd starve anyway, wouldn't we?' Margaret, holding herself together desperately, tried to speak lightly.

'Not necessarily. That would give me time to figure out something else to do.'

'You wouldn't have to figure anything else,' Dorothy declared. 'Maybe you won't, anyway. You said we have two days?'

'My observations were crude, but it's a little over two days – about forty-nine and a half hours now. Why?'

'Because Dick and Martin Crane will find us before very long. Quite possibly within two days.'

'Not in this life. If they tried to follow us they're both dead now.'

'That's where even *you* are wrong!' she flashed. 'They knew all the time exactly what you were doing to our old *Skylark*, so they built another one that you never knew anything about. And they know a lot about this new metal that you never heard of, too, because it wasn't in those plans you stole!'

DuQuesne went directly to the heart of the matter, paying no attention to her barbs. 'Can they follow us in space without seeing us?' he demanded.

'Yes. At least, I think they can.'

'How do they do it?'

'I don't know. I wouldn't tell you, if I did!'

'You think not? I won't argue the point at the moment. If they can find us – which I doubt – I hope they detect this dead star in time to keep away from it – and us.'

'But why?' Dorothy gasped. 'You've been trying to kill both of them – wouldn't you be glad to take them with us?'

'*Please* try to be logical. Far from it. There's no connection.'

'I tried to kill them, yes, because they stood in the way of my development of this new metal. If, however, I am not going to be the one to do it – I certainly hope Seaton goes ahead with it. It's the greatest discovery ever made, bar none; and if both Seaton and I, the only two men able to develop it properly, get killed, it will be lost, perhaps for hundreds of years.'

'If he must go, too, I hope he doesn't find us … but I don't believe it. I simply know he could get us away from here.'

She continued more slowly, almost speaking to herself, her heart sinking with her voice, 'He's following us and he won't stop even if he knows he can't get away.'

'There's no denying the fact that our situation is critical; but as long as I'm alive I can think. I'm going to dope out *some* way of getting that copper.'

'I hope you do.' Dorothy kept her voice from breaking only by a tremendous effort. 'I see Peggy's fainted. I wish I could. I'm worn out.'

She drew herself down upon one of the seats and stared at the ceiling, fighting an almost overpowering impulse to scream.

Thus time wore on – Perkins dead; Margaret unconscious; Dorothy lying in her seat, her thoughts a formless prayer, buoyed only by her faith in God and in her lover; DuQuesne self-possessed, smoking innumerable cigarettes, his keen mind at grips with its most desperate problem, grimly fighting until the very last instant of life – while the powerless spaceship fell with an appalling velocity, and faster and yet faster, toward that cold and desolate monster of the heavens.

XIII

Seaton and Crane drove the *Skylark* at high acceleration in the direction indicated by the unwavering compass, each man taking a twelve-hour trick at the board. The *Skylark* justified the faith of her builders, and the two inventors, with an exultant certainty of success, flew out beyond man's wildest imaginings. Had it not been for the haunting fear for Dorothy's safety, the journey would have been one of pure triumph, and even that anxiety did not preclude a profound joy in the enterprise.

'If that misguided ape thinks he can pull a stunt like that and get away with it he's got another thing coming,' Seaton declared, after making a reading on the other ship after a few days of flight. 'He went off half-cocked for sure this time, and we've got him right where the hair is short. Only about a hundred light-years now. Better we reverse pretty quick, you think?'

'It's hard to say – very hard. By our dead reckoning he seems to have started back; but dead reckoning is notoriously poor reckoning and we have no reference points.'

'Well, dead reckoning's the only thing we've got, and anyway you can't be a precisionist out here. A light-year plus or minus won't make any difference.'

'No, I suppose not,' and Crane read off the settings which, had his data been exact, would put the *Skylark* in exactly the same spot with, and having exactly the same velocity as, the other spaceship at the point of meeting.

The big ship spun, with a sickening lurch, through a half-circle as the bar was reversed. They knew that they were travelling in a direction that seemed 'down,' even though they still seemed to be going 'up.'

'Mart! C'mere.'

'Here.'

'We're getting a deflection. Too big for a star – unless it's another S-Doradus – and I can't see a thing – theoretically, of course, it could be anywhere to starboard. I want a check, fast, on true course and velocity. Is there any way to measure a gravity field you're falling freely in without knowing any distances? *Any* kind of an approximation would help.'

Crane observed, computed, and reported that the *Skylark* was being very strongly attracted by some object almost straight ahead.

'We'd better break out the big night-glasses and take a good look – as you said, this optical system could have more power. But how far away are they?'

'A few minutes over ten hours.'

'Ouch! Not good … *veree* ungood, in fact. By pouring it on, we could make it three or four hours … but … even so … you …

'Even so. Me. We're in this together, Dick; all the way. Just pour it on.'

As the time of meeting drew near they took readings every minute. Seaton juggled the power until they were very close to the other vessel and riding with it, then killed his engine. Both men hurried to the bottom port with their night-glasses and stared into star-studded blackness.

'Of course,' Seaton argued as he stared, 'it is theoretically possible that a body can exist large enough to exert this much force and not show a disk, but I don't believe it. Give me four or five minutes of visual angle and I'll buy it, but—'

'There!' Crane broke in. 'At least half a degree of visual angle. Eleven o'clock, fairly high. Not bright, but dark. Almost invisible.'

'Got it. And that little black spot, just inside the edge at half past four – DuQuesne's job?'

'I think so. Nothing else in sight.'

'Let's grab it and get out of here while we're all in one piece!'

In seconds they reduced the distance until they could plainly see the other vessel: a small black circle against the somewhat lighter black of the dead star. Crane turned on the searchlight. Seaton focused their heaviest attractor and gave it everything it would take. Crane loaded a belt of solid ammunition and began to fire peculiarly-spaced bursts.

After an interminable silence DuQuesne drew himself out of his seat. He took a long drag at his cigarette, deposited the butt carefully in an ashtray, and put on his space-suit; leaving the faceplates open.

'I'm going after that copper, Miss Vaneman. I don't know exactly how much of it I'll be able to recover, but I hope ...'

Light flooded in through a port. DuQuesne was thrown flat as the ship was jerked out of free fall. They heard an insistent metallic tapping, which DuQuesne recognized instantly.

'A machine gun!' he blurted in amazement. 'What in ... wait a minute, that's Morse! A – R – E – are ... Y-O-U – you ... A-L-I-V-E – alive ...'

'It's Dick!' Dorothy screamed. 'He's found us – I knew he would! You couldn't beat Dick and Martin in a thousand years!'

The two girls locked their arms around each other in a hysterical outburst of relief; Margaret's incoherent words and Dorothy's praises of her lover mingled with their racking sobs.

DuQuesne had climbed to the upper port; had unshielded it. 'S-O-S' he signaled with his flashlight.

The searchlight died. 'W-E K-N-O-W. P-A-R-T-Y O-K-?' It was a light this time, not bullets.

'O-K.' DuQuesne knew what 'Party' meant – Perkins did not count.

'S-U-I-T-S-?'

'Y-E-S.'

'W-I-L-L T-O-U-C-H T-O L-O-C-K B-R-A-C-E S-E-L-V-E-S.'

'O-K.'

DuQuesne reported briefly to the two girls. All three put on space-suits and crowded into the tiny airlock. The lock was pumped down. There was a terrific jar as the two ships of space were brought together and held together. Outer valves opened; residual air screamed into the interstellar void. Moisture condensed upon glass, rendering sight useless.

'Blast!' Seaton's voice came tinnily over the helmet radios. 'I can't see a foot. Can you, DuQuesne?'

'No, and these joints don't move more than a couple of inches.'

'These suits need a lot more work. We'll have to go by feel. Pass 'em along.'

DuQuesne grabbed the girl nearest him and shoved her toward the spot where Seaton would have to be. Seaton seized her, straightened her up, and did his heroic best to compress that suit until he could at least feel his sweetheart's form.

He was very much astonished to feel motions of resistance and to hear a strange voice cry out, 'Don't! It's me! Dottie's next!'

She was, and she put as much fervor into the reunion as he did. As a lovers' embrace it was unsatisfactory; but it was an eager, if distant, contact.

DuQuesne dived through the opening; Crane groped for the controls that closed the lock. Pressure and temperature came back up to normal. The clumsy suits were taken off. Seaton and Dorothy went into each other's arms.

And this time it was a real lovers' embrace.

'We'd better start doing something,' came DuQuesne's incisive voice. 'Every minute counts.'

'One thing first,' Crane said. 'Dick, what shall we do with this murderer?'

Seaton, who had temporarily forgotten all about DuQuesne, whirled around.

'Chuck him back into his own tub and let him go to the devil!' he said, savagely.

'Oh, no, Dick!' Dorothy protested, seizing his arm. 'He treated us very well, and saved my life once. Besides, you *can't* become a cold-blooded murderer just because he is. You know you can't.'

'Maybe not ... O.K., I won't kill him – unless *he* gives me about half an excuse ... maybe.'

'Out of the question, Dick,' Crane decided. 'Perhaps he can earn his way?'

'Could be.' Seaton thought for a moment, his face still grim and hard. 'He's smart as Satan and strong as a bull ... and if there's any possible one thing he is not, it's a liar.'

He faced DuQuesne squarely, gray eyes boring into eyes of midnight black. 'Will you give us your word to act as one of the party?'

'Yes.' DuQuesne stared back unflinchingly. His expression of cold unconcern had not changed throughout the conversation: it did not change now. 'With the understanding that I reserve the right to leave you at any time – "escape" is a melodramatic word, but fits the facts closely enough – provided I can do so without affecting unfavorably your ship, your project then in work, or your persons collectively or individually.'

'You're the lawyer, Mart. Does that cover it?'

'Admirably,' Crane said. 'Fully yet concisely. Also, the fact of the reservation indicates that he means it.'

'You're in, then,' Seaton said to DuQuesne, but he did not offer to shake hands. 'You've got the dope. What'll we have to put on to get away?'

'You can't pull straight away – and live – but ...'

'Sure we can. *Our* power-plant can be doubled in emergencies.'

'I said "and live".' Seaton, remembering what one full power was like, kept still.

'The best you can do is a hyperbolic orbit, and my guess is that it'll take full power to make that. Ten pounds more copper might have given me a graze, but we're a lot closer now. You've got more and larger tools that I had, Crane.

Do you want to recompute it now, or give it a good, heavy shot and then figure it?'

'A shot, I think. What do you suggest?'

'Set your engine to roll for a hyperbolic and give it full drive for … say an hour.'

'Full power,' Crane said, thoughtfully. 'I can't take that much. But if –'

'I can't, either,' Dorothy said, foreboding in her eyes. 'Nor Margaret.'

'– full power is necessary,' Crane continued as though the girl had not spoken, 'full power it shall be. Is it really of the essence, DuQuesne?'

'Definitely. More than full would be better. And it's getting worse every minute.'

'How much power can you take?' Seaton asked.

'More than full. Not much more, but a little.'

'If you can, I can.' Seaton was not boasting, merely stating a fact. 'So here's what let's do. Double the engines up. DuQuesne and I will notch the power up until one of us has to quit. Run an hour on that, and then read the news. Check?'

'Check,' said Crane and DuQuesne simultaneously, and the three men set furiously to work. Crane went to the engines, DuQuesne to the observatory. Seaton rigged helmets to air- and oxygen-tanks through valves on his board.

Seaton placed Margaret upon a seat, fitted a helmet over her head, strapped her in, and turned to Dorothy.

Instantly they were in each other's arms. He felt her labored breathing and the hard beating of her heart; saw the fear of the unknown in the violet depths of her eyes; but she looked at him steadily as she said: 'Dick, sweetheart, if this is goodbye …'

'It isn't, Dottie – yet– but I know …'

Crane and DuQuesne had finished their tasks, so Seaton hastily finished his job on Dorothy. Crane put himself to bed; Seaton and DuQuesne put on their helmets and took their places at the twin boards.

In quick succession twenty notches of power went on. The *Skylark* leaped away from the other ship, which continued its mad fall – a helpless hulk, manned by a corpse, falling to destruction upon the bleak surface of a dead star.

Notch by notch, slower now, the power went up. Seaton turned the mixing valve, a little with each notch, until the oxygen concentration was as high as they had dared to risk.

As each of the two men was determined that he would make the last advance, the duel continued longer than either would have believed possible. Seaton made what he was sure was his final effort and waited – only to feel, after a minute, the surge of the vessel that told him that DuQuesne was still able to move.

He could not move any part of his body, which was oppressed by a sickening weight. His utmost efforts to breathe forced only a little oxygen into his lungs. He wondered how long he could retain consciousness under such stress. Nevertheless, he put out everything he had and got one more notch. Then he stared at the clock-face above his head, knowing that he was all done and wondering whether DuQuesne could put on one more notch.

Minute after minute went by and the acceleration remained constant. Seaton, knowing that he was now in sole charge of the situation, fought off unconsciousness while the sweep-hand of the clock went around and around.

After an eternity of time sixty minutes had passed and Seaton tried to cut down his power, only to find that the long strain had so weakened him that he could not reverse the ratchet. He was barely able to give the lever the backward jerk which broke contact completely. Safety straps creaked as, half the power shut off, the suddenly released springs tried to hurl five bodies upward.

DuQuesne revived and shut down his engine. 'You're a better man than I am, Gunga Din,' he said, as he began to make observations.

'Because you were so badly bunged up, is all – one more notch would've pulled my cork,' and Seaton went over to liberate Dorothy and the stranger.

Crane and DuQuesne finished their computations.

'Did we gain enough?' Seaton asked.

'More than enough. One engine will take us past it.'

Then, as Crane still frowned in thought, DuQuesne went on:

'Don't you check me, Crane?'

'Yes and no. Past it, yes, but not safely past. One thing neither of us thought of, apparently – Roche's Limit.'

'That wouldn't apply to this ship,' Seaton said, positively. 'High-tensile alloy steel wouldn't crumble.'

'It might,' DuQuesne said. 'Close enough, it would … What mass would you assume, Crane – the theoretical maximum?'

'I would. That star may not be that, quite, but it isn't far from it.' Both men bent over their computers.

'I make it thirty-nine point seven notches of power, doubled,' DuQuesne said, when he had finished. 'Check?'

'Closely enough – point six five,' Crane replied.

'Forty notches … Ummm … DuQuesne paused. 'I went out at thirty-two … That means an automatic advance. It'll take time, but it's the only …'

'We've got it already – all we have to do is set it. But that'll take an ungodly lot of copper and what'll we do to live through it? Plus-pressure on the oxygen? Or what?'

After a short but intense consultation the men took all the steps they could to enable the whole party to live through what was coming. Whether they could do enough no one knew. Where they might lie at the end of this wild dash for safety; how they were to retrace their way with their depleted supply of copper, what other dangers of dead star, sun, or planet lay in their path, were terrifying questions that had to be ignored.

DuQuesne was the only member of the party who actually felt any calmness, the quiet of the others expressing their courage in facing fear.

The men took their places. Seaton started the motor which would automatically advance both power levers exactly forty notches and then stop.

Margaret Spencer was the first to lose consciousness. Soon afterward, Dorothy stifled an impulse to scream as she felt herself going under. A half-minute later and Crane went out, calmly analyzing his sensations to the last. Shortly thereafter DuQuesne also lapsed into unconsciousness, making no effort to avoid it, as he knew that it would make no difference in the end.

Seaton, though he knew it was useless, fought to keep his senses as long as possible, counting the impulses as the levers were advanced.

Thirty-two. He felt the same as when he had advanced his lever for the last time.

Thirty-three. A giant hand shut off his breath, although he was fighting to the utmost for air. An intolerable weight rested upon his eyeballs, forcing them back into his head. The universe whirled about him in dizzy circles; orange and black and green stars flashed before his bursting eyes.

Thirty-four. The stars became more brilliant and of more wildly variegated colors, and a giant pen dipped in fire wrote equations and symbols upon his quivering brain.

Thirty-five. The stars and the fiery pen exploded in pyrotechnic coruscation of searing, blinding light and he plunged into a black abyss.

Faster and faster the *Skylark* hurtled downward in her not-quite-hyperbolic path. Faster and faster, as minute by minute went by, she came closer and closer to that huge dead star. Eighteen hours from the start of that fantastic drop she swung around it in the tightest, hardest conceivable arc. Beyond Roche's Limit, it is true, but so very little beyond it that Martin Crane's hair would have stood on end if he had known.

Then, on the back leg of that incomprehensibly gigantic swing, the forty notches of doubled power began really to take hold. At thirty-six hours her path was no longer even approximately hyperbolic. Instead of slowing down, relative to the dead star that held her in an ever-weakening grip, she was speeding up at a tremendous rate.

At two days, that grip was very weak.

At three days the monster she had left was having no measurable effect.

Hurtled upward, onward, outward by the inconceivable power of the unleashed copper demons in her center, the *Skylark* tore through the reaches of interstellar space with an unthinkable, almost incalculable velocity, beside which the velocity of light was as that of a snail to that of a rifle bullet.

XIV

Seaton opened his eyes and gazed about him wonderingly. Only half conscious, bruised and sore in every part, he could not remember what had happened. Instinctively drawing a deep breath, he coughed as the plus-pressure gas filled his lungs, bringing with it a complete understanding of the situation. He tore off his helmet and drew himself across to Dorothy's couch.

She was still alive!

He placed her face downward upon the floor and began artificial respiration. Soon he was rewarded by the coughing he had longed to hear. Snatching off her helmet, he seized her in his arms, while she sobbed convulsively on his shoulder. The first ecstasy of their greeting over, she started guiltily.

'Oh, Dick! See about Peggy – I wonder if …'

'Never mind,' Crane said. 'She is doing nicely.'

Crane had already revived the stranger. DuQuesne was nowhere in sight. Dorothy blushed vividly and disengaged her arms from around Seaton's neck. Seaton, also blushing, dropped his arms and Dorothy floated away, clutching frantically at a hand-hold just out of her reach.

'Pull me down, Dick!' Dorothy laughed.

Seaton grabbed her ankle unthinkingly, neglecting his own anchorage, and they floated in the air together. Martin and Margaret, each holding a line, laughed heartily.

'Tweet, tweet – I'm a canary,' Seaton said, flapping his arms.

'Toss us a line, Mart.'

'A Dicky-bird, you mean,' Dorothy said.

Crane studied the floating pair with mock gravity.

'That is a peculiar pose, Dick. What is it supposed to represent – Zeus sitting on his throne?'

'I'll sit on your neck, you lug, if you don't get a wiggle on with that rope!'

As he spoke, however, he came within reach of the ceiling, and could push himself and his companion to a line.

Seaton put a bar into one of the engines and, after flashing the warning light, applied a little power. The *Skylark* seemed to leap under them; then everything had its normal weight once more.

'Now that things have settled down a little,' Dorothy said, 'I'll introduce you two to Miss Margaret Spencer, a very good friend of mine. These are the boys I told you so much about, Peggy. This is Dr Dick Seaton, my fiancé. He knows everything there is to be known about atoms, electrons, neutrons, and so forth. And this is Mr Martin Crane, who is a simply wonderful inventor. He made all these engines and things.'

'I may have heard of Mr Crane,' Margaret said, eagerly. 'My father was an inventor, too, and he used to talk about a man named Crane who invented a lot of instruments for supersonic planes. He said they revolutionized flying. I wonder if you are that Mr Crane?'

'That is unjustifiably high praise, Miss Spencer,' Crane replied, uncomfortable, 'but as I have done a few things along that line I could be the man he referred to.'

'If I may change the subject,' Seaton said, 'where's DuQuesne?'

'He went to clean up. Then he was going to the galley to check damage and see about something to eat.'

'Stout fella!' Dorothy applauded. 'Food! And *especially* about cleaning up – if you know what I mean and I think you do. Come on, Peggy, I know where our room is.'

'What a girl!' Seaton said as the women left, Dorothy half-supporting her companion. 'She's bruised and beat up from one end to the other. She's more than half dead yet – she didn't have enough life left in her to flag a hand-car. She can't even walk; she can just barely hobble. And did she let out one single yip? I ask to know. "Business as usual," all the way, if it kills her. *What* a girl!'

'Include Miss Spencer in that, too, Dick. Did she "let out any yips"? And she was not in nearly as good shape as Dorothy was to start with.'

'That's right,' Seaton agreed, wonderingly. 'She's got plenty of guts, too. Those two women, Marty my old and stinky chum, are blinding flashes and deafening reports … Well, let's go get a bath and shave. And shove the air-conditioners up a couple of notches, will you?'

When they came back they found the two girls seated at one of the ports. 'Did you dope yourself up, Dot?' Seaton asked.

'Yes, both of us. With amylophene. I'm getting to be a slave to the stuff.' She made a wry face.

Seaton grimaced too. 'So did we. Ouch! Nice stuff that amylophene.'

'But come over here and look out of this window. Did you *ever* see anything like it?'

As the four heads bent, so close together, an awed silence fell upon the little group. For the blackness of the black of the interstellar void is not the darkness of an Earthly night, but the absolute absence of light – a black beside which that of platinum dust is merely gray. Upon this indescribably black backdrop there glowed faint patches which were nebulae; there blazed hard, brilliant, multi-colored, dimensionless points of light which were stars.

'Jewels on black velvet,' Dorothy breathed. 'Oh, gorgeous ... wonderful!'

Through their wonder a thought struck Seaton. He leaped to the board. 'Look here, Mart. I didn't recognize a thing out there and I wondered why. We're heading away from the Earth and we must be making plenty of light-speeds. The swing around that big dud was really something, of course, but the engine should have ... or should it?'

'I think not ... Unexpected, but not a surprise. That close to Roche's Limit, anything might happen.'

'And did, I guess. We'll have to check for permanent deformations. But this object-compass still works – let's see how far we are away from home.'

They took a reading and both men figured the distance.

'What d'you make it, Mart? I'm afraid to tell you my result.'

'Forty-six point twenty-seven light-centuries. Check?'

'Check. We're up the well-known creek without a paddle ... The time was twenty-three thirty-two by the chronometer – good thing you built it to stand going through a stone-crusher. My watch's a total loss. They all are, I imagine. We'll read it again in an hour or so and see how fast we're going. I'll be scared witless to say that figure out loud, too.'

'Dinner is announced,' said DuQuesne, who had been standing at the door, listening.

The wanderers, battered, stiff and sore, seated themselves at a folding table. While eating, Seaton watched the engine – when he was not watching Dorothy – and talked to her. Crane and Margaret chatted easily. DuQuesne, except when addressed directly, maintained a self-sufficient silence.

After another observation Seaton said, 'DuQuesne, we're almost five thousand light-years away from Earth, and getting farther away at about one light-year per minute.'

'It'd be poor technique to ask how you know?'

'It would. Those figures are right. But we've got only four bars of copper left. Enough to stop us and some to spare, but not nearly enough to get us back, even by drifting – too many lifetimes on the way.'

'So we land somewhere and dig us some copper.'

'Check. What I wanted to ask you – isn't a copper-bearing sun apt to have copper-bearing planets?'

'I'd say so.'

'Then take the spectroscope, will you, and pick out a sun somewhere up ahead – down ahead, I mean – for us to shoot at? And Mart, I s'pose we'd better take our regular twelve-hour tricks – no, eight; we've got to either trust the guy or kill him – I'll take the first watch. Beat it to bed.'

'Not so fast.' Crane said. 'If I remember correctly, it's my turn.'

'Ancient history doesn't count. I'll flip you a nickel for it. Heads, I win.'

Seaton won, and the worn-out travelers went to their rooms – all except Dorothy, who lingered to bid her lover a more intimate goodnight.

Seated beside him, his arm around her and her head on his shoulder, she sat blissfully until she noticed, for the first time, her bare left hand. She caught her breath and her eyes grew round.

'Smatter, Red?'

'Oh, Dick!' she exclaimed in dismay, 'I simply forgot *everything* about taking what was left of my ring out of the doctor's engine!'

'Huh? What are you talking about?'

She told him; and he told her about Martin and himself.

'Oh, Dick – Dick– it's so wonderful to be with you again!' she concluded. 'I lived as many years as we covered miles!'

'It was tough … you had it a lot worse than we did … but it makes me ashamed all over to think of the way I blew my stack at Wilson's. If it hadn't been for Martin's cautious old bean we'd've … we owe him a lot, Dimples.'

'Yes, we do … but don't worry about the debt, Dick. Just don't ever let slip a word to Peggy about Martin being rich, is all.'

'Oh, a matchmaker now? But why not? She wouldn't think any less of him – that's one reason I'm marrying you, you know – for your money.'

Dorothy snickered sunnily. 'I know. But listen, my poor, dumb, fortune-hunting darling – if Peggy had any idea that Martin is the one and only M. Reynolds Crane she'd curl right up into a ball. She'd think he'd think she was chasing him and then he *would* think so. As it is, he acts perfectly natural. He hasn't talked that way to any girl except me for five years, and he wouldn't talk to me until he found out for sure I wasn't out after him.'

'Could be, pet,' Seaton agreed. 'On one thing you really chirped it – he's been shot at so much he's wilder than a hawk!'

At the end of eight hours Crane took over and Seaton stumbled to his room, where he slept for over ten hours like a man in a trance. Then, rising, he exercised and went out into the saloon.

Dorothy, Peggy and Crane were at breakfast; Seaton joined them. They ate the gayest, most carefree meal they had had since leaving Earth. Some of the worst bruises still showed a little, but, under the influence of the potent if painful amylophene, all soreness, stiffness, and pain had disappeared.

After they had finished eating, Seaton said, 'You suggested, Mart, that those gyroscope bearings may have been stressed beyond the yield-point. I'll take an integrating goniomete …'

'Break that down to our size, Dick – Peggy's and mine,' Dorothy said.

'Can do. Take some tools and see if anything got bent out of shape back there. It might be an idea, Dot, to come along and hold my head while I think.'

'That *is* an idea – if you never have another one.'

Crane and Margaret went over and sat down at one of the crystal-clear ports. She told him her story frankly and fully, shuddering with horror as she recalled the awful, helpless fall during which Perkins had been killed.

'We have a heavy score to settle with that Steel crowd and with DuQuesne,' Crane said, slowly. 'We can convict him of abduction now ... Perkins's death wasn't murder, then?'

'Oh, no. He was just like a mad animal. He had to kill him. But the doctor, as they call him, is just as bad. He's so utterly heartless and ruthless, so cold and scientific, it gives me the compound shivers, just to think about him.'

'And yet Dorothy said he saved her life?'

'He did, from Perkins; but that was just as strictly pragmatic as everything else he has ever done. He wanted her alive: dead, she wouldn't have been any use to him. He's as nearly a robot as any human being can be, that's what I think.'

'I'm inclined to agree with you ... Nothing would please Dick better than a good excuse for killing him.'

'He isn't the only one. And the way he ignores what we all feel shows what a machine he is ... What's that?' The *Skylark* had lurched slightly.

'Just a swing around a star, probably.' He looked at the board, then led her to a lower port. 'We are passing the star Dick was heading for, far too fast to stop. DuQuesne will pick out another. See that planet over there'– he pointed – 'and that smaller one, there?'

She saw the two planets – one like a small moon, the other much smaller – and watched the sun increase rapidly in size as the *Skylark* flew on at such a pace that any Earthly distance would have been covered as soon as it was begun. So appalling was their velocity that the ship was bathed in the light of that strange sun only for moments, then was surrounded again by darkness.

Their seventy-two-hour flight without a pilot had seemed a miracle; now it seemed entirely possible that they could fly in a straight line for weeks without encountering any obstacle, so vast was the emptiness in comparison with the points of light scattered about in it. Now and then they passed closely enough to a star so that it seemed to move fairly rapidly; but for the most part the stars stood, like distant mountain peaks to travelers in a train, in the same position for many minutes.

Awed by the immensity of the universe, the two at the window were silent, not with the silence of embarrassment but with that of two friends in the presence of a thing far beyond the reach of words. As they stared out into infinity, each felt as never before the pitiful smallness of the whole world they had known, and the insignificance of human beings and their works. Silently their minds reached out to each other in understanding.

Unconsciously Margaret half shuddered and moved closer to Crane; and a tender look came over Crane's face as he looked down at the beautiful young woman at his side. For she was beautiful. Rest and food had erased the marks of her imprisonment. Dorothy's deep and unassumed faith in the ability of Seaton and Crane had quieted her fears. And finally, a costume of Dorothy's well-made – and exceedingly expensive! – clothes, which fitted her very well and in which she looked her best and knew it, had completely restored her self-possession.

He looked up quickly and again studied the stars; but now, in addition to the wonders of space, he saw a mass of wavy black hair, high-piled upon a queenly head; deep brown eyes veiled by long, black lashes; sweet, sensitive lips; a firmly rounded, dimpled chin; and a beautifully formed young body.

'How stupendous … how unbelievably great this is … Margaret whispered. 'How vastly greater than any perception one could possibly get on Earth … and yet …

She paused, with her lip caught under two white teeth, then went on, hesitatingly, 'But doesn't it seem to you, Mr Crane, that there is something in man as great as even all this? That there must be, or Dorothy and I could not be sailing out here in such a wonderful thing as this *Skylark,* which you and Dick Seaton have made?'

Days passed. Dorothy timed her waking hours with those of Seaton – preparing his meals and lightening the tedium of his long vigils at the board – and Margaret did the same thing for Crane. But often they assembled in the saloon, while DuQuesne was on watch, and there was much fun and laughter, as well as serious discussion, among the four. Margaret, already adopted as a friend, proved a delightful companion. Her ready tongue, her quick, delicate wit, and her facility of expression delighted all three.

One day Crane suggested to Seaton that they should take notes, in addition to the photographs they had been taking.

'I know comparatively little of astronomy, but, with the instruments we have, we should be able to get data, especially on planetary systems, which would be of interest to astronomers. Miss Spencer, being a secretary, could help us?'

'Sure,' Seaton said. 'That's an idea – nobody else ever had a chance to do it before.'

'I'll be glad to – taking notes is the best thing I do!' Margaret cried, and called for pad and pencils.

After that, the two worked together for several hours on each of Martin's off shifts.

The *Skylark* passed one solar system after another, with a velocity so great that it was impossible to land. Margaret's association with Crane, begun as a duty, became a very real pleasure for them both. Working together in research, sitting together at the board in easy conversation or in equally easy silence, they compressed into days more real companionship than is usually possible in months.

Oftener and oftener, as time went on, Crane found the vision of his dream home floating in his mind as he steered the *Skylark* in her meteoric flight or as he lay strapped into his narrow bunk. Now, however, the central figure of the vision, instead of being a blur, was clear and sharply defined. And for her part, Margaret was drawn more and more to the quiet and unassuming, but steadfast young inventor, with his wide knowledge and his keen, incisive mind.

The *Skylark* finally slowed down enough to make a landing possible, and course was laid toward the nearest planet of a copper-bearing sun. As vessel neared planet a wave of excitement swept through four of the five. They watched the globe grow larger, glowing white, its outline softened by the atmosphere surrounding it. It had two satellites; its sun, a great, blazing orb, looked so big and so hot that Margaret became uneasy.

'Isn't it dangerous to get so close, Dick?'

'Uh-uh. Watching the pyrometers is part of the pilot's job. Any overheating and he'd snatch us away in a hurry.'

They dropped into the atmosphere and on down, almost to the surface. The air was breathable, its composition being very similar to that of Earth's air, except that the carbon dioxide was substantially higher. Its pressure was somewhat high, but not too much; its temperature, while high, was endurable. The planet's gravitational pull was about ten per cent higher than Earth's. The ground was almost hidden by a rank growth of vegetation, but here and there appeared glade-like openings.

Landing upon one of the open spaces, they found the ground solid and stepped out. What appeared to be a glade was in reality a rock; or rather a ledge of apparently solid metal, with scarcely a loose fragment to be seen. At one end of the ledge rose a giant tree, wonderfully symmetrical, but of a peculiar form, its branches being longer at the top than at the bottom, and having broad, dark-green leaves, long horns, and odd, flexible, shoot-like tendrils. It stood as an outpost of the dense vegetation beyond. The fern-trees, towering two hundred feet or more into the air were totally unlike the forests of Earth. They were an intensely vivid green and stood motionless in the still, hot air. Not a sign of animal life was to be seen; the whole landscape seemed to be asleep.

'A younger planet than ours,' DuQuesne said. 'In the Carboniferous, or about. Aren't those fern-trees like those in the coal measures, Seaton?'

'Check – I was just trying to think what they reminded me of. But it's this ledge that interests me no end. Who ever heard of a chunk of noble metal this big?'

'How do you know it's noble?' Dorothy asked.

'No corrosion, and it's probably been sitting here for a million years.' Seaton, who had walked over to one of the loose lumps, kicked it with his heavy shoe. It did not move.

He bent over to pick it up, with one hand. It still did not move. With both hands and all the strength of his back he could lift it, but that was all.

'What do you make of this, DuQuesne?'

DuQuesne lifted the mass, then took out his knife and scraped. He studied the freshly-exposed metal and the scrapings, then scraped and studied again.

'Hmm. Platinum group, almost certainly … and the only known member of that group with that peculiar bluish sheen is your X.'

'But didn't we agree that free X and copper couldn't exist on the same planet, and that planets of copper-bearing suns carry copper?'

'Yes, but that doesn't make it true. If this stuff is X, it'll give the cosmologists something to fight about for the next twenty years. I'll take these scrapings and run a couple of quickies.'

'Do that, and I'll gather in these loose nuggets. If it's X – and I'm pretty sure it mostly is – that'll be enough to run all the power-plants of Earth for ten thousand years.'

Crane and Seaton, accompanied by the two girls, rolled the nearer pieces of metal up to the ship. Then, as the quest led them farther and farther afield, Crane protested.

'This is none too safe, Dick.'

'It looks perfectly safe to me. Quiet as a—'

Margaret screamed. Her head was turned, looking backward at the *Skylark*; her face was a mask of horror.

Seaton drew his pistol as he whirled, only to check his finger on the trigger and lower his hand. 'Nothing but X-plosive bullets,' he said, and the four watched a thing come out slowly from behind their ship.

Its four huge, squat legs supported a body at least a hundred feet long, pursy and ungainly; at the end of a long, sinuous neck a small head seemed composed entirely of cavernous mouth armed with row upon row of carnivorous teeth. Dorothy gasped with terror; both girls shrank closer to the two men, who maintained a baffled silence as the huge beast slid its hideous neck along the hull of the vessel.

'I can't shoot, Mart – it'd wreck the boat – and if I had any solids they wouldn't be any good.'

'No. We had better hide until it goes away. You two take that ledge, we'll take this one.'

'Or gets far enough away from the *Skylark* so we can blow him apart,' Seaton added as, with Dorothy close beside him, he dropped behind the low bulwark.

Margaret, her staring eyes fixed upon the monster, remained motionless until Crane touched her gently and drew her down to his side. 'Don't be frightened, Peggy. It will go away soon.'

'I'm not now – much.' She drew a deep breath. 'If you weren't here, though, Martin, I'd be dead of pure fright.'

His arm tightened around her; then he forced it to relax. This was neither the time nor the place …

A roll of gunfire came from the *Skylark*. The creature roared in pain and rage, but was quickly silenced by the stream of .50-caliber machine-gun bullets.

'DuQuesne's on the job – let's go! Seaton cried, and the four rushed up the slope. Making a detour to avoid the writhing body, they plunged through the opening door. DuQuesne closed the lock. They huddled together in overwhelming relief as an apparent tumult arose outside.

The scene, so quiet a few moments before, was horribly changed. The air seemed filled with hideous monsters. Winged lizards of prodigious size hurtled through the air to crash against the *Skylark*'s armored hull. Flying monstrosities, with the fangs of tigers, attacked viciously. Dorothy screamed and started back as a scorpion-like thing ten feet in length leaped at the window in front of her, its terrible sting spraying the quartz with venom. As it fell to the ground a spider – if an eight-legged creature with spines instead of hair, faceted eyes, and a bloated, globular body weighing hundreds of pounds may be called a spider – leaped upon it; and, mighty mandibles against terrible sting, a furious battle raged. Twelve-foot cockroaches climbed nimbly across the fallen timber of the morass and began feeding voraciously on the carcass of the creature DuQuesne had killed. They were promptly driven away by another animal, a living nightmare of that reptilian age which apparently combined the nature and disposition of *Tyrannosaurus rex* with a physical shape approximating that of the saber-tooth tiger. This newcomer towered fifteen feet high at the shoulders and had a mouth disproportionate even to his great size; a mouth armed with sharp fangs three feet in length. He had barely begun his meal, however, when he was challenged by another nightmare, a thing shaped more or less like a crocodile.

The crocodile charged. The tiger met him head on, fangs front and rending claws outstretched. Clawing, striking, tearing savagely, an avalanche of bloodthirsty rage, the combatants stormed up and down the little island.

Suddenly the great tree bent over and lashed out against both animals. It transfixed them with its thorns, which the watchers now saw were both needle-pointed and barbed. It ripped at them with its long branches, which were in fact highly lethal spears. The broad leaves, equipped with sucking disks, wrapped themselves around the hopelessly impaled victims. The long, slender twigs or tendrils, each of which now had an eye at its extremity, waved about at a safe distance.

After absorbing all of the two gladiators that was absorbable, the tree resumed its former position, motionless in all its strange, outlandish beauty.

Dorothy licked her lips, which were almost as white as her face. 'I think I'm going to be sick,' she remarked, conversationally.

'No you aren't.' Seaton tightened his arm. 'Chin up, ace.'

'O.K., chief. Maybe not – this time.' Color began to reappear on her cheeks. 'But Dick, will you please blow up that horrible tree? It wouldn't be so bad if it were ugly, like the rest of the things, but it's *so* beautiful!'

'I sure will. I think we'd better get out of here. This is *no* place to start a copper mine, even if there's any copper here, which there probably isn't … It is X, DuQuesne, isn't it?'

'Yes. Ninety-nine plus per cent, at least.'

'That reminds me.' Seaton turned to DuQuesne, hand outstretched. 'You squared it, Blackie. Say the word and the war's all off.'

DuQuesne ignored the hand. 'Not on my side,' he said, evenly. 'I act as one of the party as long as I'm with you. When we get back, however, I still intend to take both of you out of circulation.' He went to his room.

'Well, I'll be a …' Seaton bit off *a* word. 'He ain't a man – he's a cold-blooded fish!'

'He's a machine – a robot.' Margaret declared. 'I always thought so, and now I know it!'

'We'll pull his cork when we get back,' Seaton said. 'He asked for it – we'll give him both barrels!'

Crane went to the board, and soon they were approaching another planet, which was surrounded by a dense fog. Descending slowly, they found it to be a mass of boiling-hot steam and rank vapor, under enormous pressure.

The next planet looked barren and dead. Its atmosphere was clear, but of a peculiar yellowish-green color. Analysis showed over ninety per cent chlorine. No life of any Earthly type could exist naturally upon such a world and a search for copper, even in space-suits, would be extremely difficult if not impossible.

'Well,' Seaton said, as they were once more in space, 'we've got copper enough to visit quite a few more solar systems if we have to. But there's a nice, hopeful-looking planet right over there. It may be the one we're looking for.'

Arriving in the belt of atmosphere, they tested it as before and found it satisfactory.

XV

They descended rapidly, over a large city set in the middle of a vast, level, beautifully planted plain. As they watched, the city vanished, and became a mountain summit, with valleys fading away on all sides as far as the eye could reach.

'Huh! I never saw a mirage like *that* before!' Seaton exclaimed. 'But we'll land, if we finally have to swim!'

The ship landed gently upon the summit, its occupants more than half expecting the mountain to disappear beneath them. Nothing happened, however, and the five clustered in the lock, wondering whether or not to disembark. They could see no sign of life; but each felt the pressure of a vast, invisible something.

Suddenly a man materialized in the air before them; a man identical with Seaton in every detail, down to the smudge of grease under one eye and the exact design of his Hawaiian sport shirt.

'Hello, folks,' he said, in Seaton's tone and style. 'S'prised that I know your language – huh, you would be. Don't even understand telepathy, or the ether, or the relationship between time and space. Not even the fourth dimension.'

Changing instantaneously from Seaton's form to Dorothy's, the stranger went on without a break. 'Electrons and neutrons and things – nothing here, either.'

The form became DuQuesne's. 'Ah, a freer type, but blind, dull, stupid; another nothing. As Martin Crane; the same. As Peggy, still the same, as was of course to be expected. Since you are all nothings in essence, of a race so low in the scale that it will be millions of years before it will rise even above death and death's clumsy attendant necessity, sex, it is of course necessary for me to make of you nothings in fact: to dematerialize you.'

In Seaton's form the being stared at Seaton, who felt his senses reel under the impact of an awful, if unsubstantial, blow. Seaton fought back with all his mind and remained standing.

'What's this?' the stranger exclaimed in surprise. 'This is the first time in millions of cycles that mere matter, which is only a manifestation of mind, has refused to obey a mind of power.

There's something screwy somewhere.' He switched to Crane's shape.

'Ah, I am not a perfect reproduction – there is some subtle difference. The external form is the same; the internal structure likewise. The molecules of substance are arranged properly, as are the atoms in the molecules. The electrons, neutrons, protons, positrons, neutrinos, mesons … nothing amiss on that level. On the third level …'

'Let's go!' Seaton exclaimed, drawing Dorothy backward and reaching for the airlock switch. 'This dematerialization stuff may be pie for him, but believe me, it's *none* of my dish.'

'No, no!' the stranger remonstrated, 'You really *must* stay and be dematerialized – alive or dead.'

He drew his pistol. Being in Crane's form, he drew slowly, as Crane did; and Seaton's Mark I shell struck him before the pistol cleared his pocket. The pseudo-body was volatilized; but, just to make sure, Crane fired a Mark V into the ground through the last open chink of the closing lock.

Seaton leaped to the board. As he did so, a creature materialized in the air in front of him – and crashed to the floor as he threw on the power. It was a frightful thing – outrageous teeth, long claws, and an automatic pistol held in a human hand. Forced flat by the fierce acceleration, it was unable to lift either itself or the weapon.

'We take one trick!' Seaton blazed. 'Stick to matter and I'll run along with you 'til my ankles catch fire!'

'That is a childish defiance. It speaks well for your courage, but not for your intelligence,' the animal said, and vanished.

A moment later Seaton's hair stood on end as a pistol appeared upon his board, clamped to it by bands of steel. The slide jerked; the trigger moved; the hammer came down. However, there was no explosion, but merely a click. Seaton paralyzed by the rapid succession of stunning events, was surprised to find himself still alive.

'Oh, I was almost sure it wouldn't explode,' the gun-barrel said, chattily, in a harsh, metallic voice. 'You see, I haven't derived the formula of your subnuclear structure yet, hence I could not make an actual explosive. By the use of crude force I could kill you in any one of many different ways …'

'Name one!' Seaton snapped.

'Two, if you like. I could materialize as five masses of metal directly over your heads, and fall. I could, by a sufficient concentration of effort, materialize a sun in your immediate path. Either method would succeed, would it not?'

'I … I guess it would!' Seaton admitted, grudgingly.

'But such crude work is distasteful in the extreme, and is never, under any conditions, mandatory. Furthermore, you are not quite the complete nothings that my first rough analysis seemed to indicate. In particular, the DuQuesne of you has the rudiments of a quality which, while it cannot be called mental ability, may in time develop into a quality which may just possibly make him assimilable into the purely intellectual stratum.

'Furthermore, you have given me a notable and entirely unexpected amount of exercise and enjoyment and can be made to give me more – much more – as follows: I will spend the next sixty of your minutes at work upon that formula – your sub-nuclear structure. Its derivation is comparatively simple, requiring only the solution of ninety-seven simultaneous differential equations and an integration in ninety-seven dimensions. If you can interfere with my computations sufficiently to prevent me from deriving that formula within the stipulated period of time you may return to your fellow nothings exactly as you now are. The first minute begins when the sweep-hand of your chronometer touches zero; that is … now.'

Seaton cut the power to one gravity and sat up, eyes closed tight and frowning in the intensity of his mental effort.

'You can't do it, you immaterial lug!' he thought, savagely. 'There are too many variables. No mind, however inhuman, can handle more than ninety-one differentials at once … you're wrong; that's theta, not epsilon … It's X, not Y or Z. Alpha! Beta! Ha, there's a slip; a bad one – got to go back and start all over … Nobody can integrate above ninety-six brackets … no body and no thing or mind in this whole, entire, cock-eyed universe! …'

Seaton cast aside any thought of the horror of their position. He denied any feeling of suspense. He refused to consider the fact that both he and his beloved Dorothy might at any instant be hurled into nothingness. Closing his mind deliberately to everything else, he fought that weirdly inimical entity with everything he had: with all his single-mindedness of purpose; with all his power of concentration; with all the massed and directed strength of his keen, highly-trained brain.

The hour passed.

'You win,' the gun-barrel said. 'More particularly, I should say that the DuQuesne of you won. To my surprise and delight that one developed his nascent quality very markedly during this short hour. Keep on going as you have been going, my potential kinsman; keep on studying under those eastern masters as you have been studying; and it is within the realm of possibility that, even in your short lifetime, you may become capable of withstanding the stresses concomitant with induction into our ranks.'

The pistol vanished. So did the planet behind them. The enveloping, pervading field of mental force disappeared. All five knew surely, without any trace of doubt, that that entity, whatever it had been, had gone.

'Did all that really happen, Dick?' Dorothy asked, tremulously, 'or have I been having the great-great-grandfather of all nightmares?'

'It hap … that is, I guess it happened … or maybe … Mart, if you could code that and shove it into a mechanical brain, what answer do you think would come out?'

'I don't know. I – simply– do – not– know.' Crane's mind, the mind of a highly-trained engineer, rebelled. No part of this whole fantastic episode could be explained by anything he knew. None of it could possibly have happened. Nevertheless—

'Either it happened or we were hypnotized. If so, who was the hypnotist, and where? Above all, why? It must have happened, Dick.'

'I'll buy that, wild as it sounds. Now, DuQuesne, how about you?'

'It happened. I don't know how or why it did, but I believe that it did. I've quit denying the impossibility of anything. If I had believed that your steam-bath flew out of the window by itself, that day, none of us would be out here now.'

'If it happened, you were apparently the prime operator in saving our bacon. Who in blazes are those eastern masters you've been studying under, and what did you study?'

'I don't know.' He lit a cigarette, took two deep inhalations. 'I wish I did. I've studied several esoteric philosophies … perhaps I can find out which one it was. I'll certainly try … for that, gentleman, would be my idea of heaven.' He left the room.

It took some time for the four to recover from the shock of that encounter. In fact, they had not yet fully recovered from it when Crane found a close cluster of stars, each emitting a peculiar greenish light which, in the spectro-scope, blazed with copper lines. When they had approached so close that the suns were widely spaced in the heavens Crane asked Seaton to take his place at the board while he and Margaret tried to locate a planet.

They went down to the observatory, but found that they were still too far away and began taking notes. Crane's mind was not upon his work, however, but was filled with thoughts of the girl at his side. The intervals between comments became much longer and longer, until the two were standing in silence.

The *Skylark* lurched a little, as she had done hundreds of times before. As usual, Crane put out a steadying arm. This time, however, in that highly charged atmosphere, the gesture took on a new significance. Both blushed hotly; and, as their eyes met, each saw what they had both wanted most to see.

Slowly, almost as though without volition, Crane put his other arm around her. A wave of deeper crimson flooded her face; but her lips lifted to his and her arms went up around his neck.

'Margaret – Peggy – I had intended to wait – but why should we wait? You know how much I love you, my dearest!'

'I think I do … I *know* I do … my Martin!'

Presently they made their way back to the engine-room, hoping that their singing joy was inaudible, their new status invisible. They might have kept their secret for a time had not Seaton promptly asked, 'What did you find, Mart?'

The always self-possessed Crane looked panicky; Margaret's fair face glowed a deeper and deeper pink.

'Yes, what *did* you *find*?' Dorothy demanded, with a sudden, vivid smile of understanding.

'My future wife,' Crane answered, steadily.

The two girls hugged each other and the two men gripped hands, each of the four knowing that in these two unions there was nothing whatever of passing fancy.

A planet was located and the *Skylark* flew toward it.

'It's pretty deep in, Mart. DuQuesne and I haven't got enough dope yet to plot this mess of suns, so we don't know exactly where any of them really are, but that planet's somewhere down in the middle. Would that make any difference?'

'No. There are many closer ones, but they are too big or too small or lack water or atmosphere or have some other drawback. Go ahead.'

When they neared atmosphere and cut the drive, there were seventeen great suns, scattered in all directions in the sky.

'Air-pressure at the surface, thirty pounds per square inch.

'Composition, approximately normal except for three-tenths of one per cent of a fragrant, non-poisonous gas with which I am not familiar. Temperature, one hundred degrees Fahrenheit. Surface gravity, four-tenths Earth,' came the various reports.

Seaton let the vessel settle slowly toward the ocean beneath them; the water was an intensely deep blue. He took a sample, ran it through the machine, and yelled.

'Ammoniacal copper sulphate! Hot dog! Let's go!' Seaton laid a course toward the nearest continent.

XVI

As the *Skylark* approached the shore its occupants heard a rapid succession of detonations, apparently coming from the direction in which they were traveling.

'Wonder what that racket is,' Seaton said. 'Sounds like big guns and high explosive – not atomic, though.'

'Check,' DuQuesne said. 'Even allowing for the density of this air, that kind of noise is not made by pop-guns.'

Seaton closed the lock to keep out the noise, and advanced the speed lever until the vessel tilted sharply under the pull of the engine.

'Go easy, Seaton,' DuQuesne cautioned. 'We don't want to stop one of their shells – they may not be like ours.'

'Easy it is. I'll stay high.'

As the *Skylark* closed up, the sound grew heavier and clearer. It was one practically continuous explosion.

'There they are,' said Seaton, who, from his board, could scan the whole field of vision. 'From port six, five o'clock low.'

While the other four were making their way to the indicated viewpoint Seaton went on. 'Aerial battleships, eight of 'em. Four are about the shape of ours – no wings, act like 'copters – but I never saw anything like the other four.'

Neither had either Crane or DuQuesne.

'They must be animals,' Crane decided, finally. 'I do not believe that any engineer, anywhere, would design machines like that.'

Four of the contestants were animals. Here indeed was a new kind of animal – an animal able and eager to engage a first-class battleship.

Each had an enormous, torpedo-shape body, with scores of long tentacles and a dozen or so immense wings. Each had a row of eyes along each side and a sharp, prow-like beak. Each was covered with scale-like plates of transparent armor; wings and tentacles were made of the same substance.

That it was real and highly effective armor there was no doubt, for each battleship bristled with guns and each gun was putting out an almost continuous stream of fire. Shells bursting against the creatures filled the region with flame and haze, and produced an uninterrupted roll of sound appalling in its intensity.

In spite of that desperate concentration of fire, however, the animals went straight in. Beaks tore yards-wide openings in hulls; flailing wings smashed superstructures flat; writhing, searching tentacles wrenched guns from their mounts and seized personnel. Out of action, one battleship was held while tentacles sought out and snatched its crew. Then it was dropped, to crash some twenty thousand feet below. One animal was blown apart. Two more battleships and two more animals went down.

The remaining battleship was half wrecked; the animal was as good as new. Thus the final duel did not last long.

The monster darted away after something, which the observers in the *Skylark* saw for the first time – a fleet of small airships in full flight away from the scene of battle. Fast as they were, the animal was covering three miles to their one.

'We can't stand for anything like that!' Seaton cried, as he threw on power and the *Skylark* leaped ahead. 'When I yank him away, Mart, sock him with a Mark Ten!'

The monster seized the largest, most gaily decorated plane just as the *Skylark* came within sighting distance. In four almost simultaneous motions

Seaton focused the attractor on the huge beak of the thing, shoved on its power, pointed the engine straight up and gave it five notches.

There was a crash of rending metal as the monster was torn loose from its prey. Seaton hauled it straight up for a hundred miles, while it struggled so savagely in that invisible and in-comprehensible grip that the thousands of tons of mass of the *Skylark* tossed and pitched like a rowboat in a storm at sea.

Crane fired. There was a blare of sound that paralyzed their senses, even inside the vessel and in the thin air of that enormous elevation. There was a furiously-boiling, furiously-expanding ball of ... of what? The detonation of a Mark Ten load cannot be described. It must be seen; and even then, it cannot be understood. It can scarcely be believed.

No bit large enough to be seen remained of that mass of almost indestructible armor.

Seaton reversed the bar and drove straight down, catching the crippled flagship at about five thousand feet. He focused the attractor and lowered the plane gently to the ground. The other airships, which had been clustering around their leader in near-suicidal attempts at rescue, landed nearby.

As the *Skylark* landed beside the wrecked plane, the Earthmen saw that it was surrounded by a crowd of people – men and women identical in form and feature with themselves. They were a superbly-molded race. The men were almost as big as Seaton and DuQuesne; the women were noticeably taller than the two Earthwomen. The men wore collars of metal, numerous metallic ornaments, and heavily-jeweled belts and shoulder-straps which were hung with weapons. The women were not armed, but were even more highly decorated than the men. They fairly scintillated with jewels.

The natives wore no clothing, and their smooth skins shone a dark, livid, utterly strange color in the yellowish-bluish-green glare of the light. Their skins were green, undoubtedly; but it was no green known to Earth. The 'whites' of their eyes were a light yellowish-green. The heavy hair of the women and the close-cropped locks of the men were a very dark green – almost black – as were also their eyes.

'*What* a color,' Seaton said, wonderingly. 'They're human, I guess ... except for the color ... but Great Cat, what a *color*!'

'How much of that is pigment and how much is due to this light is a question,' said Crane. 'If we were outside, away from our daylight lamps, we might look like that, too.'

'Horrors, I hope not!' Dorothy exclaimed. 'If I'm going to I won't take a step out of this ship, so there!'

'Sure you will,' Seaton said. 'You'll look like a choice piece of modern art and your hair will be jet black. Come on and give the natives a treat.'

'Then what color will mine be?' Margaret asked.

'I'm not quite sure. Probably a very dark and very beautiful green,' he grinned gleefully. 'My hunch is that this is going to be *some* visit. Wait 'till I get a couple of props … Shall we go? Come on, Dot.'

'Roger. I'll try anything, once.'

'Margaret?'

'Onward, men of Earth!'

Seaton opened the lock and the five stood in the chamber, looking at the throng outside. Seaton raised both arms above his head, in what he hoped was the universal sign of peaceful intent. In response a man of Herculean build, so splendidly decorated that his harness was one gleaming mass of jewels, waved one arm and shouted a command. The crowd promptly fell back, leaving a clear space of a hundred yards. The man unbuckled his harness, let everything drop, and advanced naked toward the *Skylark,* both arms aloft in Seaton's own gesture.

Seaton started down.

'No, Dick, talk to him from here,' Crane advised.

'Nix,' Seaton said. 'What he can do, I can. Except undress in mixed company. He won't know that I've got a gun in my pocket, and it won't take me more than half an hour to pull it if I have to.'

'Go on, then. DuQuesne and I will come along.'

'Double nix. He's alone, so I've got to be. Some of his boys are covering the field, though, so you might draw your gats and hold them so they show.'

Seaton stepped down and went to meet the stranger. When they had approached to within a few feet of each other the stranger stopped, stood erect, flexed his left arm smartly, so that the finger-tips touched his left ear, and smiled broadly, exposing clean, shining, green teeth. He spoke – a meaningless jumble of sound. His voice, coming from so big a man, seemed light and thin.

Seaton smiled in return and saluted as the other had done.

'Hail and greetings, Oh High Panjandrum,' Seaton said, cordially, his deep voice fairly booming out in the dense, heavy air. 'I get the drift, and I'm glad you're peaceable; I wish I could tell you so.'

The native tapped himself upon the chest. 'Nalboon,' he said, distinctly and impressively.

'Nalboon,' Seaton repeated; then said, in the other's tone and manner, while pointing to himself, 'Seaton.'

'See Tin,' Nalboon said, and smiled again. Again indicating himself, he said, 'Domak gok Mardonale.'

That was evidently a title, so Seaton had to give himself one. 'Boss of the Road,' he said, drawing himself up with pride.

Thus properly introduced to his visitor, Nalboon pointed to the crippled plane, inclined his royal head slightly in thanks or in acknowledgement of the service rendered – Seaton could not tell which – then turned to face his people with one arm upraised. He shouted an order in which Seaton could distinguish something that sounded like 'See Tin Basz Uvvy Roagd.'

Instantly every right arm in the crowd was aloft, that of each man bearing a weapon, while the left arms snapped into that peculiar salute. A mighty cry arose as all repeated the name and title of the distinguished visitor.

Seaton turned. 'Bring out one of those big four-color signal rockets, Mart!' he called. 'We've got to acknowledge a reception like this!'

The party appeared, DuQuesne carrying the rocket with an exaggerated deference. Seaton shrugged one shoulder and a cigarette-case appeared in his hand. Nalboon started and, in spite of his self-control, glanced at it in surprise. The case flew open and Seaton, after taking a cigarette, pointed to another.

'Smoke?' he asked, affably. Nalboon took one, but had no idea whatever of what to do with it. This astonishment at simple sleight-of-hand and ignorance of tobacco emboldened Seaton. Reaching into his mouth, he pulled out a flaming match – at which Nalboon jumped straight backward at least a foot. Then, while Nalboon and his people watched in straining attention, Seaton lit the weed, half-consumed it in two long drags, swallowed the half, regurgitated it still alight, took another puff, and swallowed the butt.

'I'm good, I admit, but not *that* good,' Seaton said to Crane. 'I never laid 'em in the aisles like that before. This rocket'll tie 'em up like pretzels. Keep clear, everybody.'

He bowed deeply to Nalboon, pulling a lighted match from his ear as he did so, and lighted the fuse. There was a roar, a shower of sparks, a blaze of colored fire as the rocket flew upward; but, to Seaton's surprise, Nalboon took it quite as a matter of course, merely saluting gravely in acknowledgement of the courtesy.

Seaton motioned his party to come up and turned to Crane. 'Better not, Dick. Let him keep on thinking that one Boss is all there is.'

'Not by a long shot. There's only one of him – two of us bosses would be twice as good.' He introduced Crane, with great ceremony, as 'Boss of the *Skylark*,' whereupon the grand salute of the people was repeated.

Nalboon gave an order, and a squad of soldiers brought up a group of people, apparently prisoners. Seven men and seven women, they were of a much lighter color than the natives. They were naked, except for jeweled collars worn by all and a thick metal belt worn by one of the men. They all walked proudly, scorn for their captors in every step.

Nalboon barked an order. Thirteen of the prisoners stared back at him, motionlessly defiant. The man wearing the belt, who had been studying Seaton closely, said something, whereupon they all prostrated themselves. Nalboon waved his hand – giving the group to Seaton and Crane. They accepted the gift with due thanks and the slaves placed themselves behind their new masters.

Seaton and Crane then tried to make Nalboon understand that they wanted copper, but failed dismally. Finally Seaton led the native into the ship and showed him the remnant of the power-bar, indicating its original size and giving information as to the number desired by counting to sixteen upon his fingers. Nalboon understood, and, going outside, pointed upward toward the largest of the eleven suns visible, and swung his arm four times in a rising-and-setting arc. He then invited the visitors to get into his plane, but Seaton refused. They would follow, he explained, in their own vessel.

As they entered the *Skylark,* the slaves followed.

'We don't want them aboard, Dick,' Dorothy protested. There are too many of them. Not that I'm exactly scared, but …

'We've got to,' Seaton decided. 'We're stuck with 'em. And besides – when in Rome, you've got to be a Roman candle, you know.'

Nalboon's newly-invested flagship led the way; the *Skylark* followed, a few hundred yards behind and above it.

'I don't get these folks at all,' Seaton said, thoughtfully. 'They've got next century's machines, but never heard of sleight-of-hand. Class Nine rockets are old stuff, but matches scare them. Funny.'

'It is surprising enough that their physical shape is the same as ours,' Crane said. 'It would be altogether too much to expect that all the details of development would be parallel.'

The fleet approached a large city and the visitors from Earth studied with interest this metropolis of an unknown world. The buildings were all of the same height, flat-topped, arranged in random squares, rectangles, and triangles. There were no streets, the spaces between the buildings being park-like areas.

All traffic was in the air. Flying vehicles darted in all directions, but the confusion was only apparent, not real, each class and each direction having its own level.

The fleet descended toward an immense building just outside the city proper and all landed upon its roof except the flagship, which led the *Skylark* to a landing-dock nearby.

As they disembarked Seaton said, 'Don't be surprised at anything I pull off – I'm a walking storehouse of all kinds of small junk.'

Nalboon led the way into an elevator, which dropped to the ground floor. Gates opened, and through ranks of prostrate people the party went out into the palace grounds of the emperor of the great nation of Mardonale.

It was a scene of unearthly splendor. Every shade of their peculiar spectrum was there, in solid, liquid, and gas. Trees were of all colors, as were grasses and flowers along the walks. Fountains played streams of various and constantly-changing hues. The air was tinted and perfumed, swirling through metal arches in billows of ever-varying colors and scents. Colors and combinations of colors impossible to describe were upon every hand, fantastically beautiful in that strong, steady, peculiar light.

'Isn't this gorgeous, Dick?' Dorothy whispered. 'But I wish I had a mirror – you look simply awful – what kind of a scarecrow am I?'

'You've been under a mercury arc? Like that, only worse. Your hair isn't as black as I thought it would be, there's some funny green in it. Your lips, though, are really black. Your teeth are green …'

'Stop it! Green teeth and black lips! That's enough – and I don't want a mirror!'

Nalboon led the way into the palace proper and into a dining hall, where a table was ready. This room had many windows, each of which was festooned with sparkling, scintillating gems. The walls were hung with a cloth resembling spun glass or nylon, which fell to the floor in shimmering waves of color.

There was no woodwork whatever. Doors, panels, tables and chairs were made of metal. A closer inspection of one of the tapestries showed that it, too, was of metal, its threads numbering thousands to the inch. Of vivid but harmonious colors, of a strange and intricate design, it seemed to writhe as its colors changed with every variation in the color of the light.

'Oh … isn't that stuff just too perfectly gorgeous?' Dorothy breathed. 'I'd give *anything* for a dress made out of it.'

'Order noted,' Seaton said. 'I'll pick up ten yards of it when we get the copper.'

'We'd better watch the chow pretty close, Seaton,' DuQuesne said, as Nalboon waved them to the table.

'You chirped it. Copper, arsenic, and so forth. Very little here we *can* eat much of, I'd say.'

'The girls and I will wait for you two chemists to approve each dish, then,' Crane said.

The guests sat down, the light-skinned slaves standing behind them, and servants brought in heaping trays of food. There were joints and cuts of many kinds of meat; birds and fish, raw and cooked in various ways; green, pink, brown, purple, black and near-white vegetables and fruits. Slaves handed the diners peculiar instruments – knives with razor edges, needle-pointed stilettos, and wide, flexible spatulas which evidently were to serve as both forks and spoons.

'I simply *can't* eat with these things!' Dorothy exclaimed.

'That's where my lumberjack training comes in handy,' Seaton grinned. 'I can eat with a spatula four times as fast as you can with a fork. But we'll fix that.'

Reaching out, apparently into the girl's hair, he brought out forks and spoons, much to the surprise of the natives.

DuQuesne and Seaton waved away most of the proffered foods without discussion. Then, tasting cautiously and discussing fully, they approved a few of the others. The approval, however, was very strictly limited.

'These probably won't poison us too much,' DuQuesne said, pointing out the selected few. 'That is, if we don't eat much now and don't eat any of it again too soon. I don't like this one little bit, Seaton.'

'You and me both,' Seaton agreed. 'I don't think there'll be any next time.'

Nalboon took a bowl full of blue crystals, sprinkled his food liberally with the substance, and passed the bowl to Seaton.

'Copper sulphate,' Seaton said. 'Good thing they put it on at the table instead of the kitchen, or we couldn't eat a bit of anything.'

Seaton, returning the bowl, reached behind him and came up with a pair of salt- and pepper-shakers which, after seasoning his own food with them, he passed to his host. Nalboon tasted the pepper cautiously, then smiled in delight and half-emptied the shaker onto his plate. He then sprinkled a few grains of salt into his palm, studied them closely with growing amazement, and after a few rapid sentences poured them into a dish held by an officer who had sprung to his side. The officer also studied the few small crystals, then carefully washed Nalboon's hand. Nalboon turned to Seaton, plainly asking for the salt-cellar.

'Sure, my ripe and old.' In the same mysterious way he produced another set, which he handed to Crane.

The meal progressed merrily, with much sign-language conversation between the two parties, a little of which was understood. It was evident that Nalboon, usually stern and reticent, was in an unusually pleasant and jovial mood.

After the meal Nalboon bade them a courteous farewell; and they were escorted to a suite of five connecting rooms by the royal usher and a company of soldiers, who mounted guard outside the suite.

Gathered in one room, they discussed sleeping arrangements. The girls insisted that they would sleep together, and that the men should occupy the rooms on either side. As the girls turned away, four slaves followed.

'I don't want these people and I can't make them go away,' she protested again. 'Can't you do something, Dick?'

'I don't think so. I think we're stuck with 'em as long as we're here. Don't you think so, Mart?'

'Yes. And from what I have seen of this culture, I infer that they will be executed if we discard them.'

'Huh? How do ... could be. We keep 'em, then, Dot.'

'Of course, in that case. You keep the men and we'll take the women.'

'Hmmm.' He turned to Crane, saying under his breath, 'They don't want us sleeping in the same room with any of these gorgeous gals, huh? I *wonder* why?'

Seaton waved all the women into the girls' room; but they hung back. One of them ran up to the man wearing the belt and spoke rapidly as she threw her arms around his neck in a perfectly human gesture. He shook his head, pointing toward Seaton several times as he reassured her. He then led her tenderly into the girls' room and the other women followed. Crane and

DuQuesne having gone to their rooms with their attendants, the man with the belt started to help Seaton take off his clothes.

Stripped, Seaton stretched vigorously, the muscles writhing and rippling under the skin of mighty arms and broad shoulders as he twisted about, working off the stiffness of comparative confinement. The slaves stared in amazement at the display of musculature and talked rapidly among themselves as they gathered up Seaton's discarded clothing. Their chief picked up a salt-shaker, a silver fork, and a few other items that had fallen from the garments, apparently asking permission to do something with them. Seaton nodded and turned to his bed. He heard a slight clank of arms in the hall and began to wonder. Going to the window, he saw that there were guards outside as well. Were they honored guests or prisoners?

Three of the slaves, at a word from their leader, threw themselves on the floor and slept; but he himself did not rest. Opening the apparently solid metal belt he took out a great number of small tools, many tiny instruments, and several spools of insulated wire. He then took the articles Seaton had given him, taking extreme pains not to spill a single crystal of salt, and set to work. As he worked, hour after hour, a strange, exceedingly complex device took form under his flying fingers.

XVII

Seaton did not sleep well. It was too hot. He was glad after eight hours to get up. No sooner had he started to shave, however, than one of the slaves touched his arm, motioning him into a reclining chair and showing him a keen blade, long and slightly curved. Seaton lay down and the slave shaved him with a rapidity and smoothness he had never before experienced, so wonderfully sharp was the peculiar razor. Then the barber began to shave his superior, with no preliminary treatment save rubbing his face with a perfumed oil.

'Hold on a minute,' said Seaton. 'Here's something that helps a lot. Soap.' He lathered the face with his brush, and the man with the belt looked up in surprised pleasure as his stiff beard was swept away with no pulling at all.

Seaton called to the others and soon the party was assembled in his room. All were dressed very lightly because of the unrelieved and unvarying heat, which was constant at one hundred degrees. A gong sounded and one of the slaves opened the door, ushering in servants bearing a table, ready set. The Earthlings did not eat anything, deciding that they would rather wait an hour or so and then eat in the *Skylark*. Hence the slaves had a much better meal than they otherwise would have had.

During that meal, Seaton was very much surprised at hearing Dorothy carrying on a labored conversation with one of the women.

'I knew you were a language shark, Dottie, but I didn't s'pose you could pick one up in a day.'

'Oh, I can't. Just a few words. I can understand very little of what they're trying to tell me.'

The woman spoke rapidly to the man with the belt, who immediately asked Seaton's permission to speak to Dorothy. Running across to her, he bowed and poured out such a stream of words that she held up her hand to silence him.

'Go slower, please,' she said, and added a couple of words in his own language.

There ensued a very strange conversation between the slave couple and Dorothy, with much talking between the man and the woman, both talking at once to Dorothy, and much use of signs and sketches. Dorothy finally turned to Seaton with a frown.

'I can't make out half of what he tried to tell me, and I'm guessing at part of that. He wants you to take him somewhere, another room of the palace here, I think. He wants to get something. I can't quite make out what it is, or whether it was his and they took it away from him, or whether it's something of theirs that he wants to steal. He can't go alone. Martin was right, any of them will be shot if they stir without us. And he says – I'm pretty sure of this part – when you get there don't let any guards come inside.'

'What do you think, Mart? I'm inclined to string along with this bunch, at least part way. I don't like Nalboon's "honor guard" set-up a bit – it smells. Like over-ripe fish.'

Crane concurred. Seaton and his slave started for the door. Dorothy went along.

'Better stay back, Dottie. We won't be gone long.'

'I will not go back,' she said, for his ears alone. 'On this damn world I'm not going to be away from you one minute more than I absolutely have to.'

'Hokay, ace,' he replied, in the same tone. 'You'd be amazed to find out how little there is in that idea for me to squawk about.'

Preceded by the man with the belt and followed by half a dozen other slaves, they went out into the hall. No opposition was made to their going; but half a company of armed guards fell in with them as an escort, most of them looking at Seaton with a mixture of reverence and fear. The slave led the way to a room in a distant wing of the palace and opened the door. As Seaton stepped into it he saw that it was an audience chamber or courtroom and that it was now empty.

The guards approached the door. Seaton waved them back. All retreated across the hall except the officer in charge, who refused to move. Seaton, the personification of offended dignity, stared haughtily at the offender, who returned the stare with interest and stepped forward, fully intending to be the first to enter the room. Seaton, with the flat of his right hand on the officer's chest, pushed him back roughly, forgetting that his strength, great upon Earth, would be gigantic upon this smaller world. The officer spun across the corridor, knocking down three of his men in his flight. Picking himself up, he drew his sword and rushed, while his men fled in panic to the extreme end of the corridor.

Seaton did not wait for him, but leaped to meet him. With his vastly super-ior agility he dodged the falling broadsword and drove his right fist into the fellow's throat, with all the strength of arm and shoulder and all the momen-tum of his body behind the blow. Bones broke audibly as the officer's head snapped back. The body went high in the air, turned two complete somer-saults, crashed against the far wall and dropped to the floor.

At this outrage, some of the guards started to lift their peculiar guns. Dor-othy screamed a warning. Seaton drew and fired in one incredibly fast motion, the Mark One load obliterating the clustered soldiers and demolish-ing that end of the palace.

In the meantime the slave had taken several pieces of apparatus from a cabinet and had placed them in his belt. Stopping only to observe for a few moments a small instrument which he clamped to the head of the dead man, he led the party back to the room they had left and set to work upon the device he had built during the sleeping period. He connected it, in an extremely intricate network of wiring, with the pieces of apparatus he had just obtained.

'Whatever that is, it's a nice job,' DuQuesne said, admiringly. 'I've built com-plex stuff myself, but he's got me completely lost. It'd take a week to find out where some of the stuff is going and what it's going to do when it gets there.'

Straightening up, the slave clamped several electrodes to his head and motioned to Seaton and the others, speaking to Dorothy as he did so.

'He wants to put those things on our heads,' she translated, 'but I can't make out what they're for. Shall we let him?'

'Yes,' he decided instantly. 'There's going to be hell to pay any minute now, and no pitch hot. I got us in too deep to back out now. Besides, I've got a hunch. But of course I'm not trying to decide for any of you. In fact, Dot, it might be smart if you …'

'I'm not smart, Dick. Where you go, I go,' Dorothy said quietly, and bent her auburn head to be fitted.

'I do not relish the idea,' Crane said. 'In fact, I do not like it at all. But, under present circumstances, it seems the thing to do.'

Margaret followed Crane's lead, but DuQuesne said, with a sneer, 'Go ahead; let him make zombies of you. Nobody wires *me* up to a machine I can't understand.'

The slave closed a switch, and – instantly– the four visitors acquired a completely detailed knowledge of the languages and customs of both Mardonale, the nation in which they now were, and of Kondal, the nation to which the slaves belonged, the only two civilized nations upon Osnome.

While amazement at this method of instruction was still upon the Earthmen's faces the slave – or, as they now knew him, Dunark, the kofedix or crown prince of Kondal – began to remove the helmets. He took off the girls', and Crane's. He was reaching for Seaton's when there was a flash, a crackle, and a puff of smoke from the machine. Dunark and Seaton both fell flat.

Before Crane could reach them, however, they both recovered and Dunark said, 'This is a mechanical educator, something entirely new. We've been working on it several years, but it is still very crude. I didn't like to use it, but I had to, to warn you of what Nalboon is going to do and to convince you that saving your own lives would save ours as well. But something went wrong, probably because of my hasty work in assembly. Instead of stopping at teaching you our languages it shorted me and Dick together – completely.'

'What would such a short do?' Crane asked.

'I'll answer that, Dunark.' Seaton had not recovered quite as fast as the Kondalian, but was now back to normal. 'All it did was to print in the brain of each of us, down to the finest detail, everything that the other had ever learned. It was the completeness of the transfer that put us both out for a minute.'

'I'm sorry, Seaton, believe me ...'

'Why?' Seaton grinned. 'It's taken each of us all our lives to learn what we know, and now it's doubled. We're both way ahead, aren't we?'

'I certainly am, and I'm very glad that you take it that way. But time presses ...'

'Let me tell 'em,' Seaton said. 'You aren't exactly sure which English to use yet, the one I talk or the one I write, and neither you nor we can think very fast, yet, in the other's language. I'll boil it down.'

'This is Crown Prince Dunark of Kondal. The other thirteen are relatives of his, princes and princesses. Nalboon's raiders got them while they were out hunting – used a new kind of nerve-gas so they couldn't kill themselves, which is good technique in these parts.

'Kondal and Mardonale have been at war for over six thousand years, a war with no holds barred. No prisoners, except to find out what they know; no niceties. Having found out what these Kondalians knew, Nalboon threw a party – a Roman circus, really – and was going to feed them to some pet devil-fish of his when those armored flying animals – karlono, they call them – smelled them and came into the picture.

'You know what happened then. These people were aboard Nalboon's plane, the one we eased down to the ground. You'd think Nalboon would think he owed us something, but …'

'Let me finish,' Dunark cut in. 'You simply will not do yourself justice. Having saved his life, you should have been guests of the most honored kind. You would have been, anywhere else in the universe. But no Mardona- lian has, or even has had, either honor or conscience. At first, Nalboon was afraid of you, as were we all. We thought you were from the fifteenth sun, now at its closest possible distance, and after seeing your power we expected annihilation.

'However, after seeing the *Skylark* as a machine, learning that you are short of power, and finding you gentle – weak, he thinks that is; how wrong he is! – instead bloodthirsty Nalboon decided to kill you and take your ship, with its wonderful new power. For, while we Osnomians are ignorant of chemistry, we know machines and we know electricity. No Osnomian has ever had any inkling that such a thing as atomic energy exists. Nevertheless, after his study of your engines, Nalboon knows how to liberate it and how to control it. With the *Skylark* he could obliterate Kondal; and to do that, he would do anything.

'Also, he or any other Osnomian scientist, including myself, would go to any length, would challenge First Cause itself, to secure even one of those small containers of the chemical you call *salt*. It is the scarcest, most precious substance in our world. You actually had more of it at the table than the total previously known to exist upon all Osnome. Its immense value is due, not to its rarity, but to the fact that it is the only known catalyst for our hardest metals.

'You know now why Nalboon intends to kill you; and nothing you can do or not do will alter that intent. His plan is this: during the next sleeping period – I simply can't use your word "night," since there is no such thing on Osnome – he will cut into the *Skylark* and take all the salt you have in it. The interrupted circus will be resumed, with you Tellurians as principal guests. We Kondalians will be given to the karlono. Then you five will be killed and your bodies smelted to recover the salt that is in them.

'This is the warning I had to give you. Its urgency explains why I used my crude educator. In self-defense, I must add this – the lives of you five Tellurians are not of paramount importance, the lives of us fourteen Kondalians much less so. We are all expendable. The *Skylark*, however, is not. If Nalboon gets her, every living Kondalian will die within a year. That fact, and that fact alone, explains why you saw me, the kofedix of Kondal, prostrate myself before Nal- boon of Mardonale, and heard me order my kinsmen to do the same.'

'How do you, a prince of another nation, know all these things?' Crane asked.

'Some are common knowledge. I heard much while aboard Nalboon's plane. I read Nalboon's plan from the brain of the officer Dick killed. He was a … a colonel of the guard, and high in Nalboon's favor. He was to have been in charge of cutting into the *Skylark* and of killing and smelting you five.'

'That clears things up,' Seaton said. 'Thanks, Dunark. The big question now is, what do we do about it?'

'I suggest that you take us into the *Skylark* and get away from here – as soon as you can. I'll pilot you to Kondalek, our capital city. There, I can assure you, you will be welcomed as you deserve. My father will treat you as a visiting karfedix should be treated. As far as I am concerned, if you can succeed in getting us back to Kondal – or in getting the *Skylark* there without any of us – nothing I can ever do will lighten the burden of my indebtedness; but I promise you all the copper you want, and anything else you may desire that is within the power of all Kondal to give.'

Seaton scowled in thought.

'Our best chance is with you,' he said, finally. 'But if we give you atomic power, which we would be doing if we take you back home, Kondal will obliterate Mardonale – if you can.'

'Of course.'

'So, ethically, perhaps we should leave you all here and try to blast our own way to the *Skylark*. Then go on about our own business.'

'That is your right.'

'But I couldn't do it. And if I did, Dottie would skin me alive and rub salt in, every day from now on … and Nalboon and his crowd *are* the scum of the universe … Maybe I'm prejudiced by having your whole mind in mine, but I think I'd have to come to the same decision if I had Nalboon's whole mind in there as well. When will we make the break – the hour after the second meal?'

'The strolling hour, yes. You are using my knowledge, I see, just as I am using yours.'

'Mart and DuQuesne, we'll make our break just after the next meal, when everybody is strolling around talking to everybody else. That's when the guards are most lax, and our best chance, since we haven't got armor and no good way of getting any.'

'But how about your killing his guards and blowing the end out of his palace?' DuQuesne asked. 'He isn't the type to take much of that sitting down. Won't that make him hurry things along?'

'We don't quite know, either Dunark or I. It depends pretty much on which emotion is governing, anger or fear. But we'll know pretty quick. He'll be paying us a call of state pretty soon now and we'll see what he acts like and how he talks. However, he's quite a diplomat and may conceal his real feelings entirely. But remember, he thinks gentleness is fear, so don't be surprised if I open up on him. If he gets the least bit tough I'll cut him down to size right then.'

'Well,' Crane said, 'if we have some time to wait, we may as well wait in comfort instead of standing up in the middle of the room. I, for one, would like to ask a few questions.'

The Tellurians seated themselves upon divans and Dunark began to dismantle the machine he had built. The Kondalians remained standing behind their 'masters,' until Seaton protested.

'Please sit down, everybody. There's no need of keeping up this farce of your being slaves as long as we're alone.'

'Perhaps not, but at the first sign of a visitor we must all be in our places. Now that we have a little time and are able to understand each other, I will introduce my party to yours.

'Fellow Kondalians, greet Karfedix Seaton and Karfedix Crane, of a strange and extremely distant planet called Earth.' He and his group saluted formally. 'Greet also the noble ladies, Miss Vaneman and Miss Spencer, soon to become Karfedir Seaton and Karfedir Crane, respectively.' They saluted again.

'Guests from Earth, allow me to present the Kofedir Sitar, the only one of my wives who was unfortunate enough to be with me on our ill-fated hunting expedition.' One of the women stepped forward and bowed deeply to the four, who returned the compliment in kind.

Ignoring DuQuesne as a captive, he went on to introduce the other Kondalians as his brothers, sisters, half-brothers, half-sisters, and cousins – all members of the ruling house of Kondal.

'Now, after I have had a word with you in private, Dr Seaton, I will be glad to give the others any information I can.'

'I want a word with you, too, Junior. I didn't want to break up your ceremony by arguing about it out there, but I am not, never was, and never will be a karfedix – which word, as you know, translates quite closely into "emperor." I'm merely a plain citizen.'

'I know that ... that is, I know it, in a way, from your own knowledge; but I find it impossible to understand it or to relate it to anything in my own experience. Nor can I understand your government; I fail entirely to see how it could function for even one of your years without breaking down. On Osnome, Dick, men of your attainments, and Martin's, are karfedo. You will be, whether you want to or not. Ph.D ... Doctor of Philosophy ... Karfedix of Knowledge ...'

'Pipe down, Dunark – forget it! What was it you wanted to talk to me about away from the mob?'

'Dorothy and Margaret. You already have it in your mind somewhere,

94

from mine, but you might find it as impossible to understand as I do much of yours. Your women are so different from ours, so startlingly beautiful, that Nalboon will not kill either of them – for a time. So, if worst comes to worst, be sure to kill them both while you still can.'

'I see … yes, I find it now.' Seaton's voice was cold, his eyes hard. 'Thanks. I'll remember that, and charge it to Nalboon's personal account.'

Rejoining the others, they found Dorothy and Sitar deep in conversation.

'So a man has half a dozen or so wives?' Dorothy was asking in surprise. 'How can you get along – I'd fight like a wildcat if Dick got any such funny ideas as that!'

'Why, splendidly, of course. I wouldn't *think* of *ever* marrying a man if he was such a … a … a *louse* that only one woman would have him!'

'I've got a cheerful thought for you and Peg, Red-top. Dunark here thinks you two are beautiful. "Startlingly beautiful" was the exact description.'

'What? In this light? Green, black, yellow, and mudcolor? We're positively hideous! And if that's your idea of a joke …'

'Oh, no, Dorthee,' Sitar interposed. 'You two *are* beautiful – really lovely. And you have such a rich, smoothly-blending color-flow. It's a shame to hide so much of it with robes.'

'Yes, why do you?' Dunark asked; as both girls blushed hotly, he paused, obviously searching in Dick's mind for an answer he could not find in his own. 'I mean, I see the sense of covering as a protection, or for certain ceremonials in which covering is ritual; but when not needed, in fact, when you are too warm, as you are now …' He broke off in embarrassment and went on, 'Help, Dick. I seem to be getting my foot in it deeper and deeper. What have I done to offend?'

'Nothing. It isn't you at all; it's just that our race has worn clothing for centuries, and can't … Mart, how would you explain "modesty" to a race like that?' He swept his arm to cover the group of perfectly poised, completely un-self-conscious, naked men and women.

'I could explain it, after a fashion, but I doubt very much if even you, Dunark, with your heredity, could understand it. Sometime, when we have a few hours to spare, I will try to, if you like. But in the meantime, what are those collars and what do they mean?'

'Identifications. When a child is nearly grown, it is cast about his neck. It bears his name, national number, and the device of his house. Being made of arenak, it cannot be altered without killing the person. Any Osnomian not wearing a collar is unthinkable; but if it should ever happen he would be killed.'

'Is that belt something similar? No, it …'

'No. Merely a pouch. But even Nalboon thought it was opaque arenak, so didn't try to open it.'

'Is that transparent armor made of the same thing?'

'Yes, except that nothing is added to the matrix to make it colored or opaque. It is in the preparation of this metal that salt is indispensable. It acts only as a catalyst, being recovered afterward, but neither nation has ever had enough salt to make all the armor they want.'

'Aren't those monsters – karlono, I think you called them – covered with the same thing? And what are they, anyway?' Dorothy asked.

'Yes. It is thought that the beasts grow it, just as fishes grow scales. But no one knows how they do it – or even how they can possibly do it. Very little is known about them, however, except that they are the worst scourge of Osnome. Various scientists have described the karlon as a bird, a beast, a fish, and a vegetable; sexual, asexual, and hermaphroditic. Its habitat is—'

The gong sounded and the Kondalians leaped to their positions. The kofe-dix went to the door. Nalboon brushed him aside and entered, escorted by a squad of heavily-armed full-armored soldiers. A scowl of anger was on his face; he was plainly in an ugly mood.

'Stop, Nalboon of Mardonale!' Seaton thundered, in the Mardonalian tongue and at the top of his powerful voice. 'Dare you invade privacy without invitation?'

The escort shrank back, but the emperor stood his ground, although he was plainly taken by surprise. With a heroic effort he smoothed his face into lines of cordiality.

'May I inquire why my guards are slain and my palace destroyed by my honored guest?'

'You may. I permit it, to point out your errors. Your guards, at your order, no doubt, sought to invade my privacy. Being forbearing, I warned them once, but one of them was foolhardy enough to challenge me, and was of course destroyed. Then the others attempted to raise their childish weapons against me, and I of course destroyed them. The wall merely chanced to be inside the field of action of the force I chanced to be employing at the time.

'An honored guest? Bah! Know, Nalboon, that when you seek to treat as captive a visiting domak of my race, you lose not only your own life, but the lives of all your nation as well. Do you perceive your errors?'

Anger and fear fought for supremacy on Nalboon's face; but a third emotion, wonder, won. He, Nalboon, was armed; he had with him a score of armed and armored men. This stranger had nothing; the slaves were less than nothing. Yet he stood there, arrogantly confident, master of the planet, the solar system, and the universe, by his bearing ... and how ... how had he completely obliterated fifty armed and armored men and a thousand tons of stone and ultra-hard metal? Nalboon temporized.

'May I ask how you, so recently ignorant, know our language?'

'You may not. You may go.'

XVIII

That was a beautiful bluff, Dick!' Dunark exclaimed, as the door closed behind Nalboon and his guards. 'Exactly the right tone – you've got him guessing plenty.'

'It got him, all right – for the moment – but I'm wondering how long it will hold him. He's a big-time operator, and smart. The smart thing for us to do, I think, would be to take off for the *Skylark* right now, before he can get organized. What do you think, Mart?'

'I think so. We're altogether too vulnerable here.'

The Earthpeople quickly secured the few personal things they had brought with them. Seaton stepped out into the hall, waved the guards away, and motioned Dunark to lead the way. The other Kondalians fell in behind, as usual, and the group walked boldly toward the exit nearest the landing dock. The guards offered no opposition, but stood at attention and saluted as they passed. The officer lifted his microphone, however, and Seaton knew that Nalboon was being kept informed of every development.

Outside the palace, Dunark turned his head.

'Run!' he snapped. All did so. 'If they get a flyer into the air before we reach the dock it'll be just too bad. There'll be no pursuit from the palace – it isn't expendable – but the dock will be tough.'

Rounding a metal statue some fifty feet from the base of the towering dock they saw that the door of one of the elevators was open and that two guards stood just inside it. At sight of the party the guards raised their guns; but, fast as they were Seaton was faster. At first sight of the open door he had taken two quick steps and hurled himself across the intervening forty feet in a football plunge. Before the two soldiers could bring their guns to bear he crashed into them, hurling them across the cage and crushing them against its metal wall.

'Good work,' Dunark said. He stripped the unconscious guards of their weapons and, after asking Seaton's permission, distributed them among the men of his party. 'Now, perhaps, we can surprise whoever is on the roof. That was why you didn't shoot?'

'No,' Seaton grunted. 'We need this elevator. It wouldn't be much good after taking even a Mark One load.' He threw the two Mardonalians out of the elevator and closed the door.

Dunark took the controls. The elevator shot upward, stopping at a level well below the top. He took a tubular device from his belt and fitted it over the muzzle of the Mardonalian pistol.

'We get out here,' Dunark said, 'and go up the rest of the way by side stairs that aren't used much. We'll meet a few guards, probably, but I can take care of them. Stay behind me, please, everybody.'

Seaton promptly objected and Dunark went on, 'No, Dick, stay back. You know as much about this as I do, I know, but you can't get at the knowledge as fast. I'll let you take over when we reach the top.'

Dunark took the lead, his pistol resting lightly against his hip. At the first turn of the corridor they came upon four guards. The pistol did not leave Dunark's hip, but there were four subdued clicks, in faster succession than a man could count, and four men dropped.

'What a silencer!' DuQuesne whispered to Seaton. 'I didn't suppose a silencer could work that fast.'

'They don't use powder,' Seaton replied absently, all his faculties pinned to the next corner. 'Force-field projection.'

Dunark disposed of several more groups of guards before the head of the last stairway was reached. He stopped there.

'Now, Dick, you take over. I'm speaking English so I won't have to order each of my men individually – command them, literally – not to take my place at your side. We'll need all the speed and all the fire-power you have. There are hundreds of men on the roof outside, with rapid-fire cannon throwing a thousand shells a minute. If Crane will give me his pistols you can kick that door open as soon as you're ready.'

'I've got a lot better idea than that,' DuQuesne said. 'I'm as fast as you are, Seaton, and, like you, I can use both hands. Give me the guns and we'll have 'em cleaned out before the door gets fully open.'

'That's a thought, brother – that's *really* a thought,' Seaton said. 'Hand 'em over, Mart. Ready, Blackie? On your mark – get set – go!'

He kicked the door open and there was a stuttering crash as the four weapons burst into almost continuous flame – a crash obliterated by an over-whelming concatenation of sound as the X-plosive bullets, sweeping the roof with a rapidly-opening fan of death, struck their marks and exploded.

It was well that the two men in the doorway were past masters in the art of handling their weapons – and that they had in their bullets the force of giant shells! For rank upon rank of soldiery were massed there; engines of destruction covered elevators, doorways, and approaches.

So fast and fierce was the attack that trained gunners had no time to press their switches. The battle lasted approximately one second. It was over while shattered remnants of the guns and fragments of the metal and stone of the dock were still falling, through a fine mist of what had once been men.

Assured that not a single Mardonalian remained upon the dock, Seaton waved emphatically to the others.

'Snap it up!' he yelled. 'This is going to be hotter than the middle tail-race of Hades in exactly one minute.'

He led the way across the dock toward the *Skylark,* choosing the path with care between yawning holes. The ship was still in place, still held immovable by the attractor, but what a sight she was! Her quartz windows were shattered, her Norwegian-armor skin was dented and warped and fissured, half her plating was gone.

Not a shot had struck her. All this damage had been done by flying fragments of the guns and of the dock itself; and Seaton and Crane, who had developed the new explosive, were aghast at its awful power.

They climbed hastily into the vessel and Seaton ran toward the controls.

'I hear battleships,' Dunark said. 'Is it permitted that I operate one of your machine guns?'

'Go as far as you like!'

While Seaton was reaching for the speed-lever the first ranging shell from the first warship exploded against the side of the dock, just below them. His hand grasped the lever just as the second shell screamed through the air, scant yards above them; and as he shot the *Skylark* into the air under five notches of power a stream of the huge projectiles poured through the spot where she had just been.

Crane and DuQuesne aimed several shots at the battleships, but the range was so extreme that no damage was done. Dunark's rifle, however, was making a continuous chatter and they turned toward him. He was shooting, not at the warships, but at the city growing so rapidly smaller beneath them. He was moving the gun's muzzle in a small spiral, spraying the entire city with death and destruction. As they looked, the first of the shells reached the ground, just as Dunark ceased firing for lack of ammunition. The palace disappeared, blotted out in a cloud of dust; a cloud which spiraled outward until it obscured the area where the city had been.

High enough to be safe, Seaton stopped climbing and went out to confer with the others.

'It sure feels good to get a cool breath,' he said, inhaling deeply the thin, cold air of that altitude. Then he saw the kondalians, who, besides having taken a beating from the – to them – atrocious acceleration, were gasping for breath and were shivering, pale with cold.

'If *this* is what you like,' Dunark said, trying manfully to grin, 'I see at last why you wear clothes.'

Apologizing quickly, Seaton went back to the board and laid a course, on a downward slant, toward the ocean. Then he asked DuQuesne to take over and rejoined the group.

'There's no accounting for tastes,' he said to Dunark, 'but I can't hand your climate a thing. It's hotter and muggier than Washington in August; "and that," as the poet feelingly remarked, "is going some." But there's no sense to sitting here in the dark. Snap the switch, will you, Dottie?'

'Be glad to … now we'll see what they *really* look like … Why, they *are* beautiful … in spite of being sort of greenish like, they *really are*!'

But Sitar took one look at the woman by her side, shut both eyes, and screamed, 'What a *horrible* light! Shut it off; *please!* I'd rather be in darkness all my—'

'Did you ever see any darkness?' Seaton interrupted.

'Yes, I shut myself into a dark closet once, when I was a girl … and it scared me half out of my senses. I'll take back what I started to say; but that light'– Dorothy had already turned it off – 'was the most *terrible* thing I ever saw!'

'Why, Sitar,' Dorothy said, 'you looked perfectly stunning!'

'They see things differently from the way we do,' Seaton explained. 'Their optic nerves respond differently, send a different message to the brain. The same stimulus produces two entirely different end sensations. Am I making myself clear?'

'Sort of. Not very.' Dorothy said, doubtfully.

'Take a concrete example, the Kondalian color "map." Can you describe it?'

'It's a kind of greenish orange … but it shouldn't be. By what we learned from Dunark, it's brilliant purple.'

'That's what I mean. Well, get set, everybody, and we'll tear off a few knots for Kondalek.'

As they neared the ocean several Mardonalian battleships tried to intercept them; but the *Skylark* hopped over them and her speed was such that pursuit was not attempted. The ocean was crossed at the same high speed.

Dunark, who had already tuned the *Skylark*'s powerful transmitter to his father's private frequency, reported to him everything that had happened; and emperor and crown prince worked out a modified version which was to be broadcast throughout the nation.

Crane drew Seaton aside.

'Do you think we can really trust these Kondalians, any more than we should have trusted the Mardonalians? It might be better for us to stay in the *Skylark* instead of going to the palace at all.'

'Yes to the first; no to the second,' Seaton replied. 'I went off half-cocked last time, I admit; but I've got his whole mind inside my skull, so I know him a lot better than I know you. They've got some mighty funny ideas, and they're bloodthirsty and hard as tungsten carbide; but, basically, they're just as decent as we are.

'As for staying in here, what good would that do? Steel is as soft as mush to the stuff they've got. And we can't go anywhere, anyway. No copper – we're down to the plating in spots. And we couldn't if we were full of copper. The old bus is a wreck; she's got to be completely rebuilt. But you don't have to worry this time, Mart. I *know* they're friends of ours.'

'You don't say that very often,' Crane conceded, 'and when you do, I believe you. All objections are withdrawn.'

Flying over an immense city, the *Skylark* came to a halt directly above the palace, which, with its landing dock nearby, was very similar to that of Nalboon, the Mardonalian potentate.

From the city beneath the *Skylark* hundreds of big guns roared in welcome. Banners and streamers hung from every point. The air became tinted and perfumed with a bewildering variety of colors and scents. Ether and air alike were full of messages of welcome and hymns of joy.

A fleet of giant warships came up, to escort the battered little globe with impressive ceremony down to the landing dock; while around them great numbers of smaller aircraft flitted. Tiny one-man machines darted here and there, apparently always in imminent danger of collision with each other or with their larger fellows, but always escaping as though by a miracle. Beautiful pleasure-planes soared and dipped and wheeled like great gulls; and, cleaving their stately way through the hordes of lesser craft, immense multiplane passenger liners partially supported by helicopter screws turned aside from their scheduled courses to pay homage to the half of the Kondalian royal family so miraculously returned from the dead.

As the *Skylark* approached the roof of the dock, all the escorting vessels dropped away. On the roof, instead of the brilliant assemblage the Earthmen had expected to see, there was only a small group of persons, all of whom were as completely unadorned as were Dunark and the other erstwhile captives.

In answer to Seaton's look of surprise, Dunark said, with feeling, 'My father, mother, and the rest of the family. They knew we'd be stripped; they are meeting us that way.'

Seaton landed the ship. He and his four stayed inside while the family reunion, which was very similar to an Earthly one under similar circumstances, took place. Dunark then led his father up to the *Skylark* and the Tellurians disembarked.

'Friends, I have told you of my father; I present you to Roban, the Karfedix of Kondal. Father, it is an honor to present to you those who rescued us from Nalboon and from Mardonale. Seaton, Karfedix of Knowledge; Crane, Karfedix of Wealth; Miss Vaneman, and Miss Spencer. The Karfedelix DuQuesne' – waving his hand at him – 'is a lesser authority of knowledge and is captive to the others.'

'The Kofedix Dunark exaggerates our services,' Seaton said, 'and does not mention the fact that he saved all our lives.'

Disregarding Seaton's remark, Roban thanked them in the name of Kondal and introduced them to the rest of his party. As they all walked toward the elevator the emperor turned to his son with a puzzled expression.

'I know that our guests are from a very distant world, and I understand your accident with the educator, but I cannot understand the titles of these men. Knowledge and wealth are not – cannot be – ruled over. Are you sure that you have translated their titles correctly?'

'No translation is possible. Crane has no title, and was not at all willing for me to apply any title to him. Seaton's title, one of learnedness, has no equivalent in our language. What I did was to call them what each one would certainly become if he had been born one of us. Their government is not a government at all, but stark madness, the rulers being chosen by the people themselves, who change their minds and their rulers every year or two. And, everyone being equal before the law, does just about as he pleases ...'

'Incredible!' exclaimed Roban. 'How, then, is anything done?'

'I do not know. I simply do not understand it at all. They do not seem to care, as a nation, whether anything worthwhile gets done or not, as long as each man has what he calls his liberty. But that isn't the worst, or the most unreasonable. Listen to this.'

Dunark told his father all about the Seaton-Crane versus DuQuesne conflict. 'Then, in spite of all that, Crane gave DuQuesne both his pistols and DuQuesne stood at Seaton's side in that doorway and the two of them killed every Mardonalian on that roof before I could fire a single shot. DuQuesne fired every bullet in both his pistols and made no attempt whatever to kill either Seaton or Crane. And he is *still* their captive!'

'Incredible! What an incomprehensibly distorted sense of honor! If it were anyone except you saying this, I would deem it the ravings of a maniac. Are you sure, son, that these are facts?'

'I am sure. I saw them happen; so did the others. But in many other respects they are ... well, they are *not* insane ... Incomprehensible. The tenets of reason as we know reason simply are not applicable to many of their ideas, concepts, and actions. Clothing, for instance. Their values, their ethics, are in some respects absolutely incommensurate with ours. However, their sense of honor is, at bottom, as sound as ours, and as strong. And, since Nalboon tried to kill them, they are definitely on our side.'

'That, at least, I can understand, and it is well.' The older man shook his head. 'My mind is full of cobwebs. An enemy who is a friend. Or vice versa. Or both. A master who arms a slave. An armed slave who does not kill his master. That, my son, is simple, plain, stark lunacy!'

During this conversation they had reached the palace, after traversing grounds even more sumptuous and splendid than those surrounding the palace of Nalboon. Inside the building, Dunark himself led the guests to their rooms, accompanied by the major-domo and an escort of guards. The rooms were intercommunicating and each had a completely equipped bathroom, with a small swimming pool, built of polished metal, in lieu of a tub.

'This'd be nice,' Seaton said, indicating the pool, 'if you had some cold water.'

'There is cold water.' Dunark turned on a ten-inch stream of lukewarm water, then shut it off and smiled sheepishly. 'But I keep forgetting what you mean by the word "cold." We will install refrigerating machines at once.'

'Oh, don't bother about that; we won't be here long enough. One thing, though. I forgot to tell you. We'll eat our own food, not yours.'

'Of course. We'll take care of it. I'll be back in half an hour to take you to fourth-meal.'

Scarcely had the Earthlings freshened themselves than he was back; but he was no longer the Dunark they had known. He now wore a metal-and-leather harness that was one blaze of gems. A belt hung with resplendent weapons replaced the familiar hollow one of metal. His right arm, between the wrist and the elbow, was almost covered by six bracelets of a transparent, deep cobalt-blue metal; each set with in incredibly brilliant stone of the same color. On his left wrist he wore a Kondalian chronometer. This was an instrument resembling an odometer, whose numerous revolving segments showed a large and constantly-increasing number – the date and time of the Osomian day expressed in a decimal number of the years of Kondalian history.

'Greetings, oh guests from Tellus! I feel more like myself, now that I am again in my trappings and have my weapons at my side.' He attached a time-piece to the wrist of each of the guests, with a bracelet of the blue metal. 'Will you accompany me to fourth-meal or aren't you hungry?'

'We accept with thanks,' Dorothy replied, promptly. 'I, for one, am starving by inches.'

As they walked toward the dining-hall Dunark noticed that Dorothy's eyes kept straying to his bracelets.

'They are our wedding rings. Man and wife exchange bracelets as part of the ceremony.'

'Then you can always tell whether a man is married, and how many wives he has, just by looking at his arm. Nice. Some men on Earth wear wedding rings, but not many.'

Roban met them at the door of the hall, and Dorothy counted ten of the peculiar bracelets upon his right arm as he led them to places near his own. The room was a replica of the other Osnomian dining-hall they had seen; and the women were decorated with the same barbaric splendor of scintillating gems.

After the meal, which was a happy one, taking on the nature of a celebration in honor of the return of the children, DuQuesne went directly to his room, while the others spent the time until zero hour in strolling about the grounds. Upon returning to the room occupied by the two girls, the couples separated, each girl accompanying her lover to the door of his room.

Margaret was ill at ease.

'What's the matter, sweetheart?' Crane asked, solicitously. She twisted nervously at a button on his shirt.

'I didn't know that you ... I wasn't ... I mean I didn't ...' She broke off, then went on with a rush. 'What did Dunark mean by calling you the Karfedix of Wealth?'

'Well, you see, I happen to have some money ...' he began.

'Then you really *are* M. Reynolds Crane!'

Crane put his other arm around her, kissed her, and held her close.

'Is *that* all that was bothering you? What does money amount to between you and me?'

'Nothing – to me – but I'm awfully glad I didn't know anything about it before.' She returned his kisses with fervor. 'That is, it doesn't mean a thing if you are *perfectly* sure that I'm not after—'

Crane, the imperturbable, broke a hard and fast rule and interrupted her. 'Don't say that, dear. Don't even think of it, ever again. We both know that between you and me there never have been, are not now, and never shall be, any doubts or any questions.'

'If I could have that tank full of good cold water right now,' Seaton said, as he stood with Dorothy in the door of his room, 'I'd throw you in, clothes and all, dive in with you, and we'd soak in it all night. Night? What do I mean, night? This constant daylight, constant heat, and supersaturated humidity are pulling my cork. You don't look up to snuff, either.' He lifted her gorgeous auburn head from his shoulder and studied her face. 'You look like you'd been pulled through a knothole – you're starting to get black circles under your eyes.'

'I know it.' She nestled even closer against him. 'I'm scared blue half the time. I always thought I had good nerves, but everything here is so perfectly *horrible* that I can't sleep – and I always used to go to sleep in the air, two or three inches before I hit the sheets. When I'm with you it isn't too bad – I really enjoy a lot of the things – but the sleeping-periods – Ugh!' She shivered in the circle of his arms. 'You can say anything about them you can think of, and I'll back you to your proverbial nineteen decimals. I just lie there, tenser and tighter, and my mind goes up like a skyrocket. Peggy and I just huddle up to each other in a ghastly purple funk. I'm ashamed of both of us, but that's the way it is and we can't help it.'

'I'm sorry, ace.' He tightened his arms. 'Sorrier than I can say. You've got nerve, and you aren't going to fall apart; I know that. It's just that you haven't roughed it away from home enough to be able to feel at home wherever your hat is. The reason you feel safe with me is probably that I feel perfectly at home here myself – except for the temperature and so on.'

'Uh-huh … probably.' Dorothy gnawed at her lower lip. 'I never thought I was a clinging-vine type, but I'm getting to be. I'm simply scared to death to go to bed.'

'Chin up, sweetheart.' An interlude. 'I wish I could be with you all the time – you know how much I wish it – but it won't be long. We'll fix the chariot and snap back to Earth in a hurry.'

She pushed him into his room, followed him inside, closed the door, and put both hands on his shoulders.

'Dick Seaton,' she said, blushing hotly, 'you're not as dumb as I thought you were – you're dumber! But if you won't say it, even after such a sob-story as that, I will. No law says that a marriage *has* to be performed on Earth to be legal.'

He pressed her close; his emotion so great that for a minute he could not talk. Then he said, 'I never thought of anything like that, Dottie girl.' His voice was low and vibrant. 'If I had I, wouldn't have dared say it out loud. With you so far away from home, it'd seem …'

'It wouldn't seem anything of the kind,' she denied, without waiting to find out what it was that she was denying. 'Don't you see, you big, thick-headed, wonderful lug, it's the only thing to do? We need each other – at least I need you so much …'

'Say "each other"– it's right,' he declared fervently.

'The family would like to have seen me married, of course … but there are some advantages, even there. Dad would hate a grand Washington wedding, and so would you. It's better all-around to be married here.'

Seaton, who had been trying to get a word in, silenced her.

'I'm convinced, Dottie, have been ever since I came out of shock. I'm so glad I can't express it. I've been scared stiff every time I've thought about our wedding. I'll speak to the karfedix the first thing in the morning … or say, how'd it be to wake him up and have it done right now?'

'Oh, Dick, be reasonable!' Dorothy's eyes, however, danced with glee. 'That would *never* do. Tomorrow will be too awfully sudden, as it is. And Dick, please speak to Martin, will you? Peggy's scared a lot worse than I am, and Martin, the dear old stupid jerk, is a lot less likely than even you are to think of being prime mover in anything like this. And Peggy's afraid to suggest it to him. Said she'd curl right up and die and she just about would.'

'Ah. Aha!' Seaton straightened up and held her out at arm's length. 'A light dawns. I thought there was something fishy about your walking me home.

Queer – like a nine-dollar bill. I didn't register, even that "sob-story"– I thought my bad example was corrupting your English. A put-up job, eh?'

'What do *you* think? That I'd have the nerve to do it all by myself? But not all, Dick.' She snuggled up to him again blissfully content. 'Just the littlest, *teeniest* bit of it, was all.'

Seaton opened the door. 'Mart, bring Peggy over here!'

'Heavens, Dick! Be careful! You'll spoil everything!'

'No, I won't. Leave it to me – I bashfully admit that I'm a blinding flash and a deafening report at this diplomacy stuff. Smooth, like an eel.' The other two joined them.

'Dottie and I have been talking things over, and have decided that today would be the best possible day for a wedding. She's afraid of these long daylight nights, and I'd sleep a lot better if I knew where she was all the time instead of part of it. She's willing, if you two see it the same way and make it a double. So how about it? And if you say anything but "yes" I'll tie you, Mart, up like a pretzel; and take you, Peg, over my knee and spank you. I'll give you one whole second to think it over.'

Margaret blushed furiously but pressed herself closer against Crane's side.

'That's time enough for me,' Crane said. 'A marriage here would be recognized anywhere, I think … with the certificate registered … if the final court declared it invalid we could be married again … Considering all the circumstances, it would be the best thing for everyone concerned.' Crane's lean, handsome face assumed a darker color as he looked down at Margaret's sparkling eyes and happily animated face. 'Nothing else in existence is as certain as our love. It is, of course, the bride's privilege to set the date. Peggy?'

'The sooner the better,' Margaret said, blushing again. 'Did you say today, Dick?'

'That's what I said. I'll see the karfedix about it as soon as we get up,' and the two couples separated.

'I'm just too perfectly happy for words,' Dorothy whispered into Seaton's ear as he kissed her goodnight. 'I simply don't care whether I sleep a wink tonight or not.'

XIX

Seaton woke up, hot and uncomfortable, but with a great surge of joy in his heart – this was his wedding day! Springing out of bed, he released the full stream of 'cold' water, filling the pool in a few moments. Poising lightly on the edge, he made a clean, sharp dive – and yelled in surprise as he came snorting to the surface. For Dunark had made his promise good; the water was only a couple of degrees above the freezing point! After a few minutes of swimming and splashing in the icy water he rubbed himself down, shaved, put on shirt and slacks, and lifted his powerful bass voice in the wedding chorus from 'The Rose Maiden.'

'Rise, sweet maid, arise, arise;
'Rise, sweet maid, arise, arise;
''Tis the last fair morning for thy maiden eyes,'

he sang lustily, out of his sheer joy in being alive, and was surprised to hear three other voices – soprano, contralto, and tenor – continue the song from the adjoining room. He opened the door.

'Good morning, Dick, you sounded happy,' Crane said.

'So did you all, but who wouldn't be? Look what today is!' He embraced Dorothy ardently. 'Besides, I found some cold water this morning.'

'Everybody within a mile heard you discover it,' Dorothy giggled. 'We warmed ours up a little. I like a cold bath, too, but not in ice-water. B-r-r-r!'

'But I didn't know you two boys could sing,' Margaret said.

'We can't,' Seaton assured her. 'We just barber-shop it now and then, for fun. But it sounded as though *you* can really *sing*.'

'I'll say she can sing!' Dorothy exclaimed. 'I didn't know it 'til just now, but she's soprano soloist in the First Episcopal, no less!'

'Whee!' Seaton whistled. 'If she can stand the strain, we'll have to give this quartet a workout some day – when there's nobody around.'

All four became silent, thinking of the coming event of the day, until Crane said, 'They have ministers here, I know, and I know something of their religion, but my knowledge is vague. You know more about it than we do, Dick – tell us about it while we wait.'

Seaton paused a moment, an odd look on his face. As one turning the pages of an unfamiliar book of reference, he was seeking the answer to Crane's question in the vast store of Osnomian information received from Dunark. He spoke slower than usual, and used much better English, when he replied.

'As well as I can explain it, it's a very peculiar mixture, partly theology, partly Darwinian evolution or its Osnomian equivalent, and partly pure pragmatism or economic determinism. They believe in a supreme being, the First Cause being its nearest English equivalent. They recognize the existence of an immortal and unknowable life-principle, or soul. They believe that the First Cause has laid down the survival of the fittest as the fundamental law, which belief accounts for their perfect physiques …'

'Perfect physiques! Why, they're as weak as children!' Dorothy exclaimed.

'That's because of the low gravity,' Seaton explained. 'You see, a man of my size weighs only about eighty-six pounds here, on a spring balance, so he wouldn't need any more muscle than a boy of twelve or so on Earth. Either one of you girls could easily handle any two of the strongest men on Osnome. It'd probably take all the strength Dunark has, just to stand up on Earth.

'Considering that fact, they are magnificently developed. They have attained this state by centuries of weeding out the unfit. They have no hospitals for the feeble-minded or the feeble-bodied; all such are executed. The same reasoning accounts for their cleanliness, physical and moral – vice is practically unknown. Clean thinking and clean living are rewarded by the production of a better mental and physical type …'

'Especially since they correct wrong living by those terrible punishments Dunark told us about,' Margaret put in.

'Perhaps, although the point is debatable. They also believe that the higher the type, the faster the evolution and the sooner will mankind reach what they call the Ultimate Goal and know all things. Believing as they do that the fittest must survive, and of course thinking themselves the superior type, it is ordained that Mardonale must be destroyed utterly, root and branch.

'Their ministers are chosen from the very fittest, next to the royal family, which is, and must remain, tops. If it doesn't, it ceases to be the royal family and a fitter family takes over. Anyway, the ministers are strong, vigorous, and clean, and are almost always high army officers as well as ministers.'

An attendant announced the coming of the emperor and his son, to pay the call of state; and, after the ceremonious greetings had been exchanged, all went into the dining-hall for first-meal. After eating, Seaton brought up the question of the double wedding. The emperor was overjoyed.

'Karfedix Seaton, nothing could please us more than to have such a ceremony performed in our palace. Marriage between such highly-evolved persons as are you four is demanded by the First Cause, whose servants we all are. Aside from that, it is an unheard-of honor for any ruler to have even one other karfedix married under his roof, and you are granting me the honor of two! I thank you, and assure you that we will do our best to make the occasion memorable.'

'Nothing fancy, please,' Seaton said. 'Just a simple, plain wedding will do very nicely.'

'I will summon Karbix Tarnan to perform the ceremony,' Roban said, paying no attention to Seaton's remark. 'Our customary time for ceremonies is just before fourth-meal. Is that time satisfactory to all concerned?'

It was entirely satisfactory.

'Dunark, since you are more familiar than I with the customs of our illustrious visitors, you will take charge.' Emperor Roban strode out of the room.

Dunark took up his microphone and sent out call after call after call.

Dorothy's eyes sparkled. 'They must be going to make a production out of our weddings, Dick – the Karbix is the highest dignitary of the church, isn't he?'

'Yes, as well as being commander-in-chief of all the armed forces of Kondal. Next to Roban he's the most powerful man in the whole empire. They're going to throw a brawl, all right – it'll make the biggest Washington wedding you ever saw look like some small fry's birthday party. And *how* you'll hate it!'

'Uh-huh, I do already.' She laughed rapturously. 'I'll cry bitter and salty tears all over the place – I don't think. It's you that will suffer – in silence, I hope?'

'As silently as possible – check.' He grinned; and she became, all of a sudden, serious.

'I've always wanted a big wedding, Dick – but remember. I wanted to give it up and thought I had.'

'I'll remember that always, sweetheart. As I have said before and am about to say again, you're a blinding flash and a deafening report – the universe's best.'

As Dunark finished his telephoning. Seaton spoke to him.

'Dottie said, a while back, she'd like to have a few yards of that tapestry-fabric for a dress … but, say, she's going to get one anyway, only finer and fancier.'

'Just so,' Dunark agreed. 'In high state ceremonials we always wear robes of state. But you two men, for some reason or other, do not wish to wear them.'

'We'll wear white slacks and sport shirts. As you know – if you can find the knowledge – while the women of our race go in for ornamental dress, most of the men do not.'

'True.' Dunark frowned in perplexity. 'Another one of those incomprehensible oddities. However, since your dress will be something no Kondalian has ever seen, it will actually be more resplendent than the robes of your brides.

'I have called in our most expert weavers and tailors, to make the gowns. Before they arrive, let us discuss the ceremony and decide what it will be. You are all somewhat familiar with our customs, but on this I make very sure. Each couple is married twice. The first marriage is symbolized by the exchange of plain bracelets. This marriage lasts two years, during which period either may divorce the other by announcing the fact.'

'Hmmm …' Crane said. 'Some very such system of trial marriage is advocated among us every few years, but they all so surely degenerate into free love that none has found a foothold.'

'We have no such trouble. You see, before the first marriage each couple, from lowest to highest, is given a mental examination. Any person whose graphs show moral turpitude is shot.'

No questions being asked, Dunark went on, 'At the end of the two years the second marriage, which is indissoluble, is performed. Jeweled bracelets are substituted for the plain ones. In the case of highly-evolved persons, it is permitted that the two ceremonies be combined into one. Then there is a third ceremony, used only in the marriage of persons of the very highest evolution, in which eternal vows are taken and the faidon, the eternal jewel, is exchanged. I am virtually certain that all four of you are in the eternal class, but that isn't enough. I must be absolutely certain. Hence, if either couple elects the eternal ceremony, I must examine that couple here and now. Otherwise, and should one of you be rejected by Tarnan, not only would my head roll, but my father would be intolerably disgraced.'

'Huh? Why?' Seaton demanded.

'Because I am responsible,' Dunark replied, quietly. 'You heard my father give me the responsibility of seeing to it that your marriages, the first of their kind in Kondalian history, are carried out as they should be. If such a frightful thing as a rejection occurred it would be my fault. I would be decapitated, there and then, as an incompetent. My father would kill himself, because only an incompetent would delegate an important undertaking to an incompetent.'

'What a code!' Seaton whispered to Crane, under his breath. '*What* a code!' Then, to Dunark, 'But suppose you pass me and Tarnan doesn't? Then what?'

'That cannot possibly happen. Mind graphs do not lie and cannot possibly be falsified. However, there is no coercion. You are at perfect liberty to elect any one of the three marriages you choose. What is your choice?'

'I want to be married for good, the longer the better. I vote for the eternal, Dunark. Bring out your test-kit.'

'So do I, Dunark,' Dorothy said, catching her breath.

'One question first,' Crane said. 'Would that mean that my wife would be breaking her vows if she married again after my death?'

'By no means. Young men are being killed every day; their wives are expected to marry again. Most men have more than one wife. Any number of men and women may be linked that way after death – just as in your chemistry varying numbers of atoms unite to form stable compounds.'

Crane and Margaret agreed that they, too, wanted to be married forever.

'In your case rings will be substituted for bracelets. After the ceremony you men may discard them if you like.'

'Not me!' Seaton declared. 'I'll wear them all the rest of my life,' and Crane expressed the same thought.

'The preliminary examination, then. Put on these helmets, please.' He handed one each to Dorothy and Seaton, and donned one himself. He pressed a button, and instantly the two could read each other's mind to the minutest detail; and each knew that Dunark was reading the minds of both. Moreover, he was studying minutely a device he held in both hands.

'You two pass. I knew you would,' he said, and, a couple of minutes later, he said the same thing to Crane and Margaret.

'I was sure,' Dunark said, 'but in this case knowing it wasn't enough. I had to prove it, incontrovertibly. But the robe-makers have been waiting. You two girls will go with them, please.'

As the girls left Dunark said, 'While I was in Mardonale I heard scraps of talk about a military discovery, besides the gas whose effects we felt. I heard also that both secrets had been stolen from Kondal. There was some gloating, in fact, that we were to be destroyed by our own inventions. I have learned here that what I heard was true.'

'Well, that's easily fixed,' Seaton said. 'Let's get the *Skylark* fixed up and we'll hop over there and jerk Nalboon out of his palace – if there is any palace and if he's still alive – and read his mind. If not Nalboon, somebody else. Check?'

'It's worth trying, anyway,' Dunark said. 'In any event we must repair the *Skylark* and replenish her supply of copper as soon as possible.'

The three men went out to the wrecked spaceship and went through it with care. Inside damage was extensive and serious; many instruments were broken, including one of the object-compasses focused upon Earth.

'It's a good thing you had three of 'em, Mart. I've got to hand it to you for using the old think-tank,' Seaton said, as he tossed the useless equipment out upon the dock.

'Better save them, Dick,' Dunark said. 'You may have use for them later.'

'Uh-uh. All they're good for is scrap.'

'Then I'll save them. I may need that kind of scrap, some day.' He issued orders that all discarded instruments and apparatus were to be stored.

'Well, I suppose the first thing to do is to set up some hydraulic jacks and start straightening,' Seaton said.

'Why not throw away this soft stuff and build it of arenak?' Dunark suggested. 'You have plenty of salt?'

'That's really a thought. Yes, two years' supply. Around a hundred pounds, at a guess.'

Dunark's eyes widened at the amount mentioned, in spite of his knowledge of Earthly conditions. He started to say something, then stopped in confusion, but Seaton knew his thought.

'Sure, we can let you have thirty pounds or so; can't we, Mart?'

'Certainly. In view of what they are doing for us, I'd insist on it.'

Dunark acknowledged the gift with shining eyes and heartfelt, but not profuse, thanks. He himself carried the precious stuff, escorted by a small army of commissioned officers, to the palace. He returned with a full construction crew; and, after making sure that the power-bar would work as well through arenak as through steel, he fired machine-gun-like instructions at the several foremen, then turned again to Seaton.

'Just one more thing and the men can begin. How thick do you want the walls? Our battleships carry one inch. We can't make it any thicker for lack of salt. But you have salt to give away; and, since we're doing this by an exact-copy process, I'd suggest four feet, same as you have now, to save a lot of time in making drawings and redesigning your gun-mounts and so on.'

'I see. Not that we'll ever need it … but it *would* save a lot of time … and besides, we're used to it. Go ahead.'

Dunark issued more orders. Then, as the mechanics set to work without a useless motion, he stood silent, immersed in thought.

'Worrying about Mardonale, Dunark?'

'Yes. I can't help thinking about that new weapon, whatever it is, that Nalboon now has.'

'Why not build another ship, exactly like this one you're building, with four feet of arenak, and simply blow Mardonale off the map?'

'Building the ship would be easy enough, but X is completely unknown. In fact, as you know, it cannot exist here.'

'You'd have to be ungodly careful with it, that's sure. But we've got a lot of it – we can give you a chunk of it.'

'I could not accept it. It isn't like the salt.'

'Sure it is. We can get a million tons of it any time we want it.' He carried one of the lumps to the airlock and tossed it out upon the dock. 'Take this nugget and get busy.'

Seaton watched, entranced, as the Kondalian mechanics set to work with skills and with tools undreamed-of on Earth. The whole interior of the vessel was supported by a complex false-work; then the plates and members were cut away as though they were made of paper. The sphere, grooved for the repellors and with the columns and central machinery complete, was molded of a stiff, plastic substance. This soon hardened into a rock-like mass, into which all necessary openings were carefully cut.

Then the structure was washed with a very dilute solution of salt, by special experts who took extreme pains not to lose or waste any fraction of a drop. Platinum plates were clamped into place and silver cables as large as a man's leg were run to the terminals of a tight-beam power station. Current was applied and the mass became almost invisible, transformed into transparent arenak.

Then indeed the Earth people had a vehicle such as had never been seen before. A four-foot shell of a substance five hundred times as strong and hard as the strongest and hardest steel, cast in one piece with the sustaining framework designed by the world's foremost engineer – a structure that no conceivable force could injure, housing inconceivable force!

The false-work was removed. Columns, members, and braces were painted black, to render them plainly visible. The walls of the cabins were also painted, several areas being left transparent to serve as windows.

The second period of work was drawing to a close, and Seaton and Crane both marveled at what had been accomplished.

'Both vessels will be finished tomorrow, except for the instruments and so on for ours. Another crew will work during the sleeping-period, installing the guns and fittings.'

Since the wedding was to be before fourth-meal, all three went back to the palace, Crane and Seaton to get dressed, Dunark to make sure that everything was as it should be.

Seaton went into Crane's room, accompanied by an attendant carrying his suitcase.

'No dress suits – shame on you!' Seaton chided. 'I thought you'd thought of everything. You're slipping, little chum.'

'I'm afraid so,' Crane agreed, equably. 'You covered it very nicely, though. Congratulations on your quick thinking. Only Dunark will know that whites are not our most formal dress.'

'And he won't tell,' Seaton said.

Dunark came in some time later.

'Give us a look,' Seaton begged. 'See if we pass inspection. I was never so rattled in my life; and the more I think about this brainstorm I had about wearing whites the less I think of it … but can't think of anything else we've got that would look half as good.'

They were clad in spotless white, from tennis shoes to open collars. The two tall figures – Crane's slender, wiry, at perfect ease; Seaton's, broad-shouldered, powerful, prowling about with unconscious suppleness and grace – and the two highbred faces, each wearing a look of keen anticipation, fully justified Dunark's answer.

'You'll do, fellows, and I'm not just chomping my choppers either.' With Seaton's own impulsive good-will he shook hands with them both and wished them an eternity of happiness.

'The next item on the agenda is for you to talk with your brides …'

'*Before* the ceremony?' Seaton asked.

'Yes. This cannot be waived. You take them ... No, you don't. That's one detail I missed. You – especially the girls – would think our formal procedure at this point somewhat indec— anyway, not quite nice in public. You put your arms around them and kiss them, is all. Come on.'

Dorothy and Margaret had been dressed in their bridal gowns by Dunark's six wives, under the watchful eyes of his mother, the First Karfedir herself. Sitar stood the two side by side, then drew off to survey the effect.

'You are the *loveliest* things in the whole world!' she cried.

'Except for this horrible light,' Dorothy mourned. 'I wish they could see what we really look like – I'd like to, myself.'

There was a peal of delighted laughter from Sitar and she spoke to one of the maids, who drew dark curtains over the windows and pressed a switch, flooding the room with pure white light.

'Dunark made these lamps,' Sitar said, with intense satisfaction. 'I knew exactly how you'd feel.'

The two Earthmen and Dunark came in. For moments nothing was said. Seaton stared at Dorothy, hungrily and almost doubting his eyes. For white was white, pink was pink, and her gorgeous hair shone in all its natural splendor of burnished bronze.

In their wondrous Kondalian bridal costumes the girls were beautiful indeed. They wore heavily-jeweled slippers, above which were tiered anklets, each a blaze of gems. Their arms and throats were so covered with sparkling, scintillating bracelets, necklaces, and pendants that little bare skin was to be seen. And the gowns!

They were softly shimmering garments infinitely more supple than the finest silk, thick-woven of metallic threads of a fineness unknown to Earth, garments that floated about or clung to those beautifully-curved bodies in lines of exquisite grace.

For black-haired Margaret, with her ivory skin, the Kondalian princess had chosen an almost-white metal, upon which, in complicated figures, sparkled numberless jewels of pastel shades. Dorothy's gown was of a dark and lustrous green, its fabric half hidden by an intricate design of blazing green and flaming crimson gems – the strange, luminous jewels of this strange world.

Each wore her long, heavy hair almost unbound, after the Kondalian bridal fashion: brushed until it fell like a shining mist, confined only from temple to temple by a structure of jewels in rare-metal filigree.

Seaton looked from Dorothy to Margaret, then back to Dorothy. He looked into violet eyes, deep with wonder and with love, more beautiful than any jewels in all her gorgeous costume. Disregarding the notables who had been filing into the room, she placed her hands on his shoulders; he placed his on her smoothly rounded hips.

'I love you, Dick. Now and always,' she said, and her own violin had no more wonderful tones than did her voice.

I love you, Dot. Now and always,' he replied; and then they both forgot all about protocol; but the demonstration apparently satisfied Kondalian requirements.

Dorothy, her eyes shining, drew herself away from Seaton and glanced at Margaret.

'Isn't she the most *beautiful* thing you ever laid eyes on?'

'She certainly is not – but I'll let Mart keep on thinking she is.'

Accompanied by the emperor and his son, Seaton and Crane went into the chapel which, already brilliant, had been decorated anew with even greater splendor. Through wide arches the Earthmen saw for the first time Osnomians wearing clothing; the great room was filled with the highest nobility of Kondal, wearing their resplendent robes of state.

As the men entered one door Dorothy and Margaret, with the empress and Sitar, entered the other. The assemblage rose to its feet and snapped into the grand salute. Martial music crashed and the two parties marched toward each other, meeting at a raised platform on which stood the Karbix Tarnan, a handsome, stately man who carried easily his eighty years of age. Tarnan raised both arms; the music ceased.

It was a solemn and impressive spectacle. The room of burnished metal with its bizarre decorations, the constantly-changing harmony of color from invisible lamps, the group of nobles standing rigidly at attention in an utter absence of all sound as the karbix lifted his arms in invocation of the First Cause – all these things deepened the solemnity of that solemn moment.

When Tarnan spoke, his voice, deep with some great feeling inexplicable even to those who knew him best, carried clearly to every part of the great chamber.

'Friends, it is our privilege today to assist in a most notable event, the marriage of four personages from another world. For the first time in the history of Osnome has one karfedix the honor of entertaining the bridal party of another. It is not for this fact alone, however, that this occasion is to be memorable. A far deeper reason is that we are witnessing, possibly for the first time in the history of the universe, the meeting upon terms of mutual fellowship and understanding of the inhabitants of two worlds separated by unthinkable distances of trackless space and by equally great differences in evolution, conditions of life, and environment. Yet these strangers are actuated by the spirit of good faith and honor which is instilled into every worthy being by the great First Cause, in the working out of whose vast projects all things are humble instruments.

'In honor of the friendship of the two worlds, we will proceed with the ceremony.

'Richard Seaton and Martin Crane, exchange plain rings with Dorothy Vaneman and Margaret Spencer.'

They did so, and repeated, after the karbix, simple vows of love and loyalty.

'May the First Cause smile upon this temporary marriage and render it worthy of permanence. As a servant and agent of the First Cause I pronounce you two and you two husband and wife. But we must remember that the dull vision of mortal man cannot pierce the veil of the future which is as crystal to the all-beholding eyes of the First Cause. Though you love each other truly some unforeseen thing may come between you to mar the perfection of your happiness. Therefore a time is granted you during which you will discover whether or not your unions are perfect.'

After a pause, Tarnan went on.

'Martin Crane, Margaret Spencer, Richard Seaton, Dorothy Vaneman: you are before us to take the final vows which will bind your bodies together for life and your spirits together for eternity. Have you considered the gravity of this step sufficiently to enter into this marriage without reservation?'

'I have,' the four replied in unison.

'Don, for a moment, the helmets before you.'

They did so, and upon each of four oscilloscope screens there appeared hundreds of irregular lines. Dead silence held while Tarnan studied certain traces upon each of the four giant screens, which were plainly visible to everyone in the room.

'I have seen – each man and woman of this congregation has seen – that each one of you four visiting personages is of the evolutionary state required for eternal marriage. Remove the helmets … exchange the jeweled rings. Do you each individually swear, in the presence of the First Cause and before the supreme justices of Kondal, that you will be true and loyal, each helping his chosen one in all things, great and small; that never, throughout eternity, in thought or in action, will your mind or your body or your spirit stray from the path of truth and honor?'

'I do.'

'I pronounce you married with the eternal marriage. Just as the faidon which each of you wears – the eternal jewel which no force of man is able to change or to deform and which gives off its inward light without change and without end – shall endure through endless cycles of time after the metal of the ring that holds it shall have crumbled in decay: even so shall your spirits, formerly two, now one and indissoluble, progress in ever-ascending evolution throughout eternity after the base material which is your bodies shall have commingled with the base material from which it came.'

The karbix lowered his arms and the bridal party walked to the door through ranks of uplifted weapons. They were led to another room, where the contracting parties signed their names in a register. Dunark then produced two marriage certificates – plates of a brilliant purple metal, beautifully engraved in parallel columns of English and Kondalian script and heavily bordered with precious stones. The principals and witnesses signed below each column and the signatures were engraved into the metal.

They were then escorted to the dining hall, where a truly royal repast was served. Between courses the nobles welcomed the visitors and wished them happiness. After the last course Tarnan spoke, his voice again agitated by the emotion that had puzzled his hearers during the marriage service.

'All Kondal is with us here in spirit, joining us in welcoming these our guests, of whose friendship no greater warrant could be given than their willingness to grant us the privilege of their marriage. Not only have they given us a boon that will make their names revered throughout the nation as long as Kondal shall exist, but also they have been the means of showing us plainly that the First Cause is upon our side; that our ages-old institution of honor is in truth the only foundation upon which can be built a race worthy to survive. At the same time they have been the means of showing us that our hated foe, entirely without honor, building his race upon a foundation of bloodthirsty savagery alone, is building wrongly and must perish utterly from the face of Osnome.'

His hearers listened, impressed by his earnestness, but not understanding his meaning, and he went on, with a deep light shining in his eyes.

'You do not understand? It is inevitable that two peoples as different as are our two should be possessed of widely-differing knowledges and abilities. These friends, from their remote world, have already made it possible for us to construct engines of destruction which will obliterate Mardonale completely—'

A fierce shout of joy interrupted the speaker and the nobles sprang to their feet, saluting the visitors with weapons held aloft. As soon as they had reseated themselves Tarnan went on.

'That is the boon. The vindication of our evolution is as easily explained. These friends landed first in Mardonale. Had Nalboon met them in honor, he would have gained the boon. But he attempted to kill his guests and steal their treasures, with what results you already know. We, however, in exchange for the few and trifling services we have been able to render them, have received even more of value than Nalboon would have obtained, even had his plans not been nullified by their vastly higher state of evolution.'

There was a clamor of cheering as Tarnan sat down. The nobles formed themselves into an escort of honor and conducted the two couples to their apartments.

Alone in one of their rooms, Dorothy turned to her husband with tears shining in her eyes.

'Dick, sweetheart, wasn't that the most *wonderful* thing you ever heard of?

Grand, in the old meaning of the word – really grand. And that old man was simply superb. I'll never get over it.'

'It was all of that, Dot. It got down to where I lived. So much so that I stopped having the jitters as soon as it started.'

But, manlike, Seaton had had enough of solemnity for one day. 'But do you know that I haven't had a good look at you yet, under light I can see by? Stand over there, beautiful, and let me feast my eyes.'

'I will not.' She responded instantly to his mood. 'I haven't seen myself, either, and that's just as important ...'

'More so,' he said, with a wide and happy smile. 'So we'll go over to that full-length mirror and both feast our eyes.'

'Of course I saw Peggy, for about a second, but I can't tell much from that. She's su—' She broke off in the middle of a one-syllable word and stared into the mirror.

'*That*,' she gasped, 'is *me*? I, I mean? Dorothy Vaneman – I mean Seaton?'

'That is Dorothy Seaton,' he assured her. 'Yes, irrevocably so.'

She stuck out a foot, the better to examine the slipper. She lifted her gown well above her knees and studied anklets and legbands. She put her hands on her hips and wriggled, setting everything above the waist into motion. She turned around and repeated the performance, to watch the ornaments dance on her far-from-niggardly expanse of back. She studied the towering, fantastically-jeweled headdress. Then she turned to Seaton, sheer delight spreading over her expressive face.

'You know what, Dick?' she exclaimed, gleefully. 'I'm going to wear this whole regalia, just exactly as it is, to the President's Ball!'

'You wouldn't. You couldn't. Nobody could have that much nerve.'

'That's what *you* think. But you aren't a woman – thanks be! Just wait and see. You know that red-headed copy-cat, Maribel Whitcomb?'

'I've heard you mention her – unfavorably.'

'Just wait 'til she sees *this*, the be-hennaed, be-padded vixen! Her eyes will stick out as though they had stalks, and she'll die of envy and frustration right there on the floor – she can't even *try* to copy this!'

'Check – to even more than the proverbial nineteen decimals. But we've got to change, or we'll be late.'

'Uh-huh, I suppose so.' Dorothy kept on looking backward at the mirror as they walked away. 'One thing's sure, though, Dickie mine. I don't know about the "deafening report" part, but I certainly am a blinding flash!'

XX

These jewels puzzle me, Dick. What are they?' Crane asked, as the four assembled, waiting for first-meal. He held up his third finger, upon which gleamed the royal jewel of Kondal in its mounting of intensely blue transparent arenak. 'I know the name, faidon, but that is about all I seem to know.'

'That's about all anybody knows. It occurs naturally just as you see it there – deep blue, apparently but not actually transparent, constantly emitting that strong blue light. It cannot be worked, cut, ground, or even scratched. It will not burn or change in any arc Kondalians can generate – and believe you me, that's saying a mouthful. It doesn't change in liquid helium. In other words, Mart, it seems to be inert.'

'How about acids?'

'I've been wondering about that. And fusion mixtures and such. Osnomians are pretty far back in chemistry. I'm going to get hold of another one and see if I can't break it down, some way or other. I can't seem to convince myself that an atomic structure could be that big.'

'No, it would be a trifle oversize for an atom.' Crane turned to the two girls. 'How do you like your solitaires?'

'They're perfectly beautiful, and this Tiffany mounting is exquisite,' Dorothy replied, enthusiastically. 'But they're so awfully big. They're as big as ten-carat diamonds, I do believe.'

'Just about,' Seaton said, 'but at that, they're the smallest Dunark could find. They've been kicking around for years, he says, so small nobody wanted them. They like big ones, you know. Wait until you get back to Washington, Dot. People will think you're wearing a bottle-stopper until they see it shining in the dark, and then they'll think it's a misplaced tail-light. But when the news gets out – wow! Jewelers will be bidding up, a million bucks per jump, for rich old dames who want something nobody else can get. Check?'

'You are right, Dick,' Crane said, thoughtfully. 'Since we intend to wear them continuously, jewelers will see them. Any jewel expert will know at a glance that they are new, unique, and fabulously valuable. In fact, they could get us into serious trouble, as fabulous jewels do.'

'Yeah … I never thought of that … well, how about this? We'll let it out, casual-like, that they're as common as mud up here. That we're wearing them purely for sentiment – that at least, will be true – and we're going to bring in a ship load of 'em to sell for ever-lasting, no-battery-needed, automobile parking lamps. And if our girlfriends really do wear their gowns to the President's Ball, as Dot says they're going to, that'll help, too. Nobody – but *nobody* – would wear thirty-eight pounds of cut stones on a dress if they cost very much per each.'

'That would probably keep anyone from murdering our wives for their rings, at least.'

'Have you read your marriage certificate, Dick?' Margaret asked.

'No. Let's look at it, Dottie.'

She produced the massive, heavily-jeweled document, and the auburn head and the brown one were very close to each other as they read together the English side of the certificate. Their vows were there, word for word, with their own signatures beneath them, all deeply engraved into the metal. Seaton smiled as he saw the legal form engraved below the signatures, and read aloud:

I, the head of the church and the commander-in-chief of the armed forces of Kondal, upon the planet Osnome, certify that I have this day, in the city of Kondalek, of said nation and planet, joined in indissoluble bonds of matrimony, Richard Ballinger Seaton, Doctor of Philosophy, and Dorothy Lee Vaneman, Doctor of Music; both of Washington, D.C., U.S.A., upon the planet Earth, in strict compliance with the marriage laws, both of Kondal and of the District of Columbia.

Tarnan, Karbix of Kondal

Witnesses:

> *Roban, Emperor of Kondal*
> *Tural, Empress of Kondal*
> *Dunark, Crown Prince of Kondal*
> *Sitar, Crown Princess of Kondal*
> *Marc C. DuQuesne, Washington, D.C., U.S.A., Earth*

'That's *some* document,' Seaton said. 'How'd he know it complies with the marriage laws of the District? I'm wondering if it does. "Indissoluble" and "eternity" are mighty big words for American marriages. Do you think we'd better get married again when we get back?'

Both girls protested vigorously and Crane said, 'No. I think not. I intend to register this just as it is and get a court ruling on it. It will undoubtedly prove legal.'

'I'm not too sure about that,' Seaton argued. 'Is there any precedent in law that says a man can make a promise that will be binding on his immortal soul for all the rest of eternity?'

'I rather doubt it. I'm sure there will be, however, when our attorneys close the case. You forget, Dick, that The Seaton-Crane Company, Engineers has a very good legal staff.'

'That's right, I had. I'll bet they'll have fun, kicking *that* one around. I wish that bell would ring.'

'So do I,' Dorothy said. 'I just can't get used to not having any night, and ...'

'And it's such a long time between meals,' Seaton put in, 'as the two famous governors said about the drinks.'

'How did you know what I was going to say?'

'Husbandly intuition,' he grinned, 'aided and abetted by a stomach that is accustomed to only six hours between eats.'

After eating, the men hurried to the *Skylark*. During the sleeping-period the repellors had been banded on and the guns and instruments, including a full Kondalian radio system, had been installed. Except for the power-bars, she was ready to fly. The Kondalian vessel lacked both power-bars and instruments.

'How's the copper situation, Dunark?' Seaton asked.

'I don't know yet, exactly. Crews are out, scouring the city for all the metallic copper they can find, but they won't find very much. As you know, we don't use it, as platinum, iridium, silver, and gold are so much better for ordinary use. We're working full time on the copper plant, but it'll be a day or so yet before we can produce virgin copper. I'm going to work on our instruments and controls – if you two are temporarily at a loose end, you might help me.'

Both men were glad to be of assistance; Crane was delighted at the chance to learn how to work that very hard and extremely stubborn metal, iridium, from which all the Kondalian instruments were to be made.

On the way to the instrument shop Seaton said to Crane, 'But what tickles me most is this arenak; and not only for armor and so forth. I s'pose you've noticed your razor?'

'How could I help it?'

'I can't understand how anything can be that hard, Mart. Forty years on an arenak-dust abrasive machine – diamond dust won't touch it – to hone it, and then it'll shave ten men every day for a thousand years and still have *exactly* the same edge it started with. That is what I would call a contribution to science.'

Dunark's extraordinary skill and his even more extraordinary automatic machine tools made the manufacture of his instruments a comparatively short job. While it was going on, the foreman in charge of the scrap-copper drive came in to report. Enough had been found to make two bars, with a few pounds to spare. The bars were in the engines, one in each ship.

'Well done, Kolanix Melnen,' Dunark said, warmly. 'I didn't expect nearly that much.'

'We got every last bit of metallic copper in the whole city,' the foreman said, proudly.

'Fine!' Seaton applauded. 'With one bar apiece, we're ready. Let 'em come.'

'We don't want them to come here; we want to go there,' Dunark said. 'One bar apiece isn't enough for that.'

'That's right,' Seaton agreed. 'For an invasion in force, no.'

'I'd let you have ours, but two wouldn't be any better than one.'

'No. Four, at least, and I'm going to have eight. There should be some way of speeding up work on that copper plant, but I haven't been able to think of any.'

'Speed it up? It's going at fantastic speed already. On Earth it takes months, not days, to build smelters and refineries.'

'I've got half a notion to go over there … but …'

'"But" is right,' Seaton said. 'You'd be more apt to throw the boys off stride than anything else.'

'Could be … but …'

While the Kondalian prince was still standing, undecided, a call for help came in. A freight plane was being pursued by a karlon a few hundred miles away.

'Now's your time to study one, Dunark!' Seaton exclaimed. 'We'll drag him in here – get your scientists out here!'

The *Skylark* reached the monster before it reached the freighter. Seaton focused the attractor and threw on power, jerking the beast upward and backward. As it saw the puny size of the *Skylark* it opened its cavernous mouth and rushed to attack. Seaton, not wishing to have his ship stripped of repellors, turned them on. The monster was hurled backward to the point of equilibrium of the two forces, where it hung helpless, struggling frantically.

Seaton towed the captive back to the field. By judicious pushing and pulling, and by using every attractor and repellor the *Skylark* mounted, the three Earthmen finally managed to hold that monstrous body flat on the ground; but not even with the help of Dunark's vessel could all of the terrible tentacles be pinned down. The scientists studied the creature as well as they could, from battleships and from heavily-armored tanks.

'I wish we could kill it without blowing it to bits,' said Dunark, via radio. 'Do you know of any way of doing it?'

No – except maybe poison. And since we don't know what would poison it, and couldn't make it if we did, I don't see much chance. Maybe we can tire him out, though, and find out where he lives.'

After the scholars had learned all they could, Seaton yanked the animal a few miles into the air and shut off the forces holding it. There was a crash and the karlon, knowing that this apparently insignificant vessel was its master, shot away in headlong flight.

'What was that noise, Dick?' Crane asked.

'I don't know – a new one on me. Probably we cracked a few of his plates,' Seaton replied, as he drove the *Skylark* after the monster.

Pitted for the first time in its life against an antagonist who could both out-fight and outfly it, the karlon put everything it had into its giant wings. It flew back over the city of Kondalek, over the outlying country, and out over the ocean. As they neared the Mardonalian border a fleet of warships came up to meet the monster; and Seaton, not wanting to let the enemy see the rejuvenated *Skylark* too closely, jerked the captive high into the air. It headed for the ocean in a perpendicular dive. Seaton focused an object-compass upon it.

'Go to it, sport,' he said. 'We'll follow you clear to the bottom, if you want to go that far!'

There was a tremendous double splash as pursued and pursuer struck the water. Dorothy gasped, seized a hand-hold, and shut both eyes; but she could scarcely feel the shock, so tremendous was the strength of the *Skylark's* new hull and so enormous the power that drove her. Seaton turned on his searchlights and closed in. Deeper and deeper the quarry dove; it became clear that the thing was just as much at home in the water as it was in the air.

The lights revealed strange forms of life, among which were staring-eyed fishes, floundering blindly in the unaccustomed glare. As the karlon bored still deeper the living things became scarcer; but the Earthmen still saw from time to time the living nightmares that inhabited the oppressive depths of those strange seas. Continuing downward, the karlon went clear to the bottom and stopped there, stirring up a murk of ooze.

'How deep are we, Mart?'

'Something under four miles. No fine figures yet.'

'Of course not. Strain gauges O.K.?'

'Scarcely moved off their zeroes.'

'Ha! Good news, even though I knew – with my mind – that they wouldn't. With our steel hull they'd've been way up in the red. Wonderful stuff, this arenak. Well, it looks as though he wants to sit it out here and we won't find out anything that way. Come on, sport, let's go somewhere else!' Spaceship and karlon went straight up – fast.

On reaching the surface, the monster decided to grab altitude, and went so high that Seaton was amazed.

'I wouldn't have believed that such a thing could possibly fly in air so thin!' he exclaimed.

'It is thin up here,' Crane said. 'Four point one six pounds per square inch.'

'This is his ceiling, I guess. Wonder what he'll do next?'

As if in answer the karlon dived towards the lowlands of Kondal, a swampy region lush with poisonous vegetation and inhabited only by venomous reptiles. As it approached the surface Seaton slowed the *Skylark* down, remarking, 'He'll have to flatten out pretty quick or he'll bust something.'

But it did not flatten out. Diving all out, it struck the morass head-first and disappeared.

Astonished at such an un-looked-for development, Seaton brought the *Skylark* to a halt and stabbed downward with the full power of the attractor.

The first stab brought up nothing but a pillar of muck; the second, one wing and one arm; the third, the whole animal – fighting as savagely as ever.

'Seaton eased the attractor's grip. 'If he digs in here again we'll follow him.'

'Will the ship stand it?' DuQuesne asked.

'She'll stand anything. But you'd better all hang on. I don't know whether there'll be much of a jar or not.'

There was scarcely any jar at all. After the *Skylark* had been pulling herself downward, quite effortlessly, for something over one minute, Seaton glanced across at Crane; who was sitting still at his board doing nothing at all except smiling quietly to himself.

'What're you grinning about, you Cheshire cat?'

'Just wondering what you came down here for and what you're going to prove. These instruments are lying, unanimously and enthusiastically. Plastic flow, you know, not fluid.'

'Oh … uh-huh, check. No lights, radar, or … We could build a sounder, though, or a velocimeter.'

'There are quite a few things we can do, if you think it worthwhile to take the time.'

'It isn't, of course.'

After a few minutes more, Seaton again hauled the monster to the surface and into the air. Again it attacked, with unabated fury.

'Well, that's about enough of that, I guess. Apparently he isn't going home – unless his home was down there in the mud, which I can't quite believe. We can't waste much more time, so you might as well put him away.'

The Mark Five struck; the ground rocked and heaved under the concussion.

'Hey, I just thought of something!' Seaton exclaimed. 'We could have taken him out and set him into an orbit around the planet. Without air, water, or food he' d die *sometime* – I think. Then they'd have a perfect specimen to study.'

'Why, Dick, what a *horrible idea!*' Dorothy's eyes flashed as she turned on him. 'You wouldn't want even such a monster as that to die *that* way!'

'No, I guess I wouldn't really. He's a game fighter. So we'll let Dunark do it sometime, if he wants to.'

The *Skylark* reached the palace dock just before fourth-meal, and while they were all eating Dunark told Seaton that the copper plant would be in production in a few hours, and that the first finished bar would roll at point thirty-four – in other words, immediately after first-meal of the following 'day.'

'Fine!' Seaton exclaimed. 'You'll be ready in the *Kondal*. Take the first eight bars and be on your way. F-f-f-f-t! There goes Mardonale!'

'Impossible, as you already know, if you think a little.'

'Oh … I see … the code. I wouldn't want you to break it, of course … but couldn't it be … say, stretched just enough to cover a situation like this, which has never come up before?'

'It can not,' Dunark said, stiffly.

'But s'pose … Pardon me, Dunark. Ignorance – I never really scanned it before. You're right. I'll play ball.'

'Smatter, Dick?' Dorothy whispered into his ear. 'What did you do to him? I thought he was going to blow his top.'

'I said something I should have known better than to say,' he replied, loudly enough so that Dunark, too, could hear. 'Also, I shouldn't have told you the schedule I had in mind. It's been changed. The *Skylark* gets her copper first, then the *Kondal*. And Dunark doesn't leave until we do. Why, I don't know, any more than Dunark can figure out, with all he got from my mind, why you and I insist on wearing clothes. A matter of code.'

'But, just that little extra time wouldn't make any difference, would it?'

'One chance in a million, maybe, with the bars rolling off the line so fast – no, after all this time, half an hour more won't make any difference. I suppose your men are loading the platinum, Dunark?'

'Yes. They're filling Number Three Storeroom full.'

'Good work, Seaton,' DuQuesne said. 'I've often wished there was some way of getting platinum out of jewelry and into laboratories and production, and your scheme will do it. I don't think much of your judgment in passing up the chance to make a million bucks or so, but I'll be glad to see jewelers drop platinum. I wonder how they'll put it across that platinum isn't the thing for jewelry any more?'

'Oh, they can keep on using it, all they want of it,' Seaton said, innocently, 'at exactly the same price as stainless steel.'

'Who do you think you're kidding?' DuQuesne's reply was not a question, but a sneer.

On the following 'morning,' immediately after 'breakfast,' enough bars were ready to supply both vessels. The *Skylark* was fueled first, then the *Kondal*. Both ships hopped across plain and city and, timed to the split second, landed as one upon the palace dock. Both crews disembarked and stood at half-attention, the three Americans dressed in their whites, the twenty Kondalian high officers wearing their robes of state.

'This stuff is for the birds.' Seaton's lips scarcely moved, only Crane could hear him. 'We stand here for exactly so many seconds, to give the natives a treat.' His eyes flicked upward at the aircraft filling the air. 'Then we come to full attention as the grand moguls and high panjandrums appear, escorting our wives, and the battleships salute, and – blast such flummery!'

'But think of how the girls are enjoying it.' Crane said, using Seaton's own technique. 'And you are going to do it, so why gripe about it?'

'I'd like to do more than pop off – I'd like to call Dot and tell her to shake a leg – but I won't. With Dunark what he is I have to play ball, but I don't have to like it.'

XXI

Suddenly the silence was shattered. Bells rang, sirens shrieked, whistles screamed, every radio and visiset and communicator in or near the city of Kondalek began to clamor. All were giving the same dire warning, the alarm extraordinary of invasion, of imminent and catastrophic danger from the air. Seaton leaped toward the nearest elevator, but whirled back toward the *Skylark* even before Dunark spoke.

'Don't try it, Dick – you can't possibly make it. Everyone will have time to reach the bomb-proofs. They'll be safe – if we can keep the Mardonalians from landing.'

'They won't land – except in hell.' The three sprang into the *Skylark;* Seaton going to the board, Crane and DuQuesne to the guns. Crane picked up his microphone.

'Send in English, and tell the girls not to answer,' Seaton directed. 'They can locate calls to a foot. Just tell 'em we're safe and to sit tight while we wipe out this gang of high-binders that's coming.'

DuQuesne was breaking out box after box of belts of ammunition. 'What do you want first, Seaton? There's not enough of any one load to fight much of a battle.'

'Start with Mark Fives and go up to Tens. That ought to be enough. If not, follow up with Fours and so on down.'

'Fives to Tens; Fours and down. Check.'

There was a crescendo whine of enormous propellers, followed by a concussion of sound as one wing of the palace disappeared in a cloud of dust and debris.

The air was full of Mardonalian warships. They were huge vessels, each mounting hundreds of guns; and a rain of high-explosive shells was reducing the entire city to ruins.

'Hold it!' Seaton's hand, already on the lever, was checked. 'Look at the Kondal – something's up!'

Dunark sat at his board and every man of his crew was at his station; but all were writhing in agony, completely unable to control their movements. As Seaton finished speaking the Kondalians ceased their agonized struggling and hung, unconscious or dead, from whatever each was holding.

'They've got to them some way – let's go!' Seaton yelled.

The dock beneath them fell apart and all three men thought the end of the world had come as a stream of shells struck the *Skylark* and exploded. But that four-foot armor of arenak was impregnable and Seaton lifted his ship upward, directly into the Mardonalian fleet. DuQuesne and Crane fired carefully; as rapidly as each could, consistent with making every bullet count; and as each bullet struck a warship disappeared and there erupted a blast of noise in which the explosions of the Mardonalian shells, violent as they were, were completely inaudible.

'You haven't got the repellors on, Dick!' Crane snapped.

'No, dammit – what a brain!' He snapped them on, then, as the unbearable din subsided almost to a murmur, he shouted, 'Hey! They must be repelling even most of the air!'

The *Skylark* was now being attacked by every ship of the Mardonalian fleet, every unit having been diverted from its mission of destruction to the task of wiping out this appallingly deadly, appallingly invulnerable midget.

From every point of the compass, from above and below, came torrents of shells. Nor were there shells alone. There came also guided missiles – tight-beam-radio-steered airplane-torpedoes – carrying warheads of fantastic power. But none of them struck arenak. Instead, they all struck an immaterial wall of pure force and exploded a hundred feet off target, creating an almost continuous glare of fury and flame.

And Crane and DuQuesne kept on firing. Half of the invading fleet had been destroyed and they were now using Mark Sixes and Mark Sevens – and anything struck by a Seven was not merely blown to bits. It was comminuted – disintegrated– volatized – almost dematerialized.

Suddenly the shelling stopped and the *Skylark* was enveloped in a blinding glare from a thousand projectors; an intense, searching, violet-light that would burn flesh and sear its way through eyelids and eyeballs into the very brain.

'Shut your eyes!' Seaton yelled as he shoved the lever forward. 'Turn your heads!'

Then they were out in space. 'That's pretty nearly atomic-bomb flash,' DuQuesne said, incredulously. 'How can they generate that kind of stuff here?'

'I don't know,' Seaton said. 'But that isn't the question. What can we do about it?'

The three talked briefly, then put on space-suits, which they smeared liberally with thick red paint. Under their helmets they wore extra-heavy welding goggles, so dark in color as to be almost black.

'This'll stop *that* kind of monkey business,' Seaton exulted, as he again threw the *Skylark* into the Mardonalian fleet.

It took about fifteen seconds for the enemy to get their projectors focused, during which time some twenty battleships were volatized; but this time the killing light was not alone.

The men heard, or rather felt, a low, intense, vibration, like a silent wave of sound, a vibration which smote upon the eardrums as no possible sound could smite, a vibration that racked the joints and tortured the nerves as though the whole body were being disintegrated. So sudden and terrible was the effect that Seaton uttered an involuntary yelp of surprise and pain as he once more fled to the safety of space.

'What the devil was that?' DuQuesne demanded. 'Can they generate and *project* infra-sound?'

'Yes,' Seaton replied. 'They can do a lot of things that we can't.'

'If we had some fur suits ...' Crane began, then paused. 'Put on all the clothes we can, and use ear-plugs?'

'We can do better than that, I think.' Seaton studied his board. 'I'll short out this resistor, so as to put more juice through the repellors. I can get a pretty good vacuum that way; certainly good enough to stop any wave propagated through air.'

Back within range of the enemy, DuQuesne, reaching for his gun, leaped away from it with a yell. 'Beat it!'

Once more at a safe distance, DuQuesne explained.

'That gun had voltage, and plenty of it. It's lucky that I'm so used to handling hot stuff that I never really make contact with anything at first touch. That's easy, though. Thick, dry gloves and rubber shields is all we need. It's a good thing for all of us that you have those fancy handles on your levers, Seaton.'

'That must have been how they got Dunark and his crew. But why didn't they get you two, then? Oh, I see. They had it tuned to iridium. They don't know anything about steel – unless they chipped a sample off somewhere – so it took them until now to tune to it.'

'You recognize everything that happens,' Crane said. 'Can you tell what they're going to do next?'

'Not quite everything. This last one was new – it must be the big new one Dunark was worrying about. The others, yes; but the defenses against them are purely Kondalian in technique and material, so we have to roll our own as we go. As to what's coming next ...' He paused in thought, then went on. 'I wish I knew. You see, I got too many new things at once, so most of them are like dimly-remembered things that flash into real knowledge only when they happen. But maybe mentioning something would do the trick. Let's see ... what have they given us so far?'

'They've given us plenty,' DuQuesne said, admiringly. 'Light, ultra and visible; sound, infra- or sub-sound; and solid jolts of high-tension electricity. They haven't yet used X-rays, accelerated particles, Hertzian waves, infra-red heat ...

'That's it – heat!' Seaton exclaimed. 'They project a wave that sets up induced currents in arenak. They can melt armor that way – given time enough.'

'Our refrigerators can handle a lot of heat,' Crane said.

'They certainly can … the limit being the amount of water on board … and when we run out of water we can hop over to the ocean and cool the shell off. Are we ready?'

They were, and soon the *Skylark* was again dealing out death and destruction to the enemy vessels, who again turned from the devastation of the helpless city to destroy this tiny, but incredibly powerful, antagonist. And DuQuesne, considerably the faster of the two gunners, was now shooting Mark Tens – and in the starkly incomprehensible violence of *those* earth-shaking blasts ten or twelve battleships usually went into their component atoms instead of only two or three.

After only a few minutes the *Skylark*'s armor began to heat up and Seaton turned the refrigerators, already operating at full rating, up to the absolute top of fifty percent overload. Even that was not enough. Although the interior of the ship stayed comfortably cool, the armor was so thick that it simply could not conduct heat fast enough. The outer layers grew hotter and hotter – red, cherry red, white. The ends of the rifle barrels, set flush with the surfaces of the arenak globes holding them, began to soften and melt, so that firing became impossible. The copper repellors began to melt and to drip away in flaming droplets, so that exploding shells and missiles came closer and closer.

'Well, it looks as though they have us stopped for the moment,' DuQuesne said calmly, with no thought of quitting apparent in either voice or manner. 'Let's go dope out something else.'

They again went up out of range, but had only started discussing ways and means when a call came, uncoded and on the general wave.

'Karfedix Seaton – Karfedix Seaton – acknowledge, please – Karfedix Seaton – Karfed—'

'Seaton acknowledging!'

'This is Karfedelix Depar, commanding four task forces. The Karbix Tarnan has ordered me to report …'

'He has broken radio silence, then?' Seaton demanded.

'I have.' The Karbix did not go on to explain, either that it was necessary or that it was now safe to do so. Seaton knew both of these facts.

'Good!' and Seaton went on to explain to both commander-in-chief and commander the nature and deadliness of Mardonale's new weapon. 'Karfedelix Depar, continue your report.'

'The Karbix Tarnan ordered me to report to you for orders. There is a Mardonalian fleet approaching from the east. Have I your permission, sir, to attack it?'

'Can you insulate against twenty kilovolts all the iridium your men must touch?'

'I think so, sir,'

'Thinking so isn't enough. If you can't, land and get insulation before engaging with any Mardonalian vessel. Are any more of our task forces en route?'

'Yes, sir. Four within the quarter-hour, three more in one, two, and three hours respectively, sir.'

'Report acknowledged. Stand by.' Seaton frowned in thought. He *had* to appoint an admiral; but he certainly did not want to ask, with every living Kondalian listening, whether or not this Depar was a big enough man for the job.

'Karbix Tarnan, sir,' he said.

'Tarnan acknowledging.'

'Sir, which of your officers now in air is best fitted to command the defense fleet now assembling?'

'Sir, the Karfedelix Depar.'

'Sir, thank you. Karfedelix Depar, I give you authority to handle and responsibility for handling correctly the forthcoming engagement. Take command!'

'Thank you, sir.'

Seaton dropped his microphone. 'I've got it doped,' he told Crane and DuQuesne. 'The *Skylark*'s faster than any shell ever fired, and has infinitely more mass. She's got four feet of arenak, they have only an inch. Arenak doesn't begin to soften until it's radiating high in the ultra-violet. Strap down solid – this is going to be a rough party from now on.'

Again the *Skylark* went down. Instead of standing still, however, she darted directly at the nearest warship under twenty notches of power. She crashed straight through it without even slowing down. Torn wide open by the forty-foot projectile, its engines wrecked and its helicopter screws and propellors useless, the helpless hulk plunged through two miles of air to the ground.

Darting here and there, the spaceship tore through vessel after vessel of the Mardonalian fleet. Here indeed was a guided missile: an irresistible projectile housing a human brain, the brain of Richard Seaton, keyed up to highest pitch and fighting the fight of his life.

As the repellors dripped off, the silent waves of sound came in stronger and stronger. He was battered by the terrific impacts, nauseated and almost blacked out by the frightful lurches of his hairpin turns. Nevertheless, with teeth tight-locked and with eyes gray and hard as the fracture of high-carbon steel, Richard Seaton fought on. Projectile and brain were, and remained, one.

Although it was impossible for the eye to follow the flight of the spaceship, the mechanical sighting devices of the Mardonalians kept her in fair focus and the projectors continued to hurl into her a considerable fraction of their death-dealing output. Enemy guns were still emitting streams of shells; but unlike the waves, the shells moved so slowly compared to their target that very few found their mark. Many of the great vessels fell to the ground, riddled by the shells of their sister-ships.

Seaton glanced at his pyrometer. The needle had stopped climbing, well short of the red line marking the fusion-point of arenak. Even as he looked, it began, very slowly, to recede. There weren't enough Mardonalian ships left to maintain such a temperature. He felt much better, too; the sub-sound was still pretty bad, but it was bearable.

In another minute the battle was over; the few remaining battleships were driving at top speed for home. But even in flight they continued to destroy; the path of their retreat was a swath of destruction. Half-inclined at first to let them escape, Seaton's mind was changed as he saw what they were doing to the countryside beneath them. He shot after them, and not until the last vessel had been destroyed did he drop the *Skylark* into the area of ruins which had once been the palace grounds, beside the *Kondal*, which was still lying as it had fallen.

After several attempts to steady their whirling senses the three men were able to walk. They opened the lock and leaped out, through the still white-hot wall. Seaton's first act was to call Dorothy, who told him that the royal party would come up as soon as engineers could clear the way. The men then removed their helmets, revealing pale and drawn faces, and turned to the *Kondal*.

'There's no way of getting into this thing … Oh, fine! They're coming to!'

Dunark opened the lock and stumbled out. 'I have to thank you for more than my life, this time,' he said, his voice shaken as much my emotion as by the shock of his experience as he grasped the hands of all three men. 'I was conscious most of the time and saw most of what happened. You have saved all Kondal.'

'Oh, it's not that bad,' Seaton said, uncomfortably. 'Both nations have been invaded before.'

'Yes, but not with anything like this. This would have been final. But I must hurry. If you will relinquish command to me, Dick, please, I will restore it to the karbix. The *Kondal* will, of course, be his flagship.'

Seaton snapped to attention and saluted. 'Kofedix Dunark, sir, I relinquish to you my command.'

'Karfedix Seaton, sir, with thanks for what you have done, I accept your command.'

Dunark hurried away, talking as he went with surviving officers of the grounded Kondalian warships.

In a few minutes the emperor and his party rounded a heap of boulders. Dorothy and Margaret screamed in unison as they saw the haggard faces of their husbands and saw their suits dripping with red. Seaton dodged as Dorothy reached him, and tore off his suit.

'Nothing but red paint,' he assured her, as he lifted her off the ground.

Out of the corner of his eye he saw the Kondalians staring in open-mouthed amazement at the *Skylark*. He turned. She was a huge ball of frost and snow!

As Seaton came back to the girls from shutting off the refrigerators, Roban came up and gave the Earthmen thanks in the name of his nation for what they had done.

'Has it yet occurred to you, Karfedix Roban,' Margaret said, diffidently, 'that, had it not been for your rigid adherence to your Code, none of us Tellurians would have been on Osnome or near it when the Mardonalians attacked you?'

'No, my daughter … by no means … I still fail to see the connection. Will you explain, please?'

'Dick's idea was to have Dunark take the first eight bars of copper and sail for Mardonale. Then we would take the next forty bars – which would take about half an hour to make – and leave immediately for Earth. Then, when Dunark arrived over Mardonale he would have been shot down out of control wouldn't he?'

'Undoubtedly … I understand now, but go ahead.'

'How long did it take the Mardonalian fleet to get here, about?'

'About forty of your hours.'

'Then assuming that Dunark didn't take any time at all in getting over there, we would have been gone about thirty-nine and a half hours when they struck … but there wasn't that much time! They must have been well on the way while we were getting the copper!'

'Very true, daughter Margaret, but the end result would have been precisely the same. You would have been gone at least one hour – which, for us, would have been as bad as one thousand.'

The Karfedix Roban stood facing the party from Earth. Back of him stood his family, the officers and nobility, and a multitude of people.

'Is it permitted, karfedo, that I award your captive some small recognition of the service he has done my nation?' Roban asked.

'It is permitted,' Seaton and Crane replied, in unison; whereupon Roban stepped forward and, after handing DuQuesne a heavy bag, fastened about his left wrist the emblem of the Order of Kondal.

'I welcome you, Karfedelix DuQuesne, to the highest nobility of Kondal.'

He then clasped around Crane's wrist a bracelet of ruby-red metal bearing a peculiarly-wrought, heavily-jeweled disk, at the sight of which the nobles saluted and Seaton barely concealed a start of surprise.

'Karfedix Crane, I bestow upon you this symbol; which proclaims that, throughout all Kondalian Osnome, you have authority as my personal representative in all things, great and small.'

Approaching Seaton, Roban held up a bracelet of seven disks so that everyone could see it. The nobles knelt; the people prostrated themselves.

'Karfedix Seaton, no language spoken by man possesses words able to express our indebtedness to you. In small and partial recognition of that indebtedness I bestow upon you these symbols, which declare you to be our overlord, the ultimate authority upon all Osnome.'

Lifting both arms above his head he continued.

'May the great First Cause smile upon you in all your endeavors until you solve the Prime Mystery; may your descendants soon reach the Ultimate Goal. Goodbye.'

Seaton spoke a few heart-felt words in response and the five Earthpeople stepped backward toward their ship. As they reached it the standing emperor and the ranks of nobles snapped into the double salute – truly a rare gesture. 'What'll we do now?' Seaton whispered. 'I'm fresh out of Ideas.'

'Bow, of course,' Dorothy said.

They bowed, deeply and slowly, and entered their vessel and as the *Skylark* shot into the air the grand fleet of Kondalian warships fired a royal salute.

XXII

DuQuesne's first act upon gaining the privacy of his own cabin was to open the bag presented to him by the emperor. He expected to find it filled with rare metals, with perhaps some jewels, instead of which the only metal present was in a heavily-insulated tube – a full half pound of metallic radium!

The least valuable items of his prize were hundreds of diamonds, rubies, and emeralds of very large size and of flawless perfection. Merely ornamental glass to Roban, he had known their Earthly value. To this wealth of known gems Roban had added a rich and varied assortment of the strange jewels peculiar to his own world, the faidon alone being absent from the collection. DuQuesne's calmness almost deserted him as he sorted out and listed the contents of the bag.

The radium alone was worth millions of dollars; and the scientist in him exulted at the uses to which it would be put, even while he was also exulting at the price he would get for it. He counted the familiar jewels, estimating their value as he did so – a staggering total. That left the strange gems, enough to fill the bag half full – shining and glowing and scintillating in multi-colored splendor. He sorted them out and counted them, but made no effort to appraise them. He knew that he could get any price he pleased to set.

'Now,' he breathed to himself, 'I can go my own way!'

The return voyage through space was uneventful. Several times, as the days wore on, the *Skylark* came within the gravity range of gigantic suns; but her pilots had learned the most important fundamental safeguard of interstellar navigation. Automatic indicating and recording goniometers were now on watch continuously, set to give alarm at a deviation of two seconds of arc; and their dead reckoning of acceleration and velocity was checked, twice each eight-hour shift, by triangulation and the application of Schuyler's Method.

When half the distance had been covered the bar was reversed, the travelers holding an impromptu ceremony as the *Skylark* spun through an angle of one hundred eighty degrees.

A few days later Seaton, who was on watch, thought he recognized Orion. It was by no means the constellation he had known, but it seemed to be shifting, ever so slowly, toward the old, familiar configuration. It *was* Orion.

'C'mere, everybody!' he shouted, and they came.

'That, my friends, is the most gladsome sight these feeble old eyes have rested on for many a long and weary moon. Wassail!'

They 'wassailed' with glee, and from that moment on the pilot was never alone at his board. Everyone who could be there was there, looking over his shoulders to watch the firmament while it assumed a more and more familiar aspect.

They identified Sol; and, some time later, they could see Sol's planets.

Crane put on all the magnification he had, and the girls peered excitedly at the familiar outlines of continents and oceans upon the lighted half of the visible disk.

It was not long until these outlines were plainly visible to the unaided vision, the Earth appearing as a softly shining, greenish half-moon, with parts of its surface obscured by fleecy wisps of cloud, with its ice-caps making of its poles two brilliant areas of white. The wanderers stared at their world with hearts in throats as Crane made certain that they would not be going too fast to land.

The girls went to prepare a meal and DuQuesne sat down beside Seaton.

'Have you gentlemen decided what you intend to do with me?'

'No. We haven't discussed it yet, and I can't make up my own mind – except that I'd like to have you in a square ring with four-ounce gloves. You've been of altogether too much real help on this trip for either of us to enjoy seeing you hanged. At the same time, you're altogether too much of a scoundrel for us to let you go free ... I, personally, don't like anything we can do, or not do, with you. That's the fix I'm in. What would you suggest?'

'Nothing,' DuQuesne replied, calmly. 'Since I am in no danger whatever of either hanging or prison, nothing you can say or do along those lines bothers me at all. Hold me on free me, as you please. I will add that, while I have made a fortune on this trip and do not have to associate any longer with Steel unless it is to my interest to do so, I may find it desirable at some future time to obtain a monopoly of X. If so, you and Crane, and possibly a few others, would die. No matter what happens or does not happen, however, this whole thing is over as far as I'm concerned. Done with. *Fini.'*

'You kill us? You talk like a man with a paper nose. Peel off, Buster, any time you like. We can out-run you, out-jump you, throw you down, or lick you – hit harder, run faster, dive deeper and come up dryer – for fun, money, chalk on marbles ...'

A thought struck him and every trace of levity disappeared. Face hard and eyes cold, he stared at DuQuesne, who stared unmovedly back at him.

'But listen, DuQuesne,' Seaton said slowly, every word sharp, clear and glacially cold. 'That goes for Crane and me personally. Nobody else. I could be arrested for what I think of you as a man; and if anything you ever do touches either Dorothy or Margaret in any way I'll kill you like I would a snake – or rather, I'll take you apart like I would any other piece of scientific apparatus. And don't think this is a threat. It's a promise. Is that clear?'

'Perfectly. Goodnight.'

For many hours Earth had been obscured by clouds, so that the pilot had no idea of what part it was beneath them. To orient himself, Seaton dropped downward into the twilight zone until he could see the surface, finding that they were almost directly over the western end of the Panama Canal. Dropping still lower, to about ten thousand feet, he stopped and waited while Crane took bearings and calculated the course to Washington.

DuQuesne had retired, cold and reticent as usual. After making sure that he had overlooked nothing, he put on the leather suit he had worn when he left Earth. He unlocked a cubby, taking therefrom a Kondalian parachute. Then, making sure every foot of the way that he was not observed, he made his way to the airlock and entered it.

Thus, when the *Skylark* paused over the Isthmus, he was ready. Smiling sardonically, he opened the outer valve and stepped out into ten thousand feet of air. The neutral color of his parachute was lost in the twilight a few seconds after he left the vessel.

The course computed. Seaton set the bar and the *Skylark* core through the air. When about half the ground had been covered Seaton spoke suddenly.

'Forgot about DuQuesne, Mart. We'd better lock him in, don't you think? Then we'll have to decide whether we want to put him in the jail-house or turn him loose.'

'I'll see to it,' Crane said.

He returned immediately with the news.

'Hmmm. He must have picked up a Kondalian parachute. You can't quite put one in your pocket, but pretty near. But I can't say I'm sorry he got away ... Anyway, we can still get him any time we want him, because that compass is still looking right at him.'

'I think he earned his liberty,' Dorothy declared.

'He deserves to be shot,' Margaret said, 'but I'm glad he's gone. He gives me the cold, creeping shivers.'

At the end of the calculated time they saw the lights of a large city beneath them; and Crane's fingers tightened upon Seaton's arm as he pointed downward. There were the landing-lights of Crane Field – seven searchlights throwing their mighty beams upward into the night.

'Nine weeks, Dick,' he said unsteadily, 'and Shiro would have kept them burning for nine years if necessary.'

The *Skylark* dropped easily to the ground and the wanderers leaped out, to be greeted by the half-hysterical Japanese. Shiro's ready vocabulary of peculiar but sonorous words failed him completely and he bent himself double in a bow, his face one beaming smile. Crane, with one arm around his wife, seized Shiro's hand and wrung it in silence.

Seaton swept Dorothy off her feet and their arms tightened around each other.

SKYLARK THREE

1

DuQuesne Goes Traveling

In the innermost private office of Steel, Brookings and DuQuesne stared at each other across the massive desk. DuQuesne's voice was cold, his black brows were drawn together.

'Get this, Brookings, and get it straight. I'm shoving off at twelve o'clock tonight. My advice to you is to lay off Richard Seaton, absolutely. Don't do a thing. NOTHING, understand? Just engrave these two words upon your brain – HOLD EVERYTHING. Keep on holding it until I get back, no matter how long that may be.'

'I am very much surprised at your change of front, doctor. You are the last man I would have expected to be scared off after one engagement.'

'Don't be any more of a fool than you have to, Brookings. There's a lot of difference between being scared and knowing when you are simply wasting effort. As you remember, I tried to abduct Mrs Seaton by picking her off with an attractor from a spaceship. I would have bet that nothing could have stopped me. Well, when they located me – probably with an automatic Osnomian emission detector – and heated me red-hot while I was still better than two hundred miles up, I knew then and there that they had us stopped: that there was nothing we could do except go back to my plan, abandon the abduction idea, and kill them all. Since my plan would take time, you objected to it, and sent an airplane to drop a five-hundred-pound bomb on them. Airplane, bomb, and all, simply vanished. It didn't explode, you remember, just flashed into light and disappeared. Then you pulled several more of your fool ideas, such as long-range bombardment, and so on. None of them worked. Still you've got the nerve to think that you can get them with ordinary gunmen! I've drawn you diagrams and shown you figures – I've told you in great detail and in one-syllable words exactly what we're up against. Now I tell you again that they've GOT SOMETHING. If you had the brains of a louse you would know that anything I can't do with a spaceship can't be done by a mob of ordinary gangsters. I'm telling you, Brookings, that you can't do it. My way is absolutely the only way that will work.'

'But five years, doctor!'

'I may be back in six months. But on a trip of this kind anything can happen, so I am planning on being gone five years. Even that may not be enough – I am carrying supplies for ten years, and that box of mine in the vault is not to be opened until ten years from today.'

'But surely we shall be able to remove the obstructions ourselves in a few weeks. We always have.'

'Oh, quit kidding yourself, Brookings! This is no time for idiocy! You stand just as much chance of killing Seaton …'

'Please, doctor, please don't talk like that!'

'Still squeamish, eh? Your pussyfooting always did give me an acute pain. I'm for direct action, word, and deed, first, last, and all the time. I repeat, you have exactly as much chance of killing Richard Seaton as a blind kitten has.'

'How do you arrive at that conclusion, doctor? You seem very fond of belittling our abilities. Personally, I think that we shall be able to attain our objectives within a few weeks – certainly long before you can possibly return from such an extended trip as you have in mind. And since you are so fond of frankness, I will say that I think Seaton has you buffaloed, as you call it. Nine-tenths of these wonderful Osnomian things I am assured by competent authorities are scientifically impossible, and I think that the other one-tenth exists only in your own imagination. Seaton was lucky in that the airplane bomb was defective and exploded prematurely; and your spaceship got hot because of your injudicious speed through the atmosphere. We shall have everything settled by the time you get back.'

'If you have I'll make you a present of the controlling interest in Steel and buy myself a chair in some home for feeble-minded old women. Your ignorance and unwillingness to believe any new idea do not change the facts in any particular. Even before they went to Osnome, Seaton was hard to get, as you found out. On that trip he learned so much new stuff that it is now impossible to kill him by any ordinary means. You should realize that fact when he kills every gangster you send against him. At all events be very, *very* careful not to kill – nor even hurt – his wife in any of your attacks, even by accident, until after you have killed him.'

'Such an event would be regrettable, certainly, in that it would remove all possibility of the abduction.'

'It would remove more than that. Remember the explosion in our laboratory, that blew an entire mountain into impalpable dust? Draw in your mind a nice, vivid picture of one ten times the size in each of our plants and in this building. I know that you are fool enough to go ahead with your own ideas, in spite of everything I've said; and, since I do not yet actually control Steel, I can't forbid you to, officially. But you should know that I know what I'm talking about, and I say again that you're going to make an utter fool of yourself just because you won't believe anything possible that hasn't been done every day for a hundred years. I wish that I could make you understand that Seaton and Crane have got something that we haven't – but for the good of our plants, and incidentally for your own, you must remember one thing, anyway; for if you forget it we won't have a plant left and you personally will be blown into atoms. Whatever you start, kill Seaton first, and be absolutely certain that he is definitely, completely, finally, and totally dead before you touch one of Dorothy Seaton's red hairs. As long as you only attack him personally he won't do anything but kill every man you send against him. If you touch her while he's still alive, though – Blooie!' and the saturnine scientist waved both hands in an expressive pantomime of wholesale destruction.

'Probably you are right in that.' Brookings paled slightly. 'Yes, Seaton would do just that. We shall be very careful, until after we succeed in removing him.'

'Don't worry – you won't succeed. I shall attend to that detail myself, as soon as I get back. Seaton and Crane and their families, the directors and employees of their plants, the banks that by any possibility may harbor their notes or solutions – in short, every person and every thing standing between me and a monopoly of "X" – all shall disappear.'

'That is a terrible program, doctor. Wouldn't the late Perkins' plan of an abduction, such as I have in mind, be better, safer, and quicker?'

'Yes – except for the fact that it will not work. I've talked until I'm blue in the face – I've proved to you over and over that you can't abduct her now without first killing him, and that you can't even touch him. My plan is the only one that will work. Seaton isn't the only one who learned anything – I learned a lot myself. I learned one thing in particular. Only four other inhabitants of either Earth or Osnome ever had even an inkling of it, and they died, with their brains disintegrated beyond reading. That thing is my ace in the hole. I'm going after it. When I get it, and not until then, I'll be ready to take the offensive.'

'You intend starting open war upon your return?'

'The war started when I tried to pick off the women with my attractor. That is why I am leaving at midnight. He always goes to bed at eleven-thirty, and I will be out of range of his object-compass before he wakes up. Seaton and I understand each other perfectly. We both know that the next time we meet one of us is going to be resolved into his component ultra-microscopic constituents. He doesn't know that he's going to be the one, but I do. My final word to you is to lay off – if you don't, you and your "competent authorities" are going to learn a lot.'

'You do not care to inform me more fully as to your destination or your plans?'

'I do not. Goodbye.'

2

Dunark Visits Earth

Martin Crane reclined in a massive chair, the fingers of his right hand lightly touching those of his left, listening attentively. Richard Seaton strode up and down the room before his friend, his unruly brown hair on end, speaking savagely between teeth clenched upon the stem of his reeking, battered briar; brandishing a sheaf of papers.

'Mart, we're stuck – stopped dead. If my head wasn't made of solid blue mush I'd've had a way figured out of this thing before now, but I can't. With that zone of force the *Skylark* would have everything imaginable – without it, we're exactly where we were before. That zone is immense, man – terrific – its possibilities are unthinkable – and I'm so damned dumb that I can't find out how to use it intelligently – can't use it at all, for that matter. By its very nature it is impenetrable to any form of matter, however applied; and this calc here,' shaking the sheaf of papers viciously, 'shows that it must also be opaque to any wave whatever, propagated through air or through ether, clear down to cosmic rays. Behind it we would be blind and helpless, so we can't use it at all. It drives me frantic! Think of a barrier of pure force, impalpable, immaterial, and exerted along a geometrical surface of no thickness whatever – and yet actual enough to stop a radiation that travels a hundred million light-years and then goes through twenty-seven feet of solid lead just like it was so much vacuum! That's what we're up against! However, I'm going to try out that model, Mart, right now. Let's go!'

'You are getting idiotic again, Dick,' Crane rejoined calmly, without moving. 'You know, even better than I do, that you are playing with the most concentrated essence of energy that the world has ever seen. That zone of force probably can be generated—'

'Probably, nothing!' barked Seaton. 'It's just as evident a fact as that stool,' kicking the unoffending bit of furniture halfway across the room as he spoke. 'If you'd've let me I'd've shown it to you yesterday.'

'Undoubtedly, then. Grant that it is impenetrable to all matter and to all known wave-lengths. Suppose that it should prove impenetrable also to gravitation and to magnetism? Those phenomena probably depend upon the ether, but we know nothing fundamental of their nature, nor of that of the ether. Therefore your calculations, comprehensive though they are, cannot predict the effect upon them of your zone of force. Suppose that that zone actually does set up a barrier in the ether, so that it nullifies gravitation, magnetism, and all allied phenomena; so that the power-bars, the attractors, and repellors, cannot work through it? Then what? As well as showing me the zone of force, you might well have shown me yourself flying off into space, unable to use your power and helpless if you released the zone. No, we must know more of the fundamentals before you try even a small-scale experiment.'

'Oh, bugs! You're carrying caution to extremes, Mart. What can happen? Even if gravitation should be nullified, I would rise only slowly, heading south the angle of our latitude – that's thirty-nine degrees – away from the perpendicular. I couldn't shoot off on a tangent, as some of these hop-heads have been claiming. Inertia would make me keep pace, approximately, with the Earth in its rotation. I would rise slowly – only as fast as the tangent departs from the curvature of the Earth's surface. I haven't figured out how fast that is, but it must be pretty slow.'

'Pretty slow?' Crane smiled. 'Figure it out.'

'All right – but I'll bet it's slower than the rise of a toy balloon.' Seaton threw down the papers and picked up his slide rule, a twenty-inch deci-trig duplex. 'You'll concede that it is allowable to neglect the radial component of the orbital velocity of the Earth, for a first approximation, won't you – or shall I figure that in too?'

'You may neglect that factor.'

'All right – let's see. Radius of rotation here in Washington would be cosine latitude times equatorial radius, approximately – call it thirty-two hundred miles. Angular velocity, fifteen degrees an hour. I want secant fifteen less one times thirty-two hundred. Right? Secant equals one over cosine – um-m-m-m – one point oh three five. Then point oh three five times thirty-two hundred. Hundred and twelve miles first hour. Velocity constant with respect to sun, accelerated respecting point of departure. Ouch! You win, Mart – I'd step out! Well, how about this, then? I'll put on a suit and carry rations. Harness outside, with the same equipment I used in the test flights before we built *Skylark One* – plus the new stuff. Then throw on the zone, and see what happens. There can't be any jar in taking off, and with that outfit I can get back O.K. if I go clear to Jupiter!'

Crane sat in silence, his keen mind considering every aspect of the motions possible, of velocity, of acceleration, of inertia. He already knew well Seaton's resourcefulness in crises and his physical and mental strength.

'As far as I can see, that might be safe,' he admitted finally, 'and we really should know something about it besides the theory.'

'Fine! I'll get at it – be ready in five minutes. Yell at the girls, will you? They'd break us off at the ankles if we pull anything new without letting them in on it.'

A few minutes later the 'girls' strolled out into Crane Field, arms around each other – Dorothy Seaton, her gorgeous auburn hair framing violet eyes and vivid coloring; black-haired, dark-eyed Margaret Crane.

'Br-r-r, it's cold!' Dorothy shivered, wrapping her coat more closely about her. 'This must be the coldest day Washington has seen for years!'

'It is cold,' Margaret agreed. 'I wonder what they are going to do out here, this kind of weather?'

As she spoke, the two men stepped out of the 'testing shed' – the huge structure that housed their Osnomian-built space-cruiser, *Skylark Two*. Seaton waddled clumsily, wearing as he did a Crane space-suit which, built of fur, canvas, metal, and transparent silica, braced by steel netting, and equipped with air-tanks and heaters, rendered its wearer independent of outside conditions of temperature and pressure. Outside this suit he wore a heavy harness of leather, buckled about his body, shoulders, and legs, attached to which were numerous knobs, switches, dials, bakelite cases, and other pieces of apparatus. Carried by a strong aluminum framework which was in turn supported by the harness, the universal bearing of a small power-bar rose directly above his grotesque-looking helmet.

'What do you think you're going to do in that thing, Dickie?' Dorothy called. Then, thinking that he could not hear her voice, she turned to Crane. 'What are you letting that precious husband of mine do now, Martin? He looks like he's up to something.'

While she was speaking, Seaton had snapped the release of his face-plate.

'Nothing much, Dottie. Just going to show you-all the zone of force. Martin wouldn't let me turn it on unless I got all cocked and primed for a year's journey into space.'

'Dot, what is that zone of force, anyway?' asked Margaret.

'Oh, it's something Dick got into his head during that awful fight they had on Osnome. He hasn't thought of anything else since we got back. You know how the attractors and repellors work? Well, he found out something funny about the way everything acted while the Mardonalians were bombarding them with a certain kind of a wave-length. He finally figured out the exact vibration that did it, and found out that if it is made strong enough, it acts as if a repellor and attractor were working together – only so much stronger that nothing can get through the boundary, either way – in fact, it's so strong that it cuts anything in two that's in the way. And the funny thing is that there's nothing there at all, really; but Dick says that the forces meeting there, or something, make it act as though something really important were there. See?'

'Uh-huh,' assented Margaret, doubtfully, just as Crane finished the final adjustments and moved toward them. A safe distance away from Seaton, he turned and waved his hand.

Instantly Seaton disappeared from view, and around the place where he had stood there appeared a shimmering globe some twenty feet in diameter – a globe apparently a perfect spherical mirror, which darted upward and toward the south. After a moment the globe disappeared and Seaton was again seen. He was now standing upon a hemispherical mass of earth. He darted back toward the group upon the ground, while the mass of earth fell with a crash a quarter of a mile away. High above their heads the mirror again encompassed Seaton, and again shot upward and southward. Five times this maneuver was repeated before Seaton came down, landing easily in front of them and opening his helmet.

'It's just what we thought it was, only worse,' he reported tersely. 'Can't do a thing with it. Gravitation won't work through it – bars won't – nothing will. And dark? DARK! Folks, you never saw real darkness, nor heard real silence. It scared me stiff!'

'Poor little boy – afraid of the dark!' exclaimed Dorothy. 'We saw absolute blackness in space.'

'Not like this, you didn't. I just saw absolute darkness and heard absolute silence for the first time in my life. I never imagined anything like it – come on up with me and I'll show it to you.'

'No you won't!' his wife shrieked as she retreated toward Crane. 'Some other time, perhaps.'

Seaton removed the harness and glanced at the spot from which he had taken off, where now appeared a hemispherical hole in the ground.

'Let's see what kind of tracks I left, Mart,' and the two men bent over the depression. They saw with astonishment that the cut surface was perfectly smooth, with not even the slightest roughness or irregularity visible. Even the smallest grains of sand had been sheared in two along a mathematically exact hemispherical surface by the inconceivable force of the disintegrating copper bar.

'Well, that sure wins the—'

An alarm bell sounded. Without a glance around, Seaton seized Dorothy and leaped into the testing shed. Dropping her unceremoniously to the floor he stared through the telescope sight of an enormous projector which had automatically aligned itself upon the distant point of liberation of atomic energy which had caused the alarm to sound. One hand upon the switch, his face was hard and merciless as he waited to make sure of the identity of the approaching spaceship before he released the frightful power of his generators upon it.

'I've been expecting DuQuesne to try it again,' he gritted, striving to make out the visitor, yet more than two hundred miles distant. 'He's out to get you, Dot – and this time I'm not just going to warm him up and scare him away, like I did last time. I'm going to give him the works … I can't locate him with this small telescope, Mart. Line him up in the big one and give me the word, will you?'

'I see him, Dick, but it is not DuQuesne's ship. It is built of transparent arenak, like the *Kondal*. Even though it seems impossible, I believe it is the *Kondal*.'

'Maybe so, and again maybe DuQuesne built it – or stole it. On second thought, though, I don't believe that DuQuesne would be fool enough to tackle us again in the same way – but I'm taking no chances … O.K., it is the *Kondal*, I can see Dunark and Sitar myself, now.'

The transparent vessel soon neared the field and the four Terrestrials walked out to greet their Osnomian friends. Through the arenak walls they recognized Dunark, Kofedix of Kondal, at the controls, and saw Sitar, his beautiful young queen, lying in one of the seats near the wall. She attempted a friendly greeting, but her face was strained as though she were laboring under a tremendous burden.

As they watched, Dunark slipped a helmet over his head and one over Sitar's, pressed a button to open one of the doors, and supported her toward the opening.

'They mustn't come out, Dick!' exclaimed Dorothy in dismay. 'They'll freeze to death in five minutes without any clothes on!'

'Yes, and Sitar can't stand up under our gravitation, either – I doubt if Dunark can, for long,' and Seaton dashed toward the vessel, motioning the visitors back.

But misunderstanding the signal, Dunark came on. As he clambered heavily through the door he staggered, and Sitar collapsed upon the frozen ground. Trying to help her, half-kneeling over her, Dunark struggled, his green skin paling to a yellowish tinge at the touch of the bitter and unexpected cold. Seaton leaped forward and gathered Sitar up as though she were a child.

'Help Dunark back in, Mart,' he directed crisply. 'Hop in, girls – we've got to take these folks back up where they can live.'

Seaton shut the door, and as everyone lay flat in the seats Crane, who had taken the controls, applied one notch of power and the huge vessel leaped upward. Many hundreds of miles of altitude were gained before he brought the cruiser to a stop and locked her in place with an anchoring attractor.

'There,' he remarked calmly. 'Gravitation here is approximately the same as upon Osnome.'

'Yeah,' put in Seaton, standing up and shedding clothes in all directions, 'and I rise to remark that we'd better undress as far as the law allows – perhaps farther. I never did like Osnomian ideas of comfortable warmth, but we can endure it by peeling down to bedrock – they can't stand our temperatures at all.'

Sitar jumped up happily, completely restored, and the three women threw their arms around each other.

'What a horrible, terrible, frightful world!' exclaimed Sitar, her eyes widening as she thought of her first experience with our Earth. 'Much as I love you, I shall never dare to try to visit you again. I have never been able to understand why you Terrestrials wear what you call "clothes", nor why you are so terribly, brutally strong. Now I really know – I will feel the utterly cold and savage embrace of this awful world of yours as long as I live!'

'Oh, it ain't so bad, Sitar.' Seaton, who was shaking both of Dunark's hands vigorously, assured her over his shoulder. 'All depends on where you were raised. We like it that way, and Osnome gives us the pip. But you poor fish,' turning again to Dunark, 'with all my brains inside your skull you should've known what you were letting yourself in for.'

'That's true, after a fashion,' Dunark admitted, 'but your brain told me that Washington was *hot*. If I'd've thought to recalculate your actual Fahrenheit degrees into our loro … but that figures only forty-seven and, while very cold, we could have endured it – wait a minute, I'm getting it. You have what you call 'seasons'. This, then, must be your "winter". Right?'

'Right the first time. That's the way your brain works in my skull, too. I could figure anything out all right after it happened, but hardly ever beforehand – so I guess I can't blame you much, at that. But what I want to know is, how'd you get here? It'd take more than my brains – you can't see our sun from any-where near Osnome, even if you knew exactly where to look for it.'

'Easy. Remember those wrecked instruments you threw out of the *Skylark* when we built *Skylark Two*?' Having every minute detail of the configuration of Seaton's brain engraved upon his own, Dunark spoke English in Seaton's own characteristic careless fashion. Only when thinking deeply or discussing abstruse matters did Seaton employ the carefully selected and precise phrasing which he knew so well how to use. 'Well, none of them were beyond repair and the juice was still on most of them. One was an object-compass bearing on the Earth. We simply fixed the bearings, put on some minor improvements, and here we are.

'Let us all sit down and be comfortable,' he continued, changing into the Kondalian tongue without a break, 'and I will explain why we have come. We are in most desperate need of two things which you alone can supply – salt, and that strange metal, X. Salt I know you have in great abundance, but I know that you have very little of the metal. You have only the one compass upon that planet?'

'That's all – one is all we set on it. However, we've got close to half a ton of it on hand – you can have all you want.'

'Even if I took it all, which I would not like to do, that would be less than half enough. We must have at least one of your tons, and two tons would be better.'

'Two tons! Holy cat! Are you going to plate a fleet of battle cruisers?'

'More than that. We must plate an area of copper of some ten thousand square miles – in fact, the very life of our entire race depends upon it.

'It's this way,' he continued, as the four human beings stared at him in wonder. 'Shortly after you left Osnome we were invaded by the inhabitants of the third planet of our fourteenth sun. Luckily for us they landed upon Mardonale, and in less than two days there was not a single Osnomian left alive upon that half of the planet. They wiped out our grand fleet in one brief engagement, and it was only the *Kondal* and a few more like her that enabled us to keep them from crossing the ocean. Even with our full force of these vessels, we cannot defeat them. Our regular Kondalian weapons were useless. We shot explosive copper charges against them of such size as to cause earthquakes all over Osnome, without seriously crippling their defenses. Their offensive weapons are almost irresistible – they have generators that burn arenak as though it were so much paper, and a series of deadly frequencies against which only a copper-driven screen is effective, and even that does not stand up long.'

'How come you lasted till now, then?' asked Seaton.

'They have nothing like the *Skylark*, and no knowledge of atomic energy. Therefore their spaceships are of the rocket type, and for that reason they can cross only at the exact time of conjunction, or whatever you call it – no, not conjunction, exactly, either, since the two planets do not revolve around the same sun: but when they are closest together. Our solar system is so complex, you know, that unless the trips are timed exactly, to the hour, the vessels will not be able to land upon Osnome, but will be drawn aside and be lost, if not drawn into the vast central sun. Although it may not have occurred to you, a little reflection will show you that the inhabitants of all the central planets, such as Osnome, must perforce be absolutely ignorant of astronomy, and of all the wonders of outer space. Before your coming we knew nothing beyond our own solar system, and very little of that. We knew of the existence of only such of the closest planets as were brilliant enough to be seen in our continuous sunlight, and they were few. Immediately after your coming I gave your knowledge of astronomy to a group of our foremost physicists and mathematicians, and they have been working ceaselessly from spaceships – close enough so that observations could be recalculated to Osnome, and yet far enough away to afford perfect "seeing", as you call it.'

'But I don't know any more about astronomy than a pig does about Sunday,' protested Seaton.

'Your knowledge of details is, of course, incomplete,' conceded Dunark, 'but the detailed knowledge of the best of your Earthly astronomers would not help us a great deal, since we are so far removed from you in space. You, however, have a very clear and solid knowledge of the fundamentals of the science, and that is what we needed, above all things.'

'Yeah, maybe you're right, at that. I do know the general theory of the motions, and I've been exposed to celestial mechanics. I'm awfully weak on advanced theory, though, as you'll find out when you get that far.'

'Perhaps – but since our enemies have no knowledge of astronomy whatever, it is not surprising that their rocket-ships can be launched only at one particularly favorable time; for there are many planets and satellites, of which they can know nothing, to throw their vessels off the course.

'Some material essential to the operation of their war machinery apparently must come from their own planet, for they have ceased attacking, have dug in, and are simply holding their ground. It may be that they had not anticipated as much resistance as we could offer with spaceships and atomic energy. At any rate, they have apparently saved enough of that material to enable them to hold out until the next conjunction – I cannot think of a better word for it – shall occur. Our forces are attacking constantly, with all the armament at our command, but it is certain that if the next conjunction is allowed to occur, it means the end of the entire Kondalian nation.'

'What d'you mean "if the next conjunction is *allowed* to occur"?' interjected Seaton. 'Nobody can stop it.'

'I am stopping it,' Dunark stated quietly, grim purpose in every lineament. 'That conjunction shall never occur. That is why I must have the vast quantities of salt and X. We are building abutments of arenak upon the first satellite of our seventh planet, and upon our sixth planet itself. We shall cover them with plated active copper, and install chronometers to throw the switches at precisely the right moment. We have calculated the exact times, places, and magnitudes of the forces to be used. We shall throw the sixth planet some distance out of its orbit, and force the first satellite of the seventh planet clear out of that planet's influence. The two bodies whose motions we have thus changed will collide in such a way that the resultant body will meet the planet of our enemies in head-on collision, long before the next conjunction. The two bodies will be of almost equal masses, and will have opposite and approximately equal velocities; hence the resultant fused or gaseous mass will be practically without velocity and will fall directly into the fourteenth sun.'

'Wouldn't it be easier to destroy it with an explosive copper bomb?'

'Easier, yes, but much more dangerous to the rest of our solar system. We cannot calculate exactly the effect of the collisions we are planning – but it is almost certain that an explosion of sufficient violence to destroy all life upon the planet would disturb its motion sufficiently to endanger the entire system. The way we have in mind will simply allow the planet and one satellite to drop out quietly – the other planets of the same sun will soon adjust themselves to the new conditions, and the system at large will be practically unaffected – at least, so we believe.'

Seaton's eyes narrowed as his thoughts turned to the quantities of copper and X8217 required and to the engineering features of the project; Crane's first thought was of the mathematics involved in a computation of that magnitude and character; Dorothy's quick reaction was one of pure horror.

'He can't, Dick! He mustn't! It would be too ghastly! It's outrageous – it's unthinkable – it's – it's – it's just simply too perfectly damned horrible!' Her violet eyes flamed, and Margaret joined in:

'That would be awful, Martin. Think of the destruction of a whole planet – of an entire world – with all its inhabitants! It makes me shudder, even to think of it.'

Dunark leaped to his feet, ablaze. But before he could say a word, Seaton silenced him.

'Shut up, Dunark! Pipe down! Don't say anything you'll be sorry for – let *me* tell 'em! Close your pan, I tell you!' as Dunark still tried to get a word in, 'I tell you I'll tell 'em, and when *I* tell 'em they *stay* told! Now listen, you two girls – you're going off half-cocked and you're both full of little red ants. What do you think Dunark is up against? Sherman chirped it when he described war – and this is a brand of war totally unknown on our Earth. It isn't a question of whether or not to destroy a population – the only question is which population is to be destroyed. One of 'em's got to go. Remember those folks go into a war thoroughly, and there isn't a thought in any of their minds even remotely resembling our conception of mercy, on either side. If Dunark's plans go through, the enemy nation will be wiped out. That is horrible, of course. But on the other hand, if we block him off from salt and X, the entire Kondalian nation will be destroyed just as thoroughly and efficiently, and even more horribly – not one man, woman, or child would be spared. Which nation do you want saved? Play that over a couple of times on your fiddle, Dot, and don't jump at conclusions.'

Dorothy, taken aback, opened and closed her mouth twice before she found her voice.

'But, Dick, they couldn't possibly. Would they kill them *all*, Dick? Surely they wouldn't – they *couldn't.*'

'Surely they would – and could. They do – it's good technique in those parts of the galaxy. Dunark has just told us of how they killed every member of the entire race of Mardonalians, in forty hours. Kondal would go the same way. Don't kid yourself, Dimples – don't be a simp. War up there is *no* species of pink tea, believe me – half of my brain has been through thirty years of Osnomian warfare, and I know precisely what I'm talking about. Let's take a vote. Personally I'm in favor of Osnome. Mart?'

'Osnome.'

'Dottie? Peggy?' Both remained silent for some time, then Dorothy turned to Margaret.

'You tell him, Peggy – we both feel the same way.'

'Dick, you know that we wouldn't want the Kondalians destroyed – but the other is so – such a – well, such an utter *Schrecklichkeit* – isn't there some other way out?'

'I'm afraid not – but if there is any other possible way out, I'll do my da—I'll try to find it,' he promised. 'The ayes have it. Dunark, we'll skip over to that X planet and load you up.'

Dunark grasped Seaton's hand. 'Thanks, Dick,' he said, simply. 'But before you help me farther, and lest I might be in some degree sailing under false colors, I must tell you that, wearer of the seven disks though you are, Overlord of Osnome though you are, my brain brother though you are; had you decided against me, nothing but my death could have kept me away from that salt and your X compass.'

'Why sure,' assented Seaton, in surprise. 'Why not? Fair enough! Anybody would do the same – don't let that gnaw on you.'

'How is your supply of platinum?'

'Mighty low. We had about decided to hop over there after some. I want some of your textbooks on electricity and so on, too. I see you brought a load of platinum with you.'

'Yes, a few hundred tons. We also brought along an assortment of books I knew you would be interested in, a box of radium, a few small bags of gems of various kinds, and some of our fabrics Sitar thought your karfediro would like to have. While we are here, I would like to get some books on chemistry and some other things.'

'We'll get you the Congressional Library, if you want it, and anything else you think you'd like. Well, gang, let's go places and do things! What first, Mart?'

'We had better drop back to Earth, have the laborers unload the platinum, and load on the salt, books, and other things. Then both ships will go to the X planet, as we will each want compasses on it, for future use. While we are loading, I should like to begin remodeling our instruments; to make them something like these; with Dunark's permission. These instruments are wonders, Dick – vastly ahead of anything I have ever seen. Come and look at them, if you want to see something really beautiful.'

'Coming up. But say, Mart, while I think of it, we mustn't forget to install a zone-of-force apparatus on this ship, too. Even though we can't use it intelligently, it certainly would be the cat's whiskers as a defense. We couldn't hurt anybody through it, of course, but if we should happen to be getting licked anywhere all we'd have to do would be to wrap ourselves up in it. They couldn't touch us. Nothing that I know of is corkscrewy enough to get through it.'

'That's the second idea you've had since I've known you, Dicky,' Dorothy smiled at Crane. 'Do you think he should be allowed to run at large, Martin?'

'That is a real idea. We may need it – you never can tell. Even if we never find any other use for the zone of force, that one is amply sufficient to justify its installation.'

'Yeah, it would be, for you – and I'm getting to be a regular Safety-First Simon myself, since they opened up on us. What about those instruments?'

The three men gathered around the instrument board and Dunark explained the changes he had made – and to such men as Seaton and Crane it was soon evident that they were examining an installation embodying sheer perfection of instrumental control – a system which only those wonder instrument-makers, the Osnomians, could have devised. The new object-compasses were housed in arenak cases after setting, and the housings were then exhausted to the highest attainable vacuum. Oscillation was set up by means of one carefully standardized electrical impulse, instead of by the clumsy finger-touch Seaton had used. The bearings, built of arenak and Osnomian jewels, were as strong as the axles of a truck, and yet were almost perfectly motionless.

'I like them myself,' admitted Dunark. 'Without a load the needles will rotate freely more than a thousand hours on the primary impulse, as against a few minutes in the old type; and under load they are many thousands of times as sensitive.'

'You're a blinding flash and a deafening report, ace!' declared Seaton, enthusiastically. 'That compass is as far ahead of my model as the *Skylark* is ahead of Wright's first glider.'

The other instruments were no less noteworthy. Dunark had adopted the Perkins telephone system, but had improved it until it was scarcely recognizable, and had made it capable of almost unlimited range. Even the guns – heavy rapid-firers, mounted in spherical bearings in the walls – were aimed and fired by remote control, from the board. He had devised full automatic steering controls; and acceleration, velocity, distance, and flight-angle meters and recorders. He had perfected a system of periscopic vision which enabled the pilot to see the entire outside surface of the shell, and to look toward any point of the heavens without interference.

'This kind of takes my eye, too, prince,' Seaton said, as he seated himself, swung a large, concave disk in front of him, and experimented with levers and dials. 'You certainly can't call this thing a periscope – it's no more a periscope than I am a polyp. When you look through this plate it's better than looking out of a window – it subtends more than the angle of vision, so that you can't see anything but out-of-doors – I thought for a second I was going to fall out. What do you call 'em, Dunark?'

'Kraloto. That would be in English … Seeing-plate? Or rather, exactly transliterated, "visiplate".'

'That's a good word – we'll adopt it. Mart, take a look if you want to see a set of perfect lenses and prisms.'

Crane looked into the visiplate and gasped. The vessel had disappeared – he was looking directly down upon the Earth below him!

'No trace of chromatic, spherical, or astigmatic aberration,' he reported in surprise. 'The refracting system is invisible – it seems as though nothing intervenes between the eye and the object. You perfected all these things since we left Osnome, Dunark? You are in a class by yourself. I could not even copy them in less than a month, and I never could have invented them.'

'I did not do it alone, by any means. The Society of Instrument-Makers, of which I am only one member, installed and tested more than a hundred systems. This one represents the best features of all the systems tried. It will not be necessary for you to copy them. I brought along two complete duplicate sets, for the *Skylark*, as well as a dozen or so of the compasses. I thought that perhaps these particular improvements might not have occurred to you, since you Terrestrials are not as familiar as we are with complex instrumental work.'

Crane and Seaton spoke together.

'That was thoughtful of you, Dunark, and we appreciate it fully.'

'That puts four more palms on your *croix de guerre*, ace. Thanks a lot.'

'Say, Dick,' called Dorothy, from her seat near the wall. 'If we're going down to the ground, how about Sitar?'

'By lying down and not doing anything, and by staying in the vessel, where it is warm, she will be all right for the short time we must stay here,' Dunark answered for his wife. 'I will help all I can, but I do not know how much that will be.'

'It isn't so bad lying down,' Sitar agreed. 'I don't like your Earth a bit, but I can stand it a little while. Anyway, I *must* stand it, so why worry about it?'

''At-a-girl!' cheered Seaton. 'And as for you, Dunark, you'll pass the time just like Sitar does – lying down. If you do much chasing around down there where we live you're apt to get your lights and liver twisted all out of shape – so you'll stay put, horizontal. We've got men enough around the shop to eat this cargo in three hours, let alone unload it. While they unload and load you up we'll install the zone apparatus, put a compass on you, put one of yours on us, and then you can hop back up here where you're comfortable. Then as soon as we can get the *Lark* ready for the trip we'll jump up here and be on our way. Everything clear? Cut the rope, Mart – let the bucket drop!'

3

Skylark Two Sets Out

'Say, Mart, I just got conscious! It never occurred to me until just now, as Dunark left, that I'm just as good an instrument-maker as Dunark is – the same one, in fact – and I've got a hunch. You know that needle on DuQuesne hasn't been working for quite a while? Well, I don't believe it's out of commission at all. I think he's gone somewhere, so far away that it can't read on him. I'm going to house it in, re-jewel it, and find out where he is.'

'An excellent idea. He has even you worrying, and as for myself …'

'Worrying! That bird is simply pulling my cork! I'm so scared he'll get Dottie that I'm running around in circles and biting myself in the small of the back. He's working on something, you can bet your shirt on that, and what gripes me is he's aiming at the girls, not at us or the job.'

'I should say that someone had aimed at you fairly accurately, judging by the number of bullets stopped lately by that arenak armor of yours. I wish that I could take some of the strain, but they are centering all their attacks upon you.'

'Yeah – I can't stick my nose outside our yard without somebody throwing lead at it. 'Sfunny, too. You're more important to the power plant than I am.'

'You should know why. They are not afraid of me. While my spirit is willing enough, it was your skill and rapidity with a pistol that frustrated four attempts at abduction in as many days. It is positively uncanny, the way you explode into action. With all my practice, I didn't even have my pistol out until it was all over, yesterday. And besides Prescott's guards, we had four policemen with us – detailed to "guard" us because of the number of gunmen you had had to kill before that!'

'It ain't practice so much, Mart – it's a gift I've always been fast, and I react automatically. You think first, that's why you're so slow. Those cops were funny. They didn't know what it was all about until it was all over but calling the wagon. That was the worst yet. One of their slugs struck directly in front of my left eye – it was kinda funny, at that, seeing it splash – and I thought I was inside a boiler in a rivet-shop when those machine-guns cut loose. It was hectic, all right, while it lasted. But one thing I'll tell the attentive world – we ain't doing all the worrying. Very few, if any, of the gangsters they send after us are getting back – wonder what they think when they shoot at us and we don't drop?

'But I'm afraid I'm beginning to crack, Mart,' Seaton went on, his voice becoming grimly earnest. 'I don't like anything about this whole mess. I don't like all four of us wearing armor all the time. I don't like living constantly under guard. I don't like all this killing, and this constant menace of losing Dorothy if I let her out of my sight for five seconds is driving me mad. Also, to tell you the truth, I'm devilishly afraid that they'll figure out something that will work. I could grab off two women, or kill two men, if they had armor and guns enough to fight a war. I believe that DuQuesne could, too – and the rest of that bunch aren't imbeciles, either, by any means. I won't feel safe until all four of us are in the *Skylark* and a long ways from here. I'm glad we're pulling out, and I don't intend to come back until I find DuQuesne. He's the bird I'm going to get – and when I get him I'll tell the cock-eyed world that he'll *stay* got. There won't be any two atoms of his entire carcass left in the same township. I meant that promise when I gave it to him – and I didn't mean maybe.'

'He realizes that fully. He knows that it is now definitely either his life or our own, and he is really dangerous. When he took Steel over and opened war upon us, he did it with his eyes wide open. With his ideas, he must have a monopoly of X or nothing; and he knows the only possible way of getting it. However, you and I both know that he would not let either one of us live, even though we surrendered.'

'You chirped it! But that guy's going to find out that he's started something. But how about turning up a few RPM's? We don't want to keep Dunark waiting too long.'

'There is very little to do beyond installing the new instruments; and that is nearly done. We can finish pumping out the compass en route. You have already installed every weapon of offense and defense known to either Earthly or Osnomian warfare, including those generators and screens you moaned so about not having during the battle over Kondal. I believe that we have on board every article for which either of us has been able to imagine even the slightest use.'

'Yeah, we've got her so full of plunder that there's hardly room left for quarters. You ain't figuring on taking anybody but Shiro along, are you?'

'No. I suppose there is no real necessity for taking even him, but he wants very much to go, and may prove himself useful.'

'I'll say he'll be useful. None of us really enjoys polishing brass or washing dishes – and besides, he's one star cook and an A-1 housekeeper.'

The installation of the new instruments was soon completed, and while Dorothy and Margaret made last-minute preparations for departure the men called a meeting of the managing directors and department heads of the Seaton-Crane Co., Engineers. The chiefs gave brief reports in turn. Units Number One and Number Two of the immense new central super-power plant were in continuous operation. Number Three was almost ready to cut in. Number Four was being rushed to completion. Number Five was well under way. The research laboratory was keeping well up on its problems. Troubles were less than had been anticipated. Financially, it was a gold-mine. With no expense for boilers or fuel and thus with a relatively small investment in plant and a very small operating cost, they were selling power at one-sixth of prevailing rates, and still profits were almost paying for all new construction. With the completion of Number Five, rates would be reduced still further.

'In short, dad, everything's slick,' remarked Seaton to Mr Vaneman, after the others had gone.

'Yes; your plan of getting the best men possible, paying them well, and giving them complete authority and sole responsibility, has worked to perfection. I have never seen an undertaking of such size go forward so smoothly and with such fine cooperation.'

'That's the way we wanted it. We hand-picked the directors, and put it up to you, strictly. You did the same to the managers. They passed it along. Everybody knows that his end is up to him, and him alone – so he digs in.'

'However, Dick, while everything at the Works is so fine, when is this other thing going to break?'

'We've won all the way so far, but I'm afraid something's about due. That's the big reason I want to get Dot away for a while. You know what they're up to.'

'Too well,' the older man answered. 'Dottie or Mrs Crane, or both. Her mother – she is telling her goodbye now – and I agree that the danger here is greater than out there.'

'Danger out there? With the *Skylark* fixed the way she is now, Dot's a lot safer than you are, in bed. Your house might fall down, you know.'

'You're probably right, son – I know you, and I know Martin Crane. Together, and in the *Skylark*, I believe you invincible.'

'All set, Dick?' asked Dorothy, appearing in the doorway.

'All set. You've the dope for Prescott and everybody, dad. We may be back in six months, and we may see something to investigate, and have to be gone a year or so. Don't begin to lose any sleep until after we've been out – oh, say three years. We'll make it a point to be back by then.'

Farewells were said, the party embarked, and *Skylark Two* shot upward. Seaton flipped a phone set over his head and spoke.

'Dunark! ... Coming out, heading directly for X ... No, better stay quite a ways off to one side when we get going good ... Yeah, I'm accelerating twenty six point oh oh oh ... Yes, I'll call you now and then, until the radio waves get lost, to check the course with you. After that, keep on the last course, reverse at the calculated distance, and by the time we're pretty well slowed down we'll feel around for each other with the compasses and go in together ... Yeah ... Uh-huh ... Fine! So-long!'

In order that the two vessels should keep reasonably close together, it had been agreed that each should be held at an acceleration of exactly twenty-six feet per second, positive and negative. This figure represented a compromise between the gravitational forces of the two worlds upon which the different parties lived. While considerably less than the acceleration of gravitation at the surface of the Earth, the Tellurians could readily accustom themselves to it; and it was not enough greater than that of Osnome to hamper seriously the activities of the green people.

Well clear of the Earth's influence, Seaton assured himself that everything was functioning properly, then stretched to his full height, writhed his arms over his head, and heaved a deep sigh of relief.

'Folks,' he declared, 'this is the first time I've felt right since we got out of this old bottle. Why, I feel so good a cat could walk up to me and scratch me right in the eye, and I wouldn't even scratch back. Yowp! I'm a wild Siberian catamount, and this is my night to howl. Whee-ee-yerow!'

Dorothy laughed, a gay, lilting carol.

'Haven't I always told you he had cat blood in him, Peggy? Just like all tomcats, every once in a while he has to stretch his claws and yowl. But go ahead, Dickie, I like it – this is the first uproar you've made in weeks. I believe I'll join you!'

'It most certainly is a relief to get this load off our minds: I could do a little ladylike yowling myself,' Margaret said; and Crane, lying completely at ease, a thin spiral of smoke curling up from his cigarette, nodded agreement.

'Dick's yowling is quite expressive at times. All of us feel the same way, but some of us are unable to express ourselves quite so vividly. However, it is past bedtime, and we should organize our crew. Shall we do it as we did before?'

'No, it isn't necessary. Everything is automatic. The bar is held parallel to the guiding compass, and signal bells ring whenever any of the instruments show a trace of abnormal behavior. Don't forget that there is at least one meter registering and recording every factor of our flight. With this control system we can't get into any such jam as we did last trip.'

'Surely you are not suggesting that we run all night with no one at the controls?'

'Exactly that. A man camping at this board is painting the lily and gilding fine gold. Awake or asleep, nobody need be closer to it than is necessary to hear a bell if one should ring, and you can hear them all over the ship. Furthermore, I'll bet a hat we won't hear a signal a week. Simply as added precaution, though, I've run lines so that any time one of these signals lets go it sounds a buzzer on the head of our bed; so I'm automatically taking the night shift. Remember, Mart, these instruments are thousands of times as sensitive as the keenest human senses – they'll spot trouble long before we could, even if we were looking right at it.'

'Of course, you understand these instruments much better than I do, as yet. If you trust them, I am perfectly willing to do the same. Goodnight.'

Seaton sat down and Dorothy nestled beside him, her head snuggled into the curve of his shoulder.

'Sleepy?'

'Heavens, no! I couldn't sleep now – could you?'

'Not any. What's the use?'

His arm tightened around her. Apparently motionless to its passengers, the cruiser bored serenely on into space, with ever-mounting velocity. There was not the faintest sound, not the slightest vibration – only the peculiar violet glow surrounding the shining copper cylinder in its massive universal bearing gave any indication of the thousands of kilowatts being generated in that mighty atomic power plant. Seaton studied it thoughtfully.

'You know, Dottie, if that violet aura and copper bar were a little different in hue and chroma, they'd be just like your eyes and hair,' he remarked finally.

'What a comparison!' Dorothy's entrancing low chuckle bubbled through her words. 'You say the weirdest things at times! Possible they would – and if the moon were made of different stuff than it is and had a different color it might be green cheese, too! What say we go over and look at the stars?'

'As you were, Rufus!' he commanded sternly. 'Don't move a millimeter – you're a perfect fit, right where you are. I'll get you any stars you want, and bring them right in here to you. What constellation would you like? I'll even get you the Southern Cross – we never see it in Washington.'

'No, I want something familiar; the Pleiades or the Big Dipper – no, get me Canis Major – "where Sirius, brightest jewel in the diadem of the firmament, holds sway",' she quoted. 'There! Thought I'd forgotten all the astronomy you ever taught me, didn't you? Think you can find it?'

'Sure. Declination about minus twenty, as I remember it, and right ascension between six and seven hours. Let's see – where would that be from our course?'

He thought for a moment, manipulated several levers and dials, snapped off the lights, and swung number one exterior visiplate around, directly before their eyes.

'Oh … Oh … this is magnificent, Dick!' she exclaimed. 'It's stupendous. It seems as though we were right out there in space itself, and not in here at all. It's … it's perfectly wonderful!'

Although neither of them was unacquainted with deep space, it presents a spectacle that never fails to awe even the most seasoned observer; and no human being had ever before viewed the wonders of space from such a coign of vantage. Thus the two fell silent and awed as they gazed out into the abysmal depths of the interstellar void. The darkness of Earthly night is ameliorated by light-rays scattered by the atmosphere; the stars twinkle and scintillate and their light is diffused, because of the same medium. But here, what a contrast! They saw the utter, absolute darkness of the complete absence of all light; and upon that indescribable blackness they beheld superimposed the almost unbearable brilliance of enormous suns concentrated into mathematical points, dimensionless. Sirius blazed in blue-white splendor, dominating the lesser members of his constellation, a minute but intensely brilliant diamond upon a field of black velvet – his refulgence unmarred by any trace of scintillation or distortion.

As Seaton slowly shifted the field of vision, angling toward and across the celestial equator and the ecliptic, they beheld in turn mighty Rigel: the Belt, headed by dazzlingly brilliant-white Delta-Orionis; red Betelgause; storied Aldebaran, the friend of mariners; and the astronomically constant Pleiades.

Seaton's arm contracted, swinging Dorothy into his embrace; their lips met and held.

'Isn't it wonderful, lover,' she murmured, 'to be out here in space this way, together, away from all our troubles and worries? *Really* wonderful … I'm so happy, Dick.'

'So am I, sweetheart.' The man's arm tightened. 'I'm not going to try to say anything …'

'I almost died, every time they shot at you.' Dorothy's mind went back to what they had gone through. 'Suppose that your armor had cracked or something? I wouldn't want to go on living. I would simply lie down and die.'

'I'm glad it didn't crack – and I'm twice as glad that they didn't succeed in grabbing you away from me …' His jaw set rigidly, his eyes became gray ice. 'Blackie DuQuesne has got something coming to him. So far, I have always paid my debts; and I will settle with him … IN FULL.

'That was an awfully quick change of subject,' he went on, his voice changing markedly, 'but that's the penalty we pay for being human – if we lived at peak all the time, there could be no thrill in it, any time. And even though we have been married so long, I still get a tremendous kick out of those peaks.'

'So long!' Dorothy giggled. 'Of course we do, we're unique. I know that everybody thinks that they are, but you and I *really* are – and we *know* that we are. Also, Dick, I know that it's thinking of that DuQuesne that keeps on dragging you down off of the high points. Why wouldn't now be a good time to unload whatever it is that you've got on your mind besides that tangled mop of hair?'

'Nothing much …'

'Come on, 'fess up. Tell it to Red-Top.'

'Let me finish, woman! I was going to. Nothing much to go on but a hunch, but I think that DuQuesne's somewhere out here in the great open spaces, where men are sometimes schemers as well as men; and if so, I'm after him – foot, horse, and marines.'

'That object compass?'

'Yeah. You see, I built that thing myself, and I know darn well it isn't out of order. It's still on him, but doesn't indicate. Therefore he is too far away to reach – and with his mass, I could find him anywhere up to about one and a half light-years. If he wants to go that far away from home, where is his logical destination? – It can't be anywhere but Osnome, since that is the only place we stopped for any length of time – the only place where he could have learned anything. He's learned something, or found something useful to him there, just as we did. That's sure, since he is not the type of man to do anything without a purpose. Uncle Dudley is on his trail – and will be able to locate him pretty soon.'

'When you get that new compass-case exhausted to a skillionth of a whillimeter or something, whatever it is? I thought Dunark said it took five hundred hours of pumping to get it where he wanted it?'

'It did him – but while the Osnomians are wonders on some things, they ain't so hot on others. You see, I've got three pumps on that job, in series. First, a Rodebush-Michalek super-pump; then, backing that, an ordinary mercury-vapor pump; and last, backing both the others, a Cenco-Hyvac motor-driven oil pump. In less than fifty hours that case will be emptier than any Dunark ever pumped. Just to make sure of cleaning up the last infinitesimal traces, though – painting the lily, as it were – I'm going to flash a getter charge in it. After that, the atmosphere in that case will be tenuous – take my word for it.'

'I'll have to, most of that contribution to science being over my head like a circus tent. What say we let *Skylark Two* drift by herself for a while, and catch us some of Nature's sweet restorer?'

4

The Zone of Force is Tested

Seaton strode into the control room with a small oblong box in his hand. Crane was seated at the desk, poring over an abstruse mathematical treatise in *Science*. Margaret was working upon a bit of embroidery. Dorothy, seated upon a cushion on the floor with one foot tucked under her, was reading, her hand straying from time to time to a box of chocolates conveniently near.

'Well, this is a peaceful, home-like scene – too bad to break it up. Just finished sealing off and flashing out this case, Mart. Going to see if she'll read. Want to take a look?'

He placed a compass upon the plane table, so that its final bearing could be read upon the master circles controlled by the gyroscopes; then simultaneously started his stop-watch and pressed the button which caused a minute couple to be applied to the needle. Instantly the needle began to revolve, and for many minutes there was no apparent change in its motion in either the primary or secondary bearings.

'Do you suppose it is out of order, after all?' asked Crane, regretfully.

'I don't think so.' Seaton pondered. 'You see, they weren't designed to indicate such distances on such small objects as men, so I threw a million ohms in series with the impulse. That cuts down the free rotation to less than half an hour, and increases the sensitivity to the limit. There, ain't she trying to quit it?'

'Yes, it is settling down. It must be on him still.'

Finally the ultra-sensitive needle came to rest. When it had done so Seaton calculated the distance, read the direction, and made a reading upon Osnome.

'He's there, all right. Bearings agree, and distances check to within a few light-years, which is as close as we can hope to check on as small a mass as a man. Well, that's that – nothing to do about it until after we get there. One sure thing, Mart – we ain't coming straight back home from "X".'

'No, an investigation is indicated.'

'Well, that puts me out of a job. What to do? Don't want to study, like you. Can't crochet, like Peg. Darned if I'll sit cross-legged on a pillow and eat candy, like that Titian blonde over there on the floor. I know what – I'll build me a mechanical educator and teach Shiro to talk English instead of that mess of language he indulges in. How'd that be, Mart?'

'Don't do it,' put in Dorothy, positively. 'He's just too perfect, the way he is. Especially don't do it if he'd talk the way you do – or could you teach him to talk the way you write?'

'Ouch! That's a dirty dig. However, Mrs Seaton, I am able and willing to defend my customary mode of speech. You realize that the spoken word is ephemeral, whereas the thought whose nuances have once been expressed in imperishable print is not subject to revision – its crudities can never be remodeled into more subtle, more gracious shading. It is my contention that, due to these inescapable conditions, the mental effort necessitated by the employment of nice distinctions in sense and meaning of words and a slavish adherence to the dictates of the more precise grammarians should be reserved for the prin—'

He broke off as Dorothy, in one lithe motion, rose and hurled her pillow at his head.

'Choke him, somebody! Perhaps you had better build it, Dick, after all.'

'I believe that he would like it, Dick. He is trying hard to learn, and the continuous use of a dictionary is undoubtedly a nuisance to him.'

'I'll ask him. Shiro!'

'You have call, sir?' Shiro entered the room from his galley, with his unfailing bow.

'Yes. How'd you like to learn to talk English like Crane there does – without taking lessons?'

Shiro smiled doubtfully, unable to take such a thought seriously.

'Yes, it can be done,' Crane assured him. 'Dr Seaton can build a machine which will teach you all at once, if you like.'

'I like, sir, enormously, yes, sir. I years study and pore, but honorable English extraordinary difference from Nipponese – no can do. Dictionary useful but ...' he flipped pages dexterously, 'extremely cumbrous. If honorable Seaton can do, shall be extreme ... gratification.'

He bowed again, smiled, and went out.

'I'll do just that little thing. So-long, folks. I'm going up to the shop.'

Day after day the *Skylark* plunged through the vast emptiness of the interstellar reaches. At the end of each second she was traveling exactly twenty-six feet per second faster than she had been at its beginning and as day after day passed, her velocity mounted into figures which became meaningless, even when expressed in thousands of miles per second. Still she seemed stationary to her occupants, and only different from a vessel motionless upon the surface of the Earth in that objects within her hull had lost three-sixteenths of their normal weight. Only the rapidity with which the closer suns and their planets were passed gave any indication of the frightful speed at which they were being hurried along by the inconceivable power of that disintegrating copper bar.

When the vessel was nearly halfway to X, the bar was reversed in order to change the sign of their acceleration, and the hollow sphere spun through an angle of one hundred and eighty degrees around the motionless cage which housed the enormous gyroscopes. Still apparently motionless and exactly as she had been before, the *Skylark* was now actually traveling in a direction which seemed 'down', and with a velocity which was being constantly decreased by the amount of their acceleration.

A few days after the bar had been reversed Seaton announced that the mechanical educator was complete, and brought it into the control room.

In appearance it was not unlike a large radio set, but it was infinitely more complex. It possessed numerous tubes, kinolamps, and photo-electric cells, as well as many coils of peculiar design – there were dozens of dials and knobs, and a multiple set of head-harnesses.

'How can a thing like that possibly work as it does?' asked Crane. 'I know that it does work, but I could scarcely believe it, even after it had educated me.'

'That is nothing like the one Dunark used, Dick,' objected Dorothy. 'How come?'

'I'll answer you first, Dot. This is an improved model – it has quite a few gadgets of my own in it. Now, Mart, as to how it works – it isn't so funny after you understand it – it's a lot like radio in that respect. It operates on a band of frequencies lying between the longest light and heat waves and the shortest radio waves. This thing here is the generator of those waves and a very heavy power amplifier. The headsets are stereoscopic transmitters, taking or receiving a three-dimensional view. Nearly all matter is transparent to those waves; for instance bones, hair, and so on. However, cerebrin, a cerebroside peculiar to the thinking structure of the brain, is opaque to them. Dunark, not knowing chemistry, didn't know why the educator worked or what it worked on – they found out by experiment that it did work; just as we found out about electricity. This three-dimensional model, or view, or whatever you want to call it, is converted into electricity in the headsets, and the resulting modulated wave goes back to the educator. There it is heterodyned with another wave – this second frequency was found after thousands of trials and is, I believe, the exact frequency existing in the optic nerves themselves – and sent to the receiving headset. Modulated as it is, and producing after rectification in the receiver a three-dimensional picture, it of course reproduces exactly what has been "viewed", if due allowance has been made for the size and configuration of the different brains involved in the transfer. You remember a sort of flash – a sensation of seeing something – when the educator worked on you? Well, you did see it, just as though it had been transmitted to the brain by the optic nerve, but everything came at once, so the impression of sight was confused. The result in the brain, however, was clear and permanent. The only drawback is that you haven't the visual memory of what you have learned, and that sometimes makes it hard to use your knowledge. You don't know whether you know anything about a certain subject or not until after you go digging around in your brain looking for it.'

'I see,' said Crane, and Dorothy, the irrepressible, put in: 'Just as clear as so much mud. What are the improvements you added to the original design?'

'Well, you see, I had a big advantage in knowing that cerebrin was the substance involved, and with that knowledge I could carry matters considerably farther than Dunark could in his original model. I can transfer the thoughts of somebody else to a third party or onto a record. Dunark's machine couldn't work against resistance – if the subject wasn't willing to give up his thoughts he couldn't get 'em. This one can take 'em away by force. In fact, by increasing plate and grid voltages in the amplifier, I believe that I can burn out a man's brain. Yesterday, I was playing with it, transferring a section of my own brain onto a magnetized tape – for a permanent record, you know – and found out that above certain rather low voltages it becomes a form of torture that would make the best efforts of the old Inquisition seem like a petting party.'

'Did you succeed in the transfer?' Crane was intensely interested.

'Sure. Push the button for Shiro, and we'll start something.'

'Put your heads against this screen,' he directed when Shiro had come in, smiling and bowing as usual. 'I've got to caliper your brains to do a good job.'

The calipering done, he adjusted various dials and clamped the electrodes over his own head and over the heads of Crane and Shiro.

'Want to learn Japanese while we're at it, Mart? I'm going to.'

'Yes, please. I tried to learn it while I was in Japan, but it was altogether too difficult to be worthwhile.'

Seaton threw in a switch, opened it, depressed two more, opened them, and threw off the power.

'All set,' he reported crisply, and barked a series of explosive syllables at Shiro, ending upon a rising note.

'Yes, sir,' answered the Japanese. 'You speak Nipponese as though you had never spoken any other tongue. I am very grateful to you, sir, that I may now discard my dictionary.'

'How about you two girls – anything you want to learn in a hurry?'

'Not me!' declared Dorothy emphatically. 'That machine is too perfectly darned weird to suit me. Besides, if I knew as much about science as you do, we'd probably fight about it.'

'I do not believe I care to—' began Margaret.

She was interrupted by the penetrating sound of an alarm bell.

'That's a new note!' exclaimed Seaton. 'I never heard that tone before.'

He stood in surprise at the board, where a brilliant purple light was flashing slowly. 'Great Cat! That's a purely Osnomian war-gadget – kind of a battleship detector – shows that there's a boatload of bad news around here somewhere. Grab the visiplates, quick, folks,' as he rang Shiro's bell. 'I'll take visiplate and area one, dead ahead. Mart, take number two; Dot, three; Peg four; Shiro, five. Look sharp! … Nothing in front. See anything, any of you?'

None of them could discover anything amiss, but the purple light continued to flash, and the alarm to sound. Seaton cut off the bell.

'We're almost to X,' he thought aloud. 'Can't be more than a million miles or so, and we're almost stopped. Wonder if somebody's there ahead of us? Maybe Dunark is doing this, though. I'll call him and see.' He threw in a switch and said one word – 'Dunark!'

'Here!' came the voice of the Kofedix from the speaker. 'Are you generating?'

'No – just called to see if you were. What do you make of it?'

'Nothing as yet. Better close up?'

'Yes, edge over this way and I'll come over to meet you. Leave your negative as it is or we'll be stopped directly. Whatever it is, it's dead ahead. It's a long ways off yet, but we'd better get organized. Wouldn't talk much, either – they may intercept our wave, narrow as it is.'

'Better yet, shut off your radio entirely. When we get close enough together, we'll use the hand-language. You may not know that you know it, but you do. Turn your heaviest searchlight toward me – I'll do the same.'

There was a click as Dunark's power was shut off abruptly, and Seaton grinned as he cut his own.

'That's right, too, folks. In Osnomian battles we always used a sign-language when we couldn't hear anything – and that was most of the time. I know it as well as I know English, now that I am reminded of the fact.'

He shifted his course to intercept that of the Osnomian vessel. After a time the watchers picked out a minute point of light, moving comparatively rapidly against the stars, and knew it to be the searchlight of the *Kondal*. Soon the two vessels were almost side by side, moving cautiously forward, and Seaton set up a sixty-inch parabolic reflector, focused upon a coil. As they went on the purple light continued to flash more and more rapidly, but still nothing was to be seen.

'Take number six visiplate, will you, Mart? It's telescopic, equivalent to a twenty-inch refractor. I'll tell you where to look in a minute – this reflector increases the power of the regular indicator.' He studied meters and adjusted dials. 'Set on nineteen hours forty-three minutes, and two hundred seventy-one degrees. He's too far away yet to read exactly, but that'll put him in the field of vision.'

'Is this radiation harmful?' asked Margaret.

'Not yet – it's too weak. Pretty quick we may be able to feel it; then I'll throw out a screen against it. When it's strong enough it's pretty deadly stuff. See anything, Mart?'

'I see something, but it is very indistinct. It is moving in sharper now. Yes, it is a spaceship, shaped like a dirigible airship.'

'See it yet, Dunark?' Seaton signaled.

'Just sighted it. Ready to attack?'

'I am not. I'm going to run. Let's go, and go fast!'

Dunark signaled violently, and Seaton shook his head time after time, stubbornly.

'A difficulty?' asked Crane.

'Yes, he wants to go jump on it, but I'm not looking for trouble with any such craft as that – it must be a thousand feet long and is certainly neither Terrestrial nor Osnomian. I say beat it while we're all in one piece. How about it?'

'Absolutely,' concurred Crane and both women, in a breath.

The bar was reversed and the *Skylark* leaped away. The *Kondal* followed, although the observers could see that Dunark was raging. Seaton swung number six visiplate around, looked once, and switched on his radio transmitter.

'Well, Dunark,' he said grimly, 'you get your wish. That bird is coming out, with at least twice the acceleration we could get with both motors full on. He saw us all the time, and was waiting for us.'

'Go on – get away if you can. You can stand a higher acceleration that we can. We'll hold him as long as possible.'

'I would, if it would do any good, but it won't. He's so much faster than we are that he could catch us anyway, if he wanted to, no matter how much of a start we had – and it looks now as though he wanted us. Two of us stand a lot better chance than one of licking him if he's looking for trouble. Spread out a little farther apart, and pretend this is all the speed we've got. What'll we give him first?'

'Give him everything at once. Beams six, seven, eight, nine, and ten …'

Crane, with Seaton, began making contacts, rapidly but with precision. 'Heat wave two seven. Induction, five eight. Oscillation, everything under point oh six three. All the explosive copper we can get in. Right?'

'Right – and if worst comes to worst, remember the zone of force. Let him shoot first, because he may be peaceable – but it doesn't look like olive branches to me.'

'Got both your screens out?'

'Yes. Mart, you might take number two visiplate and work the guns – I'll handle the rest of this stuff. Better strap yourselves in solid, everybody – this may develop into a rough party, by the looks of things right now.'

As he spoke a pyrotechnic display enveloped the entire ship as a radiation from the foreign vessel struck the outer neutralizing screen and dissipated its force harmlessly in the ether. Instantly Seaton threw on the full power of his refrigerating system and shoved in the master switch that actuated the complex offensive armament of his dreadnought of the skies. An intense, livid violet glow hid completely main and auxiliary power bars, and long flashes leaped between metallic objects in all parts of the vessel. The passengers felt each hair striving to stand on end as the very air became more and more highly charged – and this was but the slight corona-loss of the frightful stream of destruction being hurled at the other space-cruiser, now only miles away!

Seaton stared into number one visiplate, manipulating levers and dials as he drove the *Skylark* hither and yon, dodging frantically while the automatic focusing devices remained centered upon the enemy and the enormous generators continued to pour forth their deadly frequencies. The bars glowed more fiercely as they were advanced to full working load – the stranger was one blaze of incandescent ionization, but she still fought on; and Seaton noticed that the pyrometers recording the temperature of the shell were mounting rapidly, in spite of the refrigerators.

'Dunark, put everything you've got onto one spot – right on the end of his – nose!'

As the first shell struck the mark Seaton concentrated every force at his command upon the designated point. The air in the *Skylark* crackled and hissed and intense violet flames leaped from the bars as they were driven almost to the point of disruption. From the forward end of the strange craft there erupted prominence after prominence of searing, unbearable flame as the terrific charges of explosive copper struck the mark and exploded, liberating instantaneously their millions of millions of kilowatt-hours of energy. Each prominence enveloped all three of the fighting vessels and extended for hundreds of miles out into space – but still the enemy warship continued to hurl forth solid and vibratory destruction.

A brilliant orange light flared upon the panel, and Seaton gasped as he swung his visiplate upon his defenses, which he had supposed impregnable. His outer screen was already down, although its mighty copper generator was exerting its utmost power. Black areas had already appeared and were spreading rapidly where there should have been only incandescent radiance; and the inner screen was even now radiating far into the ultra-violet and was certainly doomed. Knowing as he did the stupendous power driving those screens, he knew that there were superhuman and inconceivable forces being directed against them, and his right hand flashed to the switch controlling the zone of force. Fast as he was, much happened in the mere moment that passed before his flying hand could close the switch. In the last infinitesimal instant of time before the zone closed in, a gaping hole appeared in the incandescence of the inner screen, and a small portion of a bar of energy so stupendous as to be palpable struck, like a tangible projectile, the exposed flank of the *Skylark*. Instantly the refractory arenak turned an intense, dazzling white and more than a foot of the forty-eight-inch skin of the vessel melted away like snow before an oxy-acetylene flame, melting and flying away in molten globules and sparkling gases – the refrigerating coils lining the hull were useless against the concentrated energy of that titanic thrust. As Seaton shut off his power intense darkness and utter silence closed in, and he snapped on the lights.

'They take one trick!' he blazed, his eyes almost emitting sparks, and leaped for the generators. He had forgotten the effects of the zone of force, however, and only sprawled grotesquely in the air until he floated within reach of a line.

'Hold everything, Dick!' Crane snapped, as Seaton bent over one of the bars. 'What are you going to do?'

'I'm going to put as many heavy bars in these generators as they'll stand and go out and get that bird. We can't lick him with Osnomian beams or with our explosive copper, but I can carve that sausage into slices with a zone of force, and I'm going to do it.'

'Steady, old man – take it easy. I see your point, but remember that you must release the zone of force before you can use it as a weapon. Furthermore, you must discover his exact location, and must get close enough to him to use the zone as a weapon, all without its protection. Can those screens be made sufficiently powerful to withstand the beam they employed last, even for a second?'

'Hm … in … m. Never thought of that, Mart,' Seaton replied, the fire dying out of his eyes. 'Wonder how long the battle lasted?'

'Eight and two-tenths seconds, from first to last, but they had had that heavy ray in action only a fraction of one second when you cut in the zone of force. Either they underestimated our strength at first, or else it required about eight seconds to tune in their heavy generators – probably the former.'

'But we've got to do something, man! We can't just sit here and twiddle our thumbs!'

'Why, and why not? That course seems eminently wise and proper. In fact, at the present time, thumb-twiddling seems to me to be distinctly indicated.'

'Oh, you're full of little red ants! We can't do a thing with that zone on – and you say just sit here. Suppose they know all about that zone of force? Suppose they can crack it? Suppose they ram us?'

'I shall take up your objections in order,' Crane had lighted a cigarette and was smoking meditatively. 'First, they may or may not know about it. At present, that point is immaterial. Second, whether or not they know about it, it is almost a certainty that they cannot crack it. It has been up for more than three minutes, and they undoubtedly concentrated everything possible upon us during that time. It is still standing. I really expected it to go down in the first few seconds, but now that it has held this long it will, in all probability, continue to hold indefinitely. Third, they most certainly will not ram us, for several reasons. They probably have encountered few, if any, foreign vessels able to stand against them for a minute, and will act accordingly. Then, too, it is probably safe to assume that their vessel is damaged, to some slight extent at least; for I do not believe that any possible armament could withstand the forces we directed against them and escape entirely unscathed. Finally, if they ram us, what would happen? Would we feel the shock? That barrier in the ether seems impervious, and if so, it could not transmit a blow. I do not see exactly how it would affect the ship dealing the blow. You are the one who works out the new problems in unexplored mathematics – some time you must take a few months off and work it out.'

'Yeah, it'd take that long, too, I guess – but you're right, he can't hurt us. That's using the brain, Mart! I was going off half-cocked again, damn it! I'll pipe down, and we'll go into a huddle.'

Seaton noticed that Dorothy's face was white and that she was fighting for self-control. Drawing himself over to her, he picked her up in a tight embrace.

'Cheer up, Red-Top! This man's war ain't started yet!'

'Not started? What do you mean? Haven't you and Martin just been admitting to each other that you can't do anything? Doesn't that mean that we are beaten?'

'Beaten! Us? How do you get that way? Not on your sweet young life!' he ejaculated, and the surprise on his face was so manifest that she recovered instantly. 'We've just dug a hole and pulled the hole in after us, that's all! When we get everything *doped* out to suit us we'll snap out of it and that bird'll think he's been petting a wildcat!'

'Mart, you're the thinking end of this partnership,' he continued thoughtfully. 'You've got the analytical mind and the judicial disposition, and can think circles around me. From what little you've seen of those folks tell me who, what, and where they are. I'm getting the germ of an idea, and maybe we can make it work.'

'I will try it.' Crane paused. 'They are, of course, neither from the Earth nor from Osnome. It is also evident that they are familiar with atomic energy. Their vessels are not propelled as ours are – they have so perfected that force that it acts upon every particle of the structure and its contents …'

'How do you figure that?' blurted Seaton.

'Because of the acceleration they can stand. Nothing even semi-human, and probably nothing living, could endure it otherwise. Right?'

'Yeah – I never thought of that.'

'Furthermore, they are far from home, for if they were from anywhere nearby, the Osnomians would probably have known of them – particularly since it is evident from the size of the vessel that space travel is not a recent development with them, as it is with us. Since the green system is close to the center of the galaxy, it seems reasonable, as a working hypothesis, to assume that they are from some system far from the center, perhaps close to the outer edge. They are very evidently of a high degree of intelligence. They are also highly treacherous and merciless …'

'Why?' asked Dorothy, who was listening eagerly.

'I deduce those characteristics from their unprovoked attack upon peaceful ships, vastly smaller and supposedly of inferior armament; and also from the nature of that attack. This vessel is probably a scout or an exploring ship, since it is apparently alone. It is not altogether beyond the bounds of reason to imagine it upon a voyage of discovery, in search of new planets to be subjugated and colonized …'

'That's a sweet picture of our future neighbors – but I guess you're hitting the nail on the head, at that.'

'If these deductions are anywhere nearly correct they are terrible neighbors. For my next point, are we justified in assuming that they do or do not know about the zone of force?' That's a hard one. Knowing what they evidently do know, it's hard to see how they could have missed it. And yet, if they had known about it for a long time, wouldn't they be able to get through it? Of course it may be a real and total barrier in the ether – in that case they'd know that they couldn't do a thing as long as we keep it on. Take your choice, but I believe that they know about it, and know more than we do – that it is a total barrier set up in the ether.'

'I agree with you, and we shall proceed upon that assumption. They know, then, that neither they nor we can do anything as long as we maintain the zone – that it is a stalemate. They also know that it takes an enormous amount of power to keep the zone in place. Now we have gone as far as we can go upon the meager data we have – considerably farther than we really are justified in going. We must now try to come to some conclusion concerning their present activities. If our ideas as to their natures are even approximately correct they are waiting, probably fairly close at hand, until we shall be compelled to release the zone, no matter how long that period of waiting shall be. They know, of course, from our small size, that we cannot carry enough copper to maintain it indefinitely, as they could. Does that sound reasonable?'

'I check you to nineteen decimal places, Mart, and from your ideas I'm getting surer and surer that we can pull their corks. I can get into action in a hurry when I have to, and my idea now is to wait until they relax a trifle, and then slip a fast one over on them. One more bubble out of the old think-tank and I'll let you off for the day. At what time will their vigilance be at lowest ebb? That's a poser, I'll admit, but the answer to it may answer everything – the first shot will, of course, be the best chance we'll ever have.'

'Yes, we should succeed in the first, attempt. We have very little information to guide us in answering that question.' He studied the problem for many minutes before he resumed. 'I should say that for a time they would keep all their rays and other weapons in action against the zone of force, expecting us to release it immediately. Then, knowing that they were wasting power uselessly, they would cease attacking, but would be very watchful, with every eye fastened upon us and with every weapon ready for instant use. After this period of vigilance regular ship's routine would be resumed. Half the force, probably, would go off duty – for, if they are even remotely like any organic beings with which we are familiar, they require sleep or its equivalent at intervals. The men on duty – the normal force, that is – would be doubly careful for a time. Then habit will assert itself, if we have done nothing to create suspicion, and their watchfulness will relax to the point of ordinary careful observation. Toward the end of their watch, because of the strain of the battle and because of the unusually long period of duty, they will become careless, and their vigilance will be considerably below normal. But the exact time of all these things depends entirely upon their conception of time, concerning which we have no information whatever. Though it is purely a speculation, based upon Earthly and Osnomian experience, should say that after about twelve or thirteen hours would come the time for us to make the attack.'

'That's good enough for me. Fine, Mart, and thanks. You've probably saved the lives of the party. We will now sleep for eleven or twelve hours.'

'Sleep, Dick! How could you?' Dorothy exclaimed.

5

First Blood

The next twelve hours dragged with terrible slowness. Sleep was impossible and eating was difficult, even though all knew that they would have need of the full measure of their strength. Seaton set up various combinations of switching devices connected to electrical timers, and spent hours trying, with all his marvelous quickness of muscular control, to cut shorter and ever shorter the time between the opening and the closing of the switch. At last he arranged a powerful electro-magnetic device so that one impulse would both open and close the switch, with an open period of one thousandth of a second. Only then was he satisfied.

'A thousandth is enough to give us a look around, due to persistence of vision; and it is short enough so that they won't see it unless they have a recording observer on us. Even if they still have beams on us they can't possibly neutralize our screens in that short an exposure. All right, gang? We'll take five visiplates and cover the sphere. If any of you get a glimpse of him, mark the exact spot and outline on the glass. All set?'

He pressed the button. The stars flashed in the black void for an instant, then were again shut out.

'Here he is, Dick!' shrieked Margaret. 'Right here – he covered almost half the visiplate!'

She outlined for him, as nearly as she could, the exact position of the object she had seen, and he calculated rapidly.

'Fine business!' he exulted. 'He's within half a mile of us, three-quarters on – perfect! I thought he'd be so far away that I'd have to take photographs to locate him. He hasn't a single beam on us, either. That bird's goose is cooked right now, folks, unless every man on watch has his hand right on the controls of a generator and can get into action in less than a quarter of a second! Hang on, people – I'm going to step on the gas!'

After making sure that everyone was fastened immovably in his place he strapped himself into the pilot's seat, then set the bar toward the strange vessel and applied fully one-third of its full power. The *Skylark*, of course, did not move. Then, with bewildering rapidity, he went into action; face glued to the visiplate, hands moving faster than the eye could follow – the left closing and opening the switch controlling the zone' of force, the right swinging the steering controls to all points of the sphere. The mighty vessel staggered this way and that, jerking and straining terribly as the zone was thrown on and off, lurching sickeningly about the central bearing as the gigantic power of the driving bar was exerted, now in one direction, now in another. After a second or two of this mad gyration Seaton shut off the power. He then released the zone, after assuring himself that both inner and outer screens were operating at highest possible rating.

'There, that'll hold 'em for a while, I guess. This battle was even shorter than the other one – and a lot more decisive. Let's turn on the flood-lights and see what the pieces look like.'

The lights revealed that the zone of force had indeed sliced the enemy vessel into bits. No fragment was large enough to be navigable or dangerous and each was sharply cut, as though sheared from its neighbor by some gigantic, curved blade. Dorothy sobbed with relief in Seaton's arms as Crane, with one arm around his wife, grasped his hand.

'That was flawless, Dick. As an exhibition of perfect coordination and instantaneous timing under extreme physical difficulties, I have never seen its equal.'

'You certainly saved all our lives,' Margaret added.

'Only fifty-fifty, Peg,' Seaton protested, and blushed vividly. 'Mart did most of it, you know. I'd've gummed up everything back there if he'd've let me. Let's see what we can find out about 'em.'

He touched the lever and the *Skylark* moved slowly toward the wreckage, the scattered fragments of which were beginning to move toward and around each other under their mutual gravitational forces. Snapping on a search-light, he swung its beam around, and as it settled upon one of the larger sections he saw a group of hooded figures; some of them upon the metal, others floating slowly toward it through space.

'Poor devils – they didn't have a chance,' he remarked regretfully. 'However, it was either them or us – look out! Sweet spirits of niter!'

He leaped back to the controls and the others were hurled bodily to the floor as he applied power – for at a signal each of the hooded figures had leveled a tube and once more the outer screen had flamed into incandescence. As the *Skylark* leaped away Seaton focused an attractor upon the one who had apparently signaled the attack. Rolling the vessel over in a short loop, so that the captive was hurled off into space upon the other side, he snatched the tube from the figure's grasp with one auxiliary attractor, and anchored head and limbs with others, so that the prisoner could scarcely move a muscle. Then, while Crane and the women scrambled off the floor and hurried to the visiplates, Seaton cut in beams six, two-seven, and five-eight. Number six, 'the softener', was a band of frequencies extending from violet far up into the ultra-violet. When driven with sufficient power this ray destroyed eyesight and nervous tissue, and, its power increased still further, actually loosened the molecular structure of matter. Ray two-seven was operated in a range of frequencies far below the visible red. It was pure heat – its action matter became hotter and hotter as long as it was applied, the upper limit being only the theoretical maximum of temperature. Five-eight was high-tension, high-frequency alternating current. Any conductor in its path behaved precisely as it would in the Ajax-Northrup induction furnace, which can boil platinum in ten seconds! These three items composed the beam which Seaton directed upon the mass of metal from which the enemy had elected to continue the battle – and behind each one, instead of the small energy at the command of its Osnomian inventor, were the untold millions of kilowatts developed by a one-hundred-pound bar of disintegrating copper!

There ensured a brief but appalling demonstration of the terrible effectiveness of those Osnomian weapons against anything not protected by ultra-powered screens. Metal and men – if men they were – literally vanished. One moment they were outlined starkly in the beam, there was a moment of searing, coruscating, blinding light – the next moment the beam bored on into the void, unimpeded. Nothing was visible save an occasional tiny flash, as some condensed or solidified droplet of the volatilized metal entered the path of that ravening beam.

'We'll see if there's any more of 'em loose,' Seaton remarked, as he shut off the force and probed into the wreckage with a searchlight.

No sign of life or of activity was revealed, and the light was turned upon the captive. He was held motionless in the invisible grip of the attractors, at the point where the force of those peculiar magnets was exactly balanced by the outward thrust of the repellors. By manipulating the attractor holding it, Seaton brought the strange tubular weapon into the control room through a small airlock in the wall and examined it curiously, but did not touch it.

'I never heard of a hand-ray before, so I guess I won't play with it much until after I learn something about it.'

'So you have taken a captive?' asked Margaret. 'What are you going to do with him?'

'I'm going to drag him in here and read his mind. He's one of the officers of that ship, I believe, and I'm going to find out how to build one exactly like it. Our *Skylark* is now as obsolete as a 1910 flivver, and I'm going to make us a later model. How about it, Mart, don't we want something really up-to-date if we're going to keep on space-hopping?'

'We certainly do. Those denizens seem to be particularly venomous, and we will not be safe unless we have the most powerful and most efficient spaceship possible. However, that fellow may be dangerous, even now – in fact, it is practically certain that he is.'

'You chirped it, ace. I'd rather touch a pound of dry nitrogen iodide. I've got him spread-eagled so that he can't destroy his brain until after we've read it, though, so there's no particular hurry 'bout him. We'll leave him out there for a while, to waste his sweetness on the desert air. Let's all look around for the *Kondal*. I hope they didn't get her in that fracas.'

They diffused the rays of eight giant searchlights into a vertical fan, and with it swept slowly through almost a semicircle before anything was seen. Then there was revealed a cluster of cylindrical objects amid a mass of wreckage which Crane recognized at once.

'The *Kondal* is gone, Dick. There is what is left of her, and most of her cargo of salt, in jute bags.'

As he spoke a series of green flashes played upon the bags, and Seaton yelled in relief.

'Yes – they got the ship all right, but Dunark and Sitar got away – they're still with their salt!'

The *Skylark* moved over to the wreck and Seaton, relinquishing the controls to Crane, donned a space-suit, entered the main airlock, snapped on the motor which sealed off the lock, pumped the air into a pressure-tank, and opened the outside door. He threw a light line to the two figures and pushed himself lightly toward them. He then talked briefly to Dunark in the hand-language, and handed the end of the line to Sitar, who held it while the two men explored the fragments of the strange vessel, gathering up various things of interest as they came upon them.

Back in the control room, Dunark and Sitar let their pressure decrease gradually to that of the Terrestrial vessel and removed the face-plates from their helmets.

'Again, O Karfedo of Earth, we thank you for our lives,' Dunark began, gasping for breath, when Seaton leaped to the air-gauge with a quick apology.

'Never thought of the effect our atmospheric pressure would have on you two. We can stand yours, but you'd pretty nearly pass out on ours. There, that'll suit you better. Didn't you throw out your zone of force?'

'Yes, as soon as I saw that our screens were not going to hold.' The Osnomians' labored breathing became normal as the air-pressure increased to a value only a little below that of the dense atmosphere of their native planet. 'I then increased the power of the screens to the extreme limit and opened the zone for a moment to see how the screens would hold with the added power. That moment was enough. In that moment a concentrated beam such as I had no idea could ever be generated went through the outer and inner screens as though they were not there, through the four-foot arenak of the hull, through the entire central installation, and through the hull on the other side. Sitar and I were wearing suits …'

'Say, Mart, that's one bet we overlooked. It's a hot idea, too – those strangers wore them all the time as regular equipment, apparently. Next time we get into a jam, be sure we do it; they might come in handy. 'Scuse me, Dunark – go ahead.'

'We had suits on, so as soon as the ray was shut off, which was almost instantly, I phoned the crew to jump, and we leaped out through the hole in the hull. The air rushing out gave us an impetus that carried us many miles out into space, and it required many hours for the slight attraction of the mass here to draw us back to it. We just got back a few minutes ago. That air-blast is probably what saved us, as they destroyed our vessel and sent out a party to hunt down the four men of our crew, who stayed comparatively close to the scene. They rayed you for about an hour with the most stupendous beams imaginable – no such generators have ever been considered possible of construction – but couldn't make any impression upon you. They shut off their power and stood by waiting. I wasn't looking at you when you released your zone. One moment it was there, and the next, the stranger had been cut in pieces. The rest you know.'

'We're sure glad you two got away, Dunark. Well, Mart, what say we drag that guy in and give him the once-over?'

Seaton swung the attractors holding the prisoner until they were in line with the main airlock, then reduced the power of the repellors. As he approached the lock various controls were actuated, and soon the stranger stood in the control room, held immovable against one wall, while Crane, with a 0.50-caliber elephant gun, stood against the other.

'Perhaps you girls should go somewhere else,' suggested Crane.

'Not on your life!' protested Dorothy, who, eyes wide and flushed with excitement, stood near a door, with a heavy automatic pistol in her hand. 'I wouldn't miss this for a farm!'

'Got him solid,' declared Seaton, after a careful inspection of the various attractors and repellors he had bearing upon the prisoner. 'Now let's get him out of that suit. No – better read his air first, temperature and pressure – might analyze it, too.'

Nothing could be seen of the person of the stranger, since he was encased in space armor, but it was plainly evident that he was very short and immensely broad and thick. Drilling a hole through that armor took time and apparatus, but it was finally done. Seaton drew off a sample of the atmosphere within into an Orsat apparatus, while Crane made pressure and temperature readings.

'Temperature, one hundred ten degrees. Pressure, twenty-eight pounds – about the same as ours is, now that we have stepped it up to keep the Osnomians from suffering.' Seaton soon reported that the atmosphere was quite similar to that of the *Skylark*, except that it was much higher in carbon dioxide and carried an extremely high concentration of water vapor. He brought in a power cutter and laid the suit open full length, on both sides, while Crane at the controls of attractors and repellors held the stranger immovable. He then wrenched off the helmet and cast the whole suit aside, revealing the enemy officer, clad in a tunic of scarlet silk.

He was less than five feet tall. His legs were merely blocks, fully as great in diameter as they were in length, supporting a torso of Herculean dimensions. His arms were as large as a strong man's thigh and hung almost to the floor. His astounding shoulders, fully a yard across, merged into and supported an enormous head. The being possessed recognizable nose, ears, and mouth; and the great domed forehead and huge cranium bespoke an immense and highly-developed brain.

But it was the eyes of this strange creature that fixed and held the attention. Large they were, and black – the dull, opaque, lusterless black of platinum sponge. The pupils were a brighter black, and in them flamed ruby lights: pitiless, mocking, cold. Plainly to be read in those sinister depths were the untold wisdom of unthinkable age, sheer ruthlessness, mighty power, and ferocity unrelieved. His baleful gaze swept from one member of the party to another, and to meet the glare of those eyes was to receive a tangible physical blow – it was actually a ponderable force; that of embodied hardness and of ruthlessness incarnate, generated in that merciless brain and hurled forth through those flame-shot, Stygian orbs.

'If you don't need us for anything, Dick, I think Peggy and I will go upstairs,' Dorothy broke the long silence.

'Good idea, Dot. This isn't going to be pretty to watch – or to do, either, for that matter.'

'If I stay here another minute I'll see that thing as long as I live; and I might be very ill. Goodbye,' and, heartless and bloodthirsty Osnomian though she was, Sitar had gone to join the two Tellurian women.

'I didn't want to say much before the girls, but I want to check a couple of ideas with you. Don't you think it's a safe bet that this bird reported back to his headquarters?'

'I have been thinking that very thing,' Crane spoke gravely, and Dunark nodded agreement. 'Any race capable of developing such a vessel as this would almost certainly have developed systems of communication in proportion.'

'That's the way I doped it out – and that's why I'm going to read his mind, if I have to burn his brain to do it. We've got to know how far away from home he is, whether he has turned in any report about us, and all about it. Also, I'm going to get the plans, power, and armament of their most modem ships, if he knows them, so that your gang, Dunark, can build us one like them; because the next one that tackles us will be warned and we won't be able to take it by surprise. We won't stand a chance in the *Skylark*. With a ship like theirs, how-ever, we can run – or we can fight, if we have to. Any other ideas, fellows?'

As neither Crane nor Dunark had any other suggestions to offer, Seaton brought out the mechanical educator, watching the creature's eyes narrowly. As he placed one headset over that motionless head the captive sneered in pure contempt, but when the case was opened and the array of tubes and transformers was revealed that expression disappeared; and when he added a super-power stage by cutting in a heavy-duty transformer and a five-kilowatt transmitting tube Seaton thought that he saw an instantaneously suppressed flicker of doubt or fear.

'That headset thing was child's play to him, but he doesn't like the looks of this other stuff at all. I don't blame him a bit – I wouldn't like to be on the receiving end of this hook-up myself. I'm going to put him on the recorder and on the visualizer,' Seaton continued as he connected spools of wire and tape, lamps, and lenses in an intricate system and donned a headset. 'I'd hate to have much of that brain in my own skull – afraid I'd bite myself. I'm just going to look on, and when I see anything I want I'll grab it and put it into my own brain, I'm starting off easy, not using the big tube.'

He closed several switches, lights flashed, and the wires and tapes began to feed through the magnets.

'Well, I've got his language, folks, he seems to want me to have it. It's got a lot of stuff in it that I can't understand yet, though, so guess I'll give him some English.'

He changed several connections and the captive spoke, in a profoundly deep bass voice.

'You may as well discontinue your attempt, for you will gain no information from me. That machine of yours was out of date with us thousands of years ago.'

'Save your breath or talk sense,' said Seaton, coldly. 'I gave you English so that you can give me the information I want. You already know what it is. When you get ready to talk, say so, or throw it on the screen of your own accord. If you don't, I'll put on enough voltage to burn your brain out. Remember, I can read your dead brain as well as though it were alive, but I want your thoughts, as well as your knowledge, and I'm going to have them. If you give them voluntarily I will tinker up a lifeboat that you can navigate back to your own world and let you go; if you resist I intend getting them anyway and you shall not leave this vessel alive. You may take your choice.'

'You are childish, and that machine is impotent against my will. I could have defied it a hundred years ago, when I was barely a grown man. Know you, American, that we supermen of the Fenachrone are as far above any of the other and lesser breeds of beings who spawn in their millions in their countless myriads of races upon the numberless planets of the universe as you are above the inert metal from which this your ship was built. The universe is ours, and in due course we shall take it – just as in due course I shall take this vessel. Do your worst; I shall not speak.' The creature's eyes flamed, hurling a wave of hypnotic command through Seaton's eyes and deep into his brain. Seaton's very senses reeled for an instant under the impact of that awful mental force; but after a short, intensely bitter struggle he threw off the spell.

'That was close, fellow, but you didn't quite ring the bell,' he said grimly, staring directly into those unholy eyes. 'I may rate pretty low mentally, but I can't be hypnotized into turning you loose. Also, I can give you cards and spades in certain other lines which I am about to demonstrate. Being super-men didn't keep the rest of your men from going out in my beams, and being a superman isn't going to save your brain. I am not depending upon my intel-lectual or mental force – I've got an ace in the hole in the shape of five thousand volts to apply to the most delicate centers of your brain. Start giv-ing me what I want, and start quick, or I'll tear it out of you.'

The giant did not answer, merely glared defiance and bitter hatred.

'Take it, then!' Seaton snapped, and cut in the super-power stage and began turning dials and knobs, exploring that strange mind for the particu-lar area in which he was most interested. He soon found it, and cut in the visualizer – the stereographic device, in parallel with Seaton's own brain recorder, which projected a three-dimensional picture into the viewing-area or dark space of the cabinet. Crane and Dunark, tense and silent, looked on in strained suspense as, minute after minute, the silent battle of wills ranged. Upon one side was a horrible and gigantic brain, of undreamed-of power: upon the other side a strong man, fighting for all that life holds dear, wielding against that monstrous and frightful brain a weapon wrought of high-tension electricity, applied with all the skill that Earthly and Osnomian science could devise.

Seaton crouched over the amplifier, his jaw set and every muscle taut, his eyes leaping from one meter to another, his right hand slowly turning up the potentiometer which was driving more and ever more of the searing, tortur-ing output of his super-power tube into that stubborn brain. The captive was standing utterly rigid, eyes closed, every sense and faculty mustered to resist that cruelly penetrant attack upon the innermost recesses of his mind. Crane and Dunark scarcely breathed as the three-dimensional picture in the visual-izer varied from a blank to the hazy outlines of a giant space-cruiser. It faded out as the unknown exerted himself to withstand that poignant inquisition, only to come back in clearer outlines than before as Seaton advanced the potentiometer still farther. Finally, flesh and blood could no longer resist that lethal probe and the picture became clear and sharp. It showed the captain – for he was no less an officer than the commander of the vessel – at a great council table, seated, together with many other officers, upon very low, enor-mously strong metal stools. They were receiving orders from their Emperor;

orders plainly understood by Crane and the Osnomian alike, for thought needs no translation.

'Gentlemen of the Navy,' the ruler spoke solemnly. 'Our preliminary expedition, returned some time ago, achieved its every aim, and we are now ready to begin fulfilling our destiny, the conquest of the universe. This galaxy comes first. Our base of operations will be the largest planet of that group of brilliant green suns, for they can be seen from any point in the galaxy and are almost in the exact center of it. Our astronomers,' here the captain's thoughts shifted briefly to an observatory far out in space for perfect seeing, and portrayed a reflecting telescope with a mirror five miles in diameter, capable of penetrating unimaginable myriads of light-years into space, 'have tabulated all the suns, planets, and satellites belonging to this galaxy, and each of you has been given a complete chart and assigned a certain area which he is to explore. Remember, gentlemen, that this first major expedition is to be purely one of exploration; the one of conquest will set out after you have returned with complete information. You will each report by torpedo every tenth of the year. We do not anticipate any serious difficulty, as we are of course the highest type of life in the universe; nevertheless, in the unlikely event of trouble, report it. We shall do the rest. In conclusion, I warn you again – let no people know that we exist. Make no conquests, and destroy all who by any chance may see you. Gentlemen, go with power.'

The captain embarked in a small airboat and was shot to his vessel. He took his station at an immense control board and the warship shot off into space instantly, with unthinkable velocity, and with not the slightest physical shock.

At this point Seaton made the captain take them all over the ship. They noted its construction, its power plant, its controls – every minute detail of structure, operation, and maintenance was taken from the captain's mind and both recorded and visualized.

The journey seemed to be a very long one, but finally the cluster of green suns became visible and the Fenachrone began to explore the solar systems in the region assigned to that particular vessel. Hardly had the survey started, however, when the two globular space-cruisers were detected and located. The captain stopped the ship briefly, then attacked. They watched the attack, and saw the destruction of the *Kondal*. They looked on while the captain read the brain of one of Dunark's crew, gleaning from it all the facts concerning the two spaceships, and thought with him that the two absentees from the *Kondal* would drift back in a few hours, and would be disposed of in due course. They learned that these things were automatically impressed upon the torpedo next to issue, as was every detail of everything that happened in and around the vessel. They watched him impress a thought of his own upon the record – 'the inhabitants of planet three of sun six four seven three Pilarone show unusual development and may cause trouble, as they have already brought knowledge of the metal of power and of the impenetrable shield to the Central System, which is to be our base. Recommend volatilization of this planet by vessel sent on special mission.' They saw the raying of the *Skylark*. They sensed him issue commands:

'Beam it for a time; he will probably open the shield for a moment, as the other one did,' then, after a time skipped over by the mind under examination, 'Cease raying – no use wasting power. He must open eventually, as he runs out of power. Stand by and destroy him when he opens.'

The scene shifted. The captain was asleep and was awakened by an alarm gong – only to find himself floating in a mass of wreckage. Making his way to the fragment of his vessel containing the torpedo port, he released the messenger, which flew, with ever-increasing velocity, back to the capital city of the Fenachrone, carrying with it a record of everything that had happened.

'That's what I want,' thought Seaton. 'Those torpedoes went home, fast. I want to know how far they have to go and how long it'll take them to get there. You know what distance a parsec is, since it is purely a mathematical concept; and you must have a watch or some similar instrument with which we can translate your years into ours. I don't want to have to kill you, fellow, and if you'll give up even now, I'll spare you. I'll get it anyway, you know – and you also know that a few hundred volts more will kill you.'

They saw the thought received, and saw its answer:

'You shall learn no more. This is the most important of all, and I shall hold it to disintegration and beyond.'

Seaton advanced the potentiometer still farther, and the brain picture waxed and waned, strengthened and faded. Finally, however, it was revealed by flashes that the torpedo had about a hundred and fifty-five thousand parsecs to go and that it would take two tenths of a year to make the journey; that the warships which would come in answer to the message were as fast as the torpedo; that he did indeed have in his suit a watch – a device of seven dials, each turning ten times as fast as its successor; and that one turn of the slowest dial measured one year of his time. Seaton instantly threw off his headset and opened the power switch.

'Grab a stop-watch quick, Mart!' he called, as he leaped to the discarded vacuum suit and searched out the peculiar timepiece. They noted the exact time consumed by one complete revolution of one of the dials, and calculated rapidly.

'Better than I thought!' exclaimed Seaton. 'That makes his year about four hundred ten of our days. That gives us eighty-two days before the torpedo gets there – longer than I'd dared hope. We've got to fight, too, not run. They figure on getting the *Skylark*, then volatilizing our world. Well, we can take time enough to grab off an absolutely complete record of this guy's brain. We'll need it for what's coming, and I'm going to get it, if I have to kill him to do it.'

He resumed his place at the educator, turned on the power, and a shadow passed over his face.

'Poor devil, he's conked out – couldn't stand the gaff,' he remarked, half-regretfully. 'However, that makes it easy to get what we want, and we'd've had to've killed him anyway, I guess, bad as I would have hated to bump him off in cold blood.'

He threaded new spools into the machine, and for three hours mile after mile of tape sped between the magnets as Seaton explored every recess of that monstrous, yet stupendous brain.

'Well, that's that,' he declared finally, as, the last bit of information gleaned and recorded upon the flying tape, he removed the body of the Fenachrone captain into space and blasted it out of existence. 'Now what?'

'How can we get this salt to Osnome?' asked Dunark, whose thoughts were never far from his store of precious chemical. 'You are already crowded, and Sitar and I will crowd you still more. You have no room for additional cargo, and yet much valuable time would be lost in going to Osnome for another vessel.'

'Yeah, and we've got to get a lot of X, too. Guess we'll have to take time to get another vessel. I'd like to drag in the pieces of that ship, too – his instruments and a lot of the parts could be used.'

'Why not do it all at once?' suggested Crane. 'We can start that whole mass toward Osnome by drawing it behind us until such a velocity has been attained that it will reach there at the desired time. We could then go to X, and overtake this material near the green system.'

'Right you are, ace – that's a sound idea. But say, Dunark, it wouldn't be good technique for you to eat our food for any length of time. While we're figuring this out you'd better hop over there and bring over enough to last you two until we get you home. Give it to Shiro – after a couple of lessons, you'll find he'll be as good as any of your cooks.'

Faster and faster the *Skylark* flew, pulling behind her the mass of wreckage, held by every available attractor. When the calculated velocity had been attained the attractors were shut off and the vessel darted away toward that planet, still in the Carboniferous Age, which possessed at least one solid ledge of metallic X, the rarest metal known to Tellurian science. As the automatic controls held the cruiser upon her course the six wanderers sat long in discussion as to what should be done, what could be done, to avert the threatened destruction of all the civilization of the galaxy except the monstrous and unspeakable culture of the Fenachrone. They were approaching their destination when Seaton rose to his feet.

'As I see it, it's like this. We've got our backs to the wall. Donark has troubles of his own – if the Third Planet doesn't get him the Fenachrone will, and the Third Planet is the more pressing danger. That lets him out. We've got nearly six months before the Fenachrone can get back here …'

'But how can they possibly find us here, or wherever we'll be by that time, Dick?' asked Dorothy. 'The battle was a long way from here.'

'With that much start they probably couldn't find us,' he replied soberly. 'It's the world I'm thinking about. They've got to be stopped, and stopped cold – and we've got only six months to do it in … Osnome's got the best tools and the fastest workmen I know of …' His voice died away in thought.

'That sort of thing is in your department, Dick.' Crane was calm and judicial as always. 'I will of course do anything I can, but you probably have a plan of campaign already laid out?'

'After a fashion. We've got to find out how to work through this zone of force or we're sunk without a trace. Even with weapons, screens, and ships equal to theirs we couldn't keep them from sending a vessel to destroy the Earth; and they'd probably get us too, eventually. They've got a lot of stuff we don't know about, of course, since I took only one man's mind. While he was a very able man, he doesn't know all that all the rest of them do, any more than any one man has all the Earthly science known. Absolutely our only chance is to get control of that zone – it's the only thing I know of that they haven't got. Of course, it may be impossible, but I won't believe that until we've exhausted a lot of possibilities. Dunark, can you spare a crew to build us a duplicate of that Fenachrone ship, besides those you are going to build for yourself?'

'Certainly. I will be only too glad to do so.'

'Well, then, while Dunark is doing that, I suggest that we go to this Third Planet, abduct a few of their leading scientists, and read their minds. Then visit every other highly-advanced planet we can locate and do the same. There is a good chance that, by combining the best points of the warfare of many worlds, we can evolve something that will do us some good.'

'Why not send a copper torpedo to destroy their entire planet?' suggested Dunark.

'Wouldn't work. Their detecting screens would locate it a thousand million miles off in space, and they would detonate it long before it could do them any harm. With a zone of force that would get through their screens that'd be the first thing I'd do. You see, every thought comes back to that zone. We've got to get through it some way.'

The course alarm sounded, and they saw that a planet lay directly in their path. It was X, and enough negative acceleration was applied to make an easy landing possible.

'Isn't it going to be a long, slow job, chopping off two tons of that metal and fighting away those terrible animals besides?' asked Margaret.

'It'll take about a millionth of a second, Peg. I'm going to bite it off with the zone, just like I took that bite out of our field. The rotation of the planet will throw us away from the surface, then we'll release the zone and drag our prey off with us. See?'

The *Skylark* descended rapidly toward that well-remembered ledge of metal to which the object-compass had led them.

'This is exactly the same place we landed before,' Margaret commented in surprise, and Dorothy added:

'Yes, and here's that horrible tree that ate the dinosaur or whatever it was. I thought you blew it up for me, Dick?'

'I did, Dottie – blew it into atoms. Must be a good location for carnivorous trees – and they must grow awfully fast, too. As to its being the same place, Peg – sure it is. That's what object-compasses are for.'

Everything appeared as it had at the time of their first visit. The rank Carboniferous vegetation, intensely, vividly green, was motionless in the still, hot, heavy air; the living nightmares inhabiting that primitive world were lying in the cooler depths of the jungle, sheltered from the torrid rays of that strange and fervent sun.

'How about it, Dot? Want to see some of your little friends again? If you do I'll give 'em a shot and bring 'em out.'

'Heavens, no! I saw them once – if I never see them again it will be twenty minutes too soon!'

'All right – we'll grab us a piece of this ledge and beat it.'

Seaton lowered the vessel to the ledge, focused the main anchoring attractor upon it, and threw on the zone of force. Almost immediately he released the zone, pointed the bar parallel to the compass bearing upon Osnome, and slowly applied the power.

'How much did you take, anyway?' asked Dunark in amazement. 'It looks bigger than the *Skylark*!'

'It is; considerably bigger. Thought we might as well take enough while we're here, so I set the zone for a seventy-five-foot radius. It's probably of the order of magnitude of half a million tons, since the stuff weighs more than half a ton to the cubic foot. However, we can handle it as easily as we could a smaller bite, and that much mass will help us hold that other stuff together when we catch up with it.'

The voyage to Osnome was uneventful. They overtook the wreckage, true to schedule, as they were approaching the green system, and attached it to the mass of metal behind them by means of attractors.

'Where'll we land this junk, Dunark?' asked Seaton, as Osnome grew large beneath them. 'We'll hold this lump of metal and the fragment of the ship carrying the salt; and we'll be able to hold some of the most important of the other stuff. But a lot of it is bound to get away from us – and the Lord help anybody who's under it when it comes down! You might yell for help – and say, you might ask somebody to have that astronomical date ready for us as soon as we land.'

'The parade ground will be empty now, so we will be able to land there. We should be able to land everything in a field of that size, I should think.' Dunark touched the sender at his belt, and in the general code notified the city of their arrival and warned everyone to keep away from the parade ground. He then sent several messages in the official code, concluding by asking that one or two spaceships come out and help lower the burden to the ground. As the peculiar, pulsating chatter of the Osnomian telegraph died out Seaton called for help.

'Come here, you two, and grab some of these attractors. I need about twelve hands to keep this plunder in the straight and narrow path.'

The course had been carefully laid, with allowances for the various velocities and forces involved, to follow the easiest path to the Kondalian parade ground. The hemisphere of X and the fragment of the *Kondal* which bore the salt were held immovably in place by the main attractor and one auxiliary; and many other auxiliaries held sections of the Fenachrone vessel. However, the resistance of the air seriously affected the trajectory of many of the irregularly-shaped smaller masses of metal, and all three men were kept busy flicking attractors right and left; capturing those strays which threatened to veer off into the streets or upon the buildings of the Kondalian capital city, and shifting from one piece to another so that none of them could fall freely. Two sister ships of the Kondal appeared in answer to Dunark's call, and their attractors aided greatly in handling the unruly collection of wreckage. A few of the smaller sections and a shower of debris fell clear, however, in spite of all efforts, and their approach was heralded by a meteoric display unprecedented in that world of continuous daylight.

As the three vessels with their cumbersome convoy dropped down into the lower atmosphere the guns of the city roared a welcome; banners and pennons waved; the air became riotous with color from hundreds of projectors and odorous with a bewildering variety of scents; while all around them played numberless aircraft of all descriptions and sizes. The space below them was carefully avoided, but on all sides of them and above them the air was so full that it seemed incredible that no collision occurred. Tiny one-man helicopters, little more than single chairs flying about; beautiful pleasure-planes soaring and wheeling; immense multiplane liners and giant freighters – everything in the air found occasion to fly as near as possible to the *Skylark* in order to dip their flags in salute to Dunark, their kofedix, and to Seaton, the wearer of the seven disks – their revered Overlord.

Finally the freight was landed without serious mishap and the *Skylark* leaped to the landing dock upon the palace roof, where the royal family and many nobles were waiting, in full panoply of glittering harness. Dunark and Sitar disembarked and the four others stepped out and stood at attention as Seaton addressed Roban, the Karfedix.

'Sir, we greet you, but we cannot stop, even for a moment. You know that only the most urgent necessity would make us forgo the pleasure of a brief rest beneath your roof – the kofedix will presently give you the measure of that need. We shall endeavor to return soon. Greetings; and, for a time, farewell.'

'Overlord, we greet you, and trust that soon we may entertain you and profit from your companionship. For what you have done, we thank you. May the great First Cause smile upon you until you return. Farewell.'

6

The Peace Conference

'Here's a chart of the green system, Mart, with all the motions and the rest of the dope that they've been able to get. How'd it be for you to navigate us over to the third planet of the fourteenth sun?'

'While you build a Fenachrone super-generator?'

'Right, the first time. Your deducer is hitting on all eight, as usual. That big beam is hot stuff, and their screens are something to write home about, too.'

'How can their rays be any hotter than ours, Dick?' Dorothy asked curiously. 'I thought you said we had the very last word in rays.'

'I thought we did, but those birds we met back there spoke a couple of later words. They work on an entirely different system than ours do. They generate an extremely short carrier wave, like the Millikan cosmic ray, by recombining some of the electrons and protons of their disintegrating metal, and upon this wave they impose a pure heat frequency of terrific power. The Millikan rays will penetrate anything except a special screen or a zone of force, and carry with them – something like radio frequencies carry sound frequencies – the heat rays, which volatilize anything they touch. Their screens are a lot better than ours, too – they generate the entire spectrum. It's a sweet system, and when we revamp ours so as to be just like it, we'll be able to talk turkey to those folks on the third planet.'

'How long will it take you to build it?' asked Crane, who, dexterously turning the pages of *Vega's Handbuch*, was calculating their course.

'A day or so – three or four, maybe. I've got all the stuff, and with my Osnomian tools it won't take long. If you find you'll get there before I get done, you'll have to loaf a while – kill a little time.'

'Are you going to connect the power plant to operate on the entire vessel and all its contents?'

'No – can't do it without designing the whole thing, and that's hardly worthwhile for the short time we'll use this out-of-date ship.'

Building those generators would have been a long and difficult task for a corps of Earthly mechanics and electricians, but to Seaton it was merely a job. The 'shop' had been enlarged and had been filled to capacity with Osnomian machinery; machine tools that were capable of performing automatically and with the utmost precision and speed almost any conceivable mechanical operation. He put a dozen of them to work, and before the vessel reached its destination, the new offensive and defensive weapons had been installed and thoroughly tested. He had added a third screen-generator, so that now, in addition to the four-foot hull of arenak and the repellors, warding off any material projectile, the *Skylark* was also protected by an outer, an intermediate, and an inner ray-screen; each driven by the super-power of a four-hundred-pound bar and each covering the entire spectrum – capable of neutralizing any dangerous frequency known to those master-scientists, the Fenachrone.

As the *Skylark* approached the planet, Seaton swung number six visiplate upon it, and directed their flight toward a great army base. Darting down upon it, he snatched an officer into the airlock, closed the door, and leaped back into space. He brought the captive into the control room pinioned by auxiliary attractors, and relieved him of his weapons. He then rapidly read his mind, encountering no noticeable resistance, released the attractors, and addressed him in his own language.

'Please be seated, lieutenant,' Seaton said courteously, motioning him to one of the seats. 'We come in peace. Please pardon my discourtesy in handling you, but it was necessary in order to learn your language and thus to get in touch with your commanding officer.'

The officer, overcome with astonishment that he had not been killed instantly, sank into the seat indicated, without a reply, and Seaton went on:

'Please be kind enough to signal your commanding officer that we are coming down at once, for a peace conference. By the way, I can read your signals, and will send them myself if necessary.'

Briefly the stranger worked an instrument attached to his harness, and the *Skylark* descended slowly toward the fortress.

'I know, of course, that your vessels will attack,' Seaton remarked, as he noted a crafty gleam in the eyes of the officer. 'I intend to let them use all their power for a time, to prove to them the impotence of their weapons. After that, I shall tell you what to say to them.'

'Do you think this is altogether safe, Dick?' asked Crane as they saw a fleet of gigantic airships soaring upward to meet them.

'Nothing sure but death and taxes,' returned Seaton cheerfully, 'but don't forget that we've got Fenachrone armament now, instead of Osnomian. I'm betting that they can't begin to drive anything through even our outer screen. And even if our outer screen should begin to go into the violet – I don't think it will even go cherry-red – out goes our zone of force and we automatically go up where no possible airship can reach. Since their only spaceships are rocket-driven, and of practically no maneuverability, they stand a fat chance of getting to us. Anyway, we must get in touch with them, to find out if they know anything we don't, and this is the only way I know of to do it. Besides, I want to head Dunark off from wrecking this world. They're exactly the same kind of folks he is, you notice, and I don't like civil war. Any suggestions? Keep an eye on that bird, then, Mart, and we'll go down.'

The *Skylark* dropped down into the midst of the fleet, which instantly turned against her the full force of their giant guns and their immense ray batteries. Seaton held the *Skylark* motionless, staring into his visiplate, his right hand grasping the zone-switch.

'The outer screen isn't even getting warm!' he exulted after a moment. The repellors were hurling the shells back long before they reached even the outer screen, and they were exploding harmlessly in the air. The full power of the beam-generators, too, which had been so destructive to the Osnomian defenses, was only sufficient to bring the outer screen to a dull red glow. After fifteen minutes of passive acceptance of everything the airships could bring to bear Seaton spoke to the lieutenant.

'Sir, please signal the commanding officer of vessel seven two four that I am going to cut it in two in the middle. Have him remove all men in that part of the ship to the ends, and have parachutes in readiness, as I do not wish to cause any loss of life.'

The signal was sent, and, the officer already daunted by the fact that their utmost efforts could not even make the stranger's screens radiate, it was obeyed. Seaton then threw on the frightful power of the Fenachrone super-generators. The defensive screens of the doomed warship flashed once – a sparkling, coruscating display of incandescent brilliance – and in the same instant went down. Simultaneously the entire mid-section of the vessel exploded into radiation and disappeared; completely volatilized.

'Sir, please signal the entire fleet to cease action, and to follow me down. If they do not do so, I will destroy the rest of them.'

The *Skylark* dropped to the ground, followed by the fleet of warships, who settled in a ring about her – inactive, but ready.

'Will you please loan me your sending instrument, sir?' Seaton asked. 'From this point on I can carry on negotiations better direct than through you.'

The lieutenant found his voice as he surrendered the instrument.

'Sir, are you the Overlord of Osnome, of whom we have heard? We had supposed that one a mythical character, but you must be he – no one else would spare lives that he could take, and the Overlord is the only being reputed to have a skin the color of yours.'

'Yes, lieutenant, I am the Overlord – and I have decided to become the Overlord of the entire green system, as well as of Osnome.'

He then sent out a call to the commander-in-chief of all the armies of the planet, informing him that he was coming to visit him at once, and the *Skylark* tore through the air to the capital city. No sooner had the Earthly vessel alighted upon the palace grounds than she was surrounded by a ring of warships who, however, made no offensive move. Seaton again used the telegraph.

'Commander-in-Chief of the armed forces of the planet Urvania; greetings from the Overlord of this solar system. I invite you to come into my vessel, unarmed and alone, for a conference: I come in peace and, peace or war as you decide, no harm shall come to you until after you have returned to your own command. Think well before you reply.'

'If I refuse?'

'I shall destroy one of the vessels surrounding me, and shall continue to destroy them, one every ten seconds, until you agree to come. If you still do not agree, I shall destroy all the armed forces upon this planet, then destroy all your people who are at present upon Osnome. I wish to avoid bloodshed and destruction, but I can and I will do as I have said.'

'I will come.'

The general came out upon the field unarmed, escorted by a company of soldiers. A hundred feet from the vessel he halted the guards and came on alone, erect and soldierly. Seaton met him at the door and invited him to be seated.

'What can you have to say to me?' the general demanded, disregarding the invitation.

'Many things. First, let me say that you are not only a brave man; you are a wise general – your visit to me proves it.'

'It is a sign of weakness, but I believed when I heard those reports, and still believe, that a refusal would have resulted in a heavy loss of our men.'

'It would have. I repeat that your act was not weakness, but wisdom. The second thing I have to say is that I had not planned on taking any active part in the management of things, either upon Osnome or upon this planet, until I learned of a catastrophe that is threatening all the civilizations in this galaxy – thus threatening my own distant world as well as those of this solar system. Third, only by superior force can I make either your race or the Osnomians listen to reason sufficiently to unite against a common foe. You have been reared in unreasoning hatred for so many generations that your minds are warped. For that reason I have assumed control of this entire system, and shall give you your choice between cooperating with us or being rendered incapable of molesting us while our attention is occupied by this threatened invasion.'

'We will have no traffic with the enemy whatever. This is final.'

'You just think at present that it is final. Here is a mathematical statement of what is going to happen to your world, unless I intervene. He handed the general a drawing of Dunark's plan and described it in detail. 'That is the answer of the Osnomians to your invasion of their planet. I do not want this world destroyed, but if you refuse to make common cause with us against a common foe, it may be necessary. Have you forces at your command sufficient to frustrate this plan?'

'No; but I cannot really believe that such a deflection of celestial bodies is possible. Possible or no, you realize that I could not yield to empty threats.'

'Of course not – but you were wise enough to refuse to sacrifice a few ships and men in a useless struggle against my overwhelming armament, therefore you are certainly wise enough to refuse to sacrifice your entire race. However, before you come to any definite conclusion, I will show you what threatens the galaxy.'

He handed the other a headset and ran through the section of the record showing the plans of the invaders. He then ran a few sections showing the irresistible power at the command of the Fenachrone.

'That is what awaits us all unless we combine against them.'

'What are your requirements?'

'I request immediate withdrawal of all your armed forces now upon Osnome and full cooperation with me in this coming war against the invaders. In return, I will give you the secrets I have just given the Osnomians – the power and the offensive and defensive weapons of this vessel.'

'The Osnomians are now building vessels such as this one?'

'They are building vessels a hundred times the size of this one, with corresponding armament.'

'For myself, I would agree to your terms. However, the word of the Emperor is law.'

'I understand. Would you be willing to seek an immediate audience with him? I would suggest that both you and he accompany me, and we shall hold a peace conference with the Osnomian Emperor and Commander-in-Chief upon this vessel.'

'I shall do so at once.'

'You may accompany your general, lieutenant. Again I ask pardon for my necessary rudeness.'

As the two Urvanian officers hurried toward the palace the other Terrestrials, who had been listening in from another room, entered.

'It sounded as though you convinced him, Dick; but that language is nothing like Kondalian. Why don't you teach it to us? Teach it to Shiro, too, so he can cook for, and talk to, our distinguished guests intelligently, if they're going back with us.'

As he connected up the educator Seaton explained what had happened, and concluded:

'I want to stop this civil war, keep Dunark from destroying this planet, preserve Osnome for Osnomians, and make them all cooperate with us against the Fenachrone. That's one tall order, since these folks haven't the remotest notion of anything except killing.'

A company of soldiers approached, and Dorothy got up hastily.

'Stick around, folks, we can all talk to them.'

'I believe that it would be better for you to be alone,' Crane decided, after a moment's thought. 'They are used to autocratic power, and can understand nothing but one-man control. The girls and I will keep out of it.'

'That might be better, at that,' and Seaton went to the door to welcome the guests. Seaton instructed them to lie flat, and put on all the acceleration they could bear. It was not long until they were back in Kondal, where Roban, the karfedix, and Taman, the karbix, accepted Seaton's invitation and entered the *Skylark*, unarmed. Back out in space, the vessel stationary, Seaton introduced the emperors and commanders-in-chief to each other – introductions which were acknowledged almost imperceptibly. He then gave each a headset, and ran the complete record of the Fenachrone brain.

'Stop!' shouted Roban, after only a moment. 'Would you, the Overlord of Osnome, reveal such secrets as this to the archenemies of Osnome?'

'I would. I have taken over the Overlordship of the entire green system for the duration of this emergency, and I do not want two of its planets engaged in civil war.'

The record finished, Seaton tried for some time to bring the four green warriors to his way of thinking, but in vain. Roban and Tarnan remained contemptuous. They would have thrown themselves upon him but for the knowledge that no fifty unarmed men of the green race could have overcome his strength, to them supernatural. The two Urvanians were equally obdurate. This soft Earthbeing had given them everything, they had given him nothing and would give him nothing. Finally Seaton rose to his full height and stared at them in turn, wrath and determination blazing in his eyes.

'I have brought you four together, here in a neutral vessel in neutral space, to bring about peace between you. I have shown you the benefits to be derived from the peaceful pursuit of science, knowledge, and power, instead of continuing this utter economic waste of continual war. You close your senses to reason. You of Osnome accuse me of being an ingrate and a traitor; you of Urvania consider me a soft-headed, sentimental weakling who may safely be disregarded – all because I think the welfare of the numberless peoples of the universe more important than your narrow-minded, stubborn, selfish vanity. Think what you please. If brute force is your only logic, know now that I can, and will, use brute force. Here are the seven disks,' and he placed the bracelet upon Roban's knee.

'If you four leaders are short-sighted enough to place your petty enmity before the good of all civilization I am done forever with Overlordship and with friendship. I have deliberately given you Urvanians precisely the same information that I have given the Osnomians – no more and no less. I have given neither of you all that I know, and I shall know much more than I do now before the time of the conquest shall have arrived. Unless you four men, here and now, renounce this war and agree to a perpetual peace between your worlds, I shall leave you to your mutual destruction. You do not yet realize the power of the weapons I have given you: when you do realize it you will know that mutual destruction is inevitable if you continue this inter-necine war. I shall continue upon other worlds my search for the one secret standing between me and a complete mastery of power. That I shall find that secret I am confident; and, having found it, I shall without your aid destroy the Fenachrone.

'You have several times remarked with sneers that you are not to be swayed by empty threats. What I am about to say is no empty threat – it is a most solemn promise, given by one who has both the will and the power to fulfill his every given word. Now listen carefully to this, my final utterance. If you continue this warfare and if the victor should not be utterly destroyed in its course, I swear as I stand here, by the great First Cause, that I shall myself wipe out every trace of the surviving nation as soon as the Fenachrone shall have been obliterated. Work with each other and with me and we all will, in all probability, continue to live – fight on and both your nations, to the last person, will most certainly die. Decide now which it is to be. I am done talking.'

Roban took up the bracelet and clasped it again about Seaton's arm, saying, 'You are more than ever our Overlord. You are wiser than we are, and stronger. Issue your commands and they shall be obeyed.'

'Why did not you say those things first, Overlord?' asked the Urvanian emperor, as he saluted and smiled. 'We could not in honor submit to a weakling, no matter what the fate in store. Having convinced us of your strength, there can be no disgrace in fighting beneath your screens. An armlet of seven symbols shall be cast and ready for you when you next visit us. Roban of Osnome, you are my brother.'

The two emperors saluted each other and stared eye to eye for a long moment, and Seaton knew that the perpetual peace had been signed. Then all four spoke, in unison:

'Overlord, we await your commands.'

'Dunark of Osnome is already informed as to what Osnome is to do. Say to him that it will not be necessary for him to build the vessel for me; the Urvanians will do that. Urvan of Urvania, you will accompany Roban to Osnome, where you two will order instant cessation of hostilities. Osnome has many ships of this type, and upon some of them you will return your every soldier and engine of war to your own planet. As soon as possible you will build for me a vessel like that of the Fenachrone, except that it shall be ten times as large, in every dimension, and except that every instrument, control, and weapon is to be left out.'

'Left out? It shall be so built – but of what use will it be?'

'The empty spaces shall be filled after I have returned from my quest. You will build this vessel of dagal. You will also instruct the Osnomian commander in the manufacture of that metal, which is considerably more resistant than their arenak.'

'But, Overlord, we have—'

'I have just brought immense stores of the precious chemical and of the metal of power to Osnome. They will share with you. I also advise you to build for yourselves many ships like those of the Fenachrone, with which to do battle with the invaders in case I should fail in my quest. You will, of course, see to it that there will be a corps of your most efficient mechanics and artisans within call at all times in case I should return and have sudden need for them.'

'All these things shall be done.'

The conference ended, the four nobles were quickly landed upon Osnome and once more the *Skylark* traveled out into her element, the total vacuum and absolute zero of the outer void.

'You certainly sounded savage, Dick. I almost thought you really meant it!' Dorothy chuckled.

'I did mean it, Dot. Those fellows are mighty keen on detecting bluffs. If I hadn't meant it, and if they hadn't known that I meant it, I'd never have got away with it.'

'But you *couldn't* have meant it, Dick! You wouldn't have destroyed the Osnomians, surely – you know you wouldn't.'

'No, but I would have destroyed what was left of the Urvanians, and all five of us knew exactly how it would have turned out and exactly what I would have done about it – that's why they pulled in their horns.'

'I don't know what would have happened,' interjected Margaret. 'What would have?'

'With this new stuff the Urvanians would have wiped the Osnomians out. They are an older race, and so much better in science and mechanics that the Osnomians wouldn't have stood much chance, and knew it. Incidentally, that's why I'm having them build our new ship. They'll put a lot of stuff into it that Dunark's men would miss – maybe some stuff that even the Fenachrone haven't got. However, though it might seem that the Urvanians had all the best of it, Urvan knew that I had something up my sleeve besides my bare arm – and he knew that I'd clean up what there was left of his race if they polished off the Osnomians.'

'What a frightful chance you were taking, Dick!' gasped Dorothy.

'You have to be hard to handle those folks – and believe me, I was a forty-minute egg right then. They have such a peculiar mental and moral slant that we can hardly understand them at all. This idea of cooperation is so new to them that it actually dazed all four men, ever to consider it.'

'Do you suppose they will fight, anyway?' asked Crane.

'Absolutely not. Both nations have an inflexible code of honor, such as it is, and lying is against both codes. That's one thing I like about them – I'm sorta honest myself, and with either of these races, you need nothing signed or guaranteed.'

'What next, Dick?'

'Now the real trouble starts. Mart, did you devote the imponderable force of the massive intellect to that problem – and have you got the answer?'

'What problem?' asked Dorothy. 'You didn't tell us anything about a problem.'

'No, I told Mart. I want the best physicist in this entire solar system – and since there are only one hundred and twenty-five planets around these seventeen suns, it should be simple to yon phenomenal brain. In fact, I expect to hear him say, "Elementary, my dear Watson, elementary!" '

'Hardly that, Dick, but I have found out a few things. There are some eighty planets which are probably habitable for beings like us. Other things being equal, it seems reasonable to assume that the older the sun, the longer its planets have been habitable, and therefore the older and more intelligent the life …'

' "Ha! ha! It was elementary," says Sherlock,' Seaton interrupted. 'You're heading directly at that largest, oldest, and most intelligent planet, then, I take it, where I can catch me a physicist?'

'Not directly at it, no. I am heading for the place where it will be when we arrive there. That *is* elementary, my dear Watson.'

'Ouch! That got to me, Mart, right where I live. I'll be good.'

'But you are getting ahead of me, Dick – it is not as simple as you have assumed from what I have said so far. The Osnomian astronomers have done wonders in the short time they have had, but their data, particularly on the planets of the outer suns, is as yet necessarily very incomplete. Since the furthermost outer sun is probably the oldest, it is the one in which we are most interested. It has seven planets, four of which are probably habitable, as far as temperature and atmosphere are concerned. However, nothing exact is yet known of their masses, motions, or places. Therefore I have laid our course to intercept the closest one to us, as nearly as I can from what meager data we have. If it should prove to be inhabited by intelligent beings, they can probably give us more exact information concerning their neighboring planets. That is the best I can do.'

'That's a darn fine best, old top – narrowing down to four from a hundred and twenty-five. Well, until we get there, what to do? Let's sing us a song, to keep our fearless quartette in good voice.'

'Before you do anything,' said Margaret seriously, 'I would like to know if you really think there is a chance of defeating those monsters.'

'In all seriousness, I do. In fact, I am quite confident of it. If we had two years I know that we could lick them cold; and by shoveling on the coal I believe we can get the dope in less than the six months we have to work in.'

'I know that you are serious, Dick. Now you know that I do not want to discourage anyone, but I can see small basis for optimism.' Crane spoke slowly and thoughtfully. 'I hope that you will be able to control the zone of force – but you are not studying it yourself. You seem to be certain that somewhere in this system there is a race who already knows all about it. I too would like to know your reasons for thinking that such a race exists.'

'They may not be upon this system; they may have been outsiders, as we are – but I have reasons for believing them natives of this system, since they were green. You are as familiar with Osnomian mythology as I am – you girls in particular have read Osnomian legends to Osnomian children for hours. Also identically the same legends prevail upon Urvania. I read them in that lieutenant's brain – in fact, I looked for them. You also know that every folk-legend has some basis, however tenuous, in fact. Now, Dottie, tell teacher about the battle of the gods, when Osnome was a pup.'

'The gods came down from the sky,' Dorothy recited. 'They were green, as were men. They wore invisible armor of polished metal, which appeared and disappeared. They stayed inside the armor and fought outside it with swords and lances of fire. Men who fought against them cut them through and through with swords, and they struck the men with lances of flame so that they were stunned. So the gods fought in days long gone and vanished in their invisible armor, and ...'

'That's enough,' interrupted Seaton. 'The little red-haired girl has her lesson perfectly. Get it, Mart?'

'No, I cannot say that I do.'

'Why, it doesn't even make sense!' exclaimed Margaret.

'All right, I'll elucidate. Listen!' Seaton's voice grew tense with earnestness. 'Visitors came down out of space. They were green, as were men. They wore zones of force, which they flashed on and off. They stayed inside the zones and projected their images outside, and used weapons *through the zones*. Men who fought against the images cut them through and through with swords, but could not harm them since they were not actual substance; and the images directed forces against the men so that they were stunned. So the visitors fought in days long gone, and vanished in their zones of force. How does that sound?'

'You have the most stupendous imagination the world has ever seen – but there may be some slight basis of fact there, after all,' Crane said, slowly.

'I'm convinced of it, for one reason in particular. Notice that it says specifically that the visitors *stunned* the natives. Now that thought is absolutely foreign to all Osnomian nature – when they strike they kill, and always have. Now if that myth has come down through so many generations without having that "stunned" changed to "killed", I'm willing to bet a few weeks of time that the rest of it came down fairly straight, too. Of course, what they had may not have been the zone of force as we know it, but it must have been a pure force of some kind – and believe me, that was one educated and talented force. Somebody certainly had something, even way back in those days. And if they had anything at all back there, they must know a lot by now. That's why I want to look 'em up. As for working on this problem myself – I know just enough to realize exactly how hopeless it would be for me to try to do anything with it in six months. If a dozen of the best physicists on Earth were working on it and had twenty years, I'd say go ahead – as it is we've got to locate that race that knows all about it already.'

'But suppose they want to kill us off at sight?' objected Dorothy. 'They might be able to do it, mightn't they?'

'Sure, but they probably wouldn't want to – any more than you would step on an ant who asked you to help him move a twig. That's about how much ahead of us they probably are. Of course, we struck a pure mentality once who came darn near dematerializing us entirely, but I'm betting that these folks haven't got that far along yet. By the way, I've got a hunch about those pure intellectuals.'

'Oh, tell us about it!' laughed Margaret. 'Your hunches are the world's greatest brainstorms!'

'Well, I pumped out and re-jeweled the compass we put on that funny planet – as a last resort, I thought we might maybe visit them and ask that bozo we had the argument with to help us out. I thought maybe he – or it – would show us everything about the zone of force we want to know. I don't think that we'd be dematerialized, either, because the situation would give him something more to think about for another thousand cycles; and thinking seemed to be his main object in life. However, to get back to the subject, I found that even with the new power of the compass the entire planet was still out of reach. Unless they've dematerialized it, that means about ten billion light-years as an absolute minimum. Think about that for a minute! ... I've got a kind of a hunch that maybe they don't belong in this galaxy at all – that they might be from some other galaxy, planet and all; just riding around on it like we are riding in the *Skylark*. Is the idea conceivable to a sane mind, or not?'

'Not!' decided Dorothy, promptly. 'We' d better go to bed. One more such idea, in progression with the last two you've had, would certainly give you a compound fracture of the skull. 'Night, Cranes – sweet dreams!'

7

DuQuesne's Voyage

Far from our solar system a cigar-shaped space-cruiser slackened its terrific acceleration to a point at which human beings could walk and two men got up, exercised vigorously to restore the circulation to their numbed bodies, and went into the galley to prepare their first meal since leaving the Earth some eight hours before.

Because of the long and arduous journey he had decided upon, DuQuesne had had to abandon his custom of working alone, and had studied all the available men with great care before selecting his companion and relief pilot. He finally had chosen 'Baby Doll' Loring – so called because of his curly yellow hair, his pink and white complexion, his guileless blue eyes, his slight form of rather less than medium height. But never did outward attributes more belie the inner man! The yellow curls covered a brain agile, keen, and hard; the girlish complexion neither paled nor reddened under stress; the wide blue eyes had glanced along the barrels of so many lethal weapons that in various localities the noose yawned for him; the slender body was built of rawhide and whalebone and responded instantly to the dictates of that ruthless brain. Under the protection of Steel he flourished, and in return for that protection he performed quietly, and with neatness and despatch, such odd jobs as were in his line.

When they were seated at an excellent breakfast of ham and eggs, buttered toast, and strong, aromatic coffee, DuQuesne broke the long silence.

'Do you want to know where we are?'

'I'd say we were a long ways from home, by the way this elevator of yours has been climbing all night.'

'We are a good many millions of miles from the Earth, and we are getting farther away at a rate that would have to be measured in millions of miles per second.' DuQuesne, watching the other narrowly as he made this startling announcement and remembering the effect of a similar one upon Perkins, saw with approval that the coffee cup in mid-air did not pause or waver in its course. Loring noted the bouquet of his beverage and took an appreciative sip before he replied.

'You certainly can make coffee, doctor; and good coffee is nine-tenths of a good breakfast. As to where we are – that's all right with me. I can stand it if you can.'

'Don't you want to know where we're going, and why?'

'I've been thinking about that. Before we started I didn't want to know anything, because what a man doesn't know he can't be accused of spilling in case of a leak. Now that we are on our way, though, maybe I should know enough about things to act intelligently if something unforeseen should develop. If you'd rather keep it dark and give me orders when necessary, that's all right with me, too. It's your party, you know.'

'I brought you along because one man can't stay on duty twenty-four hours a day, continuously. Since you are in as deep as you can get, and since this trip is dangerous, you should know everything there is to know. You are one of the higher-ups now, anyway: and we understand each other pretty thoroughly, I believe?'

'I believe so.'

Back in the bow control room DuQuesne applied more power, but not enough to render movement impossible.

'You don't have to drive her as hard all the way, then, as you did last night?'

'No, I'm out of range of Seaton's instruments now, and we don't have to kill ourselves. High acceleration is punishment for anyone and we must keep ourselves fit. To begin with, I suppose that you are curious about that object-compass?'

'That and other things.'

'An object-compass is a needle of specially treated copper, so activated that it points always toward one certain object after being once set upon it. Seaton undoubtedly has one upon me; but, sensitive as they are, they can't hold on a mass as small as a man at this distance. That was why we left at midnight, after he had gone to bed – so that we'd be out of range before he woke up. I wanted to lose him, as he might interfere if he knew where I was going. Now I'll go back to the beginning and tell you the whole story.'

Tersely but vividly he recounted the tale of the first interstellar cruise, the voyage of the *Skylark of Space*. When he had finished, Loring smoked for a few minutes in silence.

'There's a lot of stuff there that's hard to understand all at once. Do you mind if I ask a few foolish questions, to get things straightened out in my mind?'

'Go ahead – ask as many as you want to. It is hard to understand a lot of that Osnomian stuff – a man can't get it all at once.'

'Osnome is so far away – how are you going to find it?'

'With one of the object-compasses I mentioned. I had planned on navigating from notes I took on the trip back to the Earth, but it wasn't necessary. They tried to keep me from finding out anything, but I learned all about the compasses, built a few of them in their own shop, and set one on Osnome. I had it, among other things, in my pocket when I landed. In fact, the control of that explosive copper bullet is the only thing they had that I wasn't able to get – and I'll get that on this trip.'

'What is that arenak armor they're wearing?'

'Arenak is a synthetic metal, almost perfectly transparent. It has practically the same refractive index as air, therefore it is, to all intents and purposes, invisible. It's about five hundred times as strong as chrome-vanadium steel, and even when you've got it to the yield-point it doesn't break, but stretches out and snaps back, like rubber, with the strength unimpaired. It's the most wonderful thing I saw on the whole trip. They make complete suits of it. Of course they aren't very comfortable, but since they are only a tenth of an inch thick they can be worn.'

'And a tenth of an inch of that stuff will stop a steel-nosed machine-gun bullet?'

'Stop it! A tenth of an inch of arenak is harder to pierce than fifty inches of our hardest, toughest armor steel. A sixteen-inch armor-piercing projectile couldn't get through it. It's hard to believe, but nevertheless it's a fact. The only way to kill Seaton with a gun would be to use one heavy enough so that the shock of the impact would kill him – and it wouldn't surprise me a bit if he had his armor anchored with an attractor against that very contingency. Even if he hasn't, you can imagine the chance of getting action against him with a gun of that size.'

'Yes, I've heard that he is fast.'

'That doesn't tell half of it. You know that I'm handy with a gun myself?'

'You're faster than I am, and that's saying something. You're chain lightning.'

'Well, Seaton is at least that much faster than I am. You've never seen him work – I have. On that Osnomian dock he shot once before I started, and shot four times to my three from then on. I must have been shooting a full second after he had his side all cleaned up. To make it worse I missed once with my left hand – he didn't. There's absolutely no use tackling Richard Seaton without something at least as good as full Osnomian equipment; but, as you know, Brookings always has been and always will be a complete damned fool. He won't believe anything new until after he has actually been shown. Well, I imagine he will be shown plenty by this evening.'

'Well, I'll never tackle Seaton with a rod. How does he get that way?'

'He's naturally fast, and has practiced sleight-of-hand work ever since he was a kid. He's one of the best amateur magicians in the country, and I will say that his ability along that line has come in handy for him more than once.'

'I see where you're right in wanting to get something, since we have only ordinary weapons and they have all that stuff. This trip is to get a little something for ourselves, I take it?'

'Exactly, and you know enough now to understand what we are after. You have guessed that we are headed for Osnome?'

'I suspected it. However, if you were going only to Osnome you would have gone alone; so I also suspect that that's only half of it. I have no idea what it is, but you've got something else on your mind.'

'You're right – I knew you were keen. When I was on Osnome I found out something that only four other men – all dead – ever knew. There is a race of men far ahead of the Osnomians in science, particularly in warfare. They live a long way beyond Osnome. It is my plan to steal an Osnomian airship and mount all its screens, generators, guns, and everything else, upon this ship, or else convert their vessel into a spaceship. Instead of using their ordinary power, however, we will do as Seaton did, and use atomic power, which is practically infinite. Then we'll have everything Seaton's got, but that isn't enough. I want enough more than he's got to wipe him out. Therefore, after we get a ship armed to suit us, we'll visit this strange planet and either come to terms with them or else steal a ship from them. Then we'll have their stuff and that of the Osnomians, as well as our own. Seaton won't last long after that.'

'Do you mind if I ask how you got that dope?'

'Not at all. Except when right with Seaton I could do pretty much as I pleased, and I used to take long walks for exercise. The Osnomians tired very easily, being so weak, and because of the light gravity of the planet I had to do a lot of work or walking to keep in any kind of condition at all. I learned Kondalian quickly, and got so friendly with the guards that pretty quick they quit trying to keep me in sight, but waited at the edge of the palace grounds until I came back and joined them. Well, on one trip I was fifteen miles or so from the city when an airship crashed down in a woods about half a mile from me. It was in an uninhabited district and nobody else saw it. I went over to investigate, on the chance that I could find out something useful. It had the whole front end cut or broken off, and that made me curious, because no imaginable fall will break an arenak hull. I walked in through the hole and saw that it was one of their fighting tenders – a combination warship and repair shop, with all of the stuff in it that I've been telling you about. The generators were mostly burned out and the propelling and lifting motors were out of commission. I prowled around, getting acquainted with it, and found a lot of useful instruments and, best of all, one of Dunark's new mechanical educators, with complete instructions for its use. Also, I found three bodies, and thought I'd try it out …'

'Just a minute. Only three bodies on a warship? And what good could a mechanical educator do you if the men were all dead?'

'Three is all I found then, but there was another one. Three men and a captain compose an Osnomian crew for any ordinary vessel. Everything is automatic, you know. As for the men being dead, that doesn't make any difference – you can read their brains just the same, if they haven't been dead too long. However, when I tried to read theirs, I found only blanks – their brains had been destroyed so that nobody could read them. That did look funny, so I ransacked the ship from truck to keelson, and finally found another body, wearing an air-helmet, in a sort of closet off the control room. I put the educator on it …'

'This is getting good. It sounds like a page out of the old "Arabian Nights" that I used to read when I was a boy. You know, it really isn't surprising that Brookings didn't believe a lot of this stuff.'

'As I've said, a lot of it is hard to take; but I'm going to show it to you – all that, and a lot more.'

'Oh, I believe it, all right. After riding in this boat and looking out of the windows I'll believe anything. Reading a dead man's brain is steep, though.'

'I'll let you do it after we get there. I don't understand exactly how it works, myself, but I know how to operate one. Well, I found out that this man's brain was in good shape, and I got a shock when I read it. Here's what he had been through. They had been flying very high on their way to the front when their ship was seized by an invisible force and thrown or pulled upward. He must have thought faster than the others, because he put on an air-helmet and dived into this locker where he hid under a pile of gear, fixing things so that he could see out through the transparent arenak of the wall. No sooner was he hidden than the front end of the ship went up in a blaze of light, in spite of their ray screens going full blast. They were up so high by that time that when the bow was burned off the other three fainted from lack of air. Then their generators went out, and pretty soon two peculiar-looking strangers entered. They were wearing vacuum suits and were very short and stocky, giving the impression of enormous strength. They brought an educator of their own with them and read the brains of the three men. They then dropped the ship a few thousand feet and revived the three with a drink of something out of a flask.'

'Potent, eh? Find out what it was? The stuff we've been getting lately would make a man more unconscious than ever.'

'Some powerful drug, probably, but the Osnomian didn't know anything about it. After the men revived, the strangers, apparently from sheer cruelty and love of torturing their victims, informed them in the Osnomian language that they were from another world, near the edge of the galaxy. They even told them, knowing that the Osnomians knew nothing of astronomy, exactly where they were from. Then they went on to say that they wanted the entire green system for themselves, and that in something like two years of our time they were going to wipe out all the present inhabitants of the system and take it over, as a base for further operations. After that they amused themselves by describing exactly the kinds of death and destruction they were going to use. They described most of it in great detail. It's too involved to tell you about now, but they've got rays, force-weapons, generators, and screens that even the Osnomians never heard of. And of course they've got atomic energy, the same as we have. After telling them all this and watching them suffer they put a machine up to their heads and they dropped dead. That's probably what disintegrated their brains. Then they looked the ship over rather casually, as though they didn't see anything they were interested in; crippled the motors; and went away. The vessel was then released, and crashed. This man, of course, was killed by the fall. I buried the men – I didn't want anybody else reading that brain – hid some of the stuff I wanted most, and camouflaged the ship so that I'm fairly sure that it's there yet. I decided then to make this trip.'

'I see.' Loring's mind was grappling with these new and strange facts. 'That news is staggering, doctor. Think of it! Everybody thinks our own world is everything there is!'

'Our world is simply a grain of dust in the universe. Most people know it, academically, but very few ever give the fact any actual consideration. But now that you've had a little time to get used to the idea of there being other worlds, and some of them as far ahead of us in science as we are ahead of the monkeys, what do you think of it?'

'I agree with you that we've got to get their stuff. However, it occurs to me as a possibility that they may have so much stuff that we won't be able to make the approach. However, if the Osnomian fittings we're going to get are as good as you say they are, I think that two such men as you and I can get at least a lunch while any other crew, no matter who they are, are getting a square meal.'

'I like your style, Loring. You and I will have the world eating out of our hands shortly after we get back. As far as actual procedure over there is concerned, of course I haven't made any definite plans. We'll have to size up the situation after we get there before we can know exactly what we'll have to do. However, we are not coming back empty-handed.'

'You said something, Chief!' and the two men, so startlingly unlike physically but so alike inwardly, shook hands in token of their mutual dedication to a single purpose.

Loring was then instructed in the simple navigation of the ship of space, and thereafter the two men took their regular shifts at the controls. In due time they approached Osnome, and DuQuesne studied the planet carefully through a telescope before he ventured down into the atmosphere.

'This half of it used to be Mardonale. I suppose it's all Kondal now. No, there's a war on down there yet – at least, there's a disturbance of some kind, and on this planet that means a war.'

'What are you looking for, exactly?' asked Loring, who was also examining the terrain with a telescope.

'They've got some spherical space-ships, like Seaton's. I know they had one, and they've probably built more of them since that time. Their airships can't touch us, but those ball-shaped fighters would be pure poison for us, the way we are fixed now. Can you see any of them?'

'Not yet. Too far away to make out details. They're certainly having a hot time down there, though, in that one spot.'

They dropped lower, toward the stronghold which was being so stubbornly defended by the inhabitants of the third planet of the fourteenth sun, and so savagely attacked by the Kondalian forces.

'There, we can see what they're doing now,' and DuQuesne anchored the vessel with an attractor. 'I want to see if they've got many of those spaceships in action, and you will want to see what war is like when it is fought by people who have been making war steadily for ten thousand years.'

Poised at the limit of clear visibility the two men studied the incessant battle being waged beneath them. They saw not one, but fully a thousand of the globular craft, high in the air and grouped in a great circle around an immense fortification upon the ground below. They saw no airships in the line of battle, but noticed that many such vessels were flying to and from the front, apparently carrying supplies. The fortress was an immense dome of some glassy, transparent material, partially covered with slag, through which they saw that the central space was occupied by orderly groups of barracks, and that around the circumference were arranged gigantic generators, projectors, and other machinery at whose purposes they could not even guess. From the base of the dome, a twenty-mile-wide apron of the same glassy substance spread over the ground, and above this apron and around the dome were thrown the mighty defensive screens, visible now and then in scintillating violet splendor as one of the copper-driven Kondalian projectors sought in vain for an opening. But the Earthmen saw with surprise that the main attack was not being directed at the dome; that only an occasional beam was thrown against it in order to make the defenders keep their screens up continuously. The edge of the apron was bearing the brunt of that vicious and never-ceasing attack, and most concerned the desperate defense.

For miles beyond the edge, and as deep under it as frightful beams and enormous charges of explosive copper could penetrate, the ground was one seething, flaming volcano of molten lava; lava constantly being volatilized by the unimaginable heat of those forces and being hurled for miles in all directions by the inconceivable power of those explosive copper projectiles – the heaviest projectiles that could be used without endangering the planet itself –

being directed under the exposed edge of that unbreakable apron, which was in actuality anchored to the solid core of the planet itself; lava flowing into and filling up the vast craters caused by the explosions. The attack seemed fiercest at certain points, perhaps a quarter of a mile apart around the circle, and after a time the watchers perceived that at those points, under the edge of the apron, in that indescribable inferno of boiling lava, destructive rays, and disintegrating copper there were enemy machines at work. These machines were strengthening the protecting apron and extending it, very slowly, but ever wider and ever deeper as the ground under it and before it was volatilized or hurled away by the awful forces of the Kondalian attack. So much destruction had already been wrought that the edge of the apron and its molten moat were already fully a mile below the normal level of that cratered, torn, and tortured plain.

Now and then one of the mechanical moles would cease its labors, overcome by the concentrated fury of destruction centered upon it. Its shattered remnants would be withdrawn and shortly, repaired or replaced, it would be back at work. But it was not the defenders who had suffered most heavily. The fortress was literally ringed about with the shattered remnants of airships, and the riddled hulls of hundreds of those mighty globular cruisers of the void bore mute testimony to the deadliness and efficiency of the warfare of the invaders.

Even as they watched, one of the spheres, unable for some reason to maintain its screens or overcome by the awful forces playing upon it, flared from white into and through violet and was hurled upward as though shot from the mouth of some Brobdingnagian howitzer. A door opened, and from its flaming interior four figures leaped out into the air, followed by a puff of orange-colored smoke. At the first sign of trouble the ship next to it in line leaped in front of it and the four figures floated gently to the ground, supported by friendly attractors and protected from enemy weapons by the bulk and by the screens of the rescuing vessel Two great airships soared upward from back of the lines and hauled the disabled vessel to the ground by means of their powerful attractors. The two observers saw with amazement that after brief attention from an ant-like ground-crew the original four men climbed back into their warship and she again shot into the fray, apparently as good as ever.

'What do you know about that!' exclaimed DuQuesne. 'That gives me an idea, Loring. They must get to them that way fairly often, to judge by the teamwork they use when it does happen. How about waiting until they disable another one like that, and then grabbing it while it is in the air, deserted and unable to fight back? One of those ships is worth a thousand of this one, even if we had everything known to the Osnomians mounted on it.'

'That's a real idea – those boats certainly are brutes for punishment,' agreed

Loring, and as both men again settled down to watch the battle he went on: 'So this is war out this way? You're right. Seaton, with half this stuff, could whip the combined armies and navies of the world. I don't blame Brookings much, though, at that – nobody could believe half of this unless they could actually see it.'

'I can't understand it,' DuQuesne frowned as he considered the situation. 'The attackers are Kondalians, all right – those ships are developments of the *Skylark* – but I don't get that fort at all. Wonder if it can be the strangers already? Don't think so – they aren't due for a couple of years yet, and I don't think the Kondalians could stand against them a minute. It must be what is left of Mardonale, although I never heard of anything like that. Probably it is some new invention they dug up at the last minute. That's it, I guess,' and his brow cleared. 'It couldn't be anything else.'

They waited long for the incident to be repeated, and finally their patience was rewarded. When the next vessel was disabled and hurled upward by the concentration of enemy forces DuQuesne darted down, seized it with his most powerful attractor, and whisked it away into space at such a velocity that to the eyes of the Kondalians it simply disappeared. He took the disabled warship far out into space and allowed it to cool off for a long time before deciding that it was safe to board it. Through the transparent walls they could see no sign of life, and DuQuesne donned a space-suit and steeped into the airlock. As Loring held the steel vessel close to the stranger, DuQuesne leaped lightly through the open door into the interior. Shutting the door, he opened an auxiliary air-tank, adjusting the gauge to one atmosphere as he did so. The pressure normal, he divested himself of the suit and made a thorough examination of the vessel. He then signalled Loring to follow him, and soon both ships were over Kondal, so high as to be invisible from the ground. Plunging the vessel like a bullet toward the grove in which he had left the Kondalian airship, he slowed abruptly just in time to make a safe landing. As he stepped out upon Osnomian soil Loring landed the Earthly ship hardly less skillfully.

'This saves us a lot of trouble, Loring. This is undoubtedly one of the finest spaceships of the universe, and just about ready for anything.'

'How did they get to it?'

'One of the screen generators apparently weakened a trifle, probably from weeks of continuous use. That let some of the stuff come through, everything got hot, and the crew had to jump or roast. Nothing is hurt, though, as the ship was thrown up and out of range before the arenak melted at all. The copper repellors are gone, of course, and most of the bars that were in use are melted down, but there is enough of the main bar left to drive the ship and we can replace the melted stuff easily enough. Nothing else was hurt, as there's absolutely nothing in the structure of these vessels that can be burned. Even the insulation in the coils and generators has a melting-point higher than that of porcelain. And not all the copper was melted, either. Some of these storerooms are lined with two feet of insulation and are piled full of bars and explosive ammunition.'

'What was the smoke we saw, then?'

'That was their food-supply. It's cooked to an ash, and their water was all boiled away through the safety-valves. Those machines certainly can put out a lot of heat in a second or two!'

'Can the two of us put on those copper repellor-bands? This ship must be seventy-five feet in diameter.'

'Yes, it's a lot bigger than the *Skylark* was. It's one of their latest models, or it wouldn't have been on the front line. As to banding on the repellors – that's easy. That airship is half full of metal-working machinery that can do everything but talk. I know how to use most of it, from seeing it in use, and we can figure out the rest.'

In that unfrequented spot there was little danger of detection from the air, and none whatever of detection from the ground – of ground-travel upon Osnome there is practically none. Nevertheless, the two men camouflaged the vessels so that they were visible only to keen and direct scrutiny, and drove their task through to completion in the shortest possible time. The copper repellors were banded on, and much additional machinery was installed in the already well-equipped shop. This done, they transferred to their warship food, water, bedding, instruments, and everything else they needed or wanted from their own ship and from the disabled Kondalian airship. They made a last tour of inspection to be sure they had overlooked nothing useful, then embarked.

'Think anybody will find those ships? They could get a good line on what we've done.'

'Probably, eventually, so we'd better destroy them. We'd better take a short hop first, though, to test everything out. Since you're not familiar with the controls of a ship of this type, you need practice. Shoot us up around that moon over there and bring us back to this spot.'

'She's a sweet-handling boat – easy like a bicycle,' declared Loring as he brought the vessel lightly to a landing upon their return. 'We can burn the old one up now. We'll never need her again, any more than a snake needs his last year's skin.'

'She's good, all right. Those two hulks must be put out of existence, but we shouldn't do it here. The beams would set the woods afire, and the metal would condense all around. We don't want to leave any tracks, so we'd better pull them out into space to destroy them. We could turn them loose, but as you've never worked a ray-gun it'll be good practice for you. Also, I want you to see for yourself just what our best armor-plate amounts to compared with arenak.'

When they had towed the two vessels far out into space Loring put into practice the instruction he had received from DuQuesne concerning the complex armament of their vessel. He swung the beam-projector upon the Kondalian airship; pressed three buttons. In little more than a second the entire hull became blinding white, but it was several more seconds before the extremely refractory material began to volatilize. Though the metal was less than an inch thick, it retained its shape and strength stubbornly, and only slowly did it disappear in flaming, flaring gusts of incandescent gas.

'There, you've seen what an inch of arenak is like,' said DuQuesne when the destruction was complete. 'Now shine it on that sixty-inch chrome-vanadium armor hull of our old bus and see what happens.'

Loring did so. As the beam touched it the steel disappeared in one flare of radiance – as he swung the projector in one flashing arc from the stem to the stern there was nothing left. Loring, swinging the beam, whistled in amazement.

'Wow! What a difference! And this ship of ours has a skin of arenak six feet thick!'

'Yes. Now you understand why I didn't want to argue with anybody out here as long as we were in our own ship.'

'I understand that, all right; but I can't understand the power of these machines. Suppose I had had all twenty of them on instead of only three?'

'In that case, I think that we could have whipped even the short, thick strangers.'

'You and me both. But say, every ship's got to have a name. This new one of ours is such a sweet, harmless, inoffensive little thing, we'd better name her the *Violet*, hadn't we?'

DuQuesne started the *Violet* off in the direction of the solar system occupied by the warlike strangers, but he did not hurry. He and Loring practiced incessantly for days at the controls, darting here and there, putting on terrific acceleration until the indicators showed a velocity of hundreds of thousands of miles per second, then reversing the acceleration until the velocity was zero, or even negative. They studied the controls and alarm system until each knew perfectly every instrument, every tiny light, and the tone of each bell. They practiced with the projectors and generators, singly and in combination, with the visiplates, and with the many levers and dials, until each was so familiar with the complex installation that his handling of every control had become automatic. Not until then did DuQuesne give the word to start out in earnest toward their goal, such an unthinkable distance away.

They had not been under way long when an alarm bell sounded its warning and a brilliant green light began flashing upon the board.

'Hm ... m,' DuQuesne frowned as he reversed the bar. 'Outside atomic energy detector. Somebody's using power out here. Direction, about dead ahead – straight down. Let's see if we can see anything.'

He swung number six, the telescopic visiplate, into the lower area and both men stared into the receiver. After a long time they saw a sudden sharp flash, apparently an immense distance ahead, and simultaneously three more alarm bells rang and three colored lights flashed briefly.

'Somebody got quite a jolt then. Three forces in action at once for three or four seconds,' reported DuQuesne, as he applied still more negative acceleration.

'I'd like to know what this is all about!' he exclaimed after a time, as they saw a subdued glow, which lasted a minute or two. As the warning light was flashing more and more slowly and with diminishing intensity, the *Violet* was once more put upon her course. As she proceeded, however, the warnings of the liberation of atomic energy grew stronger and stronger, and both men scanned their path intensely for a sight of the source of the disturbance, while their velocity was cut to only a few hundred miles per hour. Suddenly the indicator swerved and pointed behind them, showing that they had passed the object, whatever it was. DuQuesne applied power and snapped on a searchlight.

'If it's so small that we couldn't see it when we passed it, it's nothing to be afraid of. We'll be able to find it with a light.'

After some search, they saw an object floating in space – a space-suit!

'Shall one of us get in the airlock, or shall we bring it in with an attractor?' asked Loring.

'An attractor, by all means. Two or three of them – repellors, too – to spread-eagle whatever it is. Never take any chances. It's probably an Osnomian, but you never can tell. It may be one of those other people. We know they were around here a few weeks ago, and they're the only ones I know of that have atomic power besides us and the Osnomians.

'That's no Osnomian,' he continued as the stranger was drawn into the airlock. 'He's big enough around for four Osnomians, and not tall enough. We'll take no chances at all with that fellow.'

The captive was brought into the control room, pinioned head, hand, and foot with attractors and repellors, before DuQuesne approached him. He then read the temperature and pressure of the stranger's air-supply, and allowed the surplus air to escape slowly before removing the stranger's suit and revealing one of the Fenachrone – eyes closed, unconscious or dead.

DuQuesne leaped for the educator and handed Loring a headset.

'Put this on quick. He may be only unconscious, and we might not be able to get a thing from him if he were awake.'

Loring donned the headset, still staring at the monstrous form with amazement, not unmixed with awe, while DuQuesne, paying no attention to anything except the knowledge he was seeking, manipulated the controls of the instrument. His first quest was for full information concerning weapons and armament. In this he was disappointed, as he learned that the stranger was one of the navigating engineers, and as such, had no detailed knowledge of the matters of prime importance to the inquisitor. He did have a complete knowledge of the marvellous Fenachrone propulsion system, however, and this DuQuesne carefully transferred to his own brain. He then rapidly explored other regions of that fearsome organ of thought.

As the gigantic and inhuman brain was spread before them DuQuesne and Loring read not only the language, customs, and culture of the Fenachrone, but all their plans for the future, as well as the events of the past. Plainly in his mind they perceived how he had been cast adrift in the emptiness of the void. They saw the Fenachrone cruiser lying in wait for the two globular vessels. Looking through an extraordinarily powerful telescope with the eyes of their prisoner they saw them approach, all unsuspecting. DuQuesne recognized all five persons in the *Skylark* and Dunark and Sitar in the *Kondal*, such was that unearthly optical instrument and so clear was the impression upon the mind before him. They saw the attack and the battle. They saw the *Skylark* throw off her zone of force and attack; saw this one survivor standing directly in line with a huge projector-spring, under thousands of pounds of tension. They saw the spring cut in two by the zone. The severed end, flying free, struck the being upon the side of the head, and the force of the blow, only partially blocked by the heavy helmet, hurled him out through the yawning gap in the wall and hundreds of miles out into space.

Suddenly the clear view of the brain of the Fenachrone became blurred and meaningless and the flow of knowledge ceased – the prisoner had regained consciousness and was trying with all his gigantic strength to break away from those intangible bonds that held him. So powerful were the forces upon him, however, that only a few twitching muscles gave evidence that he was struggling at all. Glancing about him, he recognized the attractors and repellors bearing upon him, ceased his efforts to escape, and hurled the full power of his baleful gaze into the black eyes so close to his own. But DuQuesne's mind, always under perfect control and now amply reinforced by a considerable portion of the stranger's own knowledge and power, did not waver under the force of even that hypnotic glare.

'It is useless, as you observe,' he said coldly, in the stranger's own tongue, and sneered. 'You are perfectly helpless. Unlike you of the Fenachrone, however, men of my race do not always kill strangers at sight, merely because they are strangers. I will spare your life if you can give me anything of enough value to me to make the extra time and trouble worthwhile.'

'You read my mind while I could not resist your childish efforts. I will have no traffic whatever with you who have destroyed my vessel. If you have mentality enough to understand any portion of my mind – which I doubt – you already know the fate in store for you. Do with me what you will.'

DuQuesne pondered long before he replied; considering whether or not it was to his advantage to inform this stranger of the facts of the case. Finally he decided.

'Sir, neither I nor this vessel had anything to do with the destruction of your warship. Our detectors discovered you floating in empty space; we stopped and rescued you from death. We have seen nothing else save what we saw pictured in your own brain. I know that, in common with all of your race, you possess neither conscience nor honor, as we understand the terms. An automatic liar by instinct and training whenever you think lies will best serve your purpose, you may yet have intelligence enough to recognize simple truth when you hear it. You already have observed that we are of the same race as those who destroyed your vessel, and have assumed that we are with them. In that you are wrong. It is true that I am acquainted with those others, but they are my enemies. I am here to kill them, not to aid them. You have already helped me in one way – I know as much as does my enemy concerning the impenetrable shield of force. If I will return you unharmed to your own planet, will you assist me in stealing one of your ships of space, so that I may destroy that Earth-vessel?'

The Fenachrone, paying no attention to DuQuesne's barbed comments concerning his honor and veracity, did not hesitate an instant in his reply.

'I will not. We supermen of the Fenachrone will allow no vessel of ours, with its secrets unknown to any others of the universe, to fall into the hands of any of the lesser breeds of man.'

'Well, you didn't try to lie that time, anyway. But think a minute. Seaton, my enemy, already has one of your vessels – don't think he is too much of a fool to put it back together and to learn its every secret. Then, too, remember that I have your mind, and can get along without you; even though I am willing to admit that you could be of enough help to me so that I would save your life in exchange for that help. Also, remember that, superman though you may be, your mentality cannot cope with the forces I have bearing upon you. Neither will your being a superman enable your body to retain life after I have thrown you out into space without your armor.'

'I have the normal love of life; but some things cannot be done, even with life at stake. Stealing a vessel of the Fenachrone is one of those things. I can, however, do this much – if you will return me to my own planet, you two shall be received as guests aboard one of our vessels and shall be allowed to witness the vengeance of the Fenachrone upon your enemy. Then you shall be returned to your vessel and allowed to depart unharmed.'

'Now you are lying by rote – I know just what you'd do. Get that idea out of your head right now. The attractors now holding you will not be released until after you have paid your way. Then, and then only, will I try to discover a way of returning you to your own world without risking my own neck. Incidentally, I warn you that your first attempt to play false with me in any way will also be your last.'

The prisoner remained silent, analyzing every feature of the situation, and DuQuesne continued, coldly:

'Here's something else for you to think about. If you are unwilling to help us, what is to prevent me from killing you, and then hunting up Seaton and making peace with him for the duration of this forthcoming war? With the fragments of your vessel, which he has; with my knowledge of your mind, reinforced by your own dead brain; and with the vast resources of all the planets of the green system; I do not believe that you could ever conquer us. In fact, it is quite possible – even probable – that we would be able eventually to destroy your entire race. Understand, however, that I care nothing for the green system. You are welcome to it if you do as I ask. If you do not, I shall warn them and help them simply to protect my own world, which is now my own personal property.'

'In return for our armament and equipment, you promise not to warn the green system against us? The death of your enemies takes first place in your mind?' The stranger spoke thoughtfully. 'In that I understand your view-point thoroughly. But, after I have remodeled your power plant into ours and have piloted you to our planet, what assurance have I that you will liberate me, as you have said?'

'None whatever – I have made and am making no promises, since I cannot expect you to trust me, any more than I can trust you. Enough of this argument! I am master here, and I am dictating terms. We can get along without you. Therefore you must decide quickly whether you would rather die suddenly and surely, here in space and right now, or help us as I demand and live until you get back home – enjoying meanwhile your life and whatever chance you think you may have of being liberated within the atmosphere of your own planet.'

'Just a minute, chief!' Loring said, in English, his back to the prisoner. 'Wouldn't we gain more by killing him and going back to Seaton and the green system, as you suggested?'

'No.' DuQuesne also turned away, to shield his features from the mind-reading gaze of the Fenachrone. 'That was pure bluff. I don't want to get within a million miles of Seaton until after we have the armament of this fellow's ships. I couldn't make peace with Seaton now, even if I wanted to – and I haven't the slightest intention of trying. I intend killing him on sight. Here's what we're going to do. First, we'll get what we came after. Then we'll find the *Skylark* and blow her out of space, and take over the pieces of that Fenachrone ship. After that we'll head for the green system, and with their own stuff and what we'll give them they'll be able to give the Fenachrone a hot reception. By the time they finally destroy the Osnomians – if they do – we'll have the world ready for them.' He turned to the captive. 'What is your decision?'

'I submit, in the hope that you will keep your promise, since there is no alternative but death.'

Then, still loosely held by the attractors and carefully watched by DuQuesne and Loring, the creature tore into the task of rebuilding the Osnomian power plant into the space-annihilating drive of the Fenachrone. Nor was he turning traitor, for he well knew one fact that DuQuesne's hurried inspection had failed to glean from the labyrinthine intricacies of his brain; that once within the detector screens of that distant solar system these Earth-beings would be utterly helpless before the forces which would be turned upon them. And time was precious. For the good of his own race he must drive the *Violet* so unmercifully that she would overtake even that fleeing torpedo, now many hours upon its way – the torpedo bearing news, for the first time in Fenachrone history, of the overwhelming defeat and capture of one of its mighty engines of interstellar war.

In a very short time, considering the complexity of the undertaking, the conversion of the power plant was done and the repellors, already supposed the ultimate in protection, were reinforced by a ten-thousand-pound mass of activated copper, effective for untold millions of miles. Their monstrous pilot then set the bar and advanced both levers of the dual power control out to the extreme limit of their travel.

There was no sense of motion or of acceleration, since the new system of propulsion acted upon every molecule of matter within the radius of activity of the bar, which had been set to include the entire hull. The passengers felt only the utter lack of all weight and the other peculiar sensations with which they were already familiar. But in spite of the lack of apparent motion, the *Violet* was now leaping through the unfathomable depths of interstellar space with the unthinkable acceleration of five times the velocity of light!

8

The Porpoise-Men of Dasor

'How long do you figure it's going to take us to get there, Mart?' Seaton asked from a corner, where he was bending over his apparatus-table.

'About three days at this acceleration. I set it at what I thought the safe maximum for the girls. Should we increase it?'

'Probably not – three days isn't too bad. Anyway, to save even one day we'd have to double the acceleration, so we'd better let it ride. How're you making it, Peg?'

'I'm getting used to weighing a ton now. My knees buckled only once this morning from my forgetting to watch them when I tried to walk. Don't let me interfere, though; if I am slowing us down I'll go to bed and stay there!'

'It'd hardly pay. We can use the time to good advantage. Look here, Mart – I've been looking over this stuff I got out of their ship, and here's something I know you'll eat up. They refer to it as a chart, but it's three-dimensional and almost incredible. I can't say that I understand it, but I get an awful kick out of looking at it. I've been studying it a couple of hours, and haven't started yet. I haven't found our solar system, the green one, or our own. It's too heavy to move around now, because of the acceleration we're using – come on over here and give it a look.'

The 'chart' was a strip of film, apparently miles in length, wound upon reels at each end of the machine. One section of the film was always under the viewing mechanism – an optical system projecting an undistorted image into a visiplate somewhat similar to their own – and at the touch of a lever a small motor moved the film through the projector.

It was not an ordinary star-chart: it was three-dimensional, ultra-stereo-scopic. The eye did not perceive a flat surface, but beheld an actual, extremely narrow wedge of space as seen from the center of the galaxy. Each of the closer stars was seen in its true position in space and in its true perspective, and each was clearly identified by number. In the background were faint stars and nebulous masses of light, too distant to be resolved into separate stars – a true representation of the actual sky. As both men stared, fascinated, into the visiplate, Seaton touched the lever and they apparently traveled directly along the center line of that ever-widening wedge. As they proceeded the nearer stars grew brighter and larger, soon becoming suns, with their planets and then the satellites of the planets plainly visible, and finally passing out of the picture behind the observers. The fainter stars became bright, grew into suns and solar systems, and were passed in turn. The chart still unrolled. The nebulous masses of light were approached, became composed of faint stars, which developed as had the others, and were passed.

Finally, when the picture filled the entire visiplate, they arrived at the outermost edge of the galaxy. No more stars were visible: they saw empty space stretching for inconceivably vast distances before them. But beyond that indescribable and incomprehensible vacuum they saw faint lenses and dull spots of light, which were also named, and which each man knew to be other galaxies, charted by the almost unlimited power of the Fenachrone astronomers, but not as yet explored. As the magic scroll unrolled still far-ther they found themselves back in the center of the galaxy, starting outward in the wedge adjacent to the one which they had just traversed. Seaton cut off the motor and wiped his forehead.

Wouldn't that break you off at the ankles, Mart? Did you ever conceive the possibility of such a thing?'

'I did not. There are literally miles of film in each of those reels, and I see that that cabinet is practically full of reels. There must be an index or a master-chart.'

'Yes, there's a book in this slot here, but we don't know any of their names or numbers – wait a minute! How did he report our Earth on that torpedo? Planet number three of sun six four something Pilarone, wasn't it? I'll get the record.'

'Six four seven three Pilarone, it was.'

'Pilarone … let's see …' Seaton studied the index volume. 'Reel twenty, scene fifty-one, I'd translate it.'

They found the reel, and 'scene fifty-one' did indeed show that section of space in which our solar system is. Seaton stopped the chart when star six four seven three was at its closest range, and there was our sun; with its nine planets and their many satellites accurately shown and correctly described.

'They know their stuff, all right – you've got to hand it to 'em. I've been straightening out that brain record – cutting out the hazy stretches and getting his knowledge straightened out so we can use it, and there's a lot of this kind of stuff in the record you can get. Suppose that you can figure out exactly where he comes from with this dope and with his brain record?'

'Certainly. I may be able to get more complete information upon the green system than the Osnomians have, too, which will be very useful indeed. You are right – I am intensely interested in this material, and if you do not care particularly about studying it any more at the moment, I believe that I should begin to study it now.'

'Take over. I'm going to study that record some more. Don't know whether a human brain can take it all – especially all at once – but I'm going to sort of peck around the edges and get some dope that we need pretty badly. We got a lot of information from that wampus.'

About sixty hours out, Dorothy, who had been observing the planet through number six visiplate, called Seaton away from the Fenachrone brain-record, upon which he was still concentrating.

'Come here a minute, Dickie! Haven't you got that knowledge all packed away in your skull yet?'

'I'll say I haven't. That bird's brain was three or four sizes larger than mine, and loaded Plimsoll down. I'm just nibbling around the edges yet.'

'I've always heard that the capacity of even the human brain was almost infinite. Isn't that true?' asked Margaret.

'Maybe it is, if the knowledge were built up gradually over generations. I think maybe I can get most of this stuff stowed away so that I can use it, but it's going to be an awful job.'

'Is their brain really as far ahead of ours as I gathered from what I saw of it?' asked Crane.

'That's a hard one to answer: they're so different. I wouldn't say that they are any more intelligent than we are. They know more about some things than we do; less about others. But they have very little in common with us. They don't belong to the genus "homo" at all, really. Instead of having a common ancestor with the anthropoids, as we had, they evolved from a genus which combined the worst traits of the cat tribe and the carnivorous lizards – the two most savage and bloodthirsty branches of the animal kingdom – and instead of getting better as they went along, they got worse, in those respects at least. But they do not know a lot. When you get a month or so to spare you want to put on this harness and grab his knowledge, being very careful to steer clear of his mental traits and so on. Then when we get back to Earth we'll simply tear it apart and rebuild it. You'll know what I mean when you get this stuff transplanted into your own skull. But to cut out the lecture, what's on your mind, Dottie Dimple?'

'This planet Martin picked out is all wet, literally. The visibility is fine – very few clouds – but this whole half of it is solid ocean. If there are any islands, even, they're mighty small.'

All four looked into the receiver. With the great magnification employed, the planet almost filled the visiplate. There were a few fleecy wisps of cloud, but the entire surface upon which they gazed was one sheet of the now familiar deep and glorious blue peculiar to the waters of that cuprous solar system, with no markings whatever.

'What d'you make of it, Mart? That's water, all right – copper sulphate solution, just like the Osnomian and Urvanian oceans – and nothing else visible. How big would an island have to be for us to see it from here?'

'So much depends upon the contour and nature of the island that it is hard to say. If it were low and heavily covered with their green-blue vegetation, we might not be able to see a rather large one, whereas if it were hilly and bare, we could probably see one only a few miles in diameter.'

'As it turns and as we get closer, we'll see what we can see. Better take turns watching it, hadn't we?'

It was so decided, and while the *Skylark* was still some distance away several small islands became visible, and the period of rotation of the planet was determined to be in the neighborhood of fifty hours. Margaret, then at the controls, picked out the largest island visible and directed the bar toward it. As they dropped down close to their objective, they found that the air was of the same composition as that of Osnome, but had a pressure of only seventy-eight centimeters of mercury, and that the surface gravity of the planet was ninety-five hundredths that of the Earth.

'Fine business!' exulted Seaton. 'Just about like home, but I don't see much of a place to land without getting wet, do you? Those reflectors are probably solar generators, and they cover the whole island except for that lagoon right under us.'

The island, perhaps ten miles long and half that in width, was entirely covered with great hyperbolic reflectors, arranged so closely together that little could be seen between them. Each reflector apparently focused upon an object in the center, a helix which seemed to writhe in that flaming focus, glowing with a nacreous, opalescent green light.

'Well, nothing much to see there – let's go down,' remarked Seaton as he shot the *Skylark* over to the edge of the island and down to the surface of the water. But here again nothing was to be seen of the land itself. The wall was one vertical plate of seamless metal, supporting huge metal guides, between which floated metal pontoons. From these gigantic floats metal girders and trusses went through slots in the wall into the darkness of the interior. Close scrutiny revealed that the large floats were rising steadily, although very slowly; while smaller floats bobbed up and down upon each passing wave.

'Solid generators, tide-motors, and wave-motors, all at once!' ejaculated Seaton. 'SOME power plant! Folks, I'm going to take a look at that if we have to blast our way in!'

They circumnavigated the island without finding any door or other opening – the entire thirty miles was one stupendous battery of the generators. Back at the starting point, the *Skylark* hopped over the structure and down to the surface of the small central lagoon previously noticed. Close to the water, it was seen that there was plenty of room for the vessel to move about beneath the roof of reflectors, and that the island was one solid stand of tide-motors. At one end of the lagoon was an open metal structure, the only building visible, and Seaton brought the space-cruiser up to it and through the huge opening – for door there was none. The interior of the room was lighted by long, tubular lights running around in front of the walls, which were veritable switchboards. Row after row and tier upon tier stood the instruments, plainly electrical meters of enormous capacity and equally plainly in full operation, but no wiring or bus-bar could be seen. Before each row of instruments there was a narrow walk, with steps leading down into the water of the lagoon. Every part of the great room was plainly visible, and not a living being was even watching that vast instrument board.

'What do you make of it, Dick?' asked Crane, slowly.

'No wiring – tight beam transmission. The Fenachrone do it with two matched-frequency separable units. Millions and millions of kilowatts there, if I'm any judge. Absolutely automatic too, or else …' His voice died away.

'Or else what?' asked Dorothy.

'Just a hunch. I wouldn't wonder if ...'

'Hold it, Dicky! Remember I had to put you to bed after that last hunch you had!'

'Here it is, anyway. Mart, what would be the logical line of evolution when the planet has become so old that all the land has been eroded to a level below that of the ocean? You picked us out an old one, all right – so old that there's almost no land left. Would a highly civilized people revert to fish? That seems like a backward move to me, but what other answer is possible?'

'Probably not to true fishes – although they might easily develop some fish-like traits. I do not believe, however, that they would go back to gills or to cold blood.'

'What *are* you two saying?' interrupted Margaret. 'Do you mean to say that you think *fish* live here instead of people, and that *fish* did all this?' as she waved her hand at the complicated machinery about them.

'Not fish exactly, no.' Crane paused in thought. 'Merely a people who have adjusted themselves to their environment through conscious or natural selection. We had a talk about this very thing during our first trip, shortly after I met you. Remember? I commented on the fact that there must be life throughout the universe, much of it that we could not understand; and you replied that there would be no reason to suppose them awful because incomprehensible. That may be the case here.'

'Well, I'm going to find out,' declared Seaton, as he appeared with a box full of coils, tubes, and other apparatus.

'How?' asked Dorothy, curiously.

'Fix me up a detector and follow up one of those beams. Find its frequency and direction, first, you know, then pick it up outside and follow it to where it's going. It'll go through anything, of course, but I can trap off enough of it to follow it, even if it's tight enough to choke itself. That's one thing I got from that brain record.'

He worked deftly and rapidly, and soon was rewarded by a flaring crimson color in his detector when it was located in one certain position in front of one of the meters. Noting the bearing on the great circles, he then moved the *Skylark* along that exact line, over the reflectors, and out beyond the island, where he allowed the vessel to settle directly downwards.

'Now, folks, if I've done this just right we'll get a red flash directly.'

As he spoke, the detector again burst into crimson light, and he set the bar into the line and applied a little power, keeping the light at its reddest while the other three looked on in fascinated interest.

'This beam is on something that's moving, Mart – can't take my eyes off it for a second or I'll lose it entirely. See where we're going, will you?'

'We are about to strike the water,' replied Crane quietly.

'The water!' exclaimed Margaret.

'Fair enough – why not?'

'Oh, that's right – I forgot that the *Skylark* is as good a submarine as she is an airship.'

Crane pointed number six visiplate directly into the line of flight and stared into the dark water.

'How deep are we, Mart?' asked Seaton after a time.

'Only about a hundred feet, and we do not seem to be getting any deeper.'

'That's good. Afraid this beam might be going to a station on the other side of the planet – through the ground. If so, we'd've had to go back and trace another. We can follow it any distance under water, but not through rock. Need a light?'

'Not unless we go deeper.'

For two hours, Seaton held the detector upon that tight beam of energy, travelling at a hundred miles an hour, the highest speed he could use and still hold the beam.

'I'd like to be up above, watching us. I bet we're making the water boil behind us,' remarked Dorothy.

'Yeah, we're kicking up quite a wake, I guess. It takes plenty of power to drive this unstreamlined shape through so much wetness.'

'Slow down!' commanded Crane. 'I see a submarine ahead. I thought it might be a whale at first, but it is a boat and it is what we are aiming for. You are constantly swinging with it, keeping it exactly in line.'

'O.K.' Seaton reduced the power and swung the visiplate around in front of him, whereupon the detector lamp went out. 'It's a relief to follow something I can see, instead of trying to guess which way that beam's going to wiggle next. Lead on, MacDuff – I'm right on your tail!'

The *Skylark* fell in behind the submersible craft, close enough to keep it plainly visible. Finally the stranger stopped and rose to the surface between two rows of submerged pontoons which, row upon row, extended in every direction as far as the telescope could reach.

'Well, Dot, we're where we're going, wherever that is.'

'What do you suppose it is? It looks like a floating isle-port, like it told about in that wild-story magazine you read so much.'

'Maybe – but if so they can't be fish. Let's go – I want to look it over,' and water flew in all directions as the *Skylark* burst out of the ocean and leaped into the air far above what was in truth a floating city.

Rectangular in shape, it appeared to be about six miles long and four wide. It was roofed with solar generators like those covering the island just visited, but the machines were not spaced quite so closely together, and there were numerous open lagoons. The water around the entire city was covered with wave-motors. From their great height the visitors could see an occasional submarine moving slowly under the city, and frequently small surface craft dashed across the lagoons. As they watched, a seaplane with short, thick wings, curved like those of a gull, rose from one of the lagoons and shot away over the water.

'Quite a place,' remarked Seaton as he swung a visiplate upon one of the lagoons. 'Submarines, speedboats, and fast seaplanes. Fish or not, they ain't so slow. I'm going to grab off one of those folks and see how much they know. Wonder if they're peaceable or warlike?'

'They look peaceable, but you know the proverb,' Crane cautioned his impetuous friend.

'Yes, and I'm going to be timid like mice,' Seaton returned as the *Skylark* dropped rapidly toward a lagoon near the edge of the island.

'You ought to put that in a gag book, Dick,' Dorothy chuckled. 'You forget all about being timid until an hour afterwards.'

'Watch me, Red-Top! If they even point a finger at us I'm going to run a million miles a minute.'

No hostile demonstration was made as they dropped lower and lower, however, and Seaton, with one hand upon the switch actuating the zone of force, slowly lowered the vessel down past the reflectors and to the surface of the water. Through the visiplate he saw a crowd of people coming toward them – some swimming in the lagoon, some walking along narrow runways. They seemed to be of all sizes and unarmed.

'I believe they're perfectly peaceable, and just curious, Mart. I've already got the repellors on close range – believe I'll cut them off altogether.'

'How about the ray-screens?'

'All three full out. They don't interfere with anything solid, though, and won't hurt anything. They'll stop any ray attack and this arenak hull will stop anything else we are apt to get here. Watch this board, will you, and I'll see if I can't negotiate with them.'

Seaton opened the door. As he did so, a number of the smaller beings dived headlong into the water, and a submarine rose quietly to the surface less than fifty feet away with a peculiar tubular weapon and a huge beam-projector trained upon the *Skylark*. Seaton stood motionless, his right hand raised in what he hoped was the universal sign of peace, his left holding at his hip an automatic pistol charged with X-plosive shells – while Crane, at the controls, had the Fenachrone super-gun in line and his hand lay upon the switch whose closing would volatilize the submarine and cut an incandescent path of destruction through the city lengthwise.

After a moment of inaction a hatch opened and a man stepped out upon the deck of the submarine. The two tried to converse, but with no success. Seaton then brought out the mechanical educator, held it up for the other's inspection, and waved an invitation to come aboard. Instantly the other dived, and came to the surface immediately below Seaton, who assisted him into the *Skylark*. Tall and heavy as Seaton was, the stranger was half a head taller and twice as heavy. His thick skin was of the characteristic Osnomian green and his eyes were the usual black, but he had no hair whatever. His shoulders, though broad and enormously strong, were sharply sloping, and his powerful arms were little more than half as long as would have been expected had they belonged to a human being of his size. The hands and feet were very large and very broad, and the fingers and toes were heavily webbed. His high domed forehead appeared even higher because of the total lack of hair, otherwise his features were regular and well-proportioned. He carried himself easily and gracefully, and yet with the dignity of one accustomed to command as he stepped into the control room and saluted gravely the three other Earthbeings. He glanced quickly around the room, and showed unmistakable pleasure as he saw the power plant of the cruiser of space. Languages were soon exchanged and the stranger spoke, in a bass voice vastly deeper than Seaton's own.

'In the name of our city and planet – I may say in the name of our solar system, for you are very evidently from one other than our green system – I greet you. I would offer you refreshment, as is our custom, but I fear that your chemistry is but ill adapted to our customary fare. If there be aught in which we can be of assistance to you, our resources are at your disposal – before you leave us, I shall wish to ask from you a great gift.'

'Sir, we thank you. We are in search of knowledge concerning forces which we cannot as yet control. From the power systems you employ, and from what I have learned of the composition of your suns and planets, I presume you have none of the metal of power, and it is a quantity of that element that is your greatest need?'

'Yes. Power is our only lack. We generate all we can with the materials and knowledge at our disposal, but we never have enough. Our development is hindered, our birth rate must be held down to a minimum, new cities cannot be built and new projects cannot be started, all for lack of power. For one gram of that metal I see plated upon that copper cylinder, of whose very existence no scientist upon Dasor has had even an inkling, we would do almost anything. In fact, if all else failed, I would be tempted to attack you, did I not know that our utmost power could not penetrate even your outer screen, and that you could volatilize the entire planet if you so desired.'

'Great Cat!' In his surprise Seaton lapsed from the formal language he had been employing. 'Have you figured us all out already, from a standing start?'

'We know electricity, chemistry, physics, and mathematics fairly well. You see, our race is many millions of years older than is yours.'

'You're the man I've been looking for, I guess. We have enough of this metal with us so that we can spare you some as well as not. But before I get it

I'll introduce you. Folks, this is Sacner Carfon, Chief of the Council of the planet Dasor. They saw us all the time, and when we headed for this, the Sixth City, he came over from the capital, or First City, in the flagship of his police fleet, to welcome us or to fight us, as we pleased. Carfon, this is Martin Crane … or say, better than introductions, put on the headsets, everybody, and get really acquainted.'

Acquaintance made and the apparatus put away, Seaton went to one of the store-rooms and brought out a lump of X, weighing about a hundred pounds.

'There's enough to build power plants from now on. It would save time if you were to dismiss your submarine. With you to pilot us, we can take you back to the First City a lot faster than your vessel can travel.'

Carfon took a transmitter from a pouch under his armpit and spoke briefly, then gave Seaton the course. In a few minutes the First City was reached. The *Skylark* descended rapidly to the surface of a lagoon at one end of the city. Short as had been the time consumed by their journey from the Sixth City, they found a curious and excited crowd awaiting them. The central portion of the lagoon was almost covered by the small surface craft, while the sides, separated from the sidewalks by metal curbs, were full of swimmers. The peculiar Dasorian equivalents of whistles, bells, and gongs were making a deafening uproar, and the crowd was yelling and cheering in much the same fashion as do Earthly crowds upon similar occasions. Seaton stopped the *Skylark* and took his wife by the shoulder, swinging her around in front of the visiplate.

'Look at that, Dot. Talk about rapid transit! They could give the New York Subway a flying start and beat them hands down!'

Dorothy looked into the visiplate and gasped. Six metal pipes, one above the other, ran above and parallel to each sidewalk-lane of water. The pipes were full of ocean water, water racing along at fully fifty miles an hour and discharging, each stream a small waterfall, into the lagoon. Each pipe was lighted in the interior, and each was full of people, heads almost touching feet, unconcernedly being borne along, completely immersed in that mad current. As the passenger saw daylight and felt the stream begin to drop, he righted himself, apparently selecting an objective point, and rode the current down into the ocean. A few quick strokes, and he was either at the surface or upon one of the flights of stairs leading up to the platforms. Many of the travellers did not even move as they left the orifice. If they happened to be on their backs they entered the ocean backward and did not bother about righting themselves or about selecting a destination until they were many feet below the surface.

'Good heavens, Dick! They'll kill themselves or drown!'

'Not these birds. Notice their skins? They've got a hide like a walrus, and a terrific layer of subcutaneous fat. Even their heads are protected that way –

you could hardly hit one of them hard enough with a baseball bat to hurt him. And as for drowning – they can outswim a fish, and can stay under water more than an hour without coming up for air. Even one of those youngsters can swim the full length of the city without taking a breath.'

'How do you get that velocity of flow, Carfon?' asked Crane.

'By means of pumps. These channels run all over the city, and the amount of water running in each tube and the number of tubes in use are regulated automatically by the amount of traffic. When any section of tube is empty of people, no water flows through it – thus conserving power. At each intersection there are standpipes and automatic swim-counters that regulate the volume of water and the number of tubes in use. This is ordinarily a quiet pool, as it is in a residence section, and this channel – our channels correspond to your streets, you know – has only six tubes each way. If you will look on the other side of the channel, you will see the intake end of the tubes going downtown.'

Seaton swung the visiplate around and they saw six rapidly-moving stairways, each crowded with people, leading from the ocean level up to the top of a metal tower. As the passengers reached the top of the flight, they were catapulted head-first into the chamber leading to the tube below.

'Well, that is SOME system for handling people!' exclaimed Seaton. What's the capacity of the system?'

'When running full pressure, six tubes will handle five thousand people a minute. It is only very rarely, on such occasions as this, that they are ever loaded to capacity. Some of the channels in the middle of the city have as many as twenty tubes, so that it is always possible to go from one end of the city to the other in less than ten minutes.'

'Don't they ever jam?' asked Dorothy curiously. 'I've been lost more than once in the New York Subway, and been in some perfectly frightful jams, too – and they weren't moving ten thousand people a minute either.'

'No jams ever have occurred. The tubes are perfectly smooth and well-lighted, and all turns and intersections are rounded. The controlling machines allow only so many persons to enter any tube – if more should try to enter than can be carried comfortably, the surplus passengers are slid off down a chute to the swim-ways, or sidewalks, and may either wait a while or swim to the next intersection.'

'That looks like quite a jam down there now.' Seaton pointed to the receiving pool, which was now one solid mass except for the space kept clear by the six mighty streams of humanity-laden water.

'If the newcomers can't find room to come to the surface they will swim over to some other pool.' Carfon shrugged indifferently. 'My residence is the fifth cubicle on the right side of this channel. Our custom demands that you accept the hospitality of my home, if only for a moment and only for a beaker of distilled water. Any ordinary visitor could be received in my office, but you must enter my home.'

Seaton steered the *Skylark* carefully, surrounded as she was by a tightly-packed crowd of swimmers, to the indicated dwelling, and anchored her so that one of the doors was close to a flight of steps leading from the corner of the building down into the water. Carfon stepped out, opened the door of his house, and preceded his guests within. The room was large and square, and built of synthetic, non-corroding metal, as was the entire city. The walls were tastefully decorated with striking geometrical designs in vari-colored metal, and upon the floor was a softly woven metal rug. Three doors leading into other rooms could be seen, and strange pieces of furniture stood here and there. In the center of the floor-space was a circular opening some four feet in diameter, and there, only a few inches below the level of the floor, was the surface of the ocean.

Carfon introduced his guests to his wife – a feminine replica of himself, although she was not of quite such heroic proportions.

'I don't suppose that Seven is far away, is he?' Carfon asked the woman.

'Probably he is outside, near the flying ball. If he has not been touching it ever since it came down, it is only because someone stronger than he pushed him aside. You know how boys are,' turning to Dorothy with a smile as she spoke. 'Boy nature is probably universal.'

'Pardon my curiosity, but why "Seven"?' asked Dorothy, as she returned the smile.

'He is the two thousand three hundred and forty-seventh Sacner Carfon in direct male line of descent,' she explained. 'But perhaps Six has not explained these things to you. Our population must not be allowed to increase, therefore each couple can have only two children. It is customary for the boy to be born first, and is given the name of his father. The girl is younger, and is given her mother's name.'

'That will now be changed,' said Carfon feelingly. 'These visitors have given us the secret power and we shall be able to build new cities and populate Dasor as she should be populated.'

'Really? ...' She checked herself, but a flame leaped to her eyes, and her voice was none too steady as she addressed the visitors. 'For that we Dasorians thank you more than words can express. Perhaps you strangers do not know what it means to want half a dozen children with every fiber of your being and to be allowed to have only two – we do, all too well ... I will call Seven.'

She pressed a button, and up out of the opening in the middle of the floor there shot a half-grown boy, swimming so rapidly that he scarcely touched the coaming as he came to his feet. He glanced at the four visitors, then ran up to Seaton and Crane.

'Please, sirs, may I ride, just a little short ride, in your vessel before you go away?'

'Seven!' boomed Carfon sternly, and the exuberant youth subsided.

'Pardon me, sirs, but I was so excited …'

'All right, son, no harm done at all. You bet you'll have a ride in the *Skylark* if your parents will let you.' He turned to Carfon. 'I'm not so far beyond that stage myself that I'm not in sympathy with him. Neither are you, unless I'm badly mistaken.'

'I am very glad that you feel as you do. He would be delighted to accompany us down to the office, and it will be something to remember all the rest of his life.'

'You have a little girl, too?' Dorothy asked the woman.

'Yes – would you like to see her? She is asleep now,' and without waiting for an answer the proud Dasorian mother led the way into a bedroom. Of beds there were none, for Dasorians sleep floating in thermostatically-controlled tanks, buoyed up in the water of the temperature they like best, in a fashion that no Earthly springs and mattresses can approach. In a small tank in a corner reposed a baby, apparently about a year old, over whom Dorothy and Margaret made the usual feminine ceremony of delight and approbation.

Back in the living room, after an animated conversation in which much information was exchanged concerning the two planets and their races of peoples, Carfon drew six metal goblets of distilled water and passed them around. Standing in a circle, the six touched goblets and drank.

They then embarked, and while Crane steered the *Skylark* slowly along the channel toward the offices of the Council, and while Dorothy and Margaret showed the eager Seven all over the vessel, Seaton explained to Carfon the danger that threatened the universe, what he had done, and what he was attempting to do.

'Dr Seaton, I wish to apologize to you,' the Dasorian said when Seaton had done. 'Since you are evidently still land animals, I had supposed you of inferior intelligence. It is true that your younger civilization is deficient in certain respects, but you have shown a depth of vision, a sheer power of imagination and grasp, that no member of our older civilization could approach. I believe that you are right in your conclusions. We have no such forces or screens upon this planet, and never have had; but the sixth planet of our own sun has. About fifty of your years ago, when I was a boy, such a projection visited my father. It offered to "rescue" us from our watery planet, and to show us how to build rocket-ships to move us to Three, which is half land, and which is inhabited only by lower animals.'

'And he didn't accept?'

'Certainly not. Then as now our sole lack was power, and the strangers did not show us how to increase our supply. Perhaps they had no more power than we, perhaps because of the difficulty of communication our want was not made clear to them. But of course we did not want to move to Three, and we had already had rocket-ships for hundreds of generations. We have never been able to reach Six with them, but we visited Three long ago; and everyone who went there came back as soon as he could. We detest land. It is hard, barren, unfriendly. We have everything, here upon Dasor. Food is plentiful, synthetic or natural, as we prefer. Our watery planet supplies our every need and wish, with one exception; and now that we are assured of power, even that one exception vanishes, and Dasor becomes a very Paradise. We can now lead our natural lives, work and play to our fullest capacity – we would not trade our world for all the rest of the universe.'

'I never thought of it in that way, but you're right, at that,' Seaton conceded. 'You are ideally suited to your environment. But how do I get to planet Six? Its distance is terrific, even as planetary distances go. You won't have any night until Dasor swings outside the orbit of your sun, and until then Six will be invisible, even to our most powerful telescope.'

'I do not know, myself, but I will send out a call for the Chief Astronomer. He will meet us at the office, and will give you a chart and the exact course.'

At the office the Earthly visitors were welcomed formally by the Council – the nine men in control of the entire planet. The ceremony over and their course carefully plotted, Carfon stood at the door of the *Skylark* a moment before it closed.

'We thank you with all force, Earthmen, for what you have done for us this day. Please remember, and believe that this is no idle word – if we can assist you in any way in this conflict which is to come, the resources of this planet are at your disposal. We join Osnome and the other planets of this system in declaring you, Dr Seaton, our Overlord.'

9

The Welcome to Norlamin

The *Skylark* days upon her way toward the sixth planet, Seaton gave the visiplate and the instrument board his customary careful scrutiny and rejoined the others.

'Still talking about the human fish, Dottie Dimple?' he asked, as he stoked his villainous pipe. 'Peculiar tribe of porpoises, but they made a hit with me. They're the most like our own kind of people, in everything that counts, of anybody we've seen yet – in fact, they're more like us than a lot of human beings we all know.'

'I like them immensely ...'

'You couldn't like 'em any other way, the size ...'

'Terrible, Dick, terrible! Easy as I am, I can't stand for any such pun as that. But really, I think they're just perfectly fine, in spite of their being so funny-looking. Mrs Carfon is just simply sweet, even if she does look like a walrus, and that cute little seal of a baby was just too perfectly darn cunning for words. That boy Seven is keen as mustard, too.'

'He should be,' put in Crane, dryly. 'He probably has as much intelligence now as any one of us.'

'Do you think so?' asked Margaret. 'He acted like any other boy, but he did seem to understand things remarkably well.'

'He would – they're way ahead of us in most things.' Seaton glanced at the two women quizzically and turned to Crane. 'And as for their being bald, this was one time, Mart, when those two phenomenal heads of hair our two little girl-friends are so proud of didn't make any kind of a hit at all. They probably regard that black thatch of Peg's and Dot's auburn mop as relics of a barbarous and prehistoric age – about like we would regard the hirsute hide of a Neanderthal.'

'That may be so, too,' Dorothy replied, unconcernedly, 'but we aren't planning on living there, so why worry about it? I like them, anyway, and I believe that they like us.'

'They acted that way, anyway. But say, Mart, if that planet is so old that all their land area has been eroded away, how come they've got so much water left? And they've got quite an atmosphere, too.'

'The air-pressure, while greater than that now obtaining upon Earth, was probably of the order of magnitude of three meters of mercury, originally. As to the erosion, they might have had more water to begin with than our Earth had.'

'That'd probably account for it.'

'There's one thing I want to ask you two scientists,' Margaret said. 'Everywhere we've gone, except on that one world that Dick thinks is a wandering planet, we've found the intelligent life quite remarkably like human beings. How do you account for that?'

'There, Mart, is one for the massive intellect to concentrate on,' challenged Seaton: then, as Crane considered the question in silence for some time he went on: 'I'll answer it myself, then, by asking another. Why not? Why shouldn't they be? Remember, man is the highest form of Earthly life – at least, in our own opinion and as far as we know. In our wanderings, we have picked out planets quite similar to our own in point of atmosphere and temperature and, within narrow limits, of mass as well. It stands to reason that under such similarity of conditions there would be certain similarity of results. How about it, Mart? Reasonable?'

'It seems plausible, in a way,' conceded Crane, 'but it probably is not universally true.'

'Sure not – couldn't be, hardly. No doubt we could find a lot of worlds inhabited by all kinds of intelligent things – freaks that we can't even begin to imagine now – but they probably would be occupying planets entirely different from ours in some essential feature of atmosphere, temperature, or mass.'

'But the Fenachrone world is entirely different,' Dorothy argued, 'and they're more or less human – they're bipeds, anyway, with recognizable features. I've been studying that record with you, you know, and their world has so many times more mass than ours that their gravitation is simply frightful!'

'That much difference is comparatively slight, not a real fundamental difference. I meant a hundred or so times either way – greater or less. And even their gravitation has modified their structure a lot – suppose it had been fifty times as great as it is? What would they have been like? Also, their atmosphere is very similar to ours in composition, and their temperature is bearable. It is my opinion that atmosphere and temperature have more to do with evolution than anything else, and that the mass of the planet runs a poor third.'

'You may be right,' admitted Crane, 'but it seems to me that you are arguing from insufficient premises.'

'Sure I am – almost no premises at all. I would be just about as well justified in deducting the structure of a range of mountains from a superficial study of three pebbles picked up in a creek. However, we can get an idea some time, when we have a lot of time.'

'How?'

'Remember that planet we struck on the first trip, that had an atmosphere composed mostly of gaseous chlorin? In our ignorance we assumed that life there was impossible, and didn't stop. Well, it may be just as well that we didn't. If we go back there, protected as we are with our screens and stuff, it wouldn't surprise me a bit to find life there, and lots of it – and I've got a hunch that it'll be a form of life that'd make your grandfather's whiskers curl right up into a ball!'

'You get the weirdest ideas, Dick!' protested Dorothy. 'I hope you aren't planning on exploring it, just to prove your point?'

'Never thought of it before. Can't do it now, anyway – got our hands full. However, after we get this Fenachrone mess cleaned up we'll have to do just that little thing, won't we, Mart? As that intellectual guy said while he was insisting upon dematerializing us, "Science demands it."'

'By all means. We should be in a position to make contributions to science in fields as yet untouched. Most assuredly we shall investigate those points.'

'Then they'll go alone, won't they, Peggy?'

'Absolutely! We've seen some pretty middling horrible things already, and if these two men of ours call the frightful things we have seen normal, and are planning on deliberately hunting up things that even they will consider monstrous, you and I most certainly shall stay at home!'

'Yeah? You say it easy. Bounce back, Peg, you've struck a rubber fence! Rufus, you red-haired little fraud, you know you wouldn't let me go to the corner store after a can of tobacco without insisting on tagging along!'

'You're a cockeyed …' began Dorothy hotly, but broke off in amazement and gasped, 'For Heaven's sake, what was that?'

'What was what? It missed me.'

'It went right through you! It was a kind of a funny little cloud, like smoke or something. It came right through the ceiling like a flash – went right through you and on down through the floor. There it comes back again!'

Before their startled eyes a vague, nebulous something moved rapidly upward through the floor and passed upward through the ceiling. Dorothy leaped to Seaton's side and he put his arm around her reassuringly.

"Sall right, folks – I know what that thing is.'

'Well, shoot it, quick!' Dorothy implored.

'It's one of those projections from where we're heading for, trying to get our range; and it's the most welcome sight these weary old eyes have rested upon for full many a long and dreary moon. They've probably located us from our power-plant emission. We're an awful long ways off yet, though, and going like a streak of greased lightning, so they're having trouble in holding us. They're friendly, we already know that – they probably want to talk to us. It'd make it easier for them if we'd shut off our power and drift at constant velocity, but that'd use up valuable time and throw our calculations all out. We'll let them try to match our acceleration. If they can do that, they're good.'

The apparition reappeared, oscillating back and forth irregularly – passing through the arenak walls, through the furniture and the instrument boards, and even through the mighty power plant itself, as though nothing were there. Eventually, however, it remained stationary a foot or so above the floor of the control room. Then it began to increase in density until apparently a man stood before them. His skin, like that of all the inhabitants of the planets of the green suns, was green. He was tall and well-proportioned when judged by Earthly standards except for his head, which was overly large, and which was particularly massive above the eyes and backward from the ears. He was evidently of great age, for what little of his face was visible was seamed and wrinkled, and his long, thick mane of hair and his square-cut, yard-long beard were a dazzling white, only faintly tinged with green.

While in no sense transparent, nor even translucent, it was evident that the apparition before them was not composed of flesh and blood. He looked at each of the four Earthbeings intently for a moment, then pointed toward the table upon which stood the mechanical educator, and Seaton placed it in front of the peculiar visitor. As Seaton donned a headset and handed one to the stranger, the latter stared at him, impressing upon his consciousness that he was to be given a knowledge of English. Seaton pressed the lever, receiving as he did so a sensation of an unbroken calm, a serenity profound and untroubled, and the projection spoke.

'Dr Seaton, Mr Crane, and ladies – welcome to Norlamin, the planet toward which you are now flying. We have been awaiting you for more than five thousand years of your time. It has been a mathematical certainty – it has been graven upon the very Sphere itself – that in time someone would come to us from without this system, bringing a portion, however small, of Rovolon – of the metal of power. For more than five thousand years our instruments have been set to detect the vibrations which would herald the advent of the user of that metal. Now you have come, and I perceive that you have vast stores of it. Being yourselves seekers after truth, you will share it with us gladly as we will instruct you in many things you wish to know. Allow me to operate the educator – I would gaze into your minds and reveal my own to your sight. But first I must tell you that your machine is too rudimentary to function properly, and with your permission I shall make certain minor alterations.'

Seaton nodded permission, and from the eyes and from the hands of the figure there leaped visible streams of force, which seized the transformers, coils, and tubes, and reformed and reconnected them, under Seaton's bulging eyes, into an entirely different mechanism.

'Oh, I see!' he gasped. 'Say, what are you, anyway?'

'Pardon me; in my eagerness I became forgetful. I am Orlon, the First of Astronomy of Norlamin, in my observatory upon the surface of the planet. This that you see is simply my projection, composed of forces for which you have no name in your language. You can cut it off, if you wish, with your screens, which even I can see are of a surprisingly high order of efficiency. There, this educator will now work as it should. Please put on the remodeled helmets, all four of you.'

They did so, and the pencils of force moved levers, switches, and dials as positively as human hands could have moved them, and with vastly greater speed and precision. As the dials moved, each brain received clearly and plainly a knowledge of the customs, language, and manners of the inhabitants of Norlamin. Each mind became suffused with a vast, immeasurable peace, calm power, and a depth and breadth of mental vision theretofore undreamed-of. Looking deep into his mind they sensed a quiet, placid certainty, beheld power and knowledge to them illimitable, perceived depths of wisdom to them unplumbable.

Then from his mind into theirs there flowed smoothly a mighty stream of comprehension of cosmic phenomena. They hazily saw infinitely small units grouped into planetary formations to form practically dimensionless aggregates. These in turn grouped to form slightly larger ones, and after a long succession of such groupings they knew that the comparatively gigantic bodies which then held their attention were in reality electrons, the smallest units recognized by Earthly science. They clearly understood the combinations of sub-atomic constituents into atoms. They perceived plainly the way in which atoms build up molecules, and comprehended the molecular structure of matter. In mathematical thoughts only dimly grasped, even by Seaton and Crane, were laid before them the fundamental laws of physics, of electricity, of gravitation, and of chemistry. They saw globular masses of matter, the suns and their planets, comprising solar systems; saw solar systems, in accordance with those immutable laws, grouped into galaxies. Galaxies in turn – here the flow was suddenly shut off as though a valve had been closed, and the astronomer spoke.

'Pardon me. Your brains should be stored only with the material you desire most and can use to the best advantage, for your mental capacity is even more limited than my own. Please understand that I speak in no derogatory sense; it is only that your race has many thousands of generations to go before your minds should be stored with knowledge indiscriminately. We ourselves have not reached that stage, and we are perhaps millions of years older than are you. And yet,' he continued musingly, 'I envy you. Knowledge is, of course, relative, and I can know *so* little! Time and space have yielded not an iota of their mystery to our most penetrant minds. And whether we delve baffled into the unknown smallness of the small, or whether we peer, blind and helpless, into the unknown largeness of the large, it is the same – infinity is comprehensible only to the Infinite One: the all-shaping Force directing and controlling the universe and the unknowable Sphere. The more we know, the vaster the virgin fields of investigation open to us, and the more infinitesimal becomes our knowledge. But I am perhaps keeping you from more important activities. As you approach Norlamin more nearly I shall guide you to my observatory. I am glad indeed that it is in my lifetime that you have come to us, and I await anxiously the opportunity of greeting you in the flesh. The years remaining to me of this cycle of existence are few, and I had almost ceased hoping to witness your coming.'

The projection vanished instantaneously, and the four stared at each other in an incredulous daze of astonishment. Seaton finally broke the stunned silence.

'Well, I'll be kicked to death by little red spiders!' he ejaculated. 'Mart, did you see what I saw? I thought – hoped, maybe – that I was expecting something like that, but I wasn't – it breaks me off at the ankles yet, just to think of it!'

Crane walked over to the educator in silence. He examined it, felt the changed coils and transformers, and gently shook the new insulating base of the great power-tube. Still in silence he turned his back, walked around the instrument board, read the meters, then went back and again inspected the educator.

'It was real, and not a higher development of hypnotism, as I thought at first that it must be,' he reported seriously. 'Hypnotism, if sufficiently advanced, might have affected us in that fashion, even to teaching us all a strange language, but by no possibility could it have had such an effect upon copper, steel, bakelite, and glass. It was certainly real, and while I cannot begin to understand it, I will say that your imagination has certainly vindicated itself. A race who can do such things as that can do almost anything. You have been right, from the start.'

'Then you can beat those horrible Fenachrone, after all!' cried Dorothy, and threw herself into her husband's arms.

'Do you remember, Dick, that I hailed you once as Columbus at San Salvador?' asked Margaret unsteadily from Crane's encircling arms. 'What could a man be called who from the sheer depths of his imagination called forth the means of saving from destruction all the civilizations of millions of entire worlds?'

'Don't talk that way, please, folks,' Seaton was plainly uncomfortable. He blushed, the burning red tide rising in waves up to his hair as he wriggled in embarrassment, like any schoolboy. 'Mart's done most of it, anyway, you know; and even at that, we aren't out of the woods yet, by forty-seven rows of apple trees.'

'You will admit, will you not, that we can see our way out of the woods, at least, and that you yourself feel rather relieved?' asked Crane.

'I'll say I'm relieved! We ought to be able to take 'em, with the Norlaminians backing us. If they haven't already got the stuff we need, they will know how to make it – even if that zone actually is impenetrable, I'll bet they'll be able to work out some solution. Relieved? That don't half tell it, guy – I feel like I'd just pitched off the Old Man of the Sea who's been riding on my neck! What say you girls get your fiddle and guitar and we'll sing us a little song? I feel good – they had me worried – it's the first time I've felt like singing since we cut that warship up.'

Dorothy brought out her 'fiddle' – the magnificent Stradivarius, formerly Crane's, which he had given her – Margaret her guitar, and they sang one rollicking number after another. Though by no means a Metropolitan Opera quartette, their voices were all better than mediocre, and they had sung together so much that they harmonized readily.

'Why don't you play us some real music, Dottie?' asked Margaret, after a time. 'You haven't practiced for ages.'

'Right. This quartette of ours ain't so hot,' agreed Seaton. 'If we had any audience except Shiro, they'd probably be throwing eggs by this time.'

'I haven't felt like playing lately, but I do now,' and Dorothy stood up and swept the bow over the strings. Doctor of music in violin, an accomplished musician, playing upon one of the finest instruments the world has ever known, she was lifted out of herself by relief from the dread of the Fenach-rone invasion and that splendid violin expressed every subtle nuance of her thought.

She played rhapsodies and paeans, and solos by the great masters. She played vivacious dances, then 'Traumerei' and 'Liebestraum'. At last she swept into the immortal 'Meditation', and as the last note died away Seaton held out his arms.

'You're a blinding flash and a deafening report, Dottie Dimple, and I love you,' he declared – and his eyes and his arms spoke volumes that his light utterance had left unsaid.

Norlamin close enough so that its images almost filled number six visiplate, the four wanderers studied it with interest. Partially obscured by clouds and with polar regions two glaring caps of snow – they would be green in a few months, when the planet would swing inside the orbit of its sun around that vast central luminary of that complex solar system – it made a magnificent picture. They saw sparkling blue oceans and huge green continents of unfamiliar outlines. So terrific was the velocity of the space-cruiser that the image grew larger as they watched it, and soon the field of vision could not contain the image of the whole disk.

'Well, I expect Orlon'll be showing up pretty quick now,' remarked Seaton; and it was not long until the projection appeared in the air of the control room.

'Hail, Terrestrials!' he greeted them. 'With your permission, I shall direct your flight.'

Permission granted, the figure floated across the room to the board and the rays of force centered the visiplate, changed the direction of the bar a trifle, decreased slightly their negative acceleration, and directed a stream of force upon the steering mechanism.

'We shall alight upon the grounds of my observatory upon Norlamin in seven thousand four hundred twenty-eight seconds,' he announced presently. 'The observatory will be upon the dark side of Norlamin when we arrive, but I have a force operating upon the steering mechanism which will guide the vessel along the required curved path. I shall remain with you until we land, and we may converse upon any topic of interest to you.'

'We came in search of you specifically to discuss a matter in which you will be as much interested as we are. But it would take too long to tell you about it – I'll show you.'

He brought out the magnetic brain record, threaded it into the machine and handed the astronomer a headset. Orlon put it on, touched the lever, and for an hour there was unbroken silence. There was no pause in the motion of the magnetic tape, no repetition – Orlon's brain absorbed the information as fast as it could be sent, and understood that frightful recording in every particular.

As the end of the tape was reached a shadow passed over Orlon's face.

'Truly a depraved evolution – it is sad to contemplate such a perversion of a really excellent brain. They have power, even as you have, and they have the will to destroy, which is a thing that I cannot understand. However, if it is graven upon the Sphere that we are to pass, it means only that upon the next plane we shall continue our searches – let us hope with better tools and with greater understanding than we now possess.'

"Smatter?' snapped Seaton savagely. 'Going to take it lying down, without putting up any fight at all?'

'What can we do? Violence is contrary to our very natures. No man of Norlamin could offer any but passive resistance.'

'You can do a lot if you will. Put on that headset again and get my plan, offering any suggestions your far abler mind may suggest.'

As the human scientist poured his plan of battle into the brain of the astronomer, Orlon's face cleared.

'It is graven upon the Sphere that the Fenachrone shall pass,' he said finally. 'What you ask of us we can do. I have only a general knowledge of rays, as they are not in the province of the Orlon family; but the student Rovol, of the family Rovol of Rays, has all present knowledge of such phenomena. Tomorrow I will bring you together, and I have little doubt that he will be able, with the help of your metal of power, to solve your problem.'

'I don't quite understand what you said about a whole family studying one subject, and yet having only one student in it,' said Dorothy, in perplexity.

'A little explanation is perhaps necessary. First, you must know that every man of Norlamin is a student, and most of us are students of science. With us, "labor" means mental effort, that is, study. We perform no physical or manual labor save for exercise, as all our mechanical work is done by forces. This state of things having endured for many thousands of years it long ago became evident that specialization was necessary in order to avoid duplication of effort and to insure complete coverage of the field. Soon afterward, it was discovered that very little progress was being made in any branch, because so much was known that it took a lifetime to review that which had already been accomplished, even in a narrow and highly-specialized field. Many points were studied for years before it was discovered that the identical work had been done before, and either forgotten or overlooked. To remedy this condition the mechanical educator had to be developed. Once it was perfected a new system was begun. One man was assigned to each small sub-division of scientific endeavor, to study it intensively. When he became old each man chose a successor – usually a son – and transferred his own know-ledge to the younger student. He also made a complete record of his own brain, in much the same way as you have recorded the brain of the Fenach-rone upon your metallic tape. These records are all stored in a great central library, as permanent references.

'All these things being true, now a young person need only finish an ele-mentary education – just enough to learn to think, which takes only about twenty-five or thirty years – and he is ready to begin actual work. When that time comes he receives in one day all the knowledge of his specialty which has been accumulated by his predecessors during many thousands of years of intensive study.'

'Whew!' Seaton whistled. 'No wonder you folks know something! With that start, I believe I might know something myself! As an astronomer, you may be interested in this star-chart and stuff – or do you know all about that already?'

'No, the Fenachrone are far ahead of us in that subject, because of their observatories out in open space and because of their gigantic reflectors, which cannot be used through any atmosphere. We are further hampered in having darkness for only a few hours at a time and only in winter, when our planet is outside the orbit of our sun around the great central sun of our entire system. However, with the Rovolon you have brought us, we shall have real observatories far out in space; and for that I personally will be indebted to you more than I can ever express. As for the chart, I hope to have the pleasure of examining it while you are conferring with Rovol of Rays.'

'How many families are working on rays – just one?'

'One upon each kind of rays. That is, each of the ray families knows a great deal about all kinds of vibrations of the ether, but is specializing upon one narrow field. Take, for instance, the rays you are most interested in; those able to penetrate a zone of force. From my own slight and general knowledge I know that it would of necessity be a ray of the fifth order. These rays are very new – they have been under investigation only a few thousands of years – and the Rovol is the only student who would be at all well informed upon them. Shall I explain the orders of rays more fully than I did by means of the educator?'

'Please. You assumed that we knew more than we do, so a little explanation would help.'

'All ordinary vibrations – that is, all molecular and material ones, such as light, heat, electricity, radio, and the like – were arbitrarily called waves of the first order, in order to distinguish them from waves of the second order, which are given off by particles of the second order, which you know as protons and electrons, in their combination to form atoms. Your scientist Millikan discovered these rays for you, and in your language they are known as Millikan, or Cosmic, rays.

'Some time later, when sub-electrons of the first and second levels were identified, the energies given off by their combinations or disruptions were called rays of the third and fourth orders. These rays are most interesting and most useful; in fact, they do all our mechanical work. They as a class are called protelectricity, and bear the same relation to ordinary electricity that electricity does to torque – both are pure energy, and they are interconvertible. Unlike electricity, however, it may be converted into many different forms by fields of force, in a way comparable to that in which white light is resolved into colors by a prism – or rather, more like the way alternating current is changed to direct current by a motor-generator set, with attendant changes in properties. There are two complete spectra, of about five hundred and fifteen hundred bands, respectively, each as different from the others as red is different from green. Thus, the power that propels your space-vessel, your attractors, your repellors, your object-compass, your zone of force – all these things are simply a few of the fifteen hundred wave-bands of the fourth order, all of which you doubtless would have worked out for yourselves in time. Since I know practically nothing of the fifth – the first sub-ethereal level – and since that order is to be your prime interest, I will leave it entirely to Rovol.'

'If I knew a fraction of your "practically nothing" I'd think I knew a lot. But about this fifth order – is that as far as they go?'

'My knowledge is slight and very general; only such as I must have in order to understand my own subject. The fifth order certainly is not the end – it is probably scarcely a beginning. We think now that the orders extend to infinite smallness, just as the galaxies are grouped into larger aggregations, which are probably in their turn only tiny units in a scheme infinitely large.

'Over six thousand years ago the last fourth order rays were worked out; and certain peculiarities in their behavior led the then Rovol to suspect the existence of the fifth order. Successive generations of the Rovol proved their existence, determined the conditions of their liberation, and found that this metal of power was the only catalyst able to liberate them in usable quantity. This metal, which was called Rovolon after the Rovol, was first described upon theoretical grounds and later was found, by spectroscopy, in certain stars, notably in one star only eight light-years away; and a few micrograms have been obtained from meteorites. Enough for study, and to perform a few tests, but not enough to be of any practical use.'

'Ah ... I see. Those visits, then *were* real – you Norlaminians *did* operate through a zone of force on Osnome and Urvania.'

'In a very small way, yes. On those planets and elsewhere, specifically to attract the attention of such visitors as you. And ever since that time the family Rovol have been perfecting the theory of the fifth order and waiting for your coming. The present Rovol, like myself and many others whose work is almost at a standstill, is waiting with all-consuming eagerness to greet you as soon as the *Skylark* can be landed upon our planet.'

'Neither your rocket-ships nor projections could get you any Rovolon?'

'Except for the minute quantities already mentioned, no. Every hundred years or so someone develops a new type of rocket that he thinks may stand a slight chance of making the journey to that Rovolon-bearing solar system, but not one of those venturesome youths has as yet returned. Either that sun has no planets or else the rocket-ships have failed. Our projections are useless, as they can be driven only a very short distance upon our present carrier wave. With a carrier of the fifth order we could drive a projection to any point in the galaxy, since its velocity would be millions of times that of light and the power necessary would be reduced accordingly – but as I said before, such waves cannot be generated without the metal Rovolon.'

'I hate to break this up – I'd like to listen to you talk for a week – but we're going to land pretty quick, and it looks as though we were going to land pretty hard.'

'We will land soon, but not hard,' replied Orlon confidently, and the landing was as he had foretold. The *Skylark* was falling with an ever-decreasing velocity, but so fast was the descent that it seemed to the watchers as though they must crash through the roof of the huge, brilliantly-lighted building toward which they were dropping. But they did not strike the observatory. So incredibly accurate were the calculations of the Norlaminian astronomer and so inhumanly precise were the controls he had set upon their bar that as they touched the ground after barely clearing the domed roof, the passengers felt only a sudden decrease in acceleration, like that following the coming to rest of a rapidly-moving elevator after it has completed a downward journey.

'I shall join you in person very shortly,' Orlon said, and the projection vanished.

'Well, we're here, folks, on another new world. Not quite as thrilling as the first one was, is it?' and Seaton stepped toward the door.

'How about the air composition, density, gravity, temperature, and so on?' asked Crane. 'Perhaps we should make a few tests.'

'Didn't you get that on the educator? Thought you did. Gravity a little less than seven-tenths, Air composition, same as Osnome and Dasor. Pressure, halfway between Earth and Osnome. Temperature, like Osnome most of the time, but fairly comfortable in the winter. Snow now at the poles, but this observatory is only ten degrees from the equator. They don't wear clothes enough to flag a hand-car with here, either, except when they have to. Let's go!'

He opened the door and the four travelers stepped out upon a close-cropped lawn – a turf whose blue-green softness would shame an Oriental rug. The landscape was illuminated by a soft and mellow, yet intense green light which emanated from no visible source. As they paused and glanced about them they saw that the *Skylark* had alighted in the exact center of a circular enclosure a hundred yards in diameter, walled by row upon row of shrubbery, statuary, and fountains, all bathed in ever-changing billows of light. At only one point was the circle broken. There the walls did not come together, but continued on to border a lane leading up to a massive structure of cream-and-green marble, topped by its enormous, glassy dome – the observatory of Orlon.

'Welcome to Norlamin, Terrestrials,' the deep, calm voice of the astronomer greeted them, and Orlon in the flesh shook hands cordially in the American fashion with each of them in turn and placed around each neck a crystal chain from which depended a small Norlaminian chronometer-radiophone. Behind him there stood four other old men.

'These men are already acquainted with each of you, but you do not as yet know them. I present Fodan, Chief of the Five of Norlamin. Rovol, about whom you know. Astron, the First of Energy. Satrazon, the First of Chemistry.'

Orlon fell in beside Seaton and the party turned toward the observatory. As they walked along the Earthpeople stared, held by the unearthly beauty of the grounds. The hedge of shrubbery, from ten to twenty feet high, and which shut out all sight of everything outside it, was one mass of vivid green and flaring crimson leaves; each leaf and twig groomed meticulously into its precise place in a fantastic geometrical scheme. Just inside this boundary there stood a ring of statues of heroic size. Some of them were single figures of men and women; some were busts; some were groups in natural or allegorical poses – all were done with consummate skill and feeling. Between the statues there were fountains, magnificent bronze and glass groups of the strange aquatic denizens of this strange planet, bathed in geometrically-shaped sprays, screens, and columns of water. Winding around between the statues and the fountains there was a moving, scintillating wall, and upon the waters and upon the wall there played torrents of color, cataracts of harmoniously-blended light. Reds, blues, yellows, greens – every color of their peculiar green spectrum and every conceivable combination of those colors writhed and flamed in ineffable splendor upon those deep and living screens of falling water and upon that shimmering wall.

As they entered the lane Seaton saw with amazement that what he had supposed a wall, now close at hand, was not a wall at all. It was composed of myriads of individual sparkling jewels, of every known color, for the most part self-luminous; and each gem, apparently entirely unsupported, was dashing in and out and along among its fellows, weaving and darting here and there, flying at headlong speed along an extremely tortuous, but evidently carefully-calculated course.

'What can that be, anyway, Dick?' whispered Dorothy, and Seaton turned to his guide.

'Pardon my curiosity, Orlon, but would you mind explaining that moving wall?'

'Not at all. This garden has been the private retreat of the family Orlon for many thousands of years, and women of our house have been beautifying it since its inception. You may have observed that the statuary is very old. No such work has been done for ages. Modern art has developed along the lines of color and motion, hence the lighting effects and the tapestry wall. Each gem is held upon the end of a minute pencil of force, and all the pencils are controlled by a machine which has a key for every jewel in the wall.'

Crane, the methodical, stared at the innumerable flashing jewels and asked, 'It must have taken a prodigious amount of time to complete such an undertaking?'

'It is far from complete; in fact, it is scarcely begun. It was started only about four hundred years ago.'

'Four hundred years!' exclaimed Dorothy. 'Do you live that long? How long will it take to finish it, and what will it be like when it is done?'

'No, none of us live longer than about one hundred and sixty years – at about that age most of us decide to pass. When this tapestry wall is finished, it will not be simply form and color, as it is now. It will be a portrayal of the history of Norlamin from the first cooling of the planet. It will, in all probability, require thousands of years for its completion. You see, time is of little importance to us, and workmanship is everything. My companion will continue working upon it until we decide to pass; my son's companion may continue it. In any event, many generations of the women of the Orlon will work upon it until it is complete. When it is done, it will be a thing of beauty as long as Norlamin shall endure.'

'But suppose that your son's wife isn't that kind of an artist? Suppose she would want to do music or painting or something else?' asked Dorothy, curiously.

'That is quite possible; for, fortunately, our art is not yet entirely intellectual, as is our music. There are many unfinished artistic projects in the house of Orlon, and if the companion of my son should not find one to her liking, she will be at liberty to continue anything else she may have begun, or to start an entirely new project of her own.'

'You have a family then?' asked Margaret. 'I'm afraid I didn't understand things very well when you gave them to us over the educator.'

'I send things too fast for you, not knowing that your educator was new to you; a thing with which you were not thoroughly familiar. I will therefore explain some things in language, since you are not familiar with the mechanism of thought transference. The Five do what governing is necessary for the entire planet. Their decrees are founded upon self-evident truth, and are therefore the law. Population is regulated according to the needs of the planet, and since much work is now in progress, an increase in population was recommended by the Five. My companion and I therefore had three children, instead of the customary two. By lot it fell to us to have two boys and one girl. One of the boys will assume my duties when I pass; the other will take over a part of some branch of science that has grown too complex for one man to handle as a specialist should. In fact, he has already chosen his specialty and been accepted for it – he is to be the nine hundred sixty-seventh of Chemistry, the student of the asymmetric carbon atom, which will thus be a specialty from this time henceforth.

'It was learned long ago that the most perfect children were born of parents in the full prime of mental life, that is, at about one hundred years of age. Therefore, with us each generation covers one hundred years. The first twenty-five years of a child's life are spent at home with his parents, during which time he acquires his elementary education in the common schools. Then boys and girls alike move to the Country of Youth, where they spend another twenty-five years. There they develop their brains and initiative by conducting any researches they choose. Most of us, at that age, solve the most baffling problems of the universe, only to discover later that our solutions have been fallacious. However, much really excellent work is done in the Country of Youth, primarily because of the new and unprejudiced viewpoints of the virgin minds there at work. In that country also each finds his life's companion, the one necessary to round out mere existence into a perfection of living that no person, man or woman, can ever know alone. I need not speak to you of the wonders of love or of the completion and fullness of life that it brings, for all four of you, children though you are, know love in full measure.

'At fifty years of age the man, now mentally mature, is recalled to his family home, as his father's brain is now losing some of its vigor and keenness. The father then turns over his work to the son by means of the educator – and when the weight of the accumulated knowledge of a hundred thousand generations of research is impressed upon the son's brain, his play is over.'

'What does the father do then?'

'Having made his brain record, about which I have told you, he and his companion – for she has in similar fashion turned over her work to her successor – retire to the Country of Age, where they rest and relax after their century of effort. They do whatever they care to do, for as long as they please to do it. Finally, after assuring themselves that all is well with the children, they decide that they are ready for the Change. Then, side by side as they have labored, they Pass.'

Now at the door of the observatory, Dorothy paused and shrank back against Seaton, her eyes widening as she stared at Orlon.

'No, daughter, why should we fear the Change?' he answered her unspoken question, calm serenity in every inflection of his quiet voice. 'The life-principle is unknowable to the finite mind, as is the All-Controlling Force. But even though we know nothing of the sublime goal toward which it is trending, any person ripe for the Change can, and of course does, liberate the life-principle so that its progress may be unimpeded.'

In the spacious room of the observatory, in which the Terrestrials and their Norlaminian hosts had been long engaged in study and discussion, Seaton finally rose, extended a hand toward his wife, and spoke to Orlon.

'Your Period of Sleep begins in twenty minutes – and we've been awake for thirty hours, which is a long time for us. We will go back to our *Skylark*, and when the Period of Labor begins – that will give us ten hours – I will go over to Rovol's laboratory and Crane can come back here to work with you? How would that be?'

'You need not return to your vessel – I know that its somewhat cramped quarters have become irksome. Apartments have been prepared here for you. We shall have a light meal here together, and then we shall retire, to meet again tomorrow.'

As he spoke a tray laden with appetizing dishes appeared in the air in front of each person. As Seaton resumed his seat the tray followed him, remaining always in the most convenient position.

Crane glanced at Seaton questioningly; and Satrazon, the First of Chemistry, answered his thought before he could voice it.

'The food before you, unlike that which is before us of Norlamin, is wholesome for you. It contains no copper, no arsenic, no heavy metal – in short, nothing in the least harmful to your chemistry. It is balanced as to carbohydrates, proteins, fats, and sugars, and contains the due proportion of each of the various accessory nutritional factors. You will also find that the flavors are agreeable to each of you.'

'Synthetic, eh? You've got us analyzed,' Seaton stated, rather than asked, as with knife and fork he attacked the thick, rare, and beautifully-broiled steak which, with its mushrooms and other delectable trimmings, lay upon his rigid, although unsupported tray – noticing as he did so that the Norlaminians ate with tools entirely different from those they had supplied to their Earthly guests.

'Entirely synthetic,' Satrazon made answer, 'except for the sodium chloride necessary. As you already know, sodium and chlorin are very rare throughout our system, therefore the force upon the food-supply took from your vessel the amount of salt required for the formulae. We have been unable to synthesize atoms, for the same reason that the labors of so many others have been hindered – because of the lack of Rovolon. Now, however, my science shall progress as it should; and for that I join with my fellow scientists in giving you thanks for the service you have rendered us.'

'We thank you instead, for the service we have been able to do you is slight indeed compared to what you are giving us in return. But it seems that you speak quite impersonally of the force upon the food supply. Did not you yourself direct the preparation of these meats and vegetables?'

'Oh, no. I merely analyzed your tissues, surveyed the food-supplies you carried, discovered your individual preferences, and set up the necessary integrals in the mechanism. The forces did the rest, and will continue to do so as long as you remain upon this planet.'

'Fruit salad always was my favorite dish,' Dorothy said, after a couple of bites, 'and this one is just divine! It doesn't taste like any other fruit I ever ate, either – I think it must be the same ambrosia that the old pagan gods used to eat.'

'If all you did was to set up the integrals, how do you know what you are going to have for the next meal?' asked Crane.

'We have no idea what the form, flavor, or consistency of any dish will be,' was the surprising answer. 'We know only that the flavor will be agreeable and that it will agree with the form and consistency of the substance, and that the composition will be well-balanced chemically. You see, all the details of flavor, form, texture, and so on are controlled by a device something like one of your kaleidoscopes. The integrals render impossible any unwholesome, unpleasant, or unbalanced combination of any nature, and everything else is left to the mechanism, which operates upon pure chance.'

'What a system!' Seaton exclaimed admiringly, and resumed his vigorous attack upon the long-delayed supper.

The meal over, the Earthly visitors were shown to their rooms and fell into deep, dreamless sleep.

10

Norlaminian Science

Breakfast over, Seaton watched intently as his tray, laden with empty containers, floated away from him and disappeared into an opening in the wall.

'How do you do it, Orlon?' he asked, curiously. 'I can hardly believe it, even after seeing it done.'

'Each tray is carried upon the end of a beam or rod of force, and supported rigidly by it. Since the beam is tuned to the individual wave of the instrument you wear upon your chest, your tray is of course placed in front of you, at a predetermined distance, as soon as the sending force is actuated. When you have finished your meal the beam is shortened. Thus the tray is drawn back to the food laboratory, where other forces cleanse and sterilize the various utensils and place them in readiness for the next meal. It would be an easy matter to have this same mechanism place your meals before you wherever you go upon this planet, provided only that a clear path can be plotted from the laboratory to your person.'

'Thanks, but it would scarcely be worthwhile. Besides, we'd better eat in the *Skylark* most of the time, to keep our cook good-natured. Well, I see Rovol is coming in for a landing, so I'll have to be on my way. Coming along, Dot, or have you got something else on your mind?'

'I'm going to leave you for a while. I can't really understand even a radio, and just thinking about those funny, complicated rays and things you are going after makes me dizzy in the head. Mrs Orlon is going to take us over to the Country of Youth – she says Margaret and I can play around with her daughter and her bunch and have a good time while you scientists are doing your stuff.'

'All right. 'Bye 'til tonight,' and Seaton stepped out into the grounds, where the First of Rays was waiting.

The flier was a torpedo-shaped craft of some transparent, glassy material, completely enclosed except for one circular doorway. From the midsection, which was about five feet in diameter, and provided with heavily-cushioned seats capable of carrying four passengers in comfort, the hull tapered down smoothly to a needle point at each end. As Seaton entered and settled himself into the cushions, Rovol touched a lever. Instantly a transparent door slid across the opening, locking itself into position flush with the surface of the hull, and the flier darted into the air and away. For a few minutes there was silence as Seaton studied the terrain beneath them. Fields or cities there were none; the land was covered with dense forests and vast meadows, with here and there great buildings surrounded by gracious, park-like areas. Rovol finally broke the silence.

'I understand your problem, I believe, since Orlon has transferred to me all the thought he had from you. With the aid of the Rovolon you have brought us I am confident that we shall be able to work out a satisfactory solution of the various problems involved. It will take us some few minutes to traverse the distance to my laboratory, and if there are any matters upon which your mind is not quite clear, I shall try to clarify them.'

'That's letting me down easy,' Seaton grinned, 'but you don't need to be afraid of hurting my feelings – I know just exactly how ignorant and dumb I am compared to you. There's a lot of things I don't understand at all.

First, and nearest, this airboat. It has no power plant at all. I assume that it, like so many other things hereabouts, is riding on the end of a rod of force?'

'Exactly. The beam is generated and maintained in my laboratory. All that is here in the flier is a small sender, for remote control.'

'How do you obtain your power? Solar generators and tide-motors? I know that all your work is done by protelectricity, and that you have developed all of the third order and almost all of the fourth, but Orlon did not inform us as to the sources.'

'We have not used such inefficient generators for many thousands of years. Long ago it was shown by research that energies were constantly being generated in abundance in outer space, and that they – up to and including the sixth magnitude, that is – could be collected and transmitted without loss to the surface of the planet by means of matched and synchronized units. Several million of these collectors have been built and thrown out to become tiny satellites of Norlamin.'

'How did you get them far enough out?'

'The first ones were forced out to the required distance upon beams of force produced by the conversion of electricity, which was in turn produced from turbines, solar motors, and tide-motors. With a few of them out, however, it was easy to obtain sufficient power to send out more; and now, whenever one of us requires more power than he has at his disposal, he merely sends out such additional collectors as he needs.'

'Now about those fifth-order rays, which will penetrate a zone of force. I am told that they are not ether waves at all?'

'They are not ether waves. The fourth-order rays are the shortest vibrations that can be propagated through the ether; for the ether itself is not a continuous medium. We do not know its nature exactly, but it is an actual substance, and is composed of discrete particles of the fourth order. Now the zone of force, which is itself a fourth-order phenomenon, sets up a condition of stasis in the particles composing the ether. These particles are relatively so coarse that rays and particles of the fifth order will pass through the fixed zone without retardation. Therefore, if there is anything between the particles of the ether – this matter is being debated hotly among us at the present time – it must be a sub-ether, if I may use that term. We have never been able to investigate any of these things at all fully, not even such a relatively coarse aggregation as is the ether; but now, having Rovolon, it will not be many thousands of years until we shall have extended our knowledge many orders farther, in both directions.'

'Just how will Rovolon help you?'

'It will enable us to generate an energy of the ninth magnitude – that much power is necessary to work effectively with that which you have so aptly named a zone of force – and will give us a source of fifth, and probably higher orders of vibrations which, if they are generated in space at all, are beyond our present reach. The zone of force is necessary to shield certain items of equipment from ether vibrations; as any such vibration inside the controlling fields of force renders observation or control of the higher orders of rays impossible.'

'Hm … m. I see – I'm learning something,' Seaton replied, cordially. 'Just as the higher-powered a radio set is, the more perfect must be its shielding?'

'Yes. Just as a trace of gas will destroy the usefulness of your most sensitive vacuum tubes, and just as imperfect shielding will allow interfering waves to enter sensitive electrical apparatus – in that same fashion will even the slightest ether vibration interfere with the operation of the extremely sensitive fields and lenses of force which must be used in controlling forces of the higher orders.'

'Orlon told me that you had the fifth order pretty well worked out.'

'We know exactly what the forces are, how to liberate and control them, and how to use them. In fact, in the work which we are to begin today, we shall use but little of our ordinary power: almost all our work will be done by energies liberated from copper by means of the Rovolon you have given me. But here we are at my laboratory. You already know that the best way to learn is by doing, and we shall begin at once.'

The flier alighted upon a lawn quite similar to the one before the observatory of Orlon, and the scientist led his Earthly guests into the vast, glass-lined room that was his laboratory. Great benches lined the walls. There were hundreds of dials, meters, tubes, transformers, and other instruments and mechanisms at whose uses Seaton could not even guess.

Rovol first donned a suit of transparent, flexible material, of a deep golden color, instructing Seaton to do the same; explaining that much of the work would be with dangerous frequencies and with high pressures, and that the suits were not only absolute insulators against electricity, heat, and sound, but were also ray-filters proof against any harmful radiations. As each helmet was equipped with radio-phones, conversation was not interfered with in the least.

Rovol took up a tiny flash-pencil, and with it deftly cut off a bit of Rovolon, almost microscopic in size. This he placed upon a great block of burnished copper, and upon it played a force. As he manipulated two levers, two more beams of force flattened out the particle of metal, spread it out over the copper, and forced it into the surface of the block until the thin coating was at every point in molecular contact with the copper beneath it – a perfect job of plating, and one done in the twinkling of an eye. He then cut out a piece of the treated copper the size of a pea, and other forces rapidly built around it a structure of coils and metallic tubes. This apparatus he suspended in the air at the extremity of a small beam of force. The block of copper was next cut in two, and Rovol's fingers moved rapidly over the keys of a machine which resembled slightly an overgrown and exceedingly complicated book-keeping machine. Streams and pencils of force flashed and crackled, and Seaton saw raw materials transformed into a complete power plant, in its center the two-hundred-pound lump of plated copper, where an instant before there had been only empty space upon the massive metal bench. Rovol's hands moved rapidly from keys to dials and back, and suddenly a zone of force, as large as a basketball, appeared around the apparatus poised in the air.

'But it'll fly off and we can't stop it with anything,' Seaton protested, and it did indeed dart rapidly upward.

The old man shook his head as he manipulated still more controls, and Seaton gasped as nine stupendous beams of force hurled themselves upon that brilliant spherical mirror of pure energy, seized it in mid-flight, and shaped it resistlessly, under his bulging eyes, into a complex geometrical figure of precisely the desired form.

Intense violet light filled the room, and Seaton turned toward the bar. That two-hundred-pound mass of copper was shrinking visibly, second by second, so vast were the forces being drawn from it, and the searing, blinding light would have been intolerable but for the protective color-filters of his helmet. Tremendous flashes of lightning ripped and tore from the relief-points of the bench to the ground-rods, which flared at blue-white temperature under the incessant impacts. Knowing that this corona-loss was but an infinitesimal fraction of the power being used, Seaton's mind staggered as he strove to understand the magnitude of the forces at work upon that stubborn sphere of energy.

The aged scientist used no tools whatever, as we understand the term. His laboratory was a power-house; at his command were the stupendous forces of a battery of planetoid accumulators, and added to these were the fourth-order, ninth-magnitude forces of the disintegrating copper bar. Electricity and protelectricity, under millions upon millions of kilovolts of pressure, leaped to do the bidding of that wonderful brain, stored with the accumulated knowledge of countless thousands of years of scientific research. Watching the ancient physicist work, Seaton compared himself to a schoolboy mixing chemicals indiscriminately and ignorantly, with no knowledge whatever of their properties, occasionally obtaining a reaction by pure chance. Whereas he had worked with atomic energy schoolboy fashion, the master craftsman before him knew every reagent, every reaction, and worked with known and thoroughly familiar agencies to bring about his exactly predetermined ends – just as calmly certain of the results as Seaton himself would have been in his own laboratory, mixing equivalent quantities of solutions of barium chloride and of sulphuric acid to obtain a precipitate of barium sulphate.

Hour after hour Rovol labored on, oblivious to the passage of time in his zeal of accomplishment, the while carefully instructing Seaton, who watched every step with intense interest and did everything possible for him to do. Bit by bit a towering structure arose in the middle of the laboratory. A metal foundation supported a massive compound bearing, which in turn carried a tubular network of latticed metal, mounted like an immense telescope. Near the upper, outer end of this openwork tube a group of nine forces held the field of force rigidly in place in its axis; at the lower extremity were mounted seats for two operators and the control panels necessary for the operation of the intricate system of forces and motors which would actuate and control that gigantic projector. Immense hour and declination circles could be read by optical systems from the operators' seats – circles fully forty feet in diameter, graduated with incredible delicacy and accuracy into decimal fractions of seconds of arc, and each driven by variable-speed motors through gear-trains and connections having the absolute minimum of backlash.

While Rovol was working upon one of the last instruments to be installed upon the controlling panel a mellow note sounded throughout the building, and he immediately ceased his labors and opened the master switches of his power plant.

'You have done well, youngster,' he congratulated his helper as he began to take off his protective covering. 'Without your aid I could not have accomplished nearly this much during one period of labor. The periods of exercise and of relaxation are at hand – let us return to the house of Orlon, where we all shall gather to relax and to refresh ourselves for the labors of tomorrow.'

'But it's almost done!' protested Seaton. 'Let's finish it up and shoot a little juice through it, just to try it out.'

'There speaks the rashness and impatience of youth,' rejoined the scientist, calmly removing the younger man's suit and leading him out to the waiting airboat. 'I read in your mind that you are often guilty of laboring continuously until your brain loses its keen edge. Learn now that such conduct is worse than foolish – it is criminal. We have labored the full period. Laboring for more than that length of time without recuperation results in a loss of power which, if persisted in, wreaks permanent injury to the mind, and by it you gain nothing. We have more than ample time to do that which must be done – the fifth-order projector shall be completed before the warning torpedo shall have reached the planet of the Fenachrone – therefore overexertion is unwarranted. As for testing, know now that only mechanisms built by bunglers require testing. Properly-built machines work properly.'

'But I'd've liked to've seen it work just once, anyway,' lamented Seaton as the small airship tore through the air on its way back to the observatory.

'You must cultivate calmness, my son, and the art of relaxation. With those qualities your race can easily double its present span of useful life. Physical exercise to maintain the bodily tissues at their best, and mental relaxation following mental toil – these things are the secrets of a long and productive life. Why attempt to do more than can be accomplished efficiently? There is tomorrow. I am more interested in that which we are now building than you can possibly be, since many generations of the Rovol have anticipated its construction; yet I realize that in the interest of our welfare and for the progress of civilization today's labors must not be prolonged beyond today's period of work. Furthermore, you yourself realize that there is no optimum point at which any task may be interrupted. Short of final completion of any project, one point is the same as any other. Had we continued, we would have wished to continue still farther, and so on without end.'

'I suppose so – you're probably right, at that,' the impetuous chemist conceded, as their craft came to earth before the observatory.

Crane and Orlon were already in the common room, as were the scientists Seaton already knew, as well as a group of women and children still strangers to the Terrestrials. In a few minutes Orlon's companion, a dignified, white-haired woman, entered; accompanied by Dorothy, Margaret, and a laughing, boisterous group of men and women from the Country of Youth. Introductions over, Seaton turned to Crane.

'How's every little thing, Mart?'

'Very well indeed. We are building an observatory in space – or rather, Orlon is building it and I am doing what little I can to help him. In a few days we shall be able to locate the system of the Fenachrone. How is your work progressing?'

'Smoother'n a kitten's ear. Got the big fourth-order projector about done. We're going to project a fourth-order force out to grab us some dense material, a pretty close approach to pure neutronium. There's nothing dense enough around here, even in the core of the central sun, so we're going out to a white dwarf star – one a good deal like the companion star to Sirius – get some material of the proper density from its core, and convert our sender into a fifth-order machine. Then we can really get busy – go places and do things.'

'Neutronium? Pure mass? I have been under the impression that it does not exist. Of what use can such a substance be to you?'

'Not pure neutronium – quite. Close, though – specific gravity about two and a half million. Got to have it for lenses and controls for the fifth-order forces. Those rays go right through anything less dense without measurable refraction. But I see Rovol's giving me a nasty look. He's my boss on this job, and I imagine this kind of talk's barred during the period of relaxation, as being work. That so, chief?'

'You know that it is barred,' answered Rovol, with a smile.

'All right, boss; one more little infraction and I'll shut up like a clam. I'd like to know what the girls've been doing.'

'We've been having a wonderful time!' Dorothy declared. 'We've been designing fabrics and ornaments and jewels and things. Wait 'til you see 'em – they'll knock you cold!'

'Fine! All right, Orlon, it's your party.'

'This is the time of exercise. We have many forms, most of which are unfamiliar to you. You all swim, however, and as that is one of the best of exercises, I suggest that we all swim.'

'Lead us to it!' Seaton exclaimed, then his voice changed abruptly. 'Wait a minute – I don't know about our swimming in copper sulphate solution.'

'We swim in fresh water as often as in salt, and the pool is now filled with distilled water.'

The Terrestrials quickly donned their bathing suits and all went through the observatory and down a winding path, bordered with the peculiarly beautiful scarlet and green shrubbery, to the 'pool' – an artificial lake covering a hundred acres, its polished metal bottom and sides strikingly decorated with jewels and glittering tiles in tasteful yet contrasting inlaid designs. Any desired depth of water was available and plainly marked, from the fenced-off shallows where the smallest children splashed to the twenty feet of liquid crystal which received the diver who cared to try his skill from one of the many spring-boards, flying rings, and catapults which rose high into the air a short distance away from the entrance.

Orlon and the others of the older generation plunged into the water without ado and struck out for the other shore, using a fast double-overarm stroke. Swimming in a wide circle they came out upon the apparatus and went through a series of methodical dives and gymnastic performances. It was evident that they swam, as Orlon had intimated, for exercise. To them, exercise was a necessary form of labor – labor which they performed thoroughly and well – but nothing to call forth the whole-souled enthusiasm they displayed in their chosen fields of mental effort.

The visitors from the Country of Youth, however, locked arms and sprang to surround the four Terrestrials, crying, 'Let's do a group dive.'

'I don't believe that I can swim well enough to enjoy what's coming,' whispered Margaret to Crane, and they slipped into the pool and turned around to watch. Seaton and Dorothy, both strong swimmers, locked arms and laughed as they were encircled by the green phalanx and swept out to the end of a dock-like structure and upon a catapult.

'Hold tight, everybody!' someone yelled, and interlaced, straining arms and legs held the green and white bodies in one motionless group as a gigantic force hurled them fifty feet into the air and out over the deepest part of the pool. There was a mighty splash and a miniature tidal wave as that mass of humanity struck the water headfirst and disappeared beneath the surface, still as though one multiple body. Many feet they went down before the cordon was broken and the individual units came to the surface. Then pandemonium reigned. Vigorous, informal games, having to do with floating and sinking balls and effigies; pushball, in which the players never seemed to know, or to care, upon which side they were playing; water-fights and ducking contests – all in a gale of unrestrained merriment. A green mermaid, having felt the incredible power of Seaton's arms as he tossed her away from a goal he was temporarily defending, put both her small hands around his biceps wonderingly, amazed at a strength unknown and impossible upon her world; then playfully tried to push him under. Failing, she called for help.

'He's needed a good ducking for ages!' Dorothy cried, and she and several other girls threw themselves upon him. Over and around him the lithe forms flashed, while the rest of the young people splashed water impartially over all the combatants and cheered them on. In the midst of the battle the signal sounded to end the period of exercise.

'Saved by the bell,' Seaton laughed as, almost half drowned, he was allowed to swim ashore.

When all had returned to the common room of the observatory and had seated themselves Orlon took out his miniature ray-projector, no larger than a fountain pen, and flashed it briefly upon one of the hundreds of button-like lenses upon the wall. Instantly each chair converted itself into a form-fitting divan, inviting complete repose.

'I believe that you of Earth would perhaps enjoy some of our music during this, the period of relaxation and repose – it is so different from your own,' Orlon remarked, as he again manipulated his tiny force-tube.

Every light was extinguished and there was felt a profoundly deep vibration – a note so low as to be palpable rather than audible: and simultaneously the utter darkness was relieved by a tinge of red so dark as to be barely perceptible, while a peculiar somber fragrance pervaded the atmosphere. The music rapidly ran the gamut to the limit of audibility and, in the same tempo, the lights traversed the visible spectrum and disappeared. Then came a crashing chord and a vivid flare of blended light; ushering in an indescribable symphony of sound and color, accompanied by a slower succession of shifting, blending colors.

The quality of tone was now that of a gigantic orchestra, now that of a full brass band, now that of a single unknown instrument – as though the composer had had at his command every overtone capable of being produced by any possible instrument, and with them had woven a veritable tapestry of melody upon an incredibly complex loom of sound. As went the harmony, so accompanied the play of light. Neither music nor illumination came from any apparent source; they simply pervaded the entire room. When the music was fast – and certain passages were of a rapidity impossible for any human fingers to attain – the lights flashed in vivid, tiny pencils, intersecting each other in sharply-drawn, brilliant figures which changed with dizzying speed: when the tempo was slow the beams were soft and broad, blending into each other to form sinuous, indefinite, writhing patterns whose very vagueness was infinitely soothing.

'What do you think of it, Mrs Seaton?' Orlon asked, when the symphony was ended.

'Marvelous!' breathed Dorothy, awed. 'I never imagined anything like it. I can't begin to tell you how much I like it. I never dreamed of such absolute perfection of execution, and the way the lighting accompanies the theme is just too perfectly wonderful for words! It was wonderfully, incredibly brilliant.'

'Brilliant – yes. Perfectly executed – yes. But I notice that you say nothing of depth of feeling or of emotional appeal.' Dorothy blushed uncomfortably and started to say something, but Orlon silenced her and continued: 'You need not apologize. I had a reason for speaking as I did, for in you I recognize a real musician, and our music is indeed entirely soulless. That is the result of our ancient civilization. We are so old that our music is purely intellectual, entirely mechanical, instead of emotional. It is perfect, but, like most of our other arts, it is almost completely without feeling.'

'But your statues are wonderful!'

'As I told you, those statues were made myriads of years ago. At that time we also had real music, but, unlike statuary, music at that time could not be preserved for posterity. That is another thing you have given us. Attend!'

At one end of the room, as upon a three-dimensional screen, the four Terrestrials saw themselves seated in the control room of the *Skylark*. They saw and heard Margaret take up her guitar and strike four sonorous chords in 'A'. Then, as if they had been there in person, they heard themselves sing 'The Bull-Frog' and all the other songs they had sung, far off in space. They heard Margaret suggest that Dorothy play some 'real music', and heard Seaton's comments upon the quartette.

'In that, youngster, you were entirely wrong,' said Orlon, stopping the reproduction for a moment. 'The entire planet was listening to you very attentively – we were enjoying it as no music has been enjoyed for thousands of years.'

'The whole planet!' gasped Margaret. 'Were you broadcasting it? How could you?'

'Easy,' grinned Seaton. 'They can do practically anything.'

'When you have time, in some period of labor, we would appreciate it very much if you four would sing for us again, would give us more of your vast store of youthful music, for we can now preserve it exactly as it is sung. But much as we enjoyed the quartette, Mrs Seaton, it was your work upon the violin that took us by storm. Beginning with tomorrow, my companion intends to have you spend as many periods as you will, playing for our records. We shall now have your music'

'If you like it so well, wouldn't you rather I'd play you something I hadn't played before?'

'That is labor. We could not ...'

'Piffle!' Dorothy interrupted. 'Don't you see that I could really play right now, to somebody who really enjoys music; whereas if I tried to play in front of a recorder I'd be perfectly mechanical?'

''At-a-girl, Dot! I'll get your fiddle.'

'Keep your seat, son,' instructed Orlon, as the case containing the Stradivarius appeared before Dorothy, borne by a pencil of force. 'While that temperament is incomprehensible to one of us, it is undoubtedly true that the artistic mind does operate in that manner. We listen.'

Dorothy swept into 'The Melody in F', and as the poignantly beautiful strains poured forth from that wonderful violin she knew that she had her audience with her. Though so intellectual that they themselves were incapable of producing music of real depth of feeling, they could understand and could enjoy such music with an appreciation impossible to a people of lesser mental attainments; and their profound enjoyment of her playing, burned into her mind by the telepathic, almost hypnotic power of the Norlaminian mentality, raised her to heights she had never before attained. Playing as one inspired she went through one tremendous solo after another – holding her listeners spellbound, urged on by their intense feeling to carry them further and ever further into the realm of pure emotional harmony. The bell which ordinarily signaled the end of the period of relaxation did not sound; for the first time in thousands of years the planet of Norlamin deserted its rigid schedule of life – to listen to one Earthwoman, pouring out her very soul upon her incomparable violin.

The final note of 'Memories' died away in a diminuendo wail, and the musician almost collapsed into Seaton's arms. The profound silence, more impressive far than any possible applause, was broken by Dorothy.

'There – I'm all right now, Dick. I was about out of control for a minute. I wish they could have had that on a recorder – I'll never be able to play like that again if I live to be a thousand years old.'

'It is on record, daughter. Every note and every inflection is preserved, precisely as you played it,' Orlon assured her. 'That is our only excuse for allowing you to continue as you did, almost to the point of exhaustion. While we cannot really understand an artistic mind of the peculiar type to which yours belongs, yet we realized that each time you play you are doing something no one, not even yourself, can ever do again in precisely the same subtle fashion. Therefore we allowed, in fact encouraged, you to go on as long as that creative impulse should endure – not merely for our own pleasure in hearing it, great though that pleasure was; but in the hope that our workers in music could, by a careful analysis of your product, determine quantitatively the exact vibrations or overtones which make the difference between emotional and intellectual music.'

11

Into a Sun

As Rovol and Seaton approached the physics laboratory at the beginning of the period of labor, another small airboat occupied by one man drew up beside them and followed them to the ground. The stranger, another white-bearded ancient, greeted Rovol cordially and was introduced to Seaton as 'Caslor, the First of Mechanism.'

'Truly, this is a high point in the course of Norlaminian science, my young friend,' Caslor acknowledged the introduction smilingly. 'You have enabled us to put into practice many things which our ancestors studied in theory for many a wearisome cycle of time.' Turning to Rovol he went on: 'I understand that you require a particularly precise directional mechanism? I know well that it must indeed be one of exceeding precision and delicacy, for the controls you yourself have built are able to hold upon any point, however moving, within the limits of our solar system.'

'We require controls a million times as delicate as any I have constructed, therefore, I have called your surpassing skill into cooperation. It is senseless for me to attempt a task in which I would be doomed to failure. We intend to send out a fifth-order projection, which, with its inconceivable velocity of propagation, will enable us to explore any region in the galaxy as quickly as we now visit our closest sister planet. Knowing the dimensions of this our galaxy, you can readily understand the exact degree of precision required to hold upon a point at its outermost edge.'

'Truly, a problem worthy of any man's brain,' Caslor replied after a moment's thought. 'Those small circles,' pointing to the forty-foot hour and declination circles which Seaton had thought the ultimate in precise measurement of angular magnitudes, 'are of course useless. I shall have to construct large and accurate circles, and in order to produce the slow and fast motions of the required nature, without creep, slip, play, or backlash, I shall require a pure torque, capable of being increased by infinitesimal increments ... Pure torque.'

He thought deeply for a time, then went on: 'No gear-train or chain mechanism can be built of sufficient tightness, since in any mechanism there is some freedom of motion, however slight, and for this purpose the drivers must have no freedom of motion whatever. We must have a pure torque – and the only possible force answering our requirements is band number fourteen hundred sixty-seven of the fourth order. I shall therefore be compelled to develop that band, which, having Rovolon, I can now do. The director must, of course, have a full equatorial mounting, with circles some two hundred fifty feet in diameter. Must your projector tube be longer than that, for correct design?'

'That length will be ample.'

'The mounting must be capable of rotation through the full circle of arc in either plane, and must be driven in precisely the motion required to neutralize the motion of our planet, which, as you know, is somewhat irregular. Additional fast and slow motions must of course be provided to rotate the mechanism upon each graduated circle at the will of the operator. It is my idea to make the outer supporting tube quite large, so that you will have full freedom with your inner, or projector tube proper. It seems to me that dimensions X37 B42 J867 would perhaps be as good as any.'

'Perfectly satisfactory. You have the apparatus well in mind.'

'These things will consume some time. How soon will you require this mechanism?'

'We also have much to do. Two periods of labor, let us say; or, if you require them, three.'

'It is well. Two periods will be ample time: I was afraid that you might need it today, and the work cannot be accomplished in one period of labor. The mounting will, of course, be prepared in the Area of Experiment. Farewell.'

'You aren't going to build the final projector here, then?' Seaton asked as Caslor's flier disappeared.

'We shall build it here, then transport it to the Area, where its dirigible housing will be ready to receive it. All mechanisms of that type are set up there. Not only is the location convenient to all interested, but there are to be found all necessary tools, equipment, and material. Also, and not least important for such long-range work as we contemplate, the entire Area of Experiment is anchored immovably to the solid crust of the planet, so that there can be not even the slightest vibration to affect the direction of our beams of force, which must of course be very long.'

He closed the master switches of his power-plants and the two resumed work where they had left off. The control panel was soon finished. Rovol then plated an immense cylinder of copper and placed it in the power plant. He next set up an entirely new system of refractory relief-points and installed additional ground-rods, sealed through the floor and extending deep into the ground below, explaining as he worked.

'You see, son, we must lose one-thousandth of one percent of our total energy, and provision must be made for its dissipation in order to avoid destruction of the laboratory. These air-gap resistances are the simplest means of disposing of the wasted power.'

'I understand – but how about disposing of it when we are out in space? We picked up pretty heavy charges in the *Skylark* – so heavy that I had to hold up several times in the ionized layer of an atmosphere somewhere while they leaked off – and this kind of apparatus will burn up tons of copper where ours used ounces.'

'In the projected space-vessel we shall install converters to utilize all the energy, so that there will be no loss whatever. Since such converters must be designed and built especially for each installation, and since they require a high degree of precision, it is not worthwhile to construct them for a purely temporary mechanism, such as this one.'

The walls of the laboratory were opened, ventilating blowers were built, and refrigerating coils were set up everywhere, even in the tubular structure and behind the visiplates. After assuring themselves that everything combustible had been removed the two scientists put on, under their helmets, goggles whose protecting lenses could be built up to any desired thickness. Rovol then threw a switch, and a hemisphere of flaming golden radiance surrounded the laboratory and extended for miles upon all sides.

'Why such a light?' asked Seaton.

'As a warning. This entire area will be filled with dangerous radiations, and that light is a warning for all uninsulated persons to give our theater of operations a wide berth.'

'I see. What next?'

'All that remains to be done is to take our lens-material and go,' replied Rovol, as he took from a cupboard the largest faidon that Seaton had ever seen.

'Oh, that's what you're going to use! You know, I've been wondering about that stuff. I took one back with me to the Earth to experiment on. I gave it everything I could think of, and couldn't touch it. I couldn't even make it change its temperature. What is it, anyway?'

'It is not matter at all, in the ordinary sense of the word. It is almost pure crystallized energy. You have of course noticed that it looks transparent, but that it is not. You cannot see into its substance a millionth of a micron – the illusion of transparency being purely a surface phenomenon, and peculiar to this one form of substance. I have told you that the ether is a fourth-order substance. The faidon also is a fourth-order substance, but it is crystalline, whereas the ether is probably fluid and amorphous. You might call this faidon crystallized ether without being too wrong.'

'But it should weigh tons, and it is hardly heavier than air – or no, wait a minute. Gravitation is also a fourth-order phenomenon, so it might not weigh anything at all – but it would have terrific mass – or would it, not having protons? Crystallized ether would displace fluid ether, so it might – I'll give up! It's too deep for me!'

'Its theory is abstruse, and I cannot explain it to you any more fully than I have until after we have given you at least a working knowledge of the fourth and fifth orders. Pure fourth-order material would be without weight and without mass; but these crystals as they are found are not absolutely pure. In crystallizing from the magma they entrapped sufficient numbers of particles of other orders to give them the characteristics which you have observed. The impurities, however, are not sufficient in quantity to offer any point of attack to ordinary reagents.'

'But how could such material possibly be formed?'

'It can be formed only in some such gigantic cosmic body as this, our green system, formed incalculable ages ago, when all the mass comprising it existed as one colossal sun. Picture for yourself the condition in the center of that sun. It has attained the theoretical maximum of temperature – some seventy million of your Centigrade degrees – the electrons have been stripped from the protons until the entire central core is one solid ball of neutronium and can be compressed no more without destruction of the protons themselves. Still the pressure increases. The temperature, already at the theoretical maximum, can no longer increase. What happens?'

'Disruption.'

'Precisely. And just at the instant of disruption, during the very instant of generation of the frightful forces that are to hurl suns, planets, and satellites millions of miles out into space – in that instant of time, as a result of those unimaginable temperatures and pressures, the faidon comes into being. It can be formed only by the absolute maximum of temperature and at a pressure which can exist only momentarily, even in the largest conceivable masses.'

'Then how can you make a lens of it? It must be impossible to work it in any way.'

'It cannot be worked in any ordinary way, but we shall take this crystal into the depths of that white dwarf star, into a region in which obtain pressures and temperatures only less than those giving it birth. There we shall play upon it forces which, under those conditions, will be able to work it quite readily.'

'Hm ... m ... m. That I want to see. Let's go!'

They seated themselves at the panels, and Rovol began to manipulate keys, levers, and dials. Instantly a complex structure of visible force – rods, beams, and flat areas of flaming scarlet energy – appeared at the end of the tubular, telescope-like network.

'Why red?'

'Merely to render them visible. One cannot work well with invisible tools, hence I have imposed a colored light frequency upon the invisible frequencies of the forces. We will have an assortment of colors if you prefer,' and as he spoke each force assumed a different color, so that the end of the projector was almost lost beneath a riot of color.

The structure of force, which Seaton knew was the secondary projector, swung around as if sentient. A green beam extended itself, picked up the faidon, and lengthened out, hurling the jewel a thousand yards out through the open side of the laboratory. Rovol moved more controls and the structure again righted itself, swinging back into perfect alignment with the tube and carrying the faidon upon its extremity, a thousand yards beyond the roof of the laboratory.

'We are now ready to start our projections. Be sure your suit and goggles are perfectly tight. We must see what we are doing, so the light-rays must be heterodyned upon our carrier wave. Therefore the laboratory and all its neighborhood will be flooded with dangerous frequencies from the sun we are to visit, as well as with those from our own generators.'

'O.K., chief! All tight here. You say it's ten light-years to that star. How long's it going to take us to get there?'

'About ten minutes. We could travel that far in less than ten seconds but for the fact that we must take the faidon with us. Slight as is its mass, it will require much energy in its acceleration. Our projections, of course, have no mass, and will require only the energy of propagation.'

Rovol flicked a finger, a massive pair of plunger switches shot into their sockets, and Seaton, seated at his board and staring into his visiplate, was astounded to find that he apparently possessed a dual personality. He *knew* that he was seated motionless in the operator's chair in the base of the rigidly-anchored primary projector, and by taking his eyes away from the visiplate before him he could see that nothing in the laboratory had changed, except that the pyrotechnic display from the power-bar was of unusual intensity. Yet, looking into the visiplate, he was out in space *in person*, hurtling through space at a pace beside which the best effort of the *Skylark* seemed the veriest crawl. Swinging his controls to look backward, he gasped as he saw, so stupendous was their velocity, that the green system was only barely discernible as a faint green star!

Again looking forward, it seemed as though a fierce white star had become separated from the immovable firmament and was now so close to the structure of force in which he was riding that it was already showing a disk perceptible to the unaided eye. A few moments more and the violet-white splendor became so intense that the watchers began to build up, layer by layer, the protective goggles before their eyes. As they approached still closer, falling with their unthinkable velocity into that incandescent inferno, a sight was revealed to their eyes such as man had never before been privileged to gaze upon. They were falling into a white dwarf star, could see everything visible during such an unheard-of journey, and would live to remember what they had seen! They saw the magnificent spectacle of solar prominences shooting hundreds of thousands of miles into space, and directly in their path they saw an immense sun-spot, a combined volcanic eruption and cyclonic storm in a gaseous-liquid medium of blinding incandescence.

'Better dodge that spot, hadn't we, Rovol? Mightn't it be generating interfering fourth-order frequencies?'

'It is undoubtedly generating fourth-order rays, but nothing can interfere with us, since we are controlling every component of our beam from Norlamin.'

Seaton gripped his hand-rail violently and involuntarily drew himself together into the smallest possible compass as, with their awful speed unchecked, they plunged through that flaming, incandescent photosphere and on, straight down, into the unexplored, unimaginable interior of that frightful mass. Through the protecting, golden, shielding metal, Seaton could see the structure of force in which he was, and could also see the faidon – in outline, as transparent diamonds are visible in equally transparent water. Their apparent motion slowed rapidly and the material about them thickened and became more and more opaque. The faidon drew back toward them until it was actually touching the projector, and eddy currents and striae became visible in the mass about them as their progress grew slower and slower.

''Smatter? Something wrong?' demanded Seaton.

'Not at all, everything is working perfectly. The substance is now so dense that it is becoming opaque to rays of the fourth order, so that we are now partially displacing the medium instead of moving through it without friction. At the point where we can barely see to work; that is, when our carriers will be so retarded that they can no longer carry the heterodyned light waves without complete distortion, we shall stop automatically, as the material at that depth will have the required density to refract the fifth-order rays to the correct degree.'

'How can our foundations stand it? This stuff must be a hundred times as dense as platinum already, and we must be pushing a horrible load in going through it.'

'We are exerting no force whatever upon our foundations nor upon Norlamin. The force is transmitted without loss from the power-plant in our laboratory to this secondary projector here inside the star, where it is liberated in the correct band to pull us through the mass, using all the mass ahead of us as an anchorage. When we wish to return, we shall simply change the pull into a push. Ah! We are now at a standstill – now comes the most important moment of the entire project.'

All apparent motion had ceased, and Seaton could see only dimly the outlines of the faidon, now directly before his eyes. The structure of force slowly warped around until its front portion held the faidon as in a vise. Rovol pressed a lever and behind them, in the laboratory, four enormous plunger switches drove home. A plane of pure energy, flaming radiantly even in the indescribable incandescence of the core of that seething star, bisected the faidon neatly, and ten gigantic beams, five upon each half of the jewel, rapidly molded two sections of a geometrically-perfect hollow lens. The two sections were then brought together by the closing of the jaws of the mighty vise, their edges in exact alignment. Instantly the plane and the beams of energy became transformed into two terrific opposing tubes of force – vibrant, glowing tubes whose edges in contact coincided with the almost invisible seam between the two halves of the lens.

Like a welding arc raised to the nth power those two immeasurable and irresistible forces met exactly in opposition – a meeting of such incredible violence that seismic disturbances occurred throughout the entire mass of that dense, violet-white star. Sunspots of unprecedented size appeared, prominences erupted to hundreds of times their normal distances, and although the two scientists deep in the core of the tormented star were unaware of what was happening upon its surface, convulsion after titanic convulsion wracked the mighty globe and enormous masses of molten and gaseous material were riven from it and hurled far out into space.

Seaton felt his air-supply grow hot. Suddenly it became icy cold, and knowing that Rovol had energized the refrigerator system, Seaton turned away from the fascinating welding operation for a quick look around the laboratory. As he did so he realized Rovol's vast knowledge and understood the reason for the new system of relief-points and ground-rods, as well as the necessity for the all-embracing schemes of refrigeration.

Even through the practically opaque goggles he could see that the laboratory was one mass of genuine lightning. Not only from the relief-points, but from every metallic corner and protuberance the pent-up losses from the disintegrating bar were hurling themselves upon the flaring, blue-white, rapidly-volatilizing ground-rods; and the very air of the room, renewed second by second though it was by the powerful blowers, was beginning to take on the pearly luster of the highly-ionized corona. The bar was plainly visible, a scintillating demon of pure violet radiance, and a momentary spasm of fear seized him as he saw how rapidly that great mass of copper was shrinking – fear that their power would be exhausted with their task still uncompleted.

But the calculations of the aged physicist had been accurate. The lens was completed with some hundreds of pounds of copper to spare, and that geometrical form, with its precious content of near-neutronium, was following the secondary projector back toward the green system. Rovol left his seat, discarded his armor, and signaled Seaton to do the same.

'I've got to hand it to you, ace – you're a blinding flash and a deafening report!' Seaton exclaimed, writhing out of his insulating suit. 'I feel like I'd been pulled halfway through a knothole and riveted over on both ends! How big a lens did you make, anyway? Looked like it'd hold a couple of liters, maybe three.'

'Its contents are almost exactly three liters.'

'Hm … m … m. Seven and a half million kilograms – say eight thousand tons. *Some* mass, I'd say, to put into a gallon jug. Of course, being inside the faidon it won't have any weight, and while the inertia may not be … that's why you're taking so long to bring it in?'

'Yes. The projector will now bring it here into the laboratory without any further attention from us. The period of labor is about to end, and tomorrow we shall find the lens awaiting us when we arrive to begin work.'

'How about cooling it off? It had a temperature of something like forty or fifty million degrees Centigrade before you started working on it; and when you got done with it, it must have been hot.'

'You are forgetting again, son. Remember that the hot, dense material is entirely enclosed in an envelope impervious to all vibrations longer than those of the fifth order. You could put your hand upon it now, without receiving any sensation either of heat or of cold.'

'That's right – I did forget. I noticed that I could take a faidon right out of an electric arc and it wouldn't even be warm. I couldn't explain why it was, but I see now. So that stuff inside that lens will always stay as hot as it is right now! Zowie! Here's hoping she never explodes! Well, there's the bell – for once in my life, I'm ready to quit when the whistle blows,' and arm in arm the young Terrestrial chemist and the aged Norlaminian physicist strolled out to their waiting airboat.

12

Flying Visits – Via Projection

'Now what?' asked Seaton as he and Rovol entered the laboratory. 'Tear down this fourth-order projector and tackle the big job? I see the lens is here, on schedule.'

'We shall have further use for this mechanism. We shall need at least one more lens of this dense material, and other scientists also may have need of one or two. Then, too, the new projector must be so large that it cannot be erected in this room.'

As he spoke Rovol seated himself at his control desk and ran his fingers lightly over the keys. The entire wall of the laboratory disappeared, hundreds of beams of force darted here and there, seizing and working raw materials, and in the portal there grew up, to Seaton's amazement, a keyboard and panel installation such as the Earthman, in his wildest moments, had never imagined. Bank upon bank of typewriter-like keys; row upon row of keys, pedals, and stops resembling somewhat those of the console of a gigantic pipe-organ; panel upon panel of meters, switches, and dials – all arranged about two deeply-cushioned chairs and within reach of their occupants.

'Whew! That looks like the combined mince-pie nightmares of a whole flock of linotype operators, pipe-organists, and hard-boiled radio hams!' exclaimed Seaton when the installation was complete. 'Now that you've got it, what are you going to do with it?'

'There is not a control system upon Norlamin adequate for the task we face, since the problem of the projection of rays of the fifth order has heretofore been of only academic interest. Therefore it becomes necessary to construct such a control. This mechanism will, I am confident, have a sufficiently wide range of application to perform any operation we shall require of it.'

'It looks as though it could do anything, provided the man behind it knows how to play a tune on it – but if that rumble seat is for me, you'd better count me out. I followed you for about fifteen seconds, then lost you completely.'

'That is, of course, true, and is a point I was careless enough to overlook.' Rovol thought for a moment, then got up, crossed the room to his control desk, and continued, 'We shall dismantle the machine and rebuild it at once.'

'Oh, no – too much work!' protested Seaton. 'You've got it about done, haven't you?'

'It is hardly started. Two hundred thousand bands of force must be linked to it, each in its proper place, and it is necessary that you should understand thoroughly every detail of this entire projector.'

'Why? I'm not ashamed to admit that I haven't got brains enough to understand a thing like that.'

'You have sufficient brain capacity; it is merely undeveloped. There are two reasons why you must be as familiar with this mechanism as you are with the controls of your own *Skylark*. The first is that a similar control is to be installed in your new space-vessel, since by its use you can attain a perfection of handling impossible by any other system. The second, and more important reason, is that neither I nor any other man of Norlamin could compel himself, by any force of will, to direct a ray that would take away the life of any fellow-man.'

While Rovol was speaking he had reversed his process, and soon the component parts of the new control had been disassembled and piled in orderly array about the room.

'Hm ... m ... m. Never thought of that. It's right, too,' mused Seaton. 'How're you going to get it into my thick skull – with an educator?'

'Exactly,' and Rovol sent a beam of force after his highly developed educational mechanism. Dials and electrodes were adjusted, connections were established, and the beams and pencils of force began to reconstruct the great central controlling device. But this time, instead of being merely a bewildered spectator, Seaton was an active participant in the work. As each key and meter was wrought and mounted; there were indelibly impressed upon his brain the exact reason for and function of the part; and later, when the control itself was finished and the seemingly interminable task of connecting it up to the output force bands of the transformers had begun, he had a complete understanding of everything with which he was working, and understood all the means by which the ends he had so long desired were to be attained. For to the ancient scientist the tasks he was then performing were the merest routine, to be performed in reflex fashion, and he devoted most of his attention to transferring from his own brain to that of his young assistant all of his stupendous knowledge which the smaller brain of the Terrestrial was capable of absorbing. More and more rapidly as the work progressed the mighty flood of knowledge poured into Seaton's mind. After an hour or so, when enough connections had been made so that automatic forces could be so directed as to finish the job, Rovol and Seaton left the laboratory and went into the living room. As they walked, the educator accompanied them, borne upon a beam of force.

'Your brain is behaving very nicely indeed, much better than I would have thought possible from its size. In fact, it may be possible for me to transfer to you all the knowledge I have which might be of use to you. That is why I took you away from the laboratory. What do you think of the idea?'

'Our psychologists have always maintained that none of us ever uses more than a minute fraction of the actual capacity of his brain,' Seaton replied after a moment's thought. 'If you think you can give me even a percentage of your knowledge without killing me, I don't need to tell you how glad I would be to have it.'

'Knowing that you would be, I have already requested Drasnik, the First of Psychology, to come here, and he has just arrived,' answered Rovol, and as he spoke, that personage entered the room.

When the facts had been set before him the psychologist nodded his head.

'That is quite possible,' he said with enthusiasm, 'and I will be only too glad to assist in such an operation.'

'But listen!' protested Seaton. 'You'll probably change my whole personality – Rovol's brain is three times the size of mine!'

'Tut-tut – nothing of the kind,' Drasnik reproved him. 'As you have said you are using only a minute portion of the active mass of your brain. The same thing is true with us – many millions of cycles would have to pass before we would be able to fill the brains we now have.'

'Then why are your brains so large?'

'Merely a provision of Nature that no possible accession of knowledge shall find her storehouse too small,' replied Drasnik, positively. 'Ready?'

All three donned the headsets and a wave of mental force wept into Seaton's mind, a wave of such power that the Terrestrial's every sense wilted under the impact. He did not faint, he did not lose consciousness – he simply lost all control of every nerve and fiber as his entire brain passed into the control of the immense mentality of the First of Psychology and became a purely receptive, plastic medium upon which to impress the knowledge of the aged physicist.

Hour after hour the transfer continued, Seaton lying limp as though lifeless, the two Norlaminians tense and rigid, every faculty concentrated upon the ignorant, virgin brain exposed to their gaze. Finally the operation was complete and Seaton, released from the weird, hypnotic grip of that stupendous mind, gasped, shook himself, and writhed to his feet.

'Great Cat!' he exclaimed, his eyes wide with astonishment. 'I wouldn't have believed there was as much to know in the entire universe as I know right now. Thanks, fellows, a million times – but say, did you leave any open space for more? In one way, I seem to know less than I did before, there's so much more to find out. Can I learn anything more, or did you fill me up to capacity?'

The psychologist, who had been listening to the exuberant youth with undisguised pleasure, spoke calmly.

'The mere fact that you appreciate your comparative ignorance shows that you are still capable of learning. Your capacity to learn is greater than it ever was before, even though the waste space has been reduced. Much to our surprise, Rovol and I gave you all of his knowledge that would be of any use to you, and some of my own, and still theoretically you can add to it more than nine times the total of your present knowledge.'

The psychologist departed, and Rovol and Seaton returned to the laboratory, where the forces were still merrily at work. There was nothing that could be done to hasten the connecting, and it was late in the following period of labor before they could begin the actual construction of the projector. Once started, however, it progressed with amazing rapidity. Now understanding the system, it did not seem strange to Seaton that he should merely actuate a certain combination of forces when he desired a certain operation performed; nor did it seem unusual or worthy of comment that one flick of his finger would send a force a distance of hundreds of miles to a factory where other forces were busily at work, to seize a hundred angle-bars of transparent purple metal that were to form the backbone of the fifth-order projector. Nor did it seem peculiar that the same force, with no further instruction, should bring those hundred bars back to him, in a high loop through the atmosphere; should deposit them gently in a convenient space near the site of operations; and then should disappear as though it had never existed! With such tools as that, it was a matter of only a few hours before the projector was done – a task that would have required years of planning and building upon Earth.

Two hundred and fifty feet it towered above their heads, a tubular network of braced and latticed I-beams, fifty feet in diameter at the base and tapering smoothly to a diameter of about ten feet at the top. Built of a metal thousands of times as strong and as hard as any possible steel, it was not cumbersome in appearance, and yet was strong enough to be almost absolutely rigid. Ten enormous forces held the lens of neutronium in the center of the upper end; at intervals down the shaft similar forces held variously-shaped lenses and prisms shaped from zones of force; in the center of the bottom or floor of the towering structure was the double controlling system, with a universal visiplate facing each operator.

'So far, so good,' remarked Seaton as the last connection was made. 'Now we hop in and give the baby a ride over to the Area of Experiment. Caslor must have the mounting done, and we've got time enough left in this period to try her out.'

'In a moment. I am setting the fourth-order projector to go out to the dwarf star after an additional supply of neutronium.'

Seaton, knowing that from the data of their first journey the controls could be so set as to duplicate their feat in every particular without supervision, stepped into his seat in the new controller, pressed a key, and spoke.

'Hi, Dottie, doing anything?'

'Nothing much,' Dorothy's clear voice answered. 'Got it done and can I see it?'

'Sure – sit tight and I'll send a flitabout after you.'

As he spoke Rovol's flier darted into the air and away; and in two minutes it returned, slowing abruptly as it landed. Dorothy stepped out, radiant, and returned Seaton's enthusiastic caresses with equal fervor before she spoke.

'Lover, I'm afraid you violated all known speed laws getting me here. Aren't you afraid of getting pinched?'

'Nope – not here. Besides, I didn't want to keep Rovol waiting – we're all ready to go. Hop in here with me, this left-hand control's mine.'

Rovol entered the tube, took his place, and waved his hand. Seaton's hands swept over the keys and the whole gigantic structure wafted into the air. Still upright, it was borne upon immense rods of force toward the Area of Experiment, which was soon reached. Covered as the Area was with fantastic equipment, there was no doubt as to their destination, for in plain sight, dominating all the lesser installations, there rose a stupendous telescopic mounting, with an enormous hollow tube of metallic lattice-work which could be intended for nothing else than their projector. Approaching it carefully, Seaton deftly guided the projector lengthwise into that hollow receptacle and anchored it in the optical axis. Flashing beams of force made short work of welding the two tubes together immovably with angles and lattices of the same purple metal, the terminals of the variable-speed motors were attached to the controllers, and everything was in readiness for the first trial.

'What special instruction do we need to run it, if any?' Seaton asked the First of Mechanism, who had lifted himself up into the projector.

'Very little. This control governs the hour motion, that one the right ascension. The potentiometers regulate the degree of vernier action – any ratio is possible, from direct drive up to more than a hundred million complete revolutions of that graduated dial to give you one second of arc.'

'Plenty fine, I'd say. Thanks a lot, ace. Whither away, Rovol – any choice?'

'Anywhere you please, son, since this is merely a tryout.'

'O.K. We'll hop over and tell Dunark hello.'

The tube swung around into line with that distant planet and Seaton stepped down, hard, upon a pedal. Instantly they seemed infinite myriads of miles out in space, the green system barely visible as a faint green star behind them.

'Wow, that ray's fast!' exclaimed the pilot, ruefully. 'I overshot about a hundred light years. I'll try it again, with considerably less power,' as he rearranged and reset the dials and meters before him. Adjustment after adjustment and many reductions in power had to be made before the projection ceased leaping millions of miles at a touch, but finally Seaton became familiar with the new technique and the thing became manageable. Soon they were hovering above what had been Mardonale, and saw that all signs of warfare had disappeared. Slowly turning the controls, Seaton flashed the projection over the girdling Osnomian sea and guided it through the supposedly impregnable metal walls of the palace into the throne room of Roban, where they saw the Emperor, Tarnan the Karbix, and Dunark in close conference.

'Well, here we are,' remarked Seaton. 'Now we'll put on a little visibility and give the natives a treat.'

'Sh-sh,' whispered Dorothy. 'They'll hear you, Dick – we're intruding shamefully.'

'No, they won't hear us, because I haven't heterodyned the audio in on the wave yet. And as for intruding, that's exactly what we came over here for.'

He imposed the audio system upon the inconceivably high frequency of their carrier wave and spoke in the Osnomian tongue.

'Greetings, Roban, Dunark, and Tarnan, from Seaton.' All three jumped to their feet, amazed, staring about the empty room as Seaton went on, 'I am

263

not here in person. I am simply sending you my projection. Just a moment and I will put on a little visibility.'

He brought more forces into play, and solid images of force appeared in the great hall; images of the three occupants of the controller. Introductions and greetings over, Seaton spoke briefly and to the point.

'We've got everything we came after – much more than I had any idea we could get. You need have no more fear of the Fenachrone – we have found a science superior to theirs. But much remains to be done, and we have none too much time; therefore I have come to you with certain requests.'

'The Overlord has but to command,' replied Roban.

'Not command, since we are all working together for a common cause. In the name of that cause, Dunark, I ask you to come to me at once, accompanied by Tarnan and any others you may select. You will be piloted by a force which we shall set upon your controls. Upon your way here you will visit the First City of Dasor, another planet, where you will pick up Sacner Carfon, who will be awaiting you there.'

'As you direct, so it shall be,' and Seaton flashed the projector to the neighboring planet of Urvania. There he found that the gigantic space-cruiser he had ordered had been completed, and requested Urvan and his commander-in-chief to tow it to Norlamin. He then jumped to Dasor, there interviewing Carfon and being assured of the full cooperation of the porpoise-men.

'Well, that's that, folks,' said Seaton as he shut off the power. 'We can't do much more for a few days, until they get here for the council of war. How'd it be, Rovol, for me to practice with this outfit while you are finishing up the odds and ends you want to clean up? You might suggest to Orlon, too, that it'd be a good deed for him to pilot our visitors over here.'

As Rovol wafted himself to the ground from their lofty station, Crane and Margaret appeared and were lifted up to the place formerly occupied by the physicist.

'How's tricks, Mart? I hear you're quite an astronomer?'

'Yes, thanks to Orlon and the First of Psychology. He seemed quite interested in increasing our Earthly knowledge. I certainly know much more than I had ever hoped to know of anything.'

'Me, too. You can pilot us to the Fenachrone system now without any trouble. You also absorbed some ethnology and kindred sciences. What d'you think – with Dunark and Urvan, do we know enough to go ahead or should we take a chance on holding things up while we get acquainted with some of the other peoples of these planets of the green system?'

'Delay is dangerous, as our time is already short,' Crane replied. 'We know enough, I believe. Furthermore, any additional assistance is problematical; in fact, it is more than doubtful. The Norlaminians have surveyed the system rather thoroughly, and no other planet seems to have inhabitants who have even approached the development attained here.'

'Right – that's exactly the way I dope it. As soon as the gang assembles we'll go over the top. In the meantime, I called you over to take a ride in this projector – it's a darb. I'd like to shoot for the Fenachrone system first, but I don't quite dare to.'

'Don't *dare* to? You?' scoffed Margaret. 'How come?'

'Cancel the "dare" – make it "prefer not to". Why? Because while they can't work through a zone of force, some of their real scientists – and they have lots of them – not like the bull-headed soldier we captured – may well be able to detect fifth-order stuff – even if they can't work with it intelligently – and if they detected us, it'd put them on guard.'

'Sound reasoning, Dick,' Crane agreed, 'and there speaks the Norlaminian physicist, and not my old and reckless playmate, Richard Seaton.'

'Oh, I don't know – I told you I was getting timid like a mouse. But let's not sit here twiddling our thumbs – let's go places and do things. Whither away? I want a destination a good ways off, not something in our own back yard.'

'Go back home, of course, stupe,' put in Dorothy. 'Do you have to be told every little thing?'

'Sure – never thought of that,' and Seaton, after a moment's rapid mental arithmetic, swung the great tube around, rapidly adjusted a few dials, and kicked in the energizing pedal. There was a fleeting instant of unthinkable velocity, then they found themselves poised somewhere in space.

'Well, wonder how far I missed it on my first shot?' Seaton's crisp voice broke the stunned silence. 'Guess that's our sun, over to the left ain't it, Mart?'

'Yes. You were about right for distance, and within a few tenths of a light-year laterally. That is very close, I would say.'

'Rotten, for these controls. Except for the effect of relative, proper, orbital, and other motions which I can't evaluate exactly yet for lack of precise data, I should be able to hit the left eye of a gnat at this range; and the uncertainty in my data couldn't have thrown me off more than a few hundred feet. Nope, I was too anxious – hurried too much on the settings of the slow verniers. I'll snap back and try it again.'

He did so, adjusting the verniers very carefully, and again threw on the power. There was again the sensation of the barest perceptible moment of unimaginable speed, and they were in the air some fifty feet above the ground of Crane Field, almost above the testing shed. Seaton rapidly adjusted the variable-speed motors until they were perfectly stationary relative to the surface of the Earth.

'You are improving,' commented Crane.

'Yeah – that's more like it. Guess maybe I can learn to shoot this gun, in time.'

They dropped through the roof into the laboratory, where Maxwell, now in charge, was watching a reaction and occasionally taking notes.

'Hi, Max! Seaton speaking, on a television. Got your range?'

'Exactly, chief, apparently. I can hear you perfectly, but can't see anything.' Maxwell stared about the empty laboratory.

'You will in a minute. I knew I had you, but didn't want to scare you out of a year's growth,' and Seaton thickened the image until they were plainly visible.

'Please call Mr Vaneman on the phone and tell him you're in touch with us,' directed Seaton as soon as greetings had been exchanged. 'Better yet, after you've broken it to them gently, Dot can talk to them, then we'll go over and see 'em.'

The connection established, Dorothy's image floated up to the telephone and spoke.

'Mother? This is the weirdest thing you ever imagined. We're not really here at all, you know – we're actually here in Norlamin – no, I mean Dick's just sending a kind of talking picture of us to see you on Earth here … Oh, no, I don't know anything about it – it's something like television, but much more so – I'm saying this myself right now, without any rehearsal or anything … we didn't want to burst in on you without warning, because you'd be sure to think you were seeing ghosts, and we're all perfectly all right … we're having the most perfectly gorgeous time you ever imagined … Oh, I'm so excited I can't explain anything, even if I knew anything about it to explain. We'll all four of us be over there in about a second, and tell you about it. 'Bye!'

Indeed, it was even less than a second – Mrs Vaneman was still in the act of hanging up the receiver when the image materialized in the living-room of Dorothy's girlhood home.

'Hello, mother and dad,' Seaton's voice was cheerful, but matter-of-fact. 'I'll thicken this up so you can see us better in a minute. But don't think that we are flesh and blood. You'll see simply three-dimensional force-images of us.'

For a long time Mr and Mrs Vaneman chatted with the four visitors from so far away in space, while Seaton gloried in the perfect working of that marvelous projector.

'Well, our time's about up,' Seaton finally ended the visit. 'The quitting-whistle's going to blow in five minutes, and they don't like overtime work over here where we are. We'll drop in and see you again maybe, sometime before we come back.'

'Do you know yet when you are coming back?' asked Mrs Vaneman.

'Not an idea in the world, mother, any more than we had when we started. But we're getting along fine, having the time of our lives, and are learning a lot besides. So-long!' and Seaton clicked off the power.

As they descended from the projector and walked toward the waiting air-boat Seaton fell in beside Rovol.

'You know they've got our new cruiser built of dagal, and are bring it over here. Dagal's good stuff, but it isn't as good as your inoson, which is the theoretical ultimate in strength possible for any material possessing molecular structure. Why wouldn't it be a sound idea to flash it over into inoson when it gets here?'

'That would be an excellent idea, and we shall do so. It also has occurred to me that Caslor of Mechanism, Astron of Energy, Satrazon of Chemistry, myself, and one or two others should collaborate in installing a very complete fifth-order projector in the new *Skylark*, as well as any other equipment which may seem desirable. The security of the universe may depend upon the abilities and qualities of you Terrestrials and your vessel, and therefore nothing should be left undone which it is possible for us to do.'

'That would help, and we'd appreciate it. Thanks. You might do that, while we attend to such preliminaries as wiping out the Fenachrone fleet.'

In due time the reinforcements from the other planets arrived, and the mammoth space-cruiser attracted attention even before it was landed, so enormous was she in comparison with the tiny vessels having her in tow. Resting upon the ground, it seemed absurd that such a structure could possibly move under her own power. For two miles that enormous mass of metal extended over the countryside, and while it was very narrow – for its length, still its fifteen hundred feet of diameter dwarfed everything nearby. But Rovol and his aged co-workers smiled happily as they saw it, erected their keyboards, and set to work with a will.

Meanwhile a group had gathered about a conference table – a group such as had never before been seen together upon any world. There was Fodan, the ancient Chief of the Five of Norlamin, huge-headed, with his leonine mane and flowing beard of white. There were Dunark and Tarnan of Osnome and Urvan of Urvania – smooth-faced and keen, utterly implacable and ruthless in war. There was Sacner Carfon Twenty Three Forty-Six, the immense, porpoise-like, hairless Dasorian. There were Seaton and Crane, representatives of our own Earthly civilization.

Seaton opened the meeting by handing each man a headset and running a reel showing the plans of the Fenachrone; not only as he had secured them from the captain of the marauding vessel, but also everything the First of Psychology had deduced from his own study of that inhuman brain. He then removed the reel and gave them the tentative plans of battle. Headsets removed, he threw the meeting open for discussion – and discussion there was in plenty. Each man had ideas, which were thrown upon the table and studied, for the most part calmly and dispassionately. The conference continued until only one point was left, upon which argument waxed so hot that everyone seemed shouting at once.

'Order!' commanded Seaton, banging his fist upon the table. 'Osnome and

Urvania wish to strike without warning, Norlamin and Dasor insist upon a formal declaration of war. Earth has the deciding vote. Mart, how do we vote on this?'

'I vote for formal warning, for two reasons, one of which I believe will convince even Dunark. First, because it is the fair thing to do – which reason is, of course, the one actuating the Norlaminians, but which would not be considered by Osnome, nor even remotely understood by the Fenachrone. Second, I am certain that the Fenachrone will merely be enraged by the warning and will defy us. Then what will they do? You have already said that you have been able to locate only a few of their exploring warships. As soon as we declare war upon them they will almost certainly send out torpedoes to every one of their ships of war. We can then trace the torpedoes, and thus will be enabled to find and to destroy their vessels.'

'That settles that,' declared the chairman as a shout of agreement arose. 'We shall now adjourn to the projector and send the warning. I have a tracer upon the torpedo announcing the destruction by us of their vessel, and that torpedo will arrive at its destination very shortly. It seems to me that we should make our announcement immediately after their ruler has received the news of their first defeat.'

In the projector, where they were joined by Rovol, Orlon, and several others of the various 'Firsts' of Norlamin, they flashed out to the flying torpedo, and Seaton grinned at Crane as their fifth-order carrier beam went through the far-flung screens of the Fenachrone without setting up the slightest reaction. In the wake of that speeding messenger they flew through a warm, foggy, dense atmosphere, through a receiving trap in the wall of a gigantic conical structure, and on into the telegraph room. They saw the operator remove spools of tape from the torpedo and attach them to a magnetic sender – heard him speak.

'Pardon, your majesty – we have just received a first-degree-emergency torpedo from flagship Y427W of fleet 42. In readiness.'

'Put it on, here in the council chamber,' a deep voice snapped.

'If he's broadcasting it, we're in for a spell of hunting,' Seaton remarked. 'Ah – he's putting it on a tight beam. That's fine; we can trace it,' and with a narrow detector beam he traced the invisible transmission beam into the council room.

''Sfunny. This place seems awfully familiar – I'd swear I'd seen it before, lots of times – seems like I've been in it, more than once,' Seaton remarked, puzzled, as he looked around the somber room, with its dull, paneled metal walls covered with charts, maps, screens, and speakers; and with its low, massive furniture. 'Oh, sure, I'm familiar with it from studying the brain of that Fenachrone captain. Well, while His Nibs is absorbing the bad news, we'll go over this once more. You, Carfon, having the biggest voice any of us ever heard uttering intelligible language, are to give the speech. You know about what to say. When I say "go ahead" do your stuff. Now, everybody else, listen. While he's talking I've got to have audio waves heterodyned both ways in the circuit, and they'll be able to hear any noise any of us make – so all of us except Carfon want to keep absolutely quiet, no matter what happens or what we see. As soon as he's done I'll cut off our audio and say something to let you all know we're off the air. Got it?'

'One point has occurred to me about handling the warning,' boomed Carfon. 'If it should be delivered from apparently empty air, directly at those we wish to address, it would give the enemy an insight into our methods, which might be undesirable.'

'Hm … m … m. Never thought of that … it sure would, and it would be undesirable,' agreed Seaton. 'Let's see … we can get away from that by broadcasting it. They have a very complete system of speakers, but no matter how many private-band speakers a man may have, he always has one on the general wave, which is used for very important announcements of wide interest. I'll broadcast you on that wave, so that every general-wave speaker on the planet will be energized. That way, it'll look like we're shooting from a distance. You might talk accordingly.'

'If we have a minute more, there's something I would like to ask,' Dunark broke the ensuing silence. 'Here we are, seeing everything that is happening there. Walls, planets, even suns, do not bar our vision, because of the fifth-order carrier wave. I understand that, partially, But how can we see anything there? I always thought that I knew something about communications and television hook-ups and techniques, but I see that I don't. There must be a collector or receiver, close to the object viewed, with nothing opaque to light intervening. Light from that object must be heterodyned upon the fifth-order carrier and transmitted back to us. How can you do all that from here, with neither a receiver nor a transmitter at the other end?'

'We don't,' Seaton assured him. 'At the other end there are both, and a lot of other stuff besides. Our secondary projector out there is composed of forces, visible or invisible, as we please. Part of those forces comprise the receiving, viewing, and sending instruments. They are not material, it is true, but they are nevertheless fully as actual, and far more efficient, than any other system of radio, television, or telephone in existence anywhere else. It is force, you know, that makes radio or television work – the actual copper, insulation, and other matter serve only to guide and to control the various forces employed. The Norlaminians have found out how to direct and control pure forces without using the cumbersome and hindering material substance …'

He broke off as the record from the torpedo stopped suddenly and the operator's voice came through a speaker.

'General Fenimol! Scoutship K3296, patrolling the detector zone, wishes to give you an urgent emergency report. I told them that you were in council with the Emperor, and they instructed me to interrupt it, no matter how important the council may be. They have on board a survivor of the Y427W, and have captured and killed two men of the same race as those who destroyed our vessel. They say that you will want their report without an instant's delay.'

We do!' barked the general, at a sign from his ruler. 'Put it on here. Run the rest of the torpedo report immediately afterward.'

In the projector, Seaton stared at Crane a moment, then a light of grim understanding spread over his features.

'DuQuesne, of course – I'll bet a hat no other Tellurian is this far from home. I can't help feeling sorry for the poor devil – he's a darn good man gone wrong – but we'd've had to kill him ourselves, probably, before we got done with him; so it's probably just as well they got him. Pin your ears back, everybody, and watch close – we want to get this, all of it.'

13

The Declaration of War

The capital city of the Fenachrone lay in a jungle plain surrounded by towering hills. A perfect circle of immense diameter, its buildings, of uniform height, of identical design, and constructed of the same dull gray, translucent metal, were arranged in concentric circles, like the annular rings seen upon the stump of a tree. Between each ring of buildings and the one next inside it there were lagoons, lawns, and groves – lagoons of tepid, sullenly-steaming water; lawns which were veritable carpets of lush, rank rushes and of dank mosses; groves of palms, gigantic ferns, bamboos, and numerous tropical growths unknown to Earthly botany. At the very edge of the city began jungle unrelieved and primeval; the impenetrable, unconquerable jungle possible only to such meteorological conditions as obtained there. Wind there was none, nor sunshine. Only occasionally was the sun of that reeking world visible through the omnipresent fog, a pale, wan disk; always the atmosphere was one of oppressive, hot, humid vapor. In the exact center of the city rose an immense structure, a terraced cone of buildings, as though immense disks of smaller and smaller diameter had been piled one upon the other. In these apartments dwelt the nobility and the high officials of the Fenachrone. In the highest disk of all, invisible always from the surface of the planet because of the all-enshrouding mist, were the apartments of the emperor of that monstrous race.

Seated upon low, heavily-built metal stools about the great table in the council-room were Fenor, Emperor of the Fenachrone; Fenimol, his General-in-Command; and the full Council of Eleven of the planet. Being projected in the air before them was a three-dimensional moving, talking picture – the report of the sole survivor of the warship that had attacked the *Skylark Two*. In exact accordance with the facts as the engineer knew them, the details of the battle and complete information concerning the conquerors were shown. As vividly as though the scene were being reenacted before their eyes they saw the captive revive in the *Violet,* and heard the conversation between the engineer, DuQuesne, and Loring.

In the *Violet* they sped for days and weeks, with ever-mounting velocity, toward the system of the Fenachrone. Finally, power reversed, they approached it, saw the planet looming large, passed within the detector screen.

DuQuesne tightened the control of the attractors, which had never been entirely released from their prisoner, thus again pinning the Fenachrone helplessly against the wall.

'Just to be sure you don't try to start something,' he explained coldly. 'You have done well so far, but I'll run things myself from now on, so that you can't steer us into a trap. Now tell me exactly how to go about getting one of your vessels. After we get it, I'll see about letting you go.'

'Fools, you are too late! You would have been too late, even had you killed me out there in space and had fled at your utmost acceleration. Did you but know it, you are as dead, even now – our patrol is upon you!'

DuQuesne whirled, snarling, and his automatic and that of Loring were leaping out when an awful acceleration threw them flat upon the floor, a magnetic force snatched away their weapons, and a heat-beam reduced them to two small piles of gray ash. Immediately thereafter a force from the patrolling cruiser neutralized the attractors bearing upon the captive, and he was transferred to the rescuing vessel.

The emergency report ended, and with a brief 'Torpedo message from flagship Y427W resumed at a point of interruption', the report from the ill-fated vessel continued the story of its destruction, but added little to the already complete knowledge of the disaster.

Fenor of the Fenachrone leaped up from the table, his terrible, flame-shot eyes glaring venomously – teetering in berserk rage upon his block-like legs – but did not for one second take his full attention from the report until it had been completed. Then he seized the nearest object, which happened to be his chair, and with all his enormous strength hurled it to the floor, where it lay, a battered, twisted, shapeless mass of metal.

'Thus shall we treat the entire race of the accursed beings who have done this!' he stormed, his heavy voice reverberating throughout the room. 'Torture, dismemberment, and annihilation to every ...'

'Fenor of the Fenachrone!' a tremendous voice, a full octave lower than

Fenor's own terrific bass, and of ear-shattering volume and timbre in that dense atmosphere, boomed from the general-wave speaker, its deafening roar drowning out Fenor's raging voice and every other lesser sound.

'Fenor of the Fenachrone! I know that you hear, for every general-wave speaker upon your reeking planet is voicing my words. Listen well, for this warning shall not be repeated. I am speaking by and with the authority of the Overlord of the Green System, which you know as the Central System of this our galaxy. Upon some of our many planets there are those who wished to destroy you without warning and out of hand, but the Overlord has ruled that you may continue to live provided you heed these his commands, which he has instructed me to lay upon you.

'You must forthwith abandon forever your vainglorious and senseless scheme of universal conquest. You must immediately withdraw your every vessel to within the boundaries of your own solar system, and you must keep them there henceforth.

'You are allowed five minutes to decide whether or not you will obey these commands. If no answer has been received at the end of the calculated time the Overlord will know that you have defied him, and your entire race will perish utterly. Well he knows that your very existence is an affront to all real civilization, but he holds that even such vileness incarnate as are the Fenachrone may perchance have some obscure place in the Great Scheme of Things, and he will not destroy you if you are content to remain in your proper place, upon your own dank and steaming world. Through me, the two thousand three hundred forty-sixth Sacner Carfon of Dasor, the Overlord has given you your first, last, and only warning. Heed its every word, or consider it the formal declaration of a war of utter and complete extinction!'

The awful voice ceased and pandemonium reigned in the council hall. Obeying a common impulse each Fenachrone leaped to his feet, raised his huge arms aloft, and roared out rage and defiance. Fenor snapped a command, and the others fell silent as he began howling out orders.

'Operator! Send recall torpedoes instantly to every out-lying vessel!' He scuttled over to one of the private-band speakers. 'X-794-PW! Radio general call for all vessels above E blank E to concentrate on battle stations! Throw out full-power defensive screens, and send the full series of detector screens out to the limit! Guards and patrols on invasion plan XB-218!

'The immediate steps are taken, gentlemen!' He turned to the Council, his rage unabated. 'Never before have we supermen of the Fenachrone been so insulted and so belittled! That upstart Overlord will regret that warning to the instant of his death, which shall be exquisitely postponed. All you of the Council know your duties in such a time as this – you are excused to perform them. General Fenimol, you will stay with me – we shall consider together such other details as may require attention.'

After the others had left the room Fenor turned to the general.

'Have you any immediate suggestions?'

'I would suggest sending at once for Ravindau, the Chief of the Laboratories of Science. He certainly heard the warning, and may be able to cast some light upon how it could have been sent and from what point it came.'

The emperor spoke into another sender, and soon the scientist entered, carrying in his hand a small instrument upon which a blue light blazed.

'Do not talk here, there is grave danger of being overheard by that self-styled Overlord,' he directed tersely, and led the way into a ray-proof compartment of his private laboratory, several floors below.

'It may interest you to know that you have sealed the doom of our planet and of all the Fenachrone upon it.' Ravindau spoke savagely.

'Dare you speak thus to me, your sovereign?' roared Fenor.

'I so dare,' replied the other, coldly. 'When all the civilization of a planet has been given to destruction by the unreasoning stupidity and insatiable rapacity of its royalty, allegiance to such royalty is at an end. SIT DOWN!' he thundered as Fenor sprang to his feet. 'You are no longer in your throne-room, surrounded by servile guards and by automatic devices. You are in *my* laboratory, and by a movement of my finger I can hurl you into eternity!'

The general, aware now that the warning was of much more serious import than he had suspected, broke into the acrimonious debate.

'Never mind questions of royalty!' he snapped. 'The safety of the race is paramount. Am I to understand that the situation is really grave?'

'It is worse than grave – it is desperate. The only hope for even ultimate triumph is for as many of us as possible to flee instantly clear out of this galaxy, in the hope that we may escape the certain destruction to be dealt out to us by the Overlord of the Green System.'

'You speak folly, surely,' returned Fenimol. 'Our science is – must be – superior to any other in the universe!'

'So thought I until this warning came in and I had an opportunity to study it. Then I knew that we are opposed to a science immeasurably higher than our own.'

'Such vermin as those two whom one of our smallest scouts captured without a battle, vessel and all? In what respects is their science even comparable to ours?'

'Not those vermin, no. The one who calls himself the Overlord. That one is our master. He can penetrate the impenetrable shield of force and can operate mechanisms of pure force beyond it; he can heterodyne, transmit, and use the infra-rays of whose very existence we were in doubt until recently. While that warning was being delivered he was, in all probability, watching you and listening to you, face to face. You in your ignorance supposed his warning borne by the ether, and thought therefore he must be close to this system. He is very probably at home in the Central System, and is at this moment preparing the forces he intends to hurl against us.'

The emperor fell back into his seat, all his pomposity gone, but the general stiffened eagerly and went straight to the point.

'How do you know these things?'

'Largely by deduction. We of the school of science have cautioned you repeatedly to postpone the Day of Conquest until we should have mastered the secrets of sub-rays and of infra-rays. Unheeding, you of war have gone ahead with your plans, while we of science have continued to study. We know little of the sub-rays, which we use every day, and practically nothing of the infra-rays. Some time ago I developed a detector for infra-rays, which come to us from outer space in small quantities and which are also liberated by our power-plants. It had been regarded as a scientific curiosity only, but this day it proved of real value. This instrument in my hand is such a detector. At normal impacts of infra-rays its light is blue, as you see it now. Some time before the warning sounded it turned a brilliant red, indicating that an intense source of infra-rays was operating in the neighborhood. By plotting lines of force I located the source as being in the air of the council hall, almost directly above the table of state. Therefore the carrier wave must have come through our whole system of screens without so much as giving an alarm. That fact alone proves it to have been an infra-ray. Furthermore, it carried through those screens and released in the council room a system of force of great complexity, as is shown by their ability to broadcast from those pure forces without material aid a modulated wave in the exact frequency required to energize our general speakers.

'As soon as I perceived these facts I threw about the council room a screen of force entirely impervious to anything longer than infra-rays. The warning continued, and I then knew that our fears were only too well grounded – that there is in this galaxy somewhere a race vastly superior to ours in science and that our destruction is only a matter of hours, perhaps only of minutes.'

'Are these infra-rays, then, of such a dangerous character?' asked the general. 'I had supposed them to be of such infinitely high frequency that they would be of no practical use whatever.'

'I have been trying for years to learn something of their nature, but beyond working out a method for their detection and analysis I can do nothing with them. It is perfectly evident, however, that they lie below the level of the ether, and therefore have a velocity of propagation infinitely greater than that of light. You may see for yourself, then, that to a science able to guide and control them, to make them act as carrier waves for any other desired frequency – to do all of which the Overlord has this day shown himself capable – they afford weapons before which our every defense would be precisely as efficacious as so much vacuum. Think a moment! You know that we know nothing fundamental concerning even our servants, the sub-rays. If we really knew them we could utilize them in thousands of ways as yet unknown to us. We work with the merest handful of forces, empirically, while it is practically certain that the enemy has at his command the entire spectrum, embracing untold thousands of bands, of unknown but terrific potentiality.'

'But he spoke of a calculated time necessary before our answer could be received. They must, then, be using vibrations in the ether.'

'Not necessarily – not even probably. Would we ourselves reveal unnecessarily to an enemy the possession of such forces? Do not be childish. No, Fenimol, and you, Fenor of the Fenachrone, instant and headlong flight is our only hope of present salvation and of ultimate triumph – flight to a far-distant galaxy, since upon no point in this one shall we be safe from the infra-beams of that self-styled Overlord.'

'You snivelling coward! You pusillanimous bookworm!' Fenor had regained his customary spirit as the scientist explained upon what grounds his fears were based. 'Upon such a tenuous fabric of evidence would you have such a people as ours turn tail like beaten hounds? Because, forsooth, you detect a peculiar vibration, will you have it that we are to be invaded and destroyed forthwith by a race of supernatural ability? Bah! Your calamity-howling clan has delayed the Day of Conquest from year to year – I more than half believe that you yourself or some other treacherous poltroon of your ignominious breed prepared and sent that warning, in a weak and rat-brained attempt to frighten us into again postponing the Day of Conquest! Know now, spineless weakling, that the time is ripe, and that the Fenachrone in their might are about to strike. But you, traducer of your emperor, shall die the death of the cur you are!' The hand within his tunic moved and a vibrator burst into operation.

'Coward I may be, and pusillanimous, and other things as well,' the scientist replied stonily, 'but, unlike you, I am not a fool. These walls, this very atmosphere, are fields of force that will transmit no forces directed by you. You weak-minded scion of a depraved and obscene house – arrogant, overbearing, rapacious, ignorant – your brain is too feeble to realize that you are clutching at the universe hundreds of years before the time has come. You by your overweening pride and folly have doomed our beloved planet – the most perfect planet in the galaxy in its grateful warmth and wonderful dampness and fogginess – and our entire race to certain destruction. Therefore you, fool and dolt that you are, shall die – far too long already have you ruled.' He flicked a finger and the body of the monarch shuddered as though an intolerable current of electricity had traversed it, collapsed, and lay still.

'It was necessary to destroy this that was our ruler,' Ravindau explained to the general. 'I have long known that you are not in favor of such precipitate action in the Conquest; hence all this talking upon my part. You know that

I hold the honor of the Fenachrone dear, and that all my plans are for the ultimate triumph of our race?'

'Yes, and I begin to suspect that those plans have not been made since the warning was received.'

'My plans have been made for many years; and ever since an immediate Conquest was decided upon I have been assembling and organizing the means to put them into effect. I would have left this planet in any event shortly after the departure of the grand fleet upon its final expedition – Fenor's senseless defiance of the Overlord has only made it necessary for me to expedite my leave-taking.'

'What do you intend to do?'

'I have a vessel twice as large as the largest warship Fenor boasted; completely provisioned, armed, and powered for a cruise of one hundred years at high acceleration. It is hidden in a remote fastness of the jungle. I am placing in that vessel a group of the finest, brainiest, most highly advanced and intelligent of our men and women, with their children. We shall journey at our highest speed to a certain distant galaxy, where we shall seek out a planet similar in atmosphere, temperature, and mass to the one upon which we now dwell. There we shall multiply and continue our studies; and from that planet, on the day when we shall have attained sufficient knowledge, there shall descend upon the Central System of this galaxy the vengeance of the Fenachrone. That vengeance will be all the sweeter for the fact that it shall have been delayed.'

'But how about libraries, apparatus, and equipment? Suppose that we do not live long enough to perfect that knowledge? And with only one vessel and a handful of men we could not cope with that accursed Overlord and his navies of the void.'

'Libraries are aboard, so are much apparatus and equipment. What we cannot take with us we can build. As for the knowledge I mentioned, it may not be attained in your lifetime or in mine. But the racial memory of the Fenachrone is long, as you know; and even if the necessary problems are not solved until our descendants are sufficiently numerous to populate an entire planet, yet will those descendants wreak the vengeance of the Fenachrone upon the races of that hated one, the Overlord, before they go on with the Conquest of the Universe. Many problems will arise, of course; but they shall be solved. Enough! Time passes rapidly, and all too long have I talked. I am using this time upon you because in my organization there is no soldier, and the Fenachrone of the future will need your great knowledge of warfare. Are you going with us?'

'Yes.'

'Very well.' Ravindau led the general through a door and into an airboat lying upon the terrace outside the laboratory. 'Drive us at speed to your home, where we shall pick up your family.'

Fenimol took the controls and laid a pencil of force to his home – a beam serving a double purpose. It held the vessel upon its predetermined course through that thick and sticky fog and also rendered collision impossible, since any two of these controllers repelled each other to such a degree that no two vessels could take paths which would bring them together. Some such provision had long since been found necessary, for all Fenachrone craft were provided with the same space-annihilating drive, to which any comprehensible distance was but a journey of a few moments, and at that frightful velocity collision meant annihilation.

'I understand that you could not take one of the military into your confidence until you were ready to put your plans into effect,' the general conceded. 'How long will it take you to get ready to leave? You have said that haste is imperative, and I therefore assume that you have already warned the other numbers of the expedition.'

'I flashed the emergency signal before I joined you and Fenor in the council room. Every man of the organization has received that signal, wherever he may have been, and by this time most of them, with their families, are on the way to the hidden cruiser. We shall leave this planet in fifteen minutes from now at the most – I dare not stay an instant longer than is absolutely necessary.'

The members of the general's family were bundled, amazed, into the airboat, which immediately set out toward the secret rendezvous.

In a remote and desolate part of the planet, concealed in the depths of the towering jungle growth, a mammoth space-cruiser was receiving her complement of passengers. Airboats, flying at their terrific velocity through the heavy, steaming fog as closely-spaced as their controller rays would permit, flashed signals along their guiding beams, dove into the apparently impenetrable jungle, and added their passengers to the throng pouring into the great vessel.

As the minute of departure drew near the feeling of tension aboard the cruiser increased and vigilance was raised to the maximum. The doors were shut, no one was allowed outside, and everything was held in readiness for instant flight at the least alarm. Finally a scientist and his family arrived from the opposite side of the planet – the last members of the organization – and, twenty-seven minutes after Ravindau had flashed his signal, the prow of that mighty spaceship reared toward the perpendicular, posing its massive length at the predetermined angle. There it halted momentarily, then disappeared utterly, only a vast column of tortured and shattered vegetation, torn from the ground and carried for miles upward into the air by the vacuum of its wake, remaining to indicate the path taken by the flying projectile.

Hour after hour the Fenachrone vessel bored on, with its frightful and ever-increasing velocity, through the ever-thinning stars, but it was not until the last star had been passed, until everything before them was entirely devoid of light, and until the galaxy behind them began to take on a well-defined lenticular aspect, that Ravindau would consent to leave the controls and to seek his hard-earned rest.

Day after day and week after week went by, and the Fenachrone vessel still held the acceleration with which she had started out. Ravindau and Fenimol sat in the control cabin, staring out through the visiplates, abstracted. There was no need of staring, and they were not really looking, for there was practically nothing at which to look. The galaxy of which our Earth is an infinitesimal mote, the galaxy which former astronomers considered the universe, was so far behind that even its immense expanse had become a tiny, dull, hazy spot of light. In all directions other galaxies – spots of light so small and so dull as to be distinguished only with difficulty from the absolute black of the void – seemed equally remote. The galaxy toward which they were making their stupendous flight was as yet so distant that it could not be seen by the unaided eye. For thousands of light-years around them there was stark emptiness. No stars, no meteoric matter, not even the smallest particle of cosmic dust – absolutely empty space. Absolute vacuum: absolute zero. Absolute nothingness – a concept intrinsically impossible for the most highly trained human mind to grasp.

Conscienceless and heartless monstrosities though they both were, by heredity and training, the immensity of the appalling lack of anything tangible oppressed them. Ravindau was stern and serious, Fenimol moody. Finally the latter spoke.

'It would be endurable if we knew what had happened, or if we ever could know definitely, one way or the other, whether all this was necessary.'

'We shall know, General, definitely. I am certain in my own mind, but after a time, when we have settled upon our new home and when the Overlord shall have relaxed his vigilance, you shall come back to the solar system of the Fenachrone in this vessel or a similar one. I know what you shall find – but the trip shall be made, and you shall yourself see what was once our home planet a seething sun, second only in brilliance to the parent sun about which she shall still be revolving.'

'Are we safe, even now – what of possible pursuit?' asked Fenimol, and the monstrous, flame-shot wells of black that were Ravindau's eyes almost emitted tangible fires as he made reply:

'We are far from safe, but we grow stronger minute by minute. Fifty of the greatest minds our world has ever known have been working from the moment of our departure upon a line of investigation suggested to me by certain things my instruments recorded during the visit of the self-styled Overlord. I cannot say anything yet, even to you – except that the Day of Conquest may not be so far in the future as we have supposed.'

14

Interstellar Extermination

'I hate to leave this meeting – it's great stuff,' Seaton remarked, as he flashed down to the torpedo room when Fenor decided to recall all outlying vessels, 'but this machine isn't designed to let me be in more than two places at once. Wish it was – maybe after this fracas is over we'll be able to incorporate something like that into it.'

The Fenachrone operator touched a lever and the chair upon which he sat, with all its control panels, slid rapidly across the floor toward an apparently blank wall. As he reached it a port opened, a metal scroll appeared, containing the numbers and last reported positions of all Fenachrone vessels outside the detector zone. A vast magazine of torpedoes came up through the floor, with an automatic loader to place a torpedo under the operator's hand the instant its predecessor had been launched.

'Get Peg here quick, Mart – we need a stenographer bad. Until she gets here, see what you can do in getting those first numbers before they roll off the end of the scroll. No, hold it – as you were! I've got controls enough to put the whole thing on a recorder, so we can study it at our leisure.'

Haste was indeed necessary, for the operator worked with uncanny quickness of hand. One fleeting glance at the scroll, a lightning adjustment of dials in the torpedo, a touch upon a tiny button, and a messenger was upon its way. But quick as he was, Seaton's flying fingers kept up with him, and before each torpedo disappeared through the ether gate there was fastened upon it a fifth-order tracer that would never leave it until the force had been disconnected at the gigantic control board of the Norlaminian projector. One flying minute passed, during which seventy torpedoes had been launched, before Seaton spoke.

'Wonder how many ships they've got out, anyway? Didn't get any idea from the brain-record. Anyway, Rovol, it might be a sound idea for you to install me some tracers on this board. I've got only a couple of hundred, and that may not be enough – and I've got both hands full.'

Rovol seated himself beside the younger man, like one organist joining another at the console of a tremendous organ. Seaton's nimble fingers would flash here and there, depressing keys and manipulating controls until he had exactly the required combination of forces centered upon the torpedo next to issue. He then would press a tiny switch and upon a panel full of red-topped, numbered plungers the one next in series would drive home, transferring to itself the assembled beam and releasing the keys for the assembly of other forces. Rovol's fingers were also flying, but the forces he directed were seizing and shaping materials, as well as other forces. The Norlaminian physicist set up one integral, stepped upon a pedal, and a new red-topped stop precisely like the others, and numbered in order, appeared as though by magic upon the panel at Seaton's left hand. Rovol then leaned back in his seat – but the red-topped stops continued to appear, at the rate of exactly seventy per minute, upon the panel, which increased in width sufficiently to accommodate another row as soon as a row was completed.

Rovol bent a quizzical glance upon the younger scientist, who blushed a fiery red, rapidly set up another integral, then also leaned back in his place, while his face burned deeper than before.

'That is better, son. Never forget that it is a waste of energy to do the same thing twice, and that if you know precisely what is to be done, you need not do it personally at all. Forces are faster than human hands, they are tireless, and they neither slip nor make mistakes.'

'Thanks, Rovol – I'll bet this lesson will make it stick in my mind, too.'

'You are not thoroughly accustomed to using all your knowledges as yet. That will come with practice, however, and in a few weeks you will be as thoroughly at home with forces as I am.'

'Hope so, chief, but it looks like a tall order to me.'

Finally the last torpedo was despatched. The tube closed. Seaton moved the projection back up into the council chamber, finding it empty.

'Well, the conference is over – besides, we've got more important fish to fry. War has been declared, on both sides, and we've got to get busy. They've got nine hundred and six vessels out, and every one of them has got to go to Davy Jones's locker before we can sleep sound of nights. My first job'll have to be untangling those nine oh six forces, getting lines on each one of them, and seeing if I can project straight enough to find the ships before the torpedoes overtake them. Mart, you and Orlon, our astronomers, had better figure out the last reported positions of each of those vessels, so we'll know about where to hunt for them, Rovol, you might send out a detector screen a few light-years in diameter, to be sure none of them slip a fast one over on us. By starting it right here and expanding it gradually, you can be sure that no Fenachrone is inside it. Then we'll find a hunk of copper on that planet somewhere, plate it with some of their own X metal, and blow them into Kingdom Come.'

'May I venture a suggestion?' asked Drasnik, the First of Psychology.

'Absolutely – nothing you've said so far has been idle chatter.'

'You know, of course, that there are real scientists among the Fenachrone; and you yourself have suggested that while they cannot penetrate the zone of force nor use fifth-order rays, yet they might know about them in theory, might even be able to know when they were being used – detect them in other words. Let us assume that such a scientist did detect your forces while you were there a short time ago. What should he do?'

'Search me ... What would he do?'

'He might do any one of several things, but if I read their nature aright, such a one would gather up a few men and women – as many as he could – and migrate to another planet. For he would of course grasp instantly the fact that you had used fifth-order rays as carrier waves, and would be able to deduce your ability to destroy. He would also realize that in the brief time allowed him, he could not hope to learn to control those unknown forces; and with his terribly savage and vengeful nature and intense pride of race, he would take every possible step both to perpetuate his race and to obtain revenge. Am I right?'

Seaton swung his controls savagely, and manipulated dials and keys.

'Right as rain, Drasnik. There – I've thrown a fifth-order detector screen, that they can't possibly neutralize, around them. Anything that goes out through it will have a tracer slapped onto it. But say, it's been half an hour or so since war was declared – suppose we're too late? Maybe some of 'em have got away already, and if one couple escapes we'll have the whole thing to do over again a thousand years or so from now. You've got the massive intellect, Drasnik. What can we do about it? We can't throw a detector screen around the whole galaxy.'

'I would suggest that since you have now guarded against further exodus, it is not necessary to destroy the planet for a time. Rovol and his co-workers have the other projector nearly done. Let them project me to the world of the Fenachrone, where I shall conduct a thorough mental investigation. By the time you have taken care of the raiding vessels, I believe that I shall have learned everything we need to know.'

'Fine – hop to it, and may there be lots of bubbles in your think-tank. Anybody else know of any other loop-holes I've left open?'

No other suggestions were made, and each man bent to his particular task. Crane at the star-chart of the galaxy and Orlon at the Fenachrone operator's despatching scroll rapidly worked out the approximate positions of the Fenachrone vessels, and marked them with tiny green lights in a vast model of the galaxy which they had already caused forces to erect in the air of the projector's base. It was soon learned that a few of the ships were exploring quite close to their home system; so close that the torpedoes, with their unthinkable acceleration, would reach them within a few hours.

Ascertaining the stop-number of the tracer upon the torpedo which should first reach its destination, Seaton followed it from his panel out to the flying messenger. Now moving with a velocity many times that of light, it of course was invisible to direct vision; but to the light waves heterodyned upon the fifth-order forces it was as plainly visible as though it were stationary.

Lining up the path of the projectile accurately, he then projected himself forward in that exact line, with a flat detector-screen thrown out for half a light-year upon each side of him. Setting the controls, he flashed ahead, the detector stopping him instantaneously upon encountering the power plant of the exploring raider. An oscillator sounded a shrill and rising note, and Seaton slowly shifted his controls until he stood in the control room of the enemy vessel.

The Fenachrone ship, a thousand feet long and more than a hundred feet in diameter, was tearing through space toward a brilliant blue-white star. Her crew were at battle stations, her navigating officers peering intently into the operating visiplates, all oblivious to the fact that a stranger stood in their very midst.

'Well, here's the first one. I hate like the devil to do this – it's altogether too much like pushing baby chickens into a creek – but it's a dirty job that's got to be done.'

As one man, Orlon and the other remaining Norlaminians leaped out of the projector and floated to the ground below.

'I expected that,' Seaton said. 'They can't even think of a thing like this without getting the blue willies – I don't blame them much, at that. How about you, Carfon? You can be excused if you like.'

'I want to watch those forces at work. I do not enjoy destruction, but like you, I can make myself endure it.'

Dunark, the fierce and bloodthirsty Osnomian prince, leaped to his feet, his eyes flashing.

'That's one thing I never could get about you, Dick!' he exclaimed in English. 'How a man with your brains can be so soft – so sloppily sentimental, gets clear past me. You remind me of a bowl of mush – you wade around in slush clear to your ears. Faugh! It's their lives or ours! Tell me what button to push and I'll be only too glad to push it. Cut out the sob-sister act and for Cat's sake, let's get busy!'

''At-a-boy, Dunark! That's tellin' 'em! But it's all right with me – I'll be glad to let you do it. When I say "shoot" throw in that plunger there – number sixty-three.'

Seaton manipulated controls until two electrodes of force were clamped in place, one at either end of the huge power-bar of the enemy vessel; adjusted rheostats and forces to send a disintegrating current through that massive copper cylinder, and gave the word. Dunark threw in the switch viciously, as though it were an actual sword which he was thrusting through the vitals of one of the hideous crew, and the very universe exploded around them – exploded into one mad, searing coruscation of blinding, dazzling light as the gigantic cylinder of copper resolved itself instantaneously into the pure energy from which its metal originally had come into being.

Seaton and Dunark staggered back from the visiplates, blinded by the intolerable glare of light, and even Crane, working at his model of the galaxy, blinked at the intensity of the radiation. Many minutes passed before the two men could see through their tortured eyes.

'Zowie! That was fierce!' exclaimed Seaton, when a slowly-returning perception of things other than dizzy spirals and balls of flame assured him that his eyesight was not permanently gone. 'It's nothing but my own fool carelessness, too. I should've known that with the visible spectrum in heterodyne, for visibility, enough of that stuff would leak through to raise hell on our plates – that bar weighed a hundred tons and would liberate energy enough to blow a planet from here to Arcturus. How're you coming, Dunark? See anything yet?'

'Coming along O.K. now, I guess – but for a couple of minutes it had me guessing.'

'I'll do better next time. I'll cut out the visible before the flash, and convert and reconvert the infra-red. That'll let us see what happens, without any direct effect. What's my force number on the next nearest one, Mart?'

'Twenty-nine.'

Seaton fastened a detector ray upon stop twenty-nine of the tracer-beam panel and followed its pencil of force out to the torpedo hastening upon its way toward the next doomed cruiser. Flashing ahead in its line as he had done before, he located the vessel and clamped the electrodes of force upon the prodigious driving bar. Again, as Dunark drove home the detonating switch, there was a frightful explosion and a wild glare of frenzied incandescence far out in that desolate region of interstellar space; but this time the eyes behind the visiplates were not torn by the high frequencies and everything that happened was plainly visible. One instant, there was an immense space-cruiser boring on through the void upon its horrid mission, with its full complement of the hellish Fenachrone performing their routine tasks. The next instant there was a flash of light extending for thousands upon untold thousands of miles in every direction. That flare of light vanished as rapidly as it had appeared – instantaneously – and throughout the entire neighborhood of the place where the Fenachrone cruiser had been, there was nothing. Not a plate nor a girder, not a fragment, not the most minute particle nor droplet of disrupted metal nor of condensed vapor. So terrific, so incredibly and incomprehensibly vast were the forces liberated by that mass of copper in its instantaneous decomposition that every atom of substance in that great vessel had gone with the power-bar – had been resolved into radiations which would at some distant time and in some far-off solitude unite with other radiations, again to form matter and thus obey Nature's immutable cyclic law.

Vessel after vessel was destroyed of that haughty fleet which until now had never suffered a reverse, and a little green light in the galactic model winked out and flashed back in rosy pink as each menace was removed. In a few hours the space surrounding the system of the Fenachrone was clear; then progress slackened as it became harder and harder to locate each vessel as the distance between it and its torpedo increased. Time after time Seaton would stab forward with his detector screen extended to its utmost possible spread, upon the most carefully plotted prolongation of the line of the torpedo's flight, only to have the projection flash far beyond the vessel's farthest possible position without a reaction from the far-flung screen. Then he would go back to the torpedo, make a minute alteration in his line, and again flash forward, only to miss it again. Finally, after thirty fruitless attempts to bring his detector screen into contact with the nearest Fenachrone ship, he gave up the attempt, rammed his battered, reeking briar full of the rank blend that was his favorite smoke, and strode up and down the floor of the projector base – his eyes unseeing, his hands jammed deep into his pockets, his jaw thrust forward, clamped upon the stem of his pipe, emitting dense, blue clouds of strangling vapor.

'The young maestro is thinking, I perceive,' remarked Dorothy sweetly, entering the projector from an airboat. 'You must all be blind, I guess – you no hear the bell blow, what? I've come after you – it's time to eat!'

''At-a-girl, Dot – never miss the eats! Thanks,' and Seaton with a visible effort, put his problem away.

'This is going to be a job, Mart,' he went back to it as soon as they were seated in the airboat, flying toward 'home'. 'I can nail them, with an increasing shift in azimuth, up to about thirty thousand light-years, but after that it gets awfully hard to get the right shift, and up around a hundred thousand it seems to be impossible – gets to be pure guesswork. It can't be the controls, because they can hold a point rigidly at five hundred thousand. Of course, we've got a pretty short back-line to sight on, but the shift is more than a hundred times as great as the possible error in my back-sight could account for, and there's apparently nothing either regular or systematic about it that I can figure out. But ... I don't know ... Space is curved in the fourth dimension, of course ... I wonder if ... hm ... m ... m.' He fell silent and Crane made a rapid signal to Dorothy, who was opening her mouth to say something. She shut it, feeling ridiculous, and nothing was said until they had disembarked at their destination.

'Did you solve the puzzle, Dickie?'

'Don't think so – got myself in deeper than ever, I'm afraid,' he answered, then went on, thinking aloud rather than addressing anyone in particular.

'Space is curved in the fourth dimension, and fifth-order tracers, with their velocity, may not follow the same path in that dimension that light does – in fact, they do not. If that path is to be plotted it requires the solution of five simultaneous equations, each complete and general, and each of the fifth degree, and also an exponential series with the unknown in the final exponent, before the fourth-dimensional concept can be derived … hm … m … m. No use – we've struck something not even Norlaminian theory can handle.'

'You surprise me,' Crane said. 'I supposed that they had everything worked out.'

'Not on fifth-order stuff. It begins to look as though we'd have to stick around until every one of those torpedoes gets somewhere near its mothership. Hate to do it, too – it'll take a long time to reach the vessels clear across the galaxy. I'll put it up to the gang at dinner – guess they'll let me talk business a couple of minutes overtime, especially after they find out what I've got to say.'

He explained the phenomenon to an interested group of white-haired scientists as they ate. Rovol, to Seaton's surprise, was elated and enthusiastic.

'Wonderful, my boy!' he breathed. 'Marvelous! A perfect subject for year after year of deepest study and the most profound thought. Perfect!'

'But what can we *do* about it?' Seaton demanded. 'We don't want to hang around here twiddling our thumbs for a year waiting for those torpedoes to get to wherever they're going!'

'We can do nothing but wait and study. That problem is one of splendid difficulty, as you yourself realize. Its solution may well be a matter of lifetimes instead of years. But what is a year more or less? You can destroy the Fenachrone eventually, so be content.'

'But content is just exactly what I *ain't!*' declared Seaton, emphatically. 'I want to do it, and do it *now!*'

'Perhaps I might volunteer a suggestion,' said Caslor, diffidently; and as both Rovol and Seaton looked at him in surprise he went on: 'Do not misunderstand me. I do not mean concerning the mathematical problem in discussion, about which I am entirely ignorant. But has it occurred to you that those torpedoes are not intelligent entities, acting upon their own volition and steering themselves as a result of their own ordered mental processes? No, they are mechanisms, in my own province, and I venture to say with the utmost confidence that they are guided to their destinations by streamers of force of some nature, emanating from the vessels upon whose tracks they are.'

'"Nobody Holme" is right!' exclaimed Seaton, tapping his temple with an admonitory forefinger. ''Sright, ace – I thought maybe I'd quit using my head for nothing but a hat rack now, but I guess that's all it's good for, yet. Thanks a lot for the idea – that gives me something I can get my teeth into, and now that Rovol's got a problem to work on for the next century or so, everybody's happy.'

'How does that help matters?' asked Crane. 'Of course it is not surprising that no lines of force were visible, but I thought that your detector screens would have found them if any such guiding beams had been present.'

'The ordinary bands, if of sufficient power, yes. But there are many possible tracer rays not reactive to a screen such as I was using. It was very light and weak, designed for terrific velocity and for instantaneous automatic arrest when in contact with the enormous forces of a power-bar. It wouldn't react at all to the minute energy of the kind of beams they'd be most likely to use for that work. Caslor's certainly right. They're steering their torpedoes with tracer beams of almost infinitesimal power, amplified in the torpedoes themselves – that's the way I'd do it myself. It may take a little while to rig up the apparatus, but we'll get it and then we'll run those birds ragged. We won't need the fourth-dimensional correction after all.'

When the bell announced the beginning of the following period of labor, Seaton and his co-workers were in the Area of Experiment waiting, and the work was soon under way.

'How are you going about this, Dick?' Crane asked.

'Going to examine the nose of one of those torpedoes first, and see what it actually works on. Then build a tracer detector that'll pick it up at high velocity. Beats the band, don't it, that neither Rovol nor I, who should have thought of it first, never did see anything as plain as that? That those things are following a lead?'

'That is easily explained. Both of you were not only devoting all your thoughts to the curvature of space, but were also too close to the problem – like the man in the woods, who cannot see the forest because of the trees.'

'Probably. It was plain enough, though, when Caslor showed it to us.'

While he was talking Seaton had projected himself into the torpedo he had lined up so many times the previous day. With the automatic motions set to hold him stationary in the tiny instrument compartment of the craft, now traveling at a velocity many thousands of times that of light, he set to work. A glance located the detector mechanism, a set of short-wave coils and amplifiers, and a brief study made plain to him the principles underlying the directional loop finders and the controls which guided the flying shell along the path of the tracer. He then built a detector structure of pure force immediately in front of the torpedo, and varied the frequency of his own apparatus until a meter upon one of the panels before his eyes informed him that his detector was in perfect resonance with the frequency of the tracer. He then moved ahead of the torpedo, along the guiding pencil of force.

'Getting it, eh?' Dunark congratulated him.

'After a fashion. My directors out there ain't so hot, though. I'm shy on control somewhere, so much so that if I put on anywhere near full velocity I lose the track. Think I can clear that up with a little experimenting, though.'

He fingered controls lightly, depressing a few more keys, and set one vernier, already at a ratio of a million to one, down to ten million. He then stepped up his velocity, and found that the guides worked well up to a speed much greater than any ever reached by the Fenachrone vessels or torpedoes, but failed utterly to hold at anything approaching the full velocity possible to his fifth-order projector. After hours and days of work and study – in the course of which hundreds of the Fenachrone vessels were destroyed – after employing all the resources of his mind, now stored with the knowledge accumulated by hundreds of generations of highly-trained research specialists in vibrations, he became convinced that it was an inherent impossibility to trace any ether wave with the velocity he desired.

'Can't be done, I guess, Mart,' he confessed, ruefully. 'You see, it works fine up to a certain point; but beyond that, nothing doing. I've just found out why – and in so doing, I think I've made a contribution to science. At velocities well below that of light, light-waves are shifted a minute amount, you know. At the velocity of light, and up to a velocity not even approached by the Fenachrone vessels on their longest trips, the distortion is still not serious – no matter how fast we want to travel in the *Skylark* I can guarantee that we will still be able to see things. That is to be expected from the generally-accepted idea that the apparent velocity of any ether vibration is independent of the velocity of either source or receiver. However, that relationship fails at velocities far below that of fifth-order propagation. At only a very small fraction of that speed the tracers I am following are so badly distorted that they disappear altogether, and I have to distort them backwards. That wouldn't be too bad, but when I get up to about one percent of the velocity I want to use I can't calculate a force that will operate to distort them back into recognizable wave-forms. That's another problem for Rovol to chew on, for another hundred years.'

'That will, of course, slow up the work of clearing the galaxy of the Fenachrone, but at the same time I see nothing about which to be alarmed,' Crane replied. 'You are working very much faster than you could have done by waiting for the torpedoes to arrive. The present condition is very satisfactory, I should say,' and he waved his hand at the galactic model, in nearly three-fourths of whose volume the green lights had been replaced by pink ones.

'Yeah, pretty fair as far as that goes – we'll clean up in ten days or so – but I hate to be licked. However, I might as well quit sobbing and get to work.'

In due time the nine hundred and sixth Fenachrone vessel was checked off on the model, and the two Tellurians went in search of Drasnik, whom they found in his study, summing up and analyzing a mass of data, facts, and ideas which were being projected in the air around him.

'Well, our first job's done,' Seaton stated. 'Did you find out anything that you feel like passing around?'

'My investigation is practically complete,' replied the First of Psychology, gravely. 'I have explored many Fenachrone minds, and without exception I have found them chambers of horror of a kind unimaginable to one of us. However, you are not interested in their psychology, but in facts bearing upon your problem. While such facts were scarce, I did discover a few interesting items. I spied upon them in public and in their most private haunts. I analyzed them individually and collectively, and from the few known facts and from the great deal of guesswork and conjecture there available to me I have formulated a theory. I shall first give you the known facts. Their scientists cannot direct nor control any ray not propagated through the ether, but they can detect one such frequency or band of frequencies which they call "infra-rays" and which are probably the fifth-order rays, since they lie in the first level below the ether. The detector proper is a type of lamp, which gives a blue light at the ordinary intensity of such rays as received from space or an ordinary power plant, but gives a red light under stronger excitation.'

'Uh-huh, I get that O.K. Rovol's great-great-great grandfather had 'em – I know all about them,' Seaton encouraged Drasnik, who had paused, with a questioning glance. 'I know exactly how and why such a detector works. We gave 'em an alarm, all right. Even though we were working on a tight beam from here to there, our secondary projector there was radiating enough to affect every such detector within a million miles.'

'Another significant fact is that a great many persons – I learned of some five hundred, and there were probably many more – have disappeared without explanation and without leaving a trace; and it seems that they disappeared very shortly after our communication was delivered. One of these was Fenor, the Emperor. His family remain, however, and his son is not only ruling in his stead, but is carrying out his father's policies. The other disappearances are all alike and are peculiar in certain respects. First, every man who vanished belonged to the Party of Postponement – the minority party of the Fenachrone, who believe that the time for the Conquest has not yet come. Second, every one of them was a leader of thought in some field of usefulness, and every such field is represented by at least one disappearance – even the army, as General Fenimol, the Commander-in-Chief, and his whole family, are among the absentees. Third, and most remarkable, each such disappearance included an entire family, clear down to children and grandchildren, however young. Another fact is that the Fenachrone Department of Navigation keeps a very close check upon all vessels, particularly vessels capable of navigating outer space. Every vessel built must be registered, and its location is always known from its individual tracer. No Fenachrone vessel is missing.

'I also sifted a mass of gossip and conjecture, some of which may bear upon the subject. One belief is that all the persons were put to death by

Fénor's secret service, and that the Emperor was assassinated in revenge. The most widespread belief, however, is that they have fled. Some hold that they are in hiding in some remote shelter in the jungle, arguing that the rigid registration of all vessels renders a journey of any great length impossible and that the detector screens would have given warning of any vessel leaving the planet. Others think that persons as powerful as Fenimol and Ravindau could have built any vessel they chose with neither the knowledge nor consent of the Department of Navigation; or that they could have stolen a Navy vessel, destroying its records; and that Ravindau certainly could have so neutralized the screens that they would have given no alarm. These believe that the absent ones have migrated to some other solar system or to some other planet of the same sun. One old general loudly gave it as his opinion that the cowardly traitors had probably fled clear out of the galaxy, and that it would be a good thing to send the rest of the Party of Postponement after them. There, in brief, are the salient points of my investigation insofar as it concerns your immediate problem.'

'A good many straws pointing this way and that,' Seaton commented. However, we know that the "postponers" are just as rabid on the idea of conquering the universe as the others are, only they are a lot more cautious and won't take even a gambler's chance of defeat. But you've formed a theory – what is it?'

'From my analysis of these facts and conjectures, in conjunction with certain purely psychological indices which we need not take time to go into now, I am certain that they have left their solar system, probably in an immense vessel built a long time ago and held in readiness for just such an emergency. I am not certain of their destination, but it is my opinion that they left this galaxy, and are planning upon starting anew upon some suitable planet in some other galaxy, from which, at some future date, the conquest of the universe shall proceed as it was originally planned.'

'Great balls of fire!' blurted Seaton. 'They couldn't – not in a million years!' He thought a moment, then continued more slowly: 'But they could – and, with their dispositions, they probably would. You're one hundred percent right, Drasnik. We've got a real job of hunting on our hands now. So long, and thanks a lot.'

Back in the projector Seaton prowled about in brown abstraction, his villainous pipe poisoning the circumambient air, while Crane sat, quiet and self-possessed as always, waiting for the nimble brain of his friend to find a way over, around, or through the obstacle confronting them.

'Got it, Mart!' Seaton yelled, darting to the board and setting up one integral after another. 'If they did leave the planet in a ship, we'll be able to watch them go – and we'll see what they did, anyway, no matter what it was!'

'How? They've been gone almost a month already,' protested Crane.

'We know within half an hour the exact time of their departure. We'll simply go out the distance light has traveled since that time, gather in the rays given off, amplify them a few billion times, and take a look at whatever went on.'

'But we have no idea of what region of the planet to study, or whether it was night or day at the point of departure when they left.'

'We'll get the council room, and trace events from there. Day or night makes no difference – we'll have to use infra-red anyway, because of the fog, and that's as good at night as in the daytime. There is no such thing as absolute darkness upon any planet, anyway, and we've got power enough to make anything visible that happened there, night or day. Mart, I've got power. enough here to see and to photograph the actual construction of the pyramids of Egypt in that same way – and they were built thousands of years ago!'

'Heavens, what astounding possibilities!' breathed Crane. 'Why, you could—'

'Yeah, I could do a lot of things,' Seaton interrupted him rudely, 'but right now we've got other fish to fry. I've just got the city we visited, at about the time we were there. General Fenimol, who disappeared, must be in the council room down there right now. I'll retard our projection, so that time will apparently pass quicker, and we'll duck down there and see what actually did happen. I can heterodyne, combine, and recombine just as though we were watching the actual scene – it's more complicated, of course, since I have to follow it and amplify it too, but it works out all right.'

'This is unbelievable, Dick. Think of actually seeing something that actually happened in the past!'

'Yeah, it's pretty stiff stuff. As Dot would say, it's just too perfectly darn outrageous. But we're doing it, ain't we? I know just how, and why. When we get some time I'll shoot the method into your brain. Here we are!'

Peering into the visiplates, the two men were poised above the immense central cone of the capital city of the Fenachrone. Viewing with infra-red light as they were, the fog presented no obstacle and the indescribable beauty of the city of concentric rings and the wonderfully luxuriant jungle growth were clearly visible. They plunged down into the council chamber, and saw Fenor, Ravindau, and Fenimol deep in conversation.

'With all the other feats of skill and sorcery you have accomplished, why don't you reconstruct their speech, also?' asked Crane, with a challenging glance.

'Well, old Doubting Thomas, it might not be absolutely impossible, at that. It would mean two projectors, however, due to the difference in speed of sound-waves and light-waves. Theoretically, sound-waves also continue indefinitely in air, but I don't believe that any possible detector and amplifier could reconstruct a voice more than an hour or so after it had spoken. It might though – we'll have to try it sometime, and see. You're fairly good at lip-reading, as I remember it. Get as much of it as you can, will you?'

As though they were watching the scene itself as it happened – which, in a sense, they were – they saw everything that had occurred. They saw Fenor die, saw the general's family board the airboat, saw the orderly embarkation of Ravindau's organization. Finally they saw the stupendous take-off of the first inter-galactic cruiser, and with that take-off Seaton went into action. Faster and faster he drove that fifth-order beam along the track of the fugitive, until a speed was attained beyond which his detecting converters could not hold the ether-rays they were following. For many minutes Seaton stared intently into the visiplate, plotting lines and calculating forces, then he swung around to Crane.

'Well, Mart, noble old bean, solving the disappearances was easier than I thought it would be; but the situation as regards wiping out the last of the Fenachrone is getting no better, fast.'

'I glean from the instruments that they are heading straight out into space away from the galaxy, and I assume that they are using their utmost acceleration?'

'It looks that way. They're out in absolute space, you know, with nothing in the way and with no intention of reversing their power or slowing down – they must've had absolute top acceleration on every minute since they left. Anyway, they're so far out already that I couldn't hold even a detector on them, let alone a force that I can control. Well, let's snap into it, fellow – on our way!'

'Just a minute, Dick. Take it easy. What are your plans?'

'Plans – hell! Why worry about plans? Blow up that planet before any more of 'em get away, and then chase 'em – chase 'em clear to Andromeda if necessary. Let's go!'

'Calm down and be reasonable – you are getting hysterical again. They have a maximum acceleration of five times the velocity of light. So have we, exactly, since we adopted their own drive. Now if our acceleration is the same as theirs, and they have a month's start, how long will it take us to catch them?'

'Right again, Mart – I was going off half-cocked again,' Seaton conceded ruefully, after a moment's thought. 'They'd always be going a million or so times as fast as we would be, and getting further ahead of us in geometrical ratio. What's your idea?'

'I agree with you that the time has come to destroy their planet. As for pursuing that vessel through inter-galactic space, that is your problem. You must figure out some method of increasing our acceleration. Highly efficient as is this system of propulsion, it seems to me that the knowledge of the

Norlaminians should be able to improve it in some detail. Even a slight increase in acceleration would enable us to overtake them eventually.'

'Hm … m … m.' Seaton, no longer impetuous, was thinking deeply. 'How far are we apt to have to go?'

'Until we get close enough to them to use your projector – say half a million light-years.'

'But surely they'll stop, sometime?'

'Of course, but not necessarily for many years. They are powered and provisioned for a hundred years, you remember, and are going to "a distant galaxy". Such a one as Ravindau would not have specified a *"distant"* galaxy idly, and the very closest galaxies are distant indeed.'

'But our astronomers believe … or are they wrong?'

'Their estimates are, without exception, far below the true values. They are scarcely of the correct order of magnitude.'

'Well, then, let's mop up on that planet and get going.'

Seaton had already located the magazines in which the power-bars of the Fenachrone war-vessels were stored, and it was a short task to erect a secondary projector of force in the Fenachrone atmosphere. Working out of that projector, beams of force seized one of the immense cylinders of plated copper and at Seaton's direction transported it rapidly to one of the poles of the planet, where electrodes of force were clamped upon it. In a similar fashion seventeen more of the frightful bombs were placed, equal-distant over the surface of the world of the Fenachrone, so that when they were simultaneously exploded the downward forces would be certain to meet sufficient resistance to secure complete demolition of the entire globe. Everything in readiness, Seaton's hand went to the plunger switch and closed upon it. Then, his face white and wet, he dropped his hand.

'No use, Mart – I can't do it. It pulls my cork. I know that you can't either – I'll yell for help.'

'Have you got it on the infra-red?' asked Dunark calmly, as he shot up into the projector in reply to Seaton's call. 'I want to see this, all of it.'

'It's on – you're welcome to it,' and, as the Terrestrials turned away, the whole projector base was illuminated by a flare of intense, though subdued light. For several minutes Dunark stared into the visiplate, savage satisfaction in every line of his fierce green face as he surveyed the havoc wrought by those eighteen enormous charges of incredible explosive.

'A nice job of clean-up, Dick,' the Osnomian prince reported, turning away from the visiplate. 'It made a sun of it – the original sun is now quite a splendid double star. Everything was volatilized, clear out, far beyond their outermost screen.'

'It had to be done, of course – it was either them or else all the rest of the universe,' Seaton said, jerkily. 'However, even that fact doesn't make it go down easy. Well, we're done with this projector. From now on it's strictly up to us and *Skylark Three*. Let's beat it over there and see if they've got her done yet – they were due to finish up today, you know.'

It was a silent group who embarked in the little airboat. Halfway to their destination, however, Seaton came out of his blue mood with a yell.

'Mart, I've got it! We can give the *Lark* a lot more acceleration than they are getting – and won't need the assistance of all the minds of Norlamin, either.'

'How?'

'By using one of the very heavy metals for fuel. The intensity of the power liberated is a function of atomic weight, atomic number, and density; but the fact of liberation depends upon atomic configuration – a fact which you and I figured out long ago. However, our figuring didn't go far enough – it couldn't we didn't know anything then. Copper happens to be the most efficient of the few metals which can be decomposed at all under ordinary excitation. But by using special exciters, sending out all the orders of force necessary to initiate the disruptive processes, we can use any metal we want to. Osnome has unlimited quantities of the heaviest metals, including radium and uranium. Of course we can't use radium and live – but we can and will use uranium, and that will give us something like four times the acceleration possible with copper. Dunark, what say you snap over there and smelt us a cubic mile of uranium? No – hold it – I'll put a flock of forces on the job. They'll do it quicker, and I'll make 'em deliver the goods. They'll deliver 'em fast, too, believe me – we'll see to that with a ten-ton bar. The uranium bars'll be ready to load tomorrow, and we'll have enough power to chase those birds all the rest of our lives!'

Returning to the projector, Seaton actuated the complex system of forces required for the smelting and transportation of the enormous amount of metal necessary, and as the three men again boarded their aerial conveyance the power-bar in the projector behind them flared into violet incandescence under the load already put upon it by the new uranium mine in distant Osnome.

The *Skylark* lay stretched out over two miles of country, exactly as they had last seen her, but now, instead of being water-white, the ten-thousand-foot cruiser of the void was one joint-less, seamless structure of sparkling, transparent, purple inoson. Entering one of the open doors they stepped into an elevator and were whisked upward into the control room, in which a dozen of the aged, white-bearded students of Norlamin were grouped about a banked and tiered mass of keyboards which Seaton knew must be the operating mechanism of the extraordinarily complete fifth-order projector he had been promised. 'Ah, youngsters, you are just in time. Everything is complete, and we are just about to begin loading.'

'Sorry, Rovol, but we'll have to make a couple of changes – have to rebuild the exciter or build another one,' and Seaton rapidly related what they had learned, and what they had decided to do.

'Of course, uranium is a much more efficient source of power,' agreed Rovol, 'and you are to be congratulated for thinking of it. It perhaps would not have occurred to one of us, since the heavy metals of that highly efficient group are very rare here. Building a new exciter for uranium is a simple task, and the converters for the corona-loss will of course require no change, since their action depends only upon the frequency of the emitted losses, not upon their magnitude.'

'Hadn't you suspected that some of the Fenachrone might be going to lead us a life-long chase?' asked Dunark seriously.

'We have not given the matter a thought, my son,' the Chief of the Five made answer. 'As your years increase, you will learn not to anticipate trouble and worry. Had we thought and worried over the matter before the time had arrived, you will note that it would have been pain wasted, for our young friend Seaton has avoided that difficulty in a truly scholarly fashion.'

'All set, then, Rovol?' asked Seaton, when the forces flying from the projector had built the compound exciter which would make possible the disruption of the atoms of uranium. 'The metal, enough of it to fill all the spare space in the hull, will be here tomorrow. You might give Crane and me the method of operating this projector, which I see is vastly more complex even than the one in the Area of Experiment.'

'It is the most complete thing ever seen upon Norlamin,' replied Rovol with a smile. 'Each of us installed everything in it that he could conceive of ever being of the slightest use, and since our combined knowledge covers a large field, the projector is accordingly quite comprehensive.'

Multiple headsets were donned, and from each of the Norlaminian brains there poured into the minds of the two Terrestrials a complete and minute knowledge of every possible application of the stupendous force-control banked in all its massed intricacy before them.

'Well, that's SOME outfit!' exulted Seaton in pleased astonishment as the instructions were concluded. 'It can do anything but lay an egg – and I'm not a darn bit sure that we couldn't make it do that! Well, let's call the girls and show them around – this ship is going to be their home for quite a while.'

While they were waiting Dunark led Seaton aside.

'Dick, will you need me on this trip?' he asked. 'Of course I knew that there was something on your mind when you didn't send me home when you let Urvan, Carfon, and the others go back.'

'No, we're going it alone – unless you want to come along. I did want you to stick around until I got a good chance to talk to you alone – now will be as good a time as any. You and I have traded brains, and besides, we've been through quite a lot of grief together, here and there – I want to apologize to you for not passing along to you all this stuff I've been getting here. In fact, I really wish I didn't have to have it myself. Get me?'

'Get you? I'm way ahead of you! Don't want it, nor any part of it – that's why I've stayed away from any chance of learning any of it, and the one reason why I am going back home instead of going with you. I have just brains enough to realize that neither I nor any other man of my race should have it. By the time we grow up to it naturally we may be able to handle it, but not until then.'

The two brain brothers grasped hands strongly, and Dunark continued in a lighter vein: 'It takes all kinds of people to make a world, you know – and all kinds of races, except the Fenachrone, to make a universe. With Mardonale gone, the evolution of Osnome shall progress rapidly, and while we may not reach the Ultimate Goal, I have learned enough from you already to speed up our progress considerably.'

'I was sure you'd understand, but I had to get it off my chest. Here're the girls – Sitar too. We'll show 'em around.'

Seaton's first thought was for the very brain of the ship – the precious lens of neutronium in its thin envelope of the eternal jewel – without which the beam of fifth-order rays could not be directed. He found it a quarter-mile back from the needle-sharp prow, exactly in the longitudinal axis of the hull, protected from any possible damage by bulkhead after bulkhead of impregnable inoson. Satisfied upon that point, he went in search of the others, who were exploring their vast new spaceship.

Huge as she was, there was no waste space – her design was as compact as that of a fine watch. The living quarters were grouped closely about the central compartment, which housed the power plants, the many generators and projectors, and the myriads of controls of the mechanisms for the projection and handling of fifth-order forces. Several large compartments were devoted to the machinery which automatically serviced the vessel – refrigerators, heaters, generators and purifiers for water and air, and the numberless other mechanisms which would make of the cruiser a comfortable and secure home, as well as an invincible battleship, in the heatless, lightless, airless, matterless waste of inter-galactic space. Many compartments were for the storage of food supplies, and these were even then being filled by forces under the able direction of the First of Chemistry.

'All the comforts of home, even to the labels,' Seaton grinned, as he read 'Dole #1' upon cans of pineapple which had never been within thousands of light-years of the Hawaiian Islands, and saw quarter after quarter of fresh meat going into the freezer room from a planet upon which no animals other than man had existed for many thousands of years. Nearly all of the remaining millions of cubic feet of space were for the storage of uranium for power, a few rooms already having been filled with ingot inoson for repairs. Between the many bulkheads that divided the ship into numberless airtight sections, and between the many concentric skins of purple metal that rendered the vessel space-worthy and sound, even though slabs hundreds of feet thick were to be shorn off in any direction – in every nook and cranny could be stored the metal to keep those voracious generators full-fed, no matter how long or how severe the demand for power. Every room was connected through a series of tubular tunnels, along which force-propelled cars or elevators slid smoothly – tubes whose walls fell together into air-tight seals at any point, in case of a rupture.

As they made their way back to the great control room of the vessel, they saw something that because of its small size they had not previously seen. Below that room, not too near the outer skin, in a specially-built spherical launching space, there was *Skylark Two*, completely equipped and ready for an interstellar journey on her own account!

'Why, hello, little stranger!' Margaret called. 'Rovol, that was a kind thought on your part. Home wouldn't quite be home without our old *Skylark*, would it, Martin?'

'A practical thought, as well as a kind one,' Crane responded. 'We undoubtedly will have occasion to visit places altogether too small for the really enormous bulk of this vessel.'

'Yes, and whoever heard of a sea-going ship without a small boat?' put in irrepressible Dorothy. 'She's just too perfectly darn kippy for words, sitting up there, isn't she?'

15

The Extra-Galactic Duel

Loaded until her outer skin almost bulged with tightly-packed bars of uranium and equipped to meet any emergency of which me combined efforts of the mightiest intellects of Norlamin could foresee even the slightest possibility, *Skylark Three* lay quiescent. Quiescent, but surcharged with power, she seemed to Seaton's tense mind to share his own eagerness to be off; seemed to be motionlessly straining at her neutral controls in a futile endeavor to leave that unnatural and unpleasant environment of atmosphere and of material substance, to soar outward into absolute zero of temperature and pressure, into the pure and undefiled ether which was her natural and familiar medium.

The five human beings were grouped near an open door of their cruiser; before them were the ancient scientists who for so many days had been laboring with them in their attempt to crush the monstrous race which was threatening the universe. With the elders were the Terrestrials' many friends from the Country of Youth, and surrounding the immense vessel in a throng covering an area to be measured only in square miles were massed myriads of Norlaminians. From their tasks everywhere had come the mental laborers; the Country of Youth had been left depopulated; even those who, their life-work done, had betaken themselves to the placid Nirvana of the Country of Age, returned briefly to the Country of Study to speed upon its way that stupendous Ship of Peace.

The majestic Fedan, Chief of the Five, was concluding his address:

'And may the Unknowable Force direct your minor forces to a successful conclusion of your task. If, upon the other hand, it should by some unforeseen chance be graven upon the Sphere that you are to pass in this supreme venture, you may pass in all tranquility, for the massed intellect of our entire race is here supporting me in my solemn affirmation that the Fenachrone shall not be allowed to prevail. In the name of all Norlamin I bid you farewell.'

Crane spoke briefly in reply and the little group of Earthly wanderers stepped into the elevator. As they sped upward toward the control room door after door shot into place behind them, establishing a manifold seal. Seaton's hand played over the controls and the great cruiser of the void tilted slowly upward until its narrow prow pointed almost directly into the zenith. Then, very slowly at first, the unimaginable mass of the vessel floated lightly upward with a slowly increasing velocity. Faster and faster she flew – out beyond measurable atmosphere, out beyond the outermost limits of the green system. Finally, in interstellar space, Seaton threw out super-powered detector and repellor screens, anchored himself at the driving console with a force, set the power control at 'molecular', so that the propulsive force affected alike every molecule of the vessel and its contents, and, all sense of weight and acceleration lost, he threw in the plunger switch which released every iota of the theoretically possible power of the driving mass of uranium.

Staring intently into the visiplate he corrected their course from time to time by minute fractions of a second of arc; then, satisfied at last, he set the automatic forces which would guide them, temporarily out of their course, around any obstacles, such as the uncounted thousands of solar systems lying in or near their path. He then removed the restraining forces from his body and legs, and wafted himself over to Crane and the two women.

'Well, people,' he stated, matter-of-fact, 'we're on our way. We'll be this way for some time, so we might as well get used to it. Any little thing you want to talk over?'

'How long will it take us to catch 'em?' asked Dorothy. 'Traveling this way isn't half as much fun as it is when you let us have some weight to hold us down.'

'Hard to tell exactly, Dottie. If we had precisely four times their acceleration and had started from the same place, we would of course overtake them in just the number of days they had the start of us. However, there are several complicating factors in the actual situation. We started out not only twenty-nine days behind them, but also a matter of some five hundred thousand light-years of distance. It will take us quite a while to get to their starting-point. I can't tell even that very close, as we will probably have to reduce this acceleration before we get out of the galaxy, in order to give our detectors and repellors time to act on stars and other loose impediments. Powerful as those screens are and fast as they react, there is a limit to the velocity we can use here in this crowded galaxy. Outside it, in free space, of course we can open her up again. Then, too, our acceleration is not exactly four times theirs, only three point nine one eight six. On the other hand, we don't have to catch them to go to work on them. We can operate very nicely at five thousand light-centuries. So there you are – it'll probably be somewhere between thirty-nine and forty-one days, but it may be a day or so more or less.'

'How do you know they are using copper?' asked Margaret. 'Maybe their scientists stored up some uranium and know how to use it.'

'Uh-uh. Practically certain. First, Mart and I saw only copper bars in their ship. Second, copper is the most efficient metal found in quantity upon their planet. Third, even if they had uranium or any metal of its class, they couldn't use it without a complete knowledge of, and ability to handle, the fourth and fifth orders.'

'It is your opinion, then, that destroying this last Fenachrone vessel is to prove as simple a matter as did the destruction of the others?' Crane queried, pointedly.

'Hm ... m ... m. Never thought about it from that angle at all, Mart ... You're still the ground-and-lofty thinker of the outfit, ain't you? Now that you mention it, though, we may find that the Last of the Mohicans ain't entirely toothless, at that. But say, Mart, how come I'm as wild and cock-eyed as I ever was? Rovol's a slow and thoughtful old codger, and with his accumulation of knowledge it looks like I'd be the same way.'

'Far from it. Your nature and mine remain unchanged. Temperament is a basic trait of heredity, and is neither affected nor acquired by increase of knowledge. You acquired knowledge from Rovol, Drasnik, and others, as did I – but you are still the flashing genius and I am still your balance wheel. As for Fenachrone toothlessness: now that you have considered it, what is your opinion?'

'Hard to say. They didn't know how to work in the fifth order, or they wouldn't have run. They've got real brains, though, and they'll have something like seventy days to work on the problem. While it doesn't stand to reason that they could find out much in seventy days, still they may have had a set-up of instruments on their detectors that would have enabled them to analyze our fields and thus compute the structure of the secondary projector we used there. If so, it wouldn't take them long to find out enough to give us plenty of grief – but I don't really believe that they knew enough. I don't quite know what to think. They may be easy and they may not; but, easy or hard to get, we're loaded for bear and I'm sure that we can take 'em'

'So am I, really, but we must consider every contingency. We know that they had at least a detector of fifth-order emanations …'

'And if they did have an analytical detector,' Seaton interrupted, 'they'll probably take a sock at us as soon as we stick our nose out of the galaxy!'

'They may – and even though I do not believe that there is any probability of them actually doing it, it will be well to be armed against the possibility.'

'Right, old top – we'll do that little thing!'

Uneventful days passed, and true to Seaton's calculations, the awful acceleration with which they had started out could not be maintained. A few days before the edge of the galaxy was reached it became necessary to cut off the molecular drive, and to proceed with an acceleration equal only to that of gravitation at the surface of the Earth. Tired of weightlessness and its attendant discomforts to everyday life, the travelers enjoyed the interlude immensely, but it was all too short – too soon the stars thinned out ahead of *Three*'s needle prow. As soon as the way ahead of them was clear Seaton again put on the maximum power of his terrific bars and, held securely at the console, set up a long and involved integral. Ready to transfer the blended and assembled forces to a plunger he stayed his hand, thought a moment, and turned to Crane.

'Want some advice, Mart. I'd thought of setting up three or four courses of five-ply screen on the board – a detector screen on the outside of each course, next it a repellor, then a full-coverage ether screen, then a zone of force, and a full-coverage fifth-order screen as a liner. Then, with them all set up on the board, but not out, throw out a wide detector. That detector would react upon the board at impact with anything hostile, and automatically throw out the courses it found necessary.'

'That sounds like ample protection, but I am not enough of a ray-specialist to pass an opinion. Upon what point are you doubtful?'

'About leaving them on board. The only trouble is that the reaction isn't absolutely instantaneous. Even fifth-order rays would require a millionth of a second or so to set the course. Now if they were using ether waves that'd be lots of time to block them, but if they *should* happen to have fifth-order stuff it'd get here the same time our own detector-impulse would, and it's just barely conceivable that they might give us a nasty jolt before the defenses went out. Nope, I'm developing a cautious streak myself now, when I take time to do it. We've got lots of uranium, and I'm going to put one course out.'

'You cannot put everything out, can you?'

'Not quite, but pretty nearly. I'll leave a hole in the ether screen to pass visible light – no, I won't either. We can see just as well even on the direct-vision wall plates, with light heterodyned on the fifth, so we'll close all ether bands, absolutely. All we'll have to leave open will be the one extremely narrow band upon which our projector is operating, and I'll protect that with a detector screen. Also, I'm going to send out all four courses, instead of only one – then I'll *know* we're all right.'

'Suppose they find our one band, narrow as it is? Of course, if that were shut off automatically by the detector, we'd be safe; but would we not be out of control?'

'Not necessarily – I see you didn't get quite all this stuff over the educator. The other projector worked that way, on one fixed band out of the many thousands possible. But this one is an ultra-projector, an improvement invented at the last minute. Its carrier wave can be shifted at will from one band of the fifth order to any other one; and I'll bet a hat that's *one* thing the Fenachrone haven't got! Any other suggestions? ... All right, I'll get at it.'

A single light, quick-acting detector was sent out ahead of four courses of five-ply screen, then Seaton's fingers again played over the keys, fabricating a detector screen so tenuous that it would react to nothing weaker than a copper power-bar in full operation and with so nearly absolute zero resistance that it could be driven at the full velocity of his ultra-projector. Then, while Crane watched the instruments closely and while Dorothy and Margaret watched the faces of their husbands with only mild interest, Seaton drove home the plunger that sent that prodigious and ever-widening fan ahead of them with a velocity unthinkable millions of times that of light. For five minutes, until that far-flung screen had gone as far as it could be thrown by the utmost power of the uranium bar, the two men stared at the unresponsive instruments, then Seaton shrugged his shoulders. 'I had a hunch,' he remarked with a grin. 'They didn't wait for us a second. "I don't care for some," says they, "I've already had any." They're running in a straight line, with full power on and don't intend to stop or slow down.'

'How do you know?' asked Dorothy. 'By the distance? How far are they?'

'I know, Red-Top, by what I didn't find out with that screen I just put out. It didn't reach them, and it went so far that the distance is absolutely meaningless, even expressed in parsecs. Well, a stern chase is proverbially a long chase, and I guess this one ain't going to be any exception.'

Every eight hours Seaton launched his all-embracing ultra-detector, but day after day passed and the instruments remained motionless after each cast of that gigantic net. For days the galaxy behind them had been dwindling; from a space-filling mass of stars it had shrunk down to a fairly bright ellipse.

At the previous cast of the detector it had still been distinctly visible. Now, as Dorothy and Seaton, alone in the control room, stared into that visiplate, they were shocked – their own galaxy was indistinguishable from numberless other tiny, dim patches of light. It was as small, as insignificant, as remote, as any other nebula!

'This is awful, Dick … horrible. It just simply scares me pea-green!' She shuddered as she drew herself to him, and he swept both arms around her.

''Sall right, Dottie; steady down. That stuff out there'd scare anybody – I'm scared purple myself. It isn't in any finite mind to understand this sort of thing. There's one redeeming feature, though – we're together.'

'I couldn't stand it, otherwise.' Dorothy returned his caress with all her old-time fervor and enthusiasm. 'I feel better now. If it gets you, too, I know it's all right – I was beginning to think maybe I was yellow, or something … but maybe you're kidding me?' She held him off at arm's length, looking deep into his eyes: then, reassured, went back into his arms. 'No, you feel it, too,' and her glorious auburn head found its natural resting-place in the curve of his shoulder.

'Yellow! … You?' Seaton pressed his wife closer still and laughed aloud. 'Maybe – but so is picric acid; so is TNT, and so is pure gold.'

'Flatterer!' Her low, entrancing chuckle bubbled over. 'But you know I just revel in it. I'll kiss you for that!

'It *is* awfully lonesome out here, without even a star to look at,' she went on, after a time, then laughed again. 'If the Cranes and Shiro weren't along, we'd be really "alone at last", wouldn't we?'

'I'll say we would! But that reminds me of something. According to my figures we might have been able to detect the Fenachrone on the last test, but we didn't. Think I'll try 'em again before we turn in.'

Once more he flung out that tenuous net of force, and as it reached the extreme limit of its travel the needle of the micro-ammeter flickered slightly, barely moving off its zero mark.

'Whee! Whoopee!' he yelled. 'Mart, we're on 'em!'

'Close?' demanded Crane, hurrying into the control room upon his beam.

'Anything but. Barely touched 'em – current something less than a thousandth of a micro-ampere on a million to one step-up. However, it proves our ideas are right.'

The next day – *Skylark Three* was running on Eastern Standard Time, of the Tellurian United States of North America – the two mathematicians covered sheet after sheet of paper with computations and curves. After checking and rechecking the figures Seaton shut off the power, released the molecular drive, and applied acceleration of twenty-nine point six-oh-two feet per second; and five human beings breathed at once a profound sigh of relief as an almost-normal force of gravitation was restored to them.

'Why the let-up?' asked Dorothy. 'They're an awful long ways off yet, aren't they? Why not hurry up and catch them?'

'Because we're going infinitely faster than they are now. If we kept up full acceleration we'd pass them so fast that we couldn't fight them at all. This way, we'll still be going a lot faster than they are when we get close to them, but not enough faster to keep us from maneuvering with them if we have to. Guess I'll take another reading on 'em.'

'I do not believe that you should,' Crane suggested, thoughtfully. 'After all, they may have perfected their instruments, and yet may not have detected that extremely light touch of our contact last night. If so, why put them on guard?'

'They're probably on guard anyway, without having to be put there – but it's a sound idea, nevertheless. Along the same line I'll release the fifth-order screens, with the fastest possible detector on guard. We're just about within reach of a light copper-driven beam right now, but they can't send anything heavy this far, and if they think we're overconfident so much the better.'

'There,' he continued, after a few minutes at the keyboard.

'All set. If they put a detector on us I've got a force set to make a noise like a fire siren. If pressed, I will very reluctantly admit that we're carrying caution to a point ten thousand degrees below the absolute zero of sanity. I'll bet my shirt that we won't hear a yip out of them before we touch them off. Furthermore—'

The rest of his sentence was lost in a crescendo bellow of sound. Seaton, still at the controls, shut off the noise, studied his meters carefully, and turned to Crane with a grin.

'You win the shirt, Mart. I'll give it to you next Wednesday, when my other one comes back from the laundry. It's a fifth-order detector, coming in beautifully on band forty-seven fifty.'

'Aren't you going to put something on 'em?' asked Dorothy in surprise.

'No – what's the use? I can read theirs as well as I could one of my own. Maybe they know that, too – if they don't we'll let 'em think we're coming along, as innocent as Mary's little lamb. That beam is much too thin to carry anything, and if they thicken it up I've got an axe set to chop it off.' Seaton whistled a merry, lilting refrain as his fingers played over the stops and keys.

'Why, Dick, you seem actually pleased about it.' Margaret was plainly ill at ease.

'Sure I am. I never did like to drown baby kittens, and it goes against the grain to stab a guy in the back, even if he is a Fenachrone. In a battle, though, I could blow them out of space without a qualm or a quiver.'

'But suppose they fight back too hard?'

'They can't – the worst that can possibly happen is that we can't lick them.

They certainly can't lick us, because we can outrun 'em. If we can't take 'em alone, we'll go back to Norlamin and bring up reinforcements.'

'I am not so sure,' Crane spoke slowly. 'There is, I believe, a theoretical possibility that sixth-order forces exist. Would an extension of the methods of detection of fifth-order rays reveal them?'

'*Sixth?* Sweet spirits of niter! Nobody knows anything about them. However, I've had one surprise already, so maybe your suggestion isn't as crazy as it sounds. We've got three or four days yet before either side can send anything except on the sixth, so I'll find out what I can do.'

He flew at the task, and for the next three days could hardly be torn from it for rest; but:

'O.K. Mart,' he finally announced. 'They exist, all right, and I can detect 'em. Look here,' and he pointed to a tiny receiver, upon which a small lamp flared in brilliant scarlet light.

'Are they sending them?'

'No, fortunately. They're coming from our bar. See, it shines blue when I shield it from the bar, and stays blue when I attach it to their detector ray.'

'Can you direct them?'

'Not a chance in the world. That means a lifetime, probably many lifetimes, of research unless somebody uses a fairly complete pattern of them close enough so that I can analyze it. It's a good deal like calculus in that respect. It took thousands of years to get it in the first place, but it's easy when somebody that already knows it shows you how it goes.'

'The Fenachrone learned to handle fifth-order rays so quickly, then, by an analysis of our fifth-order projector there?'

'Our secondary projector, yes. They must have had some neutronium in stock, too – but it would have been funny if they hadn't, at that – they've had atomic power for ages.'

Silent and grim, he seated himself at the console, and for an hour he wrote an intricate pattern of forces upon the inexhaustible supply of keys afforded by the ultra-projector before he once touched a plunger.

'What are you doing? I followed you for a few hundred steps, but could go no farther.'

'Merely a little safety-first stuff. In case they should send any real pattern of sixth-order stuff this set-up will analyze it, record the complete analysis, throw out a screen against every frequency of the pattern; throw on the molecular drive, and pull us back toward the galaxy at full acceleration, while switching the frequency of our carrier wave a thousand times a second, to keep them from shooting a hot one through our open band. It'll do it all in about a millionth of a second, too … Hm-m-m … They've shut off their ray – they know we've tapped it. Well, war's declared now – we'll see what we can see.'

Transferring the assembled beam to a plunger, he sent out a secondary projector toward the Fenachrone vessel, as fast as it could be driven, close behind a widespread detector net. He soon found the enemy cruiser, but so immense was the distance that it was impossible to hold the projection anywhere in its neighborhood. They flashed beyond it and through it and upon all sides of it, but the utmost delicacy of the controls would not permit of holding even upon the immense bulk of the vessel, to say nothing of holding upon such a relatively tiny object as the power-bar. As they flashed repeatedly through the warship they saw piecemeal and sketchily her formidable armament and the hundreds of men of her crew, each man at battle stations at the controls of some frightful engine of destruction. Suddenly they were cut off as a screen closed behind them – the Earthmen felt an instant of unreasoning terror as it seemed that one-half of their peculiar dual personalities vanished utterly. Seaton laughed.

'That was a funny sensation, wasn't it? It just means that they've climbed a tree and pulled the tree up after them.'

'I do not like the odds, Dick.' Crane's face was grave. 'They have many hundreds of men, all trained; and we are only two. Yes, only one, for I count for nothing at those controls.'

'All the better, Mart. This board more than makes up the difference. They've got a lot of stuff, of course, but they haven't got anything like this control system. Their captain's got to issue orders, whereas I've got everything right under my hands. Not so uneven as they think!'

Within battle range at last, Seaton hurled his utmost concentration of direct forces, under the impact of which three courses of Fenachrone defensive screen flared through the ultraviolet and went black. There the massed direct attack was stopped – at what cost the enemy alone knew – and the Fenachrone countered instantly and in a manner totally unexpected. Through the narrow slit in the fifth-order screen through which Seaton was operating, in the bare one-thousandth of a second that it was open, so exactly synchronized and timed that the screens did not even glow as it went through the narrow opening, a gigantic beam of heterodyned force struck full upon the bow of the *Skylark*, near the sharply-pointed prow, and the stubborn metal instantly flared blinding white and exploded outward in puffs of incandescent gas under the awful power of that titanic thrust. Through four successive skins of inoson, the theoretical ultimate of possible strength, toughness, and resistance, that frightful beam drove before the automatically-reacting detector closed the slit, and the impregnable defensive screens, driven by their mighty uranium bars, flared into incandescent defense. Driven as they were, they held, and the Fenachrone, finding that particular attack useless, shut off their power.

'Wow! They really have got something!' Seaton exclaimed in unfeigned admiration. '*What* a wallop that was! We will now take time out for repairs.

Also, I'm going to cut our slit down to a width of one kilocycle, if I can possibly figure out a way of working on that narrow band, and I'm going to step up our shifting speed to a hundred thousand. It's a good thing they built this ship in a lot of layers – if that'd got through to the interior it would have raised hell. You might weld up those holes, Mart, while I see what I can do here.'

Then Seaton noticed the women, white and trembling, upon a seat.

''Smatter? Cheer up, kids, you ain't seen nothing yet. That was just a couple of little preliminary love-taps, like two boxers feeling each other out in the first ten seconds of the first round.'

'Preliminary love-taps!' repeated Dorothy, looking into Seaton's eyes and being reassured by the serene confidence she read there. 'But they hit us, and hurt us badly – why, there's a hole in our *Skylark* as big as a house, and it goes through four or five layers!'

'Yeah, but we ain't hurt a bit. They're easily fixed, and we've lost nothing but a few tons of inoson and uranium. We've got lots of spare metal. I don't know what I did to him, any more than he knows what he did to us, but I'll bet my other shirt that he knows he's been nudged!'

Repairs completed and the changes made in the method of projection, Seaton actuated the rapidly-shifting slit and peered through it at the enemy vessel. Finding their screens still up he directed a complete-coverage attack upon them with four bars while, with the entire massed power of the remaining generators concentrated into one frequency, he shifted that frequency up and down the spectrum – probing, probing, ever probing with that gigantic beam of intolerable energy – feeling for some crack, however slight, into which he could insert that searing sheet of concentrated destruction. Although much of the available power of the Fenachrone was perforce devoted to repelling the continuous attack of the *Skylark,* they maintained an equally continuous offensive and in spite of the narrowness of the open slit and the rapidity with which that slit was changing from frequency to frequency, enough of the frightful forces came through to keep the ultra-powered defensive screens radiating far into the violet – and, the utmost power of the refrigerating system proving absolutely useless against the concentrated beams being employed, mass after mass of inoson was literally blown from the outer and secondary skins of the *Skylark* by the comparatively tiny jets of force that leaked through the momentarily open slit.

Seaton, grimly watching his instruments, glanced at Crane, who, calm but alert at his console, was repairing the damage as fast as it was done.

'They're sending more stuff, Mart, and it's getting hotter. That means they're building more projectors. We can play that game, too. They're using up their fuel reserves fast; but we're bigger than they are, carry more metal, and it's more efficient metal. Only one way out of it, I guess – what say we put in enough new generators to smother them down by brute force, no matter how much power it takes?'

'Why don't you use some of those awful copper shells? Or aren't we close enough yet?' Dorothy's low voice came clearly, so utterly silent was that frightful combat.

'Close! We're still better than two hundred thousand light-years apart! There may have been longer-range battles than this somewhere in the universe, but I doubt it. And as for copper, even if we could get it to 'em it'd be just like so many candy kisses compared to the stuff we're both using. Dear girl, there are fields of force extending for thousands of miles from each of these vessels beside which the exact center of the biggest lightning flash you ever saw would be a dead area!'

He set up a series of integrals and, machine after machine, in a space left vacant by the rapidly-vanishing store of uranium, there appeared inside the fourth skin of the *Skylark* a row of gigantic generators, each one adding its terrific output to the already inconceivable stream of energy being directed at the foe. As that frightful flow increased, the intensity of the Fenachrone attack diminished, and finally it ceased altogether as the enemy's whole power became necessary for the maintenance of his defenses. Still greater grew the stream of force from the *Skylark,* and, now that the attack had ceased, Seaton opened the slit wider and stopped its shifting, in order still further to increase the efficiency of his terrible weapon. Face set and eyes hard, deeper and deeper he drove his now irresistible forces. His flying fingers were upon the keys of his console; his keen and merciless eyes were in a secondary projector near the now doomed ship of the Fenachrone, directing masterfully his terrible attack. As the output of his generators still increased Seaton began to compress a hollow sphere of searing, seething energy upon the furiously-straining defensive screens of the Fenachrone. Course after course of the heaviest possible screen was sent out, driven by massed batteries of copper now disintegrating at the rate of tons in every second, only to flare through the ultraviolet and to go down before that dreadful, that irresistible onslaught. Finally, as the inexorable sphere still contracted, the utmost efforts of the defenders could not keep their screens away from their own vessel, and simultaneously the prow and the stern of the Fenachrone battleship were bared to that awful field of force, in which no possible substance could endure for even the most infinitesimal instant of time.

There was a sudden cessation of all resistance, and those titanic forces, all directed inward, converged upon a point with a power behind which there was the inconceivable energy of four hundred thousand tons of uranium being disintegrated at the highest possible rate short of instant disruption. In that same instant of collapse the enormous mass of power-copper in the Fenachrone cruiser and the vessel's every atom, alike of structure and of contents, also exploded into pure energy at the touch of that unimaginable field of force.

In that awful moment before Seaton could shut off his power it seemed to him that space itself must be obliterated by the very concentration of the unknowable and incalculable forces there unleashed – must be swallowed up and lost in the utterly indescribable brilliance of the field of radiance driven to a distance of millions upon incandescent millions of miles from the place where the last representatives of the monstrous civilization of the Fenach-rone had made their last stand against the forces of Universal Peace.

SKYLARK OF VALERON

1

Dr DuQuesne's Ruse

Day after day a spherical spaceship of arenak tore through the illimitable reaches of the interstellar void. She had once been a war vessel of Osnome; now, rechristened the *Violet*, she was bearing two Tellurians and a Fenachrone – Dr Marc C. DuQuesne of World Steel, 'Baby Doll' Loring, his versatile and accomplished assistant, and the squat and monstrous engineer of the flagship Y427W – from the Green System toward the solar system of the Fenachrone. The mid-point of the stupendous flight had long since been passed; the *Violet* had long been braking down with a negative acceleration of five times the velocity of light.

Much to the surprise of both DuQuesne and Loring, their prisoner had not made the slightest move against them. He had thrown all the strength of his supernaturally powerful body and all the resources of his gigantic brain into the task of converting the atomic motors of the *Violet* into the space-annihilating drive of his own race. This drive, affecting alike as it does every atom of substance within the radius of action of the power bar, entirely nullifies the effect of acceleration, so that the passengers feel no motion whatever, even when the craft is accelerating at maximum.

The engineer had not shirked a single task, however arduous. And, once under way, he had nursed those motors along with every artifice known to his knowing clan; he had performed such prodigies of adjustment and tuning as to raise by a full two per cent their already inconceivable maximum acceleration. Nor was this all. After the first moment of rebellion, he did not even once attempt to bring to bear the almost irresistible hypnotic power of his eyes; the immense, cold, ruby-lighted projectors of mental energy which, both men knew, were awful weapons indeed. Nor did he even once protest against the attractors which were set upon his giant limbs.

Immaterial bands, these, whose slight force could not be felt unless the captor so willed. But let the prisoner make one false move, and those tiny beams of force would instantly become copper-driven rods of pure energy, hurling the luckless weight against the wall of the control room and holding him motionless there, in spite of the most terrific exertions of his mighty body.

DuQuesne lay at ease in his seat; or rather, scarcely touching the seat, he floated at ease in the air above it. His black brows were drawn together, his black eyes were hard as he studied frowningly the Fenachrone engineer. As usual, that worthy was half inside the power plant, coaxing those mighty engines to do even better than their prodigious best.

Feeling his companion's eyes upon him, the doctor turned his inscrutable stare upon Loring, who had been studying his chief even as DuQuesne had been studying the outlander. Loring's cherubic countenance was as pinkly innocent as ever, his guileless blue eyes as calm and untroubled; but DuQuesne, knowing the man as he did, perceived an almost imperceptible tension and knew that the killer also was worried.

'What's the matter, Doll?' The saturnine scientist smiled mirthlessly. 'Afraid I'm going to let that ape slip one over on us?'

'Not exactly.' Loring's slight tenseness, however, disappeared. 'It's your party, and anything that's all right with you tickles me half to death. I have known all along you knew that that bird there isn't working under compulsion. You know as well as I do that nobody works that way because they're made to. He's working for himself, not for us, and I had just begun to wonder if you weren't getting a little late in clamping down on him.'

'Not at all – there are good and sufficient reasons for this apparent delay. I am going to clamp down on him in exactly' – DuQuesne glanced at his wrist watch – 'fourteen minutes. But you're keen – you've got a brain that really works – maybe I'd better give you the whole picture.'

DuQuesne, approving thoroughly of his iron-nerved, cold-blooded assistant, voiced again the thought he had expressed once before, a few hours out from Earth; and Loring answered as he had then, in almost the same words – words which revealed truly the nature of the man:

'Just as you like. Usually I don't want to know anything about anything, because what a man doesn't know he can't be accused of spilling. Out here, though, maybe I should know enough about things to act intelligently in case of a jam. But you're the doctor – if you'd rather keep it under your hat, that's all right with me, too. As I've said before, it's your party.'

'Yes; he certainly is working for himself.' DuQuesne scowled blackly. 'Or, rather, he thinks he is. You know I read his mind back there, while he was unconscious. I didn't get all I wanted to, by any means – he woke up too soon – but I got a lot more than he thinks I did.

'They have detector zones, way out in space, all around their world, that nothing can get past without being spotted; and patrolling those zones there are scout ships, carrying armament to stagger the imagination. I intend to take over one of those patrol ships and by means of it to capture one of their first-class battleships. As a first step I'm going to hypnotize that ape and find out absolutely everything he knows. When I get done with him, he'll do exactly what I tell him to, and nothing else.'

'Hypnotize him?' Curiosity was awakened in even Loring's incurious mind at this unexpected development. 'I didn't know that was one of your specialties.'

'It wasn't until recently, but the Fenachrone are all past masters, and I learned about it from his brain. Hypnosis is a wonderful science. The only drawback is that his mind is a lot stronger than mine. However, I have in my kit, among other things, a tube of something that will cut him down to my size.'

'Oh, I see – pentabarb.' With this hint, Loring's agile mind grasped instantly the essentials of DuQuesne's plan. 'That's why you had to wait so long, then, to take steps. Pentabarb kills in twenty-four hours, and he can't help us steal the ship after he's dead.'

'Right! One milligram, you know, will make a gibbering idiot out of any human being; but I imagine that it will take three or four times that much to soften *him* down to the point where I can work on him the way I want to. As I don't know the effects of such heavy dosages, since he's not really human, and since he must be alive when we go through their screens, I decided to give him the works exactly six hours before we are due to hit their outermost detector. That's about all I can tell you right now; I'll have to work out the details of seizing the ship after I have studied his brain more thoroughly.'

Precisely at the expiration of the fourteen allotted minutes, DuQuesne tightened the attractor beams, which had never been entirely released from their prisoner; thus pinning him helplessly, immovably, against the wall of the control room. He then filled a hypodermic syringe and moved the mechanical educator nearer the motionless, although violently struggling, creature. Then, avoiding carefully the baleful out-pourings of those flame-shot volcanoes of hatred that were the eyes of the Fenachrone, he set the dials of the educator, placed the headsets, and drove home the needle's hollow point. One milligram of the diabolical compound was absorbed without appreciable lessening of the blazing defiance being hurled along the educator's wires. One and one-half – two milligrams – three – four – five –

That inhumanly powerful mind at last began to weaken, but it became entirely quiescent only after the administration of the seventh milligram of that direly potent drug.

'Just as well that I allowed only six hours,' DuQuesne sighed in relief as he began to explore the labyrinthine intricacies of the frightful brain now open to his gaze. 'I don't see how any possible form of life can hold together long under seven milligrams of that stuff.'

He fell silent and for more than an hour he studied the brain of the engineer, concentrating upon the several small portions which contained knowledge of most immediate concern. Finally he removed the headsets.

'His plans were all made,' he informed Loring coldly, 'and so are mine, now. Bring out two full outfits of clothing – one of yours and one of mine. Two guns, belts, and so on. Break out a bale of waste, the emergency candles, and all that sort of stuff you can find.'

DuQuesne turned to the Fenachrone, who stood utterly lax, and stared deep into those dull and expressionless eyes.

'You,' he directed crisply, 'will build at once, as quickly as you can, two dummies which will look exactly like Loring and myself. They must be life-like in every particular, with faces capable of expressing the emotions of surprise and of anger, and with right arms able to draw weapons upon a signal – *my* signal. Also upon signal their heads and bodies will turn, they will leap toward the center of the room, and they will make certain noises and utter certain words, the records of which I shall prepare. Go to it!'

'Don't you need to control him through the headsets?' asked Loring curiously.

'I may have to control him in detail when we come to the really fine work, later on,' DuQuesne replied absently. 'This is more or less in the nature of an experiment, to find out whether I have him thoroughly under control. During the last act he'll have to do exactly what I shall have told him to do, without supervision, and I want to be absolutely certain that he will do it without a slip.'

'What's the plan – or maybe it's something that is none of my business?'

'No; you ought to know it, and I've got time to tell you about it now. Nothing material can possibly approach the planet of the Fenachrone without being seen, as it is completely surrounded by never less than two full-sphere detector screens; and to make assurance doubly sure our engineer there has installed a mechanism which, at the first touch of the outer screen, will shoot a warning along a tight communicator beam directly into the receiver of the nearest Fenachrone scout ship. As you already know, the smallest of those scouts can burn this ship out of the ether in less than a second.'

'That's a cheerful picture. You still think we can get away?'

'I'm coming to that. We can't possibly get through the detectors without being challenged, even if I tear out all his apparatus, so we're going to use his whole plan, but for our benefit instead of his. Therefore his present hypnotic state and the dummies. When we touch that screen you and I are going to be hidden. The dummies will be in sole charge, and our prisoner will be playing the part I've laid out for him.

'The scout ship that he calls will come up to investigate. They will bring apparatus and attractors to bear to liberate the prisoner, and the dummies will try to fight. They will be blown up or burned to cinders almost instantly, and our little playmate will put on his space-suit and be taken across to the capturing vessel. Once there, he will report to the commander.

'That officer will think the affair sufficiently serious to report it directly to headquarters. If he doesn't, this ape here will insist upon reporting it to general headquarters himself. As soon as that report is in, we, working through our prisoner here, will proceed to wipe out the crew of the ship and take it over.'

'And do you think he'll really do it?' Loring's guileless face showed doubt, his tone was faintly skeptical.

'I *know* he'll do it!' The chemist's voice was hard. 'He won't take any active part – I'm not psychologist enough to know whether I could drive him that far, even drugged, against an unhypnotizable subconscious or not – but he'll be carrying something along that will enable me to do it, easily and safely. But that's about enough of this chin music – we'd better start doing something.'

While Loring brought spare clothing and weapons, and rummaged through the vessel in search of material suitable for the dummies' fabrication, the Fenachrone engineer worked rapidly at his task. And not only did he work rapidly, he worked skillfully and artistically as well. This artistry should not be surprising, for to such a mentality as must necessarily be possessed by the chief engineer of a first-line vessel of the Fenachrone, the faithful reproduction of anything capable of movement was not a question of art – it was merely an elementary matter of line, form, and mechanism.

Cotton waste was molded into shape, reinforced, and wrapped in leather under pressure. To the bodies thus formed were attached the heads, cunningly constructed of masticated fiber, plastic, and wax. Tiny motors and many small pieces of apparatus were installed, and the completed effigies were dressed and armed.

DuQuesne's keen eyes studied every detail of the startlingly lifelike, almost microscopically perfect, replicas of himself and his traveling companion.

'A good job,' he commented briefly.

'Good?' exclaimed Loring. 'It's perfect! Why, that dummy would fool my own wife, if I had one – it almost fools me!'

'At least, they're good enough to pass a more critical test than any they are apt to get during this coming incident.'

Satisfied, DuQuesne turned from his scrutiny of the dummies and went to the closet in which had been stored the space-suit of the captive. To the inside of its front protector flap he attached a small and inconspicuous flat-sided case. He then measured carefully, with a filar micrometer, the apparent diameter of the planet now looming so large beneath them.

'All right, Doll; our time's getting short. Break out our suits and test them, will you, while I give the big boy his final instructions?'

Rapidly those commands flowed over the wires of the mechanical educator, from DuQuesne's hard, keen brain into the now docile mind of the captive. The Earthly scientist explained to the Fenachrone, coldly, precisely, and in minute detail, exactly what he was to do and exactly what he was to say from the moment of encountering the detector screens of his native planet until after he had reported to his superior officers.

Then the two Tellurians donned their own armor and made their way into an adjoining room, a small armory in which were hung several similar suits and which was a veritable arsenal of weapons.

'We'll hang ourselves up on a couple of these hooks, like the rest of the suits,' DuQuesne explained. 'This is the only part of the performance that may be even slightly risky, but there is no real danger that they will spot us. That fellow's message to the scout ship will tell them that there are only two of us, and we'll be out there with him, right in plain sight.

'If by any chance they should send a party aboard us they would probably not bother to search the *Violet* at all carefully, since they will already know that we haven't got a thing worthy of attention; and they would of course suppose us to be empty space-suits. Therefore keep your lens shields down, except perhaps for the merest crack to see through, and, above all, don't move a millimeter, no matter what happens.'

'But how can you manipulate your controls without moving your hands?'

'I can't; but my hands will not be in the sleeves, but inside the body of the suit – shut up! Hold everything – there's the flash!'

The flying vessel had gone through the zone of feeble radiations which comprised the outer detector screen of the Fenachrone. But, though tenuous, that screen was highly efficient, and at its touch there burst into frenzied activity the communicator built by the captive to be actuated by that very impulse. It had been built during the long flight through space, and its builder had thought that its presence would be unnoticed and would remain unsuspected by the Tellurians.

Now automatically put into action, it laid a beam to the nearest scout ship of the Fenachrone and into that vessel's receptors it passed the entire story of the *Violet* and her occupants. But DuQuesne had not been caught napping. Reading the engineer's brain and absorbing knowledge from it, he had installed a relay which would flash to his eyes an inconspicuous but unmistakable warning of the first touch of the screen of the enemy. The flash had come – they had penetrated the outer lines of the monstrous civilization of the dread and dreaded Fenachrone.

In the armory DuQuesne's hands moved slightly inside his shielding armor, and out in the control room the dummy, that was also to all outward seeming DuQuesne, moved and spoke. It tightened the controls of the attractors, which had never been entirely released from their prisoner, thus again pinning the Fenachrone helplessly against the wall.

'Just to be sure you don't try to start anything,' it explained coldly, in DuQuesne's own voice and tone. 'You have done well so far, but I'll run things myself from now on, so that you can't steer us into a trap. Now tell me exactly how to go about getting one of your vessels. After we get it I'll see about letting you go.'

'Fools, you are too late!' the prisoner roared exultantly. 'You would have been too late, even had you killed me out there in space and had fled at your utmost acceleration. Did you but know it you are as dead, even now – our patrol is upon you!'

The dummy that was DuQuesne whirled, snarling, and its automatic pistol and that of its fellow dummy were leaping out when an awful acceleration threw them flat upon the floor, a magnetic force snatched away their weapons, and a heat ray of prodigious power reduced the effigies to two small piles of gray ash. Immediately thereafter a beam of force from the patrolling cruiser neutralized the attractors bearing upon the captive and, after donning his space-suit, he was transferred to the Fenachrone vessel.

Motionless inside his cubby, DuQuesne waited until the airlocks of the Fenachrone vessel had closed behind his erstwhile prisoner; waited until that luckless monster had told his story to Fenor, his emperor, and to Fenimol, his general in command; waited until the communicator circuit had been broken and the hypnotized, drugged, and already dying creature had turned as though to engage his fellows in conversation. Then only did the saturnine scientist act. His finger closed a circuit, and in the Fenachrone vessel, inside the front protector flap of the discarded space-suit, the flat case fell apart noiselessly and from it there gushed forth volume upon volume of colorless and odorless, but intensely lethal, vapor.

'Just like killing goldfish in a bowl.' Callous, hard, and cold, DuQuesne exhibited no emotion whatever; neither pity for the vanquished foe nor elation at the perfect working out of his plans. 'Just in case some of them might have been wearing suits for emergencies, I had some explosive copper ready to detonate, but this makes it much better – the explosion might have damaged something we want.'

And aboard the vessel of the Fenachrone, DuQuesne's deadly gas diffused with extreme rapidity, and as it diffused, the hellish crew to the last man dropped in their tracks. They died not knowing what had happened to them; died with no thought of even attempting to send out an alarm; died not even knowing that they died.

2

Plan XB218

'Can you open the airlocks of that scout ship from the outside, doctor?' asked Loring, as the two adventurers came out of the armory into the control room, where DuQuesne, by means of the attractors, began to bring the two vessels together.

'Yes. I know everything that the engineer of a first-class battleship knew, To him, one of these little scouts was almost beneath notice, but he did know that much about them – the outside controls of all Fenachrone ships work the same way.'

Under the urge of the attractors the two ships of space were soon door to door. DuQuesne set the mighty beams to lock the craft immovably together and both men stepped into the *Violet*'s airlock. Pumping back the air, DuQuesne opened the outer door, then opened both outer and inner doors of the scout.

As he opened the inner door the poisoned atmosphere of the vessel screamed out into space, and as soon as the frigid gale had subsided the raiders entered the control room of the enemy craft. Hardened and conscienceless killer though Loring was, the four bloated, ghastly objects that had once been men gave him momentary pause.

'Maybe we shouldn't have let the air out so fast,' he suggested, tearing his gaze away from the grisly sight.

'The brains aren't hurt, and that's all I care about.' Unmoved, DuQuesne opened the air valves wide, and not until the roaring blast had scoured every trace of the noxious vapor from the whole ship did he close the airlock doors and allow the atmosphere to come again to normal pressure and temperature.

'Which ship are you going to use – theirs or our own?' asked Loring, as he began to remove his cumbersome armor.

'I don't know yet. That depends largely upon what I find out from the brain of the lieutenant in charge of this patrol boat. There are two methods by which we can capture a battleship; one requiring the use of the *Violet*, the other the use of this scout. The information which I am about to acquire will enable me to determine which of the two plans entails the lesser amount of risk.

'There is a third method of procedure, of course; that is, to go back to Earth and duplicate one of their battleships ourselves, from the knowledge I shall have gained from their various brains concerning the apparatus, mechanisms, materials, and weapons of the Fenachrone. But that would take a long time and would be far from certain of success, because there would almost certainly be some essential facts that I would not have secured. Besides, I came out here to get one of their first-line spaceships, and I intend to do it.'

With no sign of distaste DuQuesne coupled his brain to that of the dead lieutenant of the Fenachrone through the mechanical educator, and quite as casually as though he were merely giving Loring another lesson in Fenachrone matters did he begin systematically to explore the intricate convolutions of that fearsome brain. But after only ten minutes' study he was interrupted by the brazen clang of the emergency alarm. He flipped off the power of the educator, discarded his headset, acknowledged the call, and watched the recorder as it rapped out its short, insistent message.

'Something is going on here that was not on my program,' he announced to the alert but quiescent Loring. 'One should always be prepared for the unexpected, but this may run into something cataclysmic. The Fenachrone are being attacked from space, and all armed forces have been called into a defensive formation – Invasion Plan XB218, whatever that is. I'll have to look it up in the code.'

The desk of the commanding officer was a low, heavily built cabinet of metal. DuQuesne strode over to it, operated rapidly the levers and dials of its combination lock and took from one of the compartments the 'Code' – a polygonal framework of engraved metal bars and sliders, resembling some-what an Earthly multiplex squirrel-cage slide rule.

'X – B – Two – One – Eight.' Although DuQuesne had never before seen such an instrument, the knowledge taken from the brains of the dead officers rendered him perfectly familiar with it, and his long and powerful fingers set up the indicated defense plan as rapidly and as surely as those of any Fenach-rone could have done it. He revolved the mechanism in his hands, studying every plane surface, scowling blackly in concentration.

'Munitions plants – shall – so-and-so – We don't care about that. Reserves – zones – ordnance – commissary – defensive screens … Oh, here we are! Scout ships. Instead of patrolling a certain volume of space, each scout ship takes up a fixed post just inside the outer detector zone. Twenty times as many on duty, too – enough so that they will be only about ten thousand miles apart – and each ship is to lock high-power detector screens and visi-plate and recorder beams with all its neighbors.

'Also, there is to be a first-class battleship acting as mother ship, protector, and reserve for each twenty-five scouts. The nearest one is to be … Let's see, from here that would be only about twenty thousand miles over that way and about a hundred thousand miles down.'

'Does that change your plans, chief?'

'Since my plans were not made, I cannot say that it does – it changes the background, however, and introduces an element of danger that did not previously exist. It makes it impossible to go out through the detector zone – but it was practically impossible before, and we have no intention of going out, anyway, until we possess a vessel powerful enough to go through any barrage they can lay down. On the other hand, there is bound to be a certain amount of confusion in placing so many vessels, and that fact will operate to make the capture of our battleship much easier than it would have been otherwise.'

'What danger exists that wasn't there before?' demanded Loring.

'The danger that the whole planet may be blown up,' DuQuesne returned bluntly. 'Any nation or race attacking from space would of course have atomic power, and any one with that power could volatilize any planet by simply dropping a bomb on it from open space. They might want to colonize it, of course, in which case they wouldn't destroy it, but it is always safest to plan for the worst possible contingencies.'

'How do you figure on doing us any good if the whole world explodes?' Loring lighted a cigarette, his hand steady and his face pinkly unruffled. 'If she goes up, it looks as if we go out, like that – *puff*!' And he blew out the match.

'Not at all, Doll,' DuQuesne reassured him. 'An atomic explosion starting on the surface and propagating downward would hardly develop enough power to drive anything material much, if any, faster than light, and no explosion wave, however violent, can exceed that velocity. The *Violet*, as you know, although not to be compared with even this scout as a fighter, has an acceleration of five times that, so that we could outrun the explosion in her. However, if we stay in our own ship, we shall certainly be found and blown out of space as soon as this defensive formation is completed.

'On the other hand, this ship carries full Fenachrone power of offense and defense, and we should be safe enough from detection in it, at least for as long a time as we shall need it. Since these small ships are designed for purely local scout work, though, they are comparatively slow and would certainly be destroyed in any such cosmic explosion as is manifestly a possibility. That possibility is very remote, it is true, but it should be taken into consideration.'

'So what? You're talking yourself around a circle, right back to where you started from.'

'Only considering the thing from all angles.' DuQuesne was unruffled. 'We have lots of time, since it will take them quite a while to perfect this formation. To finish the summing up – we want to use this vessel, but is it safe? It is. Why? Because the Fenachrone, having had atomic energy themselves for a long time, are thoroughly familiar with its possibilities and have undoubtedly perfected screens through which no such bomb could penetrate.

'Furthermore, we can install the high-speed drive in this ship in a few days – I gave you all the dope on it over the educator, you know – so that we'll be safe, whatever happens. That's the safest plan, and it will work. So you move the stores and our most necessary personal belongings in here while I'm figuring out an orbit for the *Violet*. We don't want her anywhere near us, and yet we want her to be within reaching distance while we are piloting this scout ship of ours to the place where she is supposed to be in Plan XB218.'

'What are you going to do that for – to give them a chance to knock us off?'

'No. I need some time to study these brains, and it will take some time for that battleship mother ship of ours to get into her assigned position, where we can steal her most easily.' DuQuesne, however, did not at once remove his headset, but remained standing where he was, silent and thoughtful.

'Uh-huh,' agreed Loring. 'I'm thinking the same thing you are. Suppose that it *is* Seaton that's got them all hot and bothered this way?'

'The thought has occurred to me several times, and I have considered it at length,' DuQuesne admitted at last. 'However, I have concluded that it is not Seaton. For if it is, he must have a lot more stuff than I think he has. I do not believe that he can possibly have learned that much in the short time he has had to work in. I may be wrong, of course; but the immediately necessary steps toward the seizure of that battleship remain unchanged whether I am right or wrong; whether or not Seaton was the cause of this disturbance.'

The conversation definitely at an end, Loring again encased himself in his space-suit and set to work. For hours he labored, silently and efficiently, at transferring enough of their Earthly possessions and stores to render possible an extended period of living aboard the vessel of the Fenachrone.

He had completed that task and was assembling the apparatus and equipment necessary for the rebuilding of the power plant before DuQuesne finished the long and complex computations involved in determining the direction and magnitude of the force required to give the *Violet* the exact trajectory he desired. The problem was finally solved and checked, however, and DuQuesne rose to his feet, closing his book of nine-place logarithms with a snap.

'All done with the *Violet*, Doll?' he asked, donning his armor.

'Yes.'

'Fine! I'll go aboard and push her off, after we do a little stage-setting here. Take that body there – I don't need it any more, since he didn't know much of anything, anyway – and toss it into the nose compartment. Then shut that bulkhead door, tight. I'm going to drill a couple of holes through there from the *Violet* before I give her the gun.'

'I see – going to make us *look* disabled, whether we are or not, huh?'

'Exactly! We've got to have a good excuse for our visirays being out of order. I can make reports all right on the communicator, and send and receive code messages and orders, but we certainly couldn't stand a close-up inspection on a visiplate. Also, we've got to have some kind of an excuse for signaling to and approaching our mother battleship. We will have been hit and punctured by a meteorite. Pretty thin excuse, but it probably will serve for as long a time as we will need.'

After DuQuesne had made sure that the small compartment in the prow of the vessel contained nothing of use to them, the body of one of the Fenachrone was thrown carelessly into it, the air-tight bulkhead was closed and securely locked, and the chief marauder stepped into the airlock.

'As soon as I get her exactly on course and velocity, I'll step out into space and you can pick me up,' he directed briefly, and was gone.

In the *Violet's* engine room DuQuesne released the anchoring attractor beams and backed off to a few hundred yards' distance. He spun a couple of wheels briefly, pressed a switch, and from the *Violet's* heaviest needle-ray projector there flashed out against the prow of the scout patrol a pencil of incredibly condensed destruction.

Dunark, the crown prince of Kondal, had developed that stabbing ray as the culminating ultimate weapon of ten thousand years of Osnomian warfare: and, driven by even the comparatively feeble energies known to the denizens of the Green System before Seaton's advent, no known substance had been able to resist for more than a moment its corrosively, annihilatingly poignant thrust.

And now this furious stiletto of pure energy, driven by the full power of four hundred pounds of disintegrating atomic copper, at this point-blank range, was hurled against the mere inch of transparent material which comprised the skin of the tiny cruiser. DuQuesne expected no opposition, for with a beam less potent by far he had consumed utterly a vessel built of arenak – arenak, that Osnomian synthetic which is five hundred times as strong, tough, and hard as Earth's strongest, toughest, and hardest alloy steel.

Yet that annihilating needle of force struck that transparent surface and rebounded from it in scintillating torrents of fire. Struck and rebounded, struck and clung; boring in almost imperceptibly as its irresistible energy tore apart, electron by electron, the surprisingly obdurate substance of the cruiser's wall. For that substance was the ultimate synthetic – the one limiting material possessing the utmost measure of strength, hardness, tenacity, and rigidity theoretically possible to any substance built up from the building blocks of ether-borne electrons. This substance, developed by the master scientists of the Fenachrone, was in fact identical with the Norlaminian synthetic metal, ihoson, from which Rovol and his aides had constructed for Seaton his gigantic ship of space – *Skylark Three*.

For five long minutes DuQuesne held that terrific beam against the point of attack, then shut it off; for it had consumed less than half the thickness of the scout patrol's outer skin. True, the focal area of the energy was an almost invisibly violet glare of incandescence, so intensely hot that the concentric shading off through blinding white, yellow, and bright-red heat brought the zone of dull red far down the side of the vessel; but that awful force had had practically no effect upon the space-worthiness of the stanch little craft.

'No use, Loring!' DuQuesne spoke calmly into the transmitter inside his face-plate. True scientist that he was, he neither expressed nor felt anger or bafflement when an idea failed to work, but abandoned it promptly and completely, without rancor or repining. 'No possible meteorite could puncture that shell. Stand by!'

He inspected the power meters briefly, made several readings through the filar micrometer of number six visiplate, and checked the vernier readings of the great circles of the gyroscopes against the figures in his notebook. Then, assured that the *Violet* was following precisely the predetermined course, he entered the airlock, waved a bloated arm at the watchful Loring, and coolly stepped off into space. The heavy outer door clanged shut behind him, and the globular ship of space rocketed onward; while DuQuesne fell with a sickening acceleration toward the mighty planet of the Fenachrone, so many thousands of miles below.

That fall did not long endure. Loring, now a space pilot second to none, had held his vessel even with the *Violet*; matching exactly her course, pace, and acceleration at a distance of barely a hundred feet. He had cut off all his power as DuQuesne's right foot left the Osnomian vessel, and now falling man and plunging scout ship plummeted downward together at the same mad pace; the man drifting slowly toward the ship because of the slight energy of his step into space from the *Violet*'s side and beginning slowly to turn over as he fell. So good had been Loring's spacemanship that the scout did not even roll; DuQuesne was still opposite her starboard airlock when Loring stood in its portal and tossed a space line to his superior. This line – a small, tightly stranded cable of fiber capable of retaining its strength and pliability in the heatless depths of space – snapped out and curled around DuQuesne's bulging space-suit.

'I thought you'd use an attractor, but this is probably better, at that,' DuQuesne commented, as he seized the line in a mailed fist.

'Yeah. I haven't had much practice with them on delicate and accurate work. If I had missed you with this line I could have thrown it again; but if I missed this opening with you on a beam and shaved your suit off on this sharp edge, I figured it'd be just too bad.'

The two men again in the control room and the vessel once more leveled out in headlong flight, Loring broke the silence:

'That idea of being punctured by a meteorite didn't pan out so heavy. How would it be to have one of the crew go space-crazy and wreck the boat from the inside? They do that sometimes, don't they?'

'Yes, they do. That's an idea – thanks. I'll study up on the symptoms. I have a lot more studying to do, anyway – there's a lot of stuff I haven't got yet. This metal, for instance – we couldn't possibly build a Fenachrone battleship on Earth. I had no idea that any possible substance could be as resistant as the shell of this ship is. Of course, there are many unexplored areas in these brains here, and quite a few high-class brains aboard our mother ship that I haven't even seen yet. The secret of the composition of this metal must be in some of them.'

'Well, while you're getting their stuff, I suppose I'd better fly at that job of rebuilding our drive. I'll have time enough all right, you think?'

'Certain of it. I have learned that their system is ample. It's automatic and foolproof. They have warning long before anything can possibly happen. They can, and do, spot trouble over a light-week away, so their plans allow one week to perfect their defenses. You can change the power plant over in three or four days, so we're well in the clear on that. I may not be done with my studies by that time, but I shall have learned enough to take effective action. You work on the drive and keep house. I will study Fenachrone science and so on, answer calls, make reports, and arrange the details of what is to happen when we come within the volume of space assigned to our mother ship.'

Thus for days each man devoted himself to his task. Loring rebuilt the power plant of the short-ranging scout patrol into the terrific open-space drive of the first-line battleships and performed the simple routines of their spartan housekeeping. DuQuesne cut himself short on sleep and spent every possible hour in transferring to his own brain every worthwhile bit of knowledge which had been possessed by the commander and crew of the patrol ship which he had captured.

Periodically, however, he would close the sending circuit and report the position and progress of his vessel, precisely on time and observing strictly all the military minutiae called for by the manual – the while watching appreciatively and with undisguised admiration the flawless execution of that stupendous plan of defense.

The change-over finished, Loring went in search of DuQuesne, whom he found performing a strenuous setting-up exercise. The scientist's face was pale, haggard, and drawn.

'What's the matter, chief?' Loring asked. 'You look kind of peaked.'

'Peaked is good – I'm just about bushed. This thing of getting a hundred and ninety years of solid education in a few days would hardly come under the heading of light amusement. Are you done?'

'Done and checked – O.K.'

'Good! I am, too. It won't take us long to get to our destination now; our mother ship should be just about at her post by this time.'

Now that the vessel was approaching the location assigned to it in the plan, and since DuQuesne had already taken from the brains of the dead Fenachrone all that he wanted of their knowledge, he threw their bodies into space and rayed them out of existence. The other corpse he left lying, a bloated and ghastly mass, in the forward compartment as he prepared to send in what was to be his last flight report to the office of the general in command of the plan of defense.

'His high-mightiness doesn't know it, but that is the last call he is going to get from this unit,' DuQuesne remarked, leaving the sender and stepping over to the control board. 'Now we can leave our prescribed course and go where we can do ourselves some good. First, we'll find the *Violet*. I haven't heard of her being spotted and destroyed as a menace to navigation, so we'll look her up and start her off for home.'

'Why?' asked the henchman. 'Thought we were all done with her.'

'We probably are, but if it should turn out that Seaton is back of all this excitement, our having her may save us a trip back to the Earth. Ah, there she is, right on schedule! I'll bring her alongside and set her controls on a distance-squared decrement, so that when she gets out into free space she'll have a constant velocity.'

'Think she'll get out into free space through those screens?'

'They will detect her, of course, but when they see that she is an abandoned derelict and headed out of their system they'll probably let her go. It will be no great loss, of course, if they do burn her.'

Thus it came about that the spherical cruiser of the void shot away from the then feeble gravitation of the vast but distant planet of the Fenachrone. Through the outer detector screens she tore. Searching beams explored her instantly and thoroughly; but since she was so evidently a deserted hulk and since the Fenachrone cared nothing now for impediments to navigation beyond their screens, she was not pursued.

On and on she sped, her automatic controls reducing her power in exact ratio to the square of the distance attained; on and on, her automatic deflecting detectors swinging her around suns and solar systems and back upon her original right line; on and on toward the Green System, the central system of this the First Galaxy – our own native island universe.

3

DuQuesne Captures a Battleship

'Now we'll get ready to take that battleship.' DuQuesne turned to his aide as the *Violet* disappeared from their sight. 'Your suggestion that one of the crew of this ship could have gone space-crazy was sound, and I have planned our approach to the mother ship on that basis.

'We must wear Fenachrone space-suits for three reasons: First, because it is the only possible way to make us look even remotely like them, and we shall have to stand a casual inspection. Second, because it is general orders that all Fenachrone soldiers must wear suits while at their posts in space. Third, because we shall have lost most of our air. You can wear one of their suits without any difficulty – the surplus circumference will not trouble you very much. I, on the contrary, cannot even get into one, since they're almost a foot too short.

'I must have a suit on, though, before we board the battleship; so I shall wear my own, with one of theirs over it – with the feet cut off so that I can get it on. Since I shall not be able to stand up or to move around without giving everything away because of my length, I'll have to be unconscious and folded up so that my height will not be too apparent, and you will have to be the star performer during the first act.

'But this detailed instruction by word of mouth takes altogether too much time. Put on this headset and I'll shoot you the whole scheme, together with whatever additional Fenachrone knowledge you will need to put the act across.'

A brief exchange of thoughts and of ideas followed. Then, every detail made clear, the two Tellurians donned the space suits of the very short, but enormously wide and thick, monstrosities in semi-human form who were so bigotedly working toward their day of universal conquest.

DuQuesne picked up in his doubly mailed hands a massive bar of metal. 'Ready, Doll? When I swing this we cross the Rubicon.'

'It's all right by me. All or nothing – shoot the works!'

DuQuesne swung his mighty bludgeon aloft, and as it descended the telemental recorder sprang into a shower of shattered tubes, flying coils, and broken insulation. The visiray apparatus went next, followed in swift succession by the superficial air controls, the map cases, and practically everything else that was breakable; until it was clear to even the most casual observer that a madman had in truth wrought his frenzied will throughout the room. One final swing wrecked the controls of the airlocks, and the atmosphere within the vessel began to whistle out into the vacuum of space through the broken bleeder tubes.

'All right, Doll, do your stuff!' DuQuesne directed crisply, and threw himself headlong into a corner, falling into an inert, grotesque huddle.

Loring, now impersonating the dead commanding officer of the scout ship, sat down at the manual sender, which had not been seriously damaged, and in true Fenachrone fashion laid a beam to the mother ship.

'Scout ship K3296, Sublieutenant Grenimar commanding, sending emergency distress message,' he tapped out fluently. 'Am not using telemental recorder, as required by regulations, because nearly all instruments wrecked. Private 244C14, on watch, suddenly seized with space insanity, smashed air valves, instruments, and controls. Opened lock and leaped out into space. I was awake and got into suit before my room lost pressure. My other man, 397B42, was unconscious when I reached him, but believe I got him into his suit soon enough so that his life can be saved by prompt aid. 244C14 of course dead, but I recovered his body as per general orders and am saving it so that brain lesions may be studied by College of Science. Repaired this manual sender and have ship under partial control. Am coming toward you, decelerating to stop in fifteen minutes. Suggest you handle this ship with beam when approach as I have no fine controls. Signing off – K3296.'

'Superdreadnought Z12Q, acknowledging emergency distress message of scout ship K3296,' came almost instant answer. 'Will meet you and handle you as suggested. Signing off – Z12Q.'

Rapidly the two ships of space drew together; the patrol boat now stationary with respect to the planet, the huge battleship decelerating at maximum. Three enormous beams reached out and, held at prow, midsection, and stern, the tiny flier was drawn rapidly but carefully against the towering side of her mother ship. The double seals engaged and locked; the massive doors began to open.

Now came the most crucial point of DuQuesne's whole scheme. For that warship carried a complement of nearly a hundred men, and ten or a dozen of them – the lock commander, surgeons, and orderlies certainly, and possibly a corps of mechanics as well – would be massed in the airlock room behind those slowly opening barriers. But in that scheme's very audacity lay its great strength – its almost complete assurance of success. For what Fenachrone, with the inborn consciousness of superiority that was his heritage, would even dream that two members of any alien race would have the sheer, brazen effrontery to dare to attack a full-manned Class Z superdreadnought, one of the most formidable structures that had ever lifted its stupendous mass into the ether?

But DuQuesne so dared. Direct action had always been his forte. Apparently impossible odds had never daunted him. He had always planned his coups carefully, then followed those plans coldly and ruthlessly to their logical and successful conclusions. Two men could do this job very nicely, and would so do it. DuQuesne had chosen Loring with care. Therefore he lay at ease in his armor in front of the slowly opening portal, calmly certain that the iron nerves of his assassin aid would not weaken for even the instant necessary to disrupt his carefully laid plan.

As soon as the doors had opened sufficiently to permit ingress, Loring went through them slowly, carrying the supposedly unconscious man with care. But once inside the opaque walls of the lock room, that slowness became activity incarnate. DuQuesne sprang instantly to his full height, and before the clustered officers could even perceive that anything was amiss, four sure hands had trained upon them the deadliest hand weapons known to the science of their own race.

Since DuQuesne was overlooking no opportunity of acquiring knowledge, the heads were spared; but as the four furious blasts of vibratory energy tore through those massive bodies, making of their every internal organ a mass of disorganized protoplasmic pulp, every Fenachrone in the room fell lifeless to the floor before he could move a hand in self-defense.

Dropping his weapons, DuQuesne wrenched off his helmet, while Loring with deft hands bared the head of the senior officer of the group upon the floor. Headsets flashed out – were clamped into place – dials were set – the scientist shot power into the tubes, transferring into his own brain an entire section of the dead brain before him.

His senses reeled under the shock, but he recovered quickly, and even as he threw off the phones Loring slammed down over his head the helmet of the Fenachrone. DuQuesne was now commander of the airlocks, and the break in communication had been of such duration that not the slightest suspicion had been aroused. He snapped out mental orders to the distant power room, the side of the vessel opened, and the scout ship was drawn within.

'All tight, sir,' he reported to the captain, and the Z12Q began to retrace her path in space.

DuQuesne's first objective had been attained without untoward incident. The second objective, the control room, might present more difficulty, since its occupants would be scattered. However, to neutralize this difficulty, the Earthly attackers could work with bare hands and thus with the weapons with which both were thoroughly familiar. Removing their gauntlets, the two men ran lightly toward that holy of Fenachrone holies, the control room. Its door was guarded, but DuQuesne had known that it would be – wherefore the guards went down before they could voice a challenge. The door crashed open and four heavy, long-barreled automatics began vomiting forth a leaden storm of death. Those pistols were gripped in accustomed and steady hands; those hands in turn were actuated by the ruthless brains of heartless, con-scienceless, and merciless killers.

His second and major objective gained, DuQuesne proceeded at once to consolidate his position. Pausing only to learn from the brain of the dead captain the exact technique of procedure, he summoned into the sanctum, one at a time, every member of the gigantic vessel's crew. Man after man they came, in answer to the summons of their all-powerful captain – and man after man they died.

'Take the educator and get some of their surgeon's skill,' DuQuesne directed curtly, after the last member of the crew had been accounted for. 'Take off the heads and put them where they'll keep. Throw the rest of the rubbish out. Never mind about this captain – I want to study him.'

Then, while Loring busied himself at his grisly task, DuQuesne sat at the captain's bench, read the captain's brain, and sent in to general headquarters the captain's regular routine reports.

'All cleaned up. Now what?' Loring was as spick-and-span, as calmly unruffled, as though he were reporting in one of the private rooms of the Perkins Cafe. 'Start back to the Earth?'

'Not yet.' Even though DuQuesne had captured his battleship, thereby performing the almost impossible, he was not yet content. 'There are a lot of things to learn here yet, and I think that we had better stay here as long as possible and learn them; provided we can do so without incurring any extra risks. As far as actual flight goes, two men can handle this ship as well as a hundred, since her machinery is all automatic. Therefore we can run away any time.

'We could not fight, however, as it takes about thirty men to handle her weapons. But fighting would do no good, anyway, because they could outnumber us a hundred to one in a few hours. All of which means that if we go out beyond the detector screens we will not be able to come back – we had better stay here, so as to be able to take advantage of any favorable developments.'

He fell silent, frowningly concentrated upon some problem obscure to his companion. At last he went to the main control panel and busied himself with a device of photo cells, coils, and kino bulbs; whereupon Loring set about preparing a long-delayed meal.

'It's all hot, chief – come and get it,' the aide invited, when he saw that his superior's immediate task was done. 'What's the idea? Didn't they have enough controls there already?'

'The idea is, Doll, not to take any unnecessary chances. Ah, this goulash hits the spot!' DuQuesne ate appreciatively for a few minutes in silence, then went on: 'Three things may happen to interfere with the continuation of our search for knowledge. First, since we are now in command of a Fenachrone mother ship, I have to report to headquarters on the telemental recorder, and they may catch me in a slip any minute, which will mean a massed attack. Second, the enemy may break through the Fenachrone defenses and precipitate a general engagement. Third, there is still the bare possibility of that cosmic explosion I told you about.

'In that connection, it is quite obvious than an atomic explosion wave of that type would be propagated with the velocity of light. Therefore, even though our ship could run away from it, since we have an acceleration of five times that velocity, yet we could not see that such an explosion had occurred until the wave-front had reached us. Then, of course, it would be too late to do anything about it, because what an atomic explosion wave would do to the dense material of this battleship would be simply nobody's business.

'We might get away if one of us had his hands actually on the controls and had his eyes and his brain right on the job, but that is altogether too much to expect of flesh and blood. No brain can be maintained at its highest pitch for any length of time.'

'So what?' Loring said laconically. If the chief was not worried about these things, the henchman would not be worried either.

'So I rigged up a detector that is both automatic and instantaneous. At the first touch of any unusual vibration it will throw in the full space drive and will shoot us directly away from the point of disturbance. Now we shall be absolutely safe, no matter what happens.

'We are safe from any possible attack; neither the Fenachrone nor our common enemy, whoever they are, can harm us. We are safe even from the atomic explosion of the entire planet. We shall stay here until we get everything that we want. Then we shall go back to the Green System. We shall find Seaton.'

His entire being grew grim and implacable, his voice became harder and colder even than its hard and cold wont. 'We shall blow him clear out of the ether. The world – yes, whatever I want of the galaxy – shall be *mine!*'

4

A World is Destroyed

Only a few days were required for the completion of DuQuesne's Fenachrone education, since not many of the former officers of the battleship could add much to the already vast knowledge possessed by the Terrestrial scientist. Therefore the time soon came when he had nothing to occupy either his vigorous body or his voracious mind, and the self-imposed idleness irked his active spirit sorely.

'If nothing is going to happen out here we might as well get started back; this present situation is intolerable,' he declared to Loring, and proceeded to lay spy rays to various strategic points of the enormous shell of defense, and even to the sacred precincts of headquarters itself.

'They will probably catch me at this, and when they do it will blow the lid off; but since we are all ready for the break we don't care now how soon it comes. There's something gone sour somewhere, and it may do us some good to know something about it.'

'Sour? Along what line?'

'The mobilization has slowed down. The first phase went off beautifully, you know, right on schedule; but lately things have slowed down. That doesn't seem just right, since their plans are all dynamic, not static. Of course general headquarters isn't advertising it to us outlying captains, but I think I can sense an undertone of uneasiness. That's why I am doing this little job of spying, to get the low-down … Ah, I thought so! Look here, Doll! See those gaps on the defense map? Over half of their big ships are not in position – look at those tracer reports – not a battleship that was out in space has come back, and a lot of them are more than a week overdue. I'll say that's something we ought to know about—'

'Observation Officer of the Z12Q, attention!' snapped from the tight-beam headquarters communicator. 'Cut off those spy rays and report yourself under arrest for treason!'

'Not today,' DuQuesne drawled. 'Besides, I can't – I am in command here now.'

'Open your visiplate to full aperture!' The staff officer's voice was choked with fury; never in his long life had he been so grossly insulted by a mere captain of the line.

DuQuesne opened the plate, remarking to Loring as he did so, 'This is the blow-off, all right. No possible way of stalling him off now, even if I wanted to; and I really want to tell them a few things before we shove off.'

'Where are the men who should be at stations?' the furious voice demanded.

'Dead,' DuQuesne replied laconically.

'Dead! And you have reported nothing amiss?' He turned from his own microphone, but DuQuesne and Loring could hear his savage commands:

'K1427 – Order the twelfth squadron to bring in the Z12Q!'

He spoke again to the rebellious and treasonable observer: 'And you have made your helmet opaque to the rays of this plate, another violation of the code. Take it off!' The speaker fairly rattled under the bellowing voice of the outraged general. 'If you live long enough to get here, you will pay the full penalty for treason, insubordination, and conduct unbecom—'

'Oh, shut up, you yapping nincompoop!' snapped DuQuesne.

Wrenching off his helmet, he thrust his blackly forbidding face directly before the visiplate; so that the raging officer stared, from a distance of only eighteen inches, not into the cowed and frightened face of a guiltily groveling subordinate, but into the proud and sneering visage of Marc C. DuQuesne, of Earth.

And DuQuesne's whole being radiated open and supreme contempt, the most gallingly nauseous dose possible to inflict upon any member of that race of self-styled supermen, the Fenachrone. As he stared at the Earthman the general's tirade broke off in the middle of a word and he fell back speechless – robbed, it seemed, almost of consciousness by the shock.

'You asked for it – you got it – now just what are you going to do about it?' DuQuesne spoke aloud, to render even more trenchantly cutting the crackling mental comments as they leaped across space, each thought lashing the officer like the biting, tearing tip of a bull-whip.

'Better men than you have been beaten by overconfidence,' he went on, 'and better plans than yours have come to nothing through underestimating the resources in brain and power of the opposition. You are not the first race in the history of the universe to go down because of false pride, and you will not be the last. You thought that my comrade and I had been taken and killed. You thought so because I wanted you so to think. In reality we took that scout ship, and when we wanted it we took this battleship as easily.

'We have been here, in the very heart of your defense system for ten days. We have obtained everything that we set out to get; we have learned everything that we set out to learn. If we wished to take it, your entire planet could offer us no more resistance than did these vessels, but we do not want it.

'Also, after due deliberation, we have decided that the universe would be much better off without any Fenachrone in it. Therefore your race will of course soon disappear; and since we do not want your planet, we will see to it that no one else will want it, at least for some few eons of time to come. Think *that* over, as long as you are able to think. Goodbye!'

DuQuesne cut off the visiray with a vicious twist and turned to Loring. 'Pure boloney, of course!' he sneered. 'But as long as they don't know that fact it'll probably hold them for a while.'

'Better start drifting for home, hadn't we? They'll be coming out after us.'

'We certainly had.' DuQuesne strolled leisurely across the room toward the controls. 'We hit them hard, in a mighty tender spot, and they will make it highly unpleasant for us if we linger around here much longer. But we are in no danger. There is no tracer on this ship – they use them only on long-distance cruisers – so they'll have no idea where to look for us. Also, I don't believe that they'll even try to chase us, because I gave them a lot to think about for some time to come, even if it wasn't true.'

But DuQuesne had spoken far more truly than he knew – his 'boloney' was in fact a coldly precise statement of an awful truth even then about to be made manifest. For at that very moment Dunark of Osnome was reaching for the switch whose closing would send a detonating current through the thousands of tons of sensitized atomic copper already placed by Seaton in their deep-buried emplantments upon the noisome planet of the Fenachrone.

DuQuesne knew that the outlying vessels of the monsters had not returned to base, but he did not know that Seaton had destroyed them, one and all, in open space; he did not know that his arch-foe was the being who was responsible for the failure of the Fenachrone spaceships to come back from their horrible voyages.

Upon the other hand, while Seaton knew that there were battleships afloat in the ether within the protecting screens of the planet, he had no inkling that one of those very battleships was manned by his two bitterest and most vindictive enemies, the official and completely circumstantial report of whose death by cremation he had witnessed such a few days before.

DuQuesne strolled across the floor of the control room, and in mid-step became weightless, floating freely in the air. The planet had exploded, and the outermost fringe of the wave-front of the atomic disintegration, propagated outwardly into spherical space with the velocity of light, had impinged upon the all-seeing and ever-watchful mechanical eye which DuQuesne had so carefully installed. But only that outermost fringe, composed solely of light and ultra-light, had touched that eye. The relay – an electronic beam – had been deflected instantaneously, demanding of the governors their terrific . maximum of power, away from the doomed world. The governor had responded in a space of time to be measured only in fractional millionths of a second, and the vessel leaped effortlessly and almost instantaneously into an acceleration of five light-velocities, urged onward by the full power of the space-annihilating drive of the Fenachrone.

The eyes of DuQuesne and Loring had had time really to see nothing whatever. There was the barest perceptible flash of the intolerable brilliance of an exploding universe, succeeded in the very instant of its perception – yes, even before its real perception – by the utter blackness of the complete absence of all light whatever as the space drive automatically went into action and hurled the great vessel away from the all-destroying wave-front of the atomic explosion.

As has been said, there were many battleships within the screens of the planet, supporting a horde of scout ships according to Invasion Plan XB218; but of all these vessels and of all things Fenachrone, only two escaped the incredible violence of the holocaust. One was the immense space ship of Ravindau the scientist, which had for days been hurtling through space upon its way to a far-distant galaxy; the other was the first-line battleship carrying DuQuesne and his killer aide, which had been snatched from the very teeth of that indescribable cosmic cataclysm by the instantaneous operation of DuQuesne's automatic relays.

Everything on or near the planet had of course been destoyed instantly, and even the fastest battleship, farthest removed from the disintegrating world, was overwhelmed. For to living eyes, staring however attentively into ordinary visiplates, there had been practically no warning at all, since the wave-front of atomic disruption was propagated with the velocity of light and therefore followed very closely indeed behind the narrow fringe of visible light which heralded its coming.

Even if one of the dazed commanders had known the meaning of the coruscant blaze of brilliance which was the immediate forerunner of destruction, he would have been helpless to avert it, for no hands of flesh and blood, human or Fenachrone, could possibly have thrown switches rapidly enough to have escaped from the advancing wave-front of disruption; and at the touch of that frightful wave every atom of substance, alike of vessel, contents, and hellish crew, became resolved into its component electrons and added its contribution of energy to the stupendous cosmic catastrophe.

Even before his foot had left the floor in free motion, however, DuQuesne realized exactly what had happened. His keen eyes saw the flash of blinding incandescence announcing a world's ending and sent to his keen brain a picture; and in the instant of perception that brain had analyzed that picture and understood its every implication and connotation. Therefore he only grinned sardonically at the phenomena which left the slower-minded Loring dazed and breathless.

He continued to grin as the battleship hurtled onward through the void at a pace beside which that of any ether-borne wave, even that of such a titanic disturbance as the atomic explosion of an entire planet, was the veriest crawl.

At last, however, Loring comprehended what had happened. 'Oh, it exploded, huh?' he ejaculated.

'It most certainly did.' The scientist's grin grew diabolical. 'My statements to them came true, even though I did not have anything to do with their fruition. However, these events prove that caution is all right in its place – it pays big dividends at times. I'm very glad, of course, that the Fenachrone have been definitely taken out of the picture.'

Utterly callous, DuQuesne neither felt nor expressed the slightest sign of pity for the race of beings so suddenly snuffed out of existence. 'Their removal at this time will undoubtedly save me a lot of trouble later on,' he added, 'but the whole thing certainly gives me furiously to think, as the French say. It was done with a sensitized atomic copper bomb, of course; but I should like very much to know who did it, and why; and, above all, how they were able to make the approach.'

'Personally, I still think it was Seaton,' the baby-faced murderer put it calmly. 'No reason for thinking so, except that whenever anything impossible has been pulled off anywhere that I ever heard of, he was the guy that did it. Call it a hunch, if you want to.'

'It may have been Seaton, of course, even though I can't really think so.' DuQuesne frowned blackly in concentration. 'It may have been accidental – started by the explosion of an ammunition dump or something of the kind – but I believe that even less than I do the other. It couldn't have been any race of beings from any other planet of this system, since they are all bare of life, the Fenachrone having killed off all the other races ages ago and not caring to live on the other planets themselves. No; I still think that it was some enemy from outer space; although my belief that it could not have been Seaton is weakening.

'However, with this ship we can probably find out in short order who it was, whether it was Seaton or any possible outside race. We are far enough away now to be out of danger from that explosion, so we'll slow down, circle around, and find out whoever it was that touched it off.'

He slowed the mad pace of the cruiser until the firmament behind them once more became visible, to see that the system of the Fenachrone was now illuminated by a splendid double sun. Sending out a full series of ultra-powered detector screens, DuQuesne scanned the instruments narrowly. Every meter remained dead, its needle upon zero; not a sign of radiation could be detected upon any communicator or power band; the ether was empty for millions upon untold millions of miles. He then put on power and cruised at higher and higher velocities, describing a series of enormous loop-ing circles throughout the space surrounding that entire solar system.

Around and around the flaming double sun, rapidly becoming first a double star and then merely a faint point of light, DuQuesne urged the Fenachrone battleship, but his screens remained cold and unresponsive. No ship of the void was operating in all that vast volume of ether; no sign of man or of any of his works was to be found throughout it.

DuQuesne then extended his detectors to the terrific maximum of their unthinkable range, increased his already frightful acceleration to its absolute limit, and cruised madly onward in already vast and ever-widening spirals until a grim conclusion forced itself upon his consciousness. Unwilling though he was to believe it, he was forced finally to recognize an appalling fact. The enemy, whoever he might have been, must have been operating from a distance immeasurably greater than any that even DuQuesne's new-found knowledge could believe possible; abounding though it was in astounding data concerning super-scientific weapons of destruction.

He again cut their acceleration down to a touring rate, adjusted his auto-matic alarms and signals, and turned to Loring, his face grim and hard.

'They must have been farther away than even any of the Fenchrone physi-cists would have believed possible,' he stated flatly. 'It looks more and more like Seaton – he probably found some more high-class help somewhere. Temporarily, at least, I am stumped – but I do not stay stumped long. I shall find him if I have to comb the galaxy, star by star!'

Thus DuQuesne, not even dreaming what an incredibly inconceivable distance from their galaxy Seaton was to attain; nor what depths of extra-dimensional space Seaton was to traverse before they were again to stand face to face – cold black eyes staring straight into hard and level eyes of gray.

5

Thought – A Sixth-Order Wave

The mightiest spaceship that had ever lifted her stupendous mass from any planet known to the humanity of this, the First Galaxy, was hurtling onward through the hard vacuum of intergalactic space. Around the *Skylark* there was nothing – no stars, no suns, no meteorites, no smallest particle of cosmic dust. The First Galaxy lay so far behind her that even its vast lens showed only as a dimly perceptible patch of light in the visiplates.

The Fenachrone space chart placed other galaxies to right of and to left of, above and below, the flying cruiser; but they were so infinitely distant that their light could scarcely reach the eyes of the Terrestrial wanderers.

So prodigious had been the velocity of the *Skylark*, when the last vessel of the Fenachrone had been destroyed, that she could not possibly have been halted until she had covered more than half the distance separating that galaxy from our own; and Seaton and Crane had agreed that this chance to visit it was altogether too good to be missed. Therefore the velocity of their vessel had been augmented rather than lessened, and for uneventful days and weeks, she had bored her terrific way through the incomprehensible nothingness of the intergalactic void.

After a few days of impatient waiting and of eager anticipation, Seaton had settled down into the friendly and companionable routine of the flight. But inaction palled upon his vigorous nature and, physical outlet denied, he began to delve deeper and deeper into the almost-unknown, scarcely plumbed recesses of his new mind – a mind stored with the accumulated knowledge of thousands of generations of Rovol and of Drasnik; generations of specialists in research in two widely separated fields of knowledge.

Thus it was that one morning Seaton prowled about aimlessly in brown abstraction, hands jammed deep into pockets, the while there rolled from his villainously reeking pipe blue clouds of fumes that might have taxed sorely a less efficient air-purifier than that boasted by the *Skylark*. Prowled, suddenly to dash across the control room to the immense keyboards of his fifth-order projector.

There he sat, hour after hour. Hands setting up incredibly complex integrals upon its inexhaustible supply of keys and stops; gray eyes staring unseeingly into infinity he sat there; deaf, dumb, and blind to everything except the fascinatingly fathomless problem upon which he was so diligently at work.

Dinner time came and went, then supper time, then bedtime; and Dorothy strode purposefully toward the console, only to be led away, silently and quietly, by the watchful Crane.

'But he hasn't come up for air once today, Martin!' she protested, when they were in the private sitting room of the Cranes. 'And didn't you tell me yourself, that time back in Washington, to make him snap out of it whenever he started to pull off one of his wild marathon splurges of overwork?'

'Yes; I did,' Crane replied thoughtfully; 'but circumstances here and now are somewhat different from what they were then. I have no idea of what he is working out, but it is a problem of such complexity that in one process he used more than seven hundred factors, and it may well be that if he were to be interrupted now he could never recover that particular line of thought. Then, too, you must remember that he is now in such excellent physical condition that he is in no present danger. I would say to let him alone, for a while longer, at least.'

'All right, Martin, that's fine! I hated to disturb him, really – I would hate most awfully to derail an important train of thought.'

'Yes; let him concentrate a while,' urged Margaret. 'He hasn't indulged in one of those fits for weeks – Rovol wouldn't let him. I think it's a shame, too, because when he dives in like that after something he comes up with it in his teeth – when he really thinks, he does things. I don't see how those Norlaminians ever got anything done, when they always did their thinking by the clock and quit promptly at quitting time, even if it was right in the middle of an idea.'

'Dick can do more in an hour, the way he is working now, than Rovol of Rays could ever do in ten years!' Dorothy exclaimed with conviction. 'I'm going in to keep him company – he's more apt to be disturbed by my being gone than by having me there. Better come along, too, you two, just as though nothing was going on. We'll give him an hour or so yet, anyway.' The trio then strolled back into the control room.

The trio then strolled back into the control room.

But Seaton finished his computations without interruption. Some time after midnight he transferred his integrated and assembled forces to an anchoring plunger, arose from his irksome chair, stretched mightily, and turned to the others, tired but triumphant.

'Folks, I think I've got something!' he cried. 'Kinda late, but it'll only take a couple of minutes to test it out. I'll put these nets over your heads, and then you all look into that viewing cabinet over there.'

Over his own head and shoulders Seaton draped a finely woven screen of silvery metal, connected by a stranded cable to a plug in his board; and after he had similarly invested his companions he began to manipulate dials and knobs.

As he did so the dark space of the cabinet became filled with a soft glow of light – a glow which resolved itself into color and form, a three-dimensional picture. In the background towered a snow-capped, beautifully symmetrical volcanic mountain; in the foreground were to be seen cherry trees in full bloom surrounding a small structure of unmistakable architecture; and through their minds swept fleeting flashes of poignant longing, amounting almost to nostalgia.

'Good heavens, Dick, what have you done now?' Dorothy broke out. 'I feel so homesick that I want to cry – and I don't care a bit whether I *ever* see Japan again or not!'

'These nets aren't perfect insulators, of course, even though I've got them grounded. There's some leakage. They'd have to be solid to stop all radiation. Leaks both ways, of course, so we're interfering with the picture a little too; but there's some outside interference that I can't discover yet.' Seaton thought aloud, rather than explained, as he shut off the power. 'Folks, we *have* got something! That's the sixth-order pattern, and *thought* is in that level! Those were *thoughts* – *Shiro's* thoughts.'

'But he's asleep, surely, by this time,' Dorothy protested.

'Sure he is, or he wouldn't be thinking those kind of thoughts. Must be dreaming – he's contented enough when he is awake.'

'How did you work it out?' asked Crane. 'You said, yourself, that it might well take lifetimes of research.'

'It would, ordinarily. Partly a hunch, partly dumb luck, but mostly a combination of two brains that upon Norlamin would ordinarily never touch the same subject anywhere. Rovol, who knows everything there is to be known about rays, and Drasnik, probably the greatest authority upon the mind that ever lived, both gave me a good share of their knowledge; and the combination turned out to be hot stuff, particularly in connection with this fifth-order keyboard. Now we can really do something!'

'But you had a sixth-order detector before,' Margaret put in. 'Why didn't we touch it off by thinking?'

'Too coarse – I see that, now. It wouldn't react to the extremely slight power of a thought-wave; only to the powerful impulses from a bar or from cosmic radiation. But I can build one now that will react to thought, and I'm going to; particularly since there was a little interference on that picture that I couldn't quite account for.' He turned back to the projector.

'You're coming to bed,' declared Dorothy with finality. 'You've done enough for one day.'

She had her way, but early the next morning Seaton was again at the keyboard, wearing a complex headset and driving a tenuous fabric of force far out into the void. After an hour or so he tensed suddenly, every sense concentrated upon something vaguely perceptible; something which became less and less nebulous as his steady fingers rotated micrometric dials in infinitesimal arcs.

'Come get a load of this!' he called at last. 'Mart, what would a planet – an inhabited planet, at that – be doing way out here, heaven only knows how many light-centuries away from the nearest galaxy?'

The three donned headsets and seated themselves in their chairs in the base of the great projector. Instantly they felt projections of themselves hurled an incomprehensible distance out into empty space. But that weird sensation was not new; each was thoroughly accustomed to the feeling of duality incident to being in the *Skylark* in body, yet with a duplicate mentality carried by the projection to a point many light-years distant from his corporeal substance. Their mentalities, thus projected, felt a fleeting instant of unthinkable velocity, then hung poised above the surface of a small but dense planet, a planet utterly alone in that dreadful void.

But it was like no other planet with which the Terrestrial wanderers were familiar. It possessed neither air nor water, and it was entirely devoid of topographical features. It was merely a bare, mountainless, depthless sphere of rock and metal. Though sunless, it was not dark; it glowed with a strong, white light which emanated from the rocky soil itself. Nothing animate was visible, nor was there a sign that any form of life, animal or vegetable, had ever existed there.

'You can talk if you want to,' Seaton observed, noticing that Dorothy was holding back by main strength a torrent of words. 'They can't hear us – there's no audio in the circuit.'

'What do you mean by "they", Dick?' she demanded. 'You said it was an inhabited planet. That one isn't inhabited. It never was, and it can't possibly be, *ever!*'

'When I spoke I thought that it was inhabited, in the ordinary sense of the word, but I see now that it isn't,' he replied, quietly and thoughtfully. 'But they were there a minute ago, and they'll probably be back. Don't kid yourself, Dimples. It's inhabited, all right, and by somebody we don't know much about – or rather, by something that we knew once – altogether too well.'

'The pure intellectuals,' Crane stated, rather than asked.

'Yes; and that accounts for the impossible location of the planet, too. They probably materialized it out there, just for the exercise. There, they're coming back. Feel 'em?'

Vivid thoughts, for the most part incomprehensible, flashed from the headsets into their minds; and instantly the surroundings of their projections changed. With the speed of thought a building materialized upon that barren ground, and they found themselves looking into a brilliantly lighted and spacious hall. Walls of alabaster, giving forth a living, almost fluid light. Tapestries, whose fantastically intricate designs changed from moment to moment into ever new and ever more amazingly complex delineations. Gem-studded fountains, whose plumes and gorgeous sprays of dancing liquid obeyed no Earthly laws of mechanics. Chairs and benches, writhing, changing in form constantly and with no understandable rhythm. And in that hall were the intellectuals – the entities who had materialized those objects from the ultimately elemental radiant energy of open space.

Their number could not even be guessed. Sometimes only one was visible, sometimes it seemed that the great hall was crowded with them – ever-changing shapes varying in texture from the tenuousness of a wraith to a density greater than that of any Earthly metal.

So bewilderingly rapid were the changes in form that no one appearance could be intelligently grasped. Before one outlandish and unearthly shape could really be perceived it had vanished – had melted and flowed into one entirely different in form and in sense, but one equally monstrous to Terrestrial eyes. Even if grasped mentally, no one of those grotesque shapes could have been described in language, so utterly foreign were they to all human knowledge, history, and experience.

And now, the sixth-order projections in perfect synchronism, the thoughts of the Outlanders came clearly into the minds of the four watchers – thoughts cold, hard, and clear, diamond-like in polish and in definition; thoughts with the perfection of finish and detail possible only to the fleshless mentalities who for countless millions of years had done little save perfect themselves in the technique of pure and absolute thinking.

The four sat tense and strained as the awful import of those thoughts struck home; then, at another thought of horribly unmistakable meaning, Seaton snapped off his power and drove lightning fingers over his keyboard, while the two women slumped back, white-faced and trembling, into their seats.

'I thought it was funny, back there that time, that that fellow couldn't integrate in the ninety-seven dimensions necessary to dematerialize us, and I didn't know anything then.' Seaton, his preparations complete, leaned back in his operator's seat at the console. 'He was just kidding us – playing with us, just to see what we'd do, and as for not being able to think his way back – phooie! He can think his way through ninety-seven universes if he wants to. They're certainly extra-galactic and very probably extra-universal, and the one that played with us could have dematerialized us instantly if he had felt like it.'

'That is apparent, now,' Crane conceded. 'They are quite evidently patterns of sixth-order forces, and as such have a velocity of anything they want to use. They absorb force from the radiations in free space, and are capable of diverting and of utilizing those forces in any fashion they may choose. They would of course be eternal, and, so far as I can see, they would be indestructible. What are we going to do about it, Dick? What *can* we do about it?'

'We'll do *something*!' Seaton gritted. 'We're not as helpless as they think we are. I've got out five courses of six-ply screen, with full interliners of zones of force. I've got everything blocked, clear down to the sixth order. If they can think their way through those screens they're better than I think they are, and if they try anything else we'll do our darndest to block that, too – and with this Norlaminian keyboard and all the uranium we've got that'll be a mighty lot, believe me! After that last crack of theirs they'll hunt for us, of course, and I'm pretty sure they'll find us. I thought so – here they are! Materialization, huh? I told him once that if he'd stick to stuff that I could understand, I'd give him a run for his money!'

6

Mind Versus Matter

Far out in the depths of the intergalactic void there sped along upon its strange course the newly materialized planet of the intellectuals. Desolate and barren it was, and apparently destitute of life; but life was there – eternal, disembodied life, unaffected by any possible extreme of heat or cold, requiring for its continuance neither water nor air, nor, for that matter, any material substance whatsoever. And from somewhere in the vacuum above that planet's forbidding surface there emanated a thought – a thought coldly clear, abysmally hopeless.

'I have but one remaining aim in this life. While I have failed again, as I have failed innumerable times in the past, I shall keep on trying until I succeed in assembling in sufficient strength the exact forces necessary to disrupt this sixth-order pattern which is I.'

'You speak foolishly, Eight, as does each of us now and again,' came instant response. 'There is much more to perceive, much more to do, much more to learn. Why be discouraged or disheartened? An infinity of time is necessary in which to explore infinite space and to acquire infinite knowledge.'

'Foolish I may be, but this is no simple recurrent outburst of melancholia. I am definitely weary of this cycle of existence, and I wish to pass on to the next, whatever of experience or of sheer oblivion it may bring. In fact, I wish that you, One, had never worked out the particular pattern of forces that liberated our eleven minds from the so-called shackles of our material bodies. For we cannot die. We are simply patterns of force eternal, marking the passage of time only by the life cycles of the suns of the galaxies.

'Why, I envy even the creatures inhabiting the planets throughout the galaxy we visited but a moment ago. Partially intelligent though they are, struggling and groping, each individual dying after only a fleeting instant of life; born, growing old, and passing on in a minute fraction of a millionth of one cycle – yet I envy even them.'

'That was the reason you did not dematerialize those you accompanied briefly while they were flitting about in their crude spaceship?'

'Yes. Being alive for such an infinitesimal period of time, they value life highly. Why hurry them into the future that is so soon to be theirs?'

'Do not dwell upon such thoughts, Eight,' advised One. 'They lead only to greater and greater depths of despondency. Consider instead what we have done and what we shall do.'

'I have considered everything, at length,' the entity known as Eight thought back stubbornly. 'What benefit or satisfaction do we get out of this continuous sojourn in the cycle of existence from which we should have departed aeons ago? We have power, it is true, but what of it? It is barren. We create for ourselves bodies and their material surroundings, like this' – the great hall came into being, and so vast was the mentality creating it that the flow of thought continued without a break – 'but what of it? We do not enjoy them as lesser beings enjoy the bodies which to them are synonymous with life.

'We have traveled endlessly, we have seen much, we have studied much; but what of it? Fundamentally we have accomplished nothing and we know nothing. We know but little more than we knew ourselves countless thousands of cycles ago, when our home planet was still substance. We know nothing of time; we know nothing of space; we know nothing even of the fourth dimension save that the three of us who rotated themselves into it have never returned. And until one of us succeeds in building a neutralizing pattern we can never die – we must face a drab and cheerless eternity of existence as we now are.'

'An eternity, yes, but an eternity neither drab nor cheerless. We know but little, as you have said, but in that fact lies a stimulus; we can and shall go on forever, learning more and ever more. Think of it! But hold – what is that? I feel a foreign thought. It must emanate from a mind powerful indeed to have come so far.'

'I have felt them. There are four foreign minds, but they are unimportant.'

'Have you analyzed them?'

'Yes. They are the people of the spaceship which we just mentioned; projecting their mentalities to us here.'

'Projecting mentalities? Such a low form of life? They must have learned much from you, Eight.'

'Perhaps. I did give them one or two hints,' Eight returned, utterly indifferent, 'but they are of no importance to us.'

'I am not so sure of that,' One mused. 'We found no others in that galaxy capable of so projecting themselves, nor did we find any beings possessing minds strong enough to be capable of existence without the support of a material body. It may be that they are sufficiently advanced to join us. Even if they are not, if their minds should prove too weak for our company, they are undoubtedly strong enough to be of use in one of my researches.'

At this point Seaton cut off the projections and began to muster his sixth-order defenses, therefore he did not 'hear' Eight's outburst against the proposal of his leader.

'I will not allow it, One!' the disembodied intelligence protested intensely. 'Rather than have you inflict upon them the eternity of life that we have suffered I shall myself dematerialize them. Much as they love life, it would be infinitely better for them to spare a few minutes of it than to live forever.'

But there was no reply. One had vanished; had darted at utmost speed toward the *Skylark*. Eight followed him instantly.

Light-centuries of distance meant no more to them than to Seaton's own projector, and they soon reached the hurtling spaceship; a spaceship moving with all its unthinkable velocity, yet to them motionless – what is velocity when there are no reference points by which to measure it?

'Back, Eight!' commanded One abruptly. 'They are enclosed in a nullifying wall of the sixth order. They are indeed advanced in mentality.'

'A complete stasis in the subether?' Eight marveled. 'That will do as well as the pattern ...'

'Greetings, strangers!' Seaton's thought interrupted. Thoughts as clear as those require no interpretation of language. 'My projection is here, outside the wall, but I might caution you that one touch of your patterns will cut it off and stiffen that wall to absolute impenetrability. I assume that your visit is friendly?'

'Eminently so,' replied One. 'I offer you the opportunity of joining us; or, at least, the opportunity of being of assistance to science in the attempt at joining us.'

'They want us to join them as pure intellectuals, folks.' Seaton turned from the projector, toward his friends. 'How about it, Dottie? We've got quite a few things to do yet in the flesh, haven't we?'

'I'll say we have, Dickie – don't be an idiot!' she chuckled.

'Sorry, One!' Seaton thought again into space. 'Your invitation is appreciated to the full, and we thank you for it, but we have too many things to do in our own lives and upon our own world to accept it at this time. Later on, perhaps, we could do so with profit.'

'You will accept it *now*,' One declared coldly. 'Do you imagine that your puny wills can withstand *mine* for a single instant?'

'I don't know; but, aided by certain mechanical devices of ours, I do know that they'll do a terrific job of trying!' Seaton blazed back.

'There is one thing that I believe you can do,' Eight put in. 'Your barrier wall should be able to free me from this intolerable condition of eternal life!' And he hurled himself forward with all his prodigious force against that nullifying wall.

Instantly the screen flamed into incandescence; converters and generators whined and shrieked as hundreds of pounds of power uranium disappeared under that awful load. But the screens held, and in an instant it was over. Eight was gone, disrupted into the future life for which he had so longed, and the impregnable wall was once more merely a tenuous veil of sixth-order vibrations. Through that veil Seaton's projection crept warily; but the inhuman, monstrous mentality poised just beyond it made no demonstration.

'Eight committed suicide, as he has so often tried to do,' One commented coldly, 'but, after all, his loss will be felt with relief, if at all. His dissatisfaction was an actual impediment to the advancement of our entire group. And now, feeble intellect, I will let you know what is in store for you, before I direct against you the forces which will render your screens inoperative and therefore make further interchange of thought impossible. You shall be dematerialized; and, whether or not your minds are strong enough to exist in the free state, your entities shall be of some small assistance to me before you pass on to the next cycle of existence. What substance do you disintegrate for power?'

'That is none of your business, and since you cannot drive a ray through this screen you will never find out!' Seaton snapped.

'It matters little,' One rejoined, unmoved. 'Were you employing pure neutronium and were your vessel entirely filled with it, yet in a short time it would be exhausted. For, know you, I have summoned the other members of our group. We are able to direct cosmic forces which, although not infinite in magnitude, are to all intents and purposes inexhaustible. In a brief time your power will be gone, and I shall confer with you again.'

The other mentalities flashed up in response to the call of their leader, and at his direction arranged themselves all about the far-flung outer screen of the *Skylark*. Then from all space, directed inward, there converged upon the spaceship gigantic streamers of force. Invisible streamers, and impalpable, but under their fierce impacts the defensive screens of the Terrestrial vessel flared into even more frenzied displays of pyrotechnic incandescence than they had exhibited under the heaviest beams of the superdreadnought of the Fenachrone. For thousands of miles space became filled with coruscantly luminous discharges as the uranium-driven screens of the *Skylark* dissipated the awful force of the attack.

'I don't see how they can keep that up for very long.' Seaton frowned as he read his meters and saw at what an appalling rate their store of metal was decreasing. 'But he talked as though he knew his stuff. I wonder if – um – um –' He fell silent, thinking intensely, while the others watched his face in strained attention; then went on: 'Uh-huh. I see – he can do it – he wasn't kidding us.'

'How?' asked Crane tensely.

'But how can he, possibly, Dick?' cried Dorothy. 'Why, they aren't *anything*, really!'

'They can't store up power in themselves, of course, but we know that all space is pervaded by radiation – theoretically a source of power that out-classes us as much as we outclass mule power. Nobody that I know of ever tapped it before, and I can't tap it yet; but they've tapped it and can direct it. The directing is easy enough to understand – just like a kid shooting a high-power rifle. He doesn't have to furnish energy for the bullet, you know – he merely touches off the powder and tells the bullet where to go.

'But we're not sunk yet. I see one chance; and even though it's pretty slim, I'd take it before I would knuckle down to his nibs out there. Eight said some-thing a while ago, remember, about "rotating" into the fourth dimension? I've been mulling the idea around in my mind. I'd say that as a last resort we might give it a whirl and take a chance on coming through. See anything else that looks at all feasible, Mart?'

'Not at the present moment,' Crane replied calmly. 'How much time have we?'

'About forty hours at the present rate of dissipation. It's constant, so they've probably focused everything they can bring to bear on us.'

'You cannot attack them in any way? Apparently the sixth-order zone of force kills them?'

'Not a chance. If I open a slit one kilocycle wide anywhere in the band they'll find it instantly and it'll be curtains for us. And even if I could fight them off and work through that slit I couldn't drive a zone into them – their velocity is the same as that of the zone, you know, and they'd simply bounce back with it. If I could pen them up into a spherical – um – um – no use, can't do it with this equipment. If we had Rovol and Caslor and a few others of the Firsts of Norlamin here, and had a month or so of time, maybe we could work out something, but I couldn't even start it alone in the time we've got.'

'But even if we decide to try the fourth dimension, how could you do it? Surely that dimension is merely a mathematical concept, with no actual existence in nature?'

'No; it's actual enough, I think – nature's a big field, you know, and con-tains a lot of unexplored territory. Remember how casually that Eight thing out there discussed it? It isn't how to get there that's biting me; it's only that those intellectuals can stand a lot more grief than we can, and conditions in the region of the fourth dimension probably wouldn't suit us any too well.

'However, we wouldn't have to be there for more than a hundred thou-sandth of a second to dodge this gang, and we could stand almost anything that long, I imagine. As to how to do it – rotation. Three pairs of rotating, high-amperage currents, at mutual right angles, converging upon a point. Remembering that any rotating current exerts its force at a right angle, what would happen?'

'It might, at that,' Crane conceded, after minutes of narrow-eyed concentration; then, Crane-wise, began to muster objections. 'But it would not so affect this vessel. She is altogether too large, is of the wrong shape, and—'

'And you can't pull yourself up by your own boot straps,' Seaton interrupted. 'Right – you've got to have something to work from, something to anchor your forces to. We'd make the trip in little old *Skylark Two*. She's small, she's spherical and she has so little mass compared to *Three* that rotating her out of space would be easy – it wouldn't even shift *Three*'s reference planes.'

'It might prove successful,' Crane admitted at last, 'and, if so, it could not help but be a very interesting and highly informative experience. However, the chance of success seems to be none too great, as you have said, and we must exhaust every other possibility before we decide to attempt it.'

For hours then the two scientists went over every detail of their situation, but could evolve no other plan which held out even the slightest gleam of hope for a successful outcome; and Seaton seated himself before the banked and tiered keyboards of his projector.

There he worked for perhaps half an hour, then called to Crane: 'I've got everything set to spin *Two* out to where we're going, Mart. Now if you and Shiro' – for Crane's former 'man' and the *Skylark*'s factotum was now quite as thoroughly familiar with Norlaminian forces as he had formerly been with Terrestrial tools – 'will put some forces onto the job of getting her ready for anything you think we may meet up with, I'll put in the rest of the time trying to figure out a way of taking a good stiff poke at those jaspers out there.'

He knew that the zones of force surrounding his vessel were absolutely impenetrable to any wave propagated through the ether, and to any possible form of material substance. He knew also that the subether was blocked, through the fifth and sixth orders. He knew that it was hopeless to attempt to solve the problem of the seventh order in the time at his disposal.

If he were to open any of his zones, even for an instant, in order to launch a direct attack, he knew that the immense mentalities to which he was opposed would perceive the opening and through it would wreak the Terrestrials' dematerialization before he could send out a single beam.

Last and worst, he knew that not even his vast console afforded any combination of forces which could possibly destroy the besieging intellectuals. What *could* he do?

For hours he labored with all the power of his wonderful brain, now stored with all the accumulated knowledge of thousands upon thousands of years of Norlaminian research. He stopped occasionally to eat, and once, at his wife's insistence, he snatched a little troubled and uneasy sleep; but his mind drove him back to his board and at that board he worked. Worked – while the hands of the chronometer approached more and ever more nearly the zero hour. Worked – while the *Skylark*'s immense stores of uranium dwindled visibly away in the giving up of their inconceivable amounts of intra-atomic energy to brace the screens which were dissipating the inexhaustible flood of cosmic force being directed against them. Worked – in vain. At last he glanced at the chronometer and stood up. 'Twenty minutes now – time to go,' he announced. 'Dot, come here a minute!'

'Sweetheart!' Tall though Dorothy was, the top of her auburn head came scarcely higher than Seaton's chin. Tightly but tenderly held in his arms she tipped her head back, and her violet eyes held no trace of fear as they met his. 'It's all right, lover. I don't know whether it's because I think we're going to get away, or because we're together; but I'm not in the least bit afraid.'

'Neither am I, dear. Some way, I simply can't believe that we're passing out; I've got a hunch that we're going to come through. We've got a lot to live for yet, you and I, together. But I want to tell you what you already know – that, whatever happens, I love you.'

'Hurry it up, Seatons!'

Margaret's voice recalled them to reality, and all five were wafted upon beams of force into the spherical launching space of the craft in which they were to venture into the unknown.

That vessel was *Skylark Two*, the forty-foot globe of arenak which from Earth to Norlamin had served them so well and which had been carried, lifeboat-like, well inside the two-mile-long torpedo which was *Skylark Three*. The massive doors were clamped and sealed, and the five human beings strapped themselves into their seats against they knew not what emergency.

'All ready, folks?' Seaton grasped the ebonite handle of his master switch. 'I'm not going to tell you Cranes goodbye, Mart – you know my hunch. You got one, too?'

'I cannot say that I have. However, I have always had a great deal of confidence in your ability. Then, too, I have always been something of a fatalist; and, most important of all, like you and Dorothy, Margaret and I are together. You may start any time now, Dick.'

'All right – hang on. On your marks! Get set! Go!'

As the master switch was thrown, a set of gigantic plungers drove home, actuating the tremendous generators in the holds of the massive cruiser of space above and around them; generators which, bursting into instantaneous and furious activity, directed upon the spherical hull of their vessel three opposed pairs of currents of electricity; madly spinning currents, of a potential and of a density never before brought into being by human devices.

7

DuQuesne Visits Norlamin

DuQuesne did not find Seaton, nor did he quite comb the galaxy star by star, as he had declared that he would do in that event. He did, however, try; he prolonged the vain search to distances of so many light-years and through so many weeks of time that even the usually complacent Loring was moved to protest.

'Pretty much like hunting the proverbial needle in the haystack, isn't it, chief?' that worthy asked at last. 'They could be clear back home by this time, whoever they are. It looks as though maybe we could do ourselves more good by doing something else.'

'Yes; I probably am wasting time now, but I hate to give it up,' the scientist replied. 'We have pretty well covered this section of the galaxy. I wonder if it really was Seaton, after all? If he could blow up that planet through those screens he must have a lot more stuff than I have ever thought possible – certainly a lot more than I have, even now – and I would like very much to know how he did it. I couldn't have done it, nor could the Fenachrone, and if he did it without coming closer to it than a thousand light-years—'

'He may have been a lot closer than that,' Loring interrupted. 'He has had lots of time to make his get-away, you know.'

'Not so much as you think, unless he has an acceleration of the same order of magnitude as ours, which I doubt,' DuQuesne countered. 'Although it is of course possible, in the light of what we know must have happened, that he may have an acceleration as large as ours, or even larger. But the most vital question now is, where did he get his dope? We'll have to consider the probabilities and make our own plans accordingly.'

'All right! That's your dish – you're the doctor.'

'We shall have to assume that it was Seaton who did it, because if it was anyone else, we have nothing whatever to work on. Assuming Seaton, we have four very definite leads. Our first lead is that it must have been Seaton in the *Skylark* and Dunark in the *Kondal* that destroyed the Fenachrone ship from the wreck of which we rescued the engineer. I couldn't learn anything about the actual battle from his brains, since he didn't know much except that it was a zone of force that did the real damage, and that the two strange ships were small and spherical.

'The *Skylark* and the *Kondal* answer that description and, while the evidence is far from conclusive, we shall assume as a working hypothesis that the *Skylark* and the *Kondal* did in fact attack and cut up a Fenachrone battleship fully as powerful as the one we are now in. That, as I do not have to tell you, is a disquieting thought.

'If it is true, however, Seaton must have left the Earth shortly after we did. That idea squares up, because he could very well have had an object-compass on me – whose tracer, by the way, would have been cut by the Fenachrone screens, so we needn't worry about it, even if he did have it once.

'Our second lead lies in the fact that he must have got the data on the zone of force sometime between the time when we left the Earth and the time when he cut up the battleship. He either worked it out himself on Earth, got it en route, or else got it on Osnome, or at least somewhere in the Green System. If my theory is correct, he worked it out by himself, before he left the Earth. He certainly did not get it on Osnome, because they did not have it.

'The third lead is the shortness of the period of time that elapsed between his battle with the Fenachrone warship and the destruction of their planet.

'The fourth lead is the great advancement in ability shown; going as he did from the use of a zone of force as an offensive weapon, up to the use of some weapon as yet unknown to us that works *through* defensive screens fully as powerful as any possible zone of force.

'Now, from the above hypothesis, we are justified in concluding that Seaton succeeded in enlisting the help of some ultra-powerful allies in the Green System, on some planet other than Osnome ...'

'Why? I don't quite follow you there,' put in Loring.

'He didn't have this new stuff, whatever it is, when he met the battleship, or he would have used it instead of the dangerous, almost hand-to-hand fighting entailed by the use of a zone of force,' DuQuesne declared flatly. 'Therefore, he got it some time after that, but before the big explosion; and you can take it from me that no one man worked out a thing that big in such a short space of time. It can't be done. He had help, and high-class help at that.

'The time factor is also an argument in favor of the idea that he got it somewhere in the Green System – he didn't have time to go anywhere else. Also, the logical thing for him to do would be to explore the Green System first, since it has a very large number of planets, many of which undoubtedly are inhabited by highly advanced races. Does that make it clearer?'

'I've got it straight so far,' assented the aide.

'We must plan our course of action in detail before we leave this spot,' DuQuesne decided. 'Then we will be ready to start back for the Green System, to find out who Seaton's friends were and to persuade them to give us all the stuff they gave him. Now listen – carefully.

'We are not nearly as ready nor as well equipped as I thought we were – Seaton is about three laps ahead of us yet. Also, there is a lot more to psychology than I ever thought there was before I read those brains back there. Both of us had better get in training mentally to meet Seaton's friends, whoever they may be, or else we probably will not be able to get away with a thing.

'Both of us, you especially, want to clear our minds of every thought inimical to Seaton in any way or in even the slightest degree. You and I are, and always have been, two of the best friends Seaton ever had on Earth – or anywhere else, for that matter. And of course I cannot be Marc DuQuesne, for reasons that are self-evident. From now on I am Stewart Vaneman, Dorothy's brother … No, forget all that – too dangerous. They may know all about Seaton's friends and Mrs Seaton's family. Our best line is to be humble cogs in Seaton's great machine. We worship him from afar as the world's greatest hero, but we are not of sufficient importance for him to know personally.'

'Isn't that carrying caution to extremes?'

'It is not. The only thing that we are certain of concerning these postulated beings is that they know immensely more than we do; therefore our story cannot have even the slightest flaw in it – it must be bottle-tight. So I will be Stewart Donovan – fortunately I haven't my name, initials, or monogram on anything I own – and I am one of the engineers of the Seaton-Crane Co., working on the power-plant installation.

'Seaton may have given them a mental picture of DuQuesne, but I will grow a mustache and beard, and with this story they will never think of connecting Donovan with DuQuesne. You can keep your own name, since neither Seaton nor any of his crowd ever saw or heard of you. You are also an engineer – my technical assistant at the works – and my buddy.

'We struck some highly technical stuff that nobody but Seaton could handle, and nobody had heard anything from him for a long time, so we came out to hunt him up and ask him some questions. You and I came together because we are just like Damon and Pythias. That story will hold water, I believe – do you see any flaws in it?'

'Perhaps not flaws, but one or two things you forgot to mention. How about this ship? I suppose you could call her an improved model, but suppose they are familiar with Fenachrone spaceship construction?'

'We shall not be in this ship. If, as we are assuming, Seaton and his new friends were the star actors in the late drama, those friends certainly have mentalities and apparatus of high caliber and they would equally certainly recognize this vessel. I had that in mind when I shoved the *Violet* off.'

'Then you will have the *Violet* to explain – an Osnomian ship. However, the company could have imported a few of them, for runabout work, since Seaton left. It would be quicker than building them, at that, since they already have all the special tools and stuff on Osnome.'

'You're getting the idea. Anything else?'

'All this is built around the supposition that he will not be there when we arrive. Suppose he *is* there?'

'The chances are a thousand to one that he will be gone somewhere, exploring – he never did like to stick around in any one place. And even in the remote possibility that he should be on the planet, he certainly will not be at the dock when we land, so the story is still good. If he should be there, we shall simply have to arrange matters so that our meeting him face to face is delayed until after we have got what we want; that's all.'

'All right; I've got it down solid.'

'Be sure that you have. Above all, remember the mental attitude toward Seaton – hero worship. He is not only the greatest man that Earth ever produced; he is the king-pin of the entire galaxy, and we rate him just a hair below God Himself. Think that thought with every cell of your brain. Concentrate on it with all your mind. Feel it – act it – really believe it until I tell you to quit.'

'I'll do that. Now what?'

'Now we hunt up the *Violet*, transfer to her, and set this cruiser adrift on a course toward Earth. And while I think of it, we want to be sure not to use any more power than the *Skylark* could, anywhere near the Green System, and cover up anything that looks peculiar about the power plant. We're not supposed to know anything about the five-light drive of the Fenachrone, you know.'

'But suppose that you can't find the *Violet*, or that she has been destroyed?'

'In that case we'll go on to Osnome and steal another one just like her. But I'll find her – I know her exact course and velocity, we have ultrarange detectors, and her automatic instruments and machinery make her destruction-proof.'

DuQuesne's chronometers were accurate, his computations were sound, and his detectors were sensitive enough to have revealed the presence of a smaller body than the *Violet* at a distance vastly greater than the few millions of miles which constituted his unavoidable error. Therefore the Osnomian cruiser was found without trouble and the transfer was effected without untoward incident.

Then for days the *Violet* was hurled at full acceleration toward the center of the galaxy. Long before the Green System was reached, however, the globular cruiser was swung off her course and, mad acceleration reversed, was put into a great circle, so that she would approach her destination from the direction of our own solar system. Slower and slower she drove onward, the bright green star about which she was circling resolving itself first into a group of bright-green points and finally into widely spaced, tiny green suns.

Although facing the completely unknown and about to do battle, with their wits certainly, and with their every weapon possibly against overwhelming odds, neither man showed or felt either nervousness or disorganization. Loring was a fatalist. It was DuQuesne's party; he was merely the hired help. He would do his best when the time came to do something; until that time came there was nothing to worry about.

DuQuesne's, on the other hand, was the repose of conscious power. He had laid his plans as best he could with the information then at hand. If conditions changed he would change those plans; otherwise he would drive through with them ruthlessly, as was his wont. In the meantime he awaited he knew not what, poised, cool, and confident.

Since both men were really expecting the unexpected, neither betrayed surprise when something that was apparently a man materialized before them in the air of the control room. His skin was green, as was that of all the inhabitants of the Green System. He was tall and well proportioned, according to Earthly standards, except for his head, which was overlarge and particularly massive above the eyes and backward from the ears. He was evidently of advanced years, for his face was seamed and wrinkled, and both his long, heavy hair and his yard-long, square-cut beard were a snowy white, only faintly tinged with green.

The Norlaminian projection thickened instantly, with none of the oscillation and 'hunting' which had been so noticeable in the one which had visited *Skylark Two* a few months earlier, for at that comparatively short range the fifth-order keyboard handling it could hold a point, however moving, as accurately as a Terrestrial photographic telescope holds a star. And in the moment of materialization of his projection the aged Norlaminian spoke.

'I welcome you to Norlamin, Terrestrials,' he greeted the two marauders with the untroubled serenity and calm courtesy of his race. 'Since you are quite evidently of the same racial stock as our very good friends the doctors Seaton and Crane, and since you are traveling in a ship built by the Osnomians, I assume that you speak and understand the English language which I am employing. I suppose that you are close friends of Seaton and Crane and that you have come to learn why they have not communicated with you of late?'

Self-contained as DuQuesne was, this statement almost took his breath away, squaring almost perfectly as it did with the tale he had so carefully prepared. He did not show his amazed gratification, however, but spoke as gravely and as courteously as the other had done:

'We are very glad indeed to see you, sir; particularly since we know neither the name nor the location of the planet for which we are searching. Your assumptions are correct in every particular save one ...'

'You do not know even the name of Norlamin?' the Green scientist interrupted. 'How can that be? Did not Dr Seaton send the projections of all his party to you upon Earth, and did he not discuss matters with you?'

'I was about to explain that.' DuQuesne lied instantly, boldly, and convincingly. 'We heard that he had sent a talking, three-dimensional picture of his group to Earth, but after it had vanished all the real information that any one seemed to have obtained was that they were here in the Green System somewhere, but not upon Osnome, and that they had been taught much of science. Mrs Seaton did most of the talking, I gather, which may account for the dearth of pertinent details.

'Neither my friend Loring, here nor I – I am Stewart Donovan, by the way – saw the picture, or rather, projection. You assumed that we are Seaton's close friends. We are engineers in his company, but we have not the honor of his personal acquaintance. His scientific knowledge was needed so urgently that it was decided that we should come out here after him, since the chief of construction had heard nothing from him for so long.'

'I see.' A shadow passed over the seamed green face. 'I am very sorry indeed at what I have to tell you. We did not report anything of it to Earth because of the panic that would have ensued. We shall of course send the whole story as soon as we can learn what actually did take place and can deduce therefrom the probable sequence of events yet to occur.'

'What's that – an accident? Something happened to Seaton?' DuQuesne snapped. His heart leaped in joy and relief, but his face showed only strained anxiety and deep concern. 'He isn't here now? Surely nothing serious could have happened to him.'

'Alas, young friend, none of us knows yet what really occurred. It is highly probable, however, that their vessel was destroyed in intergalactic space by forces about which we have as yet been able to learn nothing; forces directed by some intelligence as yet to us unknown. There is a possibility that Seaton and his companions escaped in the vessel you knew as *Skylark Two*, but so far we have not been able to find them.

'But enough of talking; you are strained and weary and you must rest. As soon as your vessel was detected the beam was transferred to me – the student Rovol, perhaps the closest to Seaton of any of my race – so that I could give you this assurance. With your permission I shall direct upon your controls certain forces which shall so govern your flight that you shall alight safely upon the grounds of my laboratory in a few minutes more than twelve hours of your time, without any further attention or effort upon your part.

'Further explanations can wait until we meet in the flesh. Until that time, my friends, do nothing save rest. Eat and sleep without care or fear, for your flight and your landing shall be controlled with precision. Farewell!'

The projection vanished instantaneously, and Loring expelled his pent-up breath in an explosive sigh.

'Whew! But what a break, chief, what a—'

He was interrupted by DuQuesne, who spoke calmly and quietly, yet insistently: 'Yes, it is a singularly fortunate circumstance that the Norlaminians detected us and recognized us; it probably would have required weeks for us to have found their planet unaided.' DuQuesne's lightning mind found a way of covering up his companion's betraying exclamation and sought some way of warning him that could not be overheard. 'Our visitor was right in saying that we need food and rest badly, but before we eat let us put on the headsets and bring the record of our flight up to date – it will take only a minute or two.'

'What's biting you, chief?' thought Loring as soon as the power was on. 'We didn't have any—'

'Plenty!' DuQuesne interrupted him viciously. 'Don't you realize that they can probably hear every word we say, and that they can see every move we make, even in the dark? In fact, they may be able to read thoughts, for all I know; so *think straight* from now on, if you never did before! Now let's finish up this record.'

He then impressed upon a tape the record of everything that had just happened. They ate. Then they slept soundly – the first really untroubled sleep they had enjoyed for weeks. And at last, exactly as the projection had foretold, the *Violet* landed without a jar upon the spacious grounds beside the laboratory of Rovol, the foremost physicist of Norlamin.

When the door of the spaceship opened, Rovol in person was standing before it, waiting to welcome the voyagers and to escort them to his dwelling. But DuQuesne, pretending a vast impatience, would not be dissuaded from the object of his search merely to satisfy the Norlaminian amenities of hospitality and courtesy. He poured forth his prepared story in a breath, concluding with a flat demand that Rovol tell him everything he knew about Seaton, and that he tell it at once.

'It would take far too long to tell you anything in words,' the ancient scientist replied placidly. 'In the laboratory, however, I can and will inform you fully in a few minutes concerning everything that has happened.'

Utter stranger himself to deception in any form, as was his whole race, Rovol was easily and completely deceived by the consummate acting, both physical and mental, of DuQuesne and Loring. Therefore, as soon as the three had donned the headsets of the wonderfully efficient Norlaminian educator, Rovol gave to the Terrestrial adventurers without reserve his every mental image and his every stored fact concerning Seaton and his supposedly ill-fated last voyage.

Even more clearly than as if he himself had seen them all happen, DuQuesne beheld and understood Seaton's visit to Norlamin, the story of the Fenachrone peril, the building of the fifth-order projector, the demolition of Fenor's space fleet, the revenge-purposed flight of Ravindau the scientist, and the complete volatilization of the Fenachrone planet.

He saw Seaton's gigantic space cruiser *Skylark Three* come into being and, uranium-driven, speed out into the awesome void of intergalactic space in pursuit of the last survivors of the Fenachrone race. He watched the mighty *Three* overtake the fleeing vessel, and understood every detail of the epic engagement that ensued, clear to its cataclysmic end. He watched the victorious battleship speed on and on, deeper and deeper into the intergalactic void, until she began to approach the limiting range of even the stupendous fifth-order projector by means of which he knew the watching had been done.

Then, at the tantalizing limit of visibility, something began to happen; something at the very incomprehensibility of which DuQuesne strained both mind and eye, exactly as had Rovol when it had taken place so long before. The immense bulk of the *Skylark* disappeared behind zone after impenetrable zone of force, and it became increasingly evident that from behind those supposedly impervious and impregnable shields Seaton was waging a terrific battle against some unknown opponent, some foe invisible even to fifth-order vision.

For nothing was visible – nothing, that is, save the released energies which, leaping through level after level reached at last even to the visible spectrum. Yet forces of such unthinkable magnitude were warring there that space itself was being deformed visibly, moment by moment. For a long time the space strains grew more and more intense, then they disappeared instantly. Simultaneously the *Skylark*'s screens of force went down and she was for an instant starkly visible before she exploded into a vast ball of appallingly radiant, flaming vapor.

In that instant of clear visibility, however, Rovol's stupendous mind had photographed every salient visible feature of the great cruiser of the void. Being almost at the limit of range of the projector, details were of course none too plain; but certain things were evident. The human beings were no longer aboard; the little lifeboat that was *Skylark Two* was no longer in her spherical berth; and there were unmistakable signs of a purposeful and deliberate departure.

'And,' Rovol spoke aloud as he removed the headset, 'although we searched minutely and most carefully all the surrounding space we could find nothing tangible. From these observations it is all too plain that Seaton was attacked by some intelligence wielding dirigible forces of the sixth order; that he was able to set up a defensive pattern; that his supply of power uranium was insufficient to cope with the attacking forces; and that he took the last desperate means of escaping from his foes by rotating *Skylark Two* into the unknown region of the fourth dimension.'

DuQuesne's stunned mind groped for a moment in an amazement akin to stupefaction, but he recovered quickly and decided upon his course.

'Well, what are you doing about it?'

'We have done and are doing everything possible for us, in our present state of knowledge and advancement, to do,' Rovol replied placidly. 'We sent out forces, as I told you, which obtained and recorded all the phenomena to which they were sensitive. It is true that a great deal of data escaped them, because the primary impulses originated in a level beyond our present knowledge, but the fact that we cannot understand it has only intensified our interest in the problem. It shall be solved. After its solution we shall know what steps to take and those steps shall then be taken.'

'Have you any idea how long it will take to solve the problem?'

'Not the slightest. Perhaps one lifetime, perhaps many – who knows? However, rest assured that it shall be solved, and that the condition shall be dealt with in the manner which shall best serve the interest of humanity as a whole.'

'But good God!' exclaimed DuQuesne. 'In the meantime, what of Seaton and Crane?' He was now speaking his true thoughts. Upon this, his first encounter, he could in nowise understand the deep, calm, timeless trend of mind of the Norlaminians; not even dimly could he grasp or appreciate the seemingly slow but inexorably certain method in which they pursued relentlessly any given line of research to its ultimate conclusion.

'If it should be graven upon the Sphere that they shall pass they may – and will – pass in all tranquility, for they know full well that it was not in idle gesture that the massed intellect of Norlamin assured them that their passing should not be in vain. You, however, youths of an unusually youthful and turbulent race, could not be expected to view the passing of such a one as Seaton from our own mature viewpoint.'

'I'll tell the universe that I don't look at things the way you do!' barked DuQuesne scathingly. When I go back to Earth – if I go – I shall at least have tried. I've got a life-sized picture of myself standing idly by while someone else tries for seven hundred years to decipher the indecipherable!'

'There speaks the impetuousness of youth,' the old man chided. 'I have told you that we have proved that at present we can do nothing whatever for the occupants of *Skylark Two*. Be warned, my rash young friend; do not tamper with powers entirely beyond your comprehension.'

'Warning be damned!' DuQuesne snorted. We're shoving off. Come on, Loring – the quicker we get started the better our chance of getting something done. You'll be willing to give me the exact bearing and the distance, won't you Rovol?'

'We shall do more than that, son,' the patriarch replied, while a shadow came over his wrinkled visage. 'Your life is your own, to do with as you see fit. You have chosen to go in search of your friends, scorning the odds against you. But before I tell you what I have in mind, I must try once more to make you see that the courage which dictates the useless sacrifice of a life ceases to be courage at all, but becomes sheerest folly.

'Since we have had sufficient power several of our youths have been study-ing the fourth dimension. They rotated many inanimate objects into that region, but could recover none of them. Instead of waiting until they had derived the fundamental equations governing such phenomena they rashly visited that region in person, in a vain attempt to achieve a short cut to know-ledge. Not one of them has come back.

'Now I declare to you in all solemnity that the quest you wish to under-take, involving as it does not only that entirely unknown region but also the equally unknown sixth order of vibrations, is to you at present utterly impos-sible. Do you still insist upon going?'

'We certainly do. You may as well save your breath.'

'Very well; so be it. Frankly, I had but little hope of swerving you from your purpose by reason. But before you go we shall supply you with every resource at our command which may in any way operate to increase your infinitesi-mal chance of success. We shall build for you a duplicate of Seaton's own *Skylark Three*, equipped with every device known to our science, and we shall instruct you fully in the use of those devices before you set out.'

'But the time … DuQuesne began to object.

'A matter of hours only,' Rovol silenced him. 'True, it took us some little time to build *Skylark Three*, but that was because it had not been done before. Every force employed in her construction was of course recorded, and to reproduce her in every detail, without attention or supervision, it is neces-sary only to thread this tape, thus, into the integrator of my master keyboard. The actual construction will of course take place in the area of experiment, but you may watch it, if you wish, in this visiplate. I must take a short series of observations at this time. I will return in ample time to instruct you in the operation of the vessel and of everything in it.'

In stunned amazement the two men stared into the visiplate, so engrossed in what they saw there that they scarcely noticed the departure of the aged scientist. For before their eyes there had already sprung into being an enor-mous structure of laced and latticed members of purple metal, stretching over two miles of level plain. While it was very narrow for its length, yet its fifteen hundred feet of diameter dwarfed into insignificance the many out-landish structures nearby, and under their staring eyes the vessel continued to take form with unbelievable rapidity. Gigantic girders appeared in place as though by magic; skin after skin of thick, purple inoson was welded on; all without the touch of a hand, without the thought of a brain, without the application of any visible force.

'Now you can say it, Doll; there's no spy ray on us here. What a break – what a break!' exulted DuQuesne. 'The old fossil swallowed it bodily, hook, line, and sinker!'

'It may not be so good, though, at that, chief, in one way. He's going to watch us, to help us out if we get into a jam, and with that infernal telescope, or whatever it is, the Earth is right under his nose.'

'Simpler than taking milk away from a blind kitten,' the saturnine chemist gloated. 'We'll go out to where Seaton went, only farther – out beyond the reach of his projector. There, completely out of touch with him, we'll circle around the galaxy back to Earth and do our stuff. Easier than dynamiting fish in a bucket – the old sap's handing me everything I want, right on a silver platter!'

8

Into the Fourth Dimension

Six mighty rotating currents of electricity impinged simultaneously upon the spherical hull of *Skylark Two* and she disappeared utterly. No exit had been opened and the walls remained solid, but where the forty-foot globe of arenak had rested in her cradle an instant before there was nothing. Pushed against by six balancing and gigantic forces, twisted cruelly by six couples of angular force of unthinkable magnitude, the immensely strong arenak shell of the vessel had held and, following the path of least resistance – the only path in which she could escape from those irresistible forces – she had shot out of space as we know it and into the impossible reality of that hyperspace which Seaton's vast mathematical knowledge had enabled him so dimly to perceive.

As those forces smote his vessel, Seaton felt himself compressed. He was being driven together irresistibly in all three dimensions, and in those dimensions at the same time he was as irresistibly being twisted – was being corkscrewed in a monstrously obscure fashion which permitted him neither to move from his place nor to remain in it. He hung poised there for interminable hours, even though he knew that the time required for that current to build up to its inconceivable value was to be measured only in fractional millionths of a single second.

Yet he waited strainingly while that force increased at an all but imperceptible rate, until at last the vessel and all its contents were squeezed out of space, in a manner somewhat comparable to that in which an orange pip is forced out from between pressing thumb and resisting finger.

At the same time Seaton felt a painless, but unutterably horrible, transformation of his entire body – a rearrangement, a writhing, crawling distortion; a hideously revolting and incomprehensibly impossible extrusion of his bodily substance as every molecule, every atom, every ultimate particle of his physical structure was compelled to extend itself into that unknown new dimension.

He could not move his eyes, yet he saw every detail of the grotesquely altered spaceship. His Earthly mentality could not understand anything he saw, yet to his transformed brain everything was as usual and quite in order. Thus the four-dimensional physique that was Richard Seaton perceived, recognized, and admired as of yore his beloved Dorothy, in spite of the fact that her normally solid body was now quite plainly nothing but a three-dimensional surface, solid only in that logically impossible new dimension which his now four-dimensional brain accepted as a matter of course, but which his thinking mentality could neither really perceive nor even dimly comprehend.

He could not move a muscle, yet in some obscure and impossible way he leaped toward his wife. Immobile though tongue and jaws were, yet he spoke to her reassuringly, remonstratingly, as he gathered up her trembling form and silenced her hysterical outbursts.

'Steady on, girl, it's all right – everything's jake. Hold everything, dear. Pipe down, I tell you! This is nothing to let get your goat. Snap out of it, Red-Top!'

'But, Dick, it's … it's too perfectly outrageous!' Dorothy had been on the verge of hysteria, but she regained a measure of her customary spirit under Seaton's ministrations. 'In some ways it seems to be all right, but it's so … so … oh, I can't …'

'Hold it!' he commanded. 'You're going off the deep end again. I can't say that I expected anything like this, either, but when you think about things it's natural enough that they should be this way. You see, while we've apparently got four-dimensional bodies and brains now, our intellects are still three-dimensional, which complicates things considerably. We can handle things and recognize them, but we can't think about physical forms, understand them, or express them either in words or in thoughts. Peculiar, and nerve-wracking enough, especially for you girls, but quite normal – see?'

'Well, maybe – after a fashion. I was afraid that I had really gone crazy back there, at first, but if you feel that way, too, I know it's all right. But you said that we'd be gone only a skillionth of a second, and we've been here a week already, at the very least?'

'All wrong, Dot – at least, partly wrong. Time does go faster here, apparently, so that we seem to have been here quite a while; but as far as our own time is concerned we haven't been here anywhere near a millionth of a second yet. See that plunger? It's still moving in – it has barely made contact. Time is purely relative, you know, and it moves so fast here that that plunger switch, traveling so fast that the eye cannot follow it at all ordinarily, seems to us to be perfectly stationary.'

'But it *must* have been longer than that, Dick! Look at all the talking we've done. I'm a fast talker, I know, but even I can't talk that fast!'

'You aren't talking – haven't you discovered that yet? You are thinking, and we are getting your thoughts as speech; that's all. Don't believe it? All right; there's your tongue, right there – or better, take your heart. It's that funny-looking object right there – see it? It isn't beating – that is, it would seem to us to take weeks, or possibly months, to beat. Take hold of it – feel it for yourself.'

'Take *hold* of it! My own heart? Why, it's inside me, between my ribs – I couldn't possibly!'

'Sure you can! That's your intellect talking now, not your brain. You're four-dimensional now, remember, and what you used to call your body is nothing but the three-dimensional hypersurface of your new hyperbody. You can take hold of your heart or your gizzard just as easily as you used to pat yourself on the nose with a powder puff.'

'Well, I won't, then – why, I wouldn't touch that thing for a million dollars!'

'All right; watch me feel mine, then. See, it's perfectly motionless, and my tongue is, too. And there's something else that I never expected to look at – my appendix. Good thing you're in good shape, old vermiform, or I'd take a pair of scissors and snick you off while I've got such a good chance to do it without ...'

'Dick!' shrieked Dorothy. 'For the love of Heaven ...'

'Calm down, Dottie, calm down. I'm just trying to get you used to this mess – I'll try something else. Here, you know what this is – a new can of tobacco, with the lid soldered on tight. In three dimensions there's no way of getting into it without breaking metal – you've opened lots of them. But out here I simply reach *past* the metal of the container, like this, see, and put it into my pipe, thus. The can is still soldered tight, no holes in it anywhere, but the tobacco is out, nevertheless. Inexplicable in three-dimensional space, impossible for us really to understand mentally, but physically perfectly simple and perfectly natural after you get used to it. That'll straighten you out some, perhaps.'

'Well, maybe – I guess I won't get frantic again, Dickie – but just the same, it's altogether too perfectly darn weird to suit me. Why don't you pull that switch back out and stop us?'

'Wouldn't do any good – wouldn't stop us, because we have already had the impulse and are simply traveling on momentum now. When that is used up – in some extremely small fraction of a second of our time – we'll snap back into our ordinary space, but we can't do a thing about it until then.'

'But how can we move around so fast?' asked Margaret from the protecting embrace of the monstrosity that they knew to be Martin Crane. 'How about inertia? I should think we'd break our bones all to pieces.'

'You can't move a three-dimensional body that fast, as we found out when the force was coming on,' Seaton replied. 'But I don't think that we are ordinary matter any more, and apparently our three-dimensional laws no longer govern, now that we are in hyperspace. Inertia is based upon time, of course, so our motion might be all right, even at that. Mechanics seem to be different here, though, and, while we seem solid enough, we certainly aren't matter at all in the three-dimensional sense of the term, as we used it back where we came from. But it's all over my head like a circus tent – I don't know any more about most of this stuff than you do. I thought of course – if I thought at all, which I doubt – that we'd go *through* hyperspace in an instant of time, without seeing it or feeling it in any way, since a three-dimensional body cannot exist, of course, in four-dimensional space. How did we get this way, Mart? Is this space coexistent with ours or not?'

'I believe that it is.' Crane, the methodical, had been thinking deeply, considering every phase of their peculiar predicament. 'Coexistent, but different in all its attributes and properties. Since we may be said to be experiencing two different time rates simultaneously, we cannot even guess at what our velocity relation is, in either system of coordinates. As to what happened, that is now quite clear. Since a three-dimensional object cannot exist in hyperspace, it of course cannot be thrown or forced through hyperspace.

'In order to enter this region, our vessel and everything in it had to acquire the property of extension in another dimension. Your forces, calculated to rotate us here, in reality forced us to assume that extra extension, which process automatically moved us from the space in which we could no longer exist into the only one in which it is possible for us to exist. When that force is no longer operative, our extension into the fourth dimension will vanish and we shall as automatically return to our customary three-dimensional space, but probably not to our original location in that space. Is that the way you understand it?'

'That's a lot better than I understood it, and it's absolutely right, too. Thanks, old thinker! And I certainly hope we don't land back there where we took off from – that's why we left, because we wanted to get away from there. The farther the better,' Seaton laughed. 'Just so we don't get so far away that the whole galaxy is out of range of the object-compasses we've got focused on it. We'd be lost for fair, then.'

'That is a possibility, of course.' Crane took the light utterance far more seriously than did Seaton. 'Indeed, if the two time rates are sufficiently different, it becomes a probability. However, there is another matter which I think is of more immediate concern. It occurred to me, when I saw you take that pinch of tobacco without opening the tin, that everywhere we have gone, even in intergalactic space, we have found life, some friendly, some inimical. There is no real reason to suppose that hyperspace is devoid of animate and intelligent life.'

'Oh, Martin!' Margaret shuddered. 'Life! Here? In this horrible, this utterly impossible place?'

'Certainly, dearest,' he replied gravely. 'It all goes back to the conversation we had long ago, during the first trip of the old *Skylark*. Remember? Life need not be comprehensible to us to exist – compared to what we do not know and what we can never either know or understand, our knowledge is infinitesimal.'

She did not reply and he spoke again to Seaton:

'It would seem to be almost a certainty that four-dimensional life does in fact exist. Postulating its existence, the possibility of an encounter cannot be denied. Such beings could of course enter this vessel as easily as your fingers entered that tobacco can. The point of these remarks is this – would we not be at a serious disadvantage? Would they not have fourth-dimensional shields or walls about which we three-dimensional intelligences would know nothing?'

'Sweet spirits of niter!' Seaton exclaimed. 'Never thought of that at all, Mart. Don't see how they could – and yet it does stand to reason that they'd have some way of locking up their horses so they couldn't run away, or so that nobody else could steal them. We'll have to do a job of thinking on that, big fellow, and we'd better start right now. Come on – let's get busy!'

Then for what seemed hours the two scientists devoted the power of their combined intellects to the problem of an adequate fourth-dimensional defense, only and endlessly to find themselves butting helplessly against a blank wall. Their three dimensional brains in their now four-dimensional bodies told them that such extra-dimensional bulwarks and safeguards must, and in fact did, exist; that they were not only possible, but necessary in the humanly incomprehensible actuality in which the Terrestrials now found themselves: but still the immaterial and thus unaltered intelligences of the human beings, utterly unable to cope with any save three-dimensional concepts, failed miserably to envisage anything which promised to be of the slightest service.

Baffled, they drifted on through the unknowable reaches of hyperspace. All they knew of time was that it was hopelessly distorted; of space that it was hideously unrecognizable; of matter that it obeyed no familiar laws. They drifted. And drifted. Futilely.

Timelessly … aimlessly … endlessly …

9

Master of Earth

The take-off of Norlamin's second immense spaceship was not at all like that of its first. When *Skylark Three* left Norlamin in pursuit of the fleeing vessel of Ravindau, the Fenachrone scientist, the occasion had been made an event of world-wide interest. From their tasks everywhere had come the mental laborers to that portentous launching. To it had come also, practically en masse, the 'youngsters' from the Country of Youth; and even those who, their life work done, had betaken themselves to the placid Nirvana of the Country of Age, returned briefly to the Country of Study to speed upon its epoch-making way that stupendous messenger of civilization.

But in sharp contrast to the throngs of Norlaminians who had witnessed the take-off of *Three*, Rovol alone was present when DuQuesne and Loring wafted themselves into the control room of its gigantic counterpart. DuQuesne had been in a hurry, and in the driving urge of his haste to go to the rescue of his 'friend' Seaton he had so completely occupied the mind of Rovol that that aged scientist had had no time to do anything except transfer to the brain of the Terrestrial pirate the knowledge which he would so soon require.

Of the real reason for this overwhelming haste, however, Rovol had not had the slightest inkling. DuQuesne well knew what the ancient physicist did not even suspect – that if any one of several Norlaminians, particularly one Drasnik, First of Psychology, should become informed of the proposed flight, that flight would not take place. For Drasnik, that profound student of the mind, would not be satisfied with DuQuesne's story without a thorough mental examination – an examination which, DuQuesne well knew, he could not pass. Therefore Rovol alone saw them off, but what he lacked in numbers he made up in sincerity.

'I am very sorry that the exigencies of the situation did not permit a more seemly leave-taking,' he said in parting, 'but I can assure you of the cooperation of every one of us whose brain can be of any use. We shall watch you, and shall aid you in any way we can. May the Unknowable Force direct your minor forces to the successful conclusion of your task. If, however, it is graven upon the Sphere that you are to pass in this venture, you may pass in all tranquility, for I affirm in the name of all Norlamin that this problem shall not be laid aside short of complete solution. For all my race I bid you farewell.'

'Farewell to you, Rovol, my friend and my benefactor, and to all Norlamin,' DuQuesne replied solemnly. 'I thank you from the bottom of my heart for everything you have done for us and for Seaton, and for what you may yet be called upon to do for all of us.'

He touched a stud and in each of the many skins of the great cruiser a heavy door drove silently shut, establishing a manifold seal.

His hand moved over the controls, and the gigantic vessel tilted slowly upward until her narrow prow pointed almost directly into the zenith. Then, easily as a wafted feather, the unimaginable mass of the immense cruiser of space floated upward with gradually increasing velocity. Faster and faster she flew, out beyond measurable atmospheric pressure, out beyond the outermost limits of the Green System, swinging slowly into a right line toward the point in space where Seaton, his companions, and both their spaceships had disappeared.

On and on she drove, now at high acceleration; the stars, so widely spaced at first, crowding closer and closer together as her speed, long since incomprehensible to any finite mind, mounted to a value almost incalculable. Past the system of the Fenachrone she hurtled; past the last outlying fringe of stars of our galaxy; on and on into the unexplored, awesome depths of open and absolute space.

Behind her the vast assemblage of stars comprising our island universe dwindled to a huge, flaming lens, to a small but bright lenticular nebula, and finally to a mere patch of luminosity.

For days communication with Rovol had been difficult, since as the limit of projection was approached it became impossible for the most powerful forces at Rovol's command to hold a projection upon the flying vessel. In order to communicate, Rovol had to send out a transmitting and receiving projection.

As the distance grew still greater, DuQuesne had done the same thing. Now it was becoming evident, by the wavering and fading of the signals, that even the two projections, reaching out toward each other though they were, would soon be out of touch, and DuQuesne sent out his last message:

'There is no use in trying to keep in communication any longer, as our beams are falling apart fast. I am on negative acceleration now, of an amount calculated to bring us down to maneuvering velocity at the point to which the inertia of *Skylark Two* would have carried her, without power, at the time when we shall arrive there. Please keep a listening post established out this way as far as you can, and I will try to reach it if I find out anything. If I fail – goodbye!'

'The poor, dumb cluck!' DuQuesne sneered as he shut off his sender and turned to Loring. 'That was so easy that it was a shame to take it, but we're certainly set to go now.'

'I'll say so!' Loring agreed enthusiastically. 'That was a nice touch, chief, telling him to keep a lookout out here. He'll do it with forces, of course, not in person; but at that it'll keep him from thinking about the Earth until you're all set.'

'You've got the idea, Doll. If they had any suspicion at all that we were heading back for the Earth they could block us yet, easily enough; but if we can get back inside the solar system before they smell a rat it will be too late for them to do anything.'

He rotated his ship through an angle of ninety degrees upon her longitudinal axis and applied enough 'downward' acceleration to swing her around in such an immense circle that she would approach the galaxy from the side opposite to that from which she had left it.

Then, during days that lengthened into weeks and months of dull and monotonous flight, the two men occupied themselves, each in his own individual fashion. There was no piloting to do and no need of vigilance, for space to a distance of untold billions of miles was absolutely and utterly empty.

Loring, unemotional and incurious, performed what simple routine house-keeping there was to do, ate, slept, and smoked. During the remainder of the time he simply sat still, stolidly doing nothing whatever until the time should come when DuQuesne would tell him to perform some specific act.

DuQuesne, on the other hand, dynamic and energetic to his ultimate fiber, found not a single idle moment. His newly acquired knowledge was so vast that he needs must explore and catalogue his own brain, to be sure that he would be able instantly to call upon whatever infinitesimal portion of it might be needed in some emergency.

The fifth-order projector, with its almost infinitely complicated keyboard, must needs be studied until its every possible resource of integration, permutation, and combination held from him no more secrets than does his console from a master of the pipe organ. Thus it was that the galaxy loomed ahead, a stupendous lens of flame, before DuQuesne had really realized that the long voyage was almost over.

To his present mentality, working with his newly acquired fifth-order projector, the task of locating our solar system was but the work of a moment; and to the power and speed of his new spaceship the distance from the galaxy's edge to the Earth was merely a longish jaunt.

When they approached the Earth it appeared as a softly shining greenish half-moon. With fleecy wisps of cloud obscuring its surface here and there, with gleaming ice caps making of its poles two brilliant areas of white, it presented an arrestingly beautiful spectacle indeed; but DuQuesne was not interested in beauty. Driving down from the empty reaches of space north of the ecliptic, he observed that Washington was in the morning zone, and soon his great vessel was poised motionless, invisibly high above the city.

His first act was to throw out an ultra-powered detector screen, with automatic trips and tighteners, around the entire solar system; out far beyond the outermost point of the orbit of Pluto. Its every part remained unresponsive. No foreign radiation was present in all that vast volume of space, and DuQuesne turned to his henchman with cold satisfaction stamped upon his every hard lineament.

'No interference at all, Doll. No ships, no projections, no spy rays, nothing,' he said. 'I can really get to work now. I won't be needing you for a while, and I imagine that, after being out in space so long, you would like to circulate around with the boys and girls for a couple of weeks or so. How are you fixed for money?'

'Well, chief, I could do with a small binge and a few nights out among 'em, if it's all right with you,' Loring admitted. 'As for money, I've got only a couple of hundred on me, but I can get some at the office – we're quite a few pay days behind, you know.'

'Never mind about going to the office. I don't know exactly how well Brookings is going to like some of the things I'm going to tell him, and you're working for *me*, you know, not for the office. I've got plenty. Here's five thousand, and you can have three weeks to spend it in. Three weeks from today I'll tell you what to do. Until then, do as you please. Where do you want me to set you down? Perhaps the Perkins roof will be clear at this hour.'

'Good as any. Thanks, chief,' and without even a glance to assure himself that DuQuesne was at the controls Loring made his way through the manifold airlocks and calmly stepped out into ten thousand feet of empty air.

DuQuesne caught the falling man neatly with an attractor and lowered him gently to the now-deserted roof of the Perkins Cafe – that famous restaurant which had been planned and was maintained by the World Steel Corporation as a blind for its underground activities. He then seated himself at his console and drove his projection down into the innermost private office of Steel. He did not at first thicken the pattern into visibility, but remained invisible, studying Brookings, now president of that industrial octopus.

The magnate was seated as of yore in a comfortably padded chair at his massive and ornate desk, the focus and center of a maze of secret private communication bands and even more secret private wires. For Steel was a growing octopus and its voraciously insatiable maw must be fed.

Brookings had but one motto, one tenet – 'get it.' By fair play at times, although this method was employed but seldom; by bribery, corruption, and sabotage as the usual thing; by murder, arson, mayhem, and all other known forms of foul play if necessary or desirable – Steel GOT IT.

To be found out was the only sin, and that was usually only venial instead of cardinal; for it was because of that sometimes unavoidable contingency that Steel not only retained the shrewdest legal minds in the world, but also wielded subterranean forces sufficiently powerful to sway even supposedly incorruptible courts of justice.

Occasionally, of course, the sin was cardinal; the transgression irremediable; the court unreachable. In that case the octopus lost a very minor tentacle; but the men really guilty had never been brought to book.

Into the center of this web, then, DuQuesne drove his projection and listened. For a whole long week he kept at Brookings' elbow, day and night. He listened and spied, studied and planned until his now gigantic mentality not only had grasped every detail of everything that had developed during his long absence and of everything that was then going on, but also had planned meticulously the course which he would pursue. Then, late one afternoon, he cut in his audio and spoke.

'I knew of course that you would try to double-cross me, Brookings, but even I had no idea that you would make such an utter fool of yourself as you have.'

As he heard the sneering, cutting tone of the scientist's well-remembered voice, the magnate seemed to shrink bodily, his face turning a pasty gray as the blood receded from it.

'DuQuesne!' he gasped. 'Where – are you?'

'I'm right beside you, and I have been for over a week.' DuQuesne thickened his image to full visibility and grinned sardonically as the man at the desk reached hesitantly toward a button. 'Go ahead and push it – and see what happens. Surely even you are not dumb enough to suppose that a man with my brain – even the brain I had when I left here – would take any chances with such a rat as you have always shown yourself to be?'

Brookings sank back into his chair, shaking visibly. 'What are you, anyway? You look like DuQuesne, and yet …' His voice died away.

'That's better, Brookings. Don't ever start anything that you can't finish. You are and always were a physical coward. You're one of the world's best at bossing dirty work from a distance, but as soon as it gets close to you, you fold up like an accordion.

'As to what this is that I am talking and seeing from, it is technically known as a projection. You don't know enough to understand it even if I should try to explain it to you, which I have no intention of doing. It's enough for you to know that it is something that has all the advantages of an appearance in person, and none of the disadvantages. *None* of them – remember that word.

'Now I'll get down to business. When I left here I told you to hold your cockeyed ideas in check – that I would be back in less than five years, with enough stuff to do things in a big way. You didn't wait five days, but started right in with your pussyfooting and gumshoeing around, with the usual result – instead of cleaning up the mess, you made it messier than ever. You see, I've got all the dope on you – I even know that you were going to try to gyp me out of my back pay.'

'Oh, no, doctor; you are mistaken, really,' Brookings assured him, oilily. He was fast regaining his usual poise, and his mind was again functioning in its wonted devious fashion. 'We have really been trying to carry on until you got back, exactly as you told us to. And your salary has been continued in full, of course – you can draw it all at any time.'

'I know I can, in spite of you. However, I am no longer interested in money. I never cared for it except for the power it gave, and I have brought back with me power far beyond that of money. Also I have learned that knowledge is even greater than power. I have also learned, however, that in order to increase my present knowledge – yes, even to protect that which I already have – I shall soon need a supply of energy a million times greater than the present peak output of all the generators of Earth. As a first step in my project I am taking control of Steel right now, and I am going to do things the way they should be done.'

'But you can't do that, doctor!' protested Brookings volubly. 'We will give you anything you ask, of course, but ...'

'But nothing!' interrupted DuQuesne. 'I'm not asking a thing of you, Brookings – I'm *telling* you!'

'You think you are!' Brookings, goaded to action at last, pressed a button, savagely, while DuQuesne looked on in calm contempt.

Behind the desk, ports flashed open and rifles roared thunderously in the confined space. Heavy bullets tore through the peculiar substance of the projection and smashed into the plastered wall behind it, but DuQuesne's contemptuous grin did not change. He moved slowly forward, hands outthrust. Brookings screamed once – a scream that died away to a gurgle as fingers of tremendous strength closed about his flabby neck.

There had been four riflemen on guard. Two of them threw down their guns and fled in panic, amazed and terrified at the failure of their bullets to take effect. Those guards died in their tracks as they ran. The other two rushed upon DuQuesne with weapons clubbed. But steel barrel and wooden stock alike rebounded harmlessly from that pattern of force, fiercely driven knives penetrated it but left no wound, and the utmost strength of the two brawny men could not even shift the position of the weird being's inhumanly powerful fingers upon the throat of their employer. Therefore they stopped their fruitless attempts at a rescue and stood, dumbfounded.

'Good work, boys,' DuQuesne commended. 'You've got nerve – that's why I didn't bump you off. You can keep on guarding this idiot here after I get done teaching him a thing or two. As for you, Brookings,' he continued, loosening his grip sufficiently so that his victim could retain consciousness, 'I let you try that to show you the real meaning of futility. I told you particularly to remember that this projection has *none* of the disadvantages of a personal appearance, but apparently you didn't have enough brain power to grasp the thought. Now, are you going to work with me the way I want you to or not?'

'Yes, yes – I'll do anything you say,' Brookings promised.

'All right, then.' DuQuesne resumed his former position in front of the desk. 'You are wondering why I didn't finish choking you to death, since you know that I am not at all squeamish about such things. I'll tell you. I didn't kill you because I may be able to use you. I am going to make World Steel the real government of the Earth, and its president will therefore be dictator of the world. I do not want the job myself because I will be too busy extending and consolidating my authority, and with other things, to bother about the details of governing the planet. As I have said before, you are probably the best manager alive today; but when it comes to formulating policies you're a complete bust. I am giving you the job of world dictator under one condition – that you run it *exactly* as I tell you to.'

'Ah, a wonderful opportunity, doctor! I assure you that—'

'Just a minute, Brookings! I can read your mind like an open book. You are still thinking that you can slip one over on me. Know now, once and for all, that it can't be done. I am keeping on you continuously automatic devices that are recording every order that you give, every message that you receive or send, and every thought that you think. The first time that you try any more of your funny work on me, I will come back here and finish up the job I started a few minutes ago. Play along with me and you can run the Earth as you please, subject only to my direction in broad matters of policy; try to double-cross me and you pass out of the picture. Get me?'

'I understand you thoroughly.' Brookings' agile mind flashed over the possibilities of DuQuesne's stupendous plan. His eyes sparkled as he thought of his own place in that plan, and he became his usual blandly alert self. 'As world dictator, I would of course be in a higher place than any that World Steel, as at present organized, could possibly offer. Therefore I will be glad to accept your offer, without reservations. Now, if you will, go ahead and give me an outline of what you propose. I will admit that I did harbor a few mental reservations at first, but you have convinced me that you actually can deliver the goods.'

'That's better. I have prepared full plans for the rebuilding of all our stations and Seaton's into my new type of power plant, for the erection of a new plant at every strategic point throughout the world, and for interlocking all these stations into one system. Here they are.' A bound volume of data and a mass of blueprints materialized in the air and dropped upon the desk. 'As soon as I have gone you can call in the chiefs of the engineering staff and put them to work.'

'I perceive what seem to me to be obstacles,' Brookings remarked, after his practiced eye had run over the salient points of the project and he had leafed over the pile of blueprints. 'We have not been able to do anything with Seaton's plants because of their enormous reserves of power, and his number one plant is to be the key station of our new network. Also, there simply are not men enough to do this work. These are slack times, I know, but even if we could get every unemployed man we still would not have enough. And, by the way, what became of Seaton? He apparently has not been around for some time.'

'You needn't worry about Seaton's plants – I'll line them up for you myself. As for Seaton, he was chased into the fourth dimension. He hasn't got back yet, and he probably won't; as I will explain to his crowd when I take them over. As for men, we shall have the combined personnel of all the armies and navies of the world. You think that even that force won't be enough, but it will. As you go over those plans in detail, you will see that by the proper use of dirigible forces we shall have plenty of manpower.'

'How do you intend to subdue the armies and navies of the world?'

'It would take too long to go into detail. Turn on that radio there and listen, however, and you'll get it all – in fact, being on the inside, you'll be able to do a lot of reading between the lines that no one else will. Also, what I am going to do next will settle the doubt that is still in your mind as to whether I've really got the stuff.'

The projection vanished, and in a few minutes every radio receiving set throughout the world burst into stentorian voice. DuQuesne was broadcasting simultaneously upon every channel from five meters to five thousand, using a wave of such tremendous power that even two-million-watt stations were smothered at the very bases of their own transmitting towers.

'People of Earth, attention!' the speakers blared. 'I am speaking for the World Steel Corporation. From this time on the governments of all nations of the Earth will be advised and guided by the World Steel Corporation. For a long time I have sought some method of doing away with the stupidities of the present national governments. I have studied the possibilities of doing away with war and its attendant horrors. I have considered all feasible methods of correcting your present economic system, under which you have had constantly recurring cycles of boom and panic.

'Most of you have thought for years that something should be done about all these things. You are not only unorganized, however; you are and always have been racially distrustful and hence easily exploited by every self-seeking demagogue who has arisen to proclaim the dawn of a new day. Thus you have been able to do nothing to improve world conditions.

'It was not difficult to solve the problem of the welfare of mankind. It was quite another matter, however, to find a way of enforcing that solution. At last I have found it. I have developed a power sufficiently great to compel world-wide disarmament and to inaugurate productive employment of all men now bearing arms, as well as all persons now unemployed, at shorter hours and larger wages than any heretofore known. I have also developed means whereby I can trace with absolute certainty the perpetrators of any known crime, past or present; and I have both the power and the will to deal summarily with habitual criminals.

'The revolution which I am accomplishing will harm no one except parasites upon the body politic. National boundaries and customs shall remain as they are now. Governments will be overruled only when and as they impede the progress of civilization. War, however, will not be tolerated. I shall prevent it, not by killing the soldiers who would do the actual fighting, but by putting out of existence every person who attempts to foment strife. Those schemers I shall kill without mercy, long before their plans shall have matured.

'Trade shall be encouraged, and industry. Prosperity shall be world-wide and continuous, because of the high level of employment and remuneration. I do not ask you to believe all this, I am merely telling you. Wait and see – it will come true in less than thirty days.

'I shall now demonstrate my power by rendering the navy of the United States helpless, without taking a single life. I am now poised low over the city of Washington. I invite the Seventieth Bombing Squadron, which I see has already taken to the air, to drop their heaviest bombs upon me. I shall move out over the Potomac, so that the fragments will do no damage, and I shall not retaliate. I could wipe out that squadron without effort, but I have no desire to destroy brave men who are only obeying blindly the dictates of an outworn system.'

The spaceship, which had extended across the city from Chevy Chase to Anacostia, moved out over the river, followed by the relatively tiny bombers. After a time the entire countryside was shaken by the detonations of the world's heaviest projectiles, but DuQuesne's cold, clear voice went on:

'The bombers have done their best, but they have not even marred the outer plating of my ship. I will now show you what I can do if I should decide to do it. There is an obsolete battleship anchored off the Cape, which was to have been sunk by naval gunfire. I direct a force upon it – it is gone; volatilized almost instantly.

'I am now over Sandy Hook, I am not destroying the installations, as I cannot do so without killing men. Therefore I am simply uprooting them and am depositing them gently upon the mud flats of the Mississippi River, at St. Louis, Missouri. Now I am sending out a force to each armed vessel of the United States navy, wheresoever situated upon the face of the globe.

'At such speed as is compatible with the safety of the personnel, I am transporting those vessels through the air toward Salt Lake City, Utah. Tomorrow morning every unit of the American navy will float in Great Salt Lake. If you do not believe that I am doing this, read in your own newspaper tomorrow that I have done it.

'Tomorrow I shall treat similarly the navies of Great Britain, France, Italy,

Japan, and the other maritime nations. I shall deal then with the military forces and their fortifications.

'I have already taken steps to abate the nuisance of certain widely known criminals and racketeers who have been conducting, quite openly and flagrantly, a reign of terror for profit. Seven of those men have already died, and ten more are to die tonight. Your homes shall be safe from the kidnapper; your businesses shall be safe from the extortioner and his skulking aid, the dynamiter.

'In conclusion, I tell you that the often-promised new era is here; not in words, but in actuality. Goodbye until tomorrow.'

DuQuesne flashed his projection down into Brookings' office. 'Well, Brookings, that's the start. You understand now what I am going to do, and you know that I can do it.'

'Yes. You undoubtedly have immense power, and you have taken exactly the right course to give us the support of a great number of people who would ordinarily be bitterly opposed to anything we do. But that talk of wiping out gangsters and racketeers sounded funny, coming from you.'

'Why should it? We are now beyond that stage. And, while public opinion is not absolutely necessary to our success it is always a potent force. No program of despotism, however benevolent, can expect to be welcomed unanimously; but the course I have outlined will at least provide the opposition.'

DuQuesne cut off his forces and sat back at the controls, relaxed, his black eyes staring into infinity. Earth was his, to do with as he wished; and he would soon have it so armed that he could hold it against the universe. Master of Earth! His highest ambition had been attained – or had it? The world, after all, was small – merely a mote in space. Why not be master of the entire galaxy? There was Norlamin to be considered, of course …

Norlamin!

Norlamin would not like the idea and would have to be pacified.

As soon as he got the Earth straightened out he would have to see what could be done about Norlamin.

10

Captured!

'Dick!' Dorothy shrieked, flashing to Seaton's side; and, abandoning his fruitless speculations, he turned to confront two indescribable, yet vaguely recognizable, entities who had floated effortlessly into the control room of the *Skylark*. Large they were, and black – a dull, lusterless black – and each was possessed of four huge, bright lenses which apparently were eyes. 'Dick! What are they, anyway?'

'Life, probably; the intelligent, four-dimensional life that Mart fully expected to find here,' Seaton answered. 'I'll see if I can't send them a thought.'

Staring directly into those expressionless lenses the man sent out wave after wave of friendly thought, without result or reaction. He then turned on the power of the mechanical educator and donned a headset, extending another toward one of the weird visitors and indicating as clearly as he could by signs that it was to be placed back of the outlandish eyes. Nothing happened, however, and Seaton snatched off the useless phones.

'Might have known they wouldn't work!' he snorted. 'Electricity! Too slow – and those tubes probably won't be hot in less than ten years of this hypertime, besides. Probably wouldn't have been any good, anyway – their minds would of course be four-dimensional, and ours most distinctly are not. There may be some point – or rather, plane – of contact between their minds and ours, but I doubt it. They don't act warlike, though; we'll simply watch them a while and see what they do.'

But if, as Seaton had said, the intruders did not seem inimical, neither were they friendly. If any emotion at all affected them, it was apparently nothing more nor less than curiosity. They floated about, gliding here and there, their great eyes now close to this article, now that; until at last they floated *past* the arenak wall of the spherical space ship and disappeared.

Seaton turned quickly to his wife, ready to minister again to overstrained nerves, but much to his surprise he found Dorothy calm and intensely interested.

'Funny-looking things, weren't they, Dick?' she asked animatedly. 'They looked just like highly magnified chess knights with four hands; or like those funny little sea horses they have in the aquarium, only on a larger scale. Were those propellers they had instead of tails natural or artificial – could you tell?'

'Huh? What're you talking about? I didn't see any such details as that!' Seaton exclaimed.

'I couldn't, either, really,' Dorothy explained, 'until after I found out how to look at them. I don't know whether my method would appeal to a strictly scientific mind or not. I can't understand any of this fourth-dimensional, mathematical stuff of yours and Martin's anyway, so when I want to see anything out here I just pretend that the fourth dimension isn't there at all. I just look at what you call the three-dimensional surface and it looks all right. When I look at you that way, for instance, you look like my very own Dick, instead of like a cubist's four-dimensional nightmare.'

'You have hit it, Dorothy.' Crane had been visualizing four-dimensional objects as three-dimensional while she was speaking. 'That is probably the only way in which we can really perceive hyperthings at all.'

'It *does* work, at that!' Seaton exclaimed. 'Congratulations, Dot; you've made a contribution to science – but say, what's coming off now? We're going somewhere.'

For the *Skylark*, which had been floating freely in space – a motion which the senses of the wanderers had long since ceased to interpret as a sensation of falling – had been given an acceleration. Only a slight acceleration, barely enough to make the floor of the control room seem 'down,' but any acceleration at all in such circumstances was to the scientists cause for grave concern.

'Non-gravitational, of course, or we would have felt it before – what's the answer, Mart, if any?' Seaton demanded. 'Suppose that they've taken hold of us with a tractor and are taking us for a ride?'

'It would appear that way. I wonder if the visiplates are still practical?' Crane moved over to number one visiplate and turned it in every direction. Nothing was visible in the abysmal, all-engulfing, almost palpable darkness of the absolute black outside the hull of the vessel.

'It wouldn't work, hardly,' Seaton commented. 'Look at our time here – we must be way beyond light. I doubt if we could see anything, even if we had a sixth-order projector – which of course we haven't.'

'But how about our light inside here, then?' asked Margaret. 'The lamps are burning, and we can see things.'

'I don't know, Peg,' Seaton replied. 'All this stuff is way past me. Maybe it's because the lights are traveling with us – no, that's out. Probably, as I intimated before, we aren't seeing things at all – just feeling them, some way or other. That must be it, I think – it's sure that the light-waves from those lamps are almost perfectly stationary, as far as we're concerned.'

'Oh, there's something!' Dorothy called. She had remained at the visiplate, staring into the impenetrable darkness. 'See, it just flashed on! We're falling toward ground of some kind. It doesn't look like any planet I ever saw before, either – it's perfectly endless and it's perfectly flat.'

The others rushed to the plates and saw, instead of the utter blackness of a moment before, an infinite expanse of level, un-curving hyperland. Though so distant from it that any planetary curvature should have been evident, they could perceive none. Flat that land was – a geometrical plane – and sunless, but apparently self-luminous; glowing with a strong, somewhat hazy, violet light. And now they could also see the craft which had been towing them. It was a lozenge-shaped affair, glowing fiercely with the peculiarly livid 'light' of the hyperplanet; and was now apparently exerting its maximum tractive effort in a vain attempt to hold the prodigious mass of *Skylark Two* against the seemingly slight force of gravitation.

'Must be some kind of hyperlight that we're seeing by,' Seaton cogitated. 'Must be sixth- or seventh-order velocity, at least, or we'd be …'

'Never mind the light or our seeing things!' Dorothy interrupted. 'We are falling, and we shall probably hit hard. Can't you do something about it?'

'Afraid not, Kitten.' He grinned at her. 'But I'll try it. Nope, everything's dead. No power, no control, no nothing, and there won't be until we snap back where we belong. But don't worry about a crash. Even if that ground is solid enough to crash us, and I don't think it is, everything out here, including gravity, seems to be so feeble that it won't hurt us any.'

Scarcely had he finished speaking when the *Skylark* struck – or rather, floated gently downward into the ground. For, slight as was the force of gravitation, and partially counteracted as well by the pull of the towing vessel, the arenak globe did not even pause as it encountered the apparently solid rock of the surface of the planet – if planet it was. That rock billowed away upon all sides as the *Skylark* sank into it and through it, to come to a halt only after her mass had driven a vertical, smooth-sided well some hundreds of feet in depth.

Even though the Osnomian metal had been rendered much less dense than normal by its extrusion and expansion into the fourth dimension, yet it was still so much denser than the unknown material of the hyperplanet that it sank into that planet's rocky soil as a bullet sinks into thick jelly.

'Well, that's that!' Seaton declared. 'Thinness and tenuosity, as well as feebleness, seem to be characteristics of this hyper-material. Now we'll camp here peacefully for a while. Before they succeed in digging us out – if they try it, which they probably will – we'll be gone.'

Again, however, the venturesome and impetuous chemist was wrong. Feeble the hypermen were, and tenuous, but their curiosity was whetted even sharper than before. Derricks were rigged, and slings; but even before the task of hoisting the *Skylark* to the surface of the planet was begun, two of the peculiar denizens of the hyperworld were swimming down through the atmosphere of the four-dimensional well at whose bottom the Earth vessel lay. Past the arenak wall of the cruiser they dropped, and into the control room they floated.

'But I do not understand it at all, Dick,' Crane had been arguing. 'Postulating the existence of a three-dimensional object in four-dimensional space, a four-dimensional being could of course enter it at will, as your fingers entered that tobacco can. But since all objects here are in fact and of necessity four-dimensional, that condition alone should bar any such proceeding. Therefore, since you actually *did* take the contents out of that can without opening it, and since our recent visitors actually *did* enter and leave our vessel at will, I can only conclude that we must still be essentially three-dimensional in nature, even though constrained temporarily to occupy four-dimensional space.'

'Say, Mart, that's a thought! You're still the champion thinker of the universe, aren't you? That explains a lot of things I've been worrying myself black in the face about. I think I can explain it, too, by analogy. Imagine a two-dimensional man, one centimeter wide and ten or twelve centimeters long; the typical flatlander of the classical dimensional explanations. There he is, in a plane, happy as a clam and perfectly at home. Then some force takes him by one end and rolls him up into a spiral, or sort of semisolid cylinder, one centimeter long. He won't know what to make of it, but in reality he'll be a two-dimensional man occupying three-dimensional space.

'Now imagine further that we can see him, which of course is a pretty tall order, but necessary since this is a very rough analogy. We wouldn't know what to make of him, either, would we? Doesn't that square up with what we're going through now? We'd think that such a thing was quite a curiosity and want to find out about it, wouldn't we? That, I think, explains the whole thing, both our sensations and the actions of those sea horses – huh! Here they are again. Welcome to our city, strangers!'

But the intruders made no sign of understanding the message. They did not, could not, understand.

Their four-dimensional minds, conceived and reared in hyperspace and knowing nothing save hyperthings, were of course utterly incapable of receiving or of comprehending any thoughts emanating from the fundamentally three-dimensional Terrestrials.

The human beings, now using Dorothy's happily discovered method of dimensional reduction, saw that the hypermen did indeed somewhat resemble overgrown sea horses – the *hippocampus heptagonus* of Earthly zoology – but sea horses each equipped with a writhing, spinning, air-propeller tail and with four long and sinuous arms, terminating in many dexterous and prehensile fingers.

Each of those hands held a grappling trident; a peculiar, four-dimensional hyperforceps whose insulated, interlocking teeth were apparently electrodes – conductors of some hyper-equivalent of our Earthly electricity. With unmoved, expressionless 'faces' the two visitors floated about the control room, while Seaton and Crane sent out wave after wave of friendly thought and made signs of friendship in all the various pantomimic languages at their command.

'Look out, Mart, they're coming this way! I don't want to start anything hostile, but I don't particularly like the looks of those toad-stabbers of theirs, and if they start any funny business with them maybe we'd better wring their fishy little necks!'

But there was to be no neck-wringing – then. Slight of strength the hypermen were, and of but little greater density than the thin air through which they floated so easily; but they had no need of physical strength – then.

Indeed, some little time was to elapse before they were even to suspect the undreamed-of potentialities inherent in the, to them, incomprehensible Terrestrial physiques.

Four tridents shot out, and in a monstrously obscure fashion reached *past* clothing skin, and ribs; seizing upon and holding firmly, but painlessly and gently, the vital nervous centers of the human bodies. Seaton tried to leap to the attack, but even his quickness was of no avail – even before he moved, a wave of intolerable agony surged throughout his being, ceasing only and completely when he relaxed, relinquishing his pugnacious attempt. Shiro, leaping from the galley with cleaver upraised, was similarly impaled and similarly subdued.

Then a hoisting platform appeared, and Seaton and Margaret were forced to board it. They had no choice; the first tensing of the muscles to resist the will of the hypermen was quelled instantly by a blast of such intolerable torture that no human body could possibly defy it for even the slightest perceptible instant of time.

'Take it easy, Dot – Mart,' Seaton spoke rapidly as the hoist started upward. 'Do whatever they say – no use taking much of that stuff – until Peg and I get back. We'll get back, too, believe me! They'll *have* to take these meat hooks out of us sometime, and when they do they'll think a cyclone has broken loose.'

11

Hyperland

Raging but impotent, Seaton stood motionless beside his friend's wife upon the slowly rising lift; while Crane, Dorothy, and Shiro remained in the control room of the *Skylark*. All were helpless, incapable alike of making a single movement not authorized by their grotesque captors. Feeble the hypermen were, as has been said; but at the first tensing of a human muscle in revolt there shot from the insulated teeth of the grappling hypertrident such a terrific surge of unbearably poignant torture that any thought of resistance was out of the question.

Even Seaton – fighter by instinct though he was, and reckless as he was and desperate at the thought of being separated from his beloved Dorothy – had been able to endure only three such shocks. The unimaginable anguish of the third rebuke, a particularly vicious and long-continued wrenching and wringing of the most delicate nerve centers of his being, had left him limp and quivering. He was still furious, still bitterly humiliated. His spirit was willing, but he was physically unable to drive his fiendishly tortured body to further acts of rebellion.

Thus it was that the improvised elevator of the hypermen carried two docile captives as it went *past* not *through* – the spherical arenak shell of *Skylark Two* and up the mighty well which the vessel had driven in its downward plunge. The walls of that pit were glassily smooth; or, more accurately, were like slag; as though the peculiarly unsubstantial rock of the hyperplanet had been actually melted by the force of the cruiser's descent, easy and gradual as the fall had seemed to the senses of the Terrestrials.

It was apparent also that the hypermen were having difficulty in lifting the, to them, tremendous weight of the two human bodies. The platform would go up a few feet, then pause. Up and pause, up and pause; again and again. But at last they reached the top of the well, and, wretched as he was, Seaton had to grin when he perceived that they were being hoisted by a derrick, whose over-driven engine, attended though it was by a veritable corps of mechanics, could lift them only a few feet at a time. Coughing and snorting, it ran slower and slower until, released from the load, it burst again into free motion to build up sufficient momentum to lift them another foot or so.

And all about the rim of that forty-foot well there were being erected other machines. Trusses were rising into the air, immense chains were being forged, and additional motors were being assembled. It was apparent that the *Skylark* was to be raised; and it was equally evident that to the hypermen that raising presented an engineering problem of no small magnitude.

'She'll be right here when we get back, Peg, as far as those jaspers are concerned,' Seaton informed his companion. 'If they have to slip their clutches to lift the weight of just us two, they'll have one sweet job getting the old *Skylark* back up here. They haven't got the slightest idea of what they're tackling – they can't begin to pile enough of that kind of machinery in this whole part of the country to budge her.'

'You speak as though you were quite certain of our returning.' Margaret spoke somberly. 'I wish that I could feel that way.'

'Sure I'm certain of it,' Seaton assured her. 'I've got it all figured out. Nobody can maintain one hundred per cent vigilance forever, and as soon as I get back into shape from that last twisting they gave me, I'll be fast enough to take advantage of the break when it comes.'

'Yes, but suppose it doesn't come?'

'It's bound to come sometime. The only thing that bothers me is that I can't even guess at when we're due to snap back into our own three-dimensional space. Since we couldn't detect any motion in an ether wave, though, I imagine that we'll have lots of time, relatively speaking, to get back here before the *Skylark* leaves. Ah! I wondered if they were going to make us walk to wherever it is they're taking us, but I see we ride – there comes something that must be an airship. Maybe we can make our break now instead of later.'

But the hyperman did not relax his vigilance for an instant as the vast, vague bulk of the flier hovered in the air beside their elevator. A port opened, a short gangplank shot out, and under the urge of the punishing tridents the two human beings stepped aboard. A silent flurry ensued among the weird crew of the vessel as its huge volume sank downward under the unheard-of mass of the two captives, but no opportunity was afforded for escape – the gripping tridents did not relax, and at last the amazed officers succeeded in driving their motors sufficiently to lift the prodigious load into the air of the hyperplanet.

'Take a good long look around, Peg, so that you can help find our way back,' Seaton directed, and pointed out through the peculiarly transparent wall of their conveyance. 'See those three peaks over there, the only hills in sight? Our course is about twelve or fifteen degrees off the line of the right-hand two – and there's something that looks like a river down below us. The bend there is just about on line – see anything to mark it by?'

'Well, there's a funny-looking island, kind of heart-shaped, with a reddish-colored spire of rock – see it?'

'Fine – we ought to be able to recognize that. Bend, heart-island, red obelisk on what we'll call the upstream end. Now from here, what? Oh, we're turning – going upstream. Fine business! Now we'll have to notice when and where we leave this river, lake, or whatever it is.'

They did not, however, leave the course of the water. For hundreds of miles, apparently, it was almost perfectly straight, and for hours the airship of the hypermen bored through the air only a few hundred feet above its gleaming surface. Faster and faster the hypership flew onward, until it became a whistling, yelling projectile, tearing its way at a terrific but constant velocity through the complaining air.

But while that which was beneath them was apparently the fourth-dimensional counterpart of an Earthly canal, neither water nor landscape was in any sense familiar. No sun was visible, nor moon, nor the tiniest twinkling star. Where the heavens should have been there was merely a void of utter, absolute black, appalling in its uncompromising profundity. Indeed, the Terrestrials would have thought themselves blind were it not for the forbidding, Luciferean vegetation which, self-luminous with a ghastly bluish-violet pseudo-light, extended outward – flat – in every direction to infinity.

'What's the matter with it, Dick?' demanded Margaret, shivering. 'It's horrible, awful, unsettling. Surely anything that is actually seen must be capable of description? But this …' Her voice died away.

'Ordinarily, three-dimensionally, yes; but this, no,' Seaton assured her. 'Remember that our brains and eyes, now really pseudo-fourth-dimensional, are capable of seeing those things as they actually are; but that our entities – intelligences – whatever you like – are still three-dimensional and can neither comprehend nor describe them. We can grasp them only very roughly by transposing them into our own three-dimensional concepts, and that is a poor subterfuge that fails entirely to convey even an approximate idea. As for that horizon – or lack of it – it simply means that this planet is so big that it looks flat. Maybe it *is* flat in the fourth dimension – I don't know!'

Both fell silent, staring at the weird terrain over which they were being borne at such an insane pace. Along its right line above that straight water-course sped the airship, a shrieking arrow; and to the right of the observers and to left of them spread, as far as the eye could reach, a flatly unbroken expanse of the ghostly, livid, weirdly self-luminous vegetation of the unknowable hyperworld. And, slinking, leaping, or perchance flying between and among the boles and stalks of the rank forest growth could be glimpsed monstrous forms of animal life.

Seaton strained his eyes, trying to see them more clearly; but owing to the speed of the ship, the rapidity of the animals' movements, the unsatisfactory illumination, and the extreme difficulty of translating at all rapidly the incomprehensible four-dimensional forms into their three-dimensional equivalents, he could not even approximate either the size or the appearance of the creatures with which he, unarmed and defenseless, might have to deal.

'Can you make any sense out of those animals down there, Peg?' Seaton demanded. 'See, there's one just jumped out of the river and seemed to fly into that clump of bamboo-like stuff there. Get any details?'

'No. What with the poor light and everything being so awful and so distorted, I can hardly see anything at all. Why – what of them?'

'This of 'em. We're coming back this way, and we may have to come on foot. I'll try to steal a ship, of course, but the chance that we'll be able to get one – or to run it after we do get it – is mighty slim. But assuming that we are afoot, the more we know about what we're apt to go up against the better we'll be able to meet it. Oh, we're slowing down – been wondering what that thing up ahead of us is. It looks like a cross between the Pyramid of Cheops and the old castle of Bingen on the Rhine, but I guess it's a city – it seems to be where we're headed for.'

'Does this water actually flow out from the side of that wall, or am I seeing things?' the girl asked.

'It seems to – your eyes are all right, I guess. But why shouldn't it? There's a big archway, you notice – maybe they use it for power or something, and this is simply an outfall …'

'Oh, we're going in!' Margaret exclaimed, her hand flashing out to Seaton's arm.

'Looks like it, but they probably know their stuff.' He pressed her hand reassuringly. 'Now, Peg, no matter what happens, stick to me as long as you possibly can!'

As Seaton had noticed, the city toward which they were flying resembled somewhat an enormous pyramid, whose component units were themselves mighty buildings, towering one above and behind the other in crenelated majesty to an awe-inspiring height. In the wall of the foundation tier of buildings there yawned an enormous opening, spanned by a noble arch of metaled masonry, and out of this gloriously arched aqueduct there sprang the stream whose course the airship had been following so long. Toward that forbidding opening the hypership planed down, and into it she floated slowly and carefully.

Much to the surprise of the Terrestrials, however, the great tunnel of the aqueduct was not dark. Walls and arched ceiling alike glowed with the livid, bluish-violet ultra-light which they had come to regard as characteristic of all hyperthings, and through that uncanny glare the airship stole along. Once inside the tunnel its opening vanished – imperceptible, indistinguishable from its four-dimensional, black-and-livid-blue background.

Unending that tunnel stretched before and behind them. Walls and watery surface alike were smooth, featureless, and so uniformly and weirdly luminous that the eye could not fix upon any point firmly enough to determine the rate of motion of the vessel – or even to determine whether it was moving at all. No motion could be perceived or felt and the time-sense had long since failed. Seaton and Margaret may have traveled in that gigantic bore for inches or for miles of distance; for seconds or for weeks of hypertime; they did not then and never did know. But with a slight jar the hypership came to rest at last upon a metallic cradle which had in some fashion appeared beneath her keel. Doors opened and the being holding the tridents, who had not moved a muscle during the, to the Terrestrials, interminable journey, made it plain to them that they were to precede him out of the airship. They did so, quietly and without protest, utterly helpless to move save at the behest of their unhuman captor-guide.

Through a maze of corridors and passages the long way led. Each was featureless and blank, each was lighted by the same eerie, bluish light, each was paved with a material which, although stone-hard to the hypermen, yielded springily, as yields a soft peat bog, under the feet of the massive Terrestrials. Seaton, although now restored to full vigor, held himself rigorously in check. Far from resisting the controlling impulses of the trident he sought to anticipate those commands.

Indeed, recognizing the possibility that the captor might be aware, through those electrical connections, of his very ideas, he schooled his outward thoughts to complete and unquestioning submission. Yet never had his inner brain been more active, and now the immense mentality given him by the Norlaminians stood him in good stead. For every doorway, every turn, every angle and intersection of that maze of communicating passageways was being engraved indelibly upon his brain – he knew that no matter how long or how involved the way, he could retain his orientation with respect to the buried river up which they had sailed.

And, although quiescent enough and submissive enough to all outward seeming, his inner brain was keyed up to its highest pitch, ready and eager to drive his muscles into furious activity at the slightest lapse of the attention of the wielder of the mastering trident.

But there was no such lapse. The intelligence of the hyperman seemed to be concentrated in the glowing tips of the forceps and did not waver for an instant, even when an elevator into which he steered his charges refused to lift the immense weight put upon it.

A silent colloquy ensued, then Seaton and Margaret walked endlessly up a spiral ramp. Climbed, it seemed, for hours, their feet sinking to the ankles into the resilient material of the rock-and-metal floor, while their alert guardian floated effortlessly in the air behind them, propelled and guided by his swiftly revolving tail.

Eventually the ramp leveled off into a corridor. Straight ahead, two aisles – branch half right – branch half left – first turn left – third turn right – second doorway on right. They stopped. The door opened. They stepped into a large, office-like room, thronged with the peculiar, sea-horse-like hypermen of this four-dimensional civilization. Everything was indescribable, incomprehensible, but there seemed to be desks, mechanisms, and tier upon tier of shelf-like receptacles intended for the storage of they knew not what.

Most evident of all, however, were the huge, goggling, staring eyes of the creatures as they pressed in, closer and closer to the helplessly immobile bodies of the man and the woman. Eyes dull, expressionless, and unmoving to Earthly, three-dimensional intelligences; but organs of highly intelligible, flashing language, as well as of keen vision, to their possessors.

Thus it was that the very air of the chamber was full of speech and of signs, but neither Margaret nor Seaton could see or hear them. In turn the Earthman tried, with every resource at his command of voice, thought, and pantomime, to bridge the gap – in vain.

Then strange, many-lensed instruments were trundled into the room and up to the helpless prisoners. Lenses peered; multicolored rays probed; planimeters, pantographs, and plotting points traced and recorded every bodily part; the while the two sets of intelligences, each to the other so foreign, were at last compelled to acknowledge frustration. Seaton of course knew what caused the impasse and, knowing the fundamental incompatibility of the dimensions involved, had no real hope that communication could be established, even though he knew the hypermen to be of high intelligence and attainment.

The natives, however, had no inkling of the possibility of three-dimensional actualities. Therefore, when it had been made plain to them that they had no point of contact with their visitors – that the massive outlanders were and must remain unresponsive to their every message and signal – they perforce ascribed that lack of response to a complete lack of intelligence.

The chief of the council, who had been conducting the examination, released the forces of his mechanisms and directed his flashing glance upon the eyes of the Terrestrials' guard, ordering him to put the specimens away.

'... and see to it that they are watched very carefully,' the ordering eye concluded. 'The Fellows of Science will be convened and will study them in greater detail than we have been able to do here.'

'Yes, sir; as you have said, so shall it be,' the guard acknowledged, and by means of the trident he guided his captives through a high-arched exit and into another labyrinth of corridors.

Seaton laughed aloud as he tucked Margaret's hand under his arm and marched along under the urge of the admonishing trident.

'"Nobody 'ome – they ain't got no sense," says his royal nibs. "Tyke 'em awye!"' he exclaimed.

'Why so happy all of a sudden, Dick? I can't see very much change in our status.'

'You'd be surprised.' He grinned. 'There's been a lot of change. I've found out that they can't read our thoughts at all, as long as we don't express them in muscular activity. I've been guarding my thoughts and haven't been talking to you much for fear they could get my ideas some way. But now I can tell you that I'm going to start something pretty quick. I've got this trident thing pretty well solved. This bird's taking us to jail now, I think, and when he gets us there his grip will probably slip for an instant. If it does he'll never get it back, and we'll be merrily on our way.'

'To jail!' Margaret exclaimed. 'But suppose they put us – I hope they put us in the same cell!'

'Don't worry about that. If my hunch is right it won't make a bit of difference – I'll have you back before they can get you out of sight. Everything around here is thin almost to the point of being immaterial, you know – you could whip an army of them in purely physical combat, and I could tear this whole joint up by the roots.'

'A la Samson? I believe that you could, at that.' Margaret smiled.

'Yeah; or rather, you can play you're Paul Bunyan, and I'll be Babe, the big blue ox. We'll show this flock of proptailed gilli-wimpuses just how we gouged out Lake Superior to make a he-man's soup bowl!'

'You make me feel a lot better, Dick, even if I do remember that Babe was forty-seven ax handles across the horns.' Margaret laughed, but sobered quickly. 'But here we are – oh, I *do* hope that he leaves me with you!'

They stopped beside a metal grill, in front of which was poised another hyperman, his propeller tail idling slowly. He had thought that he was to be Seaton's jailer, and as he swung the barred gate open he engaged the Terrestrial's escort in optical conversation – a conversation which gave Seaton the mere instant of time for which he had been waiting.

'So these are the visitors from outer space, whose bodies are so much denser than solid metal?' he asked curiously. 'Have they given you much trouble?'

'None at all. I touched that one only once, and this one, that you are to keep here, wilted at only the third step of force. The orders are to keep them under control every minute, however. They are stupid, senseless brutes, as is of course to be expected from their mass and general make-up. They have not given a single sign of intelligence of even the lowest order, but their strength is apparently enormous, and they might do a great deal of damage if allowed to break away from the trident.'

'All right; I'll hold him constantly until I am relieved,' and the jailer, lowering his own trident, extended a long, tentacular arm toward the grooved and knobbed shaft of the one whose teeth were already imbedded in Seaton's tissues.

Seaton had neither perceived nor sensed anything of this conversation, but he was tense and alert; tight-strung to take advantage of even the slightest slackening of the grip of the grappling fingers of the controller. Thus in the bare instant of transfer of control from one weird being to the other he acted – instantaneously and highly effectively.

With a twisting leap he whirled about, wrenching himself free from the punishing teeth of the grapple. Lightning hands seized the shaft and swung the weapon in a flashing arc. Then, with all the quickness of his highly trained muscles and with all the power of his brawny right arm, Seaton brought the controller down full upon the grotesque head of the hyperman.

He had given no thought to the material character of weapon or of objective; he had simply wrenched himself free and struck instinctively, lethally, knowing that freedom had to be won then or never. But he was not wielding an Earthly club or an Osnomian bar; nor was the flesh opposing him the solid substance of a human and three-dimensional enemy.

At impact the fiercely driven implement flew into a thousand pieces, but such was the power behind it that each piece continued on, driving its relentless way through the tenuous body substance of the erstwhile guard. That body subsided instantly upon the floor, a shapeless and mangled mass of oozing, dripping flesh. Weaponless now, holding only the shattered butt of the ex-guard's trident, Seaton turned to front the other guard who, still holding Margaret helpless, was advancing upon him, wide-open trident to the fore.

He hurled the broken stump; then as the guard nimbly dodged the flying missile, he leaped to the barred door of the cell. He seized it and jerked mightily; and as the anchor bolts of the hinges tore out of the masonry he swung the entire gate in a full-sweeping circle. Through the soft body the interlaced bars tore, cutting it into grisly, ghastly dice, and on, across the hall, tearing into and demolishing the opposite wall.

'All right, Peg, or did he shock you?' Seaton demanded.

'All right, I guess – he didn't have time to do much of anything.'

'Fine, let's snap it up, then. Or wait a minute. I'd better get us a couple of shields. We've got to keep them from getting those stingarees into us again – as long as we can keep them away from us we can do about as we please around here, but if they ever get hold of us again it'll be just too bad.'

While Seaton was speaking he had broken away and torn out two great plates or doors of solid metal, and, handing one of them to his companion, he went on: 'Here, carry this in front of you and we'll go places and do things.'

But in that time, short as it was, the alarm had been given, and up the corridor down which they must go was advancing a corps of heavily armed beings. Seaton took one quick step forward, then realizing the impossibility of forcing his way through such a horde without impalement, he leaped backward to the damaged wall and wrenched out a huge chunk of masonry. Then, while the upper wall and the now unsupported ceiling collapsed upon him, their fragments touching his hard body lightly and bouncing off like so many soft pillows, he hurled that chunk of material down the hall and into the thickest ranks of the attackers.

Through the close-packed phalanx it tore as would a plunging tank through massed infantry, nor was it alone.

Mass after mass of rock was hurled as fast as the Earthman could bend and straighten his mighty back, and the hypermen broke ranks and fled in wild disorder.

For to them Seaton was not a man of flesh and blood, lightly tossing pillows of eiderdown along a corridor, through an assemblage of wraithlike creatures. He was to them a monstrous being, constructed of something harder, denser, and tougher than any imaginable metal. A being driven by engines of unthinkable power, who stood unharmed and untouched while masses of stone, brickwork, and structural steel crashed down upon his bare head. A being who caught those falling masses of granite and concrete and steel and hurled them irresistibly through rank after rank of flesh-and-blood men!

'Let's go, Peg!' Seaton gritted. 'The way's clear now, I guess – we'll show those horse-faced hippocampuses that what it takes to do things, we've got!'

Through the revolting, reeking shambles of the corpse-littered corridor they gingerly made their way. Past the scene of the battle, past intersection after intersection they retraced their course, warily and suspiciously at first. But no ambush had been laid – the hypermen were apparently only too glad to let them go in peace – and soon they were hurrying along as fast as Margaret could walk.

They were soon to learn, however, that the denizens of this city of four-dimensional space had not yet given up the chase. Suddenly the yielding floor dropped away beneath their feet and they fell, or rather, floated, easily and slowly downward. Margaret shrieked in alarm, but the man remained unmoved and calm.

''Sall right, Peg,' he assured her. 'We want to go clear down to the bottom of this dump, anyway, and this'll save us the time and trouble of walking down. All right; that is, if we don't sink into the floor so deep when we hit that we won't be able to get ourselves out of it. Better spread out that shield so you'll fall on it – it won't hurt you, and it may help a lot.'

So slowly were they falling that they had ample time in which to prepare for the landing; and, since both Seaton and Margaret were thoroughly accustomed to weightless maneuvering in free space, their metal shields were flat beneath them when they struck the lowermost floor of the citadel. Those shields were crushed, broken, warped and twisted as they were forced into the pavement by the force of the falling bodies – as would be the steel doors of a bank vault upon being driven broadside on, deep into a floor of solid concrete.

But they served their purpose; they kept the bodies of the Terrestrials from sinking beyond their depth into the floor of the hyperdungeon. As they struggled to their feet, unhurt, and saw that they were in a large, cavernous room, six searchlight-like projectors came into play, enveloping them in a flood of soft, pinkish-white light.

Seaton stared about him, uncomprehending, until he saw that one of the hypermen, caught accidentally in the beam, shriveled horribly and instantly into a few floating wisps of luminous substance which in a few seconds disappeared entirely.

'Huh! Death rays!' he exclaimed then. ''Sa good thing for us we're essentially three-dimensional yet, or we'd probably never have known what struck us. Now let's see – where's our river? Oh, yes; over this way. Wonder if we'd better take these shields along? Guess not, they're pretty well shot – we'll pick us up a couple of good ones on the way, and I'll get you a grill like this one to use as a flail.'

'But there's no door on that side!' Margaret protested.

'So what? We'll roll our own as we go along.'

His heavy boot crashed against the wall before them, and a section of it fell outward. Two more kicks and they were through, hurrying along passages which Seaton knew led toward the buried river, breaking irresistibly through solid walls whenever the corridor along which they were moving angled away from his chosen direction.

Their progress was not impeded. The hyperbeings were willing – yes, anxious – for their unmanageable prisoners to depart and made no further attempts to bar their path. Thus the river was soon reached.

The airship in which they had been brought to the hypercity was nowhere to be seen, and Seaton did not waste time looking for it. He had been unable to understand the four-dimensional controls even while watching them in operation, and he realized that even if he could find the vessel the chance of capturing it and of escaping in it were slight indeed. Therefore throwing an arm around his companion, he leaped without ado into the speeding current.

'But, Dick, we'll drown!' Margaret protested. 'This stuff is altogether too thin for us to swim in – we'll sink like rocks!'

'Sure we will, but what of it?' he returned. 'How many times have you actually breathed since we left three-dimensional space?'

'Why, thousands of times, I suppose – or, now that you mention it, I don't really know whether I'm breathing at all or not – but we've been gone so long … Oh, I don't believe that I really know *anything*!'

'You aren't breathing at all,' he informed her then. 'We have been expending energy, though, in spite of that fact, and the only way I can explain it is that there must be fourth-dimensional oxygen or we would have suffocated long ago. Being three-dimensional, of course we wouldn't have to breathe it in for the cells to get the benefit of it – they grab it direct. Incidentally, that probably accounts for the fact that I'm hungry as a wolf, but that'll have to wait until we get back into our own space again.'

True to Seaton's prediction, they suffered no inconvenience as they strode along the metaled pavement of the river's bottom, Seaton still carrying the bent and battered grating with which he had wrought such havoc in the corridor so far above.

Almost at the end of the tunnel, a shark-like creature darted upon them, dreadful jaws agape. With his left arm Seaton threw Margaret behind him, while with his right he swung the four-dimensional grating upon the monster of the deeps. Under the fierce power of the blow the creature became a pulpy mass, drifting inertly away upon the current, and Seaton stared after it ruefully.

'That particular killing was entirely unnecessary, and I'm sorry I did it,' he remarked.

'Unnecessary? Why, it was going to bite me!' she cried.

'Yeah, it *thought* it was, but it would have been just like one of our own real sharks trying to bite the chilled-steel prow off a battleship,' he replied. 'Here comes another one. I'm going to let him gnaw on my arm, and see how he likes it.'

On the monster came with a savage rush, until the dreadful outthrust snout almost touched the man's bare, extended arm. Then the creature stopped, dead still in mid-rush, touched the arm tentatively, and darted away with a quick flirt of its powerful tail.

'See, Peg, he knows we ain't good to eat. None of these hyperanimals will bother us – it's only these men with their meat hooks that we have to fight shy of. Here's the jump-off. Better we hit it easylike – I wouldn't wonder if that sandy bottom would be pretty tough going. I think maybe we'd better take to the beach as soon as we can.'

From the metaled pavement of the brilliantly lighted aqueduct they stepped out upon the natural sand bottom of the open river. Above them was only the somberly sullen intensity of velvety darkness; a darkness only slightly relieved by the bluely luminous vegetation upon the river's either bank. In spite of their care they sank waist-deep into that sand, and it was only with great difficulty that they fought their way up to the much firmer footing of the nearer shore.

Out upon the margin at last, they found that they could make good time, and they set out downstream at a fast but effortless pace. Mile after mile they traveled, until, suddenly, as though some universal switch had been opened, the ghostly radiance of all the vegetation of the countryside disappeared in an instant, and utter and unimaginable darkness descended as a pall. It was not the ordinary darkness of an Earthly night, nor yet the darkness of even an Earthly dark room; it was indescribable, completely perfect darkness of the total absence of every ray of light.

'Dick!' shrieked Margaret. 'Where are you?'

'Right here, Peg – take it easy,' he advised, and groping fingers touched and clung. 'They'll probably light up again. Maybe this is their way of having night. We can't do much, anyway, until it gets light again. We couldn't possibly find the *Skylark* in this darkness; and even if we could feel our way downriver we'd miss the island that marks our turning-off point. Here, I feel a nice soft rock. I'll sit down with my back against it and you can lie down, with my lap for a pillow, and we'll take us a nap. Wasn't it Porthos, or some other one of Dumas' characters that said, "He who sleeps, eats"?'

'Dick, you're a perfect peach to take things the way you do.' Margaret's voice was broken. 'I know what you're thinking of, too. Oh, I *do* hope that nothing has become of them!' For she well knew that, true and loyal friend though Seaton was, yet his every thought was for beloved Dorothy, presumably still in *Skylark Two* – just as Martin Crane came first with her in everything.

'Sure they're all right, Peg.' An instantly suppressed tremor shook his giant frame. 'They're figuring on keeping them in the *Lark* until they raise her, I imagine. If I had known as much then as I know now they'd never have got away with any of this stuff – but it can't be helped now. I wish I could do something, because if we don't get back to *Two* pretty quick it seems as though we may snap back into our own three dimensions and land in empty space. Or would we, necessarily? The time coordinates would change, too, of course, and that change might very well make it obligatory for us to be back in our exact original locations in the *Lark* at the instant of transfer, no matter where we happen to be in this hyperspace–hypertime continuum. Too deep for me – I can't figure it. Wish Mart was here, maybe he could see through it.'

'You don't wish half as much as I do!' Margaret exclaimed feelingly.

'Well, anyway, we'll pretend that *Two* can't run off and leave us here. That certainly is a possibility, and it's a cheerful thought to dwell on while we can't do anything else. Now close your eyes and go bye-bye.'

They fell silent. Now and again Margaret dozed, only to start awake at the coughing grunt of some near-by prowling hyper-denizen of that unknown jungle, but Seaton did not sleep. He did not even half believe in his own hypothesis of their automatic return to their spaceship; and his vivid imagination insisted upon dwelling lingeringly upon every hideous possibility of their return to three-dimensional space outside their vessel's sheltering walls. And the same imagination continually conjured up visions of what might be happening to Dorothy – to the beloved bride who, since their marriage upon far distant Osnome, had never before been separated from him for so long a time. He had to struggle against an insane urge to do something, anything; even to dash madly about in the absolute darkness of hyperspace in a mad attempt – doomed to certain failure before it was begun – to reach *Skylark Two* before she should vanish from four-dimensional space.

Thus, while Seaton grew more and more tense momently, more and ever more desperately frustrated, the abysmally oppressive hypernight wore illimitably on. Creeping – plodding – d-r-a-g-g-i-n-g endlessly along; extending itself fantastically into the infinite reaches of all eternity.

12

Reunion

As suddenly as the hyperland had become dark it at last became light. There was no gradual lightening, no dawning, no warning – in an instant, blindingly to eyes which had for so long been strained in vain to detect even the faintest ray of visible light in the platinum-black darkness of the hypervoid, the entire countryside burst into its lividly glowing luminescence. As the light appeared Seaton leaped to his feet with a yell.

'Yowp! I was never so glad to see a light before in all my life, even if it *is* blue! Didn't sleep much either, did you, Peg?'

'Sleep? I don't believe that I'll *ever* be able to sleep again! It seemed as though I was lying there for weeks!'

'It did seem long, but time is meaningless to us here, you know.'

The two set out at a rapid pace, down the narrow beach beside the hyperstream. For a long time nothing was said, then Margaret broke out, half hysterically:

'Dick, this is simply driving me mad! I think probably I *am* mad, already. We seem to be walking, yet we aren't, really; we're going altogether too fast, and yet we don't seem to be getting anywhere. Besides, it's taking forever and ever ...'

'Steady, Peg! Keep a stiff upper lip! Of course we really aren't walking, in a three-dimensional sense, but we're getting there, just the same. I'd say that we are traveling almost half as fast as that airship was, which is a distinctly cheerful thought. And don't try to think of anything in detail, because equally of course we can't understand it. Try not to think of anything at all, out here, because you can't get to first base. You can *do* it, physically – let it go at that.

'And as for time, forget it. Just remember that, as far as we are concerned, this whole episode is occupying only a thousandth of a second of our own real time, even if it seems to last a thousand years. Paste that idea in your hat and stick to it. Think of a thousandth of a second and snap your fingers at anything that happens. And, above all, get it down solid that you're not nutty – it's just that everything else around here is. It's like that wild one Sir Eustace pulled on me that time, remember? "I say, Seaton old chap, the chaps hereabout seem to regard me as a foreigner. Now really, you know, they should realize that I am simply alone in a nation of foreigners."'

Margaret laughed, recovering a measure of her customary poise at Seaton's matter-of-fact explanations and reassurance, and the seemingly endless journey went on. Indeed, so long did it seem that the high-strung and apprehensive Seaton was every moment expecting the instantaneous hypernight again to extinguish all illumination long before they came within sight of the little island, with its unmistakably identifying obelisk of reddish stone.

'Woof, but that's a relief!' he exploded at sight of the marker. 'We'll be there in a few minutes more – here's hoping it holds off for those few minutes!'

'It will,' Margaret said confidently. 'It'll have to, now that we're so close. How are you possibly going to get a line on those three peaks? We cannot possibly see over or through that jungle.'

'Easy – just like shooting fish down a well. That's one reason I was so glad to see that tall obelisk thing over there – it's big enough to hold my weight and high enough so that I can see the peaks from its top. I'm going to climb up it and wigwag you onto the line we want. Then we'll set a pole on that line and crash through the jungle, setting up back-sights as we go along. We'll be able to see the peaks in a mile or so, and once we see them it'll be easy to find *Two*.'

'But climbing Cleopatra's Needle comes first, and it's straight up and down,' Margaret objected practically. 'How are you going to do that?'

'With a couple of hypergrab-hooks – watch me!'

He wrenched off three of the bars of his cell grating and twisted them together, to form a heavy rod. One end of this rod he bent back upon itself, sharpening the end by squeezing it in his two hands. It required all of his prodigious strength, but in his grasp the metal slowly flowed together in a perfect weld and he waved in the air a sharply pointed hook some seven feet in length. In the same way he made another, and, with a word to the girl, he shot away through the almost intangible water toward the island.

He soon reached the base of the obelisk, and into its rounded surface he drove one of his hyperhooks. But he struck too hard. Though the hook was constructed of the most stubborn metal known to the denizens of that strange world, the obelisk was of hyperstone and the improvised tool rebounded, bent out of all semblance and useless.

It was quickly reshaped, however, and Seaton went more gently about his task. He soon learned exactly how much pressure his hooks would stand, and also the best method of imbedding the sharp metal points in the rock of the monument. Then, both hooks holding, he drove the toe of one heavy boot into the stone and began climbing.

Soon, however, his right-hand hook refused to bite; the stone had so dulled the point of the implement that it was useless. After a moment's thought Seaton settled both feet firmly, and, holding the shaft of the left-hand hook under his left elbow, bent the free end around behind his back. Then, both hands free, he essayed the muscle-tearing task of squeezing that point again into serviceability.

'Watch out, Dick – you'll fall!' Margaret called.

'I'll try not to,' he called back cheerfully. 'Took too much work and time to get up this far to waste it. Wouldn't hurt me if I did fall – but you might have to come over and pull me out of the ground.'

He did not fall. The hook was repointed without accident and he continued up the obelisk – a human fly walking up a vertical column. Four times he had to stop to sharpen his climbers, but at last he stood atop the lofty shaft. From that eminence he could see not only the three peaks, but even the scene of confused activity which he knew marked the mouth of the gigantic well at whose bottom the *Skylark* lay. Margaret had broken off a small tree, and from the obelisk's top Seaton directed its placing as a transitman directs the setting of his head flag.

'Left – way left!' His arm waved its hook in great circles. 'Easy now!' Left arm poised aloft. 'All right for line!' Both arms swept up and down, once.

A careful recheck ... 'Back a hair.' Right arm out, insinuatingly. 'All right for tack – down she goes!' Both arms up and down, twice, and the feminine flag-man drove the marker deep into the sand.

'You might come over here, Peg!' Seaton shouted, as he began his hasty descent. 'I'm going to climb down until my hooks get too dull to hold, and then fall the rest of the way – no time to waste sharpening them – and you may have to rally round with a helping hand.'

Scarcely a third of the way down, one hook refused to function. A few great plunging steps downward and the other also failed – would no longer even scratch the stubborn stone. Already falling, Seaton gathered himself together, twisted bars held horizontally beneath him, and floated gently downward. He came to the ground no harder than he would have landed after jumping from a five-foot Earthly fence; but even his three-ply bars of hypermetal did not keep him from plunging several feet into that strangely unsubstantial hyperground.

Margaret was there, however, with her grating and her plate of armor. With her aid Seaton struggled free, and together they waded through the river and hurried to the line post which Margaret had set. Then, along the line established by the obelisk and the post, the man crashed into the thick growth of the jungle, the woman at his heels.

Though the weirdly peculiar trees, creepers, and bamboo-like shoots com-prising the jungle's vegetation were not strong enough to bar the progress of the dense, hard, human bodies, yet they impeded that progress so terribly that the trail-breaker soon halted.

'Not so good this way, Peg,' he reflected. 'These creepers will soon pull you down, I'm afraid; and, besides, we'll be losing our line pretty quickly. What to do? Better I knock out a path with this magic wand of mine, I guess – none of this stuff seems to be very heavy.'

Again they set out; Seaton's grating, so bent and battered now that it could not be recognized as once having been the door of a prison cell, methodically sweeping from side to side; a fiercely driven scythe against which no hyper-thing could stand. Vines and creepers still wrapped around and clung to the struggling pair; shattered masses drifted down upon them from above, exud-ing in floods a viscous, gluey sap; and both masses of broken vegetation and floods of adhesive juices reinforced and rendered even more impassable the already high-piled wilderness of debris which had been accumulating there during time unthinkable. All hypernature seemed to be in league against them; feebly but clingingly attempting to hold them back and devour them.

Thus hampered, but driven to highest effort by the fear of imminent dark-ness and consequent helplessness, they struggled indomitably on. On and on; while behind them stretched an ever-lengthening, straight, sharply cut streak of blackness in the livid hyperlight of the jungle. On and on; Seaton flailing a path through the standing jungle, Margaret plowing along in his wake, fighting, struggling through and over the matted tangle of underbrush and the grasping, clinging tentacles of its parasitic inhabitants.

Seaton's great mass and prodigious strength enabled him to force his way through that fantastically inimical undergrowth, but the unremitting pull and drag of the attacking vines wore down the woman's slighter physique.

'Just a minute, Dick!' She stopped, strength almost spent. 'I hate to admit that I can't stand the pace, especially since you are doing all the work, as well as wading through the same mess that I am, but I don't believe that I can go on much longer without a rest.'

'All right ...' Seaton began, but broke off, staring ahead. 'No; keep on coming one minute more, Peg – three more jumps and we're through.'

'I can go that much farther, of course. Lead on, MacDuff!' and they struggled on.

In a few more steps they broke out of the thick growth of the jungle and into the almost-palpable darkness of a great, roughly circular area which had been cleared of the prolific growth. In the center of this circle could be seen the bluely illuminated works of the engineers who were raising *Skylark Two*. The edge of the great well was surrounded by four-dimensional machinery; and that well's wide apron and its towering derricks were swarming with hypermen.

'Stay behind me, Peg, but as close as you can without getting hit,' the man instructed his companion after a hasty but comprehensive study of the scene. 'Keep your shield up and have your grating in good swinging order. I'll be able to take care of most of them, I think, but you want to be ready to squash any of them that may get around me or who may rush us from behind. Those stickers of theirs are bad medicine, girl, and we don't want to take any chances at all of getting stuck again.'

'I'll say we don't!' she agreed feelingly, and Seaton started off over the now unencumbered ground. 'Wait a minute, Dick – where are you, anyway? I can't see you at all!'

'That's right, too. Never thought of it, but there's no light. The glimmer of those plants is pretty faint at best, and doesn't reach out here at all. We'd better hold hands, I guess, until we get close enough to the works out there so that we can see what we're doing and what's going on.'

'But I've got only two hands – I'm not a hippocampus – and they're both full of doors and clubs and things. But maybe I can carry this shield under my arm – it isn't heavy – there, where are you, anyway?'

Seeking hands found each other, and, hand in hand, the two set out boldly toward the scene of activity so starkly revealed in the center of that vast circle of darkness. So appalling was the darkness that it was a thing tangible – palpable. Seaton could not see his companion, could not see the weapons and the shield he bore, could not even faintly discern the very ground upon which he walked. Yet he plunged forward, almost dragging the girl along bodily, eyes fixed upon the bluely gleaming circle of structures which was his goal.

'But Dick!' Margaret panted. 'Let's not go so fast; I can't see a thing – not even my hand right in front of my eyes – and I'm afraid we'll bump into something – anything!'

'We've got to snap it up, Peg,' the man replied, not slackening his pace in the slightest, 'and there's nothing very big between us and the *Skylark*, or we could see it against those lights. We may stumble over something, of course, but it'll be soft enough so that it won't hurt us any. But suppose that another night clamps down on us before we get out there?'

'Oh, that's right; it did come awfully suddenly,' and Margaret leaped ahead; dread of the abysmally horrible hypernight so far outweighing her natural fear of unseen obstacles in her path that the man was hard put to it to keep up with her. 'Suppose they'll know we're coming?'

'Maybe – probably – I don't know. I don't imagine they can see us, but since we cannot understand anything about them, it's quite possible that they may have other senses that we know nothing about. They'll have to spot us mighty quick, though, if they expect to do themselves any good.'

The hypermen could not see them, but it was soon made evident that the weird beings had indeed, in some unknown fashion, been warned of their coming. Mighty searchlights projected great beams of livid blue light, beams which sought eagerly the human beings – probing, questing, searching.

As he perceived the beams Seaton knew that the hypermen could not see without lights any better than he could; and knowing what to expect, he grinned savagely into the darkness as he threw an arm around Margaret and spoke – or thought – to her.

'One of those beams'll find us pretty quick, and they may send something along it. If so, and if I yell jump, do it quick. Straight up; high, wide, and handsome – jump!'

For even as he spoke, one of the stabbing beams of light found them and had stopped full upon them. And almost instantly had come flashing along that beam a horde of hypermen, armed with peculiar weapons at whose use the Terrestrials could not even guess.

But also almost instantly had Seaton and Margaret jumped – jumped with the full power of Earthly muscles which, opposed by only the feeble gravity of hyperland, had given their bodies such a velocity that to the eyes of the hypermen their intended captives had simply and instantly disappeared.

'They knew we were there, all right, some way or other – maybe our mass jarred the ground – but they apparently can't see us without lights, and that gives us a break,' Seaton remarked conversationally, as they soared interminably upward. 'We ought to come down just about where that tallest derrick is – right where we can go to work on them.'

But the scientist was mistaken in thinking that the hypermen had discovered them through tremors of the ground. For the searching cones of light were baffled only for seconds; then, guided by some sense or by some mechanism unknown and unknowable to any three-dimensional intelligence, they darted aloft and were once more outlining the fleeing Terrestrials in the bluish glare of their livid radiance. And upward, along those illuminated ways, darted those living airplanes, the hypermen; and this time the man and the woman, with all their incredible physical strength could not leap aside.

'Not so good,' said Seaton, 'better we'd stayed on the ground, maybe. They *could* trace us, after all; and of course this air is their natural element. But now that we're up here, we'll just have to fight them off; back to back, until we land.'

'But how can we stay back to back?' asked Margaret sharply. 'We'll drift apart at our first effort. Then they'll be able to get behind us and they'll have us again!'

'That's so, too – never thought of that angle, Peg. You've got a belt on, haven't you?'

'Yes.'

'Fine! Loosen it up and I'll run mine through it. The belts and an ankle-and-knee lock'll hold us together and in position to play tunes on those sea-horses' ribs. Keep your shield up and keep that grating swinging and we'll lay them like a carpet.'

Seaton had not been idle while he was talking, and when the attackers drew near, vicious tridents outthrust, they encountered an irresistibly driven wall of crushing, tearing dismembering, and all-destroying metal. Back to back the two unknown monstrosities floated through the air; interlaced belts holding their vulnerable backs together, gripped legs holding their indestructibly dense and hard bodies in alignment.

For a time the four-dimensional creatures threw themselves upon the Terrestrials, only to be hurled away upon all sides, chopped literally to bits. For Margaret protected Seaton's back, and he himself took care of the space in front of him, to right and to left of them, above and below them; driving the closely spaced latticework of his metal grating throughout all that space so viciously and so furiously that it seemed to be omnipresent as well as omnipotent. For a time the hypermen tried, as has been said; only to be sliced by that fearsomely irresistible weapon into such grisly fragments that the appalled survivors of the hyper-horde soon abandoned the futile and suicidal attack.

Then, giving up hope of recapturing the specimens alive, the hyperbeings turned upon them their lethal beams. Soft, pinkly glowing beams which turned to a deep red and then flamed through the spectrum and into the violet as they were found to have no effect upon the human bodies. But the death rays of the hypermen, whatever the frequency, were futile – the massed battalions at the pit's mouth were as impotent as had been the armed forces of the great hypercity, whose denizens had also failed either to hold or to kill the supernatural Terrestrials.

During the hand-to-hand encounter the two had passed the apex of their flight; and now, bathed in the varicolored beams, they floated gently downward, directly toward the great derrick which Seaton had pointed out as marking their probable landing place. In fact, they grazed one of the massive corner members of the structure; but Seaton interposed his four-dimensional shield and, although the derrick trembled noticeably under the impact, neither he nor Margaret was hurt as they drifted lightly to the ground.

'Just like jumping off of and back into a feather bed!' Seaton exulted, as he straightened up, disconnected the hampering belts, and guided Margaret toward the vast hole in the ground, unopposed now save for the still-flaring beams. 'Wonder if any more of them want to argue the right of way with us? Guess not.'

'But how are we going to get down there?' asked Margaret.

'Fall down – or, better yet, we'll slide down those chains they've already got installed. You'd better carry all this junk, and I'll kind of carry you. That way you won't have to do anything – just take a ride.'

Scarcely encumbered by the girl's weight, Seaton stepped outward to the great chain cables, and hand under hand he went down, down past the huge lifting cradles which had been placed around the massive globe of arenak.

'But we'll go right through it – there's nothing to stop us in this dimension!' protested Margaret.

'No, we won't; and yes, there is,' Seaton replied. 'We swing *past* it and down, around onto level footing, on this loose end of chain – like this, see?' and they were once more in the control room of *Skylark Two*.

There stood Dorothy, Crane, and Shiro, exactly as they had left them so long before. Still held in the grip of the tridents, they were silent, immobile; their eyes were vacant and expressionless. Neither Dorothy nor Crane gave any sign of recognition, neither seemed even to realize that their loved ones, gone so long, had at last returned.

13

The Return to Space

Seaton's glance leaped to his beloved Dorothy. Drooping yet rigid she stood there, unmoving, corpselike. Accustomed now to seeing four-dimensional things by consciously examining only their three-dimensional surfaces, he perceived instantly the waxen, utterly inhuman vacuity of her normally piquant and vivacious face – perceived it, and at that perception went mad.

Clutching convulsively the length of hyperchain by which he had swung into the control room he leaped, furious and elementally savage; forgetting weapons and armor, heedless of risk and of odds, mastered completely by a seething, searing urge to wreak vengeance upon the creature who had so terribly outraged his Dorothy, the woman in whom centered his universe.

So furious was his action that the chain snapped apart at the wall of the control room; so rapid was it that the hyperguard had no time to move, nor even to think.

That guard had been peacefully controlling with his trident the paralyzed prisoner. All had been quiet and calm. Suddenly – in an instant – had appeared the two monstrosities who had been taken to the capital. And in that same fleeting instant one of the monsters was leaping at him. And ahead of that monster there came lashing out an enormous anchor chain, one of whose links of solid steel no ordinary mortal could lift; an anchor chain hurtling toward him with a velocity and a momentum upon that tenuous hyperworld unthinkable.

The almost-immaterial flesh of the hyperman could no more withstand that fiercely driven mass of metal than can a human body ward off an armor-piercing projectile in full flight. Through his body the great chain tore; cutting, battering, rending it into ghastly, pulpily indescribable fragments unrecognizable as ever having been anything animate. Indeed, so fiercely had the chain been urged that the metal itself could not stand the strain. Five links broke off at the climax of the chain's blacksnake-like stroke, and, accompanying the bleeding scraps of flesh that had been the guard, tore on past the walls of the space ship and out into the hypervoid.

The guard holding his tridents in Crane and Shiro had not much more warning. He saw his fellow obliterated, true; but that was all he lived to see, and he had time to do exactly nothing. One more quick flip of Seaton's singularly efficient weapon and the remains of that officer also disappeared into hyperspace. More of the chain went along, this time, but that did not matter. Dropping to the floor the remaining links of his hyperflail, Seaton sprang to

Dorothy, reaching her side just as the punishing trident, released by the slain guard, fell away from her.

She recovered her senses instantly and turned a surprised face to the man, who, incoherent in his relief that she was alive and apparently unharmed, was taking her into his arms.

'Why, surely, Dick, I'm all right – how could I be any other way?' she answered his first agonized question in amazement. She studied his worn face in puzzled wonder and went on: 'But you certainly are not. What has happened, dear, anyway; and how could it have, possibly?'

'I hated like sin to be gone so long, Dimples, but it couldn't be helped,' Seaton, in his eagerness to explain his long absence, did not even notice the peculiar implications in his wife's speech and manner. 'You see, it was a long trip, and we didn't get a chance to break away from those meat hooks of theirs until after they got us into their city and examined us. Then, when we finally did break away, we found that we couldn't travel at night. Their days are bad enough, with this thick blue light, but during the nights there's absolutely no light at all, of any kind. No moon, no stars, no nothing ...'

'Nights! What are you talking about, Dick, anyway?' Dorothy had been trying, to interrupt since his first question and had managed at last to break in. 'Why, you haven't been gone at all, not even a second. We've all been right here, all the time!'

'Huh?' ejaculated Seaton. 'Are you completely nuts, Red-Top, or what ...?'

'Dick and I were gone at least a week, Dottie,' Margaret, who had been embracing Crane, interrupted in turn, 'and it was awful!'

'Just a minute, folks!' Seaton listened intently and stared upward. 'We'll have to let the explanations ride a while longer. I thought they wouldn't give up that easy – here they come! I don't know how long we were gone – it seemed like a darn long time – but it was long enough so that I learned how to mop up on these folks, believe me! You take that sword and buckler of Peg's, Mart. They don't look so hot, but they're big medicine in these parts. All we've got to do is swing them fast enough to keep those stingaroos of theirs out of our gizzards and we're all set. Be careful not to hit too hard, though, or you'll bust that grating into forty pieces – it's hyperstuff, nowhere near as solid as anything we're used to. All it'll stand is about normal fly-swatting stroke, but that's enough to knock any of these fantailed humming birds into an outside loop. Ah, they've got guns or something! Duck down, girls, so we can cover you with these shields; and, Shiro, you might pull that piece of chain apart and throw the links at them – that'll be good for what ails them!'

The hypermen appeared in the control room, and battle again was joined. This time, however, the natives did not rush to the attack with their tridents; nor did they employ their futile rays of death. They had guns, shooting pellets of metal; they had improvised, crossbow-like slings and catapults; they had spears and javelins made of their densest materials, which their strongest men threw with all their power. But pellets and spears alike thudded harmlessly against four-dimensional shields – shields once the impenetrable, unbreakable doors of their mightiest prison – and the masses of metal and stone vomited forth by the catapults were caught by Seaton and Crane and hurled back through the ranks of the attackers with devastating effect. Shiro also was doing untold damage with his bits of chain and with such other items of four-dimensional matter as came to hand.

Still the hypermen came pressing in, closer and closer. Soon the three men were standing in a triangle, in the center of which were the women, their flying weapons defining a volume of space to enter which meant hideous dismemberment and death to any hypercreature. But on they came, willing, it seemed, to spend any number of lives to regain their lost control over the Terrestrials; realizing, it seemed, that even those supernaturally powerful beings must in time weaken.

While the conflict was at its height, however, it seemed to Seaton that the already tenuous hypermen were growing even more wraithlike; and at the same time he found himself fighting with greater and greater difficulty. The lethal grating, which he had been driving with such speed that it had been visible only as a solid barrier, moved more and ever more slowly, to come finally to a halt in spite of his every effort.

He could not move a muscle, and despairingly he watched a now almost-invisible warden who was approaching him, controlling trident outthrust. But to his relieved surprise the hyperforceps did not touch him, but slithered *past him* without making contact; and hyperman and hyperweapon disappeared altogether, fading out slowly into nothingness.

Then Seaton found himself moving in space. Without volition he was floating across the control room, toward the switch whose closing had ushered the Terrestrials out of their familiar space of three dimensions and into this weirdly impossible region of horror. Nor was he alone in his movement. Dorothy, the Cranes, and Shiro were all in motion, returning slowly to the identical positions they had occupied at the instant when Seaton had closed his master switch.

And as they moved, they *changed*. The *Skylark* herself changed, as did every molecule, every atom of substance, in or of the spherical cruiser of the void.

Seaton's hand reached out and grasped the ebonite handle of the switch. Then, as his entire body came to rest, he was swept by wave upon wave of almost-unbearable relief as the artificial and unnatural extension into the fourth dimension began to collapse. Slowly, as had progressed the extrusion into that dimension, so progressed the de-extrusion from it. Each ultimate particle of matter underwent an indescribable and incomprehensible foreshortening; a compression; a shrinking together; a writhing and twisting reverse rearrangement, each slow increment of which was poignantly welcome to every outraged unit of human flesh.

Suddenly seeming, and yet seemingly only after untold hours, the return to three-dimensional space was finished. Seaton's hand drove through the remaining fraction of an inch of its travel with the handle of the switch; his ears heard the click and snap of the plungers driving home against their stop blocks – the closing of the relay switches had just been completed. The familiar fittings of the control room stood out in their normal three dimensions, sharp and clear.

Dorothy sat exactly as she had sat before the transition. She was leaning slightly forward in her seat – her gorgeous red-bronze hair in perfect order, her sweetly curved lips half parted, her violet eyes widened in somewhat fearful anticipation of what the dimensional translation was to bring. She was unchanged – but Seaton!

He also sat exactly as he had sat an instant – or was it a month? – before; but his face was thin and heavily lined, his normally powerful body was now gauntly eloquent of utter fatigue. Nor was Margaret in better case. She was haggard, almost emaciated. Her clothing, like that of Seaton, had been forced to return to a semblance of order by the exigencies of interdimensional and inter-time translation, and for a moment appeared sound and whole.

The translation accomplished, however, that clothing literally fell apart. The dirt and grime of their long, hard journey and the sticky sap of the hyperplants through which they had fought their way had of course disappeared – being four-dimensional material, all such had perforce remained behind in four-dimensional space – but the thorns and sucking disks of the hypervegetation had taken toll. Now each rent and tear reappeared, to give mute but eloquent testimony to the fact that the sojourn of those two human beings in hyperland had been neither peaceful nor uneventful.

Dorothy's glance flashed in amazement from Seaton to Margaret, and she repressed a scream as she saw the ravages wrought by whatever it was that they had gone through. She could not understand it, could not reconcile it with what she herself had experienced while in the hyperspace–hypertime continuum, but moved by the ages-old instinct of all true women, she reached out to take her abused husband into the shelter of her arms. But Seaton's first thought was for the bodiless foes whom they might not have left behind.

'Did we get away, Mart?' he demanded, hand still upon the switch. Then, without waiting for a reply, he went on: 'We must've made it, though, or we'd've been dematerialized before this. Three rousing cheers! We made it – we made it!'

For several minutes all four gave way to their mixed but profound emotions, in which relief and joy predominated. They had escaped from the intellectuals; they had come alive through hyperspace!

'But Dick!' Dorothy held Seaton off at arm's length and studied his gaunt, lined face. 'Lover, you look actually thin.'

'I *am* thin,' he replied. 'We were gone a week, we told you. I'm just about starved to death, and I'm thirstier even than that. Not being able to eat is bad; but going without water is worse, believe me! My whole insides feel like a mess of desiccated blotters. Come on, Peg; let's empty us a couple of water tanks.'

They drank; lightly and intermittently at first, then deeply.

At last Seaton put down the pitcher. 'That isn't enough, by any means; but we're damp enough inside so that we can swallow food, I guess. While you're finding out where we are, Mart, Peg and I'll eat six or eight meals apiece.'

While Seaton and Margaret ate – ate as they had drunk, carefully, but with every evidence of an insatiable bodily demand for food – Dorothy's puzzled gaze went from the worn faces of the diners to a mirror which reflected her own vivid, unchanged self.

'But I don't understand it at all, Dick!' she burst out at last. '*I'm* not thirsty, nor hungry, and I haven't changed a bit. Neither has Martin; and yet you two have lost pounds and pounds and look as though you had been pulled through a knot hole. It didn't seem to us as though you were away from us at all. You were going to tell me about that back there, when we were interrupted. Now go ahead and explain things, before I explode. What happened, anyway?'

Seaton, hunger temporarily assuaged, gave a full but concise summary of everything that had happened while he and Margaret were away from the *Skylark*. He then launched into a scientific dissertation, only to be interrupted by Dorothy.

'But, Dick, it doesn't sound reasonable that all that could *possibly* have happened to you and Peggy without our even knowing that any time at all had passed!' she expostulated. 'We weren't unconscious or anything, were we, Martin? We knew what was going on all the time, didn't we?'

'We were at no time unconscious, and we knew at all times what was taking place around us,' Crane made surprising but positive answer. He was seated at a visiplate, but had been listening to the story instead of studying the almost-sheer emptiness that was space. 'And since it is a truism of Norlaminian psychology that any lapse of consciousness, of however short duration, is impressed upon the conscious of a mind of even moderate power, I feel safe in saying that for Dorothy and me, at least, no lapse of time did occur or could have occurred.'

'There!' Dorothy exulted. 'You've got to admit that Martin knows his stuff. How are you going to get around that?'

'Search me – wish I knew.' Seaton frowned in thought. 'But Mart chirped it, I think, when he said "for Dorothy and me, at least," because for us two the time certainly lapsed, and lapsed plenty. However, Mart certainly *does* know his stuff; the old think tank is full of bubbles all the time. He doesn't make positive statements very often, and when he does you can sink the bank roll on 'em. Therefore, since you were both conscious and time did not lapse – for you – it must have been time itself that was cuckoo instead of you. It must have stretched, or must have been stretched, like the very dickens – for you.

'Where does that idea get us? I might think that their time was intrinsically variable, as well as being different from ours, if it was not for the regular alternation of night and day – of light and darkness, at least – that Peg and I saw, and which affected the whole country, as far as we could see. So that's out.

'Maybe they treated you two to a dose of suspended animation or something of the kind, since you weren't going anywhere … Nope, that idea doesn't carry the right earmarks, and besides it would have registered as such on Martin's Norlaminianly psychological brain. So that's out, too. In fact, the only thing that could deliver the goods would be a sta— but that'd be a trifle strong, even for a hyperman, I'm afraid.'

'What would?' demanded Margaret. 'Anything that you would call strong ought to be worth listening to.'

'A stasis of time. Sounds a trifle far-fetched, of course, but …'

'But phooey!' Dorothy exclaimed. 'Now you *are* raving, Dick!'

'I'm not so sure of that, at all,' Seaton argued stubbornly. 'They really understand time, I think, and I picked up a couple of pointers. It would take a sixth-order field … That's it, I'm pretty sure, and that gives me an idea. If they can do it in hypertime, why can't we do it in ours?'

'I fail to see how such a stasis could be established,' argued Crane. 'It seems to me that as long as matter exists time must continue, since it is quite firmly established that time depends upon matter – or rather upon the motion in space of that which we call matter.'

'Sure – that's what I'm going on. Time and motion are both relative. Stop all motion – relative, not absolute motion – and what have you? You have duration without sequence or succession, which is what?'

'That would be a stasis of time, as you say,' Crane conceded, after due deliberation. 'How can you do it?'

'I don't know yet whether I can or not – that's another question. We already know, though, how to set up a stasis of the ether along a spherical surface, and after I have accumulated a little more data on the sixth order it should not be impossible to calculate a volume-stasis in both ether and subether, far enough down to establish complete immobility and local cessation of time in gross matter so affected.'

'But would not all matter so affected assume at once the absolute zero of temperature and thus preclude life?'

'I don't think so. The stasis would be subatomic and instantaneous, you know; there could be no loss or transfer of energy. I don't see how gross matter could be affected at all. As far as I can see it would be an absolutely perfect suspension of animation. You and Dot lived through it, anyway, and I'm positive that that's what they did to you. And I still say that if anybody can do it, we can.'

'"And that," ' put in Margaret roguishly, 'as you so feelingly remark, "is a cheerful thought to dwell on – let's dwell on it!" '

'We'll do that little thing, too, Peg, some of these times; see if we don't!' Seaton promised. 'But to get back to our knitting, what's the good word, Mart – located us yet? Are we, or are we not, heading for that justly famed "distant galaxy" of the Fenachrone?'

'We are not,' Crane replied flatly, 'nor are we heading for any other point in space covered by the charts of Ravindau's astronomers.'

'Huh? Great Cat!' Seaton joined the physicist at his visiplate, and made complete observations upon the brightest nebulae visible.

He turned then to the charts, and his findings confirmed those of Crane. They were so far away from our own galaxy that the space in which they were was unknown, even to those masters of astronomy and of intergalactic navigation, the Fenachrone.

'Well, we're not lost, anyway, thanks to your cautious old bean.' Seaton grinned as he stepped over to an object-compass mounted upon the plane table.

This particular instrument was equipped with every refinement known to the science of four great solar systems. Its exceedingly delicate needle, swinging in an almost-perfect vacuum upon practically frictionless jeweled bearings, was focused upon the unimaginable mass of the entire First Galaxy, a mass so inconceivably great that mathematics had shown – and even Crane would have stated as a fact – that it would affect that needle from any point whatever, however distant in macrocosmic space.

Seaton actuated the minute force which set the needle in motion, but it did not oscillate. For minute after minute it revolved slowly but freely, coming ultimately to rest without any indication of having been affected in the least by any external influence. He stared at the compass in stark, unbelieving amazement, then tested its current and its every other factor. The instrument was in perfect order and in perfect adjustment. Grimly, quietly, he repeated the oscillatory test – with the same utterly negative result.

'Well, that is eminently, conclusively, definitely, and unqualifiedly that.' He stared at Crane, unseeing, his mind racing. 'The most sensitive needle we've got, and she won't even register!'

'In other words, we are lost.' Crane's voice was level and calm. 'We are so far away from the First Galaxy that even that compass, supposedly reactive from any possible location in space, is useless.'

'But I don't get it, at all, Mart!' Seaton exclaimed, paying no attention to the grim meaning underlying his friend's utterance. 'With the whole mass of the galaxy as its object of attachment that needle absolutely will register from a distance greater than any possible diameter of the super-universe ...' His voice died away.

'Go on; you are beginning to see the light,' Crane prompted.

'Yeah – no wonder I couldn't plot a curve to trace those Fenachrone torpedoes – our fundamental assumptions were unsound. The fact simply is that if space is curved at all, the radius of curvature is vastly greater than any figure as yet proposed, even by the Fenachrone astronomers. We certainly weren't out of our own space a thousandth of a second – more likely only a couple of millionths – do you suppose that there really are folds in the fourth dimension?'

'That idea has been advanced, but folds are not strictly necessary, nor are they easy to defend. It has always seemed to me that the hypothesis of linear departure is much more tenable. The planes need not be parallel, you know – in fact, it is almost a mathematical certainty that they are *not* parallel.'

'That's so, too; and that hypothesis would account for everything of course. But how are—'

'What *are* you two talking about?' demanded Dorothy. 'We simply couldn't have come that far – why, the *Skylark* was stuck in the ground the whole time!'

'As a physicist, Red-Top, you're a fine little beauty-contest winner.' Seaton grinned. 'You forget that with the velocity she had, the *Lark* wouldn't have been stopped within three months, either – yet she seemed to stop. How about that, Mart?'

'I have been thinking about that. It is all a question of relative velocities, of course; but even at that, the angle of departure of the two spaces must have been extreme indeed to account for our present location in three-dimensional space.'

'Extreme is right; but there's no use yapping about it now, any more than about any other spilled milk. We'll just have to go places and do things; that's all.'

'Go where and do what?' asked Dorothy pointedly.

'Lost – lost in space!' Margaret breathed.

As the dread import of their predicament struck into her consciousness she had seized the arm rests of her chair in a spasmodic clutch; but she forced herself to relax and her deep brown eyes held no sign of panic.

'But we have been lost in space before, Dottie, apparently as badly as we are now. Worse, really, because we did not have Martin and Dick with us then.'

'At-a-girl, Peg!' Seaton cheered. 'We may be lost – guess we are, temporarily, at least – but we're not licked, not by seven thousand rows of apple trees!'

'I fail to perceive any very solid basis for your optimism,' Crane remarked quietly, 'but you have an idea, of course. What is it?'

'Pick out the galaxy nearest our line of flight and brake down for it.' Seaton's nimble mind was leaping ahead. 'The *Lark*'s so full of uranium that her skin's bulging, so we've got power to burn. In that galaxy there are – there *must* be – suns with habitable, possibly inhabited, planets. We'll find one such planet and land on it. Then we'll do with our might what our hands find to do.'

'Such as?'

'Along what lines?' queried Dorothy and Crane simultaneously.

'Spaceship, probably – *Two*'s entirely too small to be of any account in intergalactic work,' Seaton replied promptly. 'Or maybe fourth-, fifth-, and sixth-order projectors; or maybe some kind of an ultra-ultra radio or projector. How do I know, from here? But there's thousands of things that maybe we can do – we'll wait until we get there to worry about which one to try first.'

14

Wanted – A Planet

Seaton strode over to the control board and applied maximum acceleration. 'Might as well start traveling, Mart,' he remarked to Crane, who for almost an hour had been devoting the highest telescopic power of number six visiplate to spectroscopic, interferometric, and spectrophotometric studies of half a dozen selected nebulae. 'No matter which one you pick out we'll have to have quite a lot of positive acceleration yet before we reverse to negative.'

'As a preliminary measure, might it not be a good plan to gain some idea as to our present line of flight?' Crane asked dryly, bending a quizzical glance upon his friend. 'You know a great deal more than I do about the hypothesis of linear departure of incompatible and incommensurable spaces, however, and so perhaps you already know our true course.'

'Ouch! Pals, they got me!' Seaton clapped a hand over his heart; then, seizing his own ear, he led himself up to the switchboard and shut off the space drive, except for the practically negligible superimposed thirty-two feet per second which gave to the *Skylark*'s occupants a normal gravitational force.

'Why, Dick, how perfectly silly!' Dorothy chuckled. 'What's the matter? All you've got to do is …'

'Silly, says you?' Seaton, still blushing, interrupted her. 'Woman, you don't know the half of it! I'm just plain dumb, and Mart was tactfully calling my attention to the fact. Them's soft words that the slat-like string bean just spoke, but believe me, Red-Top, he packs a wicked wallop in that silken glove!'

'Keep still a minute, Dick, and look at the bar!' Dorothy protested. 'Everything's on zero, so we must still be going straight up, and all you have to do to get us back somewhere near our own galaxy is to turn it around. Why didn't one of you brilliant thinkers – or have I overlooked a bet?'

'Not exactly. You don't know about those famous linear departures, but I do. I haven't that excuse – I simply went off halfcocked again. You see, it's like this: even if those gyroscopes retained their orientation unchanged through the fourth-dimensional translation, which may or may not be the case, that line wouldn't mean a thing as far as getting back is concerned.

'We took one gosh-awful jump in going through hyperspace, you know, and we have no means at all of determining whether we jumped up, down, or sidewise. Nope, he's right, as usual – we can't do anything intelligently until he finds out, from the shifting of spectral lines and so on, in what direction we actually are traveling. How're you coming with it, Mart?'

'For really precise work we shall require photographs, but I have made six preliminary observations, as nearly on rectangular coordinates as possible, from which you can calculate a first-approximation course which will serve until we can obtain more precise data. Here are my rough notes upon the spectra.'

'All right, while you're taking your pictures I'll run them off on the calculator. From the looks of those shifts I'd say I could hit our course within five degrees, which is close enough for a few days, at least.'

Seaton soon finished his calculations. He then read off from the great graduated hour- and declination-circles of the gyroscope cage the course upon which the power-bar was then set, and turned with a grin to Crane, who had just opened the shutter for his first time exposure.

'We were off plenty, Mart,' he admitted. 'About ninety degrees minus declination and something like plus seven hours' right ascension, so we'll have to forget all our old data and start right from scratch. That won't hurt us much, though, since we haven't any idea where we are, anyway.

'We're heading about ten degrees or so to the right of that nebula over there, which is certainly a mighty long ways off from where I thought we were going. I'll put on full positive and point ten degrees to the left of it. Probably you'd better read it now, and by taking a set of observations, say a hundred hours apart, we can figure when we'll have to reverse acceleration.

'While you're doing that I thought I'd start seeing what I could do about a fourth-order projector. It'll take a long time to build, and we'll need one bad when we get inside that galaxy. What do you think?'

'I think that both of those ideas are sound,' Crane assented, and each man bent to his task.

Crane took his photographs and studied each of the six key nebulae with every resource of his ultra-refined instruments. Having determined the *Skylark*'s course and speed, and knowing her acceleration, he was able at last to set upon the power-bar an automatically varying control of such a nature that her resultant velocity was directly toward the lenticular nebula nearest her line of flight.

That done, he continued his observations at regular intervals – constantly making smaller his limit of observational error, constantly so altering the power and course of the vessel that the selected galaxy would be reached in the shortest possible space of time consistent with a permissible final velocity.

And in the meantime Seaton labored upon the projector. It had been out of the question, of course, to transfer to tiny *Two* the immense mechanism which had made of *Three* a sentient, almost living, thing; but, equally of course, he had brought along the force-band transformers and selectors, and as much as possible of the other essential apparatus. He had been obliged to leave behind, however, the very heart of the fifth-order installation – the precious lens of neutronium – and its lack was now giving him deep concern.

'What the matter, Dickie? You look as though you had lost your best friend.' Dorothy intercepted him one day as he paced about the narrow confines of the control room, face set and eyes unseeing.

'Not quite that, but ever since I finished that fourth-order outfit I've been trying to figure out something to take the place of that lens we had in *Three*, so that I can go ahead on the fifth, but that seems to be one thing for which there is absolutely no substitute. It's like trying to unscrew the inscrutable – it can't be done.'

'If you can't get along without it, why didn't you bring it along, too?'

'Couldn't.'

'Why?' she persisted.

'Nothing strong enough to hold it. In some ways it's worse than atomic energy. It's so hot and under such pressure that if that lens were to blow up in Omaha it would burn up the whole United States, from San Francisco to New York City. It takes either thirty feet of solid inoson or else a complete force-bracing to stand the pressure. We had neither, no time to build anything, and couldn't have taken it through hyperspace even if we could have held it safely.'

'Does that mean …'

'No. It simply means that we'll have to start at the fourth again and work up. I did bring along a couple of good big faidons, so that all we've got to do is find a planet heavy enough and solid enough to anchor a full-sized fourth-order projector on, within twenty light-years of a white dwarf star.'

'Oh, is that all? You two'll do that, all right.'

'Ain't it wonderful, the confidence some women have in their husbands?' Seaton asked Crane, who was studying through number six visiplate and the fourth-order projector the enormous expanse of the strange galaxy at whose edge they now were. 'I think maybe we'll be able to pull it off, though, at that. Of course we aren't close enough yet to find such minutiae as planets, but how are things shaping up in general?'

'Quite encouraging! This galaxy is certainly of the same order of magnitude as our own, and ...'

'Encouraging, huh?' Seaton broke in. 'If such a dyed-in-the-wool pessimist as you are can permit himself to use such a word as that, we're practically landed on a planet right now!'

'And shows the same types and varieties of stellar spectra,' Crane went on, unperturbed. 'I have identified with certainty no less than six white dwarf stars, and some forty yellow dwarfs of type G.'

'Fine! What did I tell you?' exulted Seaton.

'Now go over that again, in English, so that Peggy and I can feel relieved about it, too,' Dorothy directed. 'What's a type-G dwarf?'

'A sun like our own Sol, back home,' Seaton explained. 'Since we are looking for a planet as much as possible like our own Earth, it is a distinctly cheerful fact to find so many suns similar to our own. And as for the white dwarfs, I've got to have one fairly close to the planet we land on, because to get in touch with Rovol I've got to have a sixth-order projector; to build which I've first got to have one of the fifth order; for the construction of which I've got to have neutronium; to get which I'll have to be close to a white dwarf star. See?'

'Uh-huh! Clear and lucid to the point of limpidity – not.' Dorothy grimaced, then went on: 'As for me, I'm certainly glad to see those stars. It seems that we've been out there in absolutely empty space for ages, and I've been scared a pale lavender all the time. Having all these nice stars around us again is the next-best thing to being on solid ground.'

At the edge of the strange galaxy though they were, many days were required to reduce the intergalactic pace of the vessel to a value at which maneuvering was possible, and many more days passed into time before Crane announced the discovery of a sun which not only possessed a family of planets, but was also within the specified distance of a white dwarf star.

To any Earthly astronomer, whose most powerful optical instruments fail to reveal even the closest star as anything save a dimensionless point of light, such a discovery would have been impossible, but Crane was not working with Earthly instruments. For the fourth-order projector, although utterly useless at the intergalactic distances with which Seaton was principally concerned, was vastly more powerful than any conceivable telescope.

Driven by the full power of a disintegrating uranium bar, it could hold a projection so steadily at a distance of twenty light-years that a man could manipulate a welding arc as surely as though it was upon a bench before him – which, in effect, it was – and in cases in which delicacy of control was not an object, such as the present quest for such vast masses as planets, the projector was effective over distances of many hundreds of light-years.

Thus it came about that the search for a planetiferous sun near a white dwarf star was not unduly prolonged, and *Skylark Two* tore through the empty ether toward it.

Close enough so that the projector could reveal details, Seaton drove projections of all four voyagers down into the atmosphere of the first planet at hand. That atmosphere was heavy and of a pronounced greenish-yellow cast, and through it that fervent sun poured down a flood of lurid light upon a peculiarly dead and barren ground – but yet a ground upon which grew isolated clumps of a livid and monstrous vegetation.

'Of course detailed analysis at this distance is impossible, but what do you make of it, Dick?' asked Crane. 'In all our travels, this is only the second time we have encountered such an atmosphere.'

'Yes; and that's exactly twice too many.' Seaton, at the spectroscope, was scowling in thought. 'Chlorin, all right, with some fluorin and strong traces of oxide of nitrogen, nitrosyl chloride, and so on – just about like that one we saw in our own galaxy that time. I thought then and have thought ever since that there was something decidedly fishy about that planet, and I think there's something equally screwy about this one.'

'Well, let's not investigate it any further, then,' put in Dorothy. 'Let's go somewhere else, quick.'

'Yes, let's,' Margaret agreed, 'particularly if, as you said about that other one, it has a form of life on it that would make our grandfathers' whiskers curl up into a ball.'

'We'll do that little thing; we haven't got *Three*'s equipment now, and without it I'm no keener on smelling around this planet than you are,' and he flipped the projection across a few hundred million miles of space to the neighboring planet. Its air, while somewhat murky and smoky, was colorless and apparently normal, its oceans were composed of water, and its vegetation was green. 'See, Mart? I told you something was fishy. It's all wrong – a thing like that can't happen even once, let alone twice.'

'According to the accepted principles of cosmogony it is of course to be expected that all the planets of the same sun would have atmospheres of somewhat similar composition,' Crane conceded, unmoved. 'However, since we have observed two cases of this kind, it is quite evident that there are not only many more suns having planets than has been supposed, but also that suns capture planets from each other, at least occasionally.'

'Maybe – that would explain it, of course. But let's see what this world looks like – see if we can find a place to sit down on. It'll be nice to live on solid ground while I do my stuff.'

He swung the viewpoint slowly across the daylight side of the strange planet, whose surface, like that of Earth, was partially obscured by occasional masses of cloud. Much of that surface was covered by mighty oceans, and what little land there was seemed strangely flat and entirely devoid of topographical features.

The immaterial conveyance dropped straight down upon the largest visible mass of land, down through a towering jungle of fernlike and bamboo-like plants, halting only a few feet above the ground. Solid ground it certainly was not, nor did it resemble the watery muck of our Earthly swamps. The huge stems of the vegetation rose starkly from a black and seething field of viscous mud – mud unrelieved by any accumulation of humus or of debris – and in that mud there swam, crawled, and slithered teeming hordes of animals.

'What funny-looking mud-puppies!' Dorothy exclaimed. 'And isn't that the thickest, dirtiest, gooiest mud you ever saw?'

'Just about,' Seaton agreed, intensely interested. 'But those things seem perfectly adapted to it. Flat, beaver tails; short, strong legs with webbed feet; long, narrow heads with rooting noses, like pigs; and heavy, sharp incisor teeth. Bet they live on those ferns and stuff – that's why there's no underbrush or dead stuff. Look at that bunch working on the roots of that big bamboo over there. They'll have it down in a minute – there she goes!'

The great trunk fell with a crash as he spoke, and was almost instantly forced beneath the repellent surface by the weight of the massed 'mud-puppies' who flung themselves upon it.

'Ah, I thought so!' Crane remarked. 'Their molar teeth do not match their incisors, being quite Titanotheric in type. Probably they can assimilate lignin and cellulose instead of requiring our usual nutrient carbohydrates. However, this terrain does not seem to be at all suitable for our purpose.'

'I'll say it doesn't. I'll scout around and see if we can't find some high land somewhere, but I've got a hunch that we won't care for that, either. This murky air and the strong absorption lines of SO_2, seem to whisper in my ear that we'll find some plenty hot and plenty sulphurous volcanoes when we find the mountains.'

A few large islands or small continents of high and solid land were found at last, but they were without exception volcanic. Nor were those volcanoes quiescent. Each was in constant and furious eruption; not the sporadic and comparatively mild outbursts of violence which we of green Terra know, but the uninterrupted, world-shaking cataclysmic paroxysms of primeval forces embattled – an inexhaustible supply of cold water striving to quench a world-filling core of incandescent magma. Each conical peak and rugged vent where once a cone had been spouted incredible columns of steam, of smoke, of dust, of molten and vaporized rock, and of noxious vapor. Each volcano was working steadily and industriously at its appointed task of building up a habitable world.

'Well, I don't see any place around here either fit to live in or solid enough to anchor an observatory onto,' Seaton concluded, after he had surveyed the entire surface of the globe. 'I think we'd better flit across to the next one, don't you, folks?'

Suiting action to word, he shot the beam to the next nearest planet, which chanced to be the one whose orbit was nearest the blazing sun, and a mere glance showed that it would not serve the purposes of the Terrestrials. Small it was, and barren: waterless, practically airless, lifeless; a cratered, jagged, burned-out ember of what might once have been a fertile little world.

The viewpoint then leaped past the flaming inferno of the luminary and came to rest in the upper layers of an atmosphere.

'Aha!' Seaton exulted, after he had studied his instruments briefly. 'This looks like home, sweet home to me. Nitrogen, oxygen, some CO_2, a little water vapor, and traces of the old familiar rare gases. And see them oceans, them clouds, and them there hills? Hot dog!'

As the projection dropped toward the new world's surface, however, making possible a detailed study, it became evident that there was something abnormal about it. The mountains were cratered and torn; many of the valleys were simply desolate expanses of weathered lava, tuff, and breccia; and, while it seemed that climatic conditions were eminently suitable, of animal life there was none.

Everywhere there were signs of ravishment, as though that fair world had been torn and ravaged by cataclysmic storms of violence unthinkable; ravages which for centuries Nature had been trying to heal.

And it was not only the world itself that had been outraged. Near a large inland lake there spread the ruins of what once had been a great city; ruins so crumbled and razed as to be almost unrecognizable. What had been stone was dust, what had been metal was rust; and dust and rust alike were now almost completely overgrown by vegetation. For centuries Nature undisturbed had slowly but implacably been reducing to nought the once ordered and purposeful works of a high intelligence.

'Hm-m-m!' Seaton mused, subdued. 'There *was* a near-collision of planet-bearing suns, Mart; and that chlorin planet *was* captured. This world was ruined by the strains set up – but surely they must have been scientific enough to have seen it coming? Surely they must have made plans so that *some* of them could have lived through it?'

He fell silent, driving the viewpoint hither and thither, like a hound in quest of a scent. 'I thought so!' Another ruined city lay beneath them; a city whose building, works, and streets had been fused together into one vast agglomerate of glaringly glassy slag, through which could be seen unmelted fragments of strangely designed structural members. 'Those ruins are fresh – that was done with heat beams, Mart. But who did it, and why? I've got a hunch – wonder if we're too late – if they've killed them all off already?'

Hard-faced now and grim, Seaton combed the continent, finding at last what he sought.

'Ah, I thought so!' he exclaimed, his voice low but deadly. 'I'll bet my shirt that the chlorins are wiping out the civilization of that planet – probably people more or less like us. What d'you say, folks – do we declare ourselves in on this, or not?'

'I'll tell the cockeyed world ... I believe that we should ... By all means ...' came from Dorothy, Margaret, and Crane.

'I knew you'd back me up. Humanity *über alles* – *Homo sapiens* against all the vermin of the universe! Let's go, *Two* – do your stuff!'

As *Two* hurtled toward the unfortunate planet with her every iota of driving power, Seaton settled down to observe the strife and to see what he could do. That which lay beneath the viewpoint had not been a city, in the strict sense of the word. It had been an immense system of concentric fortifications, of which the outer circles had long since gone down under the irresistible attack of the two huge structures of metal which hung poised in the air above. Where those outer rings had been there was now an annular lake of boiling, seething lava. Lava from which arose gouts and slender pillars of smoke and fume; lava being volatilized by the terrific heat of the offensive beams and being hurled away in flaming cascades by the almost constant detonations of high-explosive shells; lava into which from time to time another portion of the immense fortress slagged down – put out of action, riddled, and finally fused by the awful forces of the invaders.

Even as the four Terrestrials stared in speechless awe, an intolerable blast of flame burst out above one of the flying forts and down it plunged into the raging pool, throwing molten slag far and wide as it disappeared beneath the raging surface.

'Hurray!' shrieked Dorothy, who had instinctively taken sides with the defenders. 'One down, anyway!'

But her jubilation was premature. The squat and monstrous fabrication burst upward through that flaming surface and, white-hot lava streaming from it in incandescent torrents, it was again in action, apparently uninjured.

'All fourth-order stuff, Mart,' Seaton, who had been frantically busy at his keyboard and instruments, reported to Crane. 'Can't find a trace of anything on the fifth or sixth, and that gives us a break. I don't know what we can do yet, but we'll do something, believe me!'

'Fourth order? Are you sure?' Crane doubted. 'A fourth-order screen would be a zone of force, opaque and impervious to gravitation, whereas those screens are transparent and are not affecting gravity.'

'Yeah, but they're doing something that we never tried, since we never use the fourth-order stuff in fighting. They've both left the gravity band open – it's probably too narrow for them to work through, at least with anything very heavy – and that gives us the edge.'

'Why? Do you know more about it than they do?' queried Dorothy.

'Who and what are they, Dick?' asked Margaret.

'Sure I know more about it than they do. I understand the fifth and sixth orders and you can't get the full benefit of any order until you know all about the next one. Just like mathematics – nobody can really handle trigonometry until after he has had calculus. And as to who they are, the folks in that fort are of course natives of the planet, and they may well be people more or less like us. It's dollars to doughnuts, though, that those vessels are manned by the inhabitants of that interloping planet – that form of life I was telling you about – and it's up to us to pull their corks if we can. There, I'm ready to go, I think. We'll visit the ship first.'

The visible projection disappeared and, their images now invisible patterns of force, they stood inside the control room of one of the invaders. The air bore the faint, greenish-yellow tinge of chlorin; the walls were banked and tiered with controlling dials, meters, and tubes; and sprawling, lying, standing, or hanging before those controls were denizens of the chlorin planet. No two of them were alike in form. If one of them was using eyes he had eyes everywhere; if hands, hands by the dozen, all differently fingered, sprouted from one, two, or a dozen supple and snaky arms.

But the inspection was only momentary. Scarcely had the unseen visitors glanced about the interior when the visibeam was cut off sharply. The peculiar beings had snapped on a full-coverage screen, and their vessel, now surrounded by the opaque spherical mirror of a zone of force, was darting upward and away – unaffected by gravity, unable to use any of her weapons, but impervious to any form of matter or to any ether-borne wave.

'Huh! "We didn't come over here to get peeked at," says they,' Seaton snorted. 'Amoebic! Must be handy, though, at that, to sprout eyes, arms, ears, and so on whenever and wherever you want to – and when you want to rest, to pull in all such impedimenta and subside into a senseless green blob. Well, we've seen the attackers, now let's see what the natives look like. They can't cut us off without sending their whole works sky-hooting off into space.'

Nor could they. The visibeam sped down into the deepest sanctum of the fortress without hindrance, revealing a long, narrow control table at which were seated men – men not exactly like the humanity of Earth, of Norlamin, of Osnome, or of any other planet, but undoubtedly men, of the genus *Homo*.

'You were right, Dick.' Crane the anthropologist now spoke. 'It seems that on planets similar to Earth in mass, atmosphere, and temperature, wherever situated, man develops. The ultimate genes must permeate universal space itself.'

'Maybe – sounds reasonable. But did you see that red light flash on when we came in? They've got detectors set on the gravity band – look at the expression on their faces.'

Each of the seated men had ceased his activity and was slumped down into his chair. Resignation, hopeless yet bitter, sat upon lofty, domed brows and stared out of large and kindly eyes. Fatigue, utter and profound, was graven upon lined faces and upon emaciated bodies.

'Oh, I get it!' Seaton exclaimed. 'They think the chlorins are watching them – as they probably do most of the time – and they can't do anything about it. Should think they could do the same – or could broadcast an interference – I could help them on that if I could talk to them – wish they had an educator, but I haven't seen any ...' He paused, brow knitted in concentration. 'I'm going to make myself visible to try a stunt. Don't talk to me; I'll need all the brain power I've got to pull this off.'

As Seaton's image thickened into substance its effect upon the strangers was startling indeed. First they shrank back in consternation, supposing that their enemies had at last succeeded in working a full materialization through the narrow gravity band. Then, as they perceived that Seaton's figure was human, and of a humanity different from their own, they sprang to surround him, shouting words meaningless to the Terrestrials.

For some time Seaton tried to make his meaning clear by signs, but the thoughts he was attempting to convey were far too complex for that simple medium. Communication was impossible and the time was altogether too short to permit of laborious learning of language. Therefore streamers of visible force shot from Seaton's imaged eyes, sinking deeply into the eyes of the figures at the head of the table.

'Look at me!' he commanded, and his fists clenched and drops of sweat stood out on his forehead as he threw all the power of his brain into that probing, hypnotic beam.

The native resisted with all his strength, but not for nothing had Seaton superimposed upon his already-powerful mind a large portion of the phenomenal brain of Drasnik, the First of Psychology of Norlamin. Resistance was useless. The victim soon sat relaxed and passive, his mind completely subservient to Seaton's, and as though in a trance he spoke to his fellows.

'This apparition is the force-image of one of a group of men from a distant solar system,' he intoned in his own language. 'They are friendly and intend to help us. Their spaceship is approaching us under full power, but it cannot get here for several days. They can, however, help us materially before they arrive in person. To that end, he directs that we cause to be brought into this room a full assortment of all our fields of force, transmitting tubes, controllers, force-converters – in short, the equipment of a laboratory of radiation ... No, that would take too long. He suggests that one of us escort him to such a laboratory.'

15

Valeron

As Seaton assumed, the near-collision of suns which had affected so disastrously the planet Valeron did not come unheralded to overwhelm a world unwarned, since for many hundreds of years her civilization had been of a high order indeed. Her astronomers were able, her scientists capable, the governments of her nations strong and just. Years before its occurrence the astronomers had known that the catastrophe was inevitable and had calculated dispassionately its every phase – to the gram, the centimeter, and the second.

With all their resources of knowledge and of power, however, it was pitifully little that the people of Valeron could do; for of what avail are the puny energies of man compared to the practically infinite forces of cosmic phenomena? Any attempt of the humanity of the doomed planet to swerve from their courses the incomprehensible masses of those two hurtling suns was as surely doomed to failure as would be the attempt of an ant to thrust from its rails an onrushing locomotive.

But what little could be done was done; done scientifically and logically; done, if not altogether without fear, at least in as much as was humbly possible without favor. With mathematical certainty were plotted the areas of least strain, and in those areas were constructed shelters. Shelters buried deeply enough to be unaffected by the coming upheavals of the world's crust; shelters of unbreakable metal, so designed, so latticed and braced as to withstand the seismic disturbances to which they were inevitably to be subjected.

Having determined the number of such shelters that could be built, equipped, and supplied with the necessities of life in the time allowed, the board of selection began its cold-blooded and heartless task. Scarcely one in a thousand of Valeron's teeming millions was to be given a chance for continued life, and they were to be chosen only from the children who would be in the prime of young adulthood at the time of the catastrophe.

These children were the pick of the planet: flawless in mind, body, and heredity. They were assembled in special schools near their assigned refuges, where they were instructed intensively in everything that they would have to know in order that civilization should not disappear utterly from the universe.

Such a thing could not be kept a secret long, and it is best to touch as lightly as possible upon the scenes which ensued after the certainty of doom became public knowledge. Humanity both scaled the heights of self-sacrificing courage and plumbed the very depths of cowardice and depravity.

Characters already strong were strengthened, but those already weak went to pieces entirely in orgies to a normal mind unthinkable. Almost overnight a peaceful and law-abiding world went mad – became an insane hotbed of crime, rapine, and pillage unspeakable. Martial law was declared at once, and after a few thousand maniacs had been ruthlessly shot down, the soberer inhabitants were allowed to choose between two alternatives. They could either die then and there before a firing squad, or they could wait and take whatever slight chance there might be of living through what was to come – but devoting their every effort meanwhile to the end that through those selected few the civilization of Valeron should endure.

Many chose death and were executed summarily and without formality, without regard to wealth or station. The rest worked. Some worked devotedly and with high purpose, some worked hopelessly and with resignation. Some worked stolidly and with thoughts only of the present, some worked slyly and with thoughts only of getting themselves, by hook or by crook, into one of those shelters. All, however, from the highest to the lowest, worked.

Since the human mind cannot be kept indefinitely at high tension, the new condition of things came in time to be regarded almost as normal, and as months lengthened into years the routine was scarcely broken. Now and then, of course, one went mad and was shot; another refused to continue his profitless labor and was shot; still another gave up the fight and shot himself. And always there were the sly – the self-seekers, the bribers, the corruptionists – willing to go to any lengths whatever to avoid their doom. Not openly did they carry on their machinations, but like loathsome worms eating at the heart of an outwardly fair fruit. But the scientists, almost to a man, were loyal. Trained to think, they thought clearly and logically, and surrounded themselves with soldiers and guards of the same stripe. Old men or weaklings would have no place in the post-cataclysmic world and there were accommodations for only the exactly predetermined number; therefore only those selected children and no others could be saved or would. And as for bribery, threats, blackmail, or any possible form of racketry or corruption –

of what use is wealth or power to a man under sentence of death? And what threat or force could sway him? Wherefore most of the sly were discovered, exposed, and shot.

Time went on. The shelters were finished. Into them were taken stores, libraries, tools and equipment of every sort necessary for the rebuilding of a fully civilized world. Finally the 'children,' now in the full prime of young manhood and young womanhood, were carefully checked in. Once inside those massive portals they were of a world apart.

They were completely informed and completely educated; they had for long governed themselves with neither aid nor interference; they knew precisely what they must face; they knew exactly what to do and exactly how to do it. Behind them the mighty, multi-ply seals were welded into place and broken rock by the cubic mile was blasted down upon their refuges.

Day by day the heat grew more and more intense. Cyclonic storms raged ever fiercer, accompanied by an incessant blaze of lightning and a deafeningly continuous roar of thunder. More and ever more violent became the seismic disturbances as Valeron's very core shook and trembled under the appalling might of the opposing cosmic forces.

Work was at an end and the masses were utterly beyond control. The devoted were butchered by their frantic fellows; the hopeless were stung to madness; the stolid were driven to frenzy by the realization that there was to be no future; the remaining sly ones deftly turned the unorganized fury of the mob into a purposeful attack upon the shelters, their only hope of life.

But at each refuge the rabble met an unyielding wall of guards loyal to the last, and of scientists who, their work now done, were merely waiting for the end. Guards and scientists fought with rifles, ray guns, swords, and finally with clubs, stones, fists, feet, and teeth. Outnumbered by thousands they fell and the howling mob surged over their bodies. To no purpose. Those shelters had been designed and constructed to withstand the attacks of Nature gone berserk, and futile indeed were the attempts of the frenzied hordes to tear a way into their sacred recesses.

Thus died the devoted and high-souled band who had saved their civilization; but in that death each man was granted the boon which, deep in his heart, he craved. They had died quickly and violently, fighting for a cause they knew to be good. They did not die as did the members of the insanely terror-stricken, senseless mob … in agony … lingeringly … but it is best to draw a kindly veil before the horrors attendant upon that riving, that tormenting, that cosmic outraging of a world.

The suns passed, each other upon his appointed way. The cosmic forces ceased to war and to the tortured and ravaged planet there at last came peace. The surviving children of Valeron emerged from their subterranean retreats and undauntedly took up the task of rebuilding their world. And to such good purpose did they devote themselves to the problems of rehabilitation that in a few hundred years there bloomed upon Valeron a civilization and a culture scarcely to be equaled in the universe.

For the new race had been cradled in adversity. In its ancestry there was no physical or mental taint or weakness, all dross having been burned away by the fires of cosmic catastrophe which had so nearly obliterated all the life of the planet. They were as yet perhaps inferior to the old race in point of numbers, but were immeasurably superior to it in physical, mental, moral, and intellectual worth.

Immediately after the Emergence it had been observed that the two outermost planets of the system had disappeared and that in their stead revolved a new planet. This phenomenon was recognized for what it was, an exchange of planets; something to give concern only to astronomers.

No one except sheerest romancers even gave thought to the possibility of life upon other worlds, it being an almost mathematically demonstrable fact that the Valeronians were the only life in the entire universe. And even if other planets might possibly be inhabited, what of it? The vast reaches of empty ether intervening between Valeron and even her nearest fellow planet formed an insuperable obstacle even to communication, to say nothing of physical passage. Little did anyone dream, as generation followed generation, of what hideously intelligent life that interloping planet bore, nor of how the fair world of Valeron was to suffer from it.

When the interplanetary invaders were discovered upon Valeron, Quedrin Vornel, the most brilliant physicist of the planet, and his son Quedrin Radnor, the most renowned, were among the first to be informed of the visitation.

Of these two, Quedrin Vornel had for many years been engaged in researches of the most abstruse and fundamental character upon the ultimate structure of matter. He had delved deeply into those which we know as matter, energy, and ether, and had studied exhaustively the phenomena characteristic of or associated with atomic, electronic, and photonic rearrangements.

His son, while a scientist of no mean attainments in his own right, did not possess the phenomenally powerful and profoundly analytical mind that had made the elder Quedrin the outstanding scientific genius of his time. He was, however, a synchronizer *par excellence*, possessing to a unique degree the ability to develop things and processes of great utilitarian value from concepts and discoveries of a purely scientific and academic nature.

The vibrations which we know as Hertzian waves had long been known and had long been employed in radio, both broadcast and tight-beam, in television, in beam-transmission of power, and in receiverless visirays and their blocking screens. When Quedrin the elder disrupted the atom, however, successfully and safely liberating and studying not only its stupendous energy but also an entire series of vibrations and particles theretofore unknown to science, Quedrin the younger began forthwith to turn the resulting products to the good of mankind.

Intra-atomic energy soon drove every prime mover of Valeron and shorter and shorter waves were harnessed. In beams, fans, and broadcasts Quedrin Radnor combined and heterodyned them, making of them tools and instruments immeasurably superior in power, precision, and adaptability to anything that his world had ever before known.

Due to the signal abilities of brilliant father and famous son, the laboratory in which they labored was connected by a private communication beam with the executive office of the Bardyle of Valeron. 'Bardyle,' freely translated, means 'coordinator.' He was neither king, emperor, nor president; and, while his authority was supreme, he was not a dictator.

A paradoxical statement this, but a true one; for the orders – rather, requests and suggestions – of the Bardyle merely guided the activities of men and women who had neither government nor laws, as we understand the terms, but were working of their own volition for the good of all mankind. The Bardyle could not conceivably issue an order contrary to the common weal, nor would such an order have been obeyed.

Upon the wall of the laboratory the tuned buzzer of the Bardyle's beam-communicator sounded its subdued call and Klynor Siblin, the scientist's capable assistant, took the call upon his desk instrument. A strong, youthful face appeared upon the screen.

'Radnor is not here, Siblin?' The pictured visitor glanced about the room as he spoke.

'No, sir. He is out in the spaceship, making another test flight. He is merely circling the world, however, so that I can easily get him on the plate here if you wish.'

'That would perhaps be desirable. Something very peculiar has occurred, concerning which all three of you should be informed.'

The connections were made and the Bardyle went on:

'A semicircular dome of force has been erected over the ruins of the ancient city of Mocelyn. It is impossible to say how long it has been in place, since you know the ruins lie in an entirely unpopulated area. It is, however, of an unknown composition and pattern, being opaque to vision and to our visi-beams. It is also apparently impervious to matter. Since this phenomenon seems to lie in your province I would suggest that you three men investigate it and take such steps as you deem necessary.'

'It is noted, Bardyle,' and Klynor Siblin cut the beam.

He then shot out their heaviest visiray beam, poising its viewpoint directly over what, in the days before the cataclysm, had been the populous city of Mocelyn.

Straight down the beam drove, upon the huge hemisphere of greenly glinting force; urged downward by the full power of the Quedrins' mighty generators. By the very vehemence of its thrust it tore through the barrier, but only for an instant. The watchers had time to perceive only fleetingly a greenish-yellow haze of light, but before any details could be grasped their beam was snapped – the automatically reacting screens had called for and had received enough additional power to neutralize the invading beam.

Then, to the amazement of the three physicists, a beam of visible energy thrust itself from the green barrier and began to feel its way along their own invisible visiray. Siblin cut off his power instantly and leaped toward the door.

'Whoever they are, they know something!' he shouted as he ran. 'Don't want them to find this laboratory, so I'll set up a diversion with a rocket plane. If you watch at all, Vornel, do it from a distance and with a spy ray, not a carrier beam. I'll get in touch with Radnor on the way.'

Even though he swung around in a wide circle, to approach the strange stronghold at a wide angle to his former line, such was the power of the plane that Siblin reached his destination in little more than an hour. Keying Radnor's visibeam to the visiplates of the plane, so that the distant scientist could see everything that happened, Siblin again drove a heavy beam into the unyielding pattern of green force.

This time, however, the reaction was instantaneous. A fierce tongue of green flame licked out and seized the flying plane in mid-air. One wing and side panel were sliced off neatly and Siblin was thrown out violently, but he did not fall. Surrounded by a vibrant shell of energy, he was drawn rapidly toward the huge dome. The dome merged with the shell as it touched it, but the two did not coalesce. The shell passed smoothly through the dome, which as smoothly closed behind it. Siblin inside the shell, the shell inside the dome.

16

Within the Chloran Dome

Siblin never knew exactly what happened during those first few minutes, nor exactly how it happened. One minute, in his sturdy plane, he was setting up his 'diversion' by directing a powerful beam of force upon the green dome of the invaders. Suddenly his rocket ship had been blasted apart and he had been hurled away from the madly spinning, gyrating wreckage.

He had a confused recollection of sitting down violently upon something very hard, and perceived dully that he was lying asprawl upon the inside of a greenishly shimmering globe some twenty feet in diameter. Its substance had the hardness of chilled steel, yet it was almost perfectly transparent, seemingly composed of cold green flame, pale almost to invisibility. He also observed, in an incurious, foggy fashion, that the great dome was rushing toward him at an appalling pace.

He soon recovered from his shock, however, and perceived that the peculiar ball in which he was imprisoned was a shell of force, of formula and pattern entirely different from anything known to the scientists of Valeron. Keenly alive and interested now, he noted with high appreciation exactly how the wall of force that was the dome merged with, made way for, and closed smoothly behind the relatively tiny globe.

Inside the dome he stared around him, amazed and not a little awed. Upon the ground, the center of that immense hemisphere, lay a featureless, football-shaped structure which must be the vessel of the invaders. Surrounding it there were massed machines and engineering structures of unmistakable form and purpose; drills, derricks, shaft heads, skips, hoists, and other equipment for boring and mining. From the lining of the huge dome there radiated a strong, lurid, yellowish-green light which intensified to positive ghastliness the natural color of the gaseous chlorin which replaced the familiar air in that walled-off volume so calmly appropriated to their own use by the Outlanders.

As his shell was drawn downward toward the strange scene Siblin saw many moving things beneath him, but was able neither to understand what he saw nor to correlate it with anything in his own knowledge or experience. For those beings were amorphous. Some flowed along the ground, formless blobs of matter; some rolled, like wheels or like barrels; many crawled rapidly, snakelike; others resembled animated pancakes, undulating flatly and nimbly about upon a dozen or so short, tentacular legs; only a few, vaguely manlike, walked upright.

A glass cage, some eight feet square and seven high, stood under the towering bulge of the great ship's side; and as his shell of force engulfed it and its door swung invitingly open, Siblin knew that he was expected to enter it.

Indeed, he had no choice – the fabric of cold flame that had been his conveyance and protection vanished, and he had scarcely time to leap inside the cage and slam the door before the noxious vapors of the atmosphere invaded the space from which the shell's impermeable wall had barred it. To die more slowly, but just as surely, from suffocation? No, the cage was equipped with a thoroughly efficient oxygen generator and air purifier; there were stores of Valeronian food and water; there were a chair, a table, and a narrow bunk; and wonder of wonders, there were even kits of toilet articles and of changes of clothing.

Far above a great door opened. The cage was lifted and, without any apparent means either of support or of propulsion, it moved through the doorways and along various corridors and halls, coming finally to rest upon the floor in one of the innermost compartments of the sky rover. Siblin saw masses of machinery, panels of controlling instruments, and weirdly multiform creatures at station; but he had scant time even to glance at them, his attention being attracted instantly to the middle of the room where, lying in a heavily reinforced shallow cup of metal upon an immensely strong, low table, he saw a – a *something*; and for the first time an inhabitant of Valeron saw at close range one of the invaders.

It was in no sense a solid, nor a liquid, nor yet a jelly; although it seemed to partake of certain properties of all three. In part it was murkily transparent, in part greenishly translucent, in part turbidly opaque; but in all it was intrinsically horrible. In every physical detail and in every nuance of radiant aura of conscious power it was disgusting and appalling; sickeningly, nauseously revolting to every human thought and instinct.

But that it was sentient and intelligent there could be no doubt. Not only could its malign mental radiations be felt, but its brain could be plainly seen; a huge, intricately convolute organ suspended in an unyielding but plastic medium of solid jelly. Its skin seemed thin and frail, but Siblin was later to learn that that tegument was not only stronger than rawhide, but was more pliable, more elastic, and more extensible than the finest rubber.

As the Valeronian stared in helpless horror that peculiar skin stretched locally almost to vanishing thinness and an enormous Cyclopean eye developed. More than an eye, it was a special organ for a special sense which humanity has never possessed, a sense combining ordinary vision with something infinitely deeper, more penetrant and more powerful. Vision, hypnotism, telepathy, thought-transference – something of all these, yet in essence a thing beyond any sense or faculty known to us or describable in language, had its being in the almost-visible, almost-tangible beam of force which emanated from the single, temporary 'eye' of the Thing and bored through the eyes and deep into the brain of the Valeronian. Siblin's very senses reeled under the impact of that wave of mental power, but he did not quite lose consciousness.

'So *you* are one of the ruling intelligences of this planet – one of its most advanced scientists?' The scornful thought formed itself, coldly clear, in his mind. 'We have always known, of course, that we are the highest form of life in the universe, and the fact that you are so low in the scale of mentality only confirms that knowledge. It would be surprising indeed if such a noxious atmosphere as yours could nurture any real intelligence. It will be highly gratifying to report to the Council of Great Ones that not only is this planet rich in the materials we seek, but that its inhabitants, while intelligent enough to do our bidding in securing those materials, are not sufficiently advanced to cause us any trouble.'

'Why did you not come in peace?' Siblin thought back. Neither cowed nor shaken, he was merely amazed at the truculently overbearing mien of the strange entity. 'We would have been glad to cooperate with you in every possible way. It would seem self-evident that all intelligent races, whatever their outward form or mental status, should work together harmoniously for their mutual advancement.'

'Bah!' snapped the amoebus savagely. 'That is the talk of a weakling – the whining, begging reasoning of a race of low intelligence, one which knows and acknowledges itself inferior. Know you, feeble brain, that we of Chlora' – to substitute an intelligible word for the unpronounceable and untranslatable thought-image of his native world – 'neither require nor desire cooperation. We are in no need either of assistance or of instruction from any lesser and lower form of life. We instruct. Other races, such as yours, either obey or are obliterated. I brought you aboard this vessel because I am about to return to my own planet, and had decided to take one of you with me, so that the other Great Ones of the Council may see for themselves what form of life this Valeron boasts.

'If your race obeys our commands implicitly and does not attempt to interfere with us in any way, we shall probably permit most of you to continue your futile lives in our service; such as in mining for us certain ores which, relatively abundant upon your planet, are very scarce upon ours.

'As for you personally, perhaps we shall destroy you after the other Great Ones have examined you, perhaps we shall decide to use you as a messenger to transmit our orders to your fellow creatures. Before we depart, however, I shall make a demonstration which should impress upon even such feeble minds as those of your race the futility of any thought of opposition to us. Watch carefully – everything that goes on outside is shown in the view box.'

Although Siblin had neither heard, felt, nor seen the captain issue any orders, all was in readiness for the take-off. The mining engineers were all on board, the vessel was sealed for flight, and the navigators and control officers were at their panels. Siblin stared intently into the 'view box,' the three-dimensional visiplate that mirrored faithfully every occurrence in the neighborhood of the Chloran vessel.

The lower edge of the hemisphere of force began to contract, passing smoothly through or around – the spectator could not decide which – the ruins of Mocelyn, hugging or actually penetrating the ground, allowing not even a whiff of its precious chlorin content to escape into the atmosphere of Valeron. The ship then darted into the air and the shrinking edge became an ever-decreasing circle upon the ground beneath her. That circle disappeared as the meeting edge fused and the wall of force, now a hollow sphere, contained within itself the atmosphere of the invaders.

High over the surface of the planet sped the Chloran raider toward the nearest Valeronian city, which happened to be only a small village. Above the unfortunate settlement the callous monstrosity poised its craft, to drop its dread curtain of strangling, choking death.

Down the screen dropped, rolling out to become again a hemispherical wall, sweeping before it every milliliter of the life-giving air of Valeron and drawing behind it the noxious atmosphere of Chlora. For those who have ever inhaled even a small quantity of chlorin it is unnecessary to describe in detail the manner in which those villagers of Valeron died; for those who have not, no possible description could be adequate. Suffice it to say, therefore, that they died – horribly.

Again the wall of force rolled up, coming clear up to the outer skin of the cruiser this time, in its approach liquefying the chlorin and forcing it into storage chambers. The wall then disappeared entirely, leaving the marauding vessel starkly outlined against the sky. Then, further and even more strongly to impress the raging but impotent Klynor Siblin:

'Beam it down!' the amoebus captain commanded, and various officers sent out thin, whip-like tentacles toward their controls.

Projectors swung downward and dense green pillars of flaming energy erupted from the white-hot refractories of their throats. And what those green pillars struck subsided instantly into a pool of hissing, molten glass. Methodically they swept the entire area of the village. All organic matter – vegetation, bodies, humus – burst instantly into wildly raging flame and in that same instant was consumed; only the incombustible ash being left behind to merge with the metal and stone of the buildings and with the minerals of the soil as they melted to form a hellish lake.

'You monster!' shrieked Siblin, white, shaken, almost beside himself. 'You vile, unspeakable monster! Of what use is such a slaughter of innocent men? They had not harmed you ...'

'Indeed they have not, nor could they,' the Chloran interrupted callously. 'They mean nothing whatever to me, in any way. I have gone to the trouble of wiping out this city to give you and the rest of your race an object lesson; to impress upon you how thoroughly unimportant you are to us and to bring home to you your abject helplessness. Your whole race is, as you have just shown yourself to be, childish, soft, and sentimental, and therefore incapable of real advancement. On the contrary we, the masters of the universe, do not suffer from silly inhibitions or from foolish weaknesses.'

The eye faded out, its sharp outlines blurring gradually as its highly specialized parts became transformed into or were replaced by the formless gel composing the body of the creature. The amoebus then poured himself out of the cup, assumed the shape of a doughnut, and rolled rapidly out of the room.

When the Chloran captain had gone, Siblin threw himself upon his narrow bunk, fighting savagely to retain his self-control. He *must* escape – he *must* escape – the thought repeated itself endlessly in his mind – but how? The glass walls of his prison were his only defense against hideous death. Nowhere in any Chloran thing, nowhere in any nook or cranny of the noisome planet toward which he was speeding, could he exist for a minute except inside the cell which his captors were keeping supplied with oxygen. No tools – nothing from which to make a protective covering – no way of carrying air – nowhere to go – helpless, helpless – even to break that glass meant death …

At last he slept, fitfully, and when he awoke the vessel was deep in interplanetary space. His captors paid no further attention to him – he had air, food, and water, and if he chose to kill himself that was of no concern to them – and Siblin, able to think more calmly now, studied every phase of his predicament.

There was absolutely no possibility of escape. Rescue was out of the question. He could, however, communicate with Valeron, since in his belt were a tiny sender and receiver, attached by tight beams to instruments in the laboratory of the Quedrins. Detection of that pencil beam might well mean instant death, but that was a risk which, for the good of humanity, must be run. Lying upon his side, he concealed one ear plug under his head and manipulated the tiny sender in his belt. 'Quedrin Radnor – Quedrin Vornel …' he called for minutes, with no response. However, person-to-person communication was not really necessary; his messages would be recorded. He went on to describe in detail, tersely, accurately, and scientifically, everything that he had observed and deduced concerning the Chlorans, their forces, and their mechanisms.

'We are now approaching the planet,' he continued, now an observer reporting what he saw in the view box. 'It is apparently largely land. It has two polar ice caps, the larger of which I call north. A dark area, which I take to be an ocean, is the most prominent feature visible at this time. It is diamond-shaped and its longer axis, lying north and south, is about one quarter of a circumference in length. Its shorter axis, about half that length, lies almost upon the equator. We are passing high above this ocean, going east.

'East of the ocean and distant from it about one fifth of a circumference lies quite a large lake, roughly elliptical in shape, whose major axis lies approximately northeast and southwest. We are dropping toward a large city upon the southeast shore of this lake, almost equally distant from its two ends. Since I am to be examined by a so-called "Council of Great Ones," it may be that this city is their capital.

'No matter what happens, do not attempt to rescue me, as it is entirely hopeless. Escape is likewise impossible, because of the lethal atmosphere. There is a strong possibility, furthermore, that I may be returned to Valeron as a messenger to our race. This possibility is my only hope of returning. I am sending this data and will continue to send it as long as is possible, simply to aid you in deciding what shall be done to defend civilization against these monsters.

'We are now docking, near a large, hemispherical dome of force ... My cell is being transported through the atmosphere toward that dome ... It is opening. I do not know whether my beam can pass out through it, but I shall keep on sending ... Inside the dome there is a great building, toward which I am floating ... I am inside the building, inside a glass compartment which seems to be filled with air ... Yes, it *is* air, for the creatures who are entering it are wearing protective suits of some transparent substance. Their bodies are now globular and they are walking, each upon three short legs. One of them is developing an eye, similar to the one I descr—'

Siblin's message stopped in the middle of a word. The eye had developed and in its weirdly hypnotic grip the Valeronian was helpless to do anything of his own volition. Obeying the telepathic command of the Great One, he stepped out into the larger room and divested himself of his scanty clothing. One of the monstrosities studied his belt briefly, recognized his communicator instruments for what they were, and kicked them scornfully into a corner – thus rendering it impossible for either captive or captors to know when that small receiver throbbed out its urgent message from Quedrin Radnor.

The inspection and examination finished, it did not take long for the monstrosities to decide upon a course of action.

'Take this scum back to its own planet as soon as your cargo is unloaded,' the Great One directed. 'You must pass near that planet on your way to explore the next one, and it will save time and inconvenience to let it carry our message to its fellows.'

Out in space, speeding toward distant Valeron, the captain again communicated with Siblin:

'I shall land you close to one of your inhabited cities and you will at once get in touch with your Bardyle. You already know what your race is to do, and you have in your cage a sample of the ore with which you are to supply us. You shall be given twenty of your days in which to take from the mine already established by us enough of that ore to load this ship – ten thousand tons. The full amount – and pure mineral, mind you, no base rock – must be in the loading hoppers at the appointed time or I shall proceed to destroy every populated city, village, and hamlet upon the face of your globe.'

'But that particular ore is rare!' protested Siblin. 'I do not believe that it will prove physically possible to recover such a vast amount of it in the short time you are allowing us.'

'You understand the orders – obey them or die!'

17
Quedrin Radnor Retaliates

Very near to Valeron, as space distances go, yet so far away in terms of miles that he could take no active part whatever in the proceedings, Quedrin Radnor sat tense at his controls, staring into his visiplate. Even before Klynor Siblin had lifted his rocket plane off the ground, Radnor had opened his throttle wide. Then, his ship hurtling at full drive toward home, everything done that he could do, he sat and watched.

Watched, a helpless spectator. Watched while Siblin made his futilely spectacular attack; watched the gallant plane's destruction; watched the capture of the brave but foolhardy pilot; watched the rolling up and compression of the Chloran dome; watched in agony the obliteration of everything, animate and inanimate, pertaining to the outlying village; watched in horrified relief the departure of the invading spaceship.

Screaming through the air, her outer plating white hot from its friction, her forward rocket tubes bellowing a vicious crescendo, Radnor braked his ship savagely to a landing in the dock beside the machine shop in which she had been built. During that long return voyage his mind had not been idle. Not only had he decided what to do, he had also made rough sketches and working drawings of the changes which must be made in his peaceful space ship to make of her a superdreadnought of the void.

Nor was this as difficult an undertaking as might be supposed. She already had power enough and to spare, her generators and converters being able to supply, hundreds of times over, her maximum present drain; and, because of the ever-present danger of collision with meteorites, she was already amply equipped with repeller screens and with automatically tripped zones of force. Therefore all that was necessary was the installation of the required offensive armament – beam projectors, torpedo tubes, fields of force, controls, and the like – the designing of which was a simple matter for the brain which had tamed to man's everyday use the ultimately violent explosiveness of intra-atomic energy.

Radnor first made sure that the machine-shop superintendent, master mechanic, and foreman understood the sketches fully and knew precisely what was to be done. Then, confident that the new projectors would project and that the as yet nonexistent oxygen bombs would explode with their theoretical violence, he hurried to the office of the Bardyle. Already gathered there was a portentous group. Besides the coordinator there were scientists, engineers, architects, and beam specialists, as well as artists, teachers, and philosophers. The group, while not large, was thoroughly representative of Valeron's mental, intellectual, and scientific culture. Each member of the Council Extraordinary was unwontedly serious of mien, for each knew well what horror his world was facing. Warned by the utter, unreasoning wantonness of the destruction wrought by the Chlorans, each knew that the high civilization of Valeron, so long attuned to the arts of peace that strife had become almost unthinkable, must now devote its every effort to the grim and hateful business of war.

'Greetings, Quedrin Radnor!' began the Bardyle. 'Your plan for the defense of Valeron has been adopted, with a few minor alterations and additions suggested by other technical experts. It has been decided, however, that your proposed punitive visit to Chlora cannot be approved. As matters now stand it can be only an expedition of retaliation and vengeance, and as such can in no wise advance our cause.'

'Very well, O Bardyle! It is—' Radnor, trained from infancy in cooperation, was accepting the group decision as a matter of course when he was interrupted by an emergency call from his own laboratory. An assistant, returning to the temporarily deserted building had found the message of Klynor Siblin and had known that it should be given immediate attention.

'Please relay it to us here, at once,' Radnor instructed; and, when the message had been delivered:

'Fellow councilors, I believe that this word from Klynor Siblin will operate to change your decision against my proposed flight to Chlora. With these incomplete facts and data to guide me I shall be able to study intelligently the systems of offense and of defense employed by the enemy, and shall then be in position to strengthen immeasurably our own armament. Furthermore, Siblin was alive within the hour – there may yet be some slight chance of saving his life in spite of what he has said.'

The Bardyle glanced once around the circle of tense faces, reading in them the consensus of opinion without having recourse to speech.

'Your point is well taken, Councilor Quedrin, and for the sake of acquiring knowledge your flight is approved,' he said slowly. 'Provided, however – and this is a most important proviso – that you can convince us that there is a reasonable certainty of your safe return. Klynor Siblin had, of course, no idea that he would be captured. Nevertheless, the Chlorans took him, and his life is probably forfeit. You must also agree not to jeopardize your life in any attempt to rescue your friend unless you have every reason to believe that such an attempt will prove successful. We are insisting upon these assurances because your scientific ability will be of inestimable value to Valeron in this forthcoming struggle, and therefore your life must at all hazards be preserved.'

'To the best of my belief my safe return is certain,' replied Radnor positively. 'Siblin's plane, used only for low-speed atmospheric flying, had no defenses whatever and so fell easy prey to the Chlorans' attack. My ship, however, was built to navigate space, in which it may meet at any time meteorites traveling at immensely high velocities, and is protected accordingly. She already had four courses of high-powered repeller screens, the inside course of which, upon being punctured, automatically throws around her a zone of force.

'This zone, as most of you know, sets up a stasis in the ether itself, and thus is not only absolutely impervious to and unaffected by any material substance, however applied, but is also opaque to any vibration or wave-form propagated through the ether. In addition to these defenses I am now installing screens capable of neutralizing any offensive force with which I am familiar, as well as certain other armament, the plans of all of which are already in your possession, to be employed in the general defense.

'I agree also to your second condition.'

'Such being the case your expedition is approved,' the Bardyle said, and Radnor made his way back to the machine shop.

His first care was to tap Siblin's beam, but his call elicited no response. Those ultra-instruments were then lying neglected in a corner of an air-filled room upon far Chlora, where the almost soundless voice of the tiny receiver went unheard. Setting upon his receiver a relay alarm to inform him of any communication from Siblin, Radnor joined the men who were smoothly and efficiently re-equipping his vessel.

In a short time the alterations were done, and, armed now to the teeth with vibratory and with solid and gaseous destruction, he lifted his warship into the air, grimly determined to take the war into the territory of the enemy.

He approached the inimical planet cautiously knowing that their cities would not be undefended, as were those of his own world, and fearing that they might have alarms and detector screens of which he could know nothing. Poised high above the outermost layer of that noxious atmosphere he studied for a long time every visible feature of the world before him.

In this survey he employed an ordinary, old-fashioned telescope instead of his infinitely more powerful and maneuverable visirays, because the use of the purely optical instrument obviated the necessity of sending out forces which the Chlorans might be able to detect. He found the diamond-shaped ocean and the elliptical lake without difficulty, and placed his vessel with care. He then cut off his every betraying force and his ship plunged downward, falling freely under the influence of gravity.

Directly over the city Radnor actuated his braking rockets, and as they burst into their staccato thunder his hands fairly flashed over his controls. Almost simultaneously he scattered broadcast his cargo of bombs, threw out a vast hemisphere of force to confine the gas they would release, activated his spy ray, and cut in the generators of his awful offensive beams.

The bombs were simply large flasks of metal, so built as to shatter upon impact, and they contained only oxygen under pressure – but what a pressure! Five thousand Valeronian atmospheres those flasks contained. Well over seventy-five thousand pounds to the square inch in our ordinary terms, that pressure was one handled upon Earth only in high-pressure laboratories. Spreading widely to cover almost the whole circle of the city's expanse, those terrific canisters hurtled to the ground and exploded with all the devastating might of the high-explosive shells which in effect they were.

But the havoc they wrought as demolition bombs was neither their only nor their greatest damage. The seventy-five million cubic feet of free oxygen, driven downward and prevented from escaping into the open atmosphere by Radnor's forces, quickly diffused into a killing concentration throughout the Chloran city save inside that one upstanding dome. Almost everywhere else throughout that city the natives died exactly as had died the people of the Valeronian village in the strangling chlorin of the invaders; for oxygen is as lethal to that amoebic race as is their noxious halogen to us.

Long before the bombs reached the ground Radnor was probing with his spy ray at the great central dome from within which Klynor Siblin's message had in part been sent. But now he could not get through it; either they had detected Siblin's beam and blocked that entire communication band or else they had already put up additional barriers around their headquarters against his attack, quickly though he had acted.

Snapping off the futile visiray, he concentrated his destructive beam into a cylinder of the smallest possible diameter and hurled it against the dome; but even that frightful pencil of annihilation, driven by Radnor's every resource of power, was utterly ineffective against that greenly scintillant hemisphere of force. The point of attack flared into radiant splendor, but showed no sign of overloading or of failure.

Knowing now that there was no hope at all of rescuing Siblin and that he himself had only a few minutes left in which to work, Radnor left his beam upon the dome only long enough for his recording photometers to analyze the radiations emanating from the point of contact. Then, full-driven still, but now operating at maximum aperture he drove it in a dizzying spiral outwardly from the dome, fusing the entire unprotected area of the metropolis into a glassily fluid slag of seething, smoking desolation. Those of the monstrosities who were beneath the protective hemisphere he could not touch, but all the others died. Some were riven asunder by the fragmentation of the bombs, many expired in the flood of lethal oxygen, the rest were cremated instantly in the unimaginable fury of Radnor's ravening beams.

But beneath that dome of force there was a mighty fortress indeed. It is true that her offensive weapons had not seen active service for many years; not since the last rebellion of the slaves had been crushed. It is also true that the Chloran officers whose duty it was to operate these weapons had been caught napping – as thoroughly surprised at that fierce counterattack as would be a group of Earthly hunters were the lowly rabbits to turn upon them with repeating rifles in their furry paws.

But it did not take long for those officers to tune in their offensive armament, and that armament was driven by no such puny engines as Radnor's spaceship bore. Being stationary and a part of the regular equipment of a fortress, their size and mass were of course much greater than anything ordinarily installed in any vessel, of whatever class or tonnage. Also, in addition to being superior in size and number, the Chloran generators were considerably more efficient in the conversion and utilization of interatomic energy than were any then known to the science of Valeron.

Therefore, as Radnor had rather more than expected, he was not long allowed to wreak his will. From the dome there reached out slowly, almost caressingly, a huge arm of force incredible, at whose blighting touch his first or outer screen simply vanished – flared through the visible spectrum and went down, all in the veriest twinkling of an eye. That first screen, although the weakest by far of the four, had never even radiated under the heaviest test loads that Radnor had been able to put upon it. Now he sat at his instruments, tense but intensely analytical, watching with bated breath as that titanic beam crashed through his second screen and tore madly at his third.

Well it was for Valeron that day that Radnor had armed and powered his vessel to withstand not only whatever forces he expected her to meet, but had, with the true scientific spirit and in so far as he was able, provided against any conceivable emergency. Thus, the first screen was, as has been said, sufficiently powerful to cope with anything the vessel was apt to encounter. Nevertheless, the power of the other defensive courses increased in geometrical progression; and, as a final precaution, the fourth screen, in the almost unthinkable contingency of its being overloaded, threw on automatically in the moment of its failure an ultimately impenetrable zone of force.

That scientific caution was now to save not only Radnor's life, but also the whole civilization of Valeron. For even that mighty fourth screen, employing in its generation as it did the unimaginable sum total of the power possible of production by the massed converters of the space flyer, failed to stop that awful thrust. It halted it for a few minutes, in a blazingly, flamingly pyrotechnic display of incandescence indescribable, but as the Chlorans meshed in additional units of their stupendous power plant it began to radiate higher and higher into the ultra-violet and was certainly doomed.

It failed, and in the instant of its going down, actuated a zone of force – a complete stasis in the ether itself, through which no possible manifestation, either of matter or of energy in any form, could in any circumstance pass. Or could it? Radnor clenched his teeth and waited. Whether or not there was a subether – something lying within and between the discrete particles which

431

actually composed the ether – was a matter of theoretical controversy and of some academically scientific interest.

But, postulating the existence of such a medium and even that of vibrations of such infinitely short period that they could be propagated therein, would it be even theoretically possible to heterodyne upon them waves of ordinary frequencies? And could those amorphous monstrosities be so highly advanced that they had reduced to practical application something that was as yet known to humanity only in the vaguest, most tenuous of hypotheses?

Minute after minute passed, however, during which the Valeronian remained alive within an intact ship which, he knew, was hurtling upward and away from Chlora at the absolute velocity of her inertia, unaffected by gravitation, and he began to smile in relief. Whatever might lie below the level of the ether, either of vibration or of substance, it was becoming evident that the Chlorans could no more handle it than he could.

For half an hour Radnor allowed his craft to drift within her impenetrable shield. Then, knowing that he was well beyond atmosphere, he made sure that his screens were full out and released his zone. Instantly his screens sprang into a dazzling, coruscant white under the combined attack of two spaceships which had been following him. This time, however, the Chloran beams were stopped by the third screen. Either the enemy had not had time to measure accurately his power, or they had not considered such measurement worthwhile.

They were now to pay dearly for not having gauged his strength. Radnor's beam, again a stabbing stiletto of pure energy, lashed out against the nearer vessel; and that luckless ship mounted no such generators as powered her parent fortress. That raging spear, driven as it was by all the power that Radnor had been able to pack into his cruiser, tore through screens and metal alike as though they had been so much paper; and in mere seconds what had once been a mighty spaceship was merely a cloud of drifting, expanding vapor. The furious shaft was then directed against the other enemy, but it was just too late – the canny amoebus in command had learned his lesson and had already snapped on his zone of force.

Having learned many facts vital to the defense of Valeron and knowing that his return homeward would now be unopposed, Radnor put on full touring acceleration and drove toward his native world. Motionless at his controls, face grim and hard, he devoted his entire mind to the problem of how Valeron could best wage the inevitable war of extinction against the implacable denizens of the monstrous, interloping planet Chlora.

18

Valeron Versus Chlora

As has been said, Radnor's reply to Siblin's message was unheard, for his ultraphones were not upon his person, but were lying disregarded in a corner of the room in which their owner had undergone examination by his captors. They still lay there as the Valeronian in his cage was wafted lightly back into the spaceship from which he had been taken such a short time before; lay there as that vehicle of vacuous space lifted itself from its dock and darted away toward distant Valeron.

During the earlier part of that voyage Radnor was also in the ether, traveling from Valeron to Chlora. The two vessels did not meet, however, even though each was making for the planet which the other had left and though each pilot was following the path for him the most economical of time and of power. In fact, due to the orbits, velocities, and distances involved, they were separated by such a vast distance at the time of their closest approach to each other that neither ship even affected the ultrasensitive electromagnetic detector screens of the other.

Not until the Chloran vessel was within Valeron's atmosphere did her commander deign again to notice his prisoner.

'As I told you when last I spoke to you, I am about to land you in one of your established cities,' the amoebus informed Siblin then. 'Get in touch with your Bardyle at once and convey our instructions to him. You have the sample and you know what you are to do. No excuses for non-performance will be accepted. If, however, you anticipate having any difficulty in convincing your fellow savages that we mean precisely what we say, I will take time now to destroy one or two more of your cities.'

'It will not be necessary – my people will believe what I tell them,' Siblin thought back. Then deciding to make one more effort, hopeless although it probably would be, to reason with that highly intelligent but monstrously callous creature, he went on:

'I wish to repeat, however, that your demand is entirely beyond reason. That ore is rare, and in the time you have allowed us I really fear that it will be impossible for us to mine the required amount of it. And surely, even from your own point of view, it would be more logical to grant us a reasonable extension of time than to kill us without further hearing simply because we have failed to perform a task that was from the very first impossible. You must bear it in mind that a dead community cannot work your mines at all.'

'We know exactly how abundant that ore is, and we know equally well your intelligence, and your ability,' the captain replied coldly – and mistakenly. 'With the machinery we have left in the mine and by working every possible man at all times, you can have it ready for us. I am now setting out to explore the next planet, but I shall be at the mine at sunrise, twenty of your mornings from tomorrow. Ten thousand tons of that mineral must be ready for me to load or else your entire race shall that day cease to exist. It matters nothing to us whether you live or die, since we already have slaves enough. We shall permit you to keep on living if you obey our orders in every particular, otherwise we shall not so permit.'

The vessel came easily to a landing. Siblin in his cage was picked up by the same invisible means, transported along corridors and through doorways, and was deposited, not ungently, upon the ground in the middle of a public square. When the raider darted away he opened the door of his glass prison and made his way through the gathering crowd of the curious to the nearest visiphone station, where the mere mention of his name cleared all lines of communication for an instant audience with the Bardyle of Valeron.

'We are glad indeed to see you again, Klynor Siblin.' The coordinator smiled in greeting. 'The more especially since Quedrin Radnor, even now on the way back from Chlora, has just reported that his attempt to rescue you was entirely in vain. He was met by forces of such magnitude that only by employing a zone of force was he himself able to win clear. But you undoubtedly have tidings of urgent import – you may proceed.'

Siblin told his story tersely and cogently, yet omitting nothing of importance. When he had finished his report the Bardyle said:

'Truly, a depraved evolution – a violent and unreasonable race indeed.' He thought deeply for a few seconds, then went on: 'The council extraordinary has been in session for some time. I am inviting you to join us here. Quedrin Radnor should arrive at about the same time as you do, and you both should be present to clear up any minor points which have not been covered in your visiphone report. I am instructing the transportation officer there to put at your disposal any special equipment necessary to enable you to get here as soon as possible.'

The Bardyle was no laggard, nor was the transportation officer of the city in which Siblin found himself. Therefore when he came out of the visiphone station there was awaiting him a two-wheeled automatic conveyance bearing upon its windshield in letters of orange light the legend, 'Reserved for Klynor Siblin.' He stepped into the queer looking, gyroscopically stabilized vehicle, pressed down '9-2-6-4-3-8' – the location number of the airport – upon the banked keys of a numbering machine, and touched a red button, whereupon the machine glided off of itself.

It turned corners, dived downward into subways and swung upward onto bridges, selecting unerringly and following truly the guiding pencils of force which would lead it to the airport, its destination. Its pace was fast, mounting effortlessly upon the straightaways to a hundred miles an hour and more.

There were no traffic jams and very few halts, since each direction of traffic had its own level and its own roadway, and the only necessity for stopping came in the very infrequent event that a main artery into which the machine's way led was already so full of vehicles that it had to wait momentarily for an opening. There was no disorder, and there were neither accidents nor collisions; for the forces controlling those thousands upon thousands of speeding mechanisms, unlike the drivers of Earthly automobiles, were uniformly tireless, eternally vigilant, and – sober.

Thus Siblin arrived at the airport without incident, finding his special plane ready and waiting. It also was fully automatic, robot-piloted, sealed for high flight, and equipped with everything necessary for comfort. He ate a hearty meal, and then, as the plane reached its ninety-thousand-foot ceiling and leveled out at eight hundred miles an hour toward the distant capital, undressed and went to bed, to the first real sleep he had enjoyed for many days.

As has been indicated, Siblin lost no time; but, rapidly as be had travelled and instantly as he had made connections, Quedrin Radnor was already in his seat in the council extraordinary when Siblin was ushered in to sit with that august body. The visiphone reports had been studied exhaustively by every councilor, and as soon as the newcomer had answered their many questions concerning the details of his experiences the council continued its intense, but orderly and thorough, study of what should be done, what could be done, in the present crisis.

'We are in agreement, gentlemen,' the Bardyle at last announced. 'This new development, offering as it does only the choice between death and slavery of the most abject kind, does not change the prior situation except in setting a definite date for the completion of our program of defense. The stipulated amount of tribute probably could be mined by dint of straining our every resource, but in all probability that demand is but the first of such a never-ending succession that our lives would soon become unbearable.

'We are agreed that the immediate extinction of our entire race is preferable to a precarious existence which can be earned only by incessant and grinding labor for an unfeeling and alien race; an existence even then subject to termination at any time at the whim of the Chlorans.

'Therefore the work which was begun as soon as the strangers revealed their true nature and which is now well under way shall go on. Most of you know already what that work is, but for one or two who do not and for the benefit of the news broadcasts I shall summarize our position as briefly as is consistent with clarity.

'We intend to defend this, our largest city, into which is being brought everything needed of supplies and equipment, and as many men as can work without interfering with each other. The rest of our people are to leave their houses and scatter into widely separated temporary refuges until the issue has been decided. This evacuation may not be necessary, since the enemy will center their attack upon our fortress, knowing that until it has been reduced we are still masters of our planet.

'It was decided upon, however, not only in the belief that the enemy may destroy our unprotected centers of population, either wantonly or in anger at our resistance, but also because such a dispersion will give our race the greatest possible chance of survival in the not-at-all-improbable event of the crushing of our defenses here.

'One power-driven dome of force is to protect the city proper, and around that dome are being built concentric rings of fortifications housing the most powerful mechanisms of offense and defense possible for us to construct.

'Although we have always been a peaceful people our position is not entirely hopeless. The *sine qua non* of warfare is power, and of that commodity we have no lack. True, without knowledge of how to apply that power our cause would be already lost, but we are not without knowledge of the application. Many of our peace-time tools are readily transformed into powerful engines of destruction. Quedrin Radnor, besides possessing a unique ability in the turning of old things to new purposes, has studied exhaustively the patterns of force employed by the enemy and understands thoroughly their generation, their utilization, and their neutralization.

'Finally, the mining and excavating machinery of the Chlorans has been dismantled and studied, and its novel features have been incorporated in several new mechanisms of our own devising. Twenty days is none too long a time in which to complete a program of this magnitude and scope, but that is all the time we have. You wish to ask a question, Councilor Quedrin?'

'If you please. Shall we not have more than twenty days? The ship to be loaded will return in that time, it is true, but we can deal with her easily enough. Their ordinary space ships are no match for ours. That fact was proved so conclusively during our one engagement in space that they did not even follow me back here. They undoubtedly are building vessels of vastly greater power, but it seems to me that we shall be safe until those heavier vessels can arrive.'

'I fear that you are underestimating the intelligence of our foes,' replied the coordinator. 'In all probability they know exactly what we are doing, and were their present spaceships superior to yours we would have ceased to exist ere this. It is practically certain that they will attack as soon as they have constructed craft of sufficient power to insure success. In fact, they may be able to perfect their attack before we can complete our defense, but that is a chance which we must take.

'In that connection, two facts give us ground for optimism. First, theirs is an undertaking of greater magnitude than ours, since they must of necessity be mobile and operative at a great distance from their base, whereas we are stationary and at home. Second, we started our project before they began theirs. This second fact must be allowed but little weight, however, for they may well be more efficient than we are in the construction of engines of war.

'The exploring vessel is unimportant. She may or may not call for her load of ore; she may or may not join in the attack which is now inevitable. One thing only is certain – we must and we will drive this program through to completion before she is due to dock at the mine. Everything else must be subordinated to the task; we must devote to it every iota of our mental, physical, and mechanical power. Each of you knows his part. The meeting is adjourned *sine die*.'

There ensued a world-wide activity unparalleled in the annals of the planet. During the years immediately preceding the cataclysm there had been hustle and bustle, misdirected effort, wasted energy, turmoil and confusion; and a certain measure of success had been wrested out of chaos only by the ability of a handful of men to think clearly and straight. Now, however, Valeron was facing a crisis infinitely more grave, for she had but days instead of years in which to prepare to meet it. But now, on the other hand, instead of possessing only a few men of vision, who had found it practically impossible either to direct or to control an out-and-out rabble of ignorant, muddled, and panic-stricken incompetents, she had a population composed entirely of clear thinkers, who, requiring a very little direction and no control at all, were able and eager to work together wholeheartedly for the common good.

Thus, while the city and its environs now seethed with activity, there was no confusion or disorder. Wherever there was room for a man to work, a man was working, and the workers were kept supplied with materials and with mechanisms. There were no mistakes, no delays, no friction. Each man knew his task and its relation to the whole, and performed it with a smoothly efficient speed born of a racial training in cooperation and coordination impossible to any member of a race of lesser mental attainments.

To such good purpose did every Valeronian do his part that at dawn of The Day everything was in readiness for the Chloran visitation. The immense fortress was complete and had been tested in every part, from the ranked batteries of gigantic converters and generators down to the most distant outlying visiray viewpoint. It was powered, armed, equipped, provisioned, garrisoned. Every once-populated city was devoid of life, its inhabitants having dispersed over the face of the globe, to live in isolated groups until it had been decided whether the proud civilization of Valeron was to triumph or to perish.

Promptly as that sunrise the Chloran explorer appeared at the lifeless mine, and when he found the loading hoppers empty he calmly proceeded to the nearest city and began to beam it down. Finding it deserted he cut off, and felt a powerful spy ray, upon which he set a tracer. This time the ray held

437

up and he saw the immense fortress which had been erected during his absence; a fortress which he forthwith attacked viciously, carelessly, and with the loftily arrogant contempt which seemed to characterize his breed.

But was that innate contemptuousness the real reason for that suicidal attempt? Or had that vessel's commander been ordered by the Great Ones to sacrifice himself and his command so that they could measure Valeron's defensive power? If so, why did he visit the mine at all and why did he not know beforehand the location of the fortress? Camouflage? In view of what the Great Ones of Chlora must have known, why that commander did what he did that morning no one of Valeron ever knew.

The explorer launched a beam – just one. Then Quedrin Radnor pressed a contact and out against the invader there flamed a beam of such violence that the amoebus had no time to touch his controls, that even the automatic trips of his zone of force – if he had such trips – did not have time in which to react. The defensive screens scarcely flashed, so rapidly did that terrific beam drive through them, and the vessel itself disappeared almost instantly – molten, vaporized, consumed utterly. But there was no exultation beneath Valeron's mighty dome. From the Bardyle down, the defenders of their planet knew full well that the real attack was yet to come, and knew that it would not be long delayed.

Nor was it. Nor did those which came to reduce Valeron's far-flung stronghold in any way resemble any form of spaceship with which humanity was familiar. Two stupendous structures of metal appeared, plunging stolidly along, veritable flying fortresses, of such enormous bulk and mass that it seemed scarcely conceivable for them actually to support themselves in air.

Simultaneously the two floating castles launched against the towering dome of defense the heaviest beams they could generate and project. Under that awful thrust Valeron's mighty generators shrieked a mad crescendo and her imponderable shield radiated a fierce, eye-tearing violet, but it held. Not for nothing had the mightiest minds of Valeron wrought to convert their mechanisms and forces of peace into engines of war; not for nothing had her people labored with all their mental and physical might for almost two-score days and nights, smoothly and efficiently as one mind in one body. Not easily did even Valeron's titanic defensive installations carry that frightful load, but they carried it.

Then, like mythical Jove hurling his bolt – like, that is, save that beside that Valeronian beam any possible bolt of lightning would have been as sweetly innocuous a caress as young love's first kiss – Radnor drove against the nearer structure a beam of concentrated fury; a beam behind which was every volt and every ampere that his stupendous offensive generators could yield.

The Chloran defenses in turn were loaded grievously, but in turn they also held; and for hours then there raged a furiously spectacular struggle. Beams, rods, planes, and needles of every known kind and of every usable frequency of vibratory energy were driven against impenetrable neutralizing screens. Monstrous cannon, hurling shells with a velocity and of an explosive violence far beyond anything known to us of Earth, radio-beam-dirigible torpedoes, robot-manned drill planes, and many other lethal agencies of ultra-scientific war – all these were put to use by both sides in those first few frantic hours, but neither side was able to make any impression upon the other. Then, each realizing that the other's defenses had been designed to withstand his every force, the intensive combat settled down to a war of sheer attrition.

Radnor and his scientists devoted themselves exclusively to the development of new and ever more powerful weapons of offense; the Chlorans ceased their fruitless attacks upon the central dome and concentrated all their offensive power into two semicircular arcs, which they directed vertically downward upon the outer ring of the Valeronian works in an incessant and methodical flood of energy.

They could not pierce the defensive shields against Valeron's massed power, but they could and did bring into being a vast annular lake of furiously boiling lava, into which the outer ring of fortresses began slowly to crumble and dissolve. This method of destruction, while slow, was certain; and grimly, pertinaciously, implacably, the Chlorans went about the business of reducing Valeron's only citadel.

The Bardyle wondered audibly how the enemy could possibly maintain indefinitely an attack so profligate of energy, but he soon learned that there were at least four of the floating fortresses engaged in the undertaking. Occasionally the two creations then attacking were replaced by two precisely similar structures, presumably to return to Chlora in order to renew their supplies of the substance, whatever it was, from the atomic disintegration of which they derived their incomprehensible power.

And slowly, contesting stubbornly and bitterly every foot of ground lost, the forces of Valeron were beaten back under the relentless, never-ceasing attack of the Chloran monstrosities – back and ever back toward their central dome as ring after ring of the outlying fortifications slagged down into that turbulently seething, that incandescently flaming lake of boiling lava.

19

To the Rescue

Valeron was making her last stand. Her back was against the wall. The steadily contracting ring of Chloran force had been driven inward until only one thin line of fortified works lay between it and the great dome covering the city itself. Within a week at most, perhaps within days, that voracious flood of lava would lick into and would dissolve that last line of defense. Then what of Valeron?

All the scientists of the planet had toiled and had studied, day and night, but to no avail. Each new device developed to halt the march of the encroaching constricting band of destruction had been nullified in the instant of its first trial:

'They must know every move we make, to block us so promptly,' Quedrin Radnor had mused one day. 'Since they certainly have no visiray viewpoints of material substance within our dome, they must be able to operate a spy ray using only the narrow gravity band, a thing we have never been able to accomplish. If they can project such viewpoints of pure force through such a narrow band, may they not be able to project a full materialization and thus destroy us? But, no, that band is – *must* be – altogether too narrow for that.'

Stirred by these thoughts he had built detectors to announce the appearance of any non-gravitational forces in the gravity band and had learned that his fears were only too well founded. While the enemy could not project through the open band any forces sufficiently powerful to do any material damage, they were thus in position to forestall any move which the men of Valeron made to ward off their inexorably approaching doom.

Far beneath the surface of the ground, in a room which was not only sealed but was surrounded with every possible safeguard, nine men sat at a long table, the Bardyle at its head.

'... and nothing can be done?' the coordinator was asking. 'There is no possible way of protecting the edges of the screens?'

'None.' Radnor's voice was flat, his face and body alike were eloquent of utter fatigue. He had driven himself to the point of collapse, and all his labor had proved useless. 'Without solid anchorages we cannot hold them – as the ground is fused they give way. When the fused area reaches the dome the end will come. The outlets of our absorbers will also be fused, and with no possible method of dissipating the energy being continuously radiated into the dome we shall all die, practically instantaneously.'

'But I judge you are trying something new, from the sudden cutting off of nearly all our weight,' stated another.

'Yes. I have closed the gravity band until only enough force can get through to keep us in place on the planet, in a last attempt to block their spy rays so that we can try one last resort …' He broke off as an intense red light suddenly flared into being upon a panel. 'No; even that is useless. See that red light? That is the pilot light of a detector upon the gravity band. The Chlorans are still watching us. We can do nothing more, for if we close that band any tighter we shall leave Valeron entirely and shall float away, to die in space.'

As that bleak announcement was uttered the councilors sat back limply in their seats. Nothing was said – what was there to say? After all, the now seemingly unavoidable end was not unexpected. Not a man at that table had really in his heart thought it possible for peaceful Valeron to triumph against the superior war-craftiness of Chlora.

They sat there, staring unseeing into empty air, when suddenly in that air there materialized Seaton's projection. Since its reception has already been related, nothing need be said of it except that it was the Bardyle himself who was the recipient of that terrific wave of mental force. As soon as the Terrestrial had made clear his intentions and his desires, Radnor leaped to his feet, a man transformed.

'A laboratory of radiation!' he exclaimed, his profound exhaustion forgotten in a blaze of new hope. 'Not only shall I lead him to such a laboratory, but my associates and I shall be only too glad to do his bidding in every possible way.'

Followed closely by the visitor, Radnor hurried buoyantly along a narrow hall and into a large room in which, stacked upon shelves, lying upon benches and tables, and even piled indiscriminately upon the floor, there was every conceivable type and kind of apparatus for the generation and projection of etheric forces.

Seaton's flashing glance swept once around the room, cataloguing and classifying the heterogeneous collection. Then, while Radnor looked on in a daze of incredulous astonishment, that quasi-solid figure of force made tangible wrought what was to the Valeronian a scientific miracle. It darted here and there with a speed almost impossible for the eye to follow, seizing tubes, transformers, coils, condensers, and other items of equipment, connecting them together with unbelievable rapidity into a mechanism at whose use the bewildered Radnor, able physicist though he was, could not even guess.

The mechanical educator finished, Seaton's image donned one of its sets of multiple headphones and placed another upon the unresisting head of his host. Then into Radnor's already reeling mind there surged an insistent demand for his language, and almost immediately the headsets were tossed aside.

There, that's better!' Seaton – for the image was, to all intents and purposes, Seaton himself exclaimed. 'Now that we can talk to each other we'll soon make those Chlorans wish that they had stayed at home.'

'But they are watching everything you do,' protested Radnor, 'and we cannot block them out without cutting off our gravity entirely. They will therefore be familiar with any mechanism we may construct and will be able to protect themselves against it.'

'They just think they will,' grimly. 'I can't close the gravity band without disaster, any more than you could, but I can find any spy ray they can use and send back along it a jolt that'll burn their eyes out. You see, there's a lot of stuff down on the edge of the fourth order that neither you nor the Chlorans know anything about yet, because you haven't had enough thousands of years to study it.'

While he was talking, Seaton had been furiously at work upon a small generator, and now he turned it on.

'If they can see through *that*,' he grinned, 'they're a lot smarter than I think they are. Even if they're bright enough to have figured out what I was doing while I was doing it, it won't do them any good, because this outfit will scramble any beam they can send through that band.'

'I must bow to your superior knowledge, of course,' Radnor said gravely, 'but I should like to ask one question. You are working a full materialization through less than a tenth of the gravity band – something that has always been considered impossible. Is there no danger that the Chlorans may analyze your patterns and thus duplicate your feat?'

'Not a chance,' Seaton assured him positively. 'This stuff I am using is on a tight beam, so tight that it is proof against analysis or interference. It took the Norlaminians – and they're a race of real thinkers – over eight thousand years to go from the beams you and the Chlorans are using down to what I'm showing you. Therefore I'm not afraid that the opposition will pick it up in the next week or two. But we'd better get busy in a big way. Your most urgent need, I take it, is for something – anything – that will stop that surface of force before it reaches the skirt of your defensive dome and blocks your dissipaters?'

'Exactly!'

'All right. We'll build you a four-way fourth-order projector to handle full materializations – four-way to handle four attackers in case they get desperate and double their program. With it you will send working images of yourselves into the power rooms of the Chloran ships and clamp a short-circuiting field across the secondaries of their converters. Of course they can bar you out with a zone of force if they detect you before you can kill the generators of their zones, but that will be just as good, as far as we're concerned – they can't do a thing as long as they're on, you know. Now put on the headset again and I'll give you the data on the projector. Better get a recorder, too, as there'll be some stuff that you won't be able to carry in your head.'

The recorder was brought in and from Seaton's brain there flowed into it and into the mind of Radnor the fundamental concepts and complete equations and working details of the new instrument. Upon the Valeronian's face was first blank amazement, then dawning comprehension, and lastly sheer, wondering awe as, the plan completed, he removed the headset. He began a confused panegyric of thanks, but Seaton interrupted him briskly.

'That's all right, Radnor, you'd do the same thing for us if things were reversed. Humanity has got to stick together against all the vermin of all the universes. But, say, I'd like to see this mess cleared up, myself – think I'll stick around and help you build it. You're worn out, but you won't rest until the Chlorans are whipped – I can't blame you for that, I wouldn't either – and I'm fresh as a daisy. Let's go!'

In a few hours the complex machine was done. Radnor and Siblin were seated at two of the sets of controls, associate physicists at the others.

'Since I don't know any more about their systems of conversion than you do, I can't tell you in detail what to do,' Seaton was issuing final instructions. 'But whatever you do, don't monkey with their primaries – shorting them might overload their liberators and blow this whole solar system over into the next galaxy. Take time to be dead sure that you've got the secondaries of their main converters, and slap a short circuit on as many of them as you can before they cut you off with a zone. You'll probably find a lot of liberator-converter sets on vessels of that size, but if you can kill the ones that feed the zone generators they're cold meat.'

'You are much more familiar with such things than we are,' Radnor remarked. 'Would you not like to come along?'

'I'll say I would, but I can't,' Seaton replied instantly. 'This isn't me at all, you know. Um ... um ... m ... I could tag along, of course, but it would be ... but let's see ...'

'Oh, of course,' Radnor apologized. 'In working with you so long and so cordially I forgot for the moment that you are not here in person.'

'Can't be done, I'm afraid.' Seaton frowned, still immersed in the hitherto unstudied problem of the re-projection of a projected image. 'Need over two hundred thousand relays and – um – synchronization – neuro-muscular – not on this outfit. Wonder if it can *be* done at all? Have to look into it some time – but excuse me, Radnor, I was thinking and got lost. Ready to go? I'll follow you up and be ready to offer advice – not that you'll need it. Shoot!'

Radnor snapped on the power and he and his aid shot their projections into one of the opposing fortresses, Siblin and his associate going into the other. Through compartment after compartment of the immense structures the as yet invisible projections went, searching for the power rooms. They were not hard to find, extending as they did nearly the full length of the stupendous structures; vaulted caverns filled with linked pairs of mastodontic fabrications, the liberator-converters.

Springing in graceful arcs from heavily insulated ports in the ends of one machine of each pair were five great bus-bars, which Radnor and Siblin recognized instantly as secondary leads from the converters – the gigantic mechanisms which, taking the raw intra-atomic energy from the liberators, converted it into a form in which it could be controlled and utilized.

Neither Radnor nor Siblin had ever heard of five-phase energy of any kind, but those secondaries were unmistakable. Therefore all four images drove against the fivefold bars their perfectly conducting fields of force. Four converters shrieked wildly, trying to wrench themselves from their foundations; insulation smoked and burst wildly into yellow flame; the stubs of the bars grew white-hot and began to fuse; and in a matter of seconds a full half of each prodigious machine subsided to the floor, a semi-molten, utterly useless mass.

Similarly went the next two in each fortress, and the next – then Radnor's two projections were cut off sharply as the Chlorans' impenetrable zone of force went on, and that fortress, all its beams and forces inoperative, floated off into space.

Siblin and his partner were more fortunate. When the amoebus commanding their prey threw in his zone switch nothing happened. Its source of power had already been destroyed, and the two Valeronian images went steadily down the line of converters, in spite of everything the ragingly frantic monstrosities could do to hinder their progress.

The terrible beam of destruction held steadily upon that fortress by the beamers in Valeron's mighty dome had never slackened its herculean efforts to pierce the Chloran screens. Now, as more and more of the converters of that floating citadel were burned out those screens began to radiate higher and higher into the ultraviolet. Soon they went down, exposing defenseless metal to the blasting, annihilating fury of the beam, to which any conceivable substance is but little more resistant than so much vacuum.

There was one gigantic, exploding flash, whose unbearable brilliance darkened even the incandescent radiance of the failing screen, and Valeron's mighty beam bored on, unimpeded. And where that mastodontic creation had floated an instant before there were only a few curling wisps of vapor.

'Nice job of clean-up, boys – fine!' Seaton clapped a friendly hand upon Radnor's shoulder. 'Anybody can handle them now. You'd better take a week off and catch up on sleep. I could do with a little myself, and you've been on the job a lot longer than I have.'

'But hold on – don't go yet!' Radnor exclaimed in consternation. 'Why, our whole race owes its very existence to you – wait at least until our Bardyle can have a word with you!'

'That isn't necessary, Radnor. Thanks just the same, but I don't go in for that sort of thing, any more than you would. Besides, we'll be here in the flesh in a few days and I'll talk to him then. So long!' And the projection disappeared.

In due time *Skylark Two* came lightly to a landing in a parkway near the council hall, to be examined curiously by an excited group of Valeronians who wondered audibly that such a tiny spaceship should have borne their salvation. The four Terrestrials, sure of their welcome, stepped out and were greeted by Siblin, Radnor, and the Bardyle.

'I must apologize, sir, for my cavalier treatment of you at our previous meeting.' Seaton's first words to the coordinator were in sincere apology. 'I trust that you will pardon it, realizing that something of the kind was necessary in order to establish communication.'

'Speak not of it, Richard Seaton. I suffered only a temporary inconvenience, a small thing indeed compared to the experience of encountering a mind of such stupendous power as yours. Neither words nor deeds can express to you the profound gratitude of our entire race for what you have done for Valeron.

'I am informed that you personally do not care for extravagant praise, but please believe me to be voicing the single thought of a world's people when I say that no words coined by brain of man could be just, to say nothing of being extravagant, when applied to you. I do not suppose that we can do anything, however slight, for you in return, in token that these are not entirely empty words?'

'You certainly can, sir,' Seaton made surprising answer. 'We are so completely lost in space that without a great deal of material and of mechanical aid we shall never be able to return to, nor even to locate in space, our native galaxy, to say nothing of our native planet.'

A concerted gasp of astonishment was his reply, then he was assured in no uncertain terms that the resources of Valeron were at his disposal.

A certain amount of public attention had of course to be endured; but Seaton and Crane, pleading a press of work upon their new projectors, buried themselves in Radnor's laboratory, leaving it to their wives to bear the brunt of Valeronian adulation.

'How do you like being a heroine, Dot?' Seaton asked one evening as the two women returned from an unusually demonstrative reception in another city.

'We just revel in it, since we didn't do any of the real work – it's just too perfectly gorgeous for words,' Dorothy replied shamelessly. 'Especially Peggy.' She eyed staid Margaret mischievously and winked furtively at Seaton. 'Why, you ought to see her – she could just simply roll it up on a fork and eat it, as though it were that much soft fudge!'

Since the scientific and mechanical details of the construction of a fifth-order projector have been given in full elsewhere there is no need to repeat them here. Seaton built his neutronium lens in the core of the nearby white dwarf star, precisely as Rovol had done it from distant Norlamin. He brought it to Valeron and around it there began to come into being a duplicate of the immense projector which the Terrestrials had been obliged to leave behind when they abandoned gigantic *Skylark Three* to plunge through the fourth dimension in tiny *Two*.

'Maybe it's none of my business, Radnor,' Seaton turned to the Valeronian curiously during a lull in their work, 'but how come you're still simply shooing away those Chloran vessels by making them put out their zones of force? Why didn't you hop over there on your projector and blow their whole planet over into the next solar system? I would have done that long ago if it had been me, I think.'

'We did visit Chlora once, with something like that in mind, but our attempt failed lamentably,' Radnor admitted sheepishly. 'You remember that peculiar special sense, that mental force that Siblin tried to describe to you? Well, it was altogether too strong for us. My father, possessing one of the strongest minds of Valeron, was in the chair, but they mastered him so completely that we had to recall the projection by cutting off the power to prevent them from taking from his mind by force the methods of transmission which you taught us and which we were then using.'

'Hmmm! So that's it, huh?' Seaton was greatly interested. 'As soon as I get this fifth-order outfit done I'll have to see what it can do about them.'

True to his word, Seaton's first use of the new mechanism was to assume the offensive. He first sought out and destroyed the Chloran structure then in space – now an easy task, since zones of force, while impenetrable to any ether-borne phenomena, offer no resistance whatever to forces of the fifth order, propagated as they are in that inner medium, the subether. Then, with the Quedrins standing by, to cut off the power in case he should be overcome, he invaded the *sanctum sanctorum* of all Chlora – the private office of the Supreme Great One himself – and stared unabashed and unaffected into the enormous 'eye' of the monstrous ruler of the planet.

There ensued a battle royal. Had mental forces been visible, it would have been a spectacular meeting indeed! Larger and larger grew the 'eye' until it was transmitting all the terrific power generated by that frightful, visibly palpitating brain. But Seaton was not of Valeron, nor was he handicapped by the limitations of a fourth-order projector. He was now being projected upon a full beam of the fifth, by a mechanism able to do full justice to his stupendously composite brain.

The part of that brain he was now employing was largely the contribution of Drasnik, the First of Psychology of ancient Norlamin; and from it he was hurling along that beam the irresistible sum total of mental power accumulated by ten thousand generations of the most profound students of the mind that our galaxy has ever known.

The creature, realizing that at long last it had met its mental master, must

have emitted radiations of distress, for into the room came crowding hordes
of the monstrosities, each of whom sought to add his own mind to those
already opposing the intruder. In vain – all their power could not turn Seaton's penetrating glare aside, nor could it wrest from that glare's unbreakable
grip the mind of the tortured Great One.

And now, mental means failing, they resorted to the purely physical. Hand
rays of highest power blasted at that figure uselessly; fiercely driven bars,
spears, axes, and all other weapons rebounded from it without leaving a
mark upon it, rebounded bent, broken, and twisted. For that figure was in no
sense matter as we understand the term. It was pure force – force made palpable and coherent by the incomprehensible power of disintegrating matter;
force against which any possible application of mechanical power would be
precisely as effective as would wafted thistledown against Gibraltar.

Thus the struggle was brief. Paying no attention to anything, mental or
physical, that the other monstrosities could bring to bear, Seaton compelled
his victim to assume the shape of the heretofore-despised human being.
Then, staring straight into that quivering brain through those hate-filled,
flaming eyes, he spoke aloud, the better to drive home his thought:

'Learn, so-called Great One, once and for all, that when you attack any
race of humanity anywhere, you attack not only that one race, but all the
massed humanity of all the planets of all the galaxies! As you have already
observed, I am not of the planet Valeron, nor of this solar system, nor even
of this galaxy; but I and my fellows have come to the aid of this race of
humanity whom you were bold enough to attack.

'I have proved that we are your masters, mentally as well as scientifically
and mechanically. Those of you who have been attacking Valeron have been
destroyed, ships and crews alike. Those en route there have been destroyed in
space. So also shall be destroyed any and all expeditions you may launch
beyond the limits of your own foul atmosphere.

'Since even such a repellent civilization as yours must have its place in the
great Scheme of Things, we do not intend to destroy your planet nor such of
your people as remain upon it or near it, unless such destruction shall
become necessary for the welfare of the human race. While we are considering what we shall do about you, I advise you to heed well this warning!'

20

The First Universe is Mapped

The four Tellurians had discussed at some length the subject of Chlora and her outlandish population.

'It looks as though you were perched upon the horns of a first-class dilemma,' Dorothy remarked at last. 'If you let them alone there is no telling what harm they will do to these people here, and yet it would be a perfect shame to kill them all – they can't help being what they are. Do you suppose you can figure a way out of it, Dick?'

'Maybe – I've got a kind of hunch, but it hasn't jelled into a workable idea yet. It's tied in with the sixth-order projector that we'll have to have, anyway, to find our way back home. Until we get that working I guess we'll just let the amoebuses stew in their own juice.'

'Well, and then what?' Dorothy prompted.

'I told you it's nebulous yet, with a lot of essential details yet to be filled in …' Seaton paused, then went on, doubtfully: 'It's pretty wild – I don't know whether …'

'Now you *must* tell us about it, Dick,' Margaret urged.

'I'll say you've got to,' Dorothy agreed. 'You've had a lot of ideas wild enough to make any sane creature's head spin around in circles, but not one of them was so hair-raising that you were backward in talking about it. This one must be the prize brainstorm of the universe – spill it to Red-Top!'

'All right, but remember that it's only half-baked and that you asked for it. I'm doping out a way to send them back to their own solar system, planet and all.'

'What!' exclaimed Margaret.

Dorothy simply whistled – a long, low whistle highly eloquent of incredulity.

'Maintenance of temperature? Time? Power? Control?' Crane, the imperturbable, picked out unerringly the four key factors of the stupendous feat.

'Your first three objections can be taken care of easily enough,' Seaton replied positively. 'No loss of temperature is possible through a zone of force – our own discovery. We can stop time with a stasis – we learned that from watching those four-dimensional folks work. The power of cosmic radiation is practically infinite and eternal – we learned how to use that from pure intellectuals. Control is the sticker, since it calls for computations and calculations at present impossible; but I believe that when we get our mechanical brain done, it will be able to work out even such a problem as that.'

'What d'you mean, mechanical brain?' demanded Dorothy.

'The thing that is going to run our sixth-order projector,' Seaton explained. 'You see, it'll be altogether too big and too complicated to be controlled manually, and thought – human thought, at least – is on one band of the sixth order. Therefore the logical thing to do is to build an artificial brain capable of thinking on all bands of the order instead of only one, to handle the whole projector. See?'

'No,' declared Dorothy promptly, 'but maybe I will, though, when I see it work. What's next on the program?'

'Well, it's going to be quite a job to build that brain and we'd better be getting at it, since without it there'll be no *Skylark Four* ...'

'Dick, I object!' Dorothy protested vigorously. 'The *Skylark of Space* was a nice name ...'

'Sure, you'd think so, since you named her yourself,' interrupted Seaton in turn, with his disarming grin.

'Keep still a minute, Dickie, and let me finish. *Skylark Two* was pretty bad, but I stood it; and by gritting my teeth all out of shape, I did manage to keep from squawking about *Skylark Three*, but I certainly am not going to stand for *Skylark Four*. Why, just think of giving a name like that to such a wonderful thing as she is going to be – as different as can be from anything that has ever been dreamed of before – just as though she were going to be simply one more of a long series of cup-challenging motor boats or something! Why, it's – it's just too perfectly idiotic for words!'

'But she's *got* to be some kind of a *Skylark*. Dot – you know that.'

'Yes, but give her a name that means something – that sounds like something. Name her after this planet, say – *Skylark of Valeron* – how's that?'

'O.K. by me. How about it, Peg? Mart?'

The Cranes agreed to the suggestion with enthusiasm and Seaton went on:

'Well, an onion by any other name would smell as sweet, you know, and it's going to be just as much of a job to build the *Skylark of Valeron as* it would have been to build *Skylark Four*. Therefore, as I have said before and am about to say again, we'd better get at it.'

The fifth-order projector was moved to the edge of the city, since nowhere within its limits was there room for the structure to be built, and the two men seated themselves at its twin consoles and their hands flew over its massed banks of keyboards. For a few minutes nothing happened; then on the vast, level plain before them – a plain which had been a lake of fluid lava a few weeks before – there sprang into being an immense foundation structure of trussed and latticed girder frames of inoson, the hardest, strongest, and toughest form of matter possible to molecular structure. One square mile of ground it covered and it was strong enough, apparently, to support a world.

When the foundation was finished, Seaton left the framework to Crane, while he devoted himself to filling the interstices and compartments as fast as they were formed. He first built one tiny structure of coils, fields, and lenses of force – one cell of the gigantic mechanical brain which was to be. He then made others, slightly different in tune, and others, and others.

He then set forces to duplicating these cells, forces which automatically increased in number until they were making and setting five hundred thousand cells per second, all that his connecting forces could handle. And everywhere, it seemed, there were projectors, fields of force, receptors and converters of cosmic energy, zones of force, and many various-shaped lenses and geometric figures of neutronium incased in sheaths of faidon.

From each cell led tiny insulated wires, so fine as to be almost invisible, to the 'nerve centers' and to one of the millions of projectors. From these in turn ran other wires, joining together to form larger and larger strands until finally several hundred enormous cables, each larger than a man's body, reached and merged into an enormous, glittering, hemispherical, mechano-electrical inner brain.

For forty long Valeronian days – more than a thousand of our Earthly hours – the work went on ceaselessly, day and night. Then it ceased of itself and there dangled from the center of the glowing, gleaming hemisphere a something which is only very vaguely described by calling it either a heavily wired helmet or an incredibly complex headset. It was to be placed over Seaton's head, it is true – it *was* a headset, but one raised to the millionth power.

It was the energizer and controller of the inner brain, which was in turn the activating agency of that entire cubic mile of as yet inert substance, that assemblage of thousands of billions of cells, so soon to become the most stupendous force ever to be conceived by the mind of man.

When that headset appeared Seaton donned it and sat motionless. For hour after hour he sat there, his eyes closed, his face white and strained, his entire body eloquent of a concentration so intense as to be a veritable trance. At the end of four hours Dorothy came up resolutely, but Crane waved her back.

'This is far and away the most crucial point of the work, Dorothy,' he cautioned her gravely. 'While I do not think that anything short of physical violence could distract his attention now, it is best not to run any risk of disturbing him. An interruption now would mean that everything would have to be done over again from the beginning.'

Something over an hour later Seaton opened his eyes, stretched prodigiously, and got up. He was white and trembling, but tremendously relieved and triumphant.

'Why, Dick, what have you been doing? You look like a ghost!' Dorothy was now an all-solicitous wife.

'I've been *thinking*, Rufus, and if you don't believe that it's hard work you'd better try it some time! I won't have to do it any more though – got a machine to do my thinking for me now.'

'Oh, is it all done?'

'Nowhere near, but it's far enough along so that it can finish itself. I've just been telling it what to do.'

'*Telling* it! Why, you talk as though it were human!'

'Human? It's a lot more than that. It can outthink and outperform even those pure intellectuals – "and that," as the poet feelingly remarked, "is going some"! And if you think that riding in that fifth-order projector was a thrill, wait until you see what this one can do. Think of it' – even the mind that had conceived the thing was awed – 'it is an extension of my own brain, using waves that traverse even intergalactic distances practically instantaneously. With it I can see anything I want to look at, anywhere; can hear anything I want to hear. It can build, make, do, or perform anything that my brain can think of.'

'That is all true, of course,' Crane said slowly, his sober mien dampening Dorothy's ardor instantly, 'but still – I can not help wondering …' He gazed at Seaton thoughtfully.

'I know it, Mart, and I'm working up my speed as fast as I possibly can,' Seaton answered the unspoken thought, rather than the words. 'But let them come – we'll take 'em. I'll have everything on the trips, ready to spring.'

'What *are* you two talking about?' Dorothy demanded.

'Mart pointed out to me the regrettable fact that my mental processes are in the same class as the proverbial molasses in January, or as a troop of old and decrepit snails racing across a lawn. I agreed with him, but added that I would have my thoughts all thunk up ahead of time when the pure intellectuals tackle us – which they certainly will.'

'Slow!' she exclaimed. 'When you planned the whole *Skylark of Valeron* and nobody knows what else, in five hours?'

'Yes, dear heart, *slow*. Remember when we first met our dear departed friend Eight, back in the original *Skylark*? You saw him materialize exact duplicates of each of our bodies, clear down to the molecular structures of our chemistry, in less than one second, from a cold standing start. Compared to that job, the one I have just done is elementary. It took me over five hours – he could have done it in nothing flat.

'However, don't let it bother you too much. I'll never be able to equal their speed, since I'll not live enough millions of years to get the required practice, but our being material gives us big advantages in other respects that Mart isn't mentioning because, as usual, he is primarily concerned with our weaknesses – yes? No?'

'Yes; I will concede that being material does yield advantages which may perhaps make up for our slower rate of thinking,' Crane conceded.

'Hear that? If he admits that much, you know that we're as good as in, right now,' Seaton declared. 'Well, while our new brain is finishing itself up, we might as well go back to the hall and chase the Chlorans back where they belong – the Brain worked out the equations for me this morning.'

From the ancient records of Valeron, Radnor and the Bardyle had secured complete observational data of the cataclysm, which had made the task of finding the present whereabouts of the Chlorans' original sun a simple task. The calculations and computations involved in the application of forces of precisely the required quantities to insure the correct final orbit were complex in the extreme; but, as Seaton had foretold, they had presented no insurmountable difficulties to the vast resources of the Brain.

Therefore, everything in readiness, the two Terrestrial scientists surrounded the inimical planet with a zone of force and with a stasis of time. They then erected force-control stations around it, adjusted with such delicacy and precision that they would direct the planet into the exact orbit it had formerly occupied around its parent sun. Then, at the instant of correct velocity and position, the control stations would go out of existence and the forces would disappear.

As the immense ball of dazzlingly opaque mirror which now hid the unwanted world swung away with ever-increasing velocity, the Bardyle, who had watched the proceedings in incredulous wonder, heaved a profound sigh of relaxation.

'What a relief – what a relief!' he exclaimed.

'How long will it take?' asked Dorothy curiously.

'Quite a while – something over four hundred years of our time. But don't let it bother you – they won't know a thing about it. When the forces let go they'll simply go right on, from exactly where they left off, without realizing that any time at all has lapsed – in fact, for them, no time at all shall have lapsed. All of a sudden they will find themselves circling around a different sun, that's all.

'If their old records are clear enough they may be able to recognize it as their original sun and they'll probably do a lot of wondering as to how they got back there. One instant they were in a certain orbit around this sun here, the next instant they will be in another orbit around an entirely different sun! They'll know, of course, that we did it, but they'll have a sweet job figuring out how and what we did – some of it is really deep stuff. Also, they will be a few hundred years off in their time, but since nobody in the world will know it, it won't make any difference.'

'How perfectly weird!' Dorothy exclaimed. 'Just think of losing a four-hundred-year chunk right out of the middle of your life and not even knowing it!'

'I would rather think of the arrest of development,' meditated Crane. 'Of the opportunity of comparing the evolution of the planets already there with that of the returned wanderer.'

'Yeah, it would be interesting – it's a shame we won't be alive then,' Seaton responded, 'but in the meantime we've got a lot of work to do for ourselves. Now that we've got this mess straightened out I think we had better tell these folks goodbye, get into *Two*, and hop out to where Dot's *Skylark of Valeron* is going to materialize.'

The farewell to the people of Valeron was brief, but sincere.

'This is in no sense goodbye,' Crane concluded. 'By the aid of these newly discovered forces of the sixth order there shall soon be worked out a system of communication by means of which all the inhabited planets of the galaxies shall be linked as closely as are now the cities of any one world.'

Skylark Two shot upward and outward, to settle into an orbit well outside that of Valeron. Seaton then sent his projection back to the capital city, fitted over his imaged head the controller of the inner brain, and turned to Crane with a grin.

'That's timing it, old son – she finished herself up less than an hour ago. Better cluster around and watch this, folks, it's going to be good.'

At Seaton's signal the structure which was to be the nucleus of the new space traveler lifted effortlessly into the air its millions of tons of dead weight and soared, as lightly as little *Two* had done, out into the airless void. Taking up a position a few hundred miles away from the Terrestrial cruiser, it shot out a spherical screen of force to clear the ether of chance bits of debris. Then inside that screen there came into being a structure of gleaming inoson, so vast in size that to the startled onlookers it appeared almost of planetary dimensions.

'Good heavens – it's stupendous!' Dorothy exclaimed. 'What did you boys make it so big for – just to show us you could, or what?'

'Hardly! She's just as small as she can be and still do the work. You see, to find our own galaxy we will have to project a beam to a distance greater than any heretofore assigned diameter of the universe, and to control it really accurately its working base and the diameter of its hour and declination circles would each have to be something like four light-years long. Since a ship of that size is of course impracticable, Mart and I did some figuring and decided that with circles one thousand kilometers in diameter we could chart galaxies accurately enough to find the one we're looking for – if you think of it, you'll realize that there are a lot of hundredth-millimeter marks around the circumference of circles of that size – and that they would probably be big enough to hold a broadcasting projection somewhere near a volume of space as large as that occupied by the Green System. Therefore we built the *Skylark of Valeron* just large enough to contain those thousand-kilometer circles.'

As *Skylark Two* approached the looming planetoid the doors of vast airlocks opened. Fifty of those massive gates swung aside before her and closed behind her before she swam free in the cool, sweet air and bright artificial sunlight of the interior. She then floated along above an immense grassy park toward two well-remembered and beloved buildings.

'Oh, Dick!' Dorothy squealed. 'There's our house – and Martin's! It's funny, though, to see them side by side. Are they the same inside, too – and what's that funny little low building between them?'

'They duplicate the originals exactly, except for some items of equipment which would be useless here. The building between them is the control room, in which are the master headsets of the Brain and its lookouts. The Brain itself is what you would think of as underground – inside the shell of the planetoid.'

The small vessel came lightly to a landing and the wanderers disembarked upon the close-clipped, springy turf of a perfect lawn. Dorothy flexed her knees in surprise.

'How come we aren't weightless, Dick?' she demanded. 'This gravity isn't – can't be – natural. I'll bet you did that too!'

'Mart and I together did, sure. We learned a lot from the intellectuals and a lot more in hyperspace, but we could neither derive the fundamental equations nor apply what knowledge we already had until we finished this sixth-order outfit. Now, though, we can give you all the gravity you want – or as little – whenever and wherever you want it.'

'Oh marvelous – this is glorious, boys!' Dorothy breathed. 'I have always just simply despised weightlessness. Now, with these houses and everything, we can have a perfectly wonderful time!'

'Here's the dining room,' Seaton said briskly. 'And here's the headset you put on to order dinner or whatever is appropriate to the culinary department. You will observe that the kitchen of this house is purely ornamental – never to be used unless you want to.'

'Just a minute, Dick.' Dorothy's voice was tensely serious. 'I have been really scared ever since you told me about the power of that Brain, and the more you tell me of it the worse scared I get. Think of the awful damage a wild, chance thought would do – and the more an ordinary mortal tries to avoid any thought the surer he is to think it, you know that. Really, I'm not ready for that yet, dear – I'd much rather not go near the headset.'

'I know, sweetheart.' His arm tightened around her. 'But you didn't let me finish. These sets around the house control forces which are capable of nothing except duties pertaining to the part of the house in which they are. This dining-room outfit, for instance, is exactly the same as the Norlaminian one you used so much, except that it is much simpler.

'Instead of using a lot of keyboards and force-tubes, you simply think into that helmet what you want for dinner and it appears. Think that you want the table cleared and it is cleared – dishes and all simply vanish. Think of anything else you want done around this room and it's done – that's all there is to it.

'To relieve your mind I'll explain some more. Mart and I both realized that that Brain could very easily become the most terrible, the most frightfully destructive thing that the universe has ever seen. Therefore, with two exceptions, every controller on this planetoid is of a strictly limited type. Of the two master controls, which are unlimited and very highly reactive, one responds only to Crane's thoughts, the other only to mine. As soon as we get some loose time we are going to build a couple of auxiliaries, with automatic stops against stray thoughts, to break you girls in on – we know as well as you do, Red-Top, that you haven't had enough practice yet to take an unlimited control.'

'I'll say I haven't!' she agreed feelingly. 'I feel a lot better now – I'm sure I can handle the rest of these things very nicely.'

'Sure you can, Well, let's call the Cranes and go into the control room,' Seaton suggested. 'The quicker we get started the quicker we'll get done.'

Accustomed as she was to the banks and tiers of keyboards, switches, dials, meters, and other operating paraphernalia of the control rooms of the previous *Skylarks*, Dorothy was taken aback when she passed through the thick, heavily insulated door into that of the *Skylark of Valeron*. For there were four gray walls, a gray ceiling, and a thick gray rug. There were low, broad double chairs and headsets. There was nothing else.

'This is your seat, Dottie, here beside me, and this is your headset – it's just a visiset, so you can see what is going on, not a controller,' he hastened to reassure her. 'You have a better illusion of seeing if your eyes are open, that's why everything is neutral in color. But better still for you girls, we'll turn off the lights.'

The illumination, which had seemed to pervade the entire room instead of emanating from any definite sources, faded out; but in spite of the fact that the room was in absolute darkness Dorothy saw with a clarity and a depth of vision impossible to any Earthly eyes. She saw at one and the same time, with infinite precision of detail, the houses and their contents; the whole immense sphere of the planetoid, inside and out; Valeron and her sister planets circling their sun; and the stupendous full sphere of the vaulted heavens.

She knew that her husband was motionless at her side, yet she saw him materialize in the control room of *Skylark Two*. There he seized the cabinet which contained the space chart of the Fenachrone – that library of films portraying all the galaxies visible to the wonderfully powerful telescopes and projectors of that horrible but highly scientific race.

That cabinet became instantly a manifold scanner, all its reels flashing through as one. Simultaneously there appeared in the air above the machine a three-dimensional model of all the galaxies there listed. A model upon such a scale that the First Galaxy was but a tiny lenticular pellet, although it was still disproportionately large; upon such a scale that the whole vast sphere of space covered by the hundreds of Fenachrone scrolls was compressed into a volume but little larger than a basketball. And yet each tiny galactic pellet bore its own peculiarly individual identifying marks.

Then Dorothy felt as though she herself had been hurled out into the unthinkable reaches of space. In a fleeting instant of time she passed through thousands of star clusters, and not only knew the declination, right ascension, and distance of each galaxy, but saw it duplicated in miniature in its exact place in an immense, three-dimensional model in the hollow interior of the space-flyer in which she actually was.

The mapping went on. To human brains and hands the task would have been one of countless years. Now, however, it was to prove only a matter of hours, for this was no human brain. Not only was it reactive and effective at distances to be expressed intelligibly in light-years or parsecs; because of the immeasurable sixth-order velocity of its carrier wave it was equally effective across reaches of space so incomprehensibly vast that the rays of visible light emitted at the birth of a sun so far away would reach the point of observation only after that sun had lived through its entire cycle of life and had disappeared.

'Well, that's about enough of that for you, for a while,' Seaton remarked in a matter-of-fact voice. 'A little of that stuff goes a long ways at first – you have to get used to it.'

'I'll say you do I Why … I … it …' Dorothy paused, even her ready tongue at a loss for words.

'You can't describe it in words – don't try,' Seaton advised. 'Let's go outdoors and watch the model grow.'

To the awe, if not to the amazement of the observers, the model had already begun to assume a lenticular pattern. Galaxies, then, really were arranged in general as were the stars composing them; there really *were* universes, and they really were lenticular – the vague speculations of the hardiest and most exploratory cosmic thinkers were being confirmed.

For hour after hour the model continued to grow and Seaton's face began to take on a look of grave concern. At last, however, when the chart was three fourths done or more, a deep-toned bell clanged out the signal for which he had been waiting – the news that there was now being plotted a configuration of galaxies identical with that portrayed by the space chart of the Fenachrone.

'Gosh!' Seaton sighed hugely. 'I was beginning to be afraid that we had escaped clear out of our own universe, and that would have been bad – very, *very* bad, believe me! The rest of the mapping can wait – let's go!'

Followed by the others he dashed into the control room, threw on his helmet, and hurled a projection into the now easily recognizable First Galaxy. He found the Green System without difficulty, but he could not hold it. It was so far away that the utmost delicacy of control of which the gigantic sixth-order installation was capable could not keep the viewpiont from leaping erratically, in fantastic bounds of hundreds of millions of miles, all through and around its objective.

But Seaton had half expected this development and was prepared for it. He had already sent out a broadcasting projection; and now, upon a band of frequencies wide enough to affect every receiving instrument in use through-out the Green System and using power sufficient to overwhelm any transmitter, however strong, that might be in operation, he sent out in a mighty voice his urgent message to the scientists of Norlamin.

21

Dunark takes a Hand

In the throne room of Kondal, with its gorgeously resplendent jeweled ceil-ing and jeweled metallic-tapestry walls, there were seated in earnest consultation the three most powerful men of the planet Osnome – Roban, the Emperor; Dunark, the Crown Prince; and Tarnan, the Commander-in-Chief. Their 'clothing' was the ordinary Osnomian regalia of straps, chains, and metallic bands, all thickly bestudded with blazing gems and for the most part supporting the full assortment of devastatingly powerful hand weapons without which any man of that race would have felt stark naked. Their fierce green faces were keenly hawk-like; the hard, clean lines of their bare green bodies bespoke the rigid physical training that every Osnomian undergoes from birth until death.

'Father, Tarnan may be right,' Dunark was saying soberly. 'We are too sav-age, too inherently bloodthirsty, too deeply interested in killing, not as a means to some really worthwhile end, but as an end in itself. Seaton the Overlord thinks so, the Norlaminians think so, the Dasorians think so, and I am beginning to think so myself. All really enlightened races look upon us as little better than barbarians, and in part I agree with them. I believe, however, that if we were really to devote ourselves to study and to productive effort we could soon equal or surpass any race in the system, except of course the Norlaminians.'

'There may be something in what you say,' the emperor admitted dubi-ously, 'but it is against all our racial teachings. What, then, of an outlet for the energies of all manhood?'

'Constructive effort instead of destructive,' argued the karbix. 'Let them build – study – learn – advance. It is all too true that we are far behind other races of the system in all really important things.'

'But what of Urvan and his people?' Roban brought up his last and strong-est argument. 'They are as savage as we are, if not more so. As you say, the necessity for continuous warfare ceased with the destruction of Mardonale, but are we to leave our whole planet defenseless against an interplanetary attack from Urvania?'

'They dare not attack us,' declared Tarnan, 'any more than we dare attack them. Seaton the Overlord decreed that the people of us two first to attack the other dies root and branch, and we all know that the word of the Over-lord is no idle, passing breath.'

'But he has not been seen for long. He may be far away and the Urvanians may decide at any time to launch their fleets against us. However, before we decide this momentous question I suggest that you two pay a visit of state to the court of Urvan. Talk to Urvan and his karbix as you have talked to me, of cooperation and of mutual advancement. If they will cooperate, we will.'

During the long voyage to Urvania, the third planet of the fourteenth sun, however, their new ardor cooled perceptibly – particularly that of the younger man – and in Urvan's palace it became clear that the love of peaceful culture inculcated upon those fierce minds by contact with more humane peoples could not supplant immediately the spirit of strife bred into bone and fiber during thousands of generations of incessant warfare.

For when the two Osomians sat down with the two Urvanians the very air seemed charged with animosity. Like strange dogs meeting with bared fangs and bristling manes, Osnomian and Urvanian alike fairly radiated hostility. Therefore Tarnan's suggestions as to cooperation and understanding were decidedly unconvincing, and were received with open scorn.

'Your race may well wish to cooperate with ours,' sneered the Emperor of Urvania, 'since but for the threats of that self-styled Overlord, you would have ceased to exist long since. And how do we know where that one is, what he is doing, whether he is paying any attention to us? Probably you have learned that he has left this system entirely and have already planned an attack upon us. In self-defense we shall probably have to wipe out your race to keep you from destroying ours. At any rate your plea is very evidently some underhanded trick of your weak and cowardly race …'

'Weak! Cowardly! *Us?* You conceited bloated toad!' stormed Dunark, who had kept himself in check thus far only by sheer power of will. He sprang to his feet, his stool flying backward. 'Here and now I demand a meeting of honor, if you know the meaning of the word honor.'

The four enraged men, all drawing weapons, were suddenly swept apart, then clutched and held immovably as a figure of force materialized among them – the form of an aged, white-bearded Norlaminian.

'Peace, children, and silence!' the image commanded sternly. 'Rest assured that there shall be no more warfare in this system and that the decrees of the Overlord shall be enforced to the letter. Calm yourselves and listen. I know well, mind you, that none of you really meant what has just been said. You of Osnome were so impressed by the benefits of mutual helpfulness that you made this journey to further its cause; you of Urvania are at heart also strongly in favor of it, but neither of you has strength enough to admit it.

'For know, vain and self-willed children, that it is weakness, not strength, which you have been displaying. It may well be, however, that your physical bravery and your love of strife can now be employed for the general good of all humanity. Would you join hands, to fight side by side in such a cause?'

'We would,' chorused the four, as one.

Each was heartily ashamed of what had just happened, and was glad indeed of the opportunity to drop it without losing face.

'Very well! We of Norlamin fear greatly that we have inadvertently given to one of the greatest foes of universal civilization weapons equal in power to the Overlord's own, and that he is even now working to undo all that has been done. Will you of Osnome and you of Urvania help in conducting an expedition against that foe?'

'We will!' they exclaimed.

Dunark added: 'Who is that enemy, and where is he to be found?'

'He is Dr Marc C. DuQuesne, of Earth.'

'DuQuesne!' barked Dunark. 'Why, I thought the Fenachrone killed him! But we shall attend to it at once – when *I* kill anyone he *stays* killed!'

'Just a moment, son,' the image cautioned. 'He has surrounded Earth with defenses against which your every arm would be entirely impotent. Come you to Norlamin, bringing each of you one hundred of his best men. We shall have prepared for you certain equipment which, although it may not enable you to emerge victorious from the engagement, will at least insure your safe return. It might be well also to stop at Dasor, which is not now far from your course of flight, and bring along Sacner Carfon, who will be of great assistance, being a man both of action and learning.'

'But *DuQuesne!*' raved Dunark, who realized immediately what must have happened. 'Why didn't you ray him on sight? Didn't you know what a liar and a thief he is, by instinct and training?'

'We had no suspicion then who he was, thinking, as did you, that DuQuesne had passed. He came under another name, as Seaton's friend. He came as one possessing knowledge, with fair and plausible words. But of that we shall inform you later. Come at once – we shall place upon your controls forces which shall pilot you accurately and with speed.'

Upon the aqueous world of Dasor they found its amphibious humanity reveling in an activity which, although dreamed of for centuries, had been impossible of realization until the *Skylark* had brought to them a supply of Rovolon, the metal of power. Now cities of metal were arising here and there above her waves, airplanes and helicopters sped through and hovered in her atmosphere, barges and pleasure craft sailed the almost unbroken expanse of ocean which was her surface, immense submarine freighters bored their serenely stolid ways through her watery depths.

Sacner Carfon, the porpoise-like, hairless, naked Dasorian councilor, heaved his six and a half feet of height and his five hundredweight of mass into Dunark's vessel and greeted the Osnomian prince with a grave and friendly courtesy.

'Yes, friend, everything is wonderfully well with Dasor,' he answered Dunark's query. 'Now that our one lack, that of power, has been supplied, our lives can at last be lived to the full, unhampered by the limitations which we have hitherto been compelled to set upon them. But this from Norlamin is terrible news. What know you of it?'

During the trip to Norlamin the three leaders not only discussed and planned among themselves, but also had many conferences with the Advisory Five of the planet toward which they were speeding, so that they arrived upon that ancient world with a complete knowledge of what they were to attempt. There Rovol and Drasnik instructed them in the use of fifth-order forces, each according to his personality and ability.

To Sacner Carfon was given command, and he was instructed minutely in every detail of the power, equipment, and performance of the vessel which was to carry the hope of civilization. To Tarnan, the best balanced of his race, was given a more limited knowledge. Dunark and Urvan, however, were informed only as to the actual operation of the armament, with no underlying knowledge of its nature or construction.

'I trust that you will not resent this necessary caution,' Drasnik said carefully. 'Your natures are as yet essentially savage and bloodthirsty; your reason is all too clouded by passion. You are, however, striving truly, and that is a great good. With a few mental operations, which we shall be glad to give you at a later time, you shall both be able to take your places as leaders in the march of your peoples toward civilization.'

Fodan, majestic chief of the Five, escorted the company of warriors to their battleship of space, and what a ship she was! Fully twice the size of *Skylark Three* in every dimension she lay there, surcharged with power and might, awaiting only her commander's touch to hurl herself away toward distant and inimical Earth.

But the vengeful expedition was too late by far. DuQuesne had long since consolidated his position. His chain of interlinked power stations encircled the globe. Governments were in name only. World Steel now ruled the entire Earth and DuQuesne's power was absolute. Nor was that rule as yet unduly onerous. The threat of war was gone, the tyranny of gangsterism was done, everybody was working for high wages – what was there to kick about? Some men of vision of course perceived the truth and were telling it, but they were being howled down by the very people they were trying to warn.

It was thus against an impregnably fortified world that Dunark and Urvan directed every force with which their flying superdreadnought was armed. Nor was she feeble, this monster of the skyways, but DuQuesne had known well what form the attack would take and, having the resources of the world upon which to draw, he had prepared to withstand the massed assault of a hundred vessels – or a thousand.

Therefore the attack not only failed; it was repulsed crushingly. For from his massed generators DuQuesne hurled out upon the Norlaminian space-ship a solid beam of such incredible intensity that in neutralizing its terrific ardor her store of power-uranium dwindled visibly, second by second. So rapidly did the metal disappear that Sacner Carfon, after waging the unequal struggle for some twenty hours, abandoned it and drove back toward the Central System, despite the raging protests of Dunark and of his equally tempestuous lieutenant.

And in his private office, which was also a complete control room, DuQuesne smiled at Brookings – a hard, cold smile. 'Now you see,' he said coldly. 'Suppose I hadn't spent all this time and money on my defenses?'

'Well, why don't you go out and chase 'em? Give 'em a scare anyway?'

'Because it would be useless,' DuQuesne stated flatly. 'That ship carries more stuff than anything we have ready to take off at present. Also, Dunark does not scare. You might kill him, but you can't scare him – it isn't in the breed.'

'Well, what is the answer, then? You have tried to take Norlamin with everything you've got – bombs, automatic ships, and projectors – and you haven't got to first base. You can't even get through their outside screens. What are you going to do – let it go on as a stalemate?'

'Hardly!' DuQuesne smiled thinly. 'While I do not make a practice of divulging my plans, I am going to tell you a few things now, so that you can go ahead with more understanding and hence with greater confidence. Seaton is out of the picture, or he would have been back here before this. The Fenachrone are all gone. Dunark and his people are unimportant. Norlamin is the only known obstacle between me and the mastery of the galaxy, therefore Norlamin must be either conquered or destroyed. Since the first alternative seems unduly difficult, I shall destroy her.'

'Destroy Norlamin – how?' The thought of wiping out that world, with all its ancient culture, did not appall – did not even affect – Brookings' callous mind. He was merely curious concerning the means to be employed.

'This whole job so far has been merely a preliminary toward that destruction,' DuQuesne informed him levelly. 'I am now ready to go ahead with the second step. The planet Pluto is, as you may or may not know, very rich in uranium. The ships which we are now building are to carry a few million tons of that metal to a large and practically uninhabited planet not too far from Norlamin. I shall install driving machinery upon that planet and, using it as a projectile which all their forces cannot stop, I shall throw Norlamin into her own sun.'

Raging but impotent, Dunark was borne back to Norlamin; and, more sub-dued now but still bitterly humiliated, he accompanied Urvan, Sacner Carfon, and the various Firsts to a consultation with the Five.

As they strolled along through the grounds, past fountains of flaming color, past fantastically geometric hedges intricately and ornately wrought of noble metal, past walls composed of self-luminous gems so moving as to form fleeting, blending pictures of exquisite line and color, Sacner Carfon eyed Drasnik in unobtrusive signal and the two dropped gradually behind.

'I trust that you were successful in whatever it was you had in mind to do while we set up the late diversion?' Carfon asked quietly, when they were out of earshot.

Dunark and Urvan, his fierce and fiery aides, had taken everything that had happened at its face value, but not so had the leader. Unlike his lieuten-ants, the massive Dasorian had known at first blast that his expedition against DuQuesne was hopeless. More, it had been clear to him that the Norlamin-ians had known from the first that their vessel, enormous as she was and superbly powerful, could not crush the defenses of Earth.

'We knew, of course, that you would perceive the truth,' the First of Psych-ology replied as quietly. 'We also knew that you would appreciate our reasons for not taking you fully into our confidence in advance. Tarnan of Osnome also had an inkling of it, and I have already explained matters to him. Yes; we succeeded. While DuQuesne's whole attention was taken up in resisting your forces and in returning them in kind, we were able to learn much that we could not have learned otherwise. Also, our young friends Dunark and Urvan, through being chastened, have learned a very helpful lesson. They have seen themselves in true perspective for the first time; and, having fought side by side in a common and so far as they know a losing cause, they have become friends instead of enemies. Thus it will now be possible to inaugurate upon those two backward planets a program leading toward true civilization.'

In the Hall of the Five the Norlaminian spokesman voiced thanks and appreciation for the effort just made, concluding:

'While as a feat of arms the expedition may not have been a success, in certain other respects it was far from being a failure. By its help we were enabled to learn much, and I can assure you now that the foe shall not be allowed to prevail – it is graven upon the Sphere that civilization is to go on.'

'May I ask a question, sir?' Urvan was for the first time in his bellicose career speaking diffidently. 'Is there no way of landing a real storming force upon Earth? Must we leave DuQuesne in possession indefinitely?'

'We must wait, son, and work,' the chief answered, with the fatalistic calm of his race. 'At present we can do nothing more, but in time …'

He was interrupted by a deafening blast of sound – the voice of Richard Seaton, tremendously amplified.

'This is the *Skylark* calling Rovol of Norlamin … *Skylark* calling Rovol of Norlamin …' it repeated over and over, rising to a roar and diminishing to a whisper as Seaton's broadcaster oscillated violently through space.

Rovol laid a beam to the nearest transmitter and spoke: 'I am here, son. What is it?'

'Fine! I'm away out here in—'

'Hold on a minute, Dick!' Dunark shouted. He had been humble and sober enough since his return to Norlamin, realizing as he never had before his own ignorance in comparison with the gigantic minds about him; the powerlessness of his entire race in comparison with the energies he had so recently seen in action. But now, as Seaton's voice came roaring in and Rovol and his brain-brother were about to indulge so naïvely and so publicly in a conversation which certainly should not reach DuQuesne's ears, his spirits rose. Here was something he could do to help.

'DuQuesne is alive, has Earth completely fortified, and is holding everything we can give him,' Dunark went on rapidly. 'He's got everything we have, maybe more, and he's undoubtedly listening to every word we're saying. Talk Mardonalian – I know for a fact that DuQuesne can't understand that. They've got an educator here and I'll give it to Rovol right now – all right, go ahead.'

'I'm clear out of the galaxy,' Seaton's voice went on, now speaking the language of the Osnomian race which had so recently been destroyed. 'So many hundreds of millions of parsecs away that none of you except Orion could understand the distance. The speed of transmission is due to the fact that we have perfected and I am using a sixth-order projector, not a fifth. Have you a ship fit for really long-distance flight – as big as *Three* was, or bigger?'

'Yes; we have a vessel twice her size.'

'Fine! Load her up and start. Head for the Great Nebula in Andromeda – Orion knows what and where it is. That isn't very close to my line, but it will do until you get some apparatus set up. I've got to have Rovol, Drasnik, and Orlon, and I would like to have Fodan; you can bring along anybody else that wants to come. I'll sign on again in an hour – you should be started by then.'

Besides the four Norlaminians mentioned, Caslor, First of Mechanism, and Astron, First of Energy, also elected to make the stupendous flight, as did many 'youngsters' from the Country of Youth. Dunark would not be left behind, nor would adventurous Urvan. And lastly there was Sacner Carfon the Dasorian, who remarked that he 'would have to go along to make the boys behave and to steer the ship in case the old professors forget to.' The spaceship was well on its way when at the end of the hour Seaton's voice again was heard.

'All right, put me on a recorder and I'll give you the data,' he instructed, when he had made sure that his signal was being received.

'DuQuesne has been trying to put a ray on us and he may try to follow us,' Dunark put in.

'Let him,' Seaton shot back grimly, then spoke in English: 'DuQuesne, Dunark says that you're listening in. You have my urgent, if not cordial, invitation to follow this Norlaminian ship. If you follow it far enough, you'll take a long, long ride, believe me!'

Again addressing the voyagers, he recounted briefly everything that had occurred since the abandonment of *Skylark Three*, then dived abruptly into the fundamental theory and practical technique of sixth-order phenomena and forces.

Of that ultra-mathematical dissertation Dunark understood not even the first sentence; Sacner Carfon perhaps grasped dimly a concept here and there. The Norlaminians, however, sat back in their seats, relaxed and smiling, their prodigious mentalities not only absorbing greedily but assimilating completely the enormous doses of mathematical and physical science being thrust upon them so rapidly. And when that epoch-making, that almost unbelievable, tale was done, not one of the aged scientists even referred to the tape of the recorder.

'Oh, wonderful – wonderful!' exclaimed Rovol in ecstasy, his transcendental imperturbability broken at last. 'Think of it! Our knowledge extended one whole order farther in each direction, both into the small and into the large. Magnificent! And by one brain, and that of a youth. Extraordinary! And we may now traverse universal space in ordinary time, because that brain has harnessed the practically infinite power of cosmic radiation, a power which exhausted the store of uranium carried by *Skylark Three* in forty hours. Phenomenal! Stupendous!'

'But do not forget that the brain of that youth is a composite of many,' said Fodan thoughtfully, 'and that in it, among others, were yours and Drasnik's. Seaton himself ascribes to that peculiar combination his successful solution of the problem of the sixth order. You know, of course, that I am in no sense belittling the native power of that brain. I am merely suggesting that perhaps other noteworthy discoveries may be made by superimposing brains in other, but equally widely divergent, fields of thought.'

'An interesting idea, truly, and one which may be fruitful of result,' assented Orlon, the First of Astronomy, 'but I would suggest that we waste no more time. I, for one, am eager to behold with my own inner consciousness the vistas of the galaxies.'

Agreeing, the five white-bearded scientists seated themselves at the multiplex console of their fifth-order installation and set happily to work. Their gigantic minds were undaunted by the task they faced – they were only thrilled with interest at the opportunity of working with magnitudes, distances, forces, objects, and events at the very contemplation of which any ordinary human mind would quail.

Steadily and contentedly they worked on, while at the behest of their nimble and unerring fingers there came into being the forces which were to build into their own vessel a duplicate of the mechano-electrical Brain which actuated and controlled the structure, almost of planetary proportions, in which Seaton was even then hurtling toward them. Hurtling with a velocity rapidly mounting to a value incalculable; driven by the power liberated by the disintegrating matter of all the suns of all the galaxies of all the universes of cosmic space!

22

Trapping the Intellectuals

With all their might of brain and skill of hand and with all the resources of their fifth-order banks of forces, it was no small task for the Norlaminians to build the sixth-order controlling system which their ship must have if they were to traverse universal space in any time short of millennia. But finally it was done.

A towering mechano-electrical Brain almost filled the midsection of their enormous sky rover, the receptors and converters of the free energy of space itself had been installed, and their intra-atomic space-drive, capable of developing an acceleration of only five light-velocities, had been replaced by Seaton's newly developed sixth-order cosmic-energy drive which could impart to the ship and its entire contents, without jolt, jar, or strain, any conceivable, almost any calculable acceleration.

For many days the Norlaminian vessel had been speeding through the void at her frightful maximum of power toward the *Skylark of Valeron*, which in turn was driving toward our galaxy at the same mad pace. Braking down now, since only a few thousand light-years of distance separated the hurtling flyers, Seaton materialized his image at the Brain control of the smaller cruiser and thought into it for minutes.

'There, we're all set!' In the control room of the *Skylark* Seaton laid aside his helmet and wiped the perspiration from his forehead in sheer relief. 'The trap is baited and ready to spring – I've been scared to death for a week that they'd tackle us before we were ready for them.'

'What difference would it have made?' asked Margaret curiously. 'Since we have our sixth-order screens out they couldn't hurt us, could they?'

'No, Peg; but keeping them from hurting us isn't enough – we've got to capture them. And they'll have to be almost directly between Rovol's ship and ours to make that capture possible. You see, we'll have to send out from each vessel a hollow hemisphere of force and to surround them. If we had only one ship, or if they don't come between our two ships, we can't bottle them up, because they have exactly the same velocity of propagation that our forces have.

'Also, you can see that our projector can't work direct on more than a hemisphere without cutting its own beams, and that we can't work through relay stations because, fast as relays are, the intellectuals would get away while the relays were cutting in. Any more questions?'

'Yes; I have one,' put in Dorothy. 'You told us that this artificial Brain of yours could do anything that your own brain could think of, and here you've got it stuck already and have to have two of them. How come?'

'Well, this is a highly exceptional case,' Seaton replied. 'What I said would be true ordinarily, but now, as I explained to Peg, it's working against some-thing that can think and act just as quickly as I can.'

'I know, dear, I was just putting you on the spot a little. What are you using for bait?'

'Thoughts. We're broadcasting them from a point midway between the two vessels. They're keen on investigating any sixth-order impulses they feel, you know – that's why we've kept all our stuff on tight beams heretofore, so that they probably couldn't detect it – so we're sending out a highly peculiar type of thought, that we are pretty sure will bring them in from wherever they are.'

'Let me listen to it, just for a minute?' she pleaded.

'W-e-l-l … I don't know.' He eyed her dubiously. 'Not for a minute – no. I haven't even tried to listen to the finished product, myself. Being of a type that not even a pure intellectual can resist, they'd burn out any human brain in mighty short order. Maybe you might for about a tenth of a second, though.'

He lowered a helmet over her expectant head and snatched it off again, but that moment had been enough for Dorothy. Her violet eyes widened terribly in an expression commingled of amazedly poignant horror and of dreadfully ecstatic fascination; her whole body trembled uncontrollably.

'Dick – Dick!' she shrieked; then, recovering slowly: 'How horrible – how ghastly – how perfectly, exquisitely damnable! What is it? Why, I actually heard babies begging to be born! And there were men who had died and gone to heaven and to hell; there were minds that had lost their bodies and didn't know what to do – were simply shrieking out their agony, despair, and utter, unreasoning terror for the whole universe to hear! And there were joys, pleasures, raptures, so condensed as to be almost as unbearable as the tortures. And there were other things – awful, terrible, utterly indescribable and unimaginable things! Oh, Dick, I was sure that I had gone stark, raving crazy!'

'Easy, dear,' Seaton reassured his overwrought wife. 'All those things are really there, and more. I told you it was bad medicine – that it would tear any human mind to pieces.'

Seaton paused, weighing in his mind how best to describe the utterly indescribable signal that was being broadcast, then went on, choosing his words with care:

'All the pangs and all the ecstasies, all the thoughts and all the emotions of all evolution of all things, animate and inanimate, are there; of all things that ever have existed from the unknowable beginning of infinite time and of all things that ever shall exist until time's unknowable end. It covers all animate life, from the first stirring of that which was to vitalize the first unicell in the slime of the first world ever to come into being in the cosmos, to the last cognition of the ultimately last intelligent entity ever to be.

'Our present humanity was of course included, from before conception through birth, through all of life, through death, and through the life beyond. It covers inanimate evolution from the ultimate particle and wave, through the birth, life, death, and rebirth of any possible manifestation of energy and of matter, up to and through the universe.

'Neither Mart nor I could do it all. We carried everything as far as we could, then the Brain went through with it to its logical conclusion, which of course we could not reach. Then the Brain systematized all the data and reduced it to a concentrated essence of pure thought. It is that essence which is being broadcast and which will certainly attract the intellectuals. In the brief flash you got of it you probably could understand only the human part – but maybe it's just as well.'

'I'll say it's just as well!' Dorothy emphatically agreed. 'I wouldn't listen to that again, even for a millionth of a second, for a million dollars – but I wouldn't have missed it for another million, either. I don't know whether to beg you to listen to it, Peggy, or to implore you not to.'

'Don't bother,' Margaret replied positively. 'Anything that could throw you into such a hysterical tantrum as that did, I don't want any of at all. None at all, in fact, would be altogether too much for—'

'Got them, folks – all done!' Seaton exclaimed 'You can put on your headsets now.'

A signal lamp had flashed brightly and he knew that those two gigantic Brains, working in perfect synchronism, had done instantaneously all that they had been set to do.

'Are you dead sure that they got them all, Dick?'

'Absolutely, and they got them in less time than it took the filament of the lamp to heat up. You can bank on it that all seven of them are in the can. I go off halfcocked and make mistakes; but those Brains don't – they can't.'

Seaton was right. Though far away, even as universal distances go, the Intellectuals had felt that broadcast thought and had shot toward its source at their highest possible speed. For in all their long lives and throughout all their cosmic wanderings they had never encountered thoughts of such wide scope, such clear cogency, such tremendous power.

The discarnate entities approached the amazing pattern of mental force which was radiating so prodigally and addressed it; and in that instant there shot out curvingly from each of the mechano-electrical Brains a gigantic, hemispherical screen.

Developing outwardly from the two vessels as poles with the unimaginable velocity possible only to sixth-order forces, the two cups were barriers impenetrable to any sixth-order force, yet neither affected nor were affected by the gross manifestations which human senses can perceive. Thus solar systems, even the neutronium cores of stars, did not hinder their instantaneous development.

Hundreds of light-years in diameter though they were, the open edges of those semi-globes of force met in perfect alignment and fused smoothly, effortlessly, instantaneously together to form a perfect, thought-tight sphere. The violently radiating thought-pattern which had so interested the intellectuals disappeared, and at the same instant the ultra-sensitive organisms of the entities were assailed by the, to them, deafening and blinding crash and flash of the welding together along its equator of the far-flung hollow globe.

These simultaneous occurrences were the first intimations that everything was not what it appeared, and the disembodied intelligences flashed instantly into furious activity, too late by the smallest possible instant of time. The trap was sprung, the sphere was impervious at its every point, and, unless they could break through that wall, the intellectuals were incarcerated until Seaton should release his screens.

Within the confines of the globe there were not a few suns and thousands of cubic parsecs of space upon whose stores of energy the intellectuals could draw. Wherefore they launched a concerted attack upon the wall, hurling against it all the force they could direct. But they were not now contending against the power of any human, organic finite brain. For Seaton's mind, powerfully composite though it was of the mightiest intellects of the First Galaxy, was only the primary impulse which was being impressed upon the grids of, and was being amplified to any desirable extent by, the almost infinite power of those two cubic miles of coldly emotionless, perfectly efficient, mechano-electrical artificial Brains.

Thus against every frantic effort of the intellectuals within it the sphere was contracted inexorably, and as it shrank, reducing the volume of space from which the prisoners could draw energy, their struggles became weaker and weaker. When the ball of force was only a few hundred miles in diameter and the two vessels were relatively at rest, Seaton erected auxiliary stations around it and assumed full control.

Rapidly then the prisoning sphere, little larger now than a toy balloon, was brought through the inoson wall of the *Skylark* and held motionless in the air above the Brain room. A complex structure of force was built around it, about which in turn there appeared a framework of inoson, supporting sixteen massive bars of uranium.

Seaton took off his helmet and sighed. 'There, that'll hold them for a while, I guess.'

'What are you going to do with them?' asked Margaret.

'Darned if I know, Peg,' he admitted ruefully. 'That's been worrying me ever since we figured out how to catch them. We can't kill them and I'm afraid to let them go, because they're entirely too hot to handle. So in the meantime, pending the hatching out of a feasible method of getting rid of them permanently, I have put them in jail.'

'Why, Dick, how positively brutal!' Dorothy exclaimed.

'Yeah? There goes your soft heart again, Red-Top, instead of your hard head. I suppose it would be positively O.K. to let them loose, so that they can dematerialize all four of us? But it isn't as bad as it sounds, because I've got a stasis of time around them. We can leave them in there for seventeen thousand million years and even their intellects won't know it, because for them no time at all shall have lapsed.'

'No-o-o – of course we can't let them go scot-free,' Dorothy admitted, 'but we – I should – well, maybe couldn't you make a bargain with them to give them their liberty if they will go away and let us alone? They're such free spirits, surely they'd rather do that than stay bottled up forever.'

'Since they are purely intellectual and hence immortal, I doubt very much if they'll dicker with us at all,' Seaton replied. 'Time doesn't mean a thing to them, you know; but since you insist I'll check the stasis and talk it over with them.'

A tenuous projection, heterodyned upon waves far below the band upon which the captives had their being, crept through the barrier screen and Seaton addressed his thoughts to the entity known as 'One.'

'Being highly intelligent, you have already perceived that we are vastly more powerful than you are. Living in the flesh possesses many advantages over an immaterial existence. One of these is that it permitted us to pass through the fourth dimension, which you cannot do because your patterns are purely three-dimensional and inextensible. While in hyperspace we learned many things. Particularly we learned much of the really fundamental natures and relationship of time, space, and matter, gaining thereby a basic knowledge of all nature which is greater, we believe, than any that has ever before been possessed by any three-dimensional being.

'Not only can we interchange matter and energy as you do in your materializations and dematerializations, but we can go much farther than you can, working in levels which you cannot reach. For instance, I am projecting myself through this screen, which you cannot do because the carrier wave is far below your lowest attainable level.

'With all my knowledge, however, I admit that I cannot destroy you, since you can shrink as nearly to a mathematical point as I can compress this zone, and its complete coalescence would of course liberate you. Upon the other hand, you realize your helplessness inside that sphere. You can do nothing since it cuts off your sources of power.

'I can keep you imprisoned therein as long as I choose. I can set upon it forces which will keep you imprisoned until this two-hundred-kilogram ingot of uranium has dwindled down to a mass of less than one milligram. Knowing that the half-life period of that element is approximately five times ten to the ninth years, you can calculate for yourself how long you shall remain incarcerated.

'My wife, however, has a purely sentimental objection to confining you thus, and wishes to make an agreement with you whereby we may set you at liberty without endangering our own present existences. We are willing to let you go if you will agree to leave this universe forever. I realize, of course, that you are beyond either sentiment or passion and are possessed of no emotions whatever. Realizing this, I give you a choice, upon purely logical grounds, thus:

'Will you leave us and our universe alone, to work out our own salvation or our own damnation, as the case may be, or shall I leave you inside that sphere of force until its monitor bars are exhausted? Think well before you reply; for, know you, we all prefer to exist for a short time as flesh and blood rather than for all eternity as fleshless and immaterial intelligences. Not only that – we intend so to exist and we shall so exist!'

'We shall make no agreements, no promises,' One replied. 'Yours is the most powerful mind I have encountered – almost the equal of one of ours – and I shall take it.'

'You just *think* you will!' Seaton blazed. 'You don't seem to get the idea at all. I am going to surround you with an absolute stasis of time, so that you will not even be conscious of imprisonment, to say nothing of being able to figure a way out of it, until certain more pressing matters have been taken care of. I shall then work out a method of removing you from this universe in such a fashion and to such a distance that if you should desire to come back here the time required would be, as far as humanity is concerned, infinite. Therefore it must be clear to you that you will not be able to get any of our minds, in any circumstances.'

'I had not supposed that a mind of such power as yours could think so muddily,' One reproved him. 'In fact, you do not so think. You know as well as I do that the time with which you threaten me is but a moment. Your galaxy is insignificant, your universe is but an ultramicroscopic mote in the cosmic all. We are not interested in them and would have left them before this had I not encountered your brain, the best I have seen in substance. That mind is highly important and that mind I shall have.'

'But I have already explained that you can't get it, ever,' protested Seaton, exasperated. 'I shall be dead long before you get out of that cage.'

'More of your purposely but uselessly confused thinking,' retorted One. 'You know well that your mind shall never perish, nor shall it diminish in vigor throughout all time to come. You have the key to knowledge, which you will hand down through all your generations. Planets, solar systems, galaxies, will come and go, as they have since time first was; but your descendants will be eternal, abandoning planets as they age to take up their abodes upon younger, pleasanter worlds, in other systems and in other galaxies – even in other universes.

'And I do not believe that I shall lose as much time as you think. You are bold indeed in assuming that your mind, able as it is, can imprison mine for even the brief period we have been discussing. At any rate, do as you please – we will make neither promises nor agreements.'

23

The Long, Long Ride

Immense as the Norlaminian vessel was, getting her inside the planetoid was a simple matter to the Brain. Inside the *Skylark* a dome bulged up, driving back the air, a circular section of the multilayered wall disappeared; Rovol's space-torpedo floated in; the wall was again intact; the dome vanished; the visitor settled lightly into the embrace of a mighty landing cradle which fitted exactly her slenderly stupendous bulk.

The Osnomian prince was the first to disembark, appearing unarmed; for the first time in his warlike life he had of his own volition laid aside his every weapon.

'Glad to see you, Dick,' he said simply, but seizing Seaton's hand in both his own, with a pressure that said far more than his words. 'We thought they got you, but you're bigger and better than ever – the worse jams you get into, the stronger you come out.'

Seaton shook the hands enthusiastically. 'Yeah, "lucky" is my middle name – I could fall into a cesspool and climb out covered with talcum powder and smelling like a bouquet of violets. But you've advanced more than I have,' glancing significantly at the other's waist, bare now of its wonted assortment of lethal weapons. 'You're going good, old son – we're all behind you!'

He turned and greeted the other newcomers in cordial and appropriate fashion, then all went into the control room.

During the long flight from Valeron to the First Galaxy no one paid any attention to course or velocity – a handful of cells in the Brain piloted the *Skylark* better than any human intelligence could have done it. Each Norlaminian scientist studied rapturously new vistas of his specialty: Orlon the charted galaxies of the First Universe, Rovol the minutely small particles and waves of the sixth order, Astron the illimitable energies of cosmic radiation, and so on.

Seaton spent day after day with the Brain, computing, calculating, thinking with a clarity and a cogency hitherto impossible, all to one end. What should he do, what *could* he do, with those confounded intellectuals? Crane, Fodan, and Drasnik spent their time in planning the perfect government – planetary, systemic, galactic, universal – for all intelligent races, wherever situated.

Sacner Carfon studied quietly but profoundly with Caslor of Mechanism, adapting many of the new concepts to the needs of his aqueous planet. Dunark and Urvan, their fiery spirits now subdued and strangely awed, devoted themselves as sedulously to the arts and industries of peace as they formerly had to those of war.

Time thus passed quickly, so quickly that, almost before the travelers were aware, the vast planetoid slowed down abruptly to feel her cautious way among the crowded stars of our galaxy. Though a mere crawl in comparison with her inconceivable intergalactic speed, her present pace was such that the stars sped past in flaming lines of light. Past the double sun, one luminary of which had been the planet of the Fenachrone, she flew; past the Central System; past the Dark Mass, whose awful attraction scarcely affected her cosmic-energy drive – hurtling toward Earth and toward Earth's now hated master, DuQuesne.

DuQuesne had perceived the planetoid long since, and his robot-manned ships rushed out into space to do battle with Seaton's new and peculiar craft. But of battle there was none; Seaton was in no mood to trifle. Far below the level of DuQuesne's screens, the cosmic energies directed by the Brain drove unopposed upon the power-bars of the space fleet of Steel and that entire fleet exploded in one space-filling flash of blinding brilliance. Then the *Skylark*, approaching the defensive screens, halted.

'I know that you're watching me, DuQuesne, and I know what you're thinking about, but you can't do it.' Seaton, at the Brain's control, spoke aloud. 'You realize, don't you, that if you clamp on a zone of force it'll throw the Earth out of its orbit?'

'Yes; but I'll do it if I have to,' came back DuQuesne's cold accents. 'I can put it back after I get done with you.'

'You don't know it yet, half-shot, but you are going to do exactly nothing at all!' Seaton snapped. 'You see, I've got a lot of stuff here that you don't know anything about because you haven't had a chance to steal it yet, and I've got you stopped cold. I'm just two jumps ahead of you, all the time. I could hypnotize you right now and make you do anything I say, but I'm not going to – I want you to be wide awake and aware of everything that goes on. Snap on your zone if you want to – I'll see to it that the Earth stays in its orbit. Well, start something, you big, black ape!'

The screens of the *Skylark* glowed redly as a beam carrying the full power of DuQuesne's installations was hurled against them – a beam behind which there was the entire massed output of Steel's world-girdling network of super-power stations. But Seaton's screens merely glowed; they did not radiate even under that titanic thrust. For, as has been said, this new *Skylark* was powered, not by intra-atomic energy, but by cosmic energy. Therefore her screens did not radiate; in fact, the furious blasts of DuQuesne's projectors only increased the stream of power being fed to her receptors and converters.

The mighty shields of the planetoid took every force that DuQuesne could send, then Seaton began to compress his zones, leaving open only the narrow band in the fourth order through which the force of gravitation makes itself manifest. Not only did he leave that band open, he so blocked it open that not even DuQuesne's zones of force, full-driven though they were, could close it.

In their closing those zones brought down over all Earth a pall of darkness of an intensity theretofore unknown. It was not the darkness of any possible night, but the appalling, absolute blackness of the utter absence of every visible wave from every heavenly body. As that unrelieved and unheralded blackness descended, millions of Earth's humanity went mad in unspeakable orgies of fright, of violence, and of crime.

But that brief hour of terror, horrible as it was, can be passed over lightly, for it ended forever any hope of world domination by any self-interested man or group, paving the way as it did for the heartiest possible reception of the government of right instead of by might so soon to be given to Earth's peoples by the sages of Norlamin.

Through the barriers both of mighty spaceship and of embattled planet

Seaton drove his sixth-order projection. Although built to be effective at universal distances the installation was equally efficient at only miles, since its control was purely mental. Therefore Seaton's image, solid and visible, materialized in DuQuesne's inner sanctum – to see DuQuesne standing behind Dorothy's father and mother, a heavy automatic pistol pressed into Mrs Vaneman's back.

'That'll be all from you, I think,' DuQuesne sneered. 'You can't touch me without hurting your beloved parents-in-law and you're too tender-hearted to do that. If you make the slightest move toward me all I've got to do is to touch the trigger. And I shall do that, anyway, right now, if you don't get out of this system and stay out. I am still master of the situation, you see.'

'You are master of nothing, you murderous baboon!'

Even before Seaton spoke the first word his projection had acted. DuQuesne was fast, as has been said, but how fast are the fastest human nervous and muscular reactions when compared with the speed of thought? DuQuesne's retina had not yet registered the fact that Seaton's image had moved when his pistol was hurled aside and he was pinioned by forces as irresistible as the cosmic might from which they sprang.

DuQuesne was snatched into the air of the room – was surrounded by a globe of energy – was jerked out of the building through a welter of crushed and broken masonry and concrete and of flailing, flying structural steel – was whipped through atmosphere, stratosphere, and empty space into the control room of the *Skylark of Valeron*. The enclosing shell of force disappeared and Seaton hurled aside his controlling helmet, for he knew that wave upon wave of passion, of sheer hate, was rising, battering at the very gates of his mind; knew that if he wore that headset one second longer the Brain, actuated by his own uncontrollable thoughts, would passionately but mercilessly exert its awful power and blast his foe into nothingness before his eyes.

Thus at long last the two men, physically so like, so unlike mentally, stood face to face; hard gray eyes staring relentlessly into unyielding eyes of midnight black. Seaton was in a towering rage; DuQuesne, cold and self-contained as ever, was calmly alert to seize any possible chance of escape from his present predicament.

'DuQuesne, I'm telling you something,' Seaton gritted through clenched teeth. 'Prop back your ears and listen. You and I are going out in that projector. You are going to issue "cease firing" orders to all your stations and tell them that you're all washed up – that a humane government is taking things over.'

'Or else?'

'Or else I'll do, here and now, what I've been wanting to do to you ever since you shot up Crane's place that night – I will scatter your component atoms all the way from here to Valeron.'

'But, Dick—' Dorothy began.

'Don't butt in, Dot!' Stern and cold, Seaton's voice was one his wife had never before heard. Never had she seen his face so hard, so bitterly implacable. 'Sympathy is all right in its place, but this is the show-down. The time for dealing tenderly with this piece of mechanism in human form is past. He has needed killing for a long time, and unless he toes the mark quick and careful he'll get it, right here and right now.

'And as for you, DuQuesne,' turning again to the prisoner, 'for your own good I'd advise you to believe that I'm not talking just to make a noise. This isn't a threat, it's a promise – get me?'

'You couldn't do it, Seaton, you're too …' Their eyes were still locked, but into DuQuesne's there had crept a doubt. 'Why, I believe you *would*!' he exclaimed.

'A damned good way to find out is to say no. Yes or no?'

'Yes.' DuQuesne knew when to back down. 'You win – temporarily at least,' he could not help adding.

The projection went out and the required orders were given. Sunlight, moonlight, and starlight again bathed the world in wonted fashion. DuQuesne sat at ease in a cushioned chair, smoking Crane's cigarettes; Seaton stood scowling blackly, hands jammed deep into pockets, addressing the jury of Norlaminians.

'You see what a jam I'm in?' he complained. 'I could be arrested for what I think of that bird. He ought to be killed, but I can't do it unless he gives me about half an excuse, and he's darn careful not to do that. So what?'

'The man has a really excellent brain, but it is slightly warped,' Drasnik offered. 'I do not believe, however, that it is beyond repair. It may well be that a series of mental operations might make of him a worthwhile member of society.'

'I doubt it.' Seaton still scowled. 'He'd never be satisfied unless he was all three rings of the circus. Being a big shot isn't enough – he's got to be Poo-Bah. He's naturally antisocial – he would always be making trouble and would never fit into a really civilized world. He *has* got a wonderful brain; but he isn't human … Say, that gives me an idea!' His corrugated brow smoothed magically, his boiling rage was forgotten.

'Blackie, how would you like to become a pure intellect? A bodiless intelligence, immaterial and immortal, pursuing pure knowledge and pure power throughout all cosmos and all time, in company with seven other such entities?'

'What are you trying to do, kid me?' DuQuesne sneered. 'I don't need any sugar coating on my pills. You are going to take me on a one-way ride – all right, go to it, but don't lie about it.'

'No; I mean it. Remember the one we met in the first *Skylark*? Well, we captured him and six others, and it's a very simple matter to dematerialize you so that you can join them. I'll bring them in, so that you can talk to them yourself.'

The intellectuals were brought into the control room, the stasis of time was released, and DuQuesne – via projection – had a long conversation with One.

'That's the life!' he exulted. 'Better a million times over than any possible life in the flesh – the ideal existence! Think you can do it without killing me, Seaton?'

'Sure can – I know both the words and the music.'

DuQuesne and the caged intellectuals poised in the air, Seaton threw a zone around cage and man, the inner zone of course disappearing as the outer one went on. DuQuesne's body disappeared – but not so his intellect.

'That was the first really bad mistake you ever made, Seaton,' the same sneering, domineering, icily cold DuQuesne informed Seaton's projection in level thought. 'It was bad because you can't ever remedy it – you *can't* kill me now! And now I *will* get you – what's to hinder me from doing anything I please?'

'I am, bucko,' Seaton informed him cheerfully. 'I told you quite a while ago that you'd be surprised at what I could do, and that still goes as it lays. But I'm surprised at your rancor and at the survival of your naughty little passions. What d'you make of it, Drasnik? Is it simply a hangover, or may it be permanent in his case?'

'Not permanent, no,' Drasnik decided. 'It is only that he has not yet become accustomed to his changed state of being. Such emotions are definitely incompatible with pure mentality and will disappear in a short time.'

'Well, I'm not going to let him think, even for a minute, that I slipped up on his case,' Seaton declared. 'Listen, you! If I hadn't been dead sure of being able to handle you I would have killed you instead of dematerializing you. And don't get too cocky about my not being able to kill you yet, either, if it comes to that. It shouldn't be impossible to calculate a zone in which there would be no free energy whatever, so that you would starve to death. But don't worry – I'm not going to do it unless I have to.'

'Just what do you think you *are* going to do?'

'See that miniature spaceship there? I am going to compress you and your new playmates into this spherical capsule and surround you with a stasis of time. Then I am going to send you on a trip. As soon as you are out of the galaxy this bar here will throw in a cosmic-energy drive – not using the power of the bar itself, you understand, but only employing its normal radiation of energy to direct and to control the energy of space – and you will depart for scenes unknown with an acceleration of approximately three times ten to the twelfth centimeters per second. You will travel at that acceleration until this small bar is gone. It will last something more than one hundred thousand million years; which, as One will assure you, is but a moment.

'Then these large bars, which will still be big enough to do the work, will rotate your capsule into the fourth dimension. This is desirable, not only to give you additional distance, but also to destroy any orientation you may have remaining, in spite of the stasis of time and not inconsiderable distance already covered. When and if your capsule gets back into three-dimensional space you will be so far away from here that you will certainly need most of what is left of eternity to find your way back here.' Then, turning to the ancient physicist of Norlamin: 'O.K., Rovol?'

'An exceedingly scholarly bit of work,' Rovol applauded.

'It is well done, son,' majestic Fodan gravely added. 'Not only is it a terrible thing indeed to take away a life, but it is certain that the unknowable force is directing these disembodied mentalities in the engraving upon the Sphere of a pattern which must forever remain hidden from our more limited senses.'

Seaton thought into the headset for a few seconds, then again projected his mind into the capsule.

'All set to go, folks?' he asked. 'Don't take it too hard – no matter how many millions of years the trip lasts, you won't know anything about it. Happy landings!'

The tiny spaceship prison shot away, to transport its contained bodiless intelligences into the indescribable immensities of the superuniverse; of the cosmic all; of that ultimately infinite space which can be knowable, if at all, only to such immortal and immaterial, to such incomprehensibly gigantic mentalities as were theirs.

The erstwhile Overlord and his wife sat upon an ordinary davenport in their own home, facing a fireplace built by human labor, within which nature-grown logs burned crackingly. Dorothy wriggled luxuriously, fitting her gorgeous auburn head even more snugly into the curve of Seaton's shoulder, her supple body even more closely into the embrace of his arm.

'It's funny, isn't it, lover, the way things turn out? Spaceships and ordinary projectors and forces and things are all right, but I'm awfully glad that you turned that horrible Brain over to the Galactic Council in Norlamin and said you'd never build another. Maybe I shouldn't say it, but it's ever so much nicer to have you just a man again, instead of a – well, a kind of a god or something.'

'I'm glad of it, too, Dot – I couldn't hold the pose. When I got so mad at DuQuesne that I had to throw away the headset I realized that I never could get good enough to be trusted with that much dynamite.'

'We're both really human, and I'm glad of it. It's funny, too,' she went on dreamily, 'the way we jumped around and how much we missed. From here across thousands of solar systems to Osnome, and from Norlamin across thousands of galaxies to Valeron. And that we haven't seen either Mars or Venus, our next-door neighbors, and there are lots of places on Earth, right in our own back yard, that we haven't seen yet, either.'

'Well, since we're going to stick around here for a while, maybe we can catch up on our local visitings.'

'I'm glad that you are getting reconciled to the idea; because where you go I go, and if I can't go you can't, either, so you've *got* to stay on Earth for a while, because Richard Ballinger Seaton Junior is going to be born right here, and not off in space somewhere!'

'Sure he is, sweetheart. I'm with you, all the way – you're a blinding flash and a deafening report; and, as I may have intimated previously, I love you.'

'Yes ... and I love you ... it's wonderful, how happy you and I are ... I wish more people could be like us ... more of them will be, too, don't you think, when they have learned what cooperation can do?'

'They're bound to. It'll take time, of course – racial hates and fears cannot be overcome in a day – but the people of good old Earth are not too dumb to learn.'

Auburn head close to brown, they stared into the flickering flames in silence; a peculiarly and wonderfully satisfying silence.

For these two the problems of life were few and small.

SKYLARK DUQUESNE

1

S.O.S.

Appearances are deceiving. A polished chunk of metal that shines like a Christmas-tree ornament may hold – and release – energy to destroy a city. A seed is quite another order of being to the murderous majesty of a toppling tree. A match flame can become a holocaust.

And the chain of events that can unseat the rulers of galaxies can begin in a cozy living room, before a hearth …

Outwardly, the comfortable (if somewhat splendidly furnished) living room of the home of the Richard Ballinger Seatons of Earth presented a peaceful scene. Peaceful? It was sheerly pastoral! Seaton and Dorothy, his spectacularly auburn-haired wife, sat on a davenport, holding hands. A fire of pine logs burned slowly, crackling occasionally and sending sparks against the fine bronze screen of the fireplace. Richard Ballinger Seaton Junior lay on the rug, trying doggedly, silently, and manfully, if unsuccessfully, to wriggle toward those entrancing flames.

Inwardly, however, it was very much otherwise. Dorothy's normally pleasant – as well as beautiful – face wore a veritable scowl.

The dinner they had just eaten had been over two hours late; wherefore not one single item of it had been fit to feed to a pig. Furthermore, and worse, Dick was not relaxed and was not paying any attention to her at all. He was still wound up tight; was still concentrating on the multitude of messages driving into his brain through the button in his left ear – messages of such urgency of drive that she herself could actually read them, even though she was wearing no apparatus whatever.

She reached up, twitched the button out of his ear, and tossed it onto a table. 'Will you please lay off of that stuff for a minute, Dick?' she demanded. 'I'm fed up to the eyeballs with this business of you killing yourself with all time work and no time sleep. You *never* had any such horrible black circles under your eyes before and you're getting positively *scrawny*. You've got to quit it. Can't you let somebody else carry some of the load? Delegate some authority?'

'I'm delegating all I possibly can already, Red-Top.' Seaton absently rubbed his ear. Until Dorothy had flipped it away, the button had been carrying to him a transcription of the taped reports of more than one hundred Planetary Observers from the planet of Norlamin, each with the IQ of an Einstein and the sagacity of an owl. The last report had had to do with plentiful supplies of X metal that had been turned up on a planet of Omicron Eridani, and the decision to dispatch a fleet of cargo-carrying ships to fetch them away.

But he admitted grudgingly to himself that that particular decision had already been made. His wife was a nearer problem. Paying full attention to her now, he put his arm around her and squeezed.

'Converting a whole planet practically all at once to use fourth-, fifth-, and sixth-order stuff is a job of work, believe me. It's all so new and so tough that not too many people can handle any part of it. It takes brains. And what makes it extra tough is that altogether too many people who are smart enough to learn it are crooks. Shysters – hoodlers – sticky-fingers generally. But I think we're just about over the hump. I wouldn't wonder if these Norlaminian Observers – snoopers, really – from the Country of Youth will turn out to be the answer to prayer.'

'They'd better,' she said, darkly. 'At least, *something* had better.'

'Besides, if you think I look like the wrath of God, take a good look at Mart sometime. He's having more grief than I am.'

'I already have; he looks like a refugee from a concentration camp. Peggy was screaming about it this morning, and we're both going to just simply …'

What the girls intended to do was not revealed, for at that moment there appeared in the air before them the projected simulacra of eight green-skinned, more-or-less-human men; the men with whom they had worked so long; the ablest thinkers of the Central System.

There was majestic Fodan, the Chief of the Five of Norlamin; there was white-bearded Orion, the First of Astronomy; Rovol, the First of Rays; Astron, the First of Energy; Drasnik, the First of Psychology; Satrazon and Caslor, the Firsts of Chemistry and of Mechanism, respectively; and – in some ways not the least – there was that powerhouse of thought, Sacner Carfon the two thousand three hundred forty-sixth: the hairless, almost porpoise-like Chief of the Council of the watery planet Dasor. They were not present in the flesh. But their energy projections were as seemingly solid as Seaton's own tall, lean body.

'We come, Overlord of the System, upon a matter of—' the Chief of the Five began.

'*Don't* call me "Overlord". Please.' Seaton broke in, with grim foreboding in his eyes, while Dorothy stiffened rigidly in the circle of his arms. Both knew that those masters of thought could scarcely be prevailed upon to leave their own worlds even via projection. For all eight of them to come *this* far – almost halfway across the galaxy! – meant that something was very wrong indeed.

'I've told you a dozen times, not only I ain't no Overlord but I don't want to be and won't be. I *don't* like to play God – I simply have not got what it takes.'

'"Coordinator", then, which is of course a far better term for all except the more primitive races,' Fodan went imperturbably on. 'We have told you, youth, not a dozen times, but once, which should have been sufficient, that your young and vigorous race possesses qualities that our immensely older peoples no longer have. You, as the ablest individual of your race, are uniquely qualified to serve total civilization. Thus, whenever your services become necessary, you will so serve. Your services have again become necessary. Orion, in whose province the matter primarily lies, will explain.'

Seaton nodded to himself. It was going to be bad, all right, he thought as the First of Astronomy took over.

'You, friend Richard, with some help from us, succeeded in encapsulating a group of malignant immaterial entities, including the disembodied personality of your fellow-scientist Dr Marc C. DuQuesne, in a stasis of time. This capsule, within which no time whatever could or can elapse, was launched into space with a linear acceleration of approximately three times ten to the twelfth centimeters per second squared. It was designed and powered to travel at that acceleration for something over one hundred thousand million Tellurian years; at the end of which lime it was to have been rotated through the fourth dimension into an unknown and unknowable location in normal three-dimensional space.'

'That's right,' Seaton said. 'And it will. It'll do just exactly that. Those pure-intellectual louses are gone for good; and so is Blackie DuQuesne.'

'You err, youth,' corrected the Norlaminian. 'You did not allow us time sufficient to consider and to evaluate all the many factors involved. Rigid analysis and extended computation show that the probability approaches unity that the capsule of stasis will, almost certainly within one Tellurian year of its launching and highly probably in much less time, encounter celestial matter of sufficient density to volatilize its uranium power-bars. This event will of course allow the stasis of time to collapse and the imprisoned immaterial entities will be liberated in precisely the same condition as in the instant of their encapsulation.'

Dorothy Seaton gasped. Even her husband showed that he was shaken. DuQuesne and the Immortals free? But –

'But it *can't?* he fairly yelled the protest. 'It'll dodge – it's built to dodge anything that dense!'

'At ordinary – or even extraordinary – velocities, yes,' the ancient sage agreed, unmoved. 'Its speed of reaction is great, yes; a rather small fraction of a trillionth of a second. That interval of time, however, while small, is very large indeed relative to zero. Compute for yourself, please, what distance that capsule will in theory traverse during that space of time at the end of only one third of one of your years.'

Seaton strode across the room and uncovered a machine that resembled somewhat a small, unpretentious desk calculator.' He picked up a helmet and thought into it briefly; then stared appalled at the figure that appeared on a tape.

'My – aunt's – cat's – kitten's – pants – buttons,' he said, slowly. 'It'd've been smarter, maybe, to've put 'em in orbit around a planetless sun … And I don't suppose there's a Chinaman's chance of catching 'em again that same way.'

'No. Those minds are competent,' agreed the Norlaminian.

'Only one point is clear. You must again activate the *Skylark of Valeron* and again wear its sixth-order controller, since we know of no other entity who either can wear it or should. We eight are here to confer and, on the basis of the few data now available, to plan.'

Seaton scowled in concentration for two long minutes.

It was a measure of the strain that had been working on him that it took that long. As he had said, he was no God, and didn't want to be. He had not gone looking for either conquest or glory. One thing at a time … but that 'one thing' had successively led him across a galaxy, into another dimension, through many a hard and desperate fight against some of the most keen-honed killers of a universe.

His gray eyes hardened. Of all those killers, it was Blackie DuQuesne who posed the greatest threat – to civilization, to Seaton himself, and above all to his wife, Dorothy. DuQuesne at large was deadly.

'All right,' he snapped at last. 'If that's all that's in the wood, I suppose that's the way it'll have to be carved.'

The Norlaminian merely nodded. He, at least, had had no doubts of how Seaton would react to the challenge. Typically, once Seaton had decided speed became of the essence. 'We'll start moving now,' he barked. 'The parameters give us up to a year – *maybe* – but from this minute we act as though DuQuesne and the intellectuals are back in circulation *right now.* So if one of you – Rovol? – will put beams on Mart and Peg and project them over here, we'll get right at it.'

And Dorothy, her face turning so white that a line of freckles stood boldly out across the bridge of her nose, picked the baby up and clasped him fiercely, protectively to her breast.

M. Reynolds ('Martin' or 'Mart') Crane was tall, slender, imperturbable; his black-haired, ivory-skinned wife Margaret was tall and whistle stacked – she and Dorothy were just about of a size and a shape. In a second or two their full working projections appeared, standing in the middle of the room

---

* Dorothy Seaton was highly averse to having the appearance of her living room ruined by office equipment. Seaton, however, was living and working under such high tension that he had to have almost instant access to the *Valeron*'s Brain, at any time of the day or night or wherever he might be. Hence this compromise – inconspicuous machines, each direct-connected to the cubic mile of ultra-miniaturization that was the Brain. E. E. S.

facing the Seatons – projections so exactly true to life and so solid-seeming as to give no indication whatever that they were not composed of fabric and of flesh and bone and blood.

Seaton stood up and half-bowed to Margaret, but wasted no time in getting down to business. 'Hi, Peg – Mart. He briefed you?'

'Up to the moment, yes,' Crane replied.

'You know, then, that some time in the indeterminate but not too distant future all hell is going to be out for noon. Any way I scan it, it looks to me as though, more or less shortly, we're going to be *spurlos versenkt* – sunk without a trace.'

'You err, youth.' Drasnik, the First of Psychology of Norlamin, spoke quite sharply, for him. 'Your thinking is loose, turbid, confused; inexcusably superficial; completely—'

'But you know what their top man said!' Seaton snapped. 'The one they called "One" – and he wasn't kidding, either, believe me!'

'I do, youth. I know more than that, since they visited us long since. They were not exactly "kidding" you, perhaps, but your several various interpretations of One's actual words and actions were inconsistent with any and every aspect of the truth. Those words and actions were in all probability designed to elicit such responses and reaction as would enable him to analyze and classify your race. Having done so, the probability approaches unity that you will not again encounter him or any of his group.'

'My – God!' Dorothy, drawing a tremendously deep breath, put Dick the Small back down on the rug and left him to his own devices. 'That makes sense ... I was scared simply witless.'

'Maybe,' Seaton admitted, 'as far as One and the rest of his original gang are concerned. But there's still DuQuesne. And if Blackie DuQuesne, even as an immaterial pattern of pure sixth-order force, thinks that way about me I'm a Digger Indian.'

'Ah, yes; DuQuesne. One question, please, to clarify my thinking. Can you, do you think, even with the fullest use of all the resources of your *Skylark of Valeron,* release the intact mind from any body?'

'Of course I ... oh, I see what you mean. Just a minute; I think probably I can find out from here.' He went over to his calculator-like instrument, put on a helmet, and stood motionless for a couple of minutes while the great Brain of the machine made its computation. Then, wearing a sheepish grin:

'A flat bust. I not only couldn't, I didn't,' he reported, cheerfully. 'So One not only did the business, but he was good enough to make me *know* that I was doing it. What an operator!' He sobered, thought intensely, then went on, 'So they sucked us in. Played with us.'

'You are now beginning to think clearly, youth,' Drasnik said. 'We come now, then, to lesser probabilities. DuQuesne's mind, of itself, is a mind of power.'

'You can broadcast *that* to the all-attentive universe,' Seaton said. 'Question: how much stuff has he got now? We know he's got the fifth order down solid. Incarnate, he didn't know any more than that. *However,* mind is a pattern of sixth-order force. Knowing what we went through to get the sixth, and that we haven't got it all yet by seven thousand rows of Christmas trees, the first sub-question asks itself: can a free mind analyze itself completely enough to work out and to handle the entire order of force in which it lies?

'We may assume, I think, that One *could* have given DuQuesne full knowledge of the sixth if he felt like it. The second sub-question, then, is; did he? If those questions aren't enough to start with I can think of plenty more.'

'They are enough, youth,' Fodan said. 'You have pointed out the crux. We will now discuss the matter. Since this first phase lies largely in your province, Drasnik, you will now take over.'

The discussion mounted, and grew, and went on and on. Silently Dorothy slipped away, and the projection of force that was Margaret Crane followed her into the kitchen.

There was no need for Dorothy to prepare coffee and sandwiches for her husband, not by hand; one thought into a controller would have produced any desired amount of any desired comestibles. But she wanted something to do. Both girls knew from experience that a conference of this sort might go on for hours; and Dorothy knew that with food placed before him, Seaton would eat; without it, he would never notice the lack.

She did not, of course, prepare anything for the others.

They were not there. Their bodies were at varying distances – a few miles for Crane and his wife, an unthinkable number of parsecs for the Norlaminians and Sacner Carfon. The distance between Earth and the Green System was so unthinkably vast that there was no point in trying to express it in numbers of miles, or even parsecs. The central green sun of the cluster that held Norlamin, Osnome, and Dasor was visible from Earth, all right – in Earth's hugest optical telescopes, as a tiny, 20th-magnitude point – but the light that reached Earth had been on its way for tens of thousands of years before Seaton's ancestors had turned from hunting to agriculture, had taken off their crude skins and begun to build houses, cities, machines, and, ultimately, spaceships.

To all of this Dorothy and Peggy Crane were no strangers; they had been themselves in such projections countless times. If they were more than usually silent, it was not because of the astonishing quality of the meeting that was taking place in the Seatons' living room, but because of the subject of that meeting. Both Dorothy and Peg knew Marc DuQuesne well. Both of them had experienced his cold, impersonal deadliness.

Neither wanted to come close to it again.

Back in the living room, Seaton was saying: 'If One gave DuQuesne all of the sixth-order force patterns, he can be anywhere and can do practically anything. So he probably didn't. On the other hand if One didn't give him any of it DuQuesne couldn't get back here in forty lifetimes. So he probably gave him some of it. The drive and the projector, at least. Maybe as much as we have, to equalize us. Maybe One figured he owed the ape that much. Whatever the truth may be, we've got to assume that DuQuesne knows as much as we do about sixth-order forces.' He paused, then corrected himself. 'If we're smart we'll assume that he knows *more* than we do. So we'll have to find somebody else who knows more than we do to learn from. Question – how do we go about doing that? Not by just wandering around the galaxy at random, looking; that's one certain damn sure thing.'

'It is indeed,' the moderator agreed. 'Sacner Carfon, you have, I think, a contribution to make at this point?'

'I have?' The Dasorian was surprised at first, but caught on quickly. 'Oh – perhaps I have, at that. By using Seaton's power and that of the Brain on the Fodan-Carfon band of the sixth, it will undoubtedly be possible to broadcast a thought that would affect selected mentalities wherever situated in any galaxy of this universe.'

'But listen!' protested Seaton. 'We don't want to *advertise* how dumb we are all over space!'

'Of course not. The thought would be very carefully built and highly selective. It would tell who we are, what we have done, and what we intend and hope to do. It would state our abilities and – by inference, and only to those we seek – our lacks; and would invite all qualified persons and entities to get in touch with us.'

Seaton looked abstracted for a moment. He was thinking. The notion of sending out a beacon of thought was probably a good one – *had* to be a good one – after all, the Norlaminians and Sacner Carfon knew what they were doing. Yet he could see complications. The Fodan-Carfon band of the sixth order was still very new and very experimental. 'Can you make it selective?' he demanded. 'I don't mind telling our prospective friends we need help – I don't want to holler it to our enemies.'

The Dasorian's deep voice chuckled. 'It can not be made selective,' he said. 'The message would of necessity be on such a carrier as to be receivable by any intelligent brain. Yet it can be hedged about with such safeguards, limitations, and compulsions that no one could or would pay attention to it except those who possess at least some ability, overt or latent, to handle the Fodan-Carfon band.'

Seaton whistled through his teeth. 'Wow! And just how are you going to clamp on such controls as *those*? I don't see how anything but magic – sheer, unadulterated, pure black magic – could swing that load.'

'Precisely. Or, rather, imprecisely. It is unfortunate that your term "magic" is so inexcusably loose and carries so many and so deplorable connotations and implications. Shall we design and build the thought we wish to send out?'

The thought was designed and was built; and was launched into space with the inconceivable, the utterly immeasurable velocity of its order of being.

A red-haired stripper called Madlyn Mannis, strutting her stuff in Tampa in Peninsula Florida, felt it and almost got it; but, not being very strongly psychic, shrugged it off and went on about the business of removing the last sequin-bedecked trifle of her costume. And, as close to the dancer as plenteous baksheesh could arrange for, a husky, good-looking young petrochemical engineer named Charles K. van der Gleiss felt a thrill like nothing he had ever felt before – but ascribed it, naturally enough, to the fact that this was the first time he had ever seen Madlyn Mannis dance. And in Washington, D.C., one Doctor Stephanie de Marigny, a nuclear physicist, pricked up her ears, tightened the muscles of her scalp, and tried for two full minutes to think of something she *ought* to think of but couldn't.

Out past the Green System the message sped, and past the dust and the incandescent gas that had once been the noisome planet of the Fenachrone. Past worlds where amphibians roared and bellowed; past planets of methane ice where crystalline life brooded sluggishly on its destiny.

In the same infinitesimal instant it reached and passed the Rim Worlds of our galaxy; touching many minds but really affecting none. Farther and farther out, with no decrease whatever in speed, it flew; past the inconceivably tiny, inconceivably fast-moving point that housed the seven greatest, most fearsome minds that the Macrocosmic All had ever spawned – minds that, knowing all about that thought already, ignored it completely.

Immensely farther out, it flashed through the galaxy in which was the solar system of Ray-See-Nee – where, for the first time, it made solid contact with a mind in a body human to the limit of classification. Kay-Lee Barlo, confidential secretary of Department Head Bay-Lay Boyn, stiffened so suddenly that she stuttered into her microphone and had to erase three words from a tape – and in that same instant her mother at home went into deep trance.

And still farther out, in a galaxy lying on the universe's Arbitrary Rim, in the Realm of the Llurdi, the message found a much larger group of receivers. While none of the practically enslaved Jelmi could do much of anything about that weirdly peculiar and inexplicably guarded thought, many of them were very much interested in it; particularly Valkyrie-like Sennlloy, a native of the planet Allondax and the master biologist of all known space; ancient Tammon, the greatest genius of the entire Jelman race; and newlyweds Mergon and Luloy, the Mallidaxian savants.

None of the monstrous Llurdi – not even their most monstrous 'director', Klazmon the Fifteenth – being monstrous – could receive the message in any part. And how well that was! For if those tremendously able aliens could have received that message, could have understood it and acted upon it, how vastly different the history of all humanity would have been!

2

Llurdi and Jelmi

The distance from Earth to the Realm of the Llurdi is such that it is worthwhile to take a moment to locate it in space.

It has been known for a long time that solar systems occur in lenticular aggregations called galaxies; each galaxy consisting of one or more thousands of millions of solar systems. And for almost as long a time, since no definite or systematic arrangement of the galaxies could be demonstrated, the terms 'Universe' and 'Cosmic All' were interchangeable; each meaning the absolute totality of all matter and all space in existence anywhere and everywhere.

There had been speculations, of course, that galaxies were arranged in lentictilar universes incomprehensibly vast in size, so that the term 'Cosmic All' should be reserved for a plurality of universes and a hyper-space of more than three spatial dimensions.

Seaton and Crane in the *Skylark of Valeron* proved that our galaxy, the Milky Way, lies in a lenticular universe by charting every galaxy in that universe. And they suggested to the various learned societies that the two celestial aggregates should be named, respectively, the First Galaxy and the First Universe.

Many millions of parsecs distant from Tellus and its First Galaxy, then, out near the Arbitrary Rim of the First Universe, there lay the Realm of the Llurdi. This Realm, which had existed for over seventy thousand Tellurian years, was made up of four hundred eighty-two planets in exactly half that many solar systems.

Two planets in each populated system were necessary because the population of the Realm was composed of two entirely different forms of highly intelligent life. Of these two races the Jelmi – the subject race, living practically in vassalage – were strictly human beings and lived on strictly Tellus-type worlds.

The master race, the Llurdi, had originated upon the harsh and hostile planet Llurdiax – Llurdiaxorb Five – with its distant, wan, almost-never-seen sun and its incessant gales of frigid, ice-laden, ammonia – and methane-impregnated, forty-pounds-to-the-square-inch air. Like mankind, they wore clothing against the rigors of their environment. Unlike mankind, however, they wore clothes only for protection, and only when protection was actually necessary. Nor was Llurdiax harsh or forbidding – to them.

It was the best of all possible worlds. They would not colonize any planet that was not as nearly as possible like the mother world of their race.

Llurdi, although they are erect, bifurcate, bi-laterally symmetrical, bi-sexual, mammalian, and have a large crania and six-digited hands each having two opposed thumbs, are not humanoids. Nor, despite their tremendous, insensitive, un-freezable wings, are they either birds or bats. Nor flying cats, although they have huge, vertically slitted eyes and needle-sharp canine teeth that protrude well below and above their upper and lower lips. Also, they have immensely strong and highly versatile tails; but there is nothing simian about them or in their ancestry.

The Realm was not exactly an empire. Nor was Llanzlan Klazmon the Fifteenth exactly an emperor. The title 'Llanzlan' translates, as nearly as possible, into 'Director'; and that was what Klazmon regarded himself as being.

It is true that what he said, went; and that if he didn't like any existing law he expunged it from all existence. But that was exactly the way things should be. How else could optimum conditions be achieved and maintained in an ever-expanding, ever-changing, ever-rising economy? He ruled, he said and thoroughly believed, with complete reason and perfect fairness and strictly in accordance with the findings of the universe's largest and most competent computers as to what was for the best good of all.

Wherefore everyone who did not agree with him was – automatically, obviously, and unquestionably – wrong.

Llurdias, the capital city of the world Llurdiax and of the Realm, had a population of just over ten million and covered more than nine hundred square miles of ground. At its geometrical center towered the mile-square, half-mile-high office-residence-palace (the Llurdan word 'Uanzlanate' has no Tellurian equivalent) of Llanzlan Klazmon the Fifteenth of the Realm of the Llurdi. And in that building's fifth sub-basement, in Hall Prime of Computation, Klazmon and his Board of Advisors were hard at work.

That vast room, the first receptor of all the reports of the Realm, was three-quarters full of receivers, recorders, analyzers – bewilderingly complex instrumentation of all kinds. From most of these devices tapes were issuing – tapes that, en route to semi-permanent storage, were being monitored by specialists in the hundreds of different fields of the Llurdan-Jelmi economy.

Klazmon the Fifteenth and his Board, seated at a long conference table in hard-upholstered 'chairs' shaped to fit the Llurdan anatomy, were paying no attention to routine affairs.

'I have called this meeting,' the ruler said, 'to decide what can be done to alleviate an intolerable situation. As you all know, we live in what could be called symbiosis with the Jelmi; who are so unstable, so illogical, so bird-brained generally that they would destroy themselves in a century were it not for our gentle but firm insistence that they conduct themselves in all matters for their own best good. This very instability of their illogical minds, however, enables them to arrive occasionally at valid conclusions from insufficient data; a thing that no logical mind can do. These conclusions – they are intuitions, really – account for practically all the advancement we Llurdi have made and explain why we have put up with the Jelmi – yes, cherished them – so long.'

He paused, contemplating the justice of the arrangement he had just described. It did not occur to him that it could in any way be described as 'wrong'.

He went on: 'What most of you do not know is that intuitions of any large worth have become less and less frequent, decade by decade, over the last few centuries. It was twelve years ago that the Jelm Jarxon elucidated the "Jarxon" band of the sixth order, and no worthwhile intuition has been achieved since that time. Beeloy, has your more rigorous analysis revealed any new fact of interest?'

A young female stood up, preened the short fur back of her left ear with the tip of her tail, and said, 'No, sir. Logic can not be applied to illogic. Statistical analysis is still the only possible tool and it cannot be made to apply to the point in question, since it is incapable of certainty and since the genius-type mind occurs in only one out of thousands of millions of Jelmi. I found a very high probability, however – point nine nine nine plus – that the techniques set up by our ancestors are wrong. In breeding for contentment by destroying the discontented we are very probably breeding out the very characteristics we wish to encourage.'

'Thank you, Beeloy. That finding was not unanticipated. Kalton, your report on Project University, please.'

'Yes, sir.' An old male, so old that his fur was almost white, stood up. 'Four hundred males and the same number of females, the most intelligent and most capable Jelmi alive, were selected and were brought here to the Llanzla-nate. They were put into quarters that were Jelm-type in every respect, even to gravity. They were given every inducement and every facility to work-study and to breed.

'First, as to work-study. They have done practically nothing except waste time. They seem to devote their every effort to what they call "escape" by means of already-well-known constructions of the fifth and sixth orders – all of which are of course promptly negated. See for yourselves what these insanely illogical malcontents are doing and know for yourselves that, in its present form, Project University is a failure as far as producing intuitions is concerned.'

Kalton picked up a fist-sized instrument between the thumbs of his left hand and a tri-di 'tank' appeared on the table's top, in plain sight of every member of the Board. Then, as he began to finger controls, a three-dimensional scene in true color appeared in the tank; a smoothly flowing, ever-shifting scene that moved from room to room and from place to place as the point of view traversed the vast volume of the prison.

It did not look like a prison. The apartments, of which there were as many as the Jelmi wanted, were furnished as luxuriously as the various occupants desired; with furniture and equipment every item of which had been selected by each occupant himself or herself. There were wonderful rugs and hangings; masterpieces of painting and of sculpture; triumphs of design in fireplaces and tables and chairs and couches. Each room or suite could be set up for individual control of gravity, temperature, pressure, and humidity. Any imaginable item of food or drink was available on fifteen seconds' notice at any hour of the day or night.

In the magnificent laboratories every known or conceivable piece of apparatus could be had for the asking; the memory banks of the library would furnish in seconds any item of information that had been stored in any one of them during all seventy thousand years of the Realm's existence.

And there were fully equipped game and exercise rooms, ranging in size from tiny card-rooms up to a full-sized football field, to suit every Jelman need or desire for play or for exercise.

But not one of the hundreds of Jelmi observed – each one a perfect specimen physically, as was plainly revealed by the complete absence of clothing – appreciated any one of these advantages! Most of the laboratories were vacant and dark. The few scientists who were apparently at work were not doing anything that made sense. The library was not in use at all; the Jelmi who were reading anything were reading works of purely Jelman authorship – mostly love stories, murder mysteries, and science fiction. Many Jelmi seemed to be busy but their activities were as pointless as cutting out paper dolls.

'The pale, frail, practically hairless, repulsive, incomplete, illogical, and insane animals refuse steadfastly to cooperate with us on my level.'

Any Earthman so frustrated would have snarled the sentence, but the Llurd merely stated it as a fact. 'You can all see for yourselves that as far as productive work is ... but hold!'

The viewpoint stopped moving and focused sharply on a young man and a young woman who, bending over a table, were working on two lengths of smooth yellow material that looked something like varnished cambric. 'Mergon and Luloy of planet Mallidax,' Kalton said into the microphone. 'What are you doing? Why are you so far away from your own laboratories?'

Mergon straightened up and glared at what he thought was the point of origin of the voice. 'If it's any of your business, funnyface, which it isn't,' he said savagely, 'I'm building a short-long whatsit, and Luloy has nothing to do with it. When I get it done I'm personally going to tear your left leg off and beat you to death with the bloody end of it.'

'You see?' Kalton dispassionately addressed the other members of the Board. 'That reaction is typical.'

He manipulated controls and both Jelmi leaped to their feet, with all four hands pressed to their buttocks. The fact that Luloy was a woman – scarcely more than a girl, in fact – was of no consequence at all to Kalton. Even Llurdan sex meant very little to the Llurdi. Jelman sex meant nothing whatever.

'Nerve-whip,' Kalton explained to his fellows. He dropped his controller into his lap and the tri-di tank vanished. 'Nothing serious – only slightly painful and producing only a little ecchymosis and extravasation. Neither of those two beasts, however, will be at all comfortable until they get back where they belong. Now, to continue my report:

'So much for failure to work-study. Failure-refusal to breed, while not possible of such simple and easy demonstration, is no less actual, effective, and determined. A purely emotional, non-logical, and ridiculous factor they call "love" seems to be involved, as does their incomprehensibly exaggerated, inexplicable craving for "liberty" or "freedom".'

The Llanzlan said thoughtfully. 'But surely, unwillingness to breed cannot possibly affect the results of artificial insemination?'

'It seems to, sir. Definitely. There is some non-physical and non-logical, but nevertheless powerful, operator involved. My assistants and I have not been able to develop any techniques that result in any except the most ephemeral pregnancies.'

'You apparently wish to comment, Velloy?' Klazmon asked.

'I certainly do!' a middle-aged female snapped, giving one tautly outstretched wing a resounding whack with her tail. 'Of course they haven't! As Prime Sociologist I said five years ago and I repeat now that no mind of the quality of those of the Jelmi here in the Uanzlanate can be coerced by any such gross physical means. Kalton talks of them and thinks of them as animals – meaning lower animals. I said five years ago and still say that they are not. Their minds, while unstable and completely illogical and in many instances unsane to the point of insanity, are nevertheless minds of tremendous power. I told this Board five years ago that the only way to make that project work – to cause selected Jelmi to produce either ideas or young or both – was to give the selectees a perfect illusion of complete freedom, and I recommended that course of action. Since I could not prove my statement mathematically, my recommendation was rejected. While I still cannot prove that statement, it is still my considered opinion that it is true; and I now repeat both statement and recommendation. I will keep on repeating them at every opportunity as long as this Board wastes time by not accepting them. I remind you that you have already wasted – lost – over five years.'

'Your statement becomes more probable year by year,' the Llanzlan admitted. 'Kalton, have you anything more to say?'

'Very little. Only that, since Project University has admittedly failed, we should of course adopt—'

Kalton was silenced in mid-sentence by a terrific explosion, which was followed by a rumbling crash as half of one wall of the hall collapsed inward.

A volume of Jelman air rushed in, enveloping a purposeful company of Jelmi in yellow coveralls and wearing gasmasks. Some of these invaders were shooting pistols; some were using or throwing knives; but all were covering and protecting eight Jelmi who were launching bombs at one great installation of sixth-order gear – the computer complex that was the very nerve center of the entire Realm.

For the Jelmi – who, as has been said, were human to the last decimal of classification – had been working on fifth- and sixth-order devices purely as a blind; their real effort had been on first-order effects so old that their use had been all but forgotten.

The Jelman plan was simple: Thirty men and thirty women would destroy the central complex of the computer system of the entire Realm. Then, if possible, the survivors of the sixty would join their fellows in taking over an already-selected Llurdan scout cruiser and taking off at max.

It was quite probable that many or even most of the attacking sixty would die. It was distinctly possible that they all would. All sixty, however, were perfectly willing to trade their lives for that particular bank of sixth-order apparatus, in order that seven hundred forty other Jelmi could escape from Llurdiax and, before control could be re-established, be beyond their masters' reach.

Theoretically, the first phase of the operation should have been successful; the Realm's nerve center should have been blown to unrecognizable bits. The Jelmi knew exactly what they were going to do, exactly how they were going to do it, and exactly how long it would take. They knew that they would have the advantage of complete surprise. There would be, they were sure, half a second or so of the paralysis of shock, followed by at least one second of utter confusion; which would give them plenty of time.

They were sure it would be as though, during a full-formal session of the Supreme Court, a gang of hoodlums should blast down a wall and come leaping into the courtroom with Tommy-guns ablaze and with long knives flying and stabbing and slashing. Grave, stately, and thoughtful, the justices could not possibly react fast enough to save their lives or their records or whatever else it was that the gangsters were after.

The Jelmi, however, had never seen any Llurd in emergency action; did not know or suspect how nearly instantaneous the Llurdan speed of reaction was; did not realize that a perfectly logical mind can not be surprised by any happening, however unusual or however outrageous.

Thus:

Yelling, shooting, throwing, stabbing, slashing, the men and women of the Jelmi rushed into battle; to be met – with no paralysis and no confusion and no loss of time whatever – by buffeting wings, flailing tails, tearing teeth, and hard, highly skilled hands and fists and feet.

Many machine operators, as agile in the air as bats, met the bombs in mid-air and hurled them out into and along the corridor through the already-breached wall, where they exploded harmlessly. Harmlessly, that is, except for a considerable increase in the relatively unimportant structural damage already wrought.

Two knives were buried to their hilts in the huge flying muscles of the Llanzlan's chest. His left wing hung useless, its bones shattered by bullets. So did his right arm. Nevertheless, he made it at speed to his console – and the battle was over.

Beams of force lashed out, immobilizing the human beings where they stood. Curtains of force closed in, pressing the Jelmi together into a tightly packed group. An impermeable membrane of force confined all the Jelman air and whatever Llurdan atmosphere had been mixed with it.

The Llanzlan, after glancing at his own wounds and at the corps of surgeons already ministering to his more seriously wounded fellows, resumed his place at the conference table.

He said, 'This meeting will resume. The places of those department heads who died will be taken by their first assistants. All department heads are hereby directed to listen, to note, and to act. Since Project University has failed, it is to be closed out immediately. All Jelmi – I perceive that none of those present is dead, or even seriously wounded – will be put aboard the ship in which they intended to leave Llurdiax. They will be given all the supplies, apparatus, and equipment that they care to requisition and will be allowed to take off for any destination they please.'

He glanced at the captured Jelmi, imprisoned in their force-bubble of atmosphere. To them it reeked of methane and halogens, but they stood proudly and coldly listening to what he said.

He dismissed them from his mind and said, 'A recess will now be taken so that those of us who are wounded may have our wounds dressed. After that we will consider in detail means of inducing the Jelmi to resume the production of breakthroughs in science.'

3

Free (?)

Some hours later, far out in deep space, the ex-Llurdan scout cruiser – now named the *Mallidax,* after the most populous Jelman planet of the Realm – bored savagely through the ether. Its crew of late revolutionaries, still dazed by the fact that they were still alive, recuperated in their various ways.

In one of the larger, more luxurious cabins Luloy of Mallidax lay prone on a three-quarter-size-bed, sobbing convulsively, uncontrollably. Her left eye was swollen shut. The left side of her face and most of her naked body bore livid black and blue bruises – bruises so brutally severe that the marks of Kalton's sense-whip punishment, incurred earlier for insubordination, were almost invisible. A dozen bandages showed white against the bronzed skin of her neck and shoulders and torso and arms and legs.

'Oh, snap out of it, Lu, *please!*' Mergon ordered, almost brusquely. He was a burly youth with crew-cut straw-colored hair; and he, too, showed plenty of evidence of having been to the wars. He had even more bruises and bandages than she did. 'Don't claim that you wanted to be a martyr any more than I did. And they can engrave it on a platinum plaque that I'm damned glad to get out of that fracas alive.'

Stopping her crying by main strength, the girl hauled herself up into a half-sitting position and glared at the man out of her one good eye.

'You ... you clod!' she stormed. 'It isn't that at all! And you know it as well as I do. It's just that we ... they ... he ... not a single *one* of them so much as ... why, we might just as well have been merely that many mosquitoes – midges – worse, exactly that many perfectly innocuous saprophytic bacilli.'

'Exactly,' he agreed, sourly, and her glare changed to a look almost of surprise. 'That's precisely what we were. It's humiliating, yes. It's devastating and it's frustrating. We tried to hit the Llurdi where it hurt, and they ignored us. Agreed. I don't like it a bit better than you do; but caterwauling and being sorry for yourself isn't going to help matters a—'

'*Caterwauling!* Being *sorry* for myself! If *that's* what you think, you can—'

'Stop it, Lu!' he broke in sharply, 'before I have to spank your fanny to a rosy blister!'

She threw up her head in defiance; then what was almost a smile began to quirk at the corners of her battered mouth. 'You can't, Merg,' she said, much more quietly than she had said anything so far. 'Look – it's all red, green, blue, yellow, and black already. That last panel I bounced off of was no pillow, friend.'

'Llenderllon's favor, sweetheart!' Bending over, he kissed her gingerly, then drew a deep breath of relief. 'You scared me like I don't know when I've been scared before,' he admitted. 'We need you too much – and I love you too much – to have you go off the deep end now. Especially now, when for the first time in our lives we're in position to do something.'

'Such as what?' Luloy's tone was more lifeless than skeptical. 'How many of our whole race are worth saving, do you think? How many Jelmi of all our worlds can be made to believe that their present way of life is anything short of perfection?'

'Very few, probably,' Mergon conceded. 'As of now. But –'

He paused, looking around their surroundings. The spaceship, which had once been one of the Llurdi's best, might have a few surprises for them. It was a matter for debate whether the Llurdi might not have put concealed spy devices in the rooms. On balance, however, Mergon thought not. The Llurdi operated on grander scales than that.

He said, 'Luloy, listen. We tried to fight our way to freedom by attacking the Llurdi right where it hurts, in the center of their power. We lost the battle. But we have what we were fighting for, don't we? Why do you think they let us go, perfectly free?'

Luloy's eye brightened a little, but not too much. 'That's plain enough. Since they couldn't make us produce either new theories or children in captivity, they're giving us what they *say* is complete freedom, so that we'll produce both. How stupid do they think we are? How stupid can they get? If we could have wrecked their long eyes, yes, we could have got away clean to a planet in some other galaxy, way out of their range; but now? If I know anything at all, it's that they'll hold a tracer beam – so weak as to be practically undetectable, of course – on us forever.'

'I think you're right,' Mergon said, and paused. Luloy looked at him questioningly and he went on, 'I'm sure you are, but I don't think it's us they are aiming at. They're probably taking the long view – betting that, with a lifelong illusion of freedom, we'll have children of our own free will.'

Luloy nodded thoughtfully. 'And we would,' she said, definitely. 'All of us would. For, after all, if we on this ship all die childless what chance is there that any other Jelmi will try it again for thousands of years? And our children would have a chance, even if we never have another.'

'True. But on the other hand, how many generations will it take for things now known to be facts to degenerate into myths? To be discredited completely, in spite of the solidest records we can make as to the truth and the danger?'

Luloy started to gnaw her lip, but winced sharply and stopped the motion. 'I see what you mean. Inevitable. But you don't seem very downcast about it, so you have an idea. Tell me, quick!'

'Yes, but I'm just hatching it; I haven't mentioned it even to Tammon yet, so I don't know whether it will work or not. At present a sixth-order breakthrough can't be hidden from even a very loose surveillance. Right?'

By now Luloy's aches and pains were forgotten. Eyes bright, she nodded. 'You're so right. Do *you* think one can be? Possibly? How?'

'By finding a solar system somewhere whose inhabitants know so much more than we do that the emanations of their sixth-order installations continuously or regularly at work will mask those of any full-scale tests we want to make. There *must* be some such race, somewhere in this universe. The Llurdi charted this universe long ago – they call it U-Prime – and I requisitioned copies of all the tapes. Second: the Llurdi are all strictly logical. Right?'

'That's right,' the girl agreed. 'Strictly. Insanely, almost, you might say.'

'So my idea is to do something as illogical as possible. They think we'll head for a new planet of our own; either in this galaxy or one not too far away. So we won't. We'll drive at absolute max for the center of the universe, with the most sensitive feelers we have full out for very strong sixth-order emanations. En route, we'll use every iota of brain-power aboard this heap in developing some new band of the sixth, being mighty careful to use so little power that the ship's emanations will mask it. Having found the hiding-place we want, we'll tear into developing and building something, not only that the Llurdi haven't got, but a thing that by use of which we can burst Llanzlan Klazmon the Fifteenth loose from his wings and tail – and through which he can't fight back. So, being absolutely – stupidly – logical about everything, what would His Supreme Omnipotence do about it?'

Luloy thought in silence for a few seconds, then tried unsuccessfully to whistle through battered, swollen lips. 'Oh, boy!' she exclaimed, delightedly. 'Slug him with a thing like that – demonstrate superiority – and the battle is over. He'll concede us everything we want, full equality, independence, you name it, without a fight – without even an argument!'

Grinning, Mergon caught her arm and led her out of the room. Throughout the great hulk of the Llurd spaceship the other battered Jelmi veterans were beginning to stir. To each of them, Mergon explained his plan and from each came the same response. 'Oh, boy!'

They began at once setting up their work plans.

The first project was to find – somewhere! – a planet generating sufficient sixth-order forces to screen what they were going to do. In the great vastnesses of the Over-Universe there were many such planets. They could have chosen that which was inhabited by Norlaminian or Dasorian peoples. They could have chosen one of a score which were comparatively nearby. They, in fact, ultimately chose and set course for the third planet of a comparatively small G-type star known to its people as Tellus, or Earth.

They could have given many reasons why this particular planet had been selected.

None of these reasons would have included the receipt of the brief pulse of telepathic communication which none of them, any longer, consciously remembered.

And back on Llurdiax the Llanzlan followed the progress of the fleeing ship of Jelm rebels with calm perception.

His great bat wings were already mending, even as the scars of the late assault on his headquarters were already nearly repaired by a host of servo-mechanisms. Deaf to the noise and commotion of the repairs, heedless of the healing wounds which any human would have devoted a month in bed to curing, the Llanzlan once again summoned his department heads and issued his pronouncement:

'War, being purely destructive, is a product of unsanity. The Jelmi are, however, unsane; many of them are insane. Thus, if allowed to do so, they commit warfare at unpredictable times and for incomprehensible, indefensible, and/ or whimsical reasons. Nevertheless, since the techniques we have been employing have been proven ineffective and therefore wrong, they will now be changed. During the tenure of this directive no more Jelmi will be executed or castrated: in fact, a certain amount of unsane thinking will not merely be tolerated but encouraged, even though it lead to the unsanity termed "war". It should not, however, be permitted to exceed that quantity of "war" which would result in the destruction of, let us say, three of their own planets.

'This course will entail a risk that we, as the "oppressors" of the Jelmi, will be attacked by them. The magnitude of this risk – the probability of such an attack – cannot be calculated with the data now available. Also, these data are rendered even less meaningful by the complete unpredictability of the actions of the group of Jelmi released from study here.

'It is therefore directed that all necessary steps be taken particularly in fifth- and sixth-order devices, that no even theoretically possible attack on this planet will succeed.

'This meeting will now adjourn.'

It did; and within fifteen minutes heavy construction began – construction that was to go on at a pace and on a scale and with an intensity of drive theretofore unknown throughout the Realm's long history. Whole worldlets were destroyed, scavenged for their minerals, their ores smelted in giant atomic space-borne foundries and cast and shaped into complex machines of offense and defense. Delicate networks of radiation surrounded every Jelm and Llurd world, ready to detect, trace, report, and home on any artifact whatsoever which might approach them. Weapons capable of blasting moons out of orbit slipped into position in great latticework spheres of defensive emplacements.

The Llurdi were preparing for anything.

Llurdan computations were never wrong. Computers, however, even Llurdan computers, are not really smart – they can't really think. Unlike the human brain, they can not arrive at valid conclusions from insufficient data. In fact, they don't even try to. They stop working and say – in words or by printing or typing or by flashing a light or by ringing a bell – 'DATA INSUF-FICIENT': and then continue to do nothing until they are fed additional information.

Thus, while the Llanzlan and his mathematicians and logicians fed enough data into their machines to obtain valid conclusions, there were many facts that no Llurd then knew. And thus those conclusions, while valid, were woe-fully incomplete; they did not cover all of actuality by far.

For, in actuality, there had already begun a chain of events that was to ren-der those mighty fortresses precisely as efficacious against one certain type of attack as that many cubic miles of sheerest vacuum.

4

Llurdi and Fenachrone

The type of attack which was about to challenge the Llurdi was from a source no civilized human would have believed still existed.

If Richard Seaton, laboring at Earth's own defenses uncountable parsecs away, had been told of it, he would flatly have declared the story a lie. He ought to know, he would have said. That particular danger to the harmony of the worlds had long since been destroyed … and he was the man who had destroyed it!

When the noisome planet of the Fenachrone was destroyed it was taken for granted that Ravindau and his faction of the Party of Postponement of Universal Conquest, who had fled from the planet just before its destruction, were the last surviving members of their monstrous race. When they in turn were destroyed it was assumed that no Fenachrone remained alive.

That assumption was wrong. There was another faction of the Party of Postponement much larger than Ravindau's, much more secretive, and much better organized.

Its leader, one Sleemet, while an extremely able scientist, had taken life-long pains that neither his name nor his ability should become known to any except a select few. He was as patriotic as was any other member of his race; he believed as implicitly as did any other that the Fenachrone should and one day would rule not only this one universe, but the entire Cosmic All. However, he believed, and as firmly, that The Day should not be set until the probability of success of the project should begin to approach unity as a limit.

According to Sleemet's exceedingly rigorous analysis, the time at which success would become virtually certain would not arrive for at least three hundred Fenachronian years.

From the day of Fenor's accession to the throne Sleemet had been grimly certain that this Emperor Fenor – headstrong, basically ignorant, and inordinately prideful even for an absolute monarch of the Fenachrone – would set The Day during his own reign; centuries before its proper time.

Therefore, for over fifty years, Sleemet had been preparing for exactly the eventuality that came about, and:

Therefore, after listening to only a few phrases of the ultimatum given to Emperor Fenor by Sacner Carfon of Dasor, speaking for the Overlord Seaton and his Forces of Universal Peace, Sleemet sent out his signal and:

Therefore, even before Ravindau's forces began to board their single vessel Sleemet's fleet of seventeen superdreadnoughts was out in deep space, blasting at full-emergency fifth-order cosmic-energy drive away from the planet so surely doomed.

Surely doomed? Yes. Knowing vastly more about the sixth order than did any other of his race, he was the only one of his race who knew anything about the Overlord of the Central System; of who and what that Overlord was and of what that Overlord had done. He, Sleemet, did not want any part of Richard Ballinger Seaton. Not then or ever.

Curse Fenor's abysmal stupidity! Since a whole new Fenachrone planet would now have to be developed, the Conquest could not be begun for *more* than three hundred years!

While Sleemet knew much more about the sixth order than Ravindau did, he did not have the sixth-order drive and it took him and his scientists and engineers several months to develop and to perfect it. Thus their fleet was still inside the First Galaxy when they finally changed drives and began really to travel – on a course that, since it was laid out to reach the most distant galaxies of the First Universe, would of necessity lie within two and a quarter hundreds of thousands of light-years of the galaxy in which the Realm of the Llurdi lay.

As has been intimated, the Llurdi were literal folk. When any Llanzlan issued a directive he meant it literally, and it was always as literally carried out.

Thus, when Llanzlan Klazmon ordered the construction of an installation of such a nature that 'no even theoretically possible attack on this planet will succeed' he meant precisely that – and that was precisely what was built. Nor, since the Llurdi had full command of the fourth and fifth orders, and some sixth-order apparatus as well, was the task overlong in the doing.

The entire one-hundred-six-mile circumference of Llurdias and a wide annulus outside the city proper were filled with tremendous fortresses; each of which was armed and powered against any contingency to which Computer Prime – almost half a cubic mile of miniaturization packed with the accumulated knowledges and happenings of some seventy thousand years – could assign a probability greater than point zero zero zero one.

Each of those fortresses covered five acres of ground; was low and flat. Each was built of super-hard, super-tough, super-refractory synthetic. Each had twenty-seven high-rising, lightning-rod-like spikes of the same material. Fortress-shell and spikes through closed spaced cast-in tubes and the entire periphery of each fortress, as well as dozens of interior relief-points, went deep into constantly water-soaked, heavily salted ground. Each fortress sprouted scores of antennae – parabolic, box, flat, and straight – and scores of heavily insulated projectors of shapes to be defined only by a professional mathematician of solid geometry.

And *how* the Llurdan detectors could now cover space! The Jelm Mergon, long before his abortive attempt to break jail, had developed a miniaturized monitor station that could detect, amplify, and retransmit on an aimed tight beam any fifth- or sixth-order signal from and to a distance of many kiloparsecs.

Hundreds of these 'mergons' were already out in deep space. Now mergons were being manufactured in lots of a thousand, and in their thousands they were being hurled outward from Llurdiax, to cover – by relays *en cascade* – not only the Llurdan galaxy and a great deal of intergalactic space, but also a good big chunk of inter-universal space as well.

The Fenachrone fleet bored on through inter-galactic space at its distance-devouring sixth-order pace. Its fourth-, fifth-, and sixth-order detector webs fanned out far – 'far' in the astronomical sense of the word – ahead of it. They were set to detect, not only the most tenuous cloud of gas, but also any manifestation whatever upon any of the known bands of any of those orders. Similar detectors reached out to an equal distance above and below and to the left of and to the right of the line of flight; so that the entire forward hemisphere was on continuous web of ultra-tenuous but ultra-sensitive detection.

And, as that fleet approached a galaxy lying well to 'starboard' – the term was still in use aboard ship except for matters of record, since the direction of action of artificial gravity, whatever its actual direction, was always 'down' – two sets of detectors tripped at once.

The squat and monstrous officer on watch reported this happening instantly, of course, to Sleemet himself; and of course Sleemet himself went instantly into action. He energized his flagship's immense fifth-order projector.

Those detections could have only one meaning. There was at least one solar system in that galaxy peopled by entities advanced enough to work with forces of at least the fifth order. They should be destroyed – that is, he corrected himself warily, unless they were allied with or belonged to that never-to-be-sufficiently-damned Overlord of the Central System of the First Galaxy … But no, at this immense distance the probability of that was vanishingly small.

They might, however, have weapons of the sixth. The fact that there were no such devices in operation at the moment did not preclude that possibility.

Very unlike the late unlamented Fenor, he, First Scientist Sleemet, was not stupidly and arrogantly sure that the Fenachrone were in fact the ablest, most intelligent, and most powerful race of beings in existence. He would investigate, of course. But he would do it cautiously.

The working projections of the Fenachrone were tight patterns of force mounted on tight beams. Thus, until they began to perform exterior work, they were virtually undetectable except by direct interception and hard-driven specific taps. Sleemet knew this to be a fact; whether the projection was on, above, or below the target planet's surface and even though that planet was so far away that it would take light hundreds of centuries to make the one-way trip.

The emanations of his vessels' sixth-order cosmic-energy drive, however, were very distinctly something else. They could not be damped out or masked and they could be detected very easily by whoever or whatever it was that was out there … Yes, an exploration would not change matters at all …

As a matter of fact, the Fenachrone Fleet's emanations had been detected a full two seconds since.

A far-outpost mergon had picked them up and passed them along to a second, which in turn had relayed them inward to its Number Three, which finally had delivered them to Computer Prime on incredibly distant Llurdiax.

There, in Hall Prime of Computation, a section supervisor had flicked the switch that had transferred the unusual bit of information to his immediate superior, Head Supervisor Klaton – who had at sight of it gone into a tizzy (for a Llurd) of worrying his left ear with the tip of his tail. He stared at the motionless bit of tape as though it were very apt indeed to bite him in the eye.

What to do? Should he disturb the Llanzlan with this or not?

This was a nose-twitching borderline case if there ever was one. If he didn't, and it turned out to be something important, he'd get his tail singed – he'd be reduced to section supervisor. But if he did, and it didn't, he'd get exactly the same treatment … However, the thing, whatever it might be, was so *terrifically* far away …

Yes, that was it! The smart thing to do would be to watch it for a few seconds – determine exact distance, direction of flight, velocity, and so forth – before reporting to the Big Boss. That would protect him either way.

Wherefore Sleemet had time to launch an analsynth projection along the indicated line.

He found a solar system containing two highly industrialized planets; one of which was cool, the other cold. One was peopled by those never-to-be-sufficiently-damned human beings; the other by a race of creatures even more monstrous and therefore even less entitled to exist.

He studied those planets and their inhabitants quickly but thoroughly, and the more he studied them the more derisive and contemptuous he became. They had no warships, no fortresses either above or below ground, no missiles, even! Their every effort and all their energies were devoted to affairs of *peace*!

Therefore, every detail having been recorded, including the gibberish being broadcast and tightbeamed by various communications satellites, Sleemet pulled in his analsynth and sent out a full working projection.

He had already located great stores of prepared power-uranium bars and blocks on both planets. Careless of detection now and working at his usual fantastic speed and with his usual perfect control, he built in seconds six tremendous pyramids upon each of the two doomed worlds – pyramids of now one-hundred-percent-convertible superatomic explosive. He assembled twenty-four exceedingly complex, carefully aimed forces and put them on trip. Then, glaring balefully into an almost opaque visiplate, he reached out without looking and rammed a plunger home – and in an instant those two distant planets became two tremendous fireballs of hellishly intolerable, mostly invisible, energies.

And almost eight thousand million highly intelligent creatures – eating, sleeping, loving, fighting, reading, thinking, working, playing – died in that utterly cataclysmic rending of two entire worlds.

Practically all of them died not knowing even that they had been hurt. A few – a *very* few – watch officers in interplanetary spaceships observed one or the other of those frightful catastrophes in time to have an instant's warning of what was coming; but only three such officers, it became known later, had enough time to throw on their faster-than-light drives and thus outrun the ravening front of annihilation.

Cosmically, however, the thing didn't amount to much. Its duration was very short indeed. While a little of each planet's substance was volatilized, practically all of it was scarcely more than melted. When equilibrium was restored they did not shine like little suns. They scarcely glowed.

Hands quietly poised, Sleemet again paused in thought.

The fact that he had murdered almost eight billion people did not bother him at all. In fact, he did not think of the action at all, as murder or as killing or as anything else. If he had, the thought would have been the Fenachrone equivalent of 'pesticide'. All space comprising the Cosmic All and every planet therein should and would belong to the Master Race; no competing race had any right whatever to live.

Should he, or should he not, explore the lines of those communications beams and destroy the other planets of this group? He should not, he decided. He would have to slow down, perhaps even change course; and it was quite possible that he was still within range of the sixth-order stuff of that self-styled Overlord. Besides, this group of queerly mixed entities would keep. After he had found a really distant Fenatype planet and had developed it, he would come back here and finish this minor chore.

But very shortly after making this decision Sleemet was given cause to know starkly that he had not investigated this civilization thoroughly enough by far; for his vessel was being assailed by forces of such incredible magnitude that his instantaneously reactive outer screen was already radiating in the high violet!

And, before he could do much more than put a hand to his construction panel, that outer screen began to show black spots of failure!

In the Hall of Prime Computation, on Llurdiax, one entire panel of instrumentation went suddenly dead. The supervisor of that section flicked two testing switches, then scanned the last couple of inches of each of two tapes. Then he paused, for a moment stunned: knocked completely out of any Llurd's calm poise. Then, licking his lips, he spoke apparently to empty air:

'Llanzlan Klazmon, sir, Blaydaxorb Three and Blaydaxorb Five stopped reporting, simultaneously, eleven seconds ago. Orbiting pyrometers of both planets reported thermonuclear temperatures at the end-points of their respective transmissions. End of report, sir.'

The supervisor did not elaborate.

While he was appalled and terribly shocked – he had never imagined such disasters possible – it was not his job to comment or to deduce or to theorize. His business – his *only* business – was to report to a higher echelon the pertinent facts of any and all unusual events or conditions; the height of the echelon to which he reported being directly proportional to the unusualness and/or magnitude of the event or condition.

Since this event was unprecedented and of very great magnitude indeed, his report went straight to the top – thus overtaking and passing the report of Head Supervisor Kalton, which was not yet ready for delivery.

Having reported the pertinent facts to the proper echelon, the section supervisor went calmly, almost unconcernedly, back to his job of supervising his section. He paid no more attention to the incident even when the Llanzlan – fully recovered now from his wounds – who had been asleep in his penthouse apartment came into the hall from the down-flyway. (Everyone rode a force-beam up, but came down on his own wings.)

While Klazmon was not hurrying any more than usual, his usual technique was to drop a full half-mile with folded wings before beginning to put on his brakes. Hence his tremendous wings and stabilizing surfaces sent blasts of cold, dense air throughout the whole end of the hall as he slowed down for a high-G landing in his seat at his master-control console. Fingers, thumbs, and tail-tip flashed over the banked and tiered keyboards of that console; and, all around the periphery of Llurdias, that miles-wide girdle of mighty fortresses came instantly to life.

A multi-layered umbrella of full-coverage screens flashed into being over the whole city and Klazmon, engineering his fifth-order projector, sent his simulacrum of pure force out to see what had happened in or to the solar system of Blaydaxorb.

He was now, to all intents and purposes, in two places at once.

He could see, hear, feel, taste, and smell exactly as well with one self as with the other. He was, however, thoroughly accustomed to the peculiar sensations of having a complete personality; he could block out at will any perceptions of either self. And his immaterial self had two tremendous advantages over his material one. It could traverse incredibly immense distances in no measurable time; and, no matter where it went or what it encountered, his physical self would remain entirely unaffected.

In a mere flick of time, then, Klazmon was in the solar system of Blaydaxorb. The Sun itself was unchanged, but in orbits three and five, where the two inhabited planets had been, there were two still-wildly-disturbed masses of liquids and gases.

He threw out a light, fast detector web, which located the marauding Fenachrone fleet in less than a second. Then, returning most of his attention to his console, he assembled seventeen exceedingly complex forces and hurled them, one at each vessel of the invading fleet.

Actually, Klazmon was little if any more affected than was Sleemet the Fenachrone about either that utterly frightful loss of life as such or the loss of those two planets as such. The Realm was big enough so that the total destruction of those two planets – of *any* two planets except of course Llurdiax itself – was unimportant to the economy of the Realm as a whole. No; what burned the Llanzlan up – made it mandatory that that fleet and the entire race whose people manned it should, after thorough study, be wiped completely out – was the brazenness, the uncivilized and illogical savagery, the incredible effrontery of this completely intolerable insult to the realm of the Llurdi and to imperial Klazmon its Llanzlan.

Klazmon knew of only one race who made a habit of performing such atrocities; such wanton, illogical, insane offenses against all sense and all reason: those chlorine-breathing, amoeboid monstrosities inhabiting Galaxy DW-427-LU. Those creatures, however, as far as any Llurd had ever learned, had always confined their activities to their own galaxy. If, Klazmon thought grimly to himself, those insanely murderous amoeboids had decided to extend their operations into the Galaxy of the Llurdi, they would find such extension a very expensive one indeed.

Wherefore, hunched now over a black-filtered visiplate, with slitted eyes narrow and cat-whiskers stiffly outthrust; with both hands manipulating high-ratio vernier knobs in infinitesimal arcs; Klazmon shoveled on the coal.

5

Combat!

As has been said, the Llurdi were a literal folk. Klazmon's directive had specified '... that no even theoretically possible attack on this planet will succeed.'

Hence that was precisely what had been built. No conceivable force or combination of forces, however applied and even at pointblank range, could crack Llurdiax's utterly impenetrable shields.

Nor was that all; for Llurdan engineers, as well as Llurdan philosophers, were thoroughly familiar with the concept that 'The best defense is a powerful offense.' Wherefore Llurdiax's offensive projectors were designed to smash down any theoretically possible threat originating anywhere within a distance that light would require one and three-quarters millions of Tellurian years to traverse.

Under the thrustings and the stabbings, the twistings and the tearings, the wrenchings and the bludgeonings of those frightful fields of force, seventeen sets of Fenachrone defensive screens – outer, intermediate, and inner – went successively upward through the visible spectrum, through the ultra-violet, and into the black of failure; baring the individual vessel's last lines of defense, the wall-shields themselves.

Then Klazmon increased the power, gouging and raving at those ultra-stubborn defenses until those defenses were just barely holding; at which point he relaxed a little, read his verniers, leaned back in his bucket seat, and took stock.

The marauding spaceships were tremendous things; cigar-shaped; flying in hollow-globe formation with one vessel – the flagship, of course – at the exact center; spaced so closely that their screens had overlapped – overlapped in such fashion that unless and until that shell of force was broken no attack could be made upon that central ship.

So far, so good. With the overwhelming superiority of ultimate-planetary over any at-all-probable mobile installations he, Llanzlan Klazmon the Fifteenth, had smashed that shell completely. He could, he was sure, destroy all those vessels as completely.

But it would not do at all to destroy even one of them without examining both it and its crew. Klazmon *had* to know the who and the what and the wherefore and the how and the why. Therefore, leaving all of his attacking beams exactly as they were, Klazmon assembled another gigantic beam – the entire output of one Llurdiaxian fortress – and hurled it against the tail-section of the flagship.

Wall-shield and tail-section vanished in a few nano-seconds of time; and not only the tail-section, but also a few hundreds of yards of the flagship's prodigious length as well, became a furiously raging fireball; a sphere of violence incredible.

Klazmon drove his projection forward then, through the now unresisting steel wall and into the control room; where it was met by blasts of force from the hand-weapons of the Fenachrone officers.

This demonstration, however, lasted for only a second or two. Then those officers, knowing what it was that was standing there so unconcernedly, abandoned their physical assault and attacked the invading projection with the full power of the huge, black, flame-shot wells of hypnotic force that were their eyes. When the mental attack also failed they merely stood there; glaring a hatred that was actually tangible.

Klazmon immobilized each one of the officers individually with pencils of force and began to study them intensively. While much shorter and thicker and wider and immensely stronger than the Jelmi of the Realm, they were definitely Jelmoid in every important respect ... yes, the two races had certainly had a common ancestry, and not too far back. Also, their thinking and conduct were precisely as was to be expected of any Jelman or Jelmoid race that had been allowed to develop in its unsane and illogical way for many thousands of years without the many benefits of Llurdan control!

They would of course have thought-exchange gear; any race of their evident advancement must have ... ah, yes; over there.

Now – which of these wights would be the admiral? That one wearing the multiplex scanner would be the pilot; that one facing the banks of dials and gauges would be the prime engineer; those six panels *had* to be battle panels, so those six monsters had to be gunnery officers ... ah!

That one there – off by himself; seated (in spite of the fact that with their short, blocky legs no Fenachrone had any need, ever, to sit) at a desk that was practically a throne; facing no gadgetry and wearing consciously an aura of power and authority – that one would be the one Klazmon wanted.

Klazmon's projection flashed up to the motionlessly straining admiral. The helmets of the 'mechanical educator' snapped onto the Llurd's quietly studious head and onto the head with the contemptuously sneering face – the head of First Scientist Fleet Admiral Sleemet of the Fenachrone.

That face, however, lost its sneer instantly, for Sleemet – even more over-weeningly and brutally and vaingloriously prideful now than were the lower echelons of his race – had never imagined the possibility of the existence of such a mind as this monstrous invader had.

Klazmon's mind, the product of seventy thousand years of coldly logical evolution, tore ruthlessly into the mind of the Fenachrone. It bored into and twisted at that straining mind's hard-held blocks; it battered and shattered them; it knocked them down flat.

Then Klazmon, omnivorous scholar that he was, set about transferring to his own brain practically everything that the Fenachrone had ever learned. Klazmon learned, as Richard Seaton had learned previously, that all Fenach-rone have authority and responsibility and were meticulous record-keepers. He learned what had happened to the civilization of the Fenachrone and to its world, and who had done it and how; he learned that each and every cap-tain knew exactly the same and had exactly the same records as did First Scientist Fleet Admiral Sleemet himself; he learned that each vessel, alone by itself, was thoroughly capable of re-creating the entire Fenachrone civiliza-tion and culture.

A few of the many other thousands of things that Klazmon learned were: that there were many Jelman and Jelmoid – human and humanoid, that is – races living in what they called the First Galaxy. That all these races were alike in destructiveness, belligerence to the point of war-lust, savagery, implacability, vengefulness, intolerance, and frightfulness generally. Not one of them (by Klazmon's light!) had any redeeming features or qualities what-ever. That all these races must be destroyed if any worthwhile civilization were ever to thrive and spread.

There was no word in any language of the Realm of the Llurdi correspond-ing even remotely to 'genocide'. If there had been, Klazmon would have regarded it as an etymological curiosity. All those surviving Fenachrone would have to die: no such race as that had any right whatever to live.

Before being destroyed, however, they would have to be studied with Llurdan thoroughness; and any and all worthwhile ideas and devices and other artifacts should be and would be incorporated into the Llurdan-Jelman way of life.

One vessel would be enough, however, to preserve temporarily for the purpose of study. In fact, what was left of the flagship would be enough.

The now-vanished tail-section had contained nothing new to Llurdan science, the encyclopedic records were intact, and the flagship's personnel – males and females, adults and adolescents and children and babies – were alive and well.

Wherefore sixteen sets of multiplex projectors doubled their drain of power from Llurdias' mighty defensive girdle, and all the Fenachrone aboard sixteen superdreadnoughts died in situ, wherever they happened to be, as those sixteen vessels became tiny sunlets.

And the Llanzlan issued orders:

1. The bulk of the Fenachrone flagship was to be brought in to the Llanzlanate at full sixth-order drive.

2. A test section of the Llanzlanate was to be converted at once to a completely authentic Fenachrone environment.

3. Every possible precaution was to be taken that no Fenachrone suffered any ill effects on the way, during transfer to their new quarters, or while in their new quarters.

Dropping the Fenachrone flagship and its personnel from his mind, Klazmon immersed himself in thought.

He had learned much. There was much more of menace than he had supposed, in many galaxies other than Galaxy DW-427-LU ... especially that so-called First Galaxy ... and particularly the Green System or Central System of that galaxy? The green-skinned Norlaminians – how of them? And how of that system's overlord, Seaton of Tellus? That one was, very evidently, a Jelm ... and, even after making all due allowance for Sleemet's bias, he was of a completely uncontrolled and therefore extremely dangerous type.

And as, evidently, his was a mind of exceeding power, he could very well be a very dangerous and quite immediate threat.

The mergons must be wider-spread even than originally planned and they must be on the lookout for this Overlord Seaton. In fact, he might be worth interviewing personally. It might be well worthwhile, some of these years, to take some time off and go to that distant galaxy, purposely to make that Jelm Seaton's acquaintance ...

Shrugging his shoulders and shaking both wings, Klazmon cut off his projection and called another meeting of his Board of Advisors.

He briefed them on what had happened; then went on:

'We must protect all our planets in the same way and to the same extent that this planet Llurdiax is protected now: a course of action now necessary because of these many Jelman and Jelmoid races that have been developing for untold millennia in their unsane and illogical ways, with no semblance of or attempt at either guidance or control.

'Second: any force of any such race that attacks us will be destroyed before it or they can do us any harm.

'Third: the manufacture and distribution of mergons will continue indefinitely at the present rate.

'Fourth: no chance or casual vessel or fleet traversing any part of the vast volume of space to be covered by our mergons is to be destroyed, or even hailed, until I myself decide what action, if any, is to be taken.'

So saying, the Llanzlan Klazmon dismissed his advisors. His great wings fanned idly as he contemplated what he had done. He was well pleased with it. He had, he reflected, scratching his head contentedly with the tip of his tail, provided for every possible contingency. Whatever this Jelm, or Jelm-like creature, named Seaton might be or do, he would pose no real threat to the Llanzlanate.

Of that Klazmon was one hundred per cent sure …

And wrong!

6

Of Disembodied Intelligences

We have now seen how the ripple of thought that began with the conference between Seaton and his advisors from the Green System had spread throughout all of recorded space, and how it had affected the lives and destinies of countless millions of persons who had never heard of him.

Yet a few threads remain to be drawn into our net. And one of these threads represents the strangest entities Seaton had encountered, ever … as well as the most deadly.

To understand what these entities are like, it is necessary to look back to their beginnings.

These are most remote, both in space and in time. In a solar system so distant from that of Sol as to be forever unknowable to anyone of Earth, and at a time an inconceivably vast number of millennia in the past, there once existed a lusty and fertile Tellus-type planet named Marghol. Over the usual millions of years mankind evolved on Marghol and thrived as usual. And finally, also as usual and according to the scheduled fate of all created material things, the planet Marghol grew old.

Whether or not a Tellus-type planet ordinarily becomes unfit to support human life before its sun goes nova is not surely known. Nor does it matter very much; for, long before either event occurs, the human race involved has developed a faster-than-light drive and has at its disposal dozens or hundreds of Earth-like planets upon which even subhuman life has not yet developed. The planet Marghol, however, while following the usual pattern in general, developed a specific thing that was, as far as is known, unique throughout all the reaches of total space and throughout all time up to the present.

On Marghol, during many, many millions of years of its prime, there had continued to exist a small, tightly inbred, self-perpetuating cult of thinkers – of men and women who devoted their every effort and their total power to thought.

They themselves did not know what freak of mind or quirk of physical environment made the ultimate outcome possible; but after those many millions of years, during which the perpetually inbreeding group grew stronger and stronger mentally and weaker and weaker physically, the seven survivors of the group succeeded finally in liberating their minds – minds perfectly intact and perfectly functioning – from the gross and perishable flesh of their physical bodies.

Then, able to travel at the immeasurable speed of thought and with all future time in which to work, they set out to learn everything there was to know. They would learn, they declared, not only all about space and time and zero and infinity and animals and people and life and death, but also everything else comprising or having anything to do with the totality of existence that is the Cosmic All.

This quest for knowledge has been going on, through universe after universe and through dimension after dimension, for a stretch of time that, given as a number in Tellurian years, would be a number utterly incomprehensible to the human mind. For what perceptible or tangible difference is there, to the human mind, between a googolplex of seconds and the same number of centuries? And, since these free minds ordinarily kept track of time only by the life-cycles of suns, the period of time during which they had already traveled and studied could have been either shorter or longer than either of the two exact figures mentioned.

Seven free minds had left the planet Marghol. They called themselves, in lieu of names, 'One' to 'Seven' in order of their liberation.

For a brief time – a mere cosmic eye-wink; a few hundreds of millions of years – there had been eight, since One had consented to dematerialize one applicant for immortality. The applicant Eight, however, sick and tired of eternal life, had committed suicide by smashing his sixth-order being out of existence against Richard Seaton's sixth-order screens.

Now those seven free minds, accompanied by the free mind of Immortality Candidate Dr Marc C. DuQuesne, were flying through ultra-deep space in a time-stasis capsule. This capsule, as has been said, was designed and powered to travel almost to infinity in both space and time. But, as the Norlaminians pointed out to Seaton, his basic assumptions were invalid.

Nothing happened, however, for week after week. Then, so immensely far out in intergalactic space that even the vast bulk of a galaxy lying there would have been invisible even to Palo-mar's 'Long Eye', the hurtling capsule struck a cloud of hydrogen gas.

That gas was, by Earthly standards, a hard vacuum; but the capsule's velocity by that time was so immensely great that that cloud might just as well have been a mountain of solid rock. The capsule's directors tried, with all their prodigious might and speed, to avoid the obstruction, but even with fullest power they did not have time enough.

Eight multi-ton power-bars of activated uranium flared practically instantaneously into ragingly incandescent gas; into molecular, atomic, and subatomic vapor and debris. A fireball brighter than a sun glared briefly; then nothing whatever was visible where that massive structure had been.

And out of that sheer emptiness came a cold, clear thought: the thought of Doctor Marc C. DuQuesne.

'One, are you familiar enough with the region of space to estimate at all closely how long we were in that stasis of time and where we now are with reference to the First Galaxy?'

Freemind One did not exactly answer the question. 'What matters it?' he asked. If the thought of an immortal and already incredibly old and incredibly knowledgeful mind can be said to show surprise, that thought did. 'It should be clear, even to you of infinitesimally short life, that any length of time expressible in any finite number of definite time periods is actually but a moment. Also, the Cosmic All is vast indeed; larger by many orders of magnitude than any that the boldest of your thinkers has as yet dared to imagine.

'Whether or not space is infinite I do not know. Whether or not my life span will be infinite I do not know. I do not as yet completely understand infinity. I do know, however, that both infinite time and infinite space are requisite for the acquisition of infinite knowledge, which is my goal; wherefore I am well content. You have no valid reason whatever for wishing to return to your Earth. Instead, you should be as eager as I am to explore and to study the as yet unknown.'

'I have unfinished business there.' DuQuesne's thought was icy cold. 'I'm going back there whether you do or not.'

'To kill beings who have at best but an instant to live? To rule an ultra-microscopic speck of cosmic dust? A speck whose fleeting existence is of but infinitesimal importance to the Great Scheme of Things? Are you still infantile enough, despite your recent transformation, to regard as valid such indefensible reasons as those?'

'They're valid enough to me. And you'd have to go back, too, I should think. Or isn't it still true that science demands the dematerialization of the whole *Skylark* party?'

'Truth is variable,' One said. 'Thus, while certain of our remarks were not true in the smaller aspects, each of them was designed to elicit a larger truth.

They aided in the initiation of chains of events by observation of which I will be able to fit many more constituent parts of this you call the First Universe precisely into place in the Great Scheme.

'Now as to you, DuQuesne. The probability was small that you were sufficiently advanced to become a worthy member of our group; but I decided to give you your chance and permitted Richard Seaton to do what he did. As a matter of fact I, not Seaton, did it. You have failed; and I now know that no member of your race can ever become a true scholar. In a very few millions of your years you would not be thinking of knowledge at all, but merely of self-destruction. I erred, one-tenth of a cycle since, in admitting Freemind Eight to our study group; an entity who was then at approximately the same stage of development as you now are. I will not repeat that error. You will be rematerialized and will be allowed to do whatever you please.'

The mind of DuQuesne almost gasped.

'Out here? Even if you re-create my ship I'd never get back!'

'You should and will have precisely the same chance as before of living out your normal instant of life in normal fashion. To that end I will construct for you a vessel that will be the replica of your former one except that it will have a sixth-order drive – what your fellow-human Seaton called the "Cosmic-Energy" drive – so that you will be able to make the journey in comparatively few of your days. I will instruct you in this drive and in certain other matters that will be required to implement what I have said. I will set your vessel's controls upon your home galaxy at the correct acceleration.

'I compute ... I construct.'

And faster by far than even an electronic eye could follow, a pattern of incredibly complex stresses formed in the empty ether.

Elemental particles, combining instantaneously, built practically instantaneously upward through electrons and protons and atoms and molecules beams and weaponry up to a million tons or more of perfectly operating super-dreadnought – and at the same time built the vastly more complex structure of the two hundred pounds or so of meat and so forth that were to enclothe Freemind DuQuesne – and did the whole job in much less time than the blink of an eye.

'... I instruct ... It is done,' and all seven freeminds vanished.

And DuQuesne, seated at a thoroughly familiar control board and feeling normal gravity on the seat of his pants, stared at that board's instruments, for a moment stunned.

According to those instruments the ship was actually travelling at an acceleration of one hundred twenty-seven lights; its internal gravity was actually nine hundred eighty-one point zero six centimeters per second squared.

He stared around the entire room, examining minutely each familiar object. Activating a visiplate, he scanned the immense skyrover, inside and out, from stem to stern, finding that it was in fact, except for the stated improvements, an exact duplicate of the mighty ship of war he had formerly owned, which, he still thought, had been one of the most powerful battleships ever built by man.

Then, and only then, did he examine the hands resting, quiescent but instantly ready, upon the board's flat, bare table. They were big, tanned, powerful hands; with long, strong, tapering, highly competent fingers. They were his hands – his own hands in every particular, clear down to the tiny scar on the side of his left index finger; where, years before, a bit of flying glass from an exploding flask had left its mark.

Shaking his head, he got up and went to his private cabin, where he strode up to a full-length mirror.

The man who stared back at him out of it was tall and powerfully built; with thick, slightly wavy hair of an intense, glossy black. The eyes, only a trifle lighter in shade, were surmounted by heavy black eyebrows growing together above his finely-chiseled aquiline beak of a nose. His saturnine face, while actually tanned, looked almost pale because of the blackness of the heavy beard always showing through, even after the closest possible shave.

'He *could* rematerialize me perfectly – and did,' he said aloud to himself, 'and the whole ship – exactly!'

Scowling in concentration, he went into his bathroom and stepped upon the platform of his weight-and-height Fairbanks. Six feet and seven-eighths of an inch. Precisely right. Two hundred two and three-quarters pounds. Ditto.

He examined the various items of equipment and of every-day use. There was his cutthroat razor, Osnomian-made of arenak – vastly sharper than any Earthly razor could possibly be honed and so incredibly hard that it could shave generation after generation of men with no loss whatever of edge.

Comb, brush, toothbrush, lotion – inside the drawers and out – every item was exactly as he had left it … clear down to the correctly printed, peculiarly distorted tubes of toothpaste and of shaving cream; each of which, when he picked it up, fitted perfectly into the grip of his left hand.

'I'll … be … totally … damned,' DuQuesne said then, aloud.

7

DuQuesne and Klazmon

The *Skylark of Valeron* swung in orbit around the sun of Earth. She was much more of worldlet than a spaceship, being a perfect sphere over a thousand kilometers in diameter. She *had* to be big. She had to house, among other things, the one-thousand-kilometers-diameter graduated circles of declination and of right ascension required to chart the thousands of millions of galaxies making up any given universe of the Cosmic All.

She was for the most part cold and dark. Even the master-control helmets, sprouting masses and mazes of thigh-thick bundles of hair-thin silver wire, hung inactivated in the neutral gray, featureless master control room. The giant computer, however – the cubic mile of ultra-miniaturization that everyone called the 'Brain' – was still in operation; and in the worldlet's miles-wide chart-room, called the 'tanks', there still glowed the enormous lenticular aggregation of points of light that was the chart of the First Universe – each tiny pool of light representing a galaxy composed of thousands of millions of solar systems.

A precisely coded thought impinged upon a receptor.

A relay clicked, whereupon a neighboring instrument, noting the passage of current through its vitals, went busily but silently to work, and an entire panel of instrumentation came to life.

Switch after switch snapped home. Field after field of time-stasis collapsed. The planetoid's artificial sun resumed its shining; breezes began again to stir the leaves of trees and of shrubbery; insects resumed their flitting from bloom to once-more-scented bloom. Worms resumed their gnawings and borings beneath the green velvet carpets that were the lawns. Brooks began again to flow; gurglingly. Birds took up their caroling and chirping and twittering precisely where they had left off so long before; and three houses – there was a house now for Shiro and his bride of a month – became comfortably warm and softly, invitingly livable.

All that activity meant, of course, that the Seaton-Crane party would soon be coming aboard.

They were in fact already on the way, in *Skylark Two*; the forty-foot globe which, made originally of Osnomian arenak and the only spaceship they owned, had been 'flashed over' into ultra-refractory inoson and now served as captain's gig, pinnace, dinghy, lifeboat, landing craft, and so forth – whatever any of the party wanted her to do. There were many other craft aboard the *Skylark of Valeron*, of course, of various shapes and sizes; but *Two* had always been the Seatons' favorite 'small boat'.

As *Two* approached the *Valeron*, directly in line with one of her huge main ports, Seaton slowed down to a dawdling crawl – a mere handful of miles per second – and thought into a helmet already on his head; and the massive gates of locks – of a miles-long succession of locks through the immensely thick skin of the planetoid – opened in front of flying *Two* and closed behind her. Clearing the last gate, Seaton put on a gee and a half of deceleration and brought the little flying sphere down to a soft and easy landing in her berth in the back yard of the Seatons' house.

Eight people disembarked; five of whom were the three Seatons and Martin and Margaret Crane. (Infant Lucile Crane rode joyously on her mother's left hip.) Seventh was short, chunky, lightning-fast Shiro, whose place in these *Skylark* annals has not been small. Originally Crane's 'man,' he had long since become Crane's firm friend; and he was now as much of a Skylarker as was any of the others.

Eighth was Lotus Blossom, Shiro's small, finely wrought, San Francisco-born and western-dressed bride, whom the others had met only that morning, just before leaving Earth. She looked like a living doll – but appearances can be *so* deceiving! She was in fact one of the most proficient female experts in unarmed combat then alive.

'Our house first, please, all of you,' Dorothy said. 'We'll eat before we do one single solitary thing else. I could eat that fabled missionary from the plains of Timbuctoo.'

Margaret laughed. 'Hat and gown and hymnbook too,' she finished. 'Me, too, Dick.'

'Okay by me; I could toy with a couple of morsels myself,' Seaton said, and pencils of force wafted the eight into the roomy kitchen of the house that was in almost every detail an exact duplicate of the Seatons' home on Earth. 'You're the chief kitchen mechanic, Red-Top; strut your stuff.'

Dorothy looked at and thought into the controller – she no longer had to wear any of the limited-control headsets to operate them – and a damask-clothed table, set for six, laden with a wide variety of food and equipped with six carved oak chairs and two high-chairs, came instantly into being in the middle of the room.

The Nisei girl jumped violently; then smiled apologetically. 'Shiro *told* me about such things, but ... well, maybe I'll get used to them sometimes, I hope.'

'Sure you will, Lotus,' Seaton assured her. 'It's pretty weird at first, but you get used to it fast.'

'I sincerely hope so,' Lotus said, and eyed the six dinner places dubiously. She had thought that she was thoroughly American, but she wasn't quite.

Traditions are strong. With an IQ that a Heidelberg student might envy, part of the crew of the most powerful vehicle man had ever seen, fully educated and trained … it was evident that Shiro's dainty little bride was more than a little doubtful about sitting at that table.

Until Dorothy took her by the hand and sat her down. 'This is where I like my friends to sit,' she announced. 'Where I can see them.'

A flush dyed the porcelain-like perfection of Lotus's skin.

'I thank you, Mrs—'

'Friends, remember?' Seaton broke in. 'Call her Dot. Now let's eat!'

Whereafter, they worked.

It may be wondered, among those historians not familiar with the saga of the *Skylarks*, why so much consternation and trouble should come from so small an event as the probabilistic speculation of a single Norlaminian sage that one mere human body, lately cast into the energy forms of the disembodied intelligences, might soon return into the universe in a viable form.

Such historians do not, of course, know Blackie DuQuesne.

While Seaton, Crane and the others were eating their meal, across distances to be measured in gigaparsecs, countless millions of persons were in one way or another busy at work on projects central to their own central concern. Seaton and Crane were not idle. They were waiting for further information … and at the same time, refurbishing the inner man with food, with rest and with pleasant company; but an hour later, after dinner, after the table and its appurtenances had vanished and the three couples were seated in the living room, more or less facing the fire, Seaton stoked up his battered black briar and Crane lighted one of his specially made cigarettes.

'Well?' Seaton demanded then. 'Have you thunk up anything you think is worth two tinker's whoops in Hades?'

Crane smiled ruefully. 'Not more than one, I'd say – if that many. Let's consider that thought or message that Carfon is sending out. It will be received, he says, only by persons or entities who not only know more than we do about one or more specific things, but also are friendly enough to be willing to share their knowledge with us. And to make the matter murkier, we have no idea either of what it is that we lack or what it, whatever it is, is supposed to be able to do. Therefore Point One would be: how are they going to get in touch with us? By what you called magic?'

Seaton did not answer at first, then only nodded. 'Magic' was still a much less than real concept to him. He said. 'If you say so – but remember the Peruvian Indian medicinemen and the cinchona bark that just happened to be full of quinine. So, whatever you want to call it – magic or extra-sensory perception or an unknown band of the sixth or what-have-you – I'll bet my last shirt it'll be *bio*. And whoever pitches it at us will be good enough at it to *know* that they can hit us with it, so all we have to do about that is wait for it to happen. However, what I'm mostly interested in right now is nothing that far out, but what we *know* that a reincarnated Blackie DuQuesne could and probably would do.'

'Such as?'

'The first thing he'll do, for all the tea in China, will be to design and set up some gadget or gizmo or technique to kill me with. Certainly me, and probably you, and quite possibly all of us.'

Dorothy and Margaret both gasped; but Crane nodded and said, 'Check. I check you to your proverbial nineteen decimals. Also, and quite possibly along with that operation, an all-out attempt to reconquer Earth. He wouldn't set out to destroy Earth, at this time, at least ... would he, do you think?'

Seaton thought for seconds, then said, 'My best guess would be no. He wants to boss it, not wipe it out. However, there are a few other things that might come ...'

'Wait up, presh!' Dorothy snapped. 'Those two will hold us for a while; especially the first one. I wish to go on record at this point to the effect that I want my husband *alive*, not dead.'

Seaton grinned. 'You and me both, pet,' he said. 'I'm in favor of it. Definitely. However, as long as I stay inside the *Valeron* here he doesn't stand the chance of a snowflake in you-know-where of getting at me ...'

How wrong Seaton was!

'... so the second point is the one that's really of over-riding importance. The rub is that we can't make even a wild guess at when he's going to get loose ... He *could* be building his ship right now ... so, Engineer Martin Crane, what's your thought as to defending Earth; as adequately as possible but in the shortest possible time?'

Crane inhaled – slowly – a deep lungful of smoke, exhaled it even more slowly, and stubbed out the butt. 'That's a tall order, Dick,' he said, finally, 'but I don't think it's hopeless. Since we know DuQuesne's exact line of departure, we know at least approximately the line of his return. As a first-approximation idea we should, I think, cover that line thoroughly with hair-triggered automation. We should occupy the fourth and the fifth completely; thus taking care of everything we *know* that he knows ... but as for the sixth ...' Crane paused in thought.

'Yeah,' Seaton agreed. 'That sixth order's an entirely different breed of cats. It's a pistol – a question with a capital Q. About all we can do on it, I'd say, is cover everything we know of it and then set up supersensitive analsynths coupled to all the automatic constructors and such-like gizmos we can dream up – with as big a gaggle of ground-and-lofty dreamers as we can round up. The Norlaminians, certainly; and Sacner Carfon for sure. If what he and Drasnik pulled off wasn't magic it certainly was a remarkably reasonable facsimile thereof. All six of us, of course, and—'

'But what can you possibly want of us?' Shiro asked, and Dorothy said, 'That goes double for Peggy and me, Dick. Of what good could we two possibly be, thinking about such stuff as that?'

Seaton flushed. "Scuse, please; my error. I switched thinking without announcing the switch. I do know, though, that our minds all work differently – especially Shiro's and double-especially Lotus's – and that when you don't have the faintest glimmering of what you're getting into you don't know what you're going to have to have to cope with it.' He grinned.

'If you can untangle that, I mean,' he said.

'I think so,' said Crane, unruffled; he had had long practice in following Seaton's lightning leaps past syntax. 'And you think that this will enable us to deal with DuQuesne?'

'It'll have to,' Seaton said positively. 'One thing we know, *something* has to. He's not going to send us a polite message asking to be friends – he's going to hit with all he's got. So,' he finished, 'let's hop to it. The Norlaminian Observers' reports are piling up on the tapes right now. And we'd all better keep our eyes peeled – as well as all the rest of our senses and instruments! – for Dr Marc C. Blackie DuQuesne!'

And DuQuesne so immensely far out in intergalactic space, at control board and computer, explored for ten solid hours the vastnesses of his new knowledge.

Then he donned a thought-helmet and thought himself up a snack; after eating which – scarcely tasting any part of it – he put in another ten solid hours of work. Then, leaning back in his form-fitting seat, he immersed himself in thought – and, being corporeal, no longer a pattern of pure force, went sound asleep.

He woke up a couple of hours later; stiff, groggy, and ravenous. He thought himself up a supper of steak and mushrooms, hashed browns, spinach, coffee, and apple pie a la mode. He ate it – with zest, this time – then sought his long-overdue bed.

In the morning, after a shower and a shave and a breakfast of crisp bacon and over-easy eggs, toast and butter and marmalade, and four cups of strong, black coffee, he sat down at his board and again went deep into thought. This time, he thought in words and sentences, the better to nail down his conclusions.

'One said I'd have precisely the same chance as before of living out my normal lifetime. Before what? Before the de-materialization or before Seaton got all that extra stuff? Since he gave me sixth order drive, offense, defense, and communications, he could have – probably did – put me on a basis of equality with Seaton as of now. Would he have given me any more than that?'

DuQuesne paused and worked for ten busy minutes at computer and control board again. What he learned was in the form of curves and quantities, not words; he did not attempt to speak them aloud, but sat staring into space.

Then, satisfied that the probabilities were adequate to base a plan on, he spoke out loud again: 'No. Why should he give me everything that Seaton's got? He didn't owe me anything.' To Blackie DuQuesne that was not a rueful complaint but a statement of fact. He went on. 'Assume we both now have a relatively small part of the spectrum of the sixth-order forces, if I keep using this drive – Ouch! What the living *hell* was *that*?'

DuQuesne leaped to his feet. 'That' had been a sixth-order probe, at the touch of which his vessel's every course of defensive screen had flared into action.

DuQuesne was not shaken, no. But he was surprised, and he didn't like to be surprised. There should have been no probes out here!

The probe had been cut off almost instantaneously; but 'almost' instantaneously is not quite zero time, and sixth-order forces operate at the speed of thought. Hence, in that not-quite-zero instant of time during which the intruding mind had been in contact with his own, DuQuesne learned a little. The creature was undoubtedly highly intelligent – and, as undoubtedly, unhuman to the point of monstrosity ... and DuQuesne had no doubt whatever in his own mind that the alien would think the same of any Tellurian.

DuQuesne studied his board and saw, much to his surprise, that only one instrument showed any drain at all above maintenance level, and that one was a milliammeter – the needle of which was steady on the scale at a reading of one point three seven *mils*! He was not being attacked at all – merely being observed – and by an observation system that was using practically no power at all!

Donning a helmet, so as to be able himself to operate at the speed of thought, DuQuesne began – very skittishly and very gingerly indeed – to soften down his spheres and zones and shells and solid fields of defensive force. He softened and softened them down; down to the point at which a working projection could come through and work.

And a working projection came through.

No one of Marc C. DuQuesne's acquaintances, friend or enemy, had ever said that he was any part of either a weakling or a coward. The consensus was that he was harder than the ultra-refractory hubs of hell itself. Nevertheless, when the simulacrum of Llanzlan Klazmon the Fifteenth of the Realm of the Llurdi came up to within three feet of him and waggled one gnarled forefinger at the helmets of a mechanical educator, even DuQuesne's burly spirit began to quail a little – but he was strong enough and hard enough not let any sign show.

With every mind-block he owned set hard, DuQuesne donned a headset and handed its mate to his visitor. He engaged that monstrous alien mind to mind. Then, releasing his blocks, he sent the Llurdi a hard, cold, sharp, diamond-clear – and lying! – thought:

'Yes? Who are you pray, and what, to obtrude your uninvited presence upon me, Foalang Kassi a' Doompf, the Highest Imperial of the Drailsen Quadrant?'

This approach was, of course, the natural one for DuQuesne to make; he did not believe in giving away truth when lies might be so much cheaper – and less dangerous. It was equally of course the worst possible approach to Klazmon: reinforcing as it did every unfavorable idea the Llurd had already formed from his lightning-fast preliminary once-over-lightly of the man and of the man's tremendous spaceship.

Klazmon did not think back at DuQuesne directly. Instead, he thought to himself and, as DuQuesne knew, for the record; thoughts that the Earthman could read like print.

To the Llurd, DuQuesne was a peculiarly and repulsively obnoxious monstrosity. Physically a Jelm, he belonged to a race of Jelmi that had never been subjected to any kind of logical, sensible, or even intelligent control.

Klazmon then thought at DuQuesne; comparing him with Mergon and Luloy on the one hand and with Sleemet of the Fenachrone on the other – and deciding that all three races were basically the same. The Llurd showed neither hatred nor detestation; he was merely contemptuous, intolerant, and utterly logical. 'Like the few remaining Fenachrone and the rebel faction of our own Jelmi and the people you think of as the Chlorans, your race is, definitely, surplus population; a nuisance that must be and shall be abated. Where –' Klazmon suddenly drove a thought – 'is the Drailsen Quadrant?'

DuQuesne, however, was not to be caught napping. His blocks held. 'You'll never know,' he sneered. 'Any task-force of yours that ever comes anywhere near us will not last long enough to energize a sixth-order communicator.'

'That's an idle boast,' Klazmon stated thoughtfully. 'It is true that you and your vessel are far out of range of any possible Llurdiaxian attacking beam. Even this projection of me is being relayed through four mergons. Nevertheless we can and we will find you easily when this becomes desirable. This point will be reached as soon as we have computed the most logical course to take in exterminating all such surplus races as yours.'

And Klazmon's projection vanished; and the helmet he had been wearing fell toward the floor.

DuQuesne was shocked as he had never been shocked before; and when he learned from his analsynths just what the range of *one* of those incredible 'mergons' was, he was starkly appalled.

One thing was crystal-clear: he was up against some truly first-class opposition here. And it had just stated, calmly and definitely, that its intention was to exterminate him, Blackie DuQuesne.

The master of lies had learned to assess the value of a truth very precisely. He knew this one to be 22-karat, crystal-clear, pure quill. Whereupon Blackie

DuQuesne turned to some very intensive thought indeed, compared with which his previous efforts might have been no more than a summer afternoon's reverie.

We know now, of course, that Blackie DuQuesne lacked major elements of information, and that his constructions could not therefore be complete. They lacked Norlaminian rigor, or the total visualization of his late companions, the disembodied intellectuals. And they lacked information.

DuQuesne knew nothing of Mergon and Luloy, now inward bound on Earth in a hideout orbit. He could not guess how his late visitor had ever heard of the Fenachrone. Nor knew he anything of that strange band of the sixth order to which Seaton referred, with more than half a worried frown, as 'magic'. In short, DuQuesne was attempting to reach the greatest conclusion of his life through less than perfect means, with only fragmentary facts to go on.

Nevertheless, Blackie C. DuQuesne, as Seaton was wont to declare, was no slouch at figuring; and so he did in time come to a plan which was perhaps the most brilliant – and also was perhaps the most witless! – of his career.

Lips curled into something much more sneer than grin, DuQuesne sat down at his construction board. He had come to the conclusion that what he needed was help, and he knew exactly where to go to get it. His ship wasn't big enough by far to hold a sixth-order projection across any important distance … but he could build, in less than an hour, a sixth-order broadcaster. It wouldn't be selective. It would be enormously wasteful of power. But it would carry a signal across half a universe.

Whereupon, in less than an hour, a signal began to pour out, into and through space:

'DuQuesne calling Seaton! Reply on tight beam of the sixth. DuQuesne calling Seaton! Reply on tight beam of the sixth. DuQuesne calling Seaton …'

8

Industrial Revolution

When Seaton and Crane had begun to supply the Earth with ridiculously cheap power, they had expected an economic boom and a significant improvement in the standard of living. Neither of them had any idea, however, of the effect upon the world's economy that their space-flights would have; but many tycoons of industry did.

They were shrewd operators, those tycoons. As one man they licked their chops at the idea of interstellar passages made in days. They gloated over thoughts of the multifold increase in productive capacity that would have to be made so soon; as soon as commerce was opened up with dozens and then with hundreds of Tellus-type worlds, inhabited by human beings as those of Earth. And when they envisioned hundreds and hundreds of uninhabited Tellus-type worlds, each begging to be grabbed and exploited by whoever got to it first with enough stuff to hold it and to develop it … they positively drooled.

These men did not think of money as money, but as their most effective and most important tool: a tool to be used as knowledgeably as the old-time lumberjack used his axe.

Thus, Earth was going through convulsions of change more revolutionary by far than any it had experienced throughout all previous history. All those pressures building up at once had blown the lid completely off. Seaton and Crane and their associates had been working fifteen hours a day for months training people in previously unimagined skills; trying to keep the literally exploding economy from degenerating into complete chaos.

They could not have done it alone, of course. In fact, it was all that a thousand Norlaminian Observers could do to keep the situation even approximately in hand. And even the Congress –*mirabile dictu!* – welcomed those aliens with open arms; for it was so hopelessly deadlocked in trying to work out any workable or enforceable laws that it was accomplishing nothing at all.

All steel mills were working at one hundred ten per cent of capacity. So were almost all other kinds of plants. Machine tools were in such demand that no estimated time of delivery could be obtained. Arenak, dagal, and inoson, those wonder-materials of the construction industry, would be in general supply some day; but that day would nor be allowed to come until the changeover could be made without disrupting the entire economy. Inoson especially was confined to the spaceship builders; and, while every pretense was being made that production was being increased as fast as possible, the demand for spaceships was so insatiable that every hulk that could leave atmosphere was out in deep space.

Multi-billion-dollar corporations were springing up all over Earth. Each sought out and began to develop a Tellus-type planet of its own, to bring up as a civilized planet or merely to exploit as it saw fit. Each was clamoring for – and using every possible artifice of persuasion, lobbying, horse-trading, and out-and-out bribery and corruption to obtain – spaceships, personnel, machinery light and heavy, office equipment, and supplies. All the employables of Earth, and many theretofore considered unemployable, were at work.

Earth was a celestial madhouse …

It is no wonder then, that Seaton and Crane were haggard and worn when they had to turn their jobs over to two upper-bracket Norlaminians and leave Earth.

Their situation thereafter was not much better.

The first steps were easy – anyway, the decisions involved were easy; the actual work involved was roughly equivalent to the energy budget of several Sol-type suns. It is an enormous project to set up a line of defense hundreds of thousands of miles long; especially when the setters-up do not know exactly what to expect in the way of attack. They knew, in fact, only one thing: that the Norlaminians had made a probabilistic statement that Marc C. DuQuesne was likely to be present among them before long.

That was excuse, reason and compulsion enough to demand the largest and most protracted effort they could make. The mere preliminaries involved laying out axes of action that embraced many solar systems, locating and developing sources of materials and energies that were enough to smother a hundred suns. As that work began to shape up, Seaton and Crane came face to face with the secondary line of problems … and at that point Seaton suddenly smote himself on the forehead and cried: 'Dunark!'

Crane looked up. 'Dunark? Why, yes, Dick. Quite right. Not only is he probably the universe's greatest strategist, but he knows the enemy almost as well as you and I do.'

'And besides,' Seaton added, 'he doesn't think like us. Not at all. And that's what we want; so I'll call him now and we'll compute a rendezvous.'

Wherefore, a few days later, Dunark's Osnomian cruiser matched velocities with the hurtling worldlet and began to negotiate its locks. Seaton shoved up the *Valeron*'s air-pressure, cut down its gravity, and reached for the master thermostat.

'Not too hot, Dick,' Dorothy said. 'Light gravity is all right, but make them wear some clothes any time they're outside their special quarters. I simply *won't* run around naked in my own house. And I won't have them doing it, either.'

Seaton laughed. 'The usual eighty-three degrees and twenty-five per cent humidity. They'll wear clothes, all right. She'll be tickled to death to wear that fur coat you gave her – she doesn't get a chance to, very often – and we can stand it easily enough,' and the four Tellurians went out to the dock to greet their green-skinned friends of old: Crown Prince Dunark and Crown Princess Sitar of Osnome, one of the planets of the enormous central sun of the Central System.

Warlike, bloodthirsty, supremely able Dunark; and Sitar, his lovely, vivacious – and equally warlike – wife. He was wearing ski-pants (Osnome's temperature, at every point on its surface and during every minute of every day of the year, is one hundred degrees Fahrenheit), a heavy sweater, wool socks, and fur-lined moccasins. She wore a sweater and slacks under her usual fantastic array of Osnomian jewelry; and over it, as Seaton had predicted, the full-length mink coat. Each was wearing only one Osnomian machine-pistol instead of the arsenal that had been their customary garb such a short time before.

The three men greeted each other warmly and executed a six-hand handshake; the while the two white women and the green one went into an arms-wrapped group; each talking two hundred words to the minute.

A couple of days later, the Norlaminian task-force arrived and a council of war was held that lasted for one full working day. Then, the defense planned in length and in depth, construction began. Seaton and Crane sat in the two master-control helmets of the Brain. Rovol worked with the brain of the Norlaminian spaceship. Dozens of other operators, men and women, worked at and with other, less powerful devices.

On the surface of a nearby planet, ten thousand square miles of land were leveled and paved to form the Area of Work. Stacks and piles and rows and assortments of hundreds of kinds of structural members appeared as though by magic. Gigantic beams of force, made visible by a thin and dusty pseudo-mist, flashed here and there; seizing this member and that and these and them and those and joining them together with fantastic speed to form enormous towers and platforms and telescope-like things and dirigible tubes and projectors.

Some of these projectors took containers of pure force out to white dwarf stars after neutronium. Others took faidons – those indestructible jewels that are the *sine qua non of* higher-order operations – out to the cores of stars to be worked into lenses of various shapes and sizes. Out into the environment of scores of millions of degrees of temperature and of scores of millions of tons per square inch of pressure that is the only environment in which the faidon can be worked by any force known to the science of man.

The base-line, which was to be built of enormous, absolutely rigid beams of force, could not be of planetary, or even of orbital dimensions. It had to extend, a precisely measured length, from the core of a star to that of another, having as nearly as possible the same proper motion, over a hundred parsecs away. Thus it took over a week to build and to calibrate that base-line; but, once that was done, the work went fast.

The most probable lines of approach were blocked by fourth-, fifth-, and sixth-order installations of tremendous range and of planetary power; less probable ones by defenses of somewhat lesser might; supersensitive detector webs fanned out everywhere. And this work, which would have required years a short time before, was only a matter of a couple of weeks for the gigantic constructor-projectors now filling the entire Area of Work.

When everything that anyone could think of doing had been done, Seaton lit his pipe, jammed both hands into his pockets, and turned to his wife.

'Well, we've got it made – now what are we going to do with it? Sit on our hands until Blackie DuQuesne trips a trigger or some Good Samaritan answers our call? I'd give three nickels to know whether he's loose yet or not, and if he is loose, just where he is at this moment.'

'I'd raise you a dime,' she said; and then, since Dorothy Seaton concealed an extremely useful brain under her red curls, she added slowly, 'And maybe ... you know what the Norlaminians deduced: that, upon liberation, he'd be rematerialized? That he'd have a very good spaceship. That, before attacking us, he would recruit personnel, both men and women, both from need of their help and from loneliness ... wait up – *loneliness!* Who – a girl, probably – would he get loneliest for?'

Seaton snapped his fingers. 'I can make an awfully good guess. Hunkie de Marigny.'

'Hunkie de Who? Oh, I remember. That big moose with the black hair and the shape.'

Seaton laughed. 'Funny, isn't it, that such an accurate description can be so misleading? But my guess is, if he's back she knows it ... I think it'd be smart to flip myself over to the Bureau and see what I can find out. Want to come along?'

'Uh-uh; she isn't my dish of tea.'

Seaton projected his solid-seeming simulacrum of pure force to distant Tellus, to Washington, and to the sidewalk in front of the Bureau. He mounted the steps, entered the building, said 'Hi, Gorgeous' to the shapely blonde receptionist, and took an elevator to the sixteenth floor; where he paused briefly in thought.

He hadn't better see Hunkie first, or only; Ferdinand Scott, the world's worst gossip, would talk about it, and Hunkie would draw her own conclusions. He'd pull Scotty's teeth first.

Wherefore he turned into the laboratory beside the one that once had been his own. 'Hi, Scotty,' he said, holding out his hand, 'don't tell me they've actually got you *working* for a change.'

Scott, a chunky youth with straw-colored hair that needed cutting, jumped off of his stool and shook hands vigorously. 'Hi, Dickie, old top! Alla time work. "Slavey" Scott; that's me. But boy oh boy, *did* I goof on that "Nobody Holme" bit! You and that bottle of waste solution, that you stirred the whole world up with like goulash! Why can't anything like that ever happen to me? But I s'pose I'd've blown the whole world to hellangone up instead of just putting it into the God-awful shape it's in now, like you and Blackie DuQuesne did. *Wow*, what a mess!'

'Yeah. Speaking of DuQuesne – seen him lately?'

'Not since the big bust. The Norlaminians probably know all about him.'

'They don't. I asked. They lost him.'

'Well, you might ask Hunkie de Marigny. She'll know if anybody does.'

'Oh – she still here?'

'Yeah. Most of us are, and will be.'

Seaton chatted for another minute, then, 'Take it easy, guy,' he said; and went up the corridor to Room 1631. The door was wide open, so he went in without knocking.

'Park it. Be with you in a moment,' a smooth contralto voice said, and Seaton sat down on a chair near the door.

The woman – Dr Stephanie de Marigny, nuclear physicist and good at her trade – kept both eyes fastened on a four-needle meter about eighteen inches in front of her nose. Her well-kept hands and red-nailed fingers, working blind with the sure precision of those of a world-champion typist, opened and closed switches, moved sliders and levers, and manipulated a dozen or so vernier knobs in tiny arcs.

There was nothing to show any uninformed observer what she was doing. Whatever it was that she was working on could have been behind that instrument-filled panel – or down in some sub-basement – or at the Proving Grounds down the Potomac – or a million miles or parsecs out in space. Whatever it was or wherever, as she worked the four needles of the master-meter closer and closer together as each needle approached the center-zero mark of the meter's scale –

Until finally the four hair-thin flat needles were exactly in line with each other and with the hair-thin zero mark. Whereupon four heavy plungers drove home and every light on the panel flashed green and went out.

'On the button,' she said then, aloud. She rose to her feet, stretched as gracefully and luxuriously and unselfconsciously as does a cat, and turned toward her visitor.

'Hi, Hunkie,' Seaton said. 'Can you spare me a minute?'

'Nice to see you again, Dick.' She came toward him, hand outstretched. 'I could probably be talked into making it two minutes.'

The word 'big', while true, was both inadequate and misleading. Stephanie de Marigny was tall – five feet ten in her nylons – and looked even taller because of her three-inch heels, her erect posture, and because of the mass of jet-black hair piled high on her head.

Her breasts jutted; her abdomen was flat and hard; her wide, flat hips flared out from a startlingly narrow waist; and her legs would have made any professional glamor-photographer drool And her face, if not as beautiful as her body, was fully as striking. Her unplucked eyebrows, as black as her hair, were too long and too thick and too bushy and grew too nearly together above a nose that was as much of a beak as DuQuesne's own. The lashes over her deep brown eyes were simply incredible. Her cheekbones were too large and too prominent. Her fire-engine-red mouth was too big. Her square chin and her hard, clean line of jaw were too outstanding; demanded too much notice. Her warm, friendly, dimple-displaying smile, however, revealed the charm that was actually hers.

Seaton said, 'As always, you're really a treat for the optic nerve.'

She ignored the compliment. 'You aren't; you look like a catastrophe looking for a place to happen. You ought to take better care of yourself, Dick. Get some sleep once in a while.'

'I'm going to, as soon as I can. But what I came in for – have you heard anything of Blackie lately?'

'No. Not since he got delusions of grandeur. Why? Should I have?'

'Not that I know of. I just thought maybe you two had enough of a thing on so you'd keep in touch.'

'Uh-uh. I ran around with him a little, is all. Nothing serious. Of all the men I know who understand and appreciate good music, he's the youngest, the best-looking, and the most fun. Also the biggest. I can wear high heels and not tower over him, which I can't do with most men ...' She paused, nibbling at her lower lip, then went on, 'My best guess is that he's out on one of the new planets somewhere, making several hundred thousand tax-free dollars per year. That's what I'm going to be doing as soon as I finish Observers' School here.'

'You're the gal who can do it, too. Luck, Hunkie.'

'Same to you, Dick. Drop in again, any time you're around.'

And aboard the *Skylark of Valeron*, Seaton turned to Dorothy with a scowl. 'Nobody's seen him or heard anything of him, so he probably isn't loose yet. I *hate* this waiting. Confound it, I wish the big black ape would get loose and start something!'

Although Seaton did not know it, DuQuesne had and was about to.

It happened that night, after Seaton had gone to bed.

The message came in loud and clear on Seaton's private all-hours receiver, monitored and directed by the unsleeping Brain:

'... Seaton reply on tight beam of the sixth stop DuQuesne calling Seaton reply on tight beam of the sixth stop DuQuesne calling ...'

Coming instantly awake at the sound of his name, Seaton kicked off the covers, thought a light on, and, setting hands and feet, made a gymnast's twisting, turning leap over Dorothy without touching her. There was plenty of room on his own side of the bed, but the direct route was quicker. He landed on his feet, took two quick steps, and slapped the remote-control helmet on his head.

'Trace this call. Hit its source with a tight beam of the sixth,' he thought into the helmet; then took it off and said aloud, You're coming in loud and clear. What gives?'

'Loud and clear here. All hell's out for noon. I just met the damndest alien any science-fiction fan ever imagined – teeth, wings, tail – the works. Klazmon

529

by name; boss of two hundred forty-one planets full of monsters just like him. He's decided that all humanity everywhere should be liquidated; and it looks as though he may have enough stuff to do just that.'

Dorothy had sat up in bed, sleepily. She made a gorgeously beautiful picture, Seaton thought; wearing a wisp of practically nothing and her hair a tousled auburn riot. As the sense of DuQuesne's words struck home, however, a look of horror spread over her face and she started to say something; but Seaton touched his lips with a forefinger and she, wide awake now, nodded.

'Nice summary, DuQuesne,' Seaton said then. 'Now break it down into smaller pieces, huh?' and DuQuesne went on to give a verbatim report of his interview with Llanzlan Klazmon of the Realm of the Llurdi.

'So much for facts,' DuQuesne said. 'Now for inferences and deductions. You know how, when you're thinking with anyone, other information, more or less relevant and more or less clear, comes along? A sort of side-band effect?'

'Yeah, always. I can see how you picked up the business about the stranger ships that way. But how sure are you that those seventeen ships were Fenachrone?'

'Positive. That thought was clear. And for that matter, there must be others running around loose somewhere. How possible is it, do you think, to wipe out completely a race that has had spaceships as long as they have?'

'Could be,' agreed Seaton. 'And this ape Klazmon figured it that we were the same race, basically, both mentally – savage, egocentric, homicidal – and physically. How could he arrive at any such bobbled-up, cockeyed conclusions as that?'

'For him, easily enough. Klazmon is just about as much like us as we are like those X-planet cockroaches. Imagine a man-sized bat, with a super-able tail, cat's eyes and teeth, humanoid arms and hands, a breastbone like the prow of a battleship, pectoral muscles the size of forty-pound hams, and—'

'Wait up a sec – this size thing. His projection?'

'That's right. Six feet tall. He wasn't the type to shrink or expand it.'

'I'll buy that. And strictly logical – with their own idea of what logic is.'

'Check. According to which logic we're surplus population and are to be done away with. So I decided to warn you as to what the human race is up against and to suggest a meeting with you that we *know* can't be listened in on. Check?'

'Definitely. We'll lock our sixths on and instruct our computers to compute and effect rendezvous at null relative velocity in minimum time. Can do?'

'Can do – am doing,' DuQuesne said; and Seaton, donning his helmet, perceived that the only fifth- or sixth-order stuff anywhere near the *Skylark of Valeron* – except what she was putting out herself, of course – was the thin, tight beam that was the base-line.

Seaton thought into his helmet for a few seconds; then, discarding it, he went around the bed, got into it on his own side, and started to kiss Dorothy a second goodnight.

'But, Dick,' she protested. 'That DuQuesne! Do you think it's safe to let him come actually aboard?'

'Yes. Not only safe, but necessary – we don't want to be blabbing that kind of stuff all over a billion parsecs of space. And safe because I still say we're better than he is at anything he wants to start, for fun, money, chalk, or marbles. So goodnight again, ace of my bosom.'

'Hadn't you better notify somebody else first? Especially the Norlaminians?'

'You said it, presh; I sure should.' Seaton put on his helmet; and it was a long time before either of the Seatons got back to sleep. Long for Dorothy, heroically keeping eyes closed and breathing regularly so that her husband would not know how shaken and terrified she really was; long for Seaton himself, who lay hour upon endless hour, hands linked behind his head, gray eyes staring fiercely up into the darkness.

It had been a long time since Richard Ballinger Seaton and Marc C. DuQuesne had locked horns last. This galaxy – this cluster – this whole First Universe was not large enough for the two of them. When they met again one of them would dispose of the other.

It was as simple as that. Yet Seaton had accepted a call for help. The whole enormous complex of defenses that he had labored so hard and long to erect against DuQuesne would now be diverted to another, perhaps even a greater, threat to the safety of civilization. It was right and proper that this should be so.

But Seaton knew that whatever the best interests of civilization in this matter, there could and would never be any greater personal threat to himself than was incarnate in the cold, hard, transcendentally logical person of Blackie DuQuesne.

9

Among the Jelmi

And half a universe away other events were moving to fruition.

As has been said, the eight hundred Jelmi aboard the ship that had once been a Llurdan cruiser were the selected pick of the teeming billions of their race inhabiting two hundred forty-one planets. The younger ones had been selected for brains, ability, and physical perfection; the older ones for a hundred years or more of outstanding scientific achievement. And of the older group, Tammon stood out head and shoulders above all the rest. He was the Einstein of his race.

He looked a vigorous, bushily gray-haired sixty; but was in fact two hundred eleven Mallidaxian years old.

Tammon was poring over a computed graph, measuring its various characteristics with vernier calipers, a filar microscope, and an integrating planimeter, when Mergon and Luloy came swinging hand in hand into his laboratory. Both were now fully recovered from the wounds they had suffered in that hand-to-hand battle with the Llurdi on now-far-distant Llurdiax. Muscles moved smoothly under the unblemished bronze of Mergon's skin; Luloy's swirling shoulder-length mop of gleaming chestnut hair was a turbulent glory.

'Hail, Tamm,' the two said in unison, and Mergon went on: 'Have you unscrewed the inscrutability of that anomalous peak yet?'

Tammon picked up another chart and scowled at a sharp spike going up almost to the top of the scale. 'This? I'm not exactly sure yet, but I may have. At least, by re-computing with an entirely new and more-than-somewhat weird set of determinors, I got this,' and he ran his fingertip along the smooth curve on the chart he had been studying.

Mergon whistled through his teeth and Luloy, after staring for a moment said, 'Wonderful! Expound, O sage, and elucidate.'

'It had to have at least one component in the sixth, on the level of thought, but no known determinors would affect it. Therefore I applied the mathematics of symbolic logic to a wide variety of hunches, dreams, I've-been-here-or-done-this-befores, premonitions, intuitions ...'

'Llenderllon's eyeballs!' Luloy broke in. 'So *that* was what you ran us all through the wringer for, a while back.'

'Precisely. Using these new determinors in various configurations – dictated not by mathematical reasoning, but by luck and by hunch and by perseverance – I finally obtained a set of uniquely manipulable determinants that yielded this final smooth curve, the exactly fitting equation of which reduces beautifully to—'

'Hold it, Tamm,' Mergon said, 'you're losing me,' and Luloy added:

'You lost *me* long ago. What does it *mean*?'

'It will take years to explore its ramifications, but one fact is clear: the fourth dimension of space does actually exist. Therefore, the conclusion seems inescapable that ...'

'Stop it!' Luloy snapped. 'This is terribly dangerous stuff to be talking about. That terrific kind of a breakthrough is just *exactly* what Klazmon – the beast! – has been after for years. And you know very well that we're not really free; that he has us under constant surveillance.'

'But by detector only,' Mergon said. 'A full working projection at this distance? Uh-uh. It might be smart, though, to be a little on the careful side, at that.'

Days lengthened into weeks. The ex-Llurdan cruiser, renamed the *Mallidax* and converted into a Jelman worldlet, still hurtled along a right-line course toward the center of the First Universe, at a positive-and-negative acceleration that would keep her – just barely! – safe against collision with intergalactic clouds of gas or dust.

The objective of their flight was a small sun, among whose quite undistinguished family of planets were a moderate-sized oxygen-bearing world and its rather large, but otherwise uninteresting companion moon.

Tammon, hot on the trail of his breakthrough in science, kept his First Assistant Mergon busy fourteen or sixteen hours per day designing and building – and sometimes inventing – new and extremely special gear; and Mergon in turn drove Luloy, his wife and Girl Friday, as hard as he drove himself.

Tammon, half the time, wore armor and billion-volt gloves against the terribly lethal forces he was tossing so nonchalantly from point to point. Mergon, only slightly less powerfully insulated, had to keep his variable-density goggles practically opaque against the eye-tearing frequencies of his welding arcs. And even Luloy, much as she detested the feel of clothing against her skin, was as armored and as insulated as was either of the men as she tested and checked and double-checked and operated, with heavily gloved flying fingers, the maze of unguarded controls that was her constructor station.

And all the other Jelmi were working just as hard; even – or especially? – Master Biologist Sennlloy: who, with her long, thick braids of Norse-goddess hair piled high on her head and held in place by a platinum-filigree net, was delving deeper and even deeper into the mystery of life.

Any research man worth his salt must not be the type to give up: he must be able to keep on butting his head against a stone wall indefinitely without hoisting the white flag. Thus, Tammon developed theory after theory after theory for, and Mergon and Luloy built model after model after model of, mechanisms to transport material objects from one place to another in normal space by moving them *through* the fourth dimension – and model after model after model failed to work.

They failed unfailingly. Unanimously. Wherefore Mergon had run somewhat low on enthusiasm when he and Luloy carried the forty-ninth model of the series into Tammon's laboratory to be put to the test. While the old savant hooked the device up into a breadboard layout of gadgetry some fifteen feet long, Mergon somewhat boredly picked up an empty steel box, dropped six large ball-bearings into it, closed and hasped its cover, grasped it firmly in his left hand, and placed an empty steel bowl on the bench.

'Now,' Tammon said, and flipped a switch – and six heavy steel balls clanged into the bowl out of nowhere.

'Huh?' Mergon's left hand had jumped upward of its own accord; and, fumbling in his haste, he opened the box in that hand and stared, jaw actually agape, at its empty interior.

'Llenderllon's eyeballs!' Luloy shrieked. '*This* one works!'

'It does indeed,' a technician agreed, and turned anxiously to Tammon. 'But sir, doesn't that fact put us into a highly dangerous position? Even though Klazmon can't operate a full working projection at this distance, he undoubtedly has had all his analytical detectors out all this time and this successful demonstration must have tripped at least some of them.'

'Not a chance,' Mergon said. 'He'll *never* find these bands – it'd be exactly like trying to analyze a pattern of fifth- or sixth-order force with a visible-light spectroscope.'

'It probably would be, at that,' the technician agreed, and Luloy said, 'But what I've been wondering about all along is, what *good* is it? What's it *for*? Except robbing a bank or something, maybe.'

'It reduces theory to practice,' Tammon told her. 'It gives us priceless data, by application of which to already-known concepts we will be able to build mechanisms and devices to perform operations hitherto deemed impossible. Operations un-thought-of, in fact.'

'Maybe we should be pretty careful about it, though, at that,' Mergon said. 'To do very much real development work, we'll have to be using a lot of fairly unusual sixth-order stuff that he can detect and analyze. That will make him wonder what we're up to and he won't stop at wondering. He'll take steps.'

'*Big* steps,' Luloy agreed.

Tammon nodded. 'That is true ... and we must land somewhere to do any worthwhile development work, since this ship is not large enough to house the projectors we will have to have. Also, we are short of certain necessities for such work, notably neutronium and faidons ... and the projectors of these ultra-bands will have to be of tremendous power, range, and scope ... you are right. We must find a solar system emanating sixth-order energies. Enough of them, if possible, to mask completely our own unavoidable emanations. We now have enough new data so that we can increase tremendously the range, delicacy, and accuracy of our own detectors. See to it, Mergon, and find a good landing place.'

'Yes, sir!' and Mergon went, with enthusiasm again soaring high, to work.

Rebuilding, and re-powering their detector systems did not take very long; but finding the kind of landing place they needed proved to be something entirely else.

They had more or less assumed that many galaxies would show as much sixth-order activity as did their own, but that assumption was wrong. In three weeks they found only three galaxies showing any at all; and not one of the three was emanating as much sixth-order stuff as their own small vessel was putting out.

After another week or so, however, the savant on watch asked Mergon to come to his station. 'There's something tremendous up ahead and off to star-board, Merg. That spot there.' He pointed. 'It's been there for almost half an hour and it hasn't increased by a thousandth of what I expected it to. I would have said that at that distance nothing could possibly register that high.'

'Did you check your circuits?' Mergon asked.

'Of course; everything's on the green.'

'Main Control!' Mergon snapped into a microphone. 'Mergon speaking. Flip one eighty immediately. Decel max.'

'Flip one eighty,' the speaker said, and the vessel turned rapidly end for end. '... ON the mark and decelerating at max.'

Mergon whirled around and sprinted for Tammon's laboratory. He yanked the door and reported, concluding, 'It's apparently emanating thousands of times as much as our whole galaxy does, so we'd better sneak up on it with care.'

'Can we stop in time or will we have to overshoot and come back to it from the other side? That may affect course, you know.'

Mergon hadn't thought of that point, but he soon found out. They couldn't stop quite in time, but the overshoot would be a matter of less than a day.

'See to it, Mergon,' Tammon said, and resumed his interrupted studies.

The approach was made. Surprise turned to consternation when it was learned that practically all of that emanation was coming from one planet instead of a thousand; but since that condition was even better than any that had been hoped for, they shielded everything that could be shielded and sneaked up on that extraordinary world – the third planet of a Type G sun. It had an unusually large satellite ... and ideal location for their proposed oper-ation ... there were two small clusters of dome-shaped structures ... abandoned ... quite recently ... with advanced technology all such things and procedures would of course be abandoned ... and there were bits and pieces of what looked like wreckage.

Seaton – who had not yet seen at close up any part of the moon! – would have recognized at a glance the American and the Russian lunar outposts, and also what was left of Ranger Seven and of several, other American and Russian moon-rockets.

As a matter of fact, the Jelmi could deduce, within fairly narrow limits, what had happened on Earth's moon.

But all they cared about was that, since the moon was not inhabited at that time, they would probably not attract undue attention if they landed on it and, thoroughly and properly screened, went to work. And Klazmon could not possibly detect them there.

Luna's mountains are high and steep. Therefore, after the *Mallidax* had come easily to ground at the foot of one such mountain, it took only a day for the *Mallidax*'s mighty construction-projectors to hollow out and finish off a sub-lunar base in that mountain's depths.

And next day, early, work was begun upon the tremendous new super-dreadnought of the void that was going to be named the *Mallidaxian*.

10

Jelmi on the Moon

Miss Madlyn Mannis – née Gretchen Schneider – stood in the shade of a huge beach umbrella (perish forbid that any single square inch of that petal-smooth, creamily flawless epidermis should be exposed to Florida's fervent sun!) on Clearwater Beach. She was digging first one set of red-nailed toes and then the other into the soft white sand, and was gazing pensively out over the wavelets of the Gulf.

She was a tall girl, and beautifully built, with artistically waved artistically red hair; and every motion she made was made with the lithe grace of the highly trained professional dancer that she in fact was. She was one of the best exotic dancers in the business. As a matter of box-office fact, she was actually almost as good as she thought she was.

She was wearing the skimpiest neo-bikini ever seen on Clearwater Beach and was paying no attention whatever, either to the outraged glares of all the other women in sight or to the distinctly outraged glances of the well-built, deeply tanned, and highly appreciative young man who was standing some twenty feet away.

She was wondering, however, and quite intensely, about the guy. He'd been following her around for a couple of weeks. Or had he? She'd seen him somewhere every day – but he couldn't *possibly* have followed her here. Not only hadn't she known she was coming here until just before she started, but she had come by speedboat and had found him on the beach when she arrived!

And the man was wondering, too. He knew that he hadn't been following her. Without hiring an eye, he wouldn't know how to. And the idea that Madlyn Mannis would be following *him* around was ridiculous – it *really* stunk. But how many times in a row could heads turn up by pure chance alone?

He didn't dare move any closer, but he kept on looking and he kept on wondering. Would she slug him or just slap him or maybe even accept it, he wondered, if he should offer to buy *the* Miss Mannis a drink …

Miss Mannis was also being studied, much more intensively and from much closer viewpoints, by two Jelmi in an immense new spaceship, the *Mallidaxian*, on the moon; and the more they studied the Mannis costume the more baffled they became.

As had been said, the Jelmi had had to build this immense new spaceship because the comparatively tiny *Mallidax*, in which they had escaped from the Realm of the Llurdi, had proved too small by far to house the outsized gear necessary for accurately controlled intergalactic work of any kind. The *Mallidaxian*, however – built as she was of inoson and sister-ship as she was to the largest, heaviest, and most powerful space-sluggers of the Realm – was not only big enough to carry any instrumentation known to the science of the age, but also powerful enough to cope with any foreseeable development or contingency.

The Jelman sub-lunar base had been dismantled and collapsed. Its every distinguishing feature had been reduced to moon-dust. The *Mallidaxian's* slimly powerful length now extended for a distance of two and one half miles from the mountain's foot out into the level-floored crater: in less than an hour she would take off for Mallidax, the home world of Tammon, Mergon, Luloy, and several other top-bracket Jelmi of the fugitive eight hundred.

The vessel's officers and crew were giving their instruments and mechanisms one last pre-flight check. Tammon was still studying the offensive and defensive capabilities of Cape Kennedy; Mergon and Luloy – among others – had been studying the human beings of this hitherto unknown world. Everyone aboard, of course, had long since mastered the principal languages of Earth.

That Madlyn Mannis should have been selected for observation was not very astonishing. Some thousands of Earthmen – and Earthwomen, Earthchildren, even Earthdogs and cats – had been. There was that about Madlyn Mannis, however, and to a lesser degree about the male with whom she seemed in some way associated, that seemed to deserve special study. For one thing, the Jelmi had been totally unable to deduce any shred of evidence that might indicate her profession – not so surprising, since the work of a stripper must seem pure fantasy to a world which habitually wears no clothes at all! Madlyn, although used to being talked about, would have been quite astonished to learn how interestedly she was being discussed on the far side of the moon.

'Oh, let's bring her up here, Merg,' Luloy said in disgust. 'I want to talk to her – find out what this idiocy *means*. We'd better bring that fellow along, too: she'd probably be scared out of her wits – if any – alone.'

'Check,' Mergon said, and the two Tellurians appeared, standing close together, in the middle of the room.

The girl screamed once; then, her eyes caught by the awesome moonscape so starkly visible through the transparent wall, she froze and stared in terror.

Then, finding that she was not being hurt, she fought her terror down. She took one fleeting glance at Mergon, blushed to the waist, and concentrated on Luloy. 'Why, you must ... you do go naked!' she gasped. 'All the time! How utterly, *utterly* shameless!'

'Shameless?' Luloy wrinkled her nose in perplexity. 'That's what I want to talk to you about, this "shame" concept. I can't understand it and its dictionary definition is senseless to the point of unsanity. I never heard of a concept before that so utterly lacked sense, reason, and logic. What significant difference can there *possibly* be between nakedness and one ribbon and two bits of gauze? And why in the name of All-Seeing Llenderllon wear any clothing at all when you don't have to? Against cold or thorns or whatever? And especially when you swim? And you take *off* your clothes too ...'

'I do no such thing!' The dancer threw herself up haughtily. 'I am an artiste. An exotic dancer's disrobing is a fine art, and I am Madlyn Mannis, *the* exotic dancer.'

'Be that as it may, just answer one question and we'll put you back where you were, on the beach. What *possible* logical, reasonable, or even comprehensible relationship can there be between clothing and sex?'

While the girl was groping for an answer, the main took one step forward and said, 'She can't answer that question. Neither can I, fully, but I can state as a fact that such a relationship is a fact of our lives; of the lives of all the people – even the least civilized peoples – of our world. It's an inbred, ages-old, worldwide sexual taboo. Based, possibly or even probably, upon the idea "out of sight, out of mind".'

'A *sexual* taboo?' Luloy shook her head in complete bafflement. 'Why, I never heard of anything so completely idiotic in my whole life! Will you wear these thought-caps with me for a moment, please, so that we may explore this weird concept in depth?'

The girl flinched away from the helmet at first, but the man reached out for his, saying, 'I've always claimed to have an open mind, but *this* I've got to see.'

Since complete non-comprehension of motivation on one side met fundamental ignorance on the other, however, thoughts were no more illuminating than words had been.

'Neither she nor I know enough about the basics of that branch of anthropology,' the man said, handing the helmet back to Luloy. 'You'd better get a book. *Mores and Customs of Tellus,* by David Lisser, in five volumes, is the most complete work I know of. You can find it in any big bookstore. It's expensive, though – it costs seventy-five dollars.'

'Oh? And we haven't any American money and we don't steal ... but I've noticed that highly refractive bits of crystalline carbon of certain shades of color are of value here.'

Turning her back on the two Tellurians, Luloy went to the laboratory bench, opened a drawer, glanced into it, and shook her head. She picked up a helmet, thought into it, and there appeared upon the palm of her hand a perfectly cut, perfectly polished, blue-white diamond half the size of an egg.

She turned back toward the two and held out her hand so that the man could inspect the gem, saying, 'I have not given any attention at all to your monetary system, but this should be worth enough, I think, to leave in the place of the book of five volumes. Or should it be bigger?'

Close up, the man goggled at blue-white fire. '*Bigger*! Than *that rock*? *Lady*! Are you *kidding*? If that thing will stand inspection it'll buy you a *library*, buildings and all!'

'That's all I wanted to know. Thank you.' Luloy turned to Mergon. 'They don't know any more than—'

'Just a minute, please,' the man broke in. 'If diamonds don't mean any more than that to you, why wouldn't it be a good idea for you to make her some? To alleviate the shock she has just had? Not as big, of course; none bigger than the end of my thumb.'

Luloy nodded. 'I know. Various sizes, for full-formal array. She's just about my size, so eleven of your quarts will do it.'

'My God, no ...' Madlyn began, but the man took smoothly over.

'Not quite, Miss Luloy. Our ladies don't decorate their formals as lavishly as you apparently do. One quart, or maybe a quart and a half, will do very nicely.'

'Very well,' Luloy looked directly at the man. 'But you won't want to be lugging them around with you all the rest of the day – they're heavy – so I'll put them in the right-hand top drawer of the bureau in your bedroom. Goodbye,' and Mergon's hands began to move toward his controls.

'Wait a minute!' the man exclaimed. 'You *can't* just dump us back where we were without a word of explanation! While spaceships aren't my specialty – I'm a petrochemical engineer T-8 – I've never imagined anything as big as this vessel actually flying, and I'm just about as much interested in that as I am in the way we got here – which *has* to be fourth-dimensional translation; it *can't* be anything else. So if everything isn't top secret, how about showing us around a little?'

'The fourth-dimension device is top secret; so much so that only three or four of us know anything about it. You may study anything else you please. Bearing in mind that we have only a few seconds over three of your minutes left, where would you like to begin?'

'The engines first, please, and the drives.'

'And you, Miss Mannis? Arts? Crafts? Sciences? There is no dancing going on at the moment.'

The dancer's right hand flashed out, seized her fellow Earthman's forearm and clung to it. 'Wherever *he* goes I go along!' she said, very positively.

Since neither of the two Earthpeople had even been projected before, they were both very much surprised at how much can be learned via projection, and in how short a time. They saw tremendous receptors and generators and propulsors; they saw the massed and banked and tiered keyboards and instrumentation of the control stations; they saw how the incredibly huge vessel's inoson structural members were trussed and latticed and braced and buttressed to make it possible for such a titanic structure to fly.

Since everything aboard the original Jelman vessel had been moved aboard this vastly larger one before the original had been reduced to moon-dust, the dancer and her companion also saw beautiful, splendid, and magnificent – if peculiarly unearthly – paintings and statues and tapestries and rugs. They heard music, ranging from vast orchestral recordings down to the squeakings and tootlings of beginners learning to play musical instruments unknown to the humanity of Earth.

And above all they saw people. Hundreds and hundreds of people; each one completely naked and each one of a physical perfection almost never to be found on Earth.

At time zero twenty seconds Mergon cut off the projectors and the Earth-man looked at Luloy.

She not only had swapped the diamond for the five-volume set of books; she had already read over a hundred pages of Volume One. She was flipping pages almost as fast as her thumb and forefinger could move, and she was absorbing the full content of the work at the rate of one glance per page.

'You people seem to be as human as we are,' Madlyn said, worriedly, 'but outside of that you're nothing like us at all in any way. *Where* did you come from anyway?'

'I can't tell you that,' Mergon said, flatly. 'Not that I don't want to, I can't. We're what you call human, yes; but our world Mallidax is a myriad of galaxies away from here – so far away that the distance is completely incomprehensible to the mind. Goodbye.'

And Madlyn Mannis found herself – with no lapse of time and with no sensation whatever of motion – standing in her former tracks under the big umbrella on the beach. The only difference was that she was now standing still instead of digging her toes into the sand.

She looked at her fellow moon-traveler. He, too, was standing in the same place as before, but he now looked as though he had been struck by lightning. She swallowed twice, then said, 'Well, I'm awfully glad I wasn't alone when *that* hap—' She broke off abruptly, licked her lips, and went on in a strangely altered tone, 'Or am I nuttier than a fruit-cake? *Vas* you dere, Sharlee?'

'I vas dere, Madlyn.' He walked toward her. He was trying to grin, but was not having much success with it. 'And my name *is* Charley – Charles K. van der Gleiss.'

'My God! That makes it even worse – or does it?'

'I don't see how anything could; very well or very much ... but I need a drink. How about you?'

'*Brother!* Do I! But we'll have to dress. You can't get anything on the beach here that's strong enough to cope with anything like *that!*'

'I know. City owned. Teetotal. I'll see you out in front in a couple of minutes. In a taxi.'

'Make it five minutes, or maybe a bit more. And if you run out on me, Charles K. van der Gleiss, I'll ... I'll hunt you up and kill you absolutely dead, so help me!'

'Okay, I'll wait, but make it snappy. I need that drink.'

She had snatched up her robe and had taken off across the sand like a startled doe; her reply came back over one shoulder. '*You* need a drink? Oh, *brother!*'

1 1

Blotto

The world had come a long way from the insular, mud-bound globe of rock and sea of the 1950s and 1970s; Seaton and Crane had seen to that. Norlaminian Observers were a familiar sight to most humans – if not in person, then surely through the medium of TV or tapefax. A thousand worlds had been photographed by Tellurian cameramen and reporters; the stories of the Osnomians, the Fenachrone, the Valeronians, even the Chlorans and other weirdly non-human races of the outer void were a matter of public record.

Nevertheless, it is a far different thing from knowing that other races exist to find yourself a guest of one of them, a quarter of a million miles from home; wherefore Madlyn and Charley's expressed intentions took immediate and tangible form.

Madlyn Mannis and Charles K. van der Gleiss were facing each other across a small table in a curtained booth; a table upon which a waiter was placing a pint of bonded hundred-proof bourbon and the various items properly accessory thereto. As soon as the curtain fell into place behind the departing waiter the girl seized the bottle, raised it to her mouth, and belted down a good two fingers – as much as she could force down before her coughing, choking, and strangling made her stop.

'Hey! Take it easy!' the man protested, taking the bottle from her hand and putting it gently down on the table. 'You're not used to guzzling it like *that*; that's for plain damn sure.'

She gulped and coughed a few times; wiped her streaming eyes. 'I'll tell the world I'm not; two little ones is always my limit, ordinarily. But I *needed* that jolt, Charley, to keep from flipping my lid completely. Don't you need one, too?'

'I certainly do. A triple, at least, with a couple of snowflakes of ice and about five drops of water.' He built the drink substantially as specified, took it down in three swallows, and drew a profoundly deep breath. 'You heard me tell them I'm a petrochemical engineer, T-8. So maybe that didn't hit me *quite* as hard as it did you, but bottled courage helps, believe me.'

He mixed another drink – single – and cocked an eyebrow at the girl. 'What'll you have as a chaser for that God-awful belt?'

'A scant jigger – three-quarters, about – in a water glass,' she said, promptly. 'Two ice-cubes and fill it up with ice-water.' He mixed the drink and she took a sip. 'Thanks, Charley. This is *much* better for *drinking* purposes. Now maybe I can talk about what happened without blowing my top. I was going to wonder why we've been running into each other all the time lately, but that doesn't amount to *anything* compared to … I actually thought … in fact, I know very well … we *were* on … weren't we? Both of us?'

'We were both on the moon,' he said flatly. 'To make things worse, we were inside a spaceship that I still don't believe can be built. Those are *facts*.'

'Uh-uh; that's what I mean. Positively *nobody* ever went to the moon or anywhere else off-Earth without being *in* something, and we didn't have even the famous paddle. And posi-damn-tively nobody – but *nobody!* – ever got into and out of a tightly closed, vacuum-tight spaceship without anybody opening any doors or ports or anything. How do you play them tunes on your piccolo, friend?'

'I don't; and the ship itself was almost as bad. Not only was it impossibly big; it was full of stuff that makes the equipment of the *General Hoyt S. Vandenberg* look like picks and shovels.' She raised an eyebrow questioningly and he went on, 'One of the missile-tracking vessels – the hairiest hunks of electronic gadgetry ever built by man. What it all adds up to is a race of people somewhere who know as much more than even the Norlaminians do as we do than grasshoppers. So I think we had better report to the cops.'

'The *cops!*' she spat the word out like an oath. 'Me? Madlyn Mannis? Squeal to the fuzz? When a great big gorilla slugs me in the brisket and heists fifteen grands' worth of diamonds off of me and I don't get …'

She broke off suddenly. Both had avoided mentioning the diamonds, but now the word was accidentally out. She shook her head vigorously, then said, 'Uh-uh. They aren't there. Who ever heard of diamonds by the quart? Anyway, even if that Luloy could have done it and did, I'll bet they evaporated or something.'

'Or they'll turn out to be glass,' he agreed. 'No use looking, hardly, I don't think. Even if they are there and are real, you couldn't sell 'em without telling where they came from – and you can't do that.'

'I couldn't? Don't be naive, Charley. Nobody ever asks me where I got any diamonds I sell – I'd slap his silly face off. I can peddle your half, too, at almost wholesale. Not all at once, of course, but a few at a time, here and there.'

'Half, Uh-uh,' he objected. 'I was acting as your agent on that deal. Ten per cent.'

'Half,' she insisted; then grinned suddenly. 'But why argue about half of nothing? To get back onto the subject of cops – the lugs! – they brushed my report off as a stripper's publicity gag and I didn't get even one line in the papers. And if I report *this* weirdie they'll give me a one-way, most-direct-route ticket to the nearest funny-farm.'

'You've got a point there.' He glowered at his drink. 'I can see us babbling about instantaneous translation through the fourth dimension and an impossible spaceship on the moon manned by people exactly like us – except that the men all look like Green Bay Packers and all the girls without exception are stacked like … like …' Words failed him.

Madlyn nodded thoughtfully. 'Uh-huh,' she agreed. 'They were certainly stacked. That Luloy … that biologist Sennlloy, who was studying all those worms and mice and things … all of 'em. And they swap hundred-carat perfect blue-white diamonds for books.'

'Yeah. We start babbling that kind of stuff and we wind up in wrap-arounds.'

'You said it. But we've got to do *something*!'

'Well, we can report to an Observer—'

'I've got a better idea. Let's tie one really on.'

Neither of them remembered very much of what happened after that, but at about three o'clock the following afternoon Charley van der Gleiss struggled upward through a million miles of foul-tasting molasses to consciousness. He was lying on the couch in his living room; fully dressed, even to his shoes. He worked himself up, very carefully, to a sitting position and shook his head as carefully. It didn't *quite* explode. Good – he'd probably live.

Walking as though on eggs, he made his cautious way to the bedroom. She was lying, also fully dressed, on his bed. On the coverlet. As he sat gingerly down on the side of the bed she opened one eye, then the other, put both hands to her head, and groaned; her features twisting in agony. 'Stop shaking me, you … *please*,' she begged. 'Oh, my poor head! It's coming clear off … right at the neck …'

Then, becoming a little more conscious, she went on, 'It didn't go back into the woodwork, Charley, did it? I'll see that horrible moonscape and that naked Luloy as long as I live.'

'And I'll see that nightmare of a spaceship. While you're taking the first shot at the bathroom I'll have 'em send up a gallon of black coffee, a couple of

543

quarts of orange juice, and whatever the pill-roller downstairs says is good for what ails us. In the meantime, would you like a hair of the dog?'

'My God, no!' She shuddered visibly. 'I never got drunk in my life before – I have to keep in shape, you know – and if I live through this I swear I'll never take another drink as long as I live!'

When they began to feel better Madlyn said, 'Why don't you peek into that drawer, Charley? There just *might* be something in it.'

He did, and there was, and he gave her the honor of lifting the soft plastic bag out of the drawer.

'My God!' she gasped. 'There's four or five *pounds* of them!' She opened the bag with trembling fingers and stood entranced for half a minute, then took out a few of the gems and examined them minutely.

'Charley,' she said then, 'if I know anything about diamonds – and I admit that I know a lot – these are not only real, but the finest things I have ever seen. I'm almost afraid to try to sell even the littlest ones. Men just simply don't give girls rocks like that. I'm not even sure that there are very many others like those around. If any.'

'Well, we would probably have had to talk to an Observer anyway, and this makes it a forced putt. Let's go, Maddy.'

'In *this* wreckage?' Expression highly scornful, she waved a hand at her rumpled and wrinkled green afternoon gown. 'Are you completely out of your mind?'

'Oh, that's easy. I'll shave and put on a clean shirt and an intelligent look and then we'll skip over to your place for you to slick up and *then* we'll go down to the Observer's office. Say, have you got a safe-deposit box?'

'No, but don't worry about that for a while, my friend. We haven't got 'em past the Observer yet!'

An hour later, looking and feeling almost human again, the two were ushered into the Observer's heavily screened private office. They told him, as nearly as they could remember, every detail of everything that had happened.

He listened attentively. He had been among the Tellurians only a few short months; in the cautious thoughtful way of Norlaminians, he was far from ready to claim that he understood them. These two in particular seemed quite non-scientific and un-logical in their attitudes … and yet, he thought, and yet there was that about them which seemed to deserve a hearing. So he heard. Then he put on a headset and saw. Visually he investigated the far side of the moon; then, frowning slightly, he increased his power to microscopic magnification and reexamined half a dozen tiny areas. He then conferred briefly with Rovol of Rays on distant Norlamin, who in turn called Seaton into a long-distance three-way.

'No doubt whatever about it,' Seaton said. 'If they hadn't been hiding from somebody or something they wouldn't have ground up that many thousands of tons of inoson into moon-dust – that's a project, you know – and I don't need to tell you that inoson does *not* occur in nature. Yes, we definitely need to know more about this one. Coming in!'

Seaton's projection appeared in the Observer's office and, after being introduced, handed thought-helmets to Madlyn and Charley. 'Put these on, please, and go over the whole thing again, in as fine detail as you possibly can. It's not that we doubt any of your statements; it's just that we want to record and to study very carefully all the side-bands of thought that can be made to appear.'

The two went over their stories again; this time being interrupted, every other second or two, by either Seaton or the Observer with sharply pertinent questions or suggestions. When, finally, both had been wrung completely dry, the Observer took off his helmet and said:

'Although much of this material is not for public dissemination, I will tell you enough to relieve your minds of stress; especially since you have already seen some of it and I know that neither of you will talk.' Being a very young Norlaminian, just graduated from the Country of Youth, he smiled at this, and the two smiled – somewhat wryly – back.

'Wait a minute,' Seaton said. 'I'm not sure we want their minds relieved of too much stress. They both ring bells – loud ones. I'd swear I know you both from somewhere, except I know darn well I've never met either of you before … it's a cinch *nobody* could ever forget meeting Madlyn Mannis …' He paused, then snapped a finger sharply. 'Idiot! Of course! Where were you, both of you, at hours twenty-three fifty-nine on the eighteenth?'

'Huh? What is this, a gag?' van der Gleiss demanded.

'Anything else but, believe me,' Seaton assured him. 'Madlyn?'

'One minute of midnight? That would be the finale of my first show … Oh-oh! Was the eighteenth a Friday?'

'Yes.'

'That's it!' The girl was visibly excited now. 'Something *did* happen. Don't ask me what – all I know is I was just finishing my routine, and I got this feeling – this feeling of *importance* about something. Why, you were in it!' She stared at Seaton's projection incredulously. 'Yes! But – you were different somehow. I don't know how. Like a – like a reflection of you, or a bad photograph …'

Through his headset Seaton thought a quick, private three-way conference with Rovol and the Norlaminian on Earth: '—clearly refers to our beacon message—' '—yes, but holy cats, Rovol, what's this about a "reflection"?—' '—conceivably some sort of triggered response from another race—'

It took less than a second, then Seaton continued with the girl and her companion, who were unaware that any interchange had taken place.

'The "something important" you're talking about, Madlyn, was a message that we broadcast. You might call it an SOS; we were looking for a response from some other race or civilization with a little more on the ball than we have. We've been hoping for an answer; it's just possible that, through you, we've got one. What was that "reflection" like?'

'I'd call it a psychic pull,' said Madlyn promptly. 'And now that you mention it, I felt it with these Jelmi too. And –' Her eyes widened, and she turned to stare at Charley.

Seaton snapped his fingers. 'Look, Madlyn. Can you take time off to spend with us? I don't know what you've got into – but I want you nearby if you get into it again!'

Why, certainly, Mr Seaton. I mean – Dr Seaton. I'll call Moe – that's my agent – and cancel Vegas, and –'

'Thanks,' grinned Seaton. 'You won't lose anything by it.'

'I'm sure I won't, judging by … but oh, yes, *how* about those diamonds –*if* they are?'

'Oh, they are,' the Norlaminian assured her, 'and they're of course yours. Would you like to have me sell them for you?'

She glanced questioningly at van der Gleiss, who nodded and gave the jewels to the Observer. Then, 'We'd like that very much, sir,' Madlyn said, 'and thanks a lot.'

'Okay,' Seaton said then. 'Now, how about you, Charley. What kind of a jolt did you get at one minute of twelve that Friday night?'

'Well, it was the first time I caught Madlyn's act, and I admit it's a sockeroo. She has the wallop of a piledriver, no question of that. But if you mean spirit-message flapdoodle or psychic poppycock, nothing. I'm not psychic myself – not a trace – and nobody can sell me that anybody else is, either. That stuff is purely bunk – it's strictly for the birds.'

'It isn't either, Mister Charles K. van der Gleiss!' Madlyn exclaimed. 'And you are too psychic – very strongly so! How else would we be stumbling over each other everywhere we go? And how else would I possibly get drunk with you?' She spread her hands out in appeal to the Observer. '*Isn't* he psychic?'

'My opinion is that he is unusually sensitive to certain forces, yes,' the Norlaminian said. 'Think carefully, youth. Wasn't there something more than the mental or esthetic appreciation of, and the physical-sexual thrill at, the work of a superb exotic dancer?'

'Of course there was!' the man snapped. 'But … but … oh, I don't know. Now that Madlyn mentions it, there *was* a sort of a feeling of a message. But I haven't got even the *foggiest* idea of what the goddam thing was!'

'And that,' Seaton said, 'is about the best definition of it I've heard. We haven't either.'

12
DuQuesne and the Jelmi

DuQuesne, who had not seen enough of the *Skylark of Valeron* to realize that it was an intergalactic spacecraft, had supposed that Seaton and his party were still aboard *Skylark Three*, which was of the same size and power as DuQuesne's own ship, the *Capital D*. Therefore, when it became clear just what it was with which the *Capital D* was making rendezvous, to say that DuQuesne was surprised is putting it very mildly indeed.

He had supposed that his vessel was one of the three most powerful super-dreadnoughts of space ever built – but *this*! This thing was not a spaceship at all! In every important respect it was a world. It was big enough to mount and to power offensive and defensive armament of full planetary capability ... and if he knew Seaton and Crane half as well as he thought he did, that monstrosity could volatilize a world as easily as it could light a firecracker.

He was second. Again. And such an insignificantly poor second as to be completely out of the competition.

Something would have to be done about this intolerable situation ... and finding out what could be done about it would take precedence over everything else until he did find out.

He scowled in thought. That worldlet of a spaceship changed everything – radically. He'd been going to let eager-beaver Seaton grab the ball and run with it while he, DuQuesne, went on about his own business. But now – could he take the risk? Ten to one – or a hundred to one? – he couldn't touch that planetoid's safety screens with anything he had. But it was worth his while to try ...

Energizing the lightest possible fifth- and sixth-order webs, he reached out with his utmost delicacy of touch to feel out the huge globe's equipment; to find out exactly what it had.

He found out exactly nothing; and in zero time. At the first, almost imperceptible touch of DuQuesne's web the mighty planetoid's every defense flared instantaneously into being.

DuQuesne cut his webbing, the defenses vanished, and Seaton said, 'No peeking, DuQuesne. Come inside and you can look around all you please, but from outside it can't be done.'

'I see it can't. How do I get inside?'

'One of your shuttles or small boats. Go neutral as soon as you clear your outer skin and I'll bring you in.'

'I'll do that,' and as DuQuesne in one of his vessel's lifeboats traversed the long series of locks through the worldlet's tremendously thick shell he kept on wrestling with his problem.

No, the idea of letting Seaton be the Big Solo Hero was out like the well-known light. Seaton and his whole party would have to die. And the sooner the better.

He'd know it all along, really; his thinking had slipped, back there, for sure. With *that* fireball of a ship – flying base, rather – by the time Seaton got the job done he would be so big that nothing could ever cut him down to size. For that matter, was there anything that could be done about Seaton and his planetoid, even at the size they already were? There was no vulnerability apparent ... on the outside, at least. But there *had* to be something; some chink or opening; all he had to do was think of it – like the time he and 'Baby Doll' Loring had taken over a fully-manned superdreadnought of the Fenachrone.

The smart thing to do, the best thing for Marc C. DuQuesne, would be to join Seaton and work hand in glove with him – for a while. Until he had a bigger, more powerful worldlet than Seaton did and knew more than all the Skylarkers put together. Then blow the *Skylark of Valeron* and everyone and everything in it into impalpable dust and go on about his own business; letting civilization worry about itself.

To get away with that, he might have to give his word to act as one of the party, as before.

He never had broken his word ... so he wouldn't give it, this time, unless he had to ... but if he had to? If it came to a choice – breaking his word or being Emperor Marc the First of a galaxy, founder of a dynasty the like of which no civilization had ever seen before?

Whatever happened, come hell or high water, Seaton and his crew must and would die. He, DuQuesne, must and would come out on top!

As soon as DuQuesne's lifeboat was inside the enormous hollow globe that was the *Skylark of Valeron,* Seaton brought it to a gentle landing in a dock behind his own home and walked out to the dock with a thought-helmet on his head and its mate in his hand.

DuQuesne opened his lifeboat's locks and Seaton joined him in the tiny craft's main compartment.

Face to face, neither man spoke in greeting or offered to shake hands; both knew that there was nothing of friendship between them or ever would be. Nor did DuQuesne wonder why Seaton was meeting him thus: outside and alone. He knew exactly what the women, especially Margaret, thought of him; but such trifles had no effect whatever upon the essence of Marc C. DuQuesne.

Seaton handed DuQuesne the spare headset. DuQuesne put it on and Seaton said in thought, 'This, you'll notice, is no ordinary mechanical educator; not by seven thousand rows of Christmas trees. I suppose you know you're in the *Skylark of Valeron*. Study it, and take your time. I'll give you her prints before you go – if we're going to have to be allies again you ought to have something better than your *Capital D* to work with.'

Seaton thought that this surprise might make DuQuesne's guard slip for an instant, but it didn't. DuQuesne studied the worldlet intensively for over an hour, then took off his headset and said:

'Nice job, Seaton. Beautiful; especially that tank-chart of the First Universe and that super-computer brain – some parts of which, I see, this headset enables me to operate. The rest of it, I suppose, is keyed to and in sync with your own mind? No others need apply?'

'That's right. So, with the prints, you'll have everything you need, I think. But before you go into detail, I may know a thing that you don't and that may have a lot of bearing, one place or another. Have you ever heard of any way of getting into or through the fourth dimension except by rotation?'

'No. Not even in theory. How sure are you that there is or can be any other way of doing it?'

'Positive. One that not even the Norlaminians know anything about,' and Seaton gave DuQuesne the full picture and the full story and all the side-bands of thought of everything that had happened to Madlyn Mannis and Charles van der Gleiss.

At the sight of Mergon and Luloy – two of the three Jelmi whom the monstrous alien Klazmon had been comparing with the Fenachrone and with the chlorine-breathing amoeboid Chlorans and with DuQuesne himself – it took every iota of DuQuesne's iron control to make no sign of the astounding burst of interest he felt; for in one blinding flash of revealment his entire course of action became pellucidly clear. He knew exactly where and what Galaxy DW-427-LU was. He knew how to get Seaton headed toward that galaxy. He knew how to kill Seaton and all his crew and take over the *Skylark of Valeron*. And, best of all, he knew how to cover his tracks!

Completely unsuspicious of any of these thoughts, Seaton went on, 'Now we're ready, I think, for the fine details of what you found out.'

After giving a precisely detailed report that lasted for twenty minutes, DuQuesne said, 'Now as to location. I have a cylindrical chart – a plug-chart, you might call it – of all the galaxies lying close to the line between the point in space where your stasis-capsule whiffed out and the First Galaxy. Those four reels there.' He pointed. 'But I have no idea whatever as to where that plug lies in the universe – its universal coordinates. But since you know where you are and I know how I got here, it can be computed – in time.'

'In practically nothing flat,' Seaton said. 'As fast as you can run your tapes through your scanner there.' Seaton put his headset back on; DuQuesne followed suit. 'They don't even have to be in order. When the end of the last tape clears the scanner your plug will be in our tank.'

And it was: a long, narrow cylinder of yellowish-green haze.

'Nice; very nice indeed.' DuQuesne paid tribute to performance. 'I started my trip right there.' He marked the spot with a tiny purple light. It was a weird sensation, this; working with that gigantic brain, in that super-gigantic tank-chart, with only a headset and at a distance of miles!

'With my artificial gravity set to exact universal north as straight up,' DuQuesne went on, 'I moved along a course as close as possible to the axis of that cylinder to this point here.' The purple point extended itself into a long line of purple light and stopped. 'Klazmon's tight beam hit me at that point there, coming in from eighty-seven point four one eight degrees starboard and three point nine two six degrees universal south.'

DuQuesne's mind, terrifically hard held for that particular statement, revealed not the faintest side-band or other indication of what a monstrous lie that was. The figures themselves were very nearly right; but the fact that the beam had actually come in from the port and the north made a tremendous difference. The purple line darted off at almost a right angle to itself and DuQuesne went on without a break:

'You'll note that there are two galaxies on that line; one about halfway out to the rim of the universe –' this galaxy actually was, in Klazmon's nomenclature, Galaxy DW-427-LU – 'the other one clear out; right on the rim itself. Under those conditions no reliable estimate of distance was possible, but if we assume that Klazmon's power is of the same order of magnitude as ours it would have to be the first one. However, I'm making no attempt to defend that assumption.'

'Sure not; but it's safe enough, I'd say, for a first approximation. So, making that assumption, that galaxy is where the Realm of the Llurdi is – where the Llurdi and the Jelmi are. Where the folks that built that big battlewagon on the moon came from.'

'While the data do not prove it, by any means, that would be my best-educated guess. But my next one – that that's where they're going back to – isn't based on anything anywhere near that solid. Side-bands only, and not too many or too strong.'

'Yeah, I got some, too. But you're having first cut at this; go ahead,' Seaton said.

'Okay. First, you have to dig up some kind of an answer to the question of why those Jelmi came such an ungodly long distance away from home to do what was, after all, a small job of work. We know that they didn't do it just for fun. We know that the whole race of Jelmi is oppressed; we know that those eight hundred rebelled. We're fairly sure that Earth alone is, right now, putting out more sixth-order emanation than all the rest of the First Universe put together.

'Okay. There were some indications that Tammon worked out the theory of that fourth-dimensional gizmo quite a while back; but they had to come this tremendous distance to find enough high-order emanation to mask their research and development work from His Nibs Llanzlan Klazmon the Fifteenth.

'Now. My argument gets pretty tenuous at this point, but isn't it a fairly safe bet that, having reduced the theory of said gizmo to practice and having built a ship big enough to handle it like toothpicks, they'd beat it right back home as fast as they could leg it, knock the living hell out of the Llurdi – they could, you know, like shooting fish in a well – and issue a star-spangled Declaration of Independence? It does to me.'

'Check. While I didn't get there by exactly the same route you did, I arrived at the same destination. So it's not only got to be investigated; it's got to be Number One on the agenda. Question: who operates? Your baby or mine?'

'You know the answer to that. I'll have other fish to fry; quite possibly until after you have the Jelman angle solved.'

'My thought exactly.' Seaton assumed that DuQuesne's first, most urgent job would be to build a worldlet of his own; DuQuesne did not correct this thought. Seaton went on, 'The other question, then, is – do we join forces again, or work independently ... or maybe table the question temporarily, until you get yourself organized and we will have made at least a stab at evaluating what this Llurdan menace actually amounts to?'

'The last ... I think.' DuQuesne scowled in thought, then his face cleared; but at no time was there the slightest seepage of side-bands to the effect that he, DuQuesne, would see to it that Seaton would be dead long before that. Or that he, DuQuesne, did not give a tinker's damn whether anything was ever done about the Llurdan menace or not.

The two men discussed less important details for perhaps ten minutes longer; then DuQuesne took his leave. And, out in deep space again, with his mighty *Captain D* again boring a hole through the protesting ether, DuQuesne allowed himself a contemptuous and highly satisfactory sneer.

Back in their own living room, Seaton asked his wife, 'Dottie, did you smell anything the least bit fishy about that?'

'Not a thing, Dick. I gave it everything I had, and everything about it rang as true as a silver bell. Did you detect anything?'

'Not a thing – curse it! Even helmet to helmet – as deep as I could go without putting the screws on and blowing everything higher than up – it was flawless. But you've got to remember the guy's case-hardened and diamond finished ... But you've also got to remember that I came to exactly the same conclusions he did – and completely independently.'

'So every indication is that he *is* acting decently. He's been known to, you know.'

'Yeah. It's possible.' Seaton did not sound at all sold on the possibility. 'But

I wouldn't trust that big black ape as far as I could drop-kick him … I'd like awfully well to know whether he's pitching us a curve or not … and if he is, what the barb-tailed devil it can possibly be … so what we'll have to do, pet, is keep our eyes peeled and look a little bit out *all* the time.'

And, still scowling and still scanning and re-scanning every tiniest bit of data for flaws, Seaton set course for Galaxy DW-427-LU, having every reason to believe it the galaxy in which the Realm of the Llurdi lay. Also, although he did not mention this fact even to Dorothy, that course 'felt right' to some deeply buried, unknown, and impossible sense in which he did not, could not, and would not believe.

For Seaton did not know that Galaxy DW-427-LU was in fact going to be highly important to him in a way that he could not foresee; if he had known, would not have believed; if he had believed, would not have understood.

For at that moment in time, not even Richard Ballinger Seaton knew what forces he had unleashed with his 'cosmic beacon'.

13

DuQuesne and Sennlloy

In the eyes of Blackie DuQuesne, Seaton was forever and helplessly trapped in the philosophy of the 'good guy'. It was difficult for DuQuesne to comprehend why a mind of as high an order of excellence as Seaton's – fully the equal of DuQuesne's own in many respects, as DuQuesne himself was prepared to concede – should subscribe to the philosophy of lending a helping hand, accepting the defeat of an enemy without rancor, refraining from personal aggrandizement when the way was so easily and temptingly clear to take over the best part of a universe.

Nevertheless, DuQuesne knew that these traits were part of Seaton's makeup. He had counted on them. He had not been disappointed. It would have been child's play for Seaton to have tricked and destroyed him as he entered that monster spaceship Seaton had somehow acquired. Instead of that, Seaton had made him a free gift of its equal!

That, however, was not good enough for Blackie DuQuesne. Seeing how far Seaton had progressed had changed things. He could not accept the status of co-belligerent. He had to be the victor.

And the one portentous hint he had gleaned from Seaton of the existence of a true fourth-dimensional system could be the tool that would make him the victor; wherefore he set out at once to get it.

Since he had misdirected Seaton as to the vector of the course of the Jelmi, sending him off on what, DuQuesne congratulated himself, was the wildest of wild-goose chases, DuQuesne need only proceed in the right direction and somehow – anyhow; DuQuesne was superbly confident that he would find a means – get from them the secret of what he needed to know. His vessel had power to spare. Therefore he cut in everything his mighty drives could take, computed a tremendous asymptotic curve into the line that the Jelmi must have taken, and took out after the intergalactic flyer that had left Earth's moon such a short time before.

DuQuesne was aware that force would be an improbably successful means of getting what he wanted. Guile was equally satisfactory. Accordingly he took off his clothes and examined himself, front and back and sides, in a full-length mirror.

He would do, he concluded. There would be nothing about his physical person which would cause him any trouble in his dealings with the Jelmi, Since he always took his sun-lamp treatments in the raw, his color gradation was right. He was too dark for a typical Caucasian Tellurian; but that was all right – he wasn't going to be a Tellurian. He would, he decided, be a native of some planet whose people went naked … the planet Xylmny, in a galaxy 'way out on the Rim somewhere … yes, he had self-control enough not to give himself away.

But his cabin wouldn't stand inspection on a usually naked basis, nor would any other private room of the ship. All had closets designed unmistakably for clothing and it wasn't worthwhile to rebuild them.

Okay, he'd be a researcher who had visited dozens of planets, and *everybody* had to wear some kind of clothing or trappings at some time or other. Protectively at least. And probably for formality or for decoration.

Wherefore DuQuesne, with a helmet on his head and a half-smile, half-sneer on his face, let his imagination run riot in filling closet after closet with the utilitarian and the decorative garmenture of world after purely imaginative world. Then, after transferring his own Tellurian clothing to an empty closet, he devoted a couple of hours to designing and constructing the apparel of his equally imaginary native world Xylmny.

In due time a call came in from the spaceship up ahead. 'You who are following us from the direction of the world Tellus: do you speak English?'

'Yes.'

'Why are you following us, Tellurian?'

'I am not a Tellurian. I am from the planet Xylmny; which, while very similar to Tellus, lies in a distant galaxy.' He told the caller, as well as he could in words, where Xylmny was. 'I am a Seeker, Sevance by name. I have visited many planets very similar to yours and to Tellus and to my own in my Seeking. Tellus itself had nothing worthy of my time, but I learned there that you have a certain knowledge as yet unknown to me; that of operating through the fourth dimension of space instantaneously, without becoming lost hopelessly therein, as is practically always the case when rotation is employed. Therefore I of course followed you.'

'Naturally. I would have done the same. I am Savant Tammon of the planet Mallidax – Llurdiaxorb Three – which is our destination. You, then, have had one or more successes in rotation? Our rotational tests all failed.'

'We had only one success. As a Seeker I will be glad to give you the specifications of the structures, computers, and forces required for any possibility of success – which is very slight at best.'

'This meeting is fortunate indeed. Have I your permission to come aboard your vessel, at such time as we approach each other nearly enough to make the fourth-dimensional transfer feasible?'

'You certainly may, sir. I'll be very glad indeed to greet you in the flesh. And until that hour, Savant Tammon, so long and thanks.'

Since Mergon braked the *Mallidaxian* down hard to help make the approach, and since the two vessels did not have to be close together even in astronomical terms, it was not long until Tammon stood facing DuQuesne in the *Capital D*'s control room.

The aged savant inhaled deeply, flexed his knees, and said, 'As I expected, our environments are very similar. We greet new friends with a four-hand clasp. Is that form satisfactory?'

'Perfectly; it's very much like our own,' DuQuesne said; and four hands clasped briefly.

'Would you like to come aboard our vessel now?' Tammon asked.

'The sooner the better,' and they were both in Tammon's laboratory, where Mergon and Luloy looked DuQuesne over with interest.

'Seeker Sevance,' Tammon said then, 'these are Savant Mergon, my first assistant, and Savant Luloy, his ... well, "wife" would be, I think, the closest possible English equivalent. You three are to become friends.'

The hand-clasp was six-fold this time, and the two Jelmi said in unison, 'I'm happy that we are to become friends.'

'May our friendship ripen and deepen,' DuQuesne improvised the formula and bowed over the cluster of hands.

'But Seeker,' Luloy said, as the cluster fell apart, 'must all Seekers do their Seeking alone? I'd go stark raving mad if I had to be alone as long as you must have been.'

'True Seekers, yes. While it is true that any normal man misses the companionship of his kind, especially that of the opposite sex –' DuQuesne gave. Luloy a cool, contained smile as his glance traversed her superb figure – 'even such a master of concentration as a true Seeker must be can concentrate better, more productively, when absolutely alone.'

Tammon nodded thoughtfully. 'That may well be true. Perhaps I shall try it myself. Now – we have some little time before dinner. Is there any other matter you would like to discuss?'

For that question DuQuesne was well prepared. A Seeker, after all, needs something to be Sought; and as he did not want to appear exclusively interested in something which even the unsuspicious Jelmi would be aware was a weapon of war, he had selected another subject about which to inquire. So he said at once:

'A minor one, yes. While I am scarcely even a tyro in biology, I have pondered the matter of many hundreds – probably many millions – of apparently identical and quite possibly inter-fertile human races spaced so immensely far apart in space that any possibility of a common ancestry is precluded.'

'Ah!' Tammon's eyes lit up. 'One of my favorite subjects; one upon which I have done much work. We Jelmi and the Tellurians are very far apart indeed in space, yet cross-breeding is successful. *In vitro*, that is, and as far as I could carry the experiment. I can not synthesize a living placenta. No *in vitro* trial was made, since we of course could not abduct a Tellurian woman and not one of our young women cared to bear a child fathered by any Tellurian male we saw.'

'From what I saw there I don't blame them,' agreed DuQuesne. It was only the truth of his feelings about Tellurians – with one important exception. 'But doesn't your success *in vitro* necessitate a common ancestry?'

'In a sense, yes; but not in the ordinary sense. It goes back to the unthinkably remote origin of all life. You can, I suppose, synthesize any non-living substance you please? Perfectly, down to what is apparently its ultimately fine structure?'

'I see what you mean.' DuQuesne, who had never thought really deeply about that fact, was hit hard. 'Steak, for instance. Perfect in every respect except in that it never has been alive. No. We can synthesize DNA-RNA complexes, the building blocks of life, but they are not alive and we can not bring them to life. And, conversely, we cannot dematerialize living flesh.'

'Precisely. Life may be an extra-dimensional attribute. Its basis may lie in some order deeper than any now known. Whatever the truth may be, it seems to be known at present only to the omnipotence who we of Mallidax call Llenderllon. All we *know* about life is that it is an immensely strong binding force and that its source – proximate, I mean, of course, not its ultimate origin – is the living spores that are drifting about in open space.'

'Wait a minute,' DuQuesne said. 'We had a theory like that long ago. So did Tellus – a scientist named Arrhenius – but all such theories were finally held to be untenable. Wishful thinking.'

'I know. Less than one year ago, however, after twenty years of search I found one such spore. Its descendants have been living and evolving ever since.'

DuQuesne's jaw dropped. 'You don't say! *That* I want to see!'

Tammon nodded. 'I have rigorous proof of authenticity. While it is entirely unlike any other form of life with which I am familiar, it is very interesting.'

'It would be, but there's one other objection. What is the chance that on any two worlds humanity would have reached exactly the same stage of evolution at any given time?'

'Ah! That is the crux of my theory, which I hope some day to prove; that when man's brain becomes large enough and complex enough to employ his hands efficiently enough, the optimum form of life for that environment has been reached and evolution stops. Thenceforth all mutants and sports are unable to compete with *Homo sapiens* and do not survive.'

DuQuesne thought for a long minute. Norlamin was very decidedly *not* a Tellus-type planet. 'Some Xylmnians have it, "Man is the ultimate creation of God." On Tellus it's "God created man in his own image." And of course the fact that I've never believed it – and I still think it's unjustifiable racial self-glorification – does not invalidate it.'

'Of course it doesn't. But to revert to the main topic, would you be willing to cooperate in an *in vivo* experiment?'

DuQuesne smiled at that, then chuckled deeply. 'I certainly would, sir; and not for purely scientific reasons, either.'

'Oh, *that* would be no problem. Nor is your present quest – it will take only a short time to install the various mechanisms in your vessel and to instruct you in their use. If my snap judgment is sound, however, this other may very well become of paramount importance and require a few days of time.' He touched a button on an intercom and said, 'Senny.'

'Yes?' came in a deep contralto from the speaker.

'Will you come in here, please? It concerns the *in vivo* experiment we have been discussing.'

'Oh? Right away, Tamm,' and in about half a minute a young woman came striding in.

DuQuesne stared, for she was a living shield-maiden – a veritable Valkyrie of flesh and blood. If she had had wings and if her pale blonde hair had been flying loose instead of being piled high on her head in thick, heavy braids, DuQuesne thought, she could have stepped right out of Wagenhorst's immortal painting *Ragnarok*.

Tammon introduced them. 'Seeker Sevance of Xylmny, Savant Sennlloy of Allondax, you two are to become friends.'

'I'm happy that we are to become friends,' the girl said, in English, extending her hands. DuQuesne took them, bowed over them, and said, 'May our friendship ripen and deepen.'

She examined him minutely, from the top of his head down to his toenails, in silence; then, turning to Tammon, she uttered a long sentence of which DuQuesne could not understand a word.

'You should speak English, my dear,' Tammon said. 'It is inurbane to exclude a guest from a conversation concerning him.'

'It is twice as inurbane,' she countered in English, 'to insult a guest, even by implication, who does not deserve it.'

'That is true,' Tammon agreed, 'but I have studied him to some little depth and it is virtually certain that the matter lies in your province rather than mine. The decision is, of course, yours. Caps-on with him, please, and decide.'

She donned a helmet and handed its mate to DuQuesne. Expecting a full-scale mental assault, he put up every block he had; but she did not think *at* him at all. Instead, she bored deep down into the most abysmal recesses of his flesh; down and down and down to depths where he – expert though he was at synthesizing perfectly any tangible article of matter – could not follow.

Eyes sparkling, she tossed both helmets onto a bench and seized both his hands in a grip very different from the casual clasp she had used a few minutes before. 'I *am* glad – very, *very* glad, friend Seeker Sevance, that we are friends!'

Although DuQuesne was amazed at this remarkable change, he played up. He bowed over her hands and, this time, kissed each of them. 'I thank you, Lady Sennlloy. My pleasure is immeasurable.' He smiled warmly and went on, 'Since I am a stranger and thus ignorant of your conventions and in particular of your taboos, may I without offense request the pleasure of your company at dinner? And my friends call me Vance.'

She returned his smile as warmly. Neither of them was paying any attention at all to anyone else in the room. 'And mine call me Senny. You may indeed, friend Vance, and I accept your invitation with joyous thanks. We go out that archway there and turn left.'

They walked slowly toward the indicated exit; side by side and so close together that hip touched hip at almost every step. In the corridor, however, Sennlloy put her hand on DuQuesne's arm and stopped. 'But hold, friend Vance,' she said. 'We should, don't you think, make this, our first meal together, one of full formality?'

'I do indeed. I would not have suggested it but I'm very much in favor of it.'

'Splendid! We'll go to my room first, then. This way,' and she steered him into and along a corridor whose blankly featureless walls were opaque instead of transparent.

Was this his cue? DuQuesne wondered. No, he decided. She wasn't the type to rush things. She was civilized ... more so than he was. If he didn't play it just about right with this girl who was very evidently a big wheel, she could and very probably would queer his whole deal.

As they strolled along DuQuesne saw that the walls were not quite feature-less. At about head height, every twenty-five feet or so, there was inset a disk of optical plastic perhaps an inch in diameter. Stopping, and turning to face one of these disks, Sennlloy pressed her right forefinger against it, explaining as she did so, 'It opens to my fingerprints only.'

There was an almost inaudible hiss of compressed air and a micrometrically fitted door – a good seven feet high and three feet wide – moved an inch out into the hall and slid smoothly aside upon tracks that certainly had not been there an instant before. DuQuesne never did find out how the thing worked. He was too busy staring into the room and watching and hearing what the girl was doing and saying.

She stepped back a half-step, bowed gracefully from the waist, and with a sweeping gesture of both hands invited him to precede her into the room. She started to say something in her own language – Allondaxian – but after a couple of words changed effortlessly to English. 'Friend Seeker Sevance, it is in earnest of our friendship that I welcome you into the privacy of my home' – and her manner made it perfectly clear that, while the phraseology was conventionally formal, in this case it was really meant.

And DuQuesne felt it; felt it so strongly that he did not bluff or coin a responsive phrase. Instead: 'Thank you, Lady Sennlloy. We of Xylmny do not have anything comparable, but I appreciate your welcome and thank you immensely.'

Inside the room, DuQuesne stared. He had wondered what this girl's private quarters would be like. She was a master scientist, true. But she was warmly human, not bookishly aloof. And what would seventy thousand years of evolution do to feminine vanity? Especially to a vanity that apparently had never been afflicted by false modesty? Or by any sexual taboos?

The furniture – heavy, solid, plain, and built of what looked like golden oak – looked ordinary and utilitarian enough. Much of it was designed for, and was completely filled with and devoted to, the tools and equipment and tapes and scanners of the top-bracket biologist which Sennlloy of Allondax in fact was. The floor was of mathematically figured, vari-colored, plastic tile. The ceiling was one vast sheet of softly glowing white light.

Three of the walls were ordinary enough. DuQuesne scarcely glanced at them because of the fourth, which was a single canvas eight feet high and over thirty feet long. One painting. What a painting! A painting of life itself; a painting that seemed actually to writhe and to crawl and to vibrate with the very essence of life itself!

One-celled life, striving fiercely upward in the primordial sea toward the light. Fiercely striving young fishes, walking determinedly ashore on their fins. Striving young mammals developing tails and climbing up into trees – losing tails, with the development of true thumbs, and coming down to earth again out of the trees – the ever-enlarging brain resulting in the appearance of true man. And finally, the development and the progress and the history of man himself.

And every being, from unicell to man, was striving with all its might upward; toward THE LIGHT. Upward! *Upward!!* UPWARD!!!

At almost the end of that heart-stopping painting there was a portrait of Sennlloy herself in the arms of a man; a yellow-haired, smooth-shaven Hercules so fantastically well-drawn, so incredibly alive-seeming, that DuQuesne stared in awe.

Beyond those two climactic figures the painting became a pure abstract of form and of line and color; an abstract, however, that was crammed full of invisible but very apparent question marks. It asked – more, it demanded and it yelled – '*What is coming next?*'

DuQuesne, who had been holding his breath, let it out and breathed deeply. 'And you painted *that* yourself,' he marveled. 'Milady Sennlloy, if you never do anything else as long as you live, you will have achieved immortality.'

She blushed to the breasts. 'Thanks, friend Vance. I'm very glad you like it: I was sure you would.'

'It's so terrific that words fail,' he said, and meant it. Then, nodding at the portrait, he went on, 'Your husband?'

She shook her head. 'Not yet. He has not the genes the Llurdi wish to propagate, so we could not marry and he had to stay on Allondax instead of becoming one of this group. But he and I love each other more than life. When we Jelmi aboard this *Mallidaxian* have taught those accursed Llurdi their lesson, we will marry and we'll never be parted again. But time presses, friend Vance; we must consider our formalities.'

Walking around the foot of her bed – the satin coverlet of which bore, in red and gold, a motif that almost made even DuQuesne blush – she went to a bureau-like piece of furniture and began to pull open its bottom drawer. Then, changing her mind, she closed it sharply; but not before the man got a glimpse of its contents that made him catch his breath. That drawer contained at least two bushels of the most fantastic jewelry DuQuesne had ever seen!

Shaking her head, Sennlloy went on, 'No. My formality should not influence yours. The fact that you appreciate and employ formality implies, does it not, that you do not materialize and dematerialize its material symbols, but cherish them?'

'Yes; you and I think very much alike on that,' DuQuesne agreed. He was still feeling his way. This *hadn't* been a cue; that was now abundantly certain. In fact, with Sennlloy so deeply in love with one man, she probably wouldn't be in the business herself at all … or would she? Were these people advanced enough – if you could call it advancement – different enough, anyway – to regard sex-for-love and sex-for-improvement-of-race as two entirely different matters; so completely unrelated as not to affect each other? He simply didn't know. Data insufficient. However the thing was to go, he'd played along so far; he'd still play along. Wherefore, without any noticeable pause, he went on:

'I intend to comply with your conventions, but I'll be glad to use my own if you prefer. So I'll ask Tammon to flip me over to my ship to put on my high-formal gear.'

'Oh, no; I'll do it.' Donning the helmet that had been lying on the beautifully grained oak-like top of the bureau, she took his left hand and compared his wristwatch briefly with the timepiece on the wall. 'I'll bring you back here in … in how many of your minutes?'

'Ten minutes will be time enough.'

'In exactly ten minutes from –' She waited until the sweep hand of his watch was exactly at the dot of twelve o'clock. 'Mark,' she said then, and DuQuesne found himself standing in his own private cabin aboard the *Capital D.*

He picked up shaving cream and brush; then, asking aloud, 'How stupid can you get, fool?' he tossed them back onto the shelf, put on his helmet, and thought his whiskers off flush with the surface of his skin. Then, partly from habit but mostly by design – its richly masculine, heady scent was supposed to 'wow the women' – he rubbed on a couple of squirts of aftershave lotion.

Opening closet doors, he looked at the just-nicely-broken-in trappings he had made such a short time before. How should he do it, jeweled or plain? She was going to be gussied up like a Christmas tree, so he'd better go plain. Showy, plenty; but no jewels. And, judging by that spectacular coverlet and other items in her room, she liked fire-engine red and gold. Okay.

Taking off his watch and donning one exactly like it except for the fact that it kept purely imaginary Xylmnian time – that had been a slip; if she'd noticed it, she'd have wondered why he was running on Tellurian time – he dressed himself in full panoply of Xylmnian finery and examined himself carefully in a full-length mirror. He now wore a winged and crested headpiece of interlaced platinum strips; the front of the crest ridging up into a three-inch platinum disk emblazoned with an intricate heraldic design in deeply inlaid massive gold. A heavy collar, two armbands, and two wristlets, all made of woven and braided platinum strands, each bore the same symbolic disk. He wore a sleeveless shirt and legless shorts of gleaming, glaringly-red silk, with knee-length hose to match – and red-leather-lined buskins of solid-gold chain mail. And lastly, a crossed-strap belt, also of massive but supple gold link, with three platinum comets on each shoulder, supported a solid-platinum scabbard containing an extremely practical knife.

He drew the blade. Basket-hilted and with fifteen inches of heavy, wickedly curved, peculiarly shaped, razor-edged and needle-pointed stainless-steel blade, it was in fact an atrocious weapon indeed – and completely unlike any item of formal dress that DuQuesne had ever heard of.

All this had taken nine and one half minutes by his watch – by his Earth-watch, lying now upon his dresser. The time was now zero minus twenty-eight seconds.

14

Seeker Sevance of Xylmny

Precisely on the tick of time DuQuesne stood again in Sennlloy's room. He glanced at her; then stood flat-footed and simply goggled. He had expected a display, but *this* was something that had to be seen to be believed – and then but barely. She was literally ablaze with every kind of gem he had ever seen and a dozen kinds completely new to him. Just as she stood, she could have supplied Tiffany and Cartier both for five years.

Yet she did *not* look barbaric. Blue-eyed, with an incredible cascade of pale blonde hair cut squarely across well below her hips, she looked both regal and virginal.

'Wow!' he exclaimed finally. 'The English has – not a word for it, but a sound,' and he executed a long-drawn-out wolf-whistle.

She laughed delightedly. 'Oh? I did not hear that on Tellus; but it sounds … appreciative.'

'It is, Milady. Very.' He took her hands and bowed over them. 'May I say, Lady Senny, that you are the most beautiful woman I have ever seen?'

'"Milady." "Lady." I have not told you how much I like those terms, friend Vance. I'm wonderfully pleased that you find me so. You're magnificently handsome yourself … and you smell nice, too.' She came squarely up to him and sniffed approvingly. 'But the … the blade of formality. May I look at it, please?'

She examined it closely, then went on, 'Tell me, Vance, how old is your recorded history? Just roughly, in Tellurian years?'

This could be a crucial question, DuQuesne realized; but, since he didn't know the score yet, he hadn't better lie too much. 'Before I answer that; you're a biologist, aren't you, and in the top bracket?'

'Yes. In English it would have to be "anthropological biologist" and yes, I know my specialty very well.'

'Okay. For better or for worse, here it is. Xylmny's recorded history goes back a little over six thousand Tellurian years.'

'Oh, wonderful!' she breathed. 'Perfect! That's what I read, but I could scarcely believe it. A *young* race. Mature, but still possessing the fire and the power and the genius that those accursed Llurdi have been breeding out of all us Jelmi for many thousands of years. They want us to produce geniuses for them, but they kill or sterilize all our aggressive, combative, rebellious young men. A few of us women carry all the necessary female genes, but without their male complements, dominant in heredity, we all might exactly as well have none of them.'

'I see … but how about Tammon?'

'He's sterile, since he was a genius before he became a rebel. And he kept on being a genius; one of the very few exceptions to the rule. But since the Llurdi are insanely logical, one exception to any rule invalidates that rule.' She glanced at the clock. 'It's time to go now.'

Walking slowly along the corridor, DuQuesne said, ' "Insanely logical" is right. I knew that there was a lot more to this than just an experiment, but I had no idea it was to put new and younger blood into an entire race. But with mothers such as you have in mind—'

'Mothers?' She broke in. 'You already know, then?'

'Of course. I am sufficiently familiar with your specialty to know what a top-bracket biologist can do and how you intend to do it. With mothers of your class some of our sons may make genius grade, but what's to keep them alive?'

'We will.' Sennlloy's voice and mien became of a sudden grim. 'This fourth-dimension device that Tammon is going to give you was developed only a few weeks ago, since we left Llurdiax. The Llurdi know nothing whatever of it. When we get back to our own galaxy with it, either the Llurdi will grant us our full freedom or we will kill every Llurdi alive. And being insanely logical, they'll grant it without a fight: without even an argument, Sancil burn their teeth, wings, and tail!'

DuQuesne did not tell the girl how interested he was in the Llurdi; especially in Llanzlan Klazmon the Fifteenth. Instead, 'That makes a weird kind of sense, at that,' he said. 'Tell me more about these Llurdi,' and she told him about them all the rest of the way to the dining hall.

They went through an archway, stepped aside, and looked around. Three or four hundred people were in the hall already, and more were streaming in from all sides. Some were eating, in couples or in groups of various numbers, at tables of various sizes. Dress varied from nothing at all up to several spectaculars as flamboyant as Sennlloy's own. Informal, semi-formal, and formal; and the people themselves were alike in only one respect – that of physical perfection. DuQuesne had never seen anything like it and said so; and Sennlloy explained, concluding:

'So, you see, we eight hundred are the very pick of two hundred forty-one planets; which makes this an ideal primary situation. The reason I wanted you to look around carefully is that perhaps I should not be the only Prime Operative.' She paused: it was quite evident that she was not at all in favor of the idea.

'Why not?' DuQuesne wasn't in favor of it, either; even though he couldn't begin to understand either her attitude or her behavior. How could any woman possibly be as deeply in love with one man as Sennlloy very evidently was, and yet act as she was acting toward such a complete stranger as himself?

It baffled him completely, but he'd *still* play along – especially since he was suffering no pain at all. 'It won't make any difference in the long run, will it?'

'Of course not. I just thought maybe you would relish diversity,' Sennlloy said.

'You can unthink it. I wouldn't. There's no tomcat blood in me – and remember what I said?'

'Do you think I don't? But you've seen some *really* beautiful women now. Much prettier than I am.'

'You know what they call that technique in English? "Fishing",' grinned DuQuesne. 'Prettier or not, Milady, you top them all by a country mile.'

'I know about fishing. I was fishing a little, perhaps.' She laughed happily and hugged his arm against her firm breast. 'But it did get you to say it again, and it means *ever* so much more, now that you've seen the competition.'

She steered him to a table for two against a wall, where he seated her meticulously – a gesture that, while evidently new to her, was evidently liked.

'You order,' she said, handing him the helmet. 'You invited me, you know.'

'But I don't know what you like to eat.'

'Oh, I like almost everything, really; and if there should be anything I don't like I won't eat it. Okay?'

'Okay,' and DuQuesne proceeded to set the table with fine linen and translucent china and sterling silver and sparkling cut glass.

The first course was a thin, clear soup; which Sennlloy liked. She also liked the crisp lettuce with Roquefort dressing; the medium rare roast beef with mushroom sauce and the asparagus in butter and the baked Idaho potato stuffed with sour cream; and she especially enjoyed the fruits-and-nuts-filled Nesselrode ice cream. She did not, however, like his corrosively strong, black, unsweetened coffee at all. Wrinkling her nose, she sniffed at it, then took a tiny sip, which she let flow back into the cup.

'How can you possibly drink such vile stuff as that?' she demanded, and replaced it with a tall glass of a fizzy, viscous concoction that looked like eggnog and reeked of something that was halfway between almond and lemon.

After dinner – DuQuesne wanted to smoke, but since no one else was doing anything of the kind he could and would get along without it as long as he was aboard the *Mallidaxian* – they milled about with the milling throng. She introduced him right and left and showed him off generally; especially to over a hundred stunning young women, with whom she discussed the 'project' in American English with a completely uninhibited frankness that made DuQuesne blush more than once.

After something over an hour of this the crowd broke up; and as the two left the hall Sennlloy said, 'Ha! We're free now, my Vance, to go about our business!'

Arms tightly around each other, savoring each contact and each motion, they walked slowly and in silence to Sennlloy's room.

Three Mallidaxian days later, DuQuesne took his leave. Of Sennlloy last, of course. She put her arms around him and rubbed her cheek against his. 'Goodbye, friend Vance. I have enjoyed our association tremendously. Scarcely ever before has work been such pleasure. So much so that I feel guilty of selfishness.'

'You needn't, Milady. That was exactly the way I wanted it, remember?'

'I remember with joy; and I have wondered why.'

'Because you are the only one of your class aboard this ship,' DuQuesne said.

'You said that, but still – well, I *am* the only Allondaxian aboard, which may account for our great compatibility. And there should be, as there has been, something more than the purely physical involved.'

DuQuesne was very glad she had said that; it gave him one last chance to explore. 'Definitely,' he agreed. 'Liking, respect, appreciation, admiration – you're a tremendous lot of woman, Milady Sennlloy. But not love. Naturally.'

'Of course not. I have my love and my work and my planet; you have yours; it would be terrible for either of us or any of ours to be hurt.'

'Our rememberings of each other should be and will be most pleasant. Goodbye, friend Vance; may All Powerful Llenderllon guard you and aid you as you Seek.'

15

DuQuesne's Assassins

Not even Marc DuQuesne was able – quite! – to put his rather astonishing, and totally pleasurable, experiences with the Jelmi – and with one Jelm in particular! – out of his mind without a second's hesitation. In another man, his mood as he set a minimum-time course and began to speed back to Earth, might have been called nostalgic … even sentimental.

But as the parsecs fled by his thoughts hardened. And just in time; for some very hard things indeed had to be done.

First and foremost, his deal with Seaton was utterly, irrevocably and permanently *off*. He no longer needed it. With the information he had received from the Jelmi, he had no further reason to worry about Seaton's offensive capabilities.

Of course, there was no reason for Seaton to know that. Or not until it was entirely too late to do Seaton any good. Let Seaton go on dawdling toward this Galaxy DW-427-LU. Seaton would be travelling at only normal max; DuQuesne would have time to make his arrangements, transact his business and *act* while Seaton was still on the way.

He did not intend to go to Earth, only to within working distance of it. Even so, he had a certain amount of time to spend. He spent it, all of it, in studying and operating the new device, which was called by the Jelm a name which Sennlloy had told him corresponded roughly to 'quad'.

And immediately he ran headlong into trouble.

To DuQuesne's keen disappointment, the confounded thing was both more and less useful than he had hoped. More: its range was enormous, much more than he had expected. Less: well, it simply didn't do *any* of the normal things that *any* machine could be made to do. And he could not tell why. He had received too much knowledge too fast; it took time to nail down all the details.

He could send himself anywhere, but he could not bring himself back. He *had* to be at the controls. Remote control wouldn't work and he couldn't find out why not. The thing – in its present state of development, at least – couldn't handle a working projection; and he couldn't explain that fact, either. There was no way at all, apparently, of coupling the two transmitters together or of automating the controls – which was absurd on the face of it. There were job lots of things it couldn't do; and in no case at all could he understand why not.

That condition was, however, perfectly natural. In fact, it was inevitable. For, as has been pointed out, the laws of the fourth-dimensional region are completely inexplicable in three-dimensional terms. Obvious impossibilities become commonplace events; many things that are inevitable in our ordinary continuum become starkly impossible there.

Tammon had told DuQuesne just that; Seaton had told him the same, and much more strongly for having been there in person; but DuQuesne could not help but boggle at such information. Of the three men, he was far and away the least able to accept an obvious impossibility as a fact and go on from there.

So Blackie DuQuesne, his face like a steel-black thundercloud, methodically and untiringly worked with his new device until he was quite sure that of all the things he could make it do, he could make it do all of them very well.

And that would be enough. Never mind the things it wouldn't do. What it would do would be plenty to get rid of Richard Ballinger Seaton once and for all.

Within range of Earth at last, DuQuesne set about the first step in that program.

The simplest and crudest methods would work – backed by the weird fourth-dimensional powers of the quad. And DuQuesne knew exactly how to go about recruiting the assistance he needed in those methods.

He launched a working projection of himself to the Safe Deposit Department of the First National Bank. He signed a name and counted out a sheaf of currency from a box. He then took a taxi to the World Building and an elevator up to the office of the president.

Brushing aside private secretaries, vice presidents, and other small fry, he strode through a succession of private offices into the *sanctum sanctorum* of President Brookings himself.

The tycoon was, as usual, alone. If he was surprised at the intrusion he did not show it. He took the big cigar from his mouth, little-fingered half an inch of ash from the end of it into a bronze tray, put it back between his teeth, and waited.

'Still thinking your usual devious, petty-larceny, half-vast thoughts, eh, Brookings?' DuQuesne sneered.

'Still thinking your usual devious, petty-larceny, half-vast sublime gall to show up around here again,' Brookings said, evenly. 'Even via projection, after the raw stuff you pulled and the ungodly flop you made of everything. Especially after the way your pal Seaton dragged you out of here with your tail between your legs. Incidentally, it took everything you had coming to repair the damage you did to the building on your way out.'

'Stupid as ever, I see. And the galaxy's tightest penny-pincher. But back pay and the law of contracts and so forth are of no importance at the moment. What I'm here about is: with all these Norlaminian so-called "Observers" looking down the back of your neck all the time, Perkins' successor and his goon squads must be eating mighty low on the hog.'

'We haven't any –' At DuQuesne's sardonically contemptuous smile Brookings changed instantly the sense of what he had been going to say – 'work for them, to speak of, at that. Why?'

'So six of your best and fastest gunnies would be interested in ten grand apiece for a month's loaf and a minute's work.'

'Don't say mine, doctor. Please! You know very well that I never have anything to do with anything like that.'

'No? But you know who took over the Perkins Cafe and the top-mobster job after I killed Perkins. So I want six off the top downstairs in the lobby at sixteen hours Eastern Daylight Time today.'

'You know I *never* handle—'

'Shut up! I'm not asking you – I'm telling you. You'll handle this, or else.'

Brookings shrugged his shoulders and sighed. He knew DuQuesne. 'If you want good men they'll have to know what the job is.'

'Naturally. Dick and Dorothy Seaton, Martin and Margaret Crane, and their Jap Shiro and his wife – Apple Blossom or whatever her name is. Seaton's fast, for an amateur, but he's no pro. Crane is slow – he thinks and aims. And the others don't count. I'll guarantee complete surprise enough for one clear shot at Seaton. Anybody who is apt to need two shots I don't want. So – no problem.'

'I'll see what I can do.'

Since DuQuesne knew that was as close as Brookings ever came to saying 'yes', he accepted it. 'In advance, of course.' Brookings held out his hand.

'Naturally.' DuQuesne took a rubber-banded sheaf of thousand-dollar bills out of his inside coat pocket and tossed it across the desk. 'Count 'em.'

'Naturally.' Brookings picked the sheaf up and riffled through it. 'Correct. Goodbye, doctor.'

'Goodbye,' DuQuesne said, and the projection vanished.

At four o'clock that afternoon DuQuesne picked up his goons – through the fourth dimension, which surprised them tremendously and scared them no little, although none of them would admit that fact – and headed for the galaxy toward which the *Skylark of Valeron* had been flying so long. The *Capital D* was of course much faster than the gigantic planetoid; and the actual difference in speed between the two intergalactic flyers was much greater than the rated one because DuQuesne was driving with all his engines at absolute max – risking burn-out, tear-out, and unavoidable collision at or near the frightful velocity of turnover – which Seaton of course was not doing. He didn't want to endanger the *Valeron*.

In the target galaxy – Galaxy DW-427-LU, according to Klazmon's chart – there was only one solar system showing really intense sixth-order activity. Almost all of that activity would be occurring on one planet; a planet whose inhabitants were highly inimical to (probably) all other forms of intelligent life.

Klazmon's side-bands of thought had been very informative on those points.

Thus it was by neither accident nor coincidence that DuQuesne came up to within long working range of the *Skylark of Valeron* well before that flying worldlet came within what DuQuesne thought was extreme range of a planet that DuQuesne *knew* to be a very dangerous planet indeed.

He had wanted it that way; he had risked his ship and his life to make it come out that way. When the *Valeron* came within range of the target planet she would be DuQuesne's not Seaton's. And DuQuesne was calmly confident that he and a *Valeron* re-tuned to his own mind could cope with any possible situation.

As a matter of fact, they couldn't. It was not, however, DuQuesne's error or fault that made it so; it was merely the way Fate's mop flopped. Neither he nor Seaton had any idea whatever of the appalling magnitude of the forces so soon to be hurled against Seaton's supposedly invulnerable flying fortress, the *Skylark of Valeron*.

Operating strictly according to plan, then, DuQuesne called his goons to attention. 'You've been briefed and you've had plenty of practice, but I'll recap the essential points.

'Guns in hands. They'll be eating dinner, with their legs under the table. Sitting ducks for one shot. But for one shot only. Especially Seaton – for an amateur he's fast. So work fast – land and shoot. I'll give you the usual three second countdown, beginning, now – Seconds! Three! Two! One! Mark!' and the six men vanished.

And in the dining room of the Seatons' home in the *Skylark of Valeron* six forty-five-caliber automatics barked viciously, practically as one.

16

The Chlorans

While much work had been done on a personal gravity control, to provide for the comfort of such visitors as Dunark and Sitar, it was still in the design stage when the *Skylark of Valeron* neared Galaxy DW-427-LU. Wherefore, when the Skylarkers sat down to dinner that evening in the Seatons' dining room that room was almost forty percent undergrav. And wherefore, when DuQuesne's six hired killers fired practically as one, all six bullets went harmlessly high.

For, at low gravity, two facts of marksmanship – unknown to or not considered by either DuQuesne or any of his men – became dominant. First, a pistol expert compensates automatically for the weight of his weapon. Second, the more expert the marksman, the more automatic this compensation is.

And one shot each was all those would-be killers had. Dunark and Sitar as has been said, went armed even to bed; and Osnomian reflexes were and are the fastest possessed by any known race of man. Each of their machine pistols clicked twice and four American hoodlums died, liquescent brains and comminuted skulls spattering abroad, before they could do anything more than begin to bring their guns back down into line for their second shots.

The other two gangsters also died; if not as quickly or as messily, just as dead. For Shiro and his bride were, for Earthmen, very fast indeed. Their chairs, too, flew away from the table the merest instant after the invaders appeared and both took off in low, flat dives.

Lotus struck her man with her left shoulder; and, using flawlessly the momentum of her mass and speed, swung him around and put her small but very hard knee exactly where it would do the most good. Then, as he doubled over in agony, she put her left arm around his head, seized her left wrist with her right hand, and twisted with all the strength of arms, shoulders, torso and legs – and the man's neck broke with a snap audible throughout the room.

And Shiro took care of his man with equal dexterity, precision and speed; and of the invaders, then there were none.

Seaton was a microsecond slower than either the Osnomians or the two Japanese; but he was fast enough to see what was happening, take in the fact that the forces already engaged were enough to handle the six hoodlums and, in mid-flight, divert his leap toward the remote-control headset. He was blindingly certain of one thing: it was Marc DuQuesne who had unleashed these killers on them. And he was equally certain of that fact's consequence: The truce was off. DuQuesne was to be destroyed.

Wherefore what happened next astonished him even more than if it had occurred at another time.

A strident roar of klaxons filled the room. It was the loudest sound any human had ever heard – without permanent damage; it was calculated to come right up to the threshold of destruction. There was to be *no* chance that anyone would fail to hear this particular signal.

His hand on the headset, Seaton paused. The bodies of the six gunmen had not yet all reached the floor, but the other Skylarkers were staring too. They had never expected to hear that sound except in test.

It was the dire warning that they were under attack – *massive* attack – attack on a scale and of a persistence that they had never expected to encounter in real combat, with whatever forces.

For that klaxon warning meant that under the fierce impact of the enemy weapons now so suddenly and mercilessly beating down on them the life of the *Valeron*'s defensive screens was to be measured only in seconds – and very few of them!

'Yipe!' he yelled then. 'Control-room *fast!*' His voice of course went unheard in the clamor of the horns; but his yelling had been purely reflexive, anyway. While uttering the first syllable he was energizing beams of force that hurtled all eight of the party through ultra-high-speed locks that snapped open in front of them and crashed shut behind them – down into the neutral-gray chamber at the base of the giant Brain.

Seaton rammed his head into his master controller and began furiously but accurately to think ... and as he sat there, face harsh and white and strained, a vast structure of inoson, interlaced with the heaviest fields of force generable by the *Valeron*'s mighty engines, came into being around the Brain and the other absolutely vital components of the worldlet's core.

After a few minutes of fantastic effort Seaton sighed gustily and tried to grin. 'We're holding 'em and we're getting away,' he said. 'But I had to let 'em whittle us down to just about a nub before I could spare power enough to grab a lunch off of them while they were getting a square meal off of us.'

He spoke the exact truth. The attack had been so incredibly violent that in order to counter it he had had to apply the full power of the *Valeron*, designed to protect a surface of over three million square kilometers, to an area of less than thirty thousand.

'But what *was* it, Dick?' Dorothy shrieked. 'What *could* it have been – possibly?'

'I don't know. But you realize, don't you, that it was two separate, unrelated attacks? Not one?'

'Why, I … I don't think I realize *anything* yet.'

'Those guns were Colts,' Seaton said, flatly. 'Forty-fives. Made in the U.S.A. So that part of it was DuQuesne's doing. He wanted – still wants – the *Valeron*. Bad. But those super-energy super-weapons were definitely something else – as sure as God made apples. No possible ship could put that much stuff out, let alone DuQuesne's *Capital D*. So the question rises and asks itself—'

'Just a minute, Dick!' Crane broke in. 'Even granting so extraordinary a coincidence as two separate attacks—'

'Coincidence, hell!' Seaton snarled. 'There is no such thing. And why postulate an impossibility when you've got Blackie DuQuesne? He sucked me in, as sure as hell's a mantrap – you can bet your case buck on that. And he outfoxed himself doing it, for all the tea in China!'

'What do you mean, Dick?' Dorothy demanded. 'How could he have?'

'Plain as the nose on … plainer! He got it from somewhere, the son of a—' Seaton bit the noun savagely off – 'probably from Klazmon, that Galaxy DW-427-LU up ahead there that we were heading for is full of bad Indians. So he honeyed up to the Jelmi, got that fourth-dimensional gadget off of them and tried to kill us with it. And he would have succeeded, except for the pure luck of our having lowered our gravity so drastically on account of Dunark and Sitar.'

'I see,' Crane said. 'And the Indians jumped us when he pulled the trigger – perhaps attracted by his use of the "gadget".'

'That's my guess, anyway,' Seaton admitted. 'DuQuesne thought he was allowing plenty of leeway in both time and space for his operation. But he wasn't. He had no more idea than we did, Mart, that any such forces as *those* could possibly be delivered at such extreme range. And one simple, easy lie – the coordinates of the Llurdan galaxy – was all he had to tell me and defend against my probe.'

DuQuesne's attention was wrenched from his timer by a glare of light from a visiplate. He glanced at it, his jaw dropping in surprise; then his hands flashed to the controls of his fourth-dimensional transmitter and his six men appeared – four of them gruesomely headless. For a moment all six stood stiffly upright; then, as the supporting forces vanished, all six bodies slumped bonelessly to the floor.

DuQuesne, after making quickly sure that the two were in fact as dead as were the four, shrugged his shoulders and flipped the bodies out into deep space. Then, donning practically opaque goggles, he studied the incandescently glaring plate – to see that the *Skylark of Valeron* now looked like a minor sun.

Involuntarily he caught his breath. The *Valeron's* screens were failing – failing fast. Course after course, including her mighty zones of force, her every defensive layer was flaring into and through the violet and going black.

DuQuesne clenched his fists; set his teeth so hard that his jaw-muscles stood out in bands and lumps. Anything to put out that much of that kind of stuff would have to be vast indeed. Incredibly vast. Nothing could *be* that big – nothing even pertaining, as far as DuQuesne knew, to any civilization or culture of the known universe.

Relaxing a little, he assembled a working projection, but before sending it out he paused in thought.

Seaton hadn't attacked; he wasn't the type to. He wouldn't have, even if he could have done so at that range. So the strangers, whoever or whatever they might be, were the aggressors, with a capital 'A'. Guilty of unprovoked and reasonless aggression; aggression in the first degree. So what Tammon had told him about that galaxy being dominated by 'inimical life-forms' was the understatement of the year. And he, DuQuesne himself, had triggered the attack; the fact that it had followed his own attack so nearly instantly made that a certainty.

How had he triggered it? Almost certainly by the use of the fourth-dimensional transmitter …

But *how*? He didn't know and he couldn't guess … and at the moment it didn't make a lick of difference. He hadn't used any sixth-order stuff since then and he sure wouldn't use any now for a good while. If he did anything at all, he'd pussyfoot it, but good. He didn't want any part of anything that could manhandle the *Skylark of Valeron* like that. His *Capital D* was small enough and far enough back – he hoped! – to avoid detection. No, he wouldn't do a single damn thing except look on.

Fascinated, DuQuesne stared into the brilliance of his plate. All the *Valeron's* screens were down now. Even the ultra-powerful innermost zone – the wall shield itself, the last line of defense of the bare synthetic of the worldlet's outer skin – was going fast. Huge black areas appeared, but they were black only momentarily. Such was the power of that incredible assault that thousands of tons of inoson flared in an instant into ragingly incandescent vapor; literally exploding; exploding with such inconceivable violence as to blast huge masses of solid inoson out of the *Valeron's* thick skin and hurl them at frightful speed out into space.

And the *Valeron* was not fighting back. She couldn't.

This fact, more than anything else, rocked DuQuesne to the core and gave him the measure of the power at the disposal of the 'inimical' entities of that galaxy. For he, knowing the *Valeron's* strength, now knew starkly that she was being attacked by forces of a magnitude never even approximated by the wildest imaginings of man.

Scowling in concentration, he kept on watching the disaster. Watched while those utterly unbelievable forces peeled the *Valeron* down like an onion, layer after kilometer-thick layer. Watched until that for which he had almost ceased to hope finally took place. The *Valeron*, down now to the merest fraction of her original size – burned and blasted down to the veriest core – struck back. And that counterstroke was no love-tap. The ether and all the subethers seethed and roiled under the vehemence of that devastating bolt of energy.

The *Skylark of Valeron* vanished from DuQuesne's plate; that plate went black; and DuQuesne stood up and stretched the kinks out of his muscles. Seaton could of course flit away on the sixth; but he, DuQuesne, couldn't. Not without being detected and getting burned to a crisp. Against the forces that he had just seen in action against the *Skylark of Valeron*, DuQuesne's own *Capital D* didn't stand the proverbial chance of the nitrocellulose dog chasing the asbestos cat in hell.

If the *Skylark of Valeron* had been hurt, half-demolished and reduced to an irreducible core of fighting muscle before it could mount one successful counter-blow against this new and unexpected enemy, then the *Capital D* would be reduced to its primitive gases. DuQuesne rapidly, soberly and accurately came to the conclusion that he simply did not own ship enough to play in this league. Not yet …

Wherefore he pussyfooted it away from there at an acceleration of only a few lights; and he put many parsecs of distance between himself and the scene of recent hostilities before he cut in his space-annihilating sixth-order drive and began really to travel. He did not know whether Seaton and his party were surviving; he did not care. He did not know the identity of the race which had hurt them so badly, so fast.

What DuQuesne knew was that, as a bare minimum, he needed something as big as the *Valeron*, plus the fourth-dimensional tricks he had learned from the Jelmi, plus a highly developed element of caution based on the scene he had just witnessed. And he knew what to do about it, and where to go to do it; wherefore his course was laid for the First Galaxy and Earth.

Hundreds of thousands of parsecs away from the scene of disaster, Seaton cut his drive and began gingerly to relax the terrific power of his defensive screens.

No young turtle, tentatively poking his head out of his shell to see if the marauding gulls had left, was more careful than Seaton. He had been caught off base twice. He did not propose to let it happen again.

Another man might have raged and sworn at DuQuesne for his treachery; or panicked at the fear inspired by the fourth-dimensional transmitter DuQuesne had come up with, or the massive blow that had fallen from nowhere. Seaton did not. The possibility – no, the virtual certainty – of treachery from DuQuesne he had accepted and discounted in the first second of receiving DuQuesne's distress call. He had accepted the risks, and grimly calculated that in any encounter, however treacherous, DuQuesne would fail; and he had been right. The sudden attack from out of nowhere, however, was something else again. What made it worse was not that Seaton had no idea of its source of reason. The thing that caused his eyes to narrow, his face to wear a hard, thoughtful scowl was that he in fact had a very good idea indeed – and he didn't like it.

But for the moment they were free. Seaton checked and double-checked every gauge and warning device and nodded at last.

'Good,' he said then, 'I was more than half expecting a kick in the pants, even way out here. The next item on our agenda is a council of war; so cluster round, everybody, and get comfortable.' He turned control over to the Brain, sat down beside Dorothy, stoked his pipe, and went on:

'Point one: DuQuesne. He got stuff somewhere – virtually certainly from the Jelmi – at least the fourth-dimensional transmitter and we don't know what else, that he didn't put out anything about. Naturally. And he sucked me in like Mary's little lamb. Also naturally. At hindsight I'm a blinding flash and a deafening report. I've got a few glimmerings, but you're the brain, Mart; so give out with analysis and synthesis.'

Crane did so; covering the essential points and concluding: 'Since the plug-chart was accurate, the course was accurate. Therefore, besides holding back vital information, DuQuesne lied about one or both of two things: the point at which the signal was received and the direction from which it came.'

'Well, you can find out about that easily enough,' Dorothy said. You know, that dingus you catch light-waves with, so as to see exactly what went on years and years ago. Or wouldn't it work, this far away?'

Seaton nodded. 'Worth a try. Dunark?'

'I say go after DuQuesne!' the Osnomian said viciously. 'Catch him and blow him and his *Capital D* to hellangone up!'

Seaton shook his head. 'I can't buy that – at the moment. Now that he's flopped again at murder, I don't think he's of first importance any more. You see, I haven't mentioned point two yet, which is a datum I didn't put into the pot because I wanted to thrash point one out first. It's about who the enemy really are. When I finally got organized to slug them a good one back, I followed the shot. They knew they'd been nudged, believe me. So much so that in the confusion I got quite a lot of information. They're Chlorans. Or, if not exactly like the Chlorans of Chlora, that we had all the trouble with, as nearly identical as makes no difference.

'*Chlorans!*' Dorothy and Margaret shrieked as one, and five minds dwelt briefly upon that hideous and ultimately terrible race of amoeboid monstrosities who, living in an atmosphere of gaseous chlorine, made it a point to enslave or to destroy all the humanity of all the planets they could reach.

All five remembered, very vividly, the starkly unalloyed ferocity with which one race of Chlorans had attacked the planet Valeron; near which the *Skylark of Valeron* had been built and after which she had been named. They remembered the horrifyingly narrow margin by which those Chlorans had been defeated. They also remembered that the Chlorans had not even then been slaughtered. The Skylarkers had merely enclosed the planet Chlora in a stasis of time and sent it back – on a trip that would last, for everyone and everything outside that stasis, some four hundred years – to its own native solar system, from which it had been torn by a near-collision of suns in the long-gone past. The Skylarkers should have blown Chlora into impalpable and invisible debris, and the men of the party had wanted to do just that, but Dorothy and Margaret and the essentially gentle Valeronians had been dead set against genocide.

Dorothy broke the short silence. 'But how *could* they be, Dick?' she asked. 'Way out here? But of course, if we human beings could do it –' She paused.

'But of course,' Seaton agreed sourly. 'Why not? Why shouldn't they be as widespread as humanity is? Or even more so, if they have killed enough of us off? And why shouldn't they be smarter than those others were? Look at how much we've learned in just months, not millennia, of time.'

Another and longer silence fell; which was broken by Seaton. 'Well, two things are certain. They're rabidly antisocial and they've got – at the moment – a lot more stuff than we have. They've got it to sell, like farmers have hay. It's also a dead-sure cinch that we can't do a thing – not *anything* – without a lot more data than we have now. It'll take all the science of Norlamin and maybe a nickel's worth besides to design and build what we'll have to have. And they can't go it blind. Nobody can. And we all know enough about Chlorans to know that we won't get one iota or one of Peg's smidgeons of information out of them by remote control. At the first touch of any kind of a high-order feeler they'll bat our ears down … to a fare-thee-well. However, other means are available.'

During this fairly long – for Seaton – speech, and during the silence that had preceded it, two things had been happening.

First the controlling Brain of the ship had been carrying out a program of Seaton's. Star by star, system by system, it had been scanning the components of the nearest galaxy to the scene of their encounter. It had in fact verified

Seaton's conclusions: the galaxy was dominated by Chlorans. Their works were everywhere. But it had also supported a – not a conclusion; a hope, more accurately – that Seaton had hardly dared put in words. Although the Chlorans ruled this galaxy, there were oxygen-breathing, warm-blooded races in it too – serfs of the Chlorans of course, but nevertheless occupying their own planets – and it was one such planet that the Brain had finally selected and was now displaying on its monitor.

The other thing was that the auburn-haired beauty who was Mrs Richard Ballinger Seaton had been eyeing her husband steadily. At first she had merely looked at him thoughtfully. Then look and mien had become heavily tinged, first with surprise and then with doubt and then with wonder; a wonder that turned into an incredulity that became more and more incredulous. Until finally, unable to hold herself in any longer, she broke in on him.

'Dick!' she cried. 'You *wouldn't*! You *know* you wouldn't!'

'I wouldn't? If not, who …?' Changing his mind between two words, Seaton cut the rest of the sentence sharply off; shrugged his shoulders; and grinned, somewhat shamefacedly, back at her.

At this point Crane, who had been looking first at one of them and then at the other, put in: 'I realize, Dorothy, that you and Dick don't need either language or headsets to communicate with each other, but how about the rest of us? What, exactly, is it that you're not as sure as you'd like to be that he wouldn't do?'

Dorothy opened her mouth to reply, but Seaton beat her to it. 'What I would do – and will because I'll have to; because it's my oyster and nobody else's – is, after we sneak up as close as we can without touching off any alarms, take a landing craft and go get the data we absolutely have to have in absolutely the only way it can be gotten.'

'And that's what I most emphatically do *not* like!' Dorothy blazed. 'Dick Seaton, you are *not* going to land on an enslaved planet, alone and unarmed and afoot, as an investigating Committee of One! For one thing, we simply don't have the time! Do we? I mean, poor old *Valeron* is simply a wreck! We've got to go somewhere and—'

But Seaton was shaking his head. 'The Brain can handle that by itself,' he said. 'All it needs is time. As a matter of fact, you've put your finger on a first-rate reason for my going in, alone. There's simply not much else we can do until the *Valeron* is back in shape again.'

'Not *your* going in.' Dorothy blazed. 'Flatly, positively *no*!'

Again Seaton shrugged his shoulders. 'I can't say I'm madly in love with the idea myself, but who's any better qualified? Or as well? Because I know that you, Dottie, aren't the type to advocate us sitting on our hands and letting them have all the races of humanity, wherever situated. So who?'

'Me,' Shiro said, promptly if ungrammatically. 'Not as good, but good enough. You can tell me what data you want and I can and will get it, just as well as—'

'Bounce back, both of you, you've struck a rubber fence!' Dunark snapped. 'That job's for Sitar and me.' The green-skinned princess waved her pistol in the air and nodded her head enthusiastically and her warlord went on, 'You and I being brain-brothers, Dick, I'd know exactly what you want. And she and I would blast—'

'Yeah, that's what I know damn well you'd do.' Seaton broke in, only to be interrupted in turn by Crane – who was not in the habit of interrupting anyone even once, to say nothing of twice.

'Excuse me, everyone,' he said, 'but you're all wrong, I think. My thought at the moment, Dick, is that your life is altogether too important to the project as a whole to be risked as you propose risking it. As to you others, with all due respect for your abilities, I do not believe that either of you is as well qualified for this kind of an investigation as I am –'

Margaret leaped to her feet in protest, but Crane went quietly on: '– in either experience or training. However, we should not decide that point yet – or at all, for that matter. We are all too biased. I therefore suggest, Dick, that we feed the Brain everything we have and keep on feeding it everything pertinent we can get hold of, until it has enough data to make that decision for us.'

'*That* makes sense,' Seaton said, and both Dorothy and Margaret nodded – but both with very evident reservations. 'The first time anything has made sense today!'

17

Ky-El Mokak the Wilder

The first thing Seaton and Crane had to do, of course, was to figure out how to get back somewhere near Galaxy DW-427-LU, within fourth-order range of that one particular extremely powerful Chloran system, without using enough sixth-order stuff to touch off any alarms – but still enough to make the trip in days instead of in months. Some sixth-order emanations could be neutralized by properly phased and properly placed counter-generators; the big question being, how much?

The answer turned out to be, according to Crane, 'Not enough' – but, according to Seaton, 'Satisfactory.' At least, it did make the trip not only possible, but feasible. And during the days of that trip each Skylarker worked – with the Brain or with a computer or with pencil and paper or with paint or

India ink and a brush, each according to his bent – on the problem of what could be done about the Chlorans.

They made little headway, if any at all. They did not have enough data. Inescapably, the attitude of each was very strongly affected by what he or she knew about the Chlorans they had already encountered. They were all smart enough to know that this was as indefensible as it was inevitable.

Thus, while each of them developed a picture completely unlike anyone else's as to what the truth probably was, none of them was convinced enough of the validity of his theory to defend it vigorously. Thus it was discussion, not argument, that went on throughout the cautious approach to the forbidden territory and the ultra-cautious investigation of the Tellus-type planet the Brain had selected through powerful optical telescopes and by means of third- and fourth-order apparatus. Then they fell silent, appalled; for that world was inhabited by highly intelligent human beings and what had been done to it was shocking indeed.

They had seen what had been done to the planet Valeron. This was worse; much worse. On Valeron the ruins had been recognizable as having once been cities. Even those that had been blown up or slagged down by nuclear energies had shown traces of what they had once been. There had been remnants and fragments of structural members, unfused portions of the largest buildings, recognizable outlines and traces of thoroughfares and so on. But here, where all of the big cities and three-fourths or more of the medium-sized ones had been, there were now only huge sheets of glass.

Sheets of glass ranging in area from ten or fifteen square miles up to several thousands of square miles, and variously from dozens up to hundreds of feet thick: level sheets of cracked and shattered, almost transparent, varicolored glass. The people of the remaining cities and towns and villages were human. In fact, they were white Caucasians – as white and as Caucasian as the citizens of Tampa or of Chicago or of Portland, Oregon or of Portland, Maine. Neither Seaton nor Shiro, search as they would, could find any evidence that any Oriental types then lived or ever had lived on that world – to Shiro's lasting regret. He, at least, was eliminated as a spy.

'Well, Dottie?' Seaton asked.

She gnawed her lip. 'Well … I suppose we'll have to do *something* – but hey!' she exclaimed, voice and expression changing markedly. 'How come you think you have to go down there at all to find out what the score is? You've snatched people right and left all over the place with ordinary beams and things, *long* before anybody ever heard of that sixth-order, fourth-dimensional gizmo.'

Seaton actually blushed. 'That's right, my pet,' he admitted. 'Once again you've got a point. I'll pick one out that's so far away from everybody else that he won't be missed for a while. Maybe two'd be better.'

Since it was an easy matter to find isolated specimens of the humanity of that world, it was less than an hour later that two men – one from a town, one found wandering alone in the mountains – were being examined by the Brain. And *what* an examination! Everything in their minds – literally everything, down to the last-least-tiniest coded 'bit' of every long-chain proteinoid molecule of every convolution of their brains – everything was being transferred to the *Valeron*'s great Brain; was being filed away in its practically unfillable memory banks.

When the transfer was complete, Sitar drew her pistol, very evidently intending to do away with the natives then and there. But Dorothy of course would not stand for that. Instead, she herself put them back into a shell of force and ran them through the *Valeron*'s locks and down into a mountain cave, which she then half-filled with food. 'I'd advise you two,' she told them then, in their own language, 'to stay put here for a few days and keep out of trouble. If you really *want* to get yourselves killed, though, that's all right with me. Go ahead any time.'

When Dorothy brought her attention back into the control room, the Brain had finished its analysis of the data it had just secured from the natives, had correlated it with all their pertinent data it had in its banks, and was beginning to put out its synthesized report.

That report came in thought; in diamond-sharp, diamond-clear thought that was not only super-intelligible and super-audible, but also was more starkly visible than any possible tri-di. It gave, as no possible other form of report could give, the entire history of the race to which those two men belonged. It described in detail and at length the Chlorons and the relationship between the two races, and went on to give, in equal detail, the most probable course of near-term events. It told Seaton that he should investigate this planet Ray-See-Nee in person. It told him in fine detail what to wear, where to go, and practically every move to make for the ensuing twenty-four hours.

At that point the report stopped, and when Seaton demanded more information, the Brain baulked. 'Data insufficient,' it thought, and everyone there would have sworn that the great Brain actually had a consciousness of self as it went on, 'This construct –' it actually meant I – 'is not built to guess, but deals only in virtual certainties; that is, with probabilities that approximate unity to twelve or more nines. With additional data, this matter can be explored to a depth quite strictly proportional to the sufficiency of the data. That is all.'

'That's the package, Dottie,' Seaton said then. 'If we want to reach the Chlorans without them reaching us first, there's how. That makes it a force, wouldn't you say?'

Dorothy wasn't sure. 'For twenty-four hours, I guess,' she agreed, dubiously. 'After which time I think I'll be screaming for you to come back here and feed that monster some more data. So be mighty darn sure to get some.'

'I'll try to, that's for sure. But the really smart thing to do might be to take this wreckage half a dozen galaxies away and put the Brain to work rebuilding her while I'm down there investigating.'

'D'you think I'll sit still for *that*?' Dorothy blazed. 'If you do, you're completely out of your mind!'

And even Crane did not subscribe to the idea. 'Why?' he asked, 'Just to tear her down again after you've found out what we'll have to have?'

'That's so, too.' Seaton thought for a moment, gray eyes narrowed and focused on infinity, translating the imperatives of the Brain into practical measures. Then he nodded. 'All right. I admit I'll feel better about the deal with you people and the Brain standing by.'

And Seaton, now lean and hard and deeply tanned, sat down in his master controller and began to manufacture the various items he would need; exactly as the Brain told him to make them.

And next morning, as the sun began to peer over the crest of the high mountain ridge directly below the *Skylark of Valeron*, Seaton came to ground, hid his tiny landing-craft in a cave at the eighteen-thousand-foot level, and hiked the fifteen miles down-mountain to the nearest town.

He now looked very little indeed like the Dr Richard B. Seaton of the Rare Metals Laboratory. He was almost gaunt. His skin was burned to a shade consistent with years of exposure to wind and weather. His hair had very evidently been cut – occasionally – with shears by his own hand; his beard had been mowed – equally occasionally – with those same shears.

He wore crudely made, heavy, hobnailed, high-laced boots; a pair of baggy, unsymmetrical breeches of untanned deerskin; and a shapeless, poor-grade leather coat that had been patched crudely and repeatedly at elbows and shoulders and across the back. He also wore what was left of a hard hat.

As he strode into the town and along its main street, more than one pair of eyes looked at him and then looked again, for the people of that town were not used to seeing anyone walk purposefully. Nor was the sloppily uniformed guard at the entrance to City Hall. This wight – who couldn't have been a day over fifteen – opened his eyes, almost straightened up and said:

'Halt, you. Who'a you? Whatcha want?'

'Business,' Seaton said, briskly. 'To see the mayor, Ree-Toe Prenk.'

'Awri'; g'wan in,' and the youth relapsed into semi-stuporous leaning on his ratty-looking rusty rifle.

It was easy enough to find His Honor's office, since it was the only one in the building doing any business at all. Seaton paused just inside the doorway and looked around. Everything was shabby and neglected. The wall-to-wall carpet was stained and dirty, worn through to the floor in several places. The divider-rail leaned drunkenly, forward here, backward there. The vacant receptionist's desk was as battered and scarred as though it had been through a war. The place hadn't been cleaned for months, and not very thoroughly then.

And the people in that office were in perfect sync with their surroundings. Half a dozen melancholy-looking people, men and women, sat listlessly on hard, straight-backed chairs; staring glumly, fixedly at nothing; completely disinterested, apparently, in whether they were called into the inner office or not.

And the secretary! She was dressed in what looked like a gunny-sack. She was scrawny. Her unkempt, straight, lank hair was dirty-mouse brown in color. She didn't look very bright. She was, however, the only secretary in sight, so Seaton strode up to her desk.

'Miss What's-your-name!' he snapped. 'Can you, without rupturing a blood-vessel, come to life long enough to do half a minute's work?'

The girl jumped, started to rise to her feet at her desk, and blushed. 'Why, yes … yes, sir, I mean. What can we do for you, Mister –'

'I'm Ky-El Mokak. I want to talk to Hizzonner about turning myself in.'

That brought her to life fast. 'About *what*?' she cried and her half-scream was followed instantly by a deeper, louder voice from the intercom.

His Honor had not been asleep after all. 'You *what*? All right, Fy-Ly, send him in; but be sure he hasn't got a gun first.'

'Gun? What would I be doing with a gun?' Seaton patted his pockets, shucked off his dilapidated coat, and made a full turn to show that he was clean. Then, seeing no coat-rack or hangers, he pitched the coat and hat into a corner and strode into the inner office.

It was, if possible, in even worse shape than the outer one. The man behind the desk was fifty-odd years old; lean and bald. He looked worried, dyspeptic and nervous. He held a hand-weapon – which was not the least bit rusty – in workmanlike fashion in a competent-looking right hand. It was not pointed directly at Seaton's midsection. It evidently did not have to be.

'What I'd ought to do right now,' the man said quietly, 'is blow your brains out without letting you say a word. You're another damn rat. A fink – a spy – maybe a revver or an under-grounder, even. You don't look like any wilder I ever saw brought in.'

The Brain had not dumped Seaton on a strange and dangerous new planet without providing him with a full 'knowledge' of its history, its mores and even its dialects. Through the educators Seaton had received enough of Ray-See-Nee's cultural patterns to be able to carry off his role. He knew what His Honor was thinking about; he knew, even, very accurately just how far the man could be pushed, where his real sympathies lay, and what he could be counted upon to do about it.

Wherefore Seaton said easily: 'Of course I don't. I've got a brain. Those lard-headed chasseurs couldn't catch me in a thousand years. None of 'em can detect a smell on a skunk. And you won't shoot me, not with the bind you're in. You aren't a damn enough fool to. You wouldn't shoot a crippled kid on crutches, let alone a full-grown, able-bodied man.'

Prenk shivered a little, but that was all. 'Who says I'm in a bind? What kind of a bind?'

'I say so,' Seaton said, flatly. 'You're hitting bottom right now. You're using half-grown kids: girls, even. How many weeks is it to be before you don't make quota and your town and everything and everybody in it get turned into a lake of lava?'

Prenk trembled visibly and his face turned white. 'You win,' he said unsteadily, and put his pistol back into the top right-hand drawer of his desk. 'Whoever you are, you know the score and aren't afraid to talk about it. You'd have no papers, of course – on you, at least … Let's see your arm.'

'No number.' Seaton rolled up his left sleeve and held his forearm out for examination. 'Look close. Scars left by good surgery are fine, but they can't be made invisible.'

'I know they can't.' His Honor looked very closely indeed, then drew a tremendously deep breath of relief. 'You *are a* wilder! You mean to say you've been up in the hills ever since the Conquest without getting caught?'

'That's right. I told you I'm smart, and the brains of a whole platoon of chasseurs, all concentrated down into one, wouldn't equip a half-witted duck.'

'But they've got *dogs*!'

'Yeah, but they aren't smart, either. Not very much smarter than the chasseurs are. Hell, I've been living on those dogs half the time. Pretty tough, fried or roasted, but boiled long enough they make mighty tasty stew.'

'Mi-Ko-Ta's beard! Who *are* you, really, and what were you, before?'

'I told you, I'm Ky-El Mokak. I am – was, rather – a Class Twelve Fellow of the Institute of Mining Engineers. Recognize the ring?' Seaton went to the desk and placed his left hand flat on its surface.

Prenk studied the massive ornament. It had been fabricated, in strict external accord with the Brain's visualization of what it should have been, from synthesized meteoric metal – metal that had actually never been in open space, to say nothing of ever having been anywhere near the gray-lichened walls of the revered institute that Seaton had never seen.

Having examined the ring minutely, Prenk looked up and nodded; his whole manner changed. 'I recognize the ring and I can read the symbols. A *Twelve*! It's a shame to register and brand you. If you say so I'll let it drop.'

'I'll say so. I'm not committing myself that deep yet.'

'All right, but why did you come in? Or is it true that whatever undergrounds spring up are smashed flat in a week?'

I don't know. I couldn't find any. Not one, and I searched every square mile for a thousand miles north, east, south, and west of here. And I didn't find anybody who wasn't too dangerous to travel with, and I'm gregarious. Also, I don't like caves and I don't like camp cooking and I don't like living off the land – and I do like music and books and art and educated people and so on – in other words, I found out that I can't revert to savagery. And, not least, I like women and there aren't any out there. What few ever make it up there die fast.'

'I'm beginning to believe you.' A little of the worry and harassment left His Honor's face. 'One more question. Why, knowing the jam we're in, did you come here instead of going somewhere where you'd be safe?'

'Because, on the basis of stuff I picked up here and there, you and I together can make it safe here. I can fix your mining machinery easily enough so you can make quota every week with no sweat; so the town won't get slagged down; not right away, anyway. You aren't a quisling, and my best guess is that most of the spies and storm-troopers have sneaked out or have been pulled out because of what's supposed to be about to happen here,' Seaton said.

Prenk stared thoughtfully at Seaton. 'You don't appear to be the suicidal type. But you know as well as I do that just making quota won't be enough for very long. What have you really got in mind, Ky-El Mokak?'

Seaton thought for a moment. Then, shrugging his shoulders, he dug down into his baggy breeches and brought out two closely folded headsets.

'Put one of these on. It isn't a player or a recorder; just a kind of super-telephone. A fast way of exchanging information.'

Prenk wore it for a couple of minutes, then took it off, staring suspiciously in turn at it and at Seaton. 'Why didn't I ever hear of anything like *that* before?' he demanded. Seaton didn't answer the question and Prenk went on, 'Oh; secret. Okay. But what makes you think you can set up an underground right out here in the open?'

'There's no reason in the world why we can't,' Seaton declared. 'Especially since we'd just be reviving one that everybody, including the Premier and you yourself, thinks is smashed flat and is about to be liquidated.'

This was the second really severe test Seaton had made of the Brain's visualizations, and it too stood solidly up. All Prenk said was, 'You're doing the talking; keep it up,' but his hands, clenching tightly into fists, showed that Seaton's shot had struck the mark.

'I've talked enough,' Seaton said then. 'From here on I'd be just guessing. It's your turn to talk.'

'All right. It's too late now, I'm afraid, for anything to make any difference. Yes, I was the leader of a faction that believed in decent, humane, civilized government, but we weren't here then, we were in the capital. Our coup failed. And those of us who were caught were exiled here and arrangements were made for us to be the next wipe-out.'

'Some of your party survived, then. Could you interest them again, do you think?'

'Without arms and equipment, no. That was why we failed.'

'Equipment would be no problem.'

'It wouldn't?' Prenk's eyes began to light up.

'No.' Seaton did not elaborate, but went on, 'The problem is people and morale. I can't supply people and we have to start here, not over in the capital. Self-preservation. We've got to make quota. Your people have been hammered down so flat that they don't give a whoop whether they live or die. As I said, I can fix the machinery, but that of itself won't be enough. We'll have to give 'em a shot in the arm of hope.'

'Okay, and thanks.'

And no one in the outer office, not even the secretary, so much as looked up as the two men, talking busily, walked out.

DuQuesne, en route to Earth, knew just what a madhouse Earth was, and in just what respects. He knew just how nearly impossible it was to buy machine tools of any kind. He also knew just what an immense job it was going to be to build a duplicate of the *Skylark of Valeron*. Or, rather, to build the tools that would build the machines that would in turn build the planetoid. With his high-order constructors he *could* build most of those primary machine tools himself; perhaps all of them in time; but time was exactly what he did not have. Time was decidedly of the essence.

DuQuesne's ex-employer, the World Steel Corporation, had billions of dollars' worth of exactly the kind of tooling he had to have. They not only used it, they manufactured it and sold it. And what of it they did not manufacture they could buy.

How they could buy! As a result of many years of intensive, highly organized, and well directed snooping, Brookings of Steel had over a thousand very effective handles upon over a thousand very important men.

And he, DuQuesne, had a perfect handle on Brookings. He was much harder and more ruthless than Brookings was, and Brookings knew it. He could make Brookings buy his primary tooling for him – enough of it to stuff the *Capital D* to her outer skin. And he would do just that.

Wherefore, as soon as he got within working range of Earth, he launched his projection directly into Brookings' private office. This time, the tycoon was neither calm nor quiet. Standing behind his desk, chair lying on its side behind him, he was leaning forward with his left hand flat on the top of his desk. He was clutching a half-smoked, half-chewed cigar in his right hand and brandishing it furiously in the air. He was yelling at his terrified secretary; who, partly standing in front of her chair and partly crouching into it, was trying to muster up courage to run.

When DuQuesne's projection appeared Brookings fell silent for a moment and goggled. Then he screamed. 'Get out of here, you!' at the girl, who scuttled frantically away. He hurled what was left of his cigar into his big bronze ashtray, where it disintegrated into a shower of sparks and a slathery mess of soggy, sticky brown leaves. And finally, exerting everything he had of self-control, he picked his chair up, sat down in it and glared at DuQuesne.

'Careful of your apoplexy, Fat,' DuQuesne sneered then. 'I've told you – you'll rupture your aorta some day and that will just about break my heart.'

Brookings' reply to that was unprintable; after which he went on, even more bitterly, 'This is all it lacks to make this a perfect day.'

'Yeah,' DuQuesne agreed, callously. 'Some days you can't lay up a cent. I suppose you've been eager to know why I didn't return your goons to you.'

'There's nothing in the world I'm less interested in.'

'I'll tell you anyway, for the record.' DuQuesne did not know what had actually happened, but Brookings was never to know that. 'They each got one free shot, as I said they would. But they missed.'

'Skip that, doctor,' Brookings said, brusquely. 'You didn't come here for that. What do you want this time?'

DuQuesne reached over, took a ballpoint out of Brookings' pocket, tore the top sheet off of the memorandum pad on Brookings' desk, and wrote out an order for one hundred twenty-five million dollars, payable to the World Steel Corporation, on a numbered account in a Swiss bank. He slid the order across the glass top of the desk and said:

'You needn't worry about whether it's good or not. It is. I want machine tools and fast deliveries.'

Brookings glanced at the paper, but did not touch it. His every muscle tensed, but he did not quite blow up again. 'Machine tools,' he grated. 'You know damn well money's no good on them'

'Money alone, no,' DuQuesne agreed equably. 'That's why I'm having you apply pressure. You'll get the details – orders, specs, times and places of delivery, and so forth – by registered mail tomorrow morning. Shall I spell out the "or else" for you?'

Brookings was quivering with rage, but there wasn't a thing in the world he could do about the situation and he knew it. 'Not for me,' he managed finally, 'but I'd better record it for certain people who will have to know.'

'Okay. Any mistake in any detail of the transaction or one second more than twenty-four hours' delay in any specified time of delivery will mean a one-hundred-kiloton superatomic on North Africa Number Eleven. Goodbye.'

And DuQuesne cut his projection. To Brookings, he seemed to vanish; to DuQuesne himself, he simply was back in his own *Capital D*, far out in space; and DuQuesne allowed himself to smile.

Things were going rather well, he thought. Seaton was tangled up with whoever the new enemy had turned out to be; might well be dead; at any rate, was not a factor he, DuQuesne, needed currently to take into his calculations. By the time Seaton was back in circulation DuQuesne should have his new ship and be ready to handle him. And from then on …

From then on, thought DuQuesne, it was only a short step to his rightful, inevitable destiny: *his* universe. No one able to contest his mastery – so thought DuQuesne, who at that point in time knew nearly every factor that bore upon his plans, and had carefully and correctly evaluated them all. He knew about the Llurdi and the Jelmi; he knew that Seaton and the Chlorans were, from his point of view, keeping each other neutralized; he knew that the Norlaminians, even, were unlikely to cause him any trouble. DuQuesne really knew all the relevant facts but one – or, you might say, two. These two facts were a very long distance away. One was a young girl. The other was her mother.

Two individuals out of a universe! Why, even if DuQuesne had known of their existence, he might have discounted their importance completely. In which he would have been – completely – wrong.

18

Humanity Triumphant, Not Inc

Since Seaton as Ky-El Mokak was not the least bit fussy, he accepted the first house that Prenk showed him. His Honor offered also – with a more than somewhat suggestive expression – to send him a housekeeper, but Seaton declined the offer with thanks; explaining that that could wait until he got himself organized and could do a little looking around for himself.

Prenk gave Seaton a handful of currency and a ground-car – one of Prenk's own, this; a beautifully streamlined, beautifully kept little three-wheeled jewel of a ground-car – told him where the shopping-centers were, and went back to City Hall.

Seaton bought a haircut and a shave, a couple of outfits of clothing, and some household supplies, which he took out to his new home and stowed away.

By that time it was the local equivalent of half-past three, and the shifts changed at four o'clock; wherefore he drove his spectacular little speedster six miles up-canyon to the uraninite mine that was the sole reason for the town's existence. Since he did not want to be shot out of hand, he did not dare to be late or to do anything unusual, either during the five-mile train-ride along the main tunnel or during the skip-ride down to the eighty-four-hundred-foot level where he was to work.

Once in the stope itself, however, he stopped – exactly thirteen feet short of the stiffly erect young overseer – and stood still while his shiftmates picked up their tools and started for the hanging wall – the something-more-than-vertical face of the cavernous stope – to begin their day's work.

The overseer was a well-fed young man, and the second native Seaton had seen who looked more than half alive. His jacket, breeches and boots were as glossily black as his crash-helmet was glossily white. He was a very proud young man, and arrogant. His side-arm hung proudly at his hip. His bull-whip coiled arrogantly ready for instant use.

This wight stared haughtily at Seaton for a moment, and began to swell up like a pouter pigeon. Then, as Seaton made an unmistakable gesture at him, he went into smoothly violent action.

'Oh, you're the wilder!' he snarled, and swung the heavy blacksnake with practiced ease.

But Seaton had known exactly what to expect and he was ready for it. He ducked and sidestepped with the speed and control of the trained gymnast that he was; he handled the short, thick club that had been in his sleeve as though it were the wand of the highly skilled prestidigitator that he was. Thus, in the instant that the end of the lash curled savagely around the hickory he swung it like a home-run hitter swings a bat – and caught the blacksnake's heavy, shot-loaded butt on the fly in his right hand.

The minion went for his gun, of course, but Seaton's right arm was already swinging around and back, and as gun cleared holster the bull-whip's vicious tip snapped around both gun and hand with a pistol-sharp report. The trooper stared, for an instant stunned, at the blood spurting from his paralyzed right hand; and that instant was enough. Seaton stepped up to him and put his left fist deep into his midsection. Then, as the half-conscious man began to double over, he sent his right fist against its preselected target. Not the jaw – he didn't want to break his hand – the throat. Nor did he hit him hard; he didn't want to kill the guy, or even damage him permanently.

As the man fell to the hard-rock floor – writhing in agony, groaning, strangling and gasping horribly for breath – the men and women and teenagers looking on burst as one into clamor. 'Stomp 'im!' they shrieked and yelled. 'Give 'im the boots! Stomp 'im! Kill 'im! Stomp 'is head clean off! Stomp 'im right down into the rock!'

'Hold it!' Seaton rasped, and the miners fell silent; but they did not relapse into their former apathy.

Seaton stood by, waiting coldly for his victim to be able to draw a breath. He picked the overseer's pistol-like weapon up and looked it over. He had never seen anything like it before, and casual inspection didn't tell him much about how it worked, but that could wait. He didn't intend to use it. In fact, he wasn't really interested in it at all.

When the overseer had partially recovered his senses, Seaton jammed a headset onto his head and thought viciously at him; as much to give him a taste of real punishment as to find out what he knew and to impress upon his mind exactly what he had to do if he hoped to keep on living. Then Seaton made what was for him a speech. First, to the now completely deflated officer:

'You – you slimy traitor, you *quisling*! Know now that a new regime has taken over. Maybe I'll let you live and maybe I'll turn you over to these boys and girls here – you know what they'd do to you. That depends on how *exactly* you stick to what I just told you. One thought of a squeal – if you ever get one millimeter out of line, and you'll be under surveillance every second of every day – you'll die a long, slow, tough death. And I mean *tough!*'

He turned to the miners; studied them narrowly. His 'shot in the arm' had done them a lot of good. Excitement was still high; none of them had relapsed into the apathy that had affected them all such a short time before. In fact, one close-clustered group of men was eyeing Seaton and the overseer in a fashion that made it perfectly clear that, had it not been for Seaton's mien and the gun and the whip, there would have been a lynching then and there.

'Take it easy, people,' Seaton told them. 'I know you all want to tear this ape apart, but what good would it do? None. Not a bit. So I won't let you do it. But I don't intend to use either whip or gun and I don't think I'll have to, because this is the first bite of a fresh kettle of fish for every civilized human being of this world. I won't go into much detail, but I represent a group of human beings, as human as yourselves, called HUMANITY TRIUMPHANT. I'm a forerunner. I'm here to bring you a message; to tell you that humanity has never been conquered permanently and never will be so conquered. Humanity has triumphed and will continue to triumph over all the vermin infesting all the planets of all the solar systems of all the galaxies of all surveyed space.

'HUMANITY TRIUMPHANT's plans have been made in full and are being put out into effect. Humanity will win here, and in not too long a time. Every Chloran in every solar system in this region of space will die. That's a promise.

'Nor do we need your help. All we ask you is that you produce the full quota of ore every week, so that no Chloran warship will come here too soon. And that production will be no problem very shortly, since I can repair your machinery and will have it all back in working order by one week from today. So in a very few weeks you women can go back to keeping house for your families; you youngsters can go back to school; and half of you men will be able to make quota in half a shift and spend the other half of it playing penny-ante. And you, Brother Rat' – he turned back to the deposed overseer – 'you can peel that pretty uniform. You're going to work, right now. You and I are going to be partners – and if you so much as begin to drag your feet I'll slap your face clear around onto the back of your neck. Let's go!'

They went. They picked up a drill – which weighed all of three hundred pounds – and lugged it across the rough rock floor of the foot of the face; which, translated from the vernacular, means the lower edge of the expanse of high-grade ore that was being worked.

It was a beautiful thing, that face; a startlingly high and wide expanse of the glossy, lustrous, submetallic pitch black of uraninite; slashed and spattered and shot through at random with the characteristic violent yellows of autunite and carnotite and the variant greens of torbernite.

But Seaton was not particularly interested in beauty at the moment. What he *hoped* was that he could keep from giving away the fact that this was the first time he had ever handled a mining machine of any kind or type. He thought he could, however, and he did.

For, after all, there are only so many ways in which holes can be made in solid rock. Second, since the hardrock men who operate the machinery to make those holes are never the greatest intellects of any world, such machinery must be essentially simple. And third, the Brain's visualizations had been very complete and Richard Seaton was, as he had admitted to Prenk, an exceptionally smart man.

Wherefore, although Seaton unobtrusively let the overseer take the lead, the two men worked very well together and the native did not once drag his feet. They set up the heavy drill and locked it in place against the face. They slipped the shortest 'twelve-inch' steel into the chuck and rammed it home. They turned on the air and put their shoulders to the stabilizing pads – and that monstrous machine, bellowing and thundering under the terrific urge of two hundred pounds to the square inch of compressed air, drove that heavy bit restlessly into the ore.

And the rest of the miners, fired by Seaton's example as well as by his 'shot in the arm,' worked as they had not worked in months; to such good purpose that when the shift ended at midnight the crew had sent out almost twice as much high-grade ore as they had delivered the night before.

It need hardly be mentioned, perhaps, that Seaton was enjoying himself very much. Although he was not, in truth, the 'big, muscle-bound ape – especially between the ears' he was wont to describe himself as, there was certainly a pleasure in being up against the sort of problem that muscle and skill could settle. For a time he was concerned about the fact that events elsewhere might be proceeding at a pace he could not control; but there was not a minute spent on the surface of this planet that was not a net gain in terms of the automatic repair of the *Valeron*. That great ship had been *hurt*. Since there was at the moment very little that Seaton could do effectively about DuQuesne, or directly about the Chlorans, or the Fenachrone – and there was a great deal he could do here on the surface of Ray-See-Nee – he put the other matters out of his mind and did what had to be done.

And enjoyed it enormously!

Seaton went 'home' to the empty and solitary house that was his temporary residence and raised the oversize ring to his lips. 'Dottie,' he said.

'Oh, Dick!' a tiny scream came from the ring. 'I *wish* you wouldn't take such horrible chances! I thought I'd *die*! Won't you, tomorrow morning, just shoot the louse out of hand? *Please?*'

'I wasn't taking any chances, Dot; a man with half my training could have done it. I *had* to do something spectacular to snap these people out of it; they're dead from the belt-buckle up, down, and back. But I've done enough, I think, so I won't have any more trouble at all. It'll get around – and *how!* – and strictly on the Q and T. All those other apes will need is a mere touch of fist.'

'You hope. Me, too, for that matter. Just a sec, here's Martin. He wants to talk to you about that machinery business,' and Crane's voice replaced Dorothy's

'I certainly do, Dick. You say you want two-hundred-fifty-pound Sullivan Sluggers, complete with variable-height mounts and inch-and-a-quarter – that's English, remember – bits. You want Ingersoll-Rand compressors and Westinghouse generators and Wilfley tables and so on, each item by name and no item resembling any of their own machinery in any particular. Since you are supposed to be repairing their own machinery, wouldn't it be better to have the Brain do just that, while you look on, making wise motions, and learn?'

'It might be better, at that,' Seaton admitted, after a moment's thought. 'My thought was that since nobody now working in the mine knows anything much about either mining or machinery it wouldn't make any difference, as long as the stuff was good and rusty on the outside, and I know how our stuff works. But I can learn theirs and it will save a lot of handling and we'll have the time. They're working only two shifts in only one stope, you know. Lack of people. But nine-tenths of their equipment is as dead as King Tut and the rest of it starts falling apart every time anybody gives any of it a stern look – I was scared spitless all shift that we'd be running out of air or power, or both, any minute. So we'll have to do one generator and at least one compressor tonight; so you might as well start getting the stuff ready for me.'

'It's ready. I'll send it down as soon as it gets good and dark. In the meantime, how about Brother Rat? Have you anyone watching him?'

'No, I didn't think it was necessary. But it might be, at that. From up there, would you say?'

'Definitely. And Shiro and Lotus haven't much to do at the moment. I'll make arrangements.'

'Do that, guy, and so long till dark.'

'Just a sec, Dick,' Dorothy said then. 'I'm not done with you yet. You remembered the no-neighbors bit, I think?'

'I sure did, Honey-Chile. No neighbors within half a mile. So, any dark of the moon, slip down here in one of the fifteen-footers and all will be well.'

'You big, nice man,' Dorothy purred. 'Comes dark, comes me! An' you can lay to that.'

Countless parsecs away, DuQuesne made proper entry into the solar system, putting his *Capital D* into a parking orbit around Earth, and began to pick up his tremendous order of machine tools and supplies. It went well; Brookings had done his job. There was, however, one job DuQuesne had to do for himself. During the loading, accordingly, he went in person to Washington, D.C., to the Rare Metals Laboratory, and to Room 1631.

That room's door was open. He tapped lightly on it as he entered the room. He closed the door gently behind him.

'Park it,' a well-remembered contralto voice said. 'Be with you in a moment.'

'No rush.' DuQuesne sat down, crossed his legs, lighted a cigarette, and gazed at the woman seated at her electronics panel. Both her eyes were buried in the light-shield of a binocular eyepiece; both her hands were manipulating vernier knobs in tiny arcs.

'Oh! Hi, Blackie! Be with you in half a moment.'

'No sweat, Hunkie. Finish your obs.'

'Natch.' Her attention had not wavered for an instant from her instruments; it did not waver then.

In a minute or so she pressed a button, her panel went dark, and she rose to her feet. 'It's been a long time, Blackie,' she said, stepping toward him and extending her hand.

'It has indeed.' He took her hand and began an encircling action with his left – a maneuver which she countered, neatly but still smilingly, by grasping his left hand and holding it firmly.

'Tsk, tsk,' she tsked. 'The merchandise is on display, Blackie, but it is not to be handled. Remember?'

'I remember. Still untouchable,' he said.

'That's right. You're a hard-nosed, possessive brute, Blackie – any man to interest me very much would have to be, I suppose – but no man born is ever going to tell me what I can or can't do. Selah. But let's skip that.' She released his hands, waved him to a chair, sat down, crossed her legs, accepted the lighted cigarette he handed her, and went on, 'Thanks. The gossip was that you were all washed up and had, as Ferdy put it, "taken it on the lam." I didn't believe it then and I don't believe it now. I've been wanting to tell you; you're a good enough man so that whatever you're really after, you'll get.'

This woman could reach DuQuesne as no other woman ever had. 'Thanks, Hunkie,' he said; and, reaching out, he pressed her right hand hard then dropped it. 'What I came up here for – have you a date for Thursday evening that you can't or won't break?'

Her smile widened; her two lovely dimples deepened. 'Don't tell me; let me guess. Louisa Vinciughi in *Lucia*.'

'Nothing else but. You like?'

'I love. With the usual stipulation – we "Dutch" it.'

'Listen, Hunkie!' he protested. 'Aren't you ever going to get off of that "Dutch" thing? Don't you think a man can take a girl out without having monkey-business primarily in mind?'

She considered the question thoughtfully, then nodded. 'As stated, yes. Eliding the one word "primarily", no. I've heard you called a lot of things, my friend, but "stupid" was never one of them. Not even once.'

'I know.' DuQuesne smiled, a trifle wryly. 'You are not going to be obligated by any jot or iota or tittle to any man living or yet to be born.'

Her head went up a little and her smile became a little less warm. 'That's precisely right, Marc. But I've never made any secret of the fact that I enjoy your company a lot. So, on that basis, okay and thanks.'

'On that basis, then, if that's the way it has to be, and thanks to you, too,' DuQuesne said, and took his leave.

And Thursday evening came; and all during that long and thoroughly pleasant evening the man was, to the girl's highly sensitive perception … well, different, although very subtly so. He was not quite, by some very small fraction, his usual completely poised and urbane self. Even Vinciughi's wonderful soprano voice did not bring him entirely back from wherever it was he was. Wherefore, just before saying goodnight at the door of her apartment, she said:

'You have something big on your mind, Blackie. Tremendously big. Would it help to come in and talk a while?' This was the first time in all their long acquaintance that she had ever invited him into her apartment. 'Or wouldn't it?'

He thought for a moment. 'No,' he decided. 'There are so many maybes and ifs and buts in the way that talking would be even more futile than thinking. But I'd like to ask you this: how much longer will you be here in Washington, do you think?'

She caught her breath. 'The Observer says it'll take me a year and a half to get what I should have.'

'That's fine,' DuQuesne said. His thoughts were racing, but none of them showed. What were those Observers doing? And why? He knew the kind of mind Stephanie de Marigny had – they were feeding with a teaspoon a mind fully capable of gulping it down by the truckload … why? *Why?* So as not to play favorites, probably – that was the only reason he could think of. DuQuesne was playing for very high stakes; he could not afford to overlook any possibility, however remote. Had his interest in Hunkie de Marigny been deduced by the Norlaminians? Was it, in fact, possible – even likely – that he was under observation even now? Was their strange slowdown in her training meaningful? He could not answer; but he decided on caution. He went on with scarcely a noticeable pause, 'I'll see you well before that – if I may?'

'Why, of course you may! I'd get an acute attack of the high dudgeons if you *ever* came to Washington without seeing me!'

He took his leave then, and she went into her apartment and closed the door ... and stood there, motionless, listening to his receding footsteps with a far-away, brooding look in her deep brown eyes.

19

The Coup

As the days had passed, more and more of the Skylarkers had come to ground in Seaton's temporary home on the planet Ray-See-Nee; until many of them, especially Dorothy, were spending most of their nights there. On this particular evening they were all there.

Since the personal gravity-controls had been perfected long since, Dunark and Sitar were comfortable enough as far as gravity was concerned. The engineers, however, had not yet succeeded in incorporating really good ambient-atmosphere temperature-controllers into them; wherefore he was swathed in wool and she wore her fabulous mink coat. They each wore two Osnomian machine pistols instead of one, and they sat a couple of feet apart – in instant readiness for any action that might become necessary.

Lotus and Shiro, a little closer together than the two Osnomians but not enough so to get into each other's way, sat cross-legged on the floor. He was listening intently, while she wasn't. Almost everything that was being said was going completely over her head.

Dorothy, Margaret, and Crane sat around a small table, fingering tall glasses in which ice-cubes tinkled faintly.

Seaton paced the floor, with his right hand in his breeches pocket and his left holding his pipe, which he brandished occasionally in the air to emphasize a point.

'Considering that we can't do anything at all on unmuffled high-order stuff except when an ore-scow is here, masking our emanations,' Seaton was saying, 'we haven't done too bad. However, I wouldn't wonder if we'd just about run out of time and we're right between the devil and the deep blue sea. Mart, what's your synthesis?'

Crane sipped his drink and cleared his throat. 'You're probably right in one respect, Dick. They apparently make a spectacle of these destructions of cities; not for the Chlorans' amusement – I doubt very much if they enjoy or abhor anything, as we understand the term – but to keep the rest of the population of this world in line. Whether or not the quisling dictator of this world arranged for this city to be the next sacrifice, it is certain that we have interfered with the expected course of events to such an extent that the powers-that-be will at least investigate. But I can't quite see the dilemma.'

'I can,' Dorothy said. They *have* to have a grisly example, once every so often; and since this one didn't develop on schedule maybe they'll go crying to mama instead of trying to handle us themselves. You see, they may know more about us than we think they do.'

'That's true, of course—' Crane began, but Seaton broke in.

'So I say it's time to let Ree-Toe Prenk in on the whole deal and add him to our Council of War,' he declared, and talk went on.

They were still discussing the situation twenty minutes later, when someone tapped gently on the front door.

The Osnomians leaped to their feet, pistols in all four hands. The two Japanese leaped to their feet and stood poised, knees and elbows slightly flexed, ready for action. Forty-five-caliber automatics appeared in the hands of the three at the table, and Crane flipped his remote control helmet onto his head. Seaton, magnum in hand, snapped on the outside lights and peered out through the recently installed one-way glass of the door.

'Speak of the devil,' he said in relief. 'It's Hizzoner.' He opened the door wide and went on, 'Come in, Your Honor. We were just talking about you.'

Prenk came in, his eyes bulging slightly at the sight of the arsenal of armaments now being put back into holsters. They bulged still more as he looked at the Japanese, and he gulped as he stared fascinatedly at the green-skinned Osnomians.

'I knew, of course, within a couple of days,' Prenk said then, quietly, 'that you who call yourself Ky-El Mokak were not confining your statements to the exact truth. No wilder could possibly have done what you were doing; but by that time I knew that you, whoever you were, were really on our side. I had no suspicion until this moment, however, that you were actually from another world. I thought that your speech to the miners was what you said it was going to be, "a shot in the arm of hope". It now seems more than slightly possible that you were talking about the very matters I came here tonight to see you about. Certain supplies, you will remember.'

'I remember. I lied to you, yes. Wholesale and retail. But how else could

I have made the approach, the mood you were in, without blowing every-thing higher than up?'

'Your technique was probably the best possible, I admit.'

'Okay. Yes, we're from a galaxy so far away from here that you could barely find it with the biggest telescope this world ever had. Our business at the moment is to wipe out every Chloran in this region of space, but we can't do it without – among other things – a lot more data than we now have. And we'll need weeks of time, mostly elsewhere, for preparation.

'But before we go too deeply into that you must meet my associates. People, this is His Honor Ree-Toe Prenk; what you might call the Mayor of the City of Ty-Ko-Ma of the Planet Ray-See-Nee. You know all about him. Ree-Toe, this is Hi-Fi Mokak, my wife – Lo-Test and Hi-Test Crane, husband and wife' – and he went on with two more pairs of coined names.

'Hi-Fi indeed!' Dorothy snorted, under her breath, in English. 'Just you wait 'til I get you alone tonight, you egregious clown!'

'Whad'ya mean "clown"?' he retorted. 'Try *your* hand sometime at invent-ing seven names on the spur of the moment!'

Seaton then put on a headset, slipped one over Prenk's head, and said in thought: 'This is what is left – the residue you might say – of our mobile base the *Skylark of Valeron*,' and went on to show him and to describe to him the great Brain, the immense tank-chart of the entire First Universe, the tremen-dous driving engines and even more tremendous engines of offense and of defense.

Prenk was held spellbound and speechless, for this 'residue', hundreds of kilometers in diameter and hundreds of millions of tons in weight, was so utterly beyond any artificial structure Prenk had ever imagined that he simply could not grasp its magnitude at all. And when Seaton went on to show him a full mental picture of what that base had been before the battle with the Chlorans and what it would have to be before they could begin to move against the Chlorans – the one-thousand kilometer control-circles, the thousands of cubic kilometers of solidly packed offensive and defensive gear, the scores of fantastically braced and buttressed layers of inoson that com-posed the worldlet's outer skin – he was so strongly affected as to be speechless in fact.

'I … I see. That is … a little, maybe …' he stammered, then subsided into silence.

'Yes, it *is* a bit big to get used to all at once,' Seaton agreed. 'It needs a lot of work. Some we're doing; some of it can't be done anywhere near here; but we don't want to leave without being reasonably sure that you and your people will be alive when we get back. So we want a lot of information from you.'

'I'll be glad to tell you everything I know or can find out.'

'Thanks. Ideas, first. How much do you think the quisling Big Shots actually know? What do you think they'll do about it? What do you think His Magnificence the Director will do? And what should we do about what he thinks he's going to do? In a few days we'll want all the information you can get – facts, names, dates, places, times, and personnel. Also one sample copy of each and every item of equipment desired; with numbers wanted and times and places of delivery. Brother Prenk, you have the floor.'

'One advantage of a small town and a group like ours,' Prenk said, slowly, 'is that everybody knows everybody else's business. Thus, we all knew who the spies were, but the people were all so low in their minds that they simply did not care whether they lived or died. We had done our best and had failed; most of us had given up hope completely. Now, however, the few remaining spies have been locked up and are under control. They and the overseers are still reporting, but' – he smiled wolfishly – 'they are saying precisely and only what I tell them to say. This condition can't last very long; but, after what you just showed me, I'm pretty sure I can make it last long enough. We have organized a really efficient force of guerrilla fighters and our plans for the capital are ...'

A couple of weeks later, then, three hundred fifty-eight highly trained men and one highly trained woman set out.

A woman? Yes. Dorothy had protested vigorously.

'But Sitar! *You* aren't going, surely? *Surely* you're staying home?'

'Staying *home!*' the green girl had blazed. 'The First Wife of a prince of Osnome goes with her prince wherever he goes. She fights beside him, at need she dies beside him. Would you have him die fighting and me live an hour? I'd blow myself to hits!'

'My God!' Dorothy had gasped, and had stared, appalled.

'That's right,' Seaton had told her. 'Their ethics, mores and customs differ more than somewhat from ours, you know.' And nothing more had been said about Sitar being a member of the Expeditionary Force.

Prenk's guerrillas had infiltrated the capital city by ones and twos; no group ever larger than two. Each one wore the costume of an easily recognizable class of citizen. They were apparently artisans and workmen, soldiers, sailors, clerks, businessmen, tycoons of industry. Nor were the watches they all wore on their wrists any more alike than were their costumes – except in one respect. They all told the same time, to the tenth of a split second, and they all were kept in sync by pulses from a tiny power-pack that had been hidden in a tree in the outskirts of the city.

At time zero minus thirty minutes, three hundred fifty-nine persons began to enter into and to distribute themselves throughout an immense building that resembled a palace or a cathedral much more than the capitol building even of a world.

At time zero minus four seconds all those persons, who had in the meantime been doing inconspicuous this and innocuous that, changed direction toward or began to walk toward or kept on walking toward their objectives.

At time zero on the tick, three hundred fifty-nine knives came out of concealment and that exact number of persons fell.

Some of the guerrillas remained on guard where their victims lay. Others went into various offices on various businesses. On the top-most floor four innocent-looking visitors blasted open the steel door of Communications and shot the four operators then on duty. The leader of the four invaders stepped up to the master-control desk, shoved a body aside, flipped three or four switches, and said:

'Your attention, please! These programs have been interrupted to announce that former Premier Da-Bay Saien and his sycophants have been executed for high treason. Premier Ree-Toe Prenk and his loyalists are now the government. Business is to go on as usual; no new orders will be issued except as they become necessary. That is all. Scheduled programs will now be resumed.'

It was not as easy everywhere, however, as that announcement indicated. By the very nature of things, the information secured by the counterspies was incomplete and sometimes, especially in fine detail, was wrong. Thus, when Seaton took his post on the fifteenth floor, standing before and admiring a heroic-size bronze statue of a woman strangling a boa constrictor whose coils enveloped half her height, he saw that there were four guards, instead of the two he had expected to find, at the door of the office that was his objective. But he couldn't – wouldn't – call for help. They hadn't had manpower enough to carry spares. He'd trip the SOS if necessary, but not until it became absolutely necessary – but that office *had* to be put out of business by time zero plus fifteen seconds. He'd just have to act twice as fast, was all.

Cursing silently the fact that his magnum was not to be used during the first few silent seconds of the engagement, he watched the four men constantly out of the corners of his eyes, planning every detail of his campaign, altering those details constantly as the guards changed ever so slightly their positions and postures. He could get three of them, he was sure, before any one of them could fire; but he'd have to be lucky as well as fast to get the fourth in time – and if the ape had time to take any kind of aim at all it would be very ungood.

On the tick of zero time Seaton shed his businessman's cloak and took off. Literally. His knife swept through the throat of the nearest guard before that luckless wight had moved a muscle. He kicked the second, who was bending over at the moment, on and through the temple with the steel-lined toe of one highly special sure-grip fighting shoe. He stabbed the third, whose throat was protected at that instant by an upflung left arm, through the left side of the rib-cage, twisting his blade as he pulled it out.

Ultra-fast as Seaton had been, the fourth guard had had time to lift his weapon, but he had not had time to aim it, or even to point it properly. He fired in panic, before his gun was pointed even waist-high. If Seaton had stayed upright the bullet would have missed him completely. But he didn't. He ducked and sidestepped and twisted – and the heavy slug tore a long and savage wound across the left side of his back.

One shot was all the fellow got, of course. Seaton kicked the door open and leaped into the room, magnum high and ready. The noise of that one shot might have torn it, but good.

'*Freeze*, everybody!' he rasped, and everyone in the big room froze. 'One move of any finger toward any button and I blast. This office is closed temporarily. Leave the building, all of you; right now and fast. Just as you are. Come back in here after lunch for business as usual. Scram!'

The office force – some nonchalantly, some wonderingly, some staring at Seaton in surprise – 'scrammed' obediently. All, that is, except one girl who came last; the girl who had been sitting at an executive-type desk beside the door of the inner office. She was a fairly tall girl; with hazel eyes and with dark brown hair arranged in up-to-the-second 'sunburst' style. Her close-fitting white nylon upper garment and her even tighter fire-engine-red tights displayed a figure that could not be described as being merely adequate.

Instead of passing him as the others had done she stopped, held out both hands in indication of having nothing except peaceable intentions, and peered around his left side. Then, bringing her eyes back to his, she said, 'You're bleeding terribly, sir. It doesn't seem to be very deep – entrance and exit holes in your shirt are only four or five inches apart – but you're losing an awful lot of blood. Won't you let me give you first aid? I'm a quite competent nurse, sir.'

'*What?*' Seaton demanded, but whatever he had intended to add to that one word was forestalled by a bellow of wrath from behind the just-opening door of the inner office.

'Kay-Lee! You shirking slut! How much more of this do you think you can get away with? When I buzz you you *jump* or I'll cut your bloody –' The man broke off sharply and goggled at what he saw. He was a pasty-faced, paunchy man of forty; very evidently self-indulgent and as evidently completely at a loss at the moment.

'Come in, Bay-Lay Boyn,' Seaton said. 'Slowly, if you don't want your brains to decorate the ceiling. Did you ever see a man shot in the head with a magnum pistol?'

The man gulped and licked his lips. The girl broke the very short silence. 'Whatever you do to that poisonous slob, sir, I hope it's nothing trivial. I'd love to see his brains spattered all over the ceiling and I'd never let them be washed off. I'd look up at them week after week and gloat.'

'Kay-Lee dear, you don't mean that! You *can't* mean it!' the man implored. 'Do something! *Please* do something! I'll double your salary – I'll make you a First – I'll give you a diamond necklace – I'll—'

'You'll shut your filthy lying mouth, *Your Exalted*,' she said – quietly, but with an icily venomous contempt that made Seaton stare. 'I've taken all the raps for you I'm ever going to.' She turned to Seaton. 'Please believe, sir, that no matter who your people are or what you do, any possible change will be for the better. And I remind you – if you don't want to fall flat on your face from weakness you'll let me dress that wound.'

'I wouldn't wonder,' Seaton admitted. 'Blood's running down into my shoes already and it's beginning to hurt like the devil. So get your kit. But before you start on me we'll use some three-inch bandage to lash that ape's hands around that pillar there.'

That done, Seaton peeled to the waist and the girl went expertly to work. She sprayed the nasty-looking wound, which was almost but not quite a deep but open groove, with antiseptic and with coagulant. She cross-taped its ragged edges together with blood-proof adhesive tape. She sponged most of the liquid blood off his back. She sprinkled half a can of curative-antiseptic powder; she taped on thick pads of sterile gauze. She wrapped – and taped into place – roll after roll of three-inch bandage around his body and up over his shoulder and around his neck. Then she stood back and examined her handiwork, eyes narrowed in concentration.

'That'll do it for a while,' she decided. 'I suppose you'll be too busy to take any time today, but you'll *have* to get that sewed up not later than tomorrow forenoon.'

'I'll do that. Thanks a million, lady; it feels a lot better already,' and Seaton bent over to pick up his shirt and undershirt.

'But you *can't* wear those bloody rags!' she protested, then went on, 'But I don't know of anything else around here that you *can* wear, at that.'

Seaton grinned. 'No quandary – I'll go the way I am. Costume or the lack of it isn't important at the moment.' He glanced at his watch and was surprised to see how very few minutes had elapsed.

'Shall I go now, sir?'

'Not yet.' Seaton was used to making fast decisions, and they were usually right. He made one now. 'I take it you were that ape's confidential secretary.'

'Yes, sir, I was.'

'So you know more about the actual workings of the department than he does and can run it as well. To make a snap judgment, can run it better than he has been running it.'

'Much better, sir,' she said, flatly. 'I've covered up for his drunken blunderings twice in the last two months. He passed the buck to me and I took it. A few lashes are much better than what he revels in doing to people; especially since he can't touch me now. He knows that after taking his floggings I'd go under hypnosis and tell everything I know about him if he tried to lay a finger on me.'

'Lashes? Floggings? I see.' Seaton's face hardened. 'Okay, you're it.' He took a badge out of his pocket, slid its slip out of its holder, and handed the slip to Kay-Lee. 'Type on this your name and his rating and title and turn your recorder on.'

She did so. He glanced at the slip, replaced it in its holder, and pinned the badge in place just above the girl's boldly outstanding left breast. 'I, Ky-El Mokak, acting for and with the authority of Premier Ree-Toe Prenk, hereby make you, Kay-Lee Barlo, an Exalted of the Twenty-Sixth and appoint you Head of the Department of Public Works. I hereby charge you, Your Exalted, to so operate your department as to prevent, not to cause, the destruction of persons and of property by those enemies of all mankind the Chlorans.' He stepped to the desk; cut the recorder off.

For the first time, the girl's taut self-control was broken. 'Do you mean I can actually clean this pig-sty up?' she demanded, tears welling into her eyes. 'That you actually *want* me to clean it up?'

'Just that. You'll be briefed at a meeting of the new department heads late this afternoon. In the meantime start your house-cleaning as soon as you like after your people get back from lunch; and I don't have to tell you now to act. Have you got or can you get a good hand-gun?'

'Yes, *sir*, there's a very good one – his – in his desk. I was trying to get up nerve enough to ask for it.'

'It's yours as of now. Can you use it? That's probably a foolish question.'

'I'll say I can use it! I made Pistol Expert One when I was eleven and I've been improving ever since.'

'Fine!' He glanced again at his watch. 'Go get it, be sure it's loaded, buckle it on and wear it. Show your badge, play the recording and lay down the law. If there's any argument, shoot to kill. We aren't fooling.' He glanced at the prisoner. 'He'll be out of your way. I'm taking him downstairs pretty soon to answer some questions.'

'I – I thank you, sir. I can't tell you how much. But you – I mean ... well, I –' The girl was a study in mixed emotions. Her nostrils flared and her whole body was tense with the beyond-imagining thrill of what had just occurred; but at the same time she was so acutely embarrassed that she could scarcely talk. 'I want to tell you, sir, that I *wasn't* trying to curry ...' She broke off in confusion and gulped twice.

'Curry? I know you weren't. You aren't the toadying type. That's one reason you got it – but just a second.'

He looked again at his watch and did not put it down; but in a few seconds raised the ring to his lips and asked, 'Are you there, Ree-Toe?'

'Here, Ky-El,' the tiny ring-voice said.

'Mission accomplished, including selection and installation of department head.'

'Splendid! Are you hurt?'

'Not badly. Scratch across my back. How're we doing?'

'Better even than expected. The Premier is dead, I don't know yet exactly how. All your people are all right except for some not-too-serious wounds. Ours, only ten dead reported so far. The army came over to a man. You have earned a world's thanks this day, Ky-El, and its eternal gratitude.'

Seaton blushed. 'Skip it, chief. Any change in schedule?'

'None.'

'Okay. Off.' Seaton, lowering his hand to his side, turned to Kay-Lee.

She, who had not quite been able to believe all along that all this was actually happening to *her*, was staring at him in wide-eyed awe. 'You *are a* biggie!' she gasped. 'A great *big* biggie, Your Exalted, to talk to the Premier himself like that! So this unbelievable appointment will stick!'

'It will stick. Definitely. So chin high and don't spare the horses, Your Exalted; and I'll see you at the meeting. Until then, so-long.'

Seaton cut his prisoner loose and half-led, half-dragged him, gibbering and begging, out of the room. Almost Seaton regretted it was over; the work on Ray-See-Nee had been pleasurable, as well as useful.

But – now he had his base of operations, unknown to the Chlorans, on a planet they thought safely their own. Now he could go on with his campaign against them. Seaton was well aware that the universe held other enemies than the Chlorans, but his motto was one thing at a time.

However, it is instructive now to see just what two of those inimical forces were up to at this one – one which knew it was in trouble ... and one which did not!

20

DuQuesne and Fenachrone

Before the world of the Fenachrone was destroyed by Civilization's superatomic bombs it was a larger world than Earth, and a denser, and with a surface gravity very much higher. It was a world of steaming jungle; of warm and reeking fog; of tepid, sullenly steaming water; of fantastically lush vegetation unknown to Earthly botany. Wind there was none, nor sunshine. Very seldom was the sun of that reeking world visible at all through the omnipresent fog, and then only as a pale, wan disk; and what of its atmosphere was not fog was hot and humid and sulphurously stinking air.

And as varied the world, so varied the people. The Fenachrone, while basically humanoid, were repulsively and monstrously short, wide and thick. They were immensely strong physically, and their mentalities were as monstrous as their civilization was many thousands of years older than that of Earth; their science was equal to ours in most respects and ahead of it in some.

Most monstrous of all the facets of Fenachrone existence, however, was their basic philosophy of life. Might was right. Power was not only the greatest good; it was the only good. The Fenachrone were the MASTER RACE, whose unquestionable destiny it was to be the unquestionable masters of the entire space-time continuum – of the summated totality of the Cosmic All.

For many thousands of years nothing had happened to shake any Fenachrone's rock-solid conviction of the destiny of their race. Progress along the Master-Race line had been uninterrupted. In fact, it had never been successfully opposed. The Fenachrone had already wiped out, without really extending themselves, all the other civilizations within a hundred parsecs or so of their solar system. But up to the time of Emperor Fenor no ruler of the Fenachrone had become convinced that the time had come to set the Day of Conquest – the day upon which the Big Push was to begin.

But rash, headstrong, egomaniacal Fenor insisted upon setting the Day in his own reign – which was why First Scientist Fleet Admiral Sleemet had set up his underground so long before. He was just as patriotic as any other member of his race; just as thoroughly sold on the idea of the inevitable ultimate supremacy over all created things wherever situated; but his computations did not indicate that success was as yet quite certain.

How right Sleemet was!

He knew that he was right after hearing the first few words of Sacner Carfon's ultimatum to Emperor Fenor: that was why he had pushed the panic button for the eighty-five-thousand-odd members of his faction to flee the planet right then.

He knew it still better when, after Fenor's foolhardy defiance of Sacner Carfon, of the Overlord, and of the Forces of Universal Peace, his native planet became a minor sun behind his flying fleet.

Even then, however, Sleemet had not learned very much – at least, nowhere nearly enough.

At first glance it might seem incredible that, after such an experience, Sleemet could have so lightly destroyed two such highly industrialized worlds about which he knew so little. It might seem as though it must have been impressed upon his mind that the Fenachrone were not the ablest, strongest, wisest, smartest, most highly advanced and most powerful form of life ever created. Deeper study will show, however, that with his heredity and conditioning he could not possibly have done anything else.

Sleemet probably did not begin to realize the truth until the Llurd Klazmon so effortlessly – apparently – wiped out sixteen of his seventeen superdread-noughts, then crippled his flagship beyond resistance or repair and sent it hurtling through space toward some completely unknown destination.

His first impulse, like that of all his fellows, was to storm and to rage and to hurl things and to fight. But there was no one to fight; and storming and raging and hurling and smashing things did not do any good. In fact, nothing they could do elicited any attention at all from their captors.

Wherefore, as days stretched out endlessly and monotonously into endless and monotonous weeks, all those five-thousand-odd Fenachrone – males and females, adults and teenagers and children and babies – were forced inexorably into a deep and very un-Fenachronian apathy.

And when the hulk of the flagship arrived at the Llanzlanate on far Llur-diax, things went immediately from bad to worse. The volume of space into which the Fenachrone were moved had a climate exactly like that of their native city on their native world. All its artifacts – its buildings, and its offices and its shops and its foods and its drinks and its everything else – were precisely what they should have been.

Ostensibly, they were encouraged to live lives even more normal than ever before (if such an expression is allowable); to breed and to develop and to evolve; and especially to perform breakthroughs in science.

Actually, however, it was practically impossible for them to do anything of their own volition; because they were being studied and analyzed and tested every minute of every day. Studied coldly and logically and minutely; with an utterly callous ferocity unknown to even such a ferocious race as the Fenach-rone themselves were.

Hundreds upon hundreds of the completely helpless captives died – died without affecting in any smallest respect the treatment received by the survivors – and as their utter helplessness struck in deeper and deeper, the Fenachrone grew steadily weaker, both physically and mentally.

This was no surprise to their captors, the Llurdi. Nor was it in any sense a disappointment. To them the Fenachrone were tools; and they were being tempered and shaped to their task …

On Earth, leaving Stephanie de Marigny's apartment, DuQuesne went back to the *Capital D* and took off on course one hundred seventy-five Universal – that is, five degrees east of Universal South. He went that way because in that direction lay the most completely unexplored sector of the First Universe and he did not want company. Earth and the First Galaxy lay on the edge of the First Quadrant. Llurdiax and its Realm lay in the Second. So did the Empire of the

Chlorans and his own imaginary planet Xylmny. The second galaxy along that false line, which might also attract Seaton, lay in the Third. He didn't want any part of Richard Ballinger Seaton – yet – and this course was mathematically the best one to take to get out of and keep out of Seaton's way. Therefore he would follow it clear out to the Fourth Quadrant rim of the First Universe.

As the *Capital D* bored a hole through the protesting ether DuQuesne took time out from his thinkings to consider women. First, he considered Stephanie de Marigny; with a new and not at all unpleasant thrill as he did so. He considered Sennlloy and Luloy and some unattached women of the Jelmi. They all left him completely cold; and he was intellectually honest enough to know why and to state that 'why' to himself. The Jelmi were so much older than the humanity of Earth that they were out of his class. He could stand equality – definitely; in fact, that was what he wanted – but he could not live with and would not try to live with any woman so demonstrably his superior.

But Hunkie – ah, *there* was a man's woman! His equal; his perfect equal in every respect; with a brain to match one of the finest bodies ever built. She didn't *play* hard to get, she *was* hard to get; but once got she'd stay got. She'd stand at a man's back till his belly caved in.

Slowed to a crawl, as Universal speed goes, the *Capital D* entered the outermost galaxy of the Rim of the Universe and DuQuesne energized his highest-powered projector. He studied the Tellus-type planets of hundreds of solar systems. Many of these planets were inhabited, but he did not reveal himself to the humanity of any of them.

He landed on an uninhabited planet and went methodically to work. He bulldozed out an Area of Work. He set up his batteries of machine tools; coupling an automatic operator of pure force to each tool as it was set up. Then he started to work on the Brain; which took longer than all the rest of the construction put together. It was an exact duplicate of that of the *Skylark of Valeron*; one cubic mile of tightly packed ultra-miniaturized components; the most tremendous and most tremendously capable super-computer known to man.

While the structure of the two brains was identical, their fillings were not. As has been said, there were certain volumes – blocks of cells – in the *Valeron's* brain that DuQuesne had not been able to understand. These blocks he left inoperative – for the time being. Conversely, DuQuesne either had or wanted powers and qualities and abilities that Seaton neither had nor wanted; hence certain blocks that were as yet inoperative in Seaton's vast, fabrication were fully operative in DuQuesne's.

It is a well-known fact that white-collar men, who sit at desks and whose fellowship with machines is limited to weekend drives in automobiles, scoff heartily at the idea that any two machines of the same make and model do or can act differently from each other except by reason of wear. With increasing knowledge of an acquaintance with machines, however – especially with mechanisms of the more complex and sophisticated sorts – this attitude changes markedly. The men and women who operate such machines swear unanimously that those machines do unquestionably have personalities; each its unique and peculiar own.

Thus, while the fact can not be explained in logical or 'common' sense terms, those two giants' brains were as different in personality as were the two men who built them.

Nor was DuQuesne's worldlet, which he named the *DQ*, very much like the *Skylark of Valeron* except in shape. It was bigger. Its skin was much thicker and much denser and much more heavily armed. The individual mechanisms were no larger – the *Valeron*'s were the biggest and most powerful that DuQuesne knew how to build – but there were so many of them that he was pretty sure of being safe from anyone. Even from whoever it was that had mauled the *Valeron* so unmercifully – whom he, DuQuesne, did not intend to approach. Ever.

It was, in fact, his prayerful hope that both mauler and maulee – Seaton himself – would ultimately emerge from the scuffle whittled down to a size where he would not have to consider them again.

He did not, in fact, consider them; nor did he consider the captive Fenach-rone in the pens of Llurdiax; nor the Jelmi; nor – and this, perhaps, was his greatest mistake – did he consider, because he did not know about, a mother and daughter of whose existence neither he nor any other Tellus-type human being had yet heard.

He simply built himself the most powerful space vessel he could imagine, armed it, launched it … and set out to recapture the universe Seaton had once taken away from him.

The revolution on the planet Ray-See-Nee was over and Richard Seaton, disguised under the identity of Ky-El Mokak, was ready to take the one tactical move for which all the effort and struggle on the planet had been only the preliminaries. But first he needed to know what had happened to his shipmates and friends; he had been busy enough fighting his own fights and taking his own prisoners to have temporarily lost sight of them.

Wherefore, in Ray-See-Nee's palatial Capitol Building, in the Room of State – which, except for the absence of an actual throne, was in effect a throne-room – Seaton turned his prisoner over to a guard and rounded up his own crew, so that they could look each other over and compare notes.

Sitar, limping badly but with fur coat still glossily immaculate, proudly displayed a left leg bandaged from the knee all the way up. 'A slash from here, clear down to there.' The Osnomian princess ran a forefinger along a line six or seven inches long. 'And a bullet right through there. That was the *gaudiest* fight I was ever in in my whole life!'

Dunark, whose right arm was in a sling, spoke up. 'She got that slash saving my life. I'd just taken this one through the shoulder' – he pointed – 'and was paralyzed for a second. So she kicked her leg up in the way – while she was flipping a gun around to blow this guy apart, you know – so his knife went into her leg instead of my neck.'

'Yes, but go on and tell them about how many times you—' Sitar began.

'Sh-h-h-h,' Dunark said, and she subsided. 'Maybe some day we'll write a book. How about you, Mart? I notice you've been standing up all the time.'

'I'll be standing up or lying on my face for a while, I guess.'

'But that wouldn't account for the cane,' Seaton objected. 'Come clean, guy.'

'One through the hip – thigh, rather, low down – no bones broken.'

Shiro, who had a broken arm, would not talk at first, but they finally got the story out of him. His last opponent had been just too big and too strong and too well trained to be easy meat, but Shiro had finally got him with a leg-lock around the neck. 'But how about you, Dick?' Shiro asked. 'Whoever wrapped you up must get hospital supplies at wholesale.'

Seaton grinned. 'She had only one patient.' He told his own story, then went on, 'Since we can all walk, let's go over and see what they're finding out.'

Ree-Toe Prenk had said that he wanted all thirty-one of the department heads taken alive if possible; but he had known that it would not be possible. He was surprised and highly pleased, in fact, that only six of the High Exalt-eds had been killed or had taken their own lives.

There is no need to go into the details of that questioning. Seaton took no part in any of it; nor did any of his group. He did not offer to help and Prenk did not ask him.

Nor is it necessary to describe the operation outside the palace. The rebels had learned much from their previous failure, and they now had all the arms, ammunition and supplies they needed. Thus, before sunset that day every known quisling had been shot and every suspect was under surveillance. Premier Ree-Toe Prenk sat firmly in the Capitol City's saddle; and whoever controlled that city always controlled the world.

Hours before control was assured, however, Prenk called Seaton. 'About the daily report to Chloran headquarters that is due in half an hour,' the new Premier said. 'I am wondering if you have any ideas. Our ordinary reports are not dangerous to make, since they are made to underlings whose only interest in the human race it to encode and file our reports properly. But, since their automatic instruments have recorded much of this change of government, it will have to be reported in detail. And a Great One, or even a Greater Great One, may become interested, in which case the reporter's mind may be searched.' Prenk looked thoughtful, then shook his head. 'There's no use trying to gloss it over. In an event like this the Greatest Great One himself will very probably become interested and the reporter will die on the spot. In any case, even with an ordinary Great One, his mind will be shattered for life.'

'I see,' Seaton said. 'I didn't think of it, but I'm not surprised. We've tangled with Chlorans before. But cheer up. I locked eyes with their Supreme Great One ...'

'You didn't!' Prenk broke in, in amazement. 'You actually did?'

'I actually did, and I knocked him – it? – loose from his teeth.' Regretfully Seaton added, 'But we can't make a battle out of this.' He scowled in concentration for a minute, then went on, 'Okay, there's more than one way to stuff a goose. I'll make the report. Let's go.'

Wherefore, twenty-five minutes later, Seaton sat at an ultra-communicator panel in Communications, ready to flip a switch.

The reporter whose shift it was stood off to one side, out of the cone of vision of the screen. Crane sat – gingerly, sidewise, and on a soft pillow – well within the cone of visibility of the screen, at what looked like an ordinary communications panel, but was in fact a battery of all the analytical instruments known to the science of Norlamin.

'But, Your Exalted,' said the highly nervous reporter. 'I'm very glad indeed that you're doing this instead of me, but won't they notice that it isn't me? And probably do something about it?'

'I'm sure they won't.' Seaton had already considered the point. 'I doubt very much, in view of their contempt for other races, if they ever bother to differentiate between any one human being and any other one. Like us and beetles.'

The reporter breathed relief. 'They probably don't, sir, at that. They *don't* seem to pay any attention to us as individuals.'

Seaton braced himself and, exactly on the tick of time, flipped the switch. Knowing that the amoeboids could assume any physical form they pleased and as a matter of course assumed the form most suitable for the job, he was not surprised to see that the filing clerk looked like an overgrown centipede with a hundred or so long, flexible tentacles ending in three-fingered 'hands' – a dozen or so of which were manipulating the gadgetry of a weirdly complex instrument-panel. He was somewhat surprised, however, in spite of what he had been told, that the thing did not develop an eye and look at him; did not even direct a thought at him. Instead:

'I am ready, slave,' a deep bass voice rolled from the speaker, in the language of Prenk's planet Ray-See-Nee. 'Start the tape.'

Seaton pressed a button; the tape began to travel through the sender. For perhaps five minutes nothing happened. Then the sender stopped and a deeper, heavier voice came from the speaker: a voice directed at the filing clerk, but using Rayseenese ...

Why? Seaton wondered to himself. *Oh, I see. Soften 'em up. Scare the pants off 'em, then put on the screws.*

'Yield, clerk,' the new voice said.

'I yield with pleasure, O Great One,' the clerk replied, and went rigidly motionless; not moving a finger or a foot.

'It pleases me to study this matter myself,' the giant voice went on as though the clerk had not spoken. 'While slight, the possibility does exist that some of these verminous creatures have dared to plot against the Race Supreme. If this is merely another squabble among themselves for place it is of no interest; but if there is any trace of non-submission, vermin and city will cease to exist. I shall learn the deepest truth. They can make lying tapes, but no entity of this or of any other galaxy can lie to a Great One mind to mind.'

While the Great One talked, the picture on the screen began to change. The clerk began to fade out and something else began to thicken in. And Seaton, knowing what was coming, set himself in earnest and brought into play that part of his multi-compartmented mind that was the contribution of Drasnik, the First of Psychology of Norlamin.

This coming interview, he knew, must be vastly different from his meeting with the Supreme Great One of Chlora One. That had been a wide-open, hammer-and-tongs battle; a battle of sheer power of mind. Here it would have to be a matter of delicacy of control; of precision and of nicety and of skill as well as of power. He would have to play his mind as exactly and as subtly as Dorothy played her Stradivarius, for if the monster came to suspect any iota of the truth all hell would be out for noon with no pitch hot.

The screen cleared and Seaton saw what he had known he would see; a large, flatly ellipsoidal mass of something that was not quite a jelly not quite a solid; a monstrosity through whose transparent outer membrane there was visible a large, intricately convoluted brain. As Seaton looked at the thing it developed an immense eye, from which there poured directly into Seaton's brain a beam of mental energy so incredibly powerful as to be almost tangible physically.

Braced as he was, every element of the man's mind quivered under the impact of that callously hard-driven probe; but by exerting all his tremendous mental might he took it. More, he was able to hold his Drasnik-taught defenses so tightly as to reveal only and precisely what the Great One expected to find – utter helplessness and abject submission.

That probe was not designed to kill. Or rather, the Great One did not care in the least whether it killed or not. It was intended to elicit the complete truth; and from any ordinary human mind it did.

'Can you lie to me, slave?' That tremendous voice resounded throughout every chamber of Seaton's mind. 'Or withhold from me any iota of the truth?'

'I cannot lie to you, O Great One; nor withhold from you any iota, however small, of the truth.' This took everything of camouflage and of defensive screen Seaton had; but he managed to reveal no sign at all of any of it.

'How much do you personally know, not of the details of the *coup d'état* itself, but of the motivation underlying it?'

'Everything, O Great One, since I was Premier Ree-Toe Prenk's right-hand man,' and Seaton reported the exact truth of Prenk's motivation and planning.

The Great One's probe vanished, the screen went dark, and the sender resumed its sending.

'Huh!' Seaton wiped his sweating face with his handkerchief. ' "This dope isn't of any interest, clerk old boy, so just file it away and forget it," His Nibs says. It's a good thing he was after Prenk's motivation, not mine. If he's really bored in after mine I don't know whether I could have kept things all nice and peaceful or not. I knew I'd been nudged, believe you me.'

'I believed you,' Crane said, looking into his friend's eyes. 'Are you sure you're all right?'

The reporter goggled in awe: 'And you can still talk intelligently, sir?'

'Yeah.' Seaton answered both questions at once, but did not elaborate. 'What did you get, Mart? Anything?'

'I learned where it is,' said Crane. Nothing else.

Small reward for weeks of effort and risk of life … and yet it was for that the entire campaign on the planet Ray-See-Nee had been waged! The whole operation had been designed to get that one fact. A people had been given new hope; some hundreds had lost their lives; many thousands had received scars they would bear a long time; a regime had been deposed and a new one put in power.

But these were only by-products, only the small change of a victory which justified all of Seaton's efforts … and would have its consequences in every part of the universe, for incalculable times to come!

21

Llanzlan Mergon

Ray-See-Nee's new department heads, in their meeting with Premier Ree-Toe Prenk in the Room of State, were in unanimous agreement that everything was under control. Some quislings and recalcitrants had been shot and a few more would probably have to be. That was only to be expected. Yes, since all of the new incumbents had been jumped many grades in status and in authority and in salary, there was and would continue to be a certain amount of jealousy; but that was not of very much importance. The jealous ones would either accept the facts of life or be shot. Period.

After the meeting was over Kay-Lee Barlo came up to Seaton. She now bore herself as though she had been born an Exalted; her ex-boss's pistol swung jauntily at one very female hip as she walked. As she came up to him and took both his hands in hers, standing so close to him that her upstanding, outstanding hair-do almost tickled his nose, it became evident that her weapon had been fired quite recently. She wore no perfume, and the faint but unmistakable acrid odor of burned smokeless powder still clung to her hair.

'O Ky-El!' she exclaimed, equal to equal now. 'I'll simply *never* be able to thank you enough. Nor will all Ray-See-Nee. This world will be an entirely different place to live on hereafter.'

'I sincerely hope so, Kay-Lee.' Seaton smiled into the girl's eager, expressive face. 'Ray-See-Nee is lucky to have had as strong, able and just a man as Ree-Toe Prenk to take over.'

'As you said a while back, "You can say *that* again." He's all of that. What he's done already is marvelous. But everyone knows – he does, too, he's put you up on a pedestal a mile high – that it's you who put him in the saddle. That's what I wanted mostly to tell you. Also, I wanted to ask you' – she paused and flushed slightly – 'you'll forget, won't you please, what I said about that louse's brains? I didn't mean that, really; I'm not the type to cherish a grudge like *that*. I was a little … well, I'd been a little put out with him, just before you came in.' With which masterpiece of understatement she gave his hands another vigorous, friendly squeeze and, swinging around, walked hip-wiggling out of the room.

She thereupon took certain steps and performed certain actions which would have astonished Seaton very much, had he known about them. But he did not – until much later.

Prenk came up to the Skylarkers a few minutes later. He shook hands with each of the off-worlders; thanked them in rounded phrases. 'I would like very much to have you stay here indefinitely, friends,' he concluded, 'but I know of course that is impossible. If all the resources of the world could be devoted to the project and if all our technical men could work on it undetected for a year, we could not build anything able to withstand those Chlorans' beams.'

'We can't either. Not here,' Seaton said. 'That's why we have to go; but we'll be back. I don't know when; but we'll be back some day.'

'I'm sure you will: and may Great My-Ko-Ta ward you and cherish you as you build.'

Back on what was left of their worldlet, now reconditioned to the extent that it was not likely to fall apart on the spot, and out in deep space once more, the Skylarkers began efficiently and expertly to put the pieces of their victory together.

They had located the Enemy. They even had an operating covert base in Chloran territory, to which they could return at any time. They had weapons which, in theory at least, could cope with anything the Chlorans were likely to own.

Yet Seaton fretted. The weapons were there, but his control was not adequate; the weapons had outgrown the control. Dealing with Chlorans was touchy business. You wanted all the space you could get between you and them. Yet, at any operating range which even Seaton, to say nothing of Crane and the others, considered safe, their striking power was simply too erratic to depend on.

'It's a bust,' Seaton said gloomily. 'Course, if worst came to worst I could go back to undercover methods. Smuggle in a bomb, maybe – just to throw their main centers off balance while the rest of you hit them with all we've got. I could stow away aboard one of those ore-scows taking the booty off Ray-See-Nee easily enough –'

'You talk like a man with a paper nose,' Dorothy scoffed. 'I have a picture of *that* expedition – of you in armor, with air-tanks strapped on your back and lugging an underwater camera or projector around. Un-noticed ... I don't think.'

And Dunark added, 'And since you haven't got any idea of what to look for, you'd have to lug around a full analsynth set-up. A couple of tons of stuff. Uh-uh.'

Seaton grinned, unperturbed. 'That's what I was coming to. Getting in would be easy, but doing anything wouldn't. And neither would getting out. But Mart, we've chopped one horn off of the dilemma, but we haven't even touched the other. We've got to master that fourth-dimension rig; and we're not even close. It's a matter of *kind,* not merely of degree.'

'I can't see that. If so, we could not have warded off their attack at all.'

'Oh, I didn't mean the energies themselves; it's the control of that much stuff. Synchronization, phasing in, combination, and so forth. Getting such stuff as that closely enough together. Look, Mart. This bit that we've got left of the *Valeron* is stuffed with machinery practically to the skin. She's so small, relatively, that you wouldn't think there'd be any trouble meshing in machines from various parts of her. But there is. Plenty. It never showed up before because we never had to use a fraction of our total power before, but it showed up plenty back there. My beam was loose as ashes, and I've figured out why.

'Sixth-order stuff moves as many times faster than light as light does faster than a snail – maybe more. But it still takes a little time to get from one machine to another, inside even as small a globe as this is. See?'

Crane frowned in thought. 'I see. I also see what the difficulties would be in anything large enough and strong enough to attack the Chlorans. It would mean timing each generator and each element of each projector; and each with a permissible variation of an infinitesimal fraction of a microsecond. That, of course, means Rovol and Caslor.'

'I suppose it does ... unless we can figure out an easier, faster way ... I don't know whether the Chlorans have got anything like that or not, but they've got *something*. There ought to be some way of snitching it off of them.'

'Why must they have?' Dunark demanded. 'It's probably just a matter of size. They have a whole planet to fortify. Dozens of 'em if they want to. So it doesn't have to be a matter of refinement at all. Just brutal, piled up, over-whelming power.'

'Could be,' Seaton agreed. 'If so, we can't match it, since the *Valeron* was as big as she could be and still have a factor of safety of two point two.' He paused in thought, then went on, 'But with such refinement, we could take a planet, no matter how loaded it was ... I think. So maybe we'd better take off for Norlamin, at that.'

'One thing we should do first, perhaps,' Dorothy suggested. 'Find out what that DuQuesne really did. He has me worried.'

'Maybe we should, at that,' Seaton agreed. 'I'd forgotten all about the big black ape.'

It was easy enough to find the line along which DuQuesne had traveled; the plug-chart was proof that he had not lied about that. They reached without incident the neighborhood of the point DuQuesne had marked on the chart. Seaton sent out a working projection of the device that, by intercepting and amplifying light-waves traversing open space, enabled him actually to see events that had happened in the not-too-distant past.

He found the scene he wanted. He studied it, analyzed and recorded it. Then:

'He lied to me almost a hundred and eighty degrees,' Sexton said. 'That beam came from that galaxy over there.' He jerked a thumb. 'The alien who bothered him was in that galaxy. That much I'll buy. But it doesn't make sense that he'd go there. That alien was nobody he wanted to monkey with, that's for dead sure. So where did he meet the Jelmi, if not in that galaxy?'

'On the moon, perhaps,' Margaret said.

'Possibly. I'll compute it ... no, the timing isn't right' – Seaton thought for a moment – 'but there's no use guessing. That galaxy may be the first place to look for signs; but I'll bet my case buck it'll be a long, cold hunt. I'd like awfully well to have that gizmo – flip bombs past the Chlorans' screens and walls with it ...'

'From a distance greater than *their* working range?' Crane asked.

'That's so, too ... or maybe so, at that, chum. Who knows *what* you can do through the fourth? But it looks as though our best bet is to beat it to

Norlamin, rebuild this wreck, and tear into that business of refinement of synchronization. So say you all?'

So said they all and Seaton, flipping on full-power sixth-order drive, set course for Norlamin.

As the student will be aware, the events of this climatic struggle between the arch-enemies, Seaton and DuQuesne, were at this point reaching an area of maximum tension. It is curious to reflect that the outer symptom of this internal disruptive stress was, in the case of nearly every major component of the events to come, a psychological state of either satisfied achievement, or contented decision, or calm resignation. It is as though each of the major operatives were suffering from a universe-wide sense of false tranquility. On Ray-See-Nee, the new government felt its problems were behind it and only a period of solid, rewarding rebuilding lay ahead. (Although Kay-Lee Barlo had taken certain prudent precautions against this hope being illusory – as we shall see.) The Chlorans, proud and scornful in their absolute supremacy, had no hint that Seaton or anyone else was making or even proposed to make any effective moves against them. The Fenachrone, such few weary survivors as remained of them, had given themselves over to – not despair, no; but a proud acceptance of the fact that they were doomed.

There was in fact no tranquility in store for any of them! But they had not yet found that out.

Meanwhile the Jelmi, for example, were just beginning to feel the first itch of new challenges. In their big new space-rover, the *Mallidaxian*, Savant Tammon was as nearly perfectly happy as it is possible for a human or humanoid to be. He had made the greatest breakthrough of his career; perhaps the greatest breakthrough of all history. Exploring its many ramifications and determining its many as yet unsuspected possibilities would keep him busy for the rest of his life. Wherefore he was working fourteen or fifteen hours every day and reveling in every minute of it. He hummed happily to himself; occasionally he burst into song – in a voice that was decidedly not of grand-operatic quality.

He had enlarged his private laboratory by tearing out four storerooms adjoining it; and the whole immense room was stacked to the ceiling with new apparatus and equipment. He was standing on a narrow catwalk, rubbing his bristly chin with the back of his hand as he wondered where he could put another two-ton tool, when Mergon and Luloy came swinging in; hand in hand as usual. Vastly different from Tammon, Mergon was not at all happy about the *status quo*.

'Listen, Tamm!' he burst out. 'I've been yapping at you for a week and a half for a decision and your time is up as of right now. If you don't pull your head out of the fourth dimension and make it right now I'll do it myself and to hell with you and your authority as Captain-Commander.'

'Huh? What? Time? Decision? What decision?' It was plain that the old savant had no idea at all of what his first assistant was so wrought up about.

'You set course for Mallidax and said we were going back to Mallidax. That's sheer idiocy and you know it. Of all places in the charted universe we should *not* go to, Mallidax is top and prime. We're too close for comfort already. Even though Klazmon must have lost us back there in Sol's system, he certainly picked us up again long ago and he'd give both wings and all his teeth for half the stuff you have here,' and Mergon waved both arms indicatively around the jam-packed room.

'Oh?' Tammon gazed owlishly at the pair. 'There was some talk … but why should I care where we go? This is the merest trifle, Mergon. Do not bother me with trivia any more,' and Tammon cut communications with them as definitely as though he had thrown a switch.

Mergon shrugged his shoulders and Luloy giggled. 'You're it, boy. That's what you get for sticking your neck out. All hail our new Captain-Commander!'

'Well, *somebody* had to. All our necks would have been in slings in another week. So pass the word, will you, and I'll skip up to the control room and change course.'

Luloy spread the word; which was received with acclaim. Practically everybody aboard who was anybody agreed with Sennlloy when she said, 'It's high time *somebody* took over and Merg's undoubtedly the best man for the job. Tammy's a nice old dear, but ever since he got bitten by that fourth-dimension germ he hasn't known what month it is or which way is up or within forty million parsecs of where he is in space.'

'You see, Merg?' Luloy crowed, when it became evident that the shift in command was heartily approved. 'I wouldn't even dream of ever saying "I told you so", but I said at the first meeting that you should be Captain-Commander, and now everybody thinks so, almost.'

'Yeah, almost,' he agreed; not at all enthusiastically. 'Everybody except the half-wits. Pass the buck. Let George do it. Nobody with a brain firing on three barrels wants the job.'

'Why, that isn't so, Merg. You *know* it isn't!' she protested, indignantly.

'Well, J don't want it,' he broke in, 'but since Tamm wished it onto me I'll take a crack at it.'

The *Mallidaxian*, swinging wide and braking down, hard, skirted the outermost edge of the Realm; the edge farthest away from Llurdiax. Mergon did not approach or signal to any planet of the Jelmi. Instead, he picked out an uninhabited Tellus-type planet four solar systems away from the border and landed on it. And there, under cover of the superdreadnought's mighty defensive screens and with Captain-Commander Mergon tensely on watch, the engineers and scientists disembarked, set up their high-order projectors, and went furiously to work building an enormous and enormously powerful dome.

The work went on uninterrupted, day after day; for so many days that both Mergon and Luloy became concerned – the girl very highly so. 'Do you suppose we've figured wrong?' she asked.

Mergon frowned. 'I can't be sure, of course, but I don't think so. Pure logic, remember. Everything we've done has been designed to keep Klazmon guessing. Off balance. He's fortified Llurdiax, that's sure, but we don't know how heavily and we can't find out.' He paused.

'Without using the gizmo, which of course is out,' said Luloy.

'Check. We haven't sent any spy-rays or anything else. They wouldn't have got us anything. But he certainly expected us to try. He'll think we don't care … which as a matter of fact, we don't … too much. It's almost a mathematical certainty that we can handle anything he can throw at us of now. But if we give him time enough to build more really big stuff it'll be just too bad.'

'And the horrible old monster is probably doing just exactly that,' Luloy said.

'I wouldn't wonder. But we can finish the dome before he can build enough stuff, and he can't let that happen. Especially since we're not interfering with his prying and spying, but are treating him with the same contempt he used to treat us. That'll bother him no end. Burn him up! Also … remember that stuff in the dome that no Llurd can possibly understand.'

Luloy laughed. 'Because it isn't anything whatever, really, except Llurd-bait? I'm scared that maybe they will understand it yet – even though I'm sure they won't.'

'They can't. Their minds won't stretch that far in that direction,' Mergon said positively. 'They knew we made a breakthrough, so they'll know that what they see is only a fraction of what the thing really is; and that'll scare 'em. As much as Llurdi can be scared, that is. Which isn't very much. So Klazmon will do something before our dome is finished. As I read the tea-leaves, he'll have to.'

'But just suppose he doesn't take the bait?'

'Then we'll have to take the initiative. I don't want to – it'd weaken our bargaining position tremendously – but I will if I have to.'

He did not have to. His analysis of the Llurdan mentality and temperament had been accurate.

Four full days before the scheduled date of completion of the dome, Klazmon's full working projection appeared in the *Mallidaxian*'s control room. Mergon had detected its coming, but had done nothing to interfere with it. The Llurd quite obviously intended parley, not violence.

'Hail, brother Llanzlan, Klazmon of the Llurdi,' Mergon greeted his visitor quietly, but in the phraseology of one ruler greeting another on the basis of unquestionable equality. 'Is there perhaps some service that I, Llanzlan Mergon of the Realm of the Jelmi, may perform for you and thus place you in my debt?'

This, to a human dictator, would have been effrontery intolerable; but Mergon had been pretty sure that it would have little or no effect, emotionally, upon Klazmon. Nor did it; to all seeming it had no effect at all. The Llurd merely said, 'You wish me to believe that you Jelmi have made a breakthrough sufficiently important to justify the establishment of an independent but coexistent Realm of the Jelmi.'

This was in no sense a question; it was a flat statement. Mergon had been eminently correct in his assumption that he would not have to draw the Llurd a blueprint. Mergon quirked an eyebrow at Luloy, who pressed the button that signaled all the savants in the dome to drop their tools and dash back into the ship.

'That is correct,' Mergon said.

Klazmon's projection remained motionless and silent; both Jelmi could almost perceive the Llurd's thoughts. And Mergon, who had tracked the Llurd's thoughts so unerringly so far, was practically certain that he was still on track.

Klazmon did not actually know whether the Jelmi had made a breakthrough or not. The Jelmi intended to make him believe that they had, and that breakthrough was something that made them either invulnerable or invincible, or both. Any of those matters or assumptions could be either true or false. One of them, the question of invulnerability, could be and should be tested without delay. If they were in fact invulnerable, no possible attack could harm them. If they were not invulnerable they were bluffing and lying and should therefore be eliminated.

Wherefore Mergon was not surprised when Klazmon's projection vanished without having said another word – nor when, an instant after that vanishment, the *Mallidaxian*'s mighty defensive screens flared white.

They did not even pause at the yellow or the yellow-white, but went directly to the blinding white; to the degree of radiance at which the vessel's spare began automatically to cut in – spare after spare after spare.

After staring in silence for two long minutes, Mergon said, 'We figured their most probable maximum offense and applied a factor of safety of three – and look at 'em!'

White-faced, Luloy licked her lips. 'Mighty Llenderllon!' she cried. 'How can they *possibly* deliver such an attack way out here?'

Then Mergon picked up his microphone and said, 'Our screens are still holding and they're protecting the dome; but we're going to need a lot more defense. So go back out there, please, and give me everything you can.'

He then sat back and stared tight-jawed at the ever-climbing needles of his meters and at the unchanging blinding-white brilliance of his vessel's screens.

22

The Geas

As the Llurd's attack mounted to higher and ever higher plateaus of fury, Mergon slid along his bench to his fourth-dimensional controls and there appeared on the floor beside him a lithium-hydride fusion bomb, armed and ready.

He stared at it, his jaw-muscles tightening into lumps. Luloy stared at the thing, too, and her face became even paler than it had been.

'But could you, Merg?' she asked, through stiff lips. 'I ... I mean, you couldn't possibly ... could you?'

'I don't know,' he said harshly, scarcely separating locked teeth. 'I may have to whether I can or not. We had a factor of safety of three. Two point nine of them are in now and the last tenth is starting up. The dome can't put out more than that.'

'I know! But if we blow the llanzlanate up, won't they kill all the Jelmi of all our worlds and start breeding a more tractable race of slaves?'

'That's the way I read it. In that case we eight hundred could get away and start a better civilization somewhere out of range.'

She shuddered. 'In that case would life be worth living?'

'It's a tough decision to make ... since the alternative could be for us to kill all the Llurdi.'

'Oh, no!' she cried. 'But don't you think, Merg, that he'll cooperate? They're absolutely logical, you know.'

'Maybe. In one way I think so, but I simply can't see any absolute ruler making such an abject surrender. However, we've got to decide right now and we'll have to stick to our decision – we both know that he can't be bluffed. If it comes right down to it we can do one of three things, First, commit suicide for one whole eight hundred by not touching the bomb off. Second, wipe them out. Third, let them wipe out all Jelmi except us. What's your vote?'

'Llenderllon help me! Put that way, there's – *oh, look*!' she screamed, in a miraculously changed tone of voice. 'The mastermeter! It's slowing down! *It's going to stop!*' She uttered an ear-splitting shriek of pure joy and hurled herself into her husband's arms.

'It's stabilized, for a fact,' Mergon said, after their emotions had subsided to something approaching normal. 'He's throwing everything he's got at us. We're holding him, but just barely, so the question is—'

'One thing first,' she broke in. 'My vote. I hate to say it, but we *can't* let them kill our race.'

He put his arm around her and squeezed. 'That's what I was sure you'd say. The question now is, how long do we let him stew in his own juice before we skip over there and talk peace terms?'

'*Not* long enough to let him build more generators than we can to fry us with,' she replied, promptly if a bit unclearly. 'One day? Half a day? A quarter?'

'But long enough to let him know he's licked,' Mergon said. 'I'd say one full day would be just about right. So let's go get us some sleep.'

'*Sleep!* Llenderllon's eyeballs! Can you even *think* of such a thing as *sleep* after all *this*?'

'Certainly I can. So can you – you're all frazzled out. Come on, girl, we're hitting the sheets.'

'Why, I won't be able to sleep a *wink* until this is all over!'

But she was wrong; in ten minutes, they were both sleeping the sleep of exhaustion.

Twelve hours later she came suddenly awake, rolled over toward him, and shook him vigorously by the shoulder. 'Wake up, you!'

He grumbled something and tried to pull away from her grip.

She shook him again. 'Wake up, you great big oaf! Suppose that beast Klazmon has got more generators built and our screens are all failing?'

He opened one eye. 'If they fail, sweet, we won't know a thing about it.' He opened the other eye and, three-quarters awake now, went on, 'Do you think I'm running this ship single-handed? What do you think the other officers are for?'

'But they aren't you,' she declared, with completely feminine illogic where her husband was concerned. 'So hurry up and get up and we'll see for ourselves.'

'Okay, but not 'til after breakfast, if I have to smack you down. So punch us up a gallon of coffee, huh? And a couple slabs of ham and six or eight eggs? Then we'll go see.'

They ate and went and saw. The screens still flared at the same blinding white, but there were no signs of overloading or of failure. They could, the Third Officer bragged, keep it up for years. Everything was under control.

'You hope,' Mergon said – but not to the officer. He said that under his breath and he and Luloy turned away toward their own station.

Much to Mergon's relief, nothing happened during the rest of the day, and at the end of the twenty-fourth hour he sent the actual bomb and working projections of himself and Luloy into the llanzlanate. Into the Llanzlan's private study, where Klazmon was hard at work.

It was an immense room, and one in which a good anthropologist could have worked delightedly for weeks. The floor was bare, hard, smooth-polished; fantastically inlaid in metal and colored quartz and turquoise and jade. The pictures – framed mostly in extruded stainless steel – portrayed scenes (?) and things (?) and events (?) never perceived by any Earthly sense and starkly incomprehensible to any Earthly mind. The furniture was … 'weird' is the only possible one-word description. Every detail of the room proclaimed that here was the private retreat of a highly talented and very eminent member of a culture that was old, wide and high.

'Hail, Llanzlan Klazmon,' Mergon said quietly, conversationally. 'You will examine this bomb, please, to make sure that, unlike us two, it is actual and practical.'

The Llurd's eyes had bulged a little and the tip of his tail had twitched slightly at the apparition. That was all. He picked up an instrument with a binocular eyepiece, peered through it for a couple of seconds, and put it down. 'It is actual and practical,' he agreed.

Whatever emotions may have been surging through the Llanzlan's mind, his control was superb. He did not ask them how they had done it, or why, or any other question. After the event he knew much and could guess more – and he was perhaps the starkest realist of the most starkly realistic race of intelligent beings yet known to live.

'You realize, of course, that we do not intend to fire it except as the ultimately last resort.'

'I do now.'

'Ah, yes. Our conduct throughout has surprised you; especially that we did not counterattack.'

'If not exactly surprised, at least did not anticipate that Jelmi would or could act with practically Llurdan logic,' the Llurd conceded.

'We can. And when we think it best, we do. We suggest that you cut off your attack. We will then put on air-suits and return here in person, to discuss recent developments as reasoning and logical entities should.'

The Llurd was fast on the uptake. He knew that, given time, he could crush this threat; but he knew that he would not have the time. He could see ahead as well as Mergon could to the total destruction of two hundred forty more planets. Wherefore he barked a couple of syllables at a com and the furiously incandescent screens of the *Mallidaxian* went cold and dark.

Jelmi and bomb disappeared. Mergon and Luloy donned gas-tight, self-contained, plastic-helmeted coveralls and reappeared in the Llanzlan's study. Klazmon seated them courteously in two Jelman easy-chairs – which looked atrociously out of place in that room – and the peace conference, which was to last for days, began.

'First,' the Llanzlan said, 'this breakthrough that you have accomplished. At what stage in the negotiations do you propose to give me the complete technical specifications of it?'

'Now,' Mergon said, and a yard-high stack of tapes appeared on the floor beside the Llurd's desk. It was the entire specs and description of the fourth-dimensional translator. Nothing was omitted or obscured.

'Oh? I see. There is, then, much work yet to be done on it. Work that only you Jelmi can do.'

'That is true, as you will learn from those tapes. Now,' said Mergon, settling down to the bargaining session, 'first, we have shown you that Jelmi capable of doing genius-type work cannot be coerced into doing it. Second, the fact is that it is psychologically impossible for us to do such work under coercion. Third, we believe firmly that free and independent Jelmi can coexist with the Llurdi. Fourth, we believe equally firmly that for the best good of both races they should so coexist ...'

And at that first day's end, after supper, Luloy said, 'Merg, I simply would not have believed it. Ever. I'm not sure I really believe it now. But you know I almost like – I actually *admire* that horrible monster in some ways!'

Seaton called Rovol of Rays, on Norlamin, as soon as he could reach him. He told him the story of what he had done on Ray-See-Nee, and what he hoped to gain by it, in detail, then went on to ask his help on the control of the fourth-dimensional translator. 'You see, Rovol, at perfect sync it would – theoretically – take zero power. I don't expect the unattainable ideal, of course' – he winked at Dorothy – 'just close enough so we can pack enough stuff into the *Valeron* to handle everything they can throw at us and still have enough left over to fight back with.'

'Ah, youth, a fascinating problem indeed. I will begin work on it at once, and will call in certain others in whose provinces some aspects of it lie. By the time you arrive here we will perhaps have determined whether or not any solution is at present possible.'

'What?' Seaton yelped. 'Why – I thought – surely' – he almost stuttered. 'I thought you'd have it done by then – maybe be sending it out to meet us, even.'

The old Norlaminian's paternally forbearing sigh was highly expressive. 'Still the heedless, thoughtless youth, in spite of all our teachings. You have not studied the problem yourself at all.'

'Well, not very much, I admit.'

'I advise you to do so. If you devote to it every period of labor between now and your arrival here you may perhaps be able to talk about it intelligently,' and Rovol cut com.

Dorothy whistled. She didn't whistle very often, but she could do it very expressively.

'Yeah,' Seaton said, ruefully. 'And the old boy wasn't kidding, either.'

'Not having a sense of humor, he can't kid. He really slapped you on the wrist, friend. But why would it be such a horrible job to sync a few generators in?'

'I don't know, but I'll find out.' He went, worked for four solid hours with the Brain, and came back wearing a sheepish grin. 'It's true,' he reported. 'I knew it'd be tricky, but I had no idea. You have to work intelligently, manipulably and re-producibly in time units of three times ten to the minus twenty-eighth of a second – the time it takes light to travel a billionth of a billionth of a centimeter.'

'Hush. You don't expect me to understand that, do you?'

'I'll say I don't. I don't expect to even really understand it myself.'

Seaton did not work on the problem every day until arrival, but he worked on it for over a hundred hours – enough so that he began to realize how difficult it was.

The *Skylark of Valeron* entered the Green System, approached Norlamin, and went into orbit around it. The travelers boarded a shuttle, which thereupon began to slide down a landing-beam toward Rovol's private dock.

The little craft settled gently into a neoprene-lined cup. The visitors disembarked and walked down a short flight of metallic steps, at the foot of which the ancient, white-bearded sage was waiting for them. He greeted them warmly – for a Norlaminian – and led them through the 'garden' toward the metal-and-quartz palace that was his home.

'Oh, Dick, isn't it *wonderful*!' Dorothy pressed his arm against her side. 'It's so much like Orion's and yet so different …'

And it was both. The acreage of velvet-short, springy grass was about the same as that upon which they had landed so long before. The imperishable-metal statuary was similar. Here also were the beds of spectacular flowers and the hedges and sculptured masses of gorgeously vari-colored plant life. The tapestry wall, however – composed of millions upon millions of independently moving, flashing, self-luminous jewels of all the colors of the rainbow – ran for a good three hundred yards beside the walk. It was evident that the women of the Rovol had been working on it for hundreds of centuries instead of for mere hundreds of years. Instead of being only form and color, as was the wall of the Orion, it was well along toward portraying the entire history of the Family Rovol.

Rovol wanted to entertain his guests instead of work, but Seaton objected. 'Shame on you, Rovol. The Period of Labor is just starting, and remember how you fellows used to bat my ears down about there being definite and non-interchangeable times for work and for play and so forth?'

'That is of course true, youth,' Rovol agreed, equably enough. 'I should not have entertained the idea for a moment. My companion will welcome the ladies and show them to your apartments. We will proceed at once to the Area of Experiment,' and he called an aircar by fingering a stud at his belt.

'I've been studying, as you suggested,' Seaton said then. 'Can the thing be solved? The more I worked on it the more dubious I got.'

'Yes, but the application of its solution will be neither easy nor simple.' The aircar settled gently to the walk a few yards ahead of the party and Rovol and Seaton boarded it; Rovol still talking. 'But you will be delighted to know that, thanks to your gift of the metal of power, what would have been a work of lifetimes can very probably be accomplished in a few mere years.'

Seaton was not delighted. Knowing what Rovol could mean by the word 'few,' he was appalled; but there was nothing whatever he could do to speed things up.

He spent a couple of weeks rebuilding the *Skylark of Valeron* – with batteries of offensive and defensive weaponry where single machines had been – then stood around and watched the Norlaminians work. And as day followed day without anything being accomplished he became more and more tense and impatient. He concealed his feelings perfectly, he thought; but he should have known that he could hide nothing from the extremely percipient mind of the girl who was in every respect his other half.

'Dick, you've been jittering like a witch,' she said one evening, 'about something I can't see any reason for. But you have a reason, or you wouldn't be doing it. So break down and tell me.'

'I can't, confound it. I know I'm always in a rush to get a thing done, but not like this. I'm all of a twitter inside. I can't sleep ...'

Dorothy snickered. 'You can't? If what you were doing last night wasn't sleeping it was the most reasonable facsimile thereof I've ever seen. Or heard.'

'Not like I ought to, I mean. Nightmares. Devils all the time sticking me with pitchforks. Do you believe in hunches?'

'No,' she said, promptly. 'I never had any. Not a one.'

'I never did, either, and if this is one I never want to have another. But it could be a hunch that we ought to be investigating that alien galaxy of DuQuesne's. Whatever it is, I want to go somewhere and I haven't the faintest idea where.'

'Oh? Listen!' Dorothy's eyes widened. 'I'll bet you're getting an answer to that message we sent out!'

He shook his head. 'Uh-uh. Can't be. Telepathy has got to be something you can understand.'

'Who besides you ever said it would have to be telepathy? And who knows what telepathy would have to be like? Come on, let's go tell Martin and Peggy!'

'Huh?' he yelped. 'Tell M. Reynolds Crane, the hardest-boiled skeptic that ever went unhung, that I want to go sky-shooting to hellangone off into the wild blue yonder just because I've got an itch that I can't scratch?'

'Why not?' She looked him steadily in the eye. 'We're exploring *terra incognita*, Dick. How much do you really know about that mind of yours, the way it is now?'

'Okay. Maybe they'll buy it; you did. Let's go.'

They went; and, a little to Seaton's surprise, Crane agreed with Dorothy. So did Margaret. Hence three hours later, the big sky-rover was on her way.

Four days out, however, Seaton said, 'This isn't the answer, I don't think. The itch is still there. So what?'

There was silence for a couple of minutes, then Dorothy chuckled suddenly. Sobering quickly, she said, with a perfectly straight face. 'I'll bet it's that new department head girl-friend of yours, Dick; the pistol-packing mama with the wiggle. She wants to see the big, hold, handsome Earthman again. And if it is, I'll scratch …'

Seaton jumped almost out of his chair. 'You're not kidding half as much as you think you are, pet. That crack took a good scratch at exactly where it itches.' He put on his remote-control helmet and changed course. 'And that helps still more.' He thought for minutes, then shrugged his shoulders and said, 'I'm not getting a thing … not anything more at all. How many of you remember either Ree-Toe Prenk or the girl well enough to picture either of them accurately in your minds?'

They all remembered one or both of the Rayseenians.

'Okay. This'll sound silly. It *is* silly, for all the tea in China, but let's try something. All join hands, picture either or both of them, and think at them as hard as we can. The thought is simply "we're coming". Okay?'

More than half sheepishly, they tried it – and it worked. At least Seaton said, 'Well, it worked, I guess. Anyway, for the first time in weeks, it's gone. But I didn't get a thing. Nothing whatever. Not even a hint either that we were being paged or that our reply was being received. Did any of you?'

None of them had.

'Huh!' Seaton snorted. 'If this is telepathy they can keep it – I'll take Morse's original telegraph!'

A week or so after the *Skylark of Valeron* left the neighborhood of Ray-See-Nee, that planet's new government began to have trouble. Ree-Toe Prenk had said and had believed that whoever controlled the capital controlled the world, but that was not true in his case. It had always been true previously because the incoming powers had always been of the same corrupt-to-the-core stripe as those who were ousted – and when corruption has been the way of life for generations it is deep-rooted indeed.

There were, of course, other factors behind the unrest. But neither Prenk nor any other human knew about them – then.

All the district bosses had always gone along with the Big Boss as a matter of course. Not one of them cared a whit who ran the world, as long as his own privileges and perquisites and powers and takes were not affected. Prenk, however, was strictly honest and strictly just. If he should succeed in taking over Ray-See-Nee's government in full, every crook and boodler on the planet would lose everything he had; possibly even his life. Thus, while the new Premier held the capital – in a rapidly deteriorating grip – his influence outside that city's limits varied inversely as about the fourth power of the distance.

This resistance, while actual enough, was in no sense overt. Every order was ostensibly obeyed to the letter; but everything deteriorated at an accelerating rate and Prenk could do nothing whatever about it. Whenever and wherever Prenk was not looking, business went on as usual – gambling, drugs, prostitution, crime and protection – but he could not prove any of it. Neither uniformed police nor detectives could find anything much amiss. They made arrests, but no suspect was ever convicted. The prosecution's cases were weak. The juries brought in verdicts of 'innocent', usually without leaving the box.

Even when, in desperation, Prenk went – supposedly top-secretly – to an outlying city, fully prepared to stage a questioning that would have made Torquemada blush, he did nothing and he learned nothing. Every person on his list had vanished tracelessly and every present incumbent had abundant proof of innocence. Nor did any of them know why they had been promoted so suddenly. They were just lucky, they guessed.

It was indeed baffling. It would have been less so if Prenk had had any notion of the universe-wide stir of mighty events just beginning to bubble – if he had been able, as we are now able, to fit together all these patchwork stories into one nearly Norlaminian fabric of universal history.

But he wasn't – and, for his peace of mind, perhaps that was just as well!

Premier Ree-Toe Prenk sat at his desk in the Room of State. Kay-Lee Barlo, shapely legs crossed and pistol at hip, sat at his left. Sy-By Takeel, the new Captain-General of the Guard, stood at ease at his right.

'Whoever is doing this is a smooth, shrewd operator,' Prenk said. 'So much so that you two are the only people I can trust. And I don't suppose either of you will ever be approached. Probably neither of you would be bought even if you offered yourselves ever so deftly for sale.'

'I wouldn't be, certainly,' Takeel said. 'Captains-General of mercenaries don't sell out. I wouldn't answer for any of my lieutenants, though, if there's loot to be had. There is here, I take it?'

'Unlimited quantities, apparently. So you, too, are subject to assassination?'

The soldier shrugged. 'Oh, yes, it's an occupational hazard How about you, Exalted Barlo? No chance either, I'd say?'

'None at all. My stand is too well known. Half my people would stab me in the back if they dared to and they all look me in the eye and lie in their Mi-Ko-Ta-cursed teeth. I wish Ky-El Mokak and his people would get back here quick,' Kay-Lee said wistfully.

'So do I,' Prenk said, glumly. 'But even if we had a sixth-order tightbeamer and could use it, we haven't the slightest idea of where he came from or where he went to.'

'That's true.' She nibbled at her lip. 'But listen. I'm a psychic. It runs in the women of some families, you know, being … well, what most people call witches, kind of. My talent isn't developed yet, but mother and I together could witch-wish at him to come back here as fast as he can and I'm sure he would.'

The soldier's face showed quite plainly what he thought of the idea, but Prenk nodded – if more than somewhat dubiously. 'I've heard of that "witch-wishing" business, and that it sometimes works. So go home right now and get at it, Kay-Lee, and give it everything you and your mother both can put out.'

Kay-Lee went home forthwith and went into executive session with her mother; a handsome, black-haired woman of forty-odd. 'And I have positive identification,' the girl concluded. 'His blood was all over the place – positively *quarts* of it – and I saved some just in case.' And, of course, she had – prudently, wisely and, as it turned out, luckily for all concerned!

The older woman's face cleared. 'That's good. Without a positive, I'm afraid it would be hopeless at what the distance probably is by this time. Run and get the witch-holly, dear, while I fix the incense.'

They each ate seven ritually preserved witch-holly berries and inhaled seven deep drafts of aromatic smoke. While they were waiting for the powerful drugs to take effect, Kay-Lee asked, 'How much of this rigamarole is chemistry, do you suppose, mother, and how much is just hocus-pocus?'

'No one knows. Some day, whatever it is that we have will be recognized as having existence and will be really studied. Until then, all we can do is follow the ancient ritual.'

'I think I'll talk to Ky-El about it. But listen. Witches with any claim at all to decency simply don't put geases on people. But what if he's so far away that we can't reach him any other way?'

The older woman frowned, then said, 'In that case, my dear, we'll never, *never* tell anyone a thing about it.'

23

Re-Seating of the Premier

As the *Skylark of Valeron* approached Galaxy DW-427-LU, Dorothy said, 'Dick, I suppose it's occurred to you more than once that I'm not much of a woman.'

'You aren't? I'd say you'd do until the real thing showed up.' Seaton, who had been thinking of the problem of synchronization instead of his wife, changed voice instantly when he really looked at her and saw what a black mood she was in. 'You're the universe's best, is all, ace. I knew you were feeling a little low in your mind, but not ... listen, sweetheart. What could possibly make you think you aren't the absolute top?'

She did not answer the question. Instead, 'What do you think you're going to get into this time?'

'Nothing much, I'm sure. Prenk's probably running out of ammunition. We can make more in five minutes than he can in five years.'

'I'm sure that isn't it. You're going into personal danger again and I'll be expected to sit up here in the *Skylark* eating my heart out wondering if you're alive or dead. You don't see Sitar going through that with Dunark.'

'Wait up, sweetheart. Mores and customs, remember?'

'Mores and customs be damned! Do you remember exactly what Sitar said and exactly how she said it? Did it sound like mores and customs to you? Was there any element whatever of suttee in it?'

'But listen, Dottie –' He took her gently in his arms.

'You listen!' she rushed on. 'If he dies she doesn't want to keep on living and she won't. And she doesn't care who knows it. Maybe it started that way – society's sanction – but that was her personal profession of faith. And I feel the same way. If you die I don't want to keep on living and won't. So next time I'm going with you.'

Being an American male, he could not accept that without an argument. 'But there's Dickie,' he said.

'There are also her three children on Osnome. I learned something from her about what the basic, rock-bottom attitude of a woman toward her man ought to be. Even from little Lotus. She's no bigger than a minute and a half, but what did *she* do? So while we're having this moment of truth let's be rock-bottom honest with each other for the first time in our lives instead of mouthing the platitudes of our society. I'm not a story-book mother, Dick. If it ever comes right down to a choice, you know how I'll decide – and how long it will take!'

Seaton could not get in touch with Ree-Toe Prenk, of course, until the *Valeron* was actually inside Galaxy DW-427-LU; but as soon as communication could be established Kay-Lee Barlo asked eagerly, 'You *did* get our thought, then, Ky-El? Mother's and mine? We didn't feel that we were quite reaching you.'

'Not exactly,' Seaton replied. 'I didn't get any real thought at all; just a feeling that I ought to be going *somewhere* that bothered me no end until I headed this way. But since it was you people calling, I'm mighty glad I got what little I did.'

The *Skylark* went into orbit around Ray-See-Nee and the Skylarkers climbed into a landing-craft that Seaton had designed and built specifically for the occasion. It was a miniature battleship – one of the deadliest fighting ships of its size and heft ever built. And this time the whole party was heavily armed. Dunark and Sitar were in full Osnomian panoply of war. Dorothy wore a pair of her long-barrelled .38 target pistols in leg-holsters under her bouffant skirt. Even little Lotus wore two .25 automatics. 'I don't know whether I can hit anybody with one of these or not,' she had said while Dorothy was rigging her. 'I'd much rather work hand to hand. But if they're too far away to get at I can at least make a lot of noise and *look* like I'm doing something.'

They were met at the spaceport by two platoons of the Premier's Guard, led by Captain-General Sy-By Takeel himself. They were guarded like visiting royalty from the spaceport to the Capitol Building and up into the Room of State, where they were greeted with informal cordiality by Prenk and by Kay-Lee, who was now an Exalted of the Thirty-Fifth, besides being First Deputy Premier.

Prenk seated his guests, not on stools in front of and below his throne-like desk, but at a long conference table with Seaton at its head. The two lieutenants posted guards outside the two immense doors at the far end of the vast room and stationed the rest of their men in position to cover both entrances. Takeel, with velvet slippers over his field-boots, stood on Prenk's desk, commanding the entire room, with a machine-gun-like weapon cradled expertly and accustomedly in the crook of his left arm.

'Are things this bad?' Seaton asked. 'I knew it was tough when you told us to come loaded for bear – but *this*?'

'They're exactly this bad. These two' – Prenk jerked a thumb at Kay-Lee and at Takeel – 'are the only two people on this whole world that I know I can trust. Until quite recently I was sure I held the city – but now I'm not at all sure of holding even this building. I can only hope that you're not too late. I'll tell you what the situation is; then you will tell me, please, if there is anything you can do about it.'

He talked for twelve minutes. Then:

'P-s-s-s-st!' Kay-Lee hissed. 'Danger! Coming – nearing us – fast! I can feel it – taste it – smell it! Get ready quick!' She sprang to her feet, drew her pistol, and arranged a dozen clips of cartridges meticulously on the table in front of her.

The Osnomians' chairs crashed backward, their heavy coats flew off, and they stood tensely ready, machine pistols in all four hands. And, seconds later, the other Skylarkers were on their feet and ready too. The Captain-General had not heard the low-voiced warning, but he had seen the action and that was enough. Trigger-nerved Dunark's chair had no sooner struck the floor on its first bounce than Takeel was going into his shooting stance, with his weapon flipping around into position as though it were sliding in a greased groove; the while glaring ferociously at his senior lieutenant – who thereupon began to have an acute attack of the jitters.

It was the commander's savage motion, actually, that ruined the attackers' split-second schedule. For, at a certain second, the two lieutenants were to shoot their captain; then to shoot Prenk and Kay-Lee Barlo; and then, as the attack proper was launched, they were to kill as many of their own men as they could. Thus, knowing what a savage performer the Captain-General was with his atrocious weapon, their hands were forced; they had to act a couple of seconds too soon. They tried – but with two short bursts so close together as to be practically one, Takeel cut them down. Cut them both almost literally in two.

Thus, when the two great doors were blasted simultaneously down and the attackers stormed in with guns ablaze, they did not find a half-dead and completely demoralized Guard and a group of surprised visitors. Instead:

The mercenaries were neither dead nor demoralized. They knew exactly what to do and were doing it. Dunark and Sitar had the fire-power of half a company of trained troops and were using it to the fullest full. The Captain-General, from his coign of vantage atop the desk, was spraying both entrances with bullets like a gardener watering two flower-beds with a hose. Kay-Lee was throwing lead almost as fast as Takeel was; changing magazines with such fluent speed and precision as to miss scarcely a shot. Dorothy, nostrils flaring and violet eyes blazing, was shooting as steadily and as accurately as though she were out on the range marking up another possible. Even tiny Lotus, with one of her .25s clutched in both hands, was shooting as fast as she could pull the trigger.

It was Seaton, however, who ended the battle. He waited long enough to be absolutely sure of what was going on, then fired twice with his left-hand magnum – through the doorways, high over the heads of the attackers, far down the corridors.

There were two terrific explosions; followed by one long rumbling crash as that whole section of the building either went somewhere else or collapsed into rubble. Falling and flying masonry and steel and razor-edged shards of structural glass killed almost everyone outside the heavily reinforced wall of the Room of State. The shock-waves of the blasts, raging through the doorways, killed half of the enemy massed there and blew the others half the length of the room. And, continuing on with rapidly decreasing force, knocked most of the Skylarkers flat and blew the Captain-General off of the desk and clear back against the wall.

'Sangram's head!' that worthy yelled, scrambling to his feet with machinegun again – or still? He had not for an instant lost control of *that* – at the ready. 'What in Japnonk's rankest hell was that?'

'X-plosive shell,' Seaton said, his voice as hard as his eyes. 'This time I came loaded for bear. Now we'll mop up and find out what's been going on. I gather, sir, that your two platoon leaders were in on it?'

'Yes. It's a shame I had to kill 'em without asking 'em a few questions.' He did not explain that he had had neither the time in which nor the weapon with which merely to wound them seriously enough so that neither of them could fight back with any sort of weapon. There was no need.

'That won't make too much difference.' Seaton looked around; first at his own crew and then at the guards, half of whom were down. Medics and first-aid men were rushing in to work on them. He looked again, more closely, at his people and at Prenk and Kay-Lee. Not one of them, apparently, had even been scratched.

That, however, was logical. The mercenaries were hard-trained fighting men, shooting was their business. Hence the attackers' orders had been to shoot the guards first, and there had been no time to evaluate the actual situation and to change the plan of attack. Hence, as far as anyone knew, not a single bullet had been aimed at the far end of the room.

Seaton took a pair of headsets out of his pocket and applied one of them, first to one of the two lieutenants' heads, then to the other.

'Un-huh,' he grunted then. 'That ape didn't know too much, but this one was going to be the new Captain-General. I suppose you've got a recorder, Ree-Toe?'

'I'll get it, sir!' Kay-Lee exclaimed; and Prenk, eyes bulging, gasped:

'Don't tell me you can read a *dead* brain, sir!'

'Oh, yes. They keep their charges, sometimes for days.' Kay-Lee handed Seaton a microphone then, and he spoke into it for ten minutes – the while three Rayseenian faces went through gamuts of emotion; each culminating in the same expression of joyous satisfaction.

When Seaton paused for breath Prenk said in awe, 'That machine is certainly a something … I don't suppose …' He stopped.

'I do suppose, yes. I'll give you a few sets, with blueprints, and show you how they work,' and Seaton went on with his reading.

A few minutes later he cut off the mike and said, 'That ape over there,' he pointed, 'is one of the Big Wheels. Have someone latch onto him, Ree-Toe; we'll read him next. He's one you'll be really interested in, so I'll hook you up in parallel with me so you can get everything he knows into your own brain.' He took a third headset from his pocket and began to adjust its settings, going on, 'It takes a different set-up … so … and goes on your head so.'

'That ape' was a fattish, sallow-faced man of fifty, who had been directing operations from outside the room and had intended to stay outside it until everything was secure within. He had been blown into the room and halfway along its length by the force of the blasts. He was pretty badly smashed up, but he was beginning to regain consciousness and was weakly trying to get to his feet.

This unlucky wight was a mine of information indeed, but Prenk stopped the mining operation after only a couple of minutes of digging.

'Sy-By,' he said. 'Two more of your officers you can shoot.' He gave two names. 'Then come back here with some men you think you can trust and we'll test 'em to make sure. By that time I'll have a list of people for you to round up and bring in for examination.'

There is no need to follow any farther the Premier's progress in cleaning up his planet. In fact, only one more incident that occurred there is of interest here – one that occurred while Seaton and Dorothy were getting ready for bed in one of the suites of honor. She put both arms around him suddenly; he pressed her close.

'Dick, I belonged there. Beside you. Every fiber of my being belonged there. That was *exactly* where I belonged.'

'I know you did, sweet. I'll have to admit it. But …'

She put her hand over his mouth. 'But nothing, my dearest. No buts. I've killed rats and rattlesnakes, and that wasn't any different. Not a bit different in any way.'

Of the more than five thousand Fenachrone who had left their noisome home planet in Sleemet's flagship, almost seven hundred had died and more were dying.

It was not that the Llurdi were physically cruel to them or abused them in any way. They didn't. Nor were they kind; they were conspicuously and insultingly neutral and indifferent to them. Conspicuous and insulting, that is, to the hypersensitive minds of the captives. In their own minds, the Llurdi were acting strictly according to logic. Every item of the subjects' environment duplicated precisely its twin on the subjects' home world. What more could logically be done? Nothing.

The Llurdi observed the mental anguish of the Fenachrone, of course, and recorded their emotions quite accurately, but with no emotional reactions whatever of their own. Practically all emotions were either illogical or unsane, or both.

To the illogical and unsane Fenachrone, however – physically, mentally, intellectually and psychologically – the situation was intolerable; one that simply could not be endured.

They were proud, haughty, intolerant; their race had always been so. Since time immemorial it had been bred into their innermost consciousnesses that they were the RACE SUPREME – destined unquestionably to be the absolute rulers of all things living or yet to live throughout all the transfinite reaches of the Cosmic All.

Holding this belief with every fiber of their beings, they had been plunged instantly into a condition of complete, utter helplessness.

Their vessel could not fight. While it was intact except for its tail-section and its power-pods, its every offensive projector was burned out; useless. Nor could they fight personally, either physically or mentally. Their physical strength, enormous as it was, was of no avail against the completely logical, completely matter-of-fact minds of the Llurdi.

Most galling condition of all, the Fenachrone were not treated as enemies; nor as menaces or threats; nor even as intelligent entities whose knowledges and abilities might be worthy of notice. These things were observed and recorded, to be sure, but only as competent parts of a newly discovered class of objects, the Fenachrone; a class of objects that happened to be alive. The Fenachrone were neither more nor less noteworthy than were birds or barnacles.

Sleemet, no longer young and perhaps the proudest and most intractable and most intransigent of the lot, could not endure that treatment very long; but he did not bend. The old adage 'Where there's life there's hope,' simply is not true where such as the Llurdi and the Fenachrone are concerned. Sleemet lost all hope and broke; broke almost completely down.

He stopped eating. That did not bother the Llurdi in any way. Why should it? They were neither squeamish nor humane, any more than they were cruel or vindictive. The fact that certain of these creatures stopped taking nourishment under certain conditions was merely a datum to be observed and recorded.

But since Sleemet was big and strong, even for a Fenachrone, and had previously eaten very well indeed, it took him a long time to die. And as he weakened – as the bindings between flesh and spirit loosened more and ever more – he regressed more and ever more back into the youth of his race. Back and back. Still farther back; back into its very childhood; back to a time when his remote ancestors ate their meat alive and communicated with each other, sometimes by grunts and gestures, but more often by means of a purely mental faculty that was later to evolve into the power of ocular hypnosis.

Half conscious or less of his surroundings but knowing well that death was very near, Sleemet half-consciously sent out his race's ages-old mental message-in-extremity of the dying.

Marc C. DuQuesne knew vastly more about the Fenachrone than did any other man alive, not excluding Richard Seaton. He and Seaton were, as far as is known, the only two men ever to meet Fenachrone mind to mind and live through the experience; but DuQuesne had been in thought-helmet contact with a Fenachrone much longer and much more intimately and very much more interestedly than Seaton ever had – because of the tremendous intrinsic differences between the personalities of the two men.

Seaton, after having crippled a war-vessel of the Fenachrone, had pinned its captain against a wall with so many beams of force that he could not move his head and could scarcely move any other part of his monstrous body. Then, by means of a pair of thought-helmets, he had taken what of that captain's knowledge he wanted. He had, however, handled that horribly unhuman brain very gingerly. He had merely read certain parts of it, as one reads an encyclopedia; at no time had his mind become *en rapport* with that of the monster. In fact, he had said to Crane:

'I'd hate to have much of that brain in my own skull – afraid I'd bite myself. I'm just going to look ... and when I see something I want I'll grab it and put it into my own brain.'

DuQuesne, however, in examining a navigating engineer of that monstrous race, had felt no such revulsion, contrariwise – although possibly not quite consciously – he had admired certain traits of Fenachrone; character so much that he had gone *en rapport* with that engineer's mind practically cell to cell; with the result that he had emerged from that mental union as nearly a Fenachrone himself as a human being could very well become.

Wherefore, as DuQuesne in his flying-planetoid-base approached the point of its course nearest to the planet Llurdiax, he began to feel the thinnest possible tendril of thought trying to make contact with one of the deepest chambers of his mind. He stiffened; shutting it off by using automatically an ability that he had not known consciously that he had. He relaxed; and, all interest now, tuned his mind to that feeler of thought, began to pull it in, and stopped – and the contact released a flood of Fenachrone knowledge completely new to him.

A Fenachrone, dying somewhere, wanted ... wanted what? Not help, exactly. Notice? Attention? To *give* something? DuQuesne was not enough of a Fenachrone to translate that one thought even approximately, and he was not interested enough to waste any time on it. It had something to do with the good of the race; that was close enough.

DuQuesne, frowning a little, sat back in his bucket seat and thought. He had supposed that the Fenachrone were all dead ... but it made sense that Seaton couldn't have killed *all* of a space-faring race, at that. But so what? He didn't care how many Fenachrone died. But a lot of their stuff was really good, and he certainly hadn't got it all yet, by any means; it might be smart to listen to what the dying monster had to say – especially since he, DuQuesne, was getting pretty close to the home grounds of Klazmon the Llurd.

Wherefore DuQuesne opened his mental shield: and, since his mind was still tuned precisely to the questing wave and since the *DQ* was now practically as close to Llurdiax as it would get on course 255U, he received a burst of thought that jarred him to the very teeth.

It is amazing how much information can be carried by a Fenachrone-compressed burst of thought. It was fortunate for DuQuesne that he had the purely Fenachrone abilities to decompress it, to spread it out and analyze it, and later, to absorb it fully.

The salient points, however, were pellucidly clear. The dying monster was First Scientist Fleet Admiral Sleemet; and he and more than four thousand other Fenachrone were helpless captives of and were being studied to death by Llurdan scientists under the personal direction of Llanzlan Klazmon.

Realizing instantly what that meant – Klazmon would be out here in seconds with a probe, if nothing stronger – DuQuesne slammed on full-coverage screens at full power, thus sealing his entire worldlet bottle-tight against any and every spy-ray, beam, probe, band, zone of force and/or order of force that he knew anything about. Since this included everything he had known before this trip began, plus everything he had learned from Freemind One and from the Jelmi and from Klazmon himself, he was grimly certain that he was just as safe as though he were in God's hip pocket from any possible form of three-dimensional observation or attack.

Cutting in his fourth-dimensional gizmo – how glad he was that he had studied it so long and so intensively that he knew more about it than its inventors did! – he flipped what he called its 'eye' into the Fenachrone Reservation on distant Llurdiax. He seized Sleemet, bed and all, in a wrapping of force and deposited the bundle gently on the floor of the *DQ*'s control room, practically at his, DuQuesne's feet. Fenachrone could breathe Earth air for hours without appreciable damage – they had proved that often enough – and if he decided to keep any of them alive he'd make them some air they liked better.

Second, he brought over a doctor, complete with kit and instruments and supplies; and third, the Fenachrone equivalent of a registered nurse.

'You, doctor!' DuQuesne snapped, in Fenachronian. 'I don't know whether this spineless weakling is too far gone to save or not. Or whether he is worth saving or not. But since he was actually in charge of your expedition-to-preserve-the-race I will listen to what he has to say instead of blasting him out of hand. So give him a shot of the strongest stuff you have – or is he in greater need of food than of stimulant?'

DuQuesne did not know whether the doctor would cooperate with a human being or not. But he did – whether from lack of spirit of his own or from desire to save his chief, DuQuesne did not care to ask.

'Both,' the doctor said, 'but nourishment first, by all means. Intravenous, nurse, please,' and doctor and nurse went to work with the skill and precision of their highly trained crafts.

And, somewhat to DuQuesne's surprise, Sleemet began immediately to rally; and in three-quarters of an hour he had regained full consciousness.

'You spineless worm!' DuQuesne shot at the erstwhile invalid, in true Fenachrone tone and spirit. 'You gutless wonder! You pusillanimous weakling, you sniveling coward! Is it the act of a noble of the Fenachrone to give up, to yield supinely, to surrender ignominiously to a fate however malign while a spark of life endures?'

Sleemet was scarcely stirred by this vicious castigation. He raised dull eyes – eyes shockingly lifeless to anyone who had ever seen the ruby-lighted, flame-shot wells of vibrant force that normal Fenachrone eyes were – and said lifelessly, 'There is a point, the certainty of death, at which struggle becomes negative instead of positive. It merely prolongs the agony. Having passed that point, I died.'

'There is no such point, idiot, while life lasts! Do I look like Klazmon of Llurdiax?'

'No, but death is no less certain at your hands than at his.'

'Why should it be, stupid?' and DuQuesne's sneer was extra-high-voltage stuff, even for Dr Marc C. DuQuesne.

Now was the crucial moment. IF he could take all those Fenachrone over, and IF he could control them after they got back to normal, *what* a crew they would make! He stared contemptuously at the ex-admiral and went on:

'Whether or not you and your four thousand die in the near future is up to you. While I do not have to have a crew, I can use one efficiently for a few weeks. If you choose to work with me I will, at the end of that time, give you a duplicate of your original spaceship and will see to it that you are allowed to resume your journey wherever you wish.'

'Sir, the Fenachrone do not—' the doctor began stiffly.

'Shut up, you poor, dumb clown!' DuQuesne snapped. 'Haven't you learned *anything*? That instead of being the strongest race in space you are one of the weakest? You have one choice merely – cooperate or die. And that is not yours, but Sleemet's. Sleemet?'

'But how do I know that if—'

'If you have any part of a brain, fool, use it! What matters it to me whether Fenachrone live or die? I'm not asking you anything; I'm telling you under what conditions I will save your lives. If you want to argue the matter I'll put you three – and the bed – back where you were and be on my way. Which do you prefer?'

Sleemet had learned something. He had been beaten down flat enough so that he could learn something – and he realized that he had much to learn from any race who could do what his rescuer had just done.

'We will work with you,' Sleemet said. 'You will, I trust, instruct us concerning how you liberated us three and propose to liberate the others?'

'I can't. It was fourth-dimensional translation.' DuQuesne lied blandly. 'Did you ever try to explain the color "blue" to a man born blind? No scientist of your race will be able to understand either the theory or the mechanics of fourth-dimensional translation for something like eleven hundred thousand of your years.'

24

DuQuesne and Sleemet

En route to the galaxy in which DuQuesne's aliens supposedly lived, Dorothy said, 'Say, Dick. I forgot to ask you something. What did you ever find out about that thought business of Kay-Lee's?'

'Huh?' Seaton was surprised. 'What was there to find out? How are you going to explain the mechanism of thought – by unscrewing the inscrutable? She said, and I quote, "We didn't feel that we were quite reaching you," unquote. So it was she and Ree-Toe Prenk. Obviously. Holding hands or something –across a Ouija board or some other focusing device, probably. Staring into each other's eyes to link minds and direct the thought.'

'But they *did* hit you with something,' she insisted, 'and it bothers me. They can do it and we can't.'

'No sweat, pet. That isn't a circumstance to what you do every time you think at a controller to order up a meal or whatever. How do you do that? Different people, different abilities, is all. Anyway, Earth mediums have done that kind of thing for ages. If you're really interested, you can take some time off and learn it, next time we're on Ray-See-Nee. But for right now, my red-headed beauty, we've got something besides that kind of monkey-business to worry about.'

'That's right, we have,' and Dorothy forgot the minor matter in thinking of the major. 'Those aliens. Have you and Martin figured out a *modus operandi*?'

'More or less. Go in openly, like tourists, but with everything we've got not only on the trips but hyped up to as nearly absolutely instantaneous reactivity as the Brain can possibly get it.'

Both DuQuesne's *DQ* and Seaton's *Skylark of Valeron* were within range of Llurdiax. DuQuesne, however, as has been said, was covering up as tightly as he could. Everything that could be muzzled or muffled was muzzled or muffled, and he was traveling comparatively slowly, so as to put out the minimum of detectable high-order emanation. Furthermore, his screens were shoved out to such a tremendous distance, and were being varied so rapidly and so radically in shape, that no real pattern existed to be read. The *DQ* was not undetectable, of course, but it would have taken a great deal of highly specialized observation and analysis to find her.

The *Skylark of Valeron*, on the other hand, was coming in wide open: 'Like a tourist,' as Seaton had told Dorothy the plan was to do.

In the llanzlanate on Llurdiax, therefore, an observer alerted Klazmon, who flew immediately to his master-control panel. He checked the figures the observer had given him, and was as nearly appalled as a Llurd could become. An artificial structure of that size and mass – it was certainly not a natural planetoid – had never even been thought of by any builder of record. He measured its acceleration – the *Valeron* was still braking down at max – and his eyes bulged. That thing, tremendous as it was, had the power-to-mass ratio of a speedster! In spite of its immense size it was actually an intergalactic flyer!

He launched a probe, as he had done so many times before – but with entirely unexpected results.

The stranger's guardian screens were a hundred times as reactive as any known Llurdan science. He was not allowed time for even the briefest of mental contacts or for any real observation at all. So infinitesimal had been the instant usable time that only one fact was clear. The entities in that mobile monstrosity were – positively – Jelmoids.

Not true Jelmi, certainly. He knew all about the Jelmi. Those tapes bore unmistakable internal evidence of being true and complete records and there was no hint anywhere in them of anything like this. If not the Jelmi, who? Ah, yes, the Fenachrone, whose fleet … no, Sleemet knew nothing of such a construction … and he was not exactly of the same race … ah, yes, that one much larger ship that had escaped. The probability was high that its one occupant belonged to precisely the same Jelmoid race as did the personnel of this planetoid. The escaped one had reported Klazmon's cursory investigation as an attack. It was a virtual certainty, therefore, that this was a battleship of that race, heading for Llurdiax to … to what? To investigate merely? No.

Nor merely to parley. They had made no attempt whatever to communicate. (It did not occur to Klazmon, then or ever, that his own fiercely driven probe could not possibly have been taken for an attempt at communication. He had fully intended to communicate, as soon as he had seized the mind of whoever was in command of the strange spacecraft.) And now, with the stranger's incredible full-coverage screen in operation, communication was and would remain impossible.

But he had data sufficient for action. These Jelmoids, like all others he knew, were rabidly anti-social, illogical, unreasoning, unsane and insane. They were – definitely – surplus population.

So thinking, Llanzlan Klazmon launched his attack.

As the *Skylark* entered that enigmatic galaxy, Seaton was not in his home, with only a remote-control helmet with which to work. He was in the control room itself, at the base of the Brain, with the tremendously complex master-control itself surrounding his head. Thus he was attuned to and in instantaneous contact with every activated cell of that gigantic Brain. It was ready to receive and to act upon with the transfinite speed of thought any order that Seaton would think. Nor would any such action interfere in any way with the automatics that Seaton had already set up.

'I'm going to stay here all day,' Seaton said, 'and all night tonight, too, if necessary.'

But he did not have to stay there even all day. In less than four hours the Llanzlan drove his probe and Seaton probed practically instantaneously back. And since Seaton's hyped-up screens were a hundred times faster than the Llurd's, Seaton 'saw' a hundred times as much as Klazmon did. He saw the city Llurdias in all its seat-of-empire pride and glory. He perceived its miles-wide girdle of fortresses. He perceived the llanzlanate; understood its functions and purposes. He entered the Hall of Computation and examined minutely the beings and the machines at work there.

How could all this be? Because the speed of thought, if not absolutely infinite, is at least transfinite; immeasurable to man. And the *Valeron*'s inorganic brain and Seaton's organic one were, absolutely and super-intimately, the two component parts of one incredibly able, efficient and proficient whole.

Thus, when the alien's attack was launched in all its fury and almost all of the *Valeron*'s mighty defensive engines went simultaneously into automatic action, the coded chirpings that the Brain employed to summon human help did not sound: that Brain's builder, fellow, boss, and perfect complement was already on the job.

And thus, since no warning had been given, the other Skylarkers were surprised when Seaton called them all down into the control room.

They were even more surprised when they saw how white and strained his face was.

'This may become *veree* unfunny,' he said. ''Tsa good thing I muscled her up or we'd be losing some skin and some of our defense. As it is, we're holding 'em and we've got a few megas in reserve. Not enough to be really happy about, but some. And we're building more, of course. *However*, that ape down there has undoubtedly got a lot of stuff otherwheres on the planet that he can hook in pretty fast, so whatever we're going to do we'd better do right now.'

'They didn't try to communicate at all?' Crane asked. 'Strange for a race of such obviously high attainments.'

'Not a lick,' Seaton said, flatly. 'Just a probe; the hardest and sharpest probe I ever saw. When I blocked it – *Whammo!*'

'You probed, too, of course,' Dorothy said. 'What did you find out? Are they really monstrous, as DuQuesne said, out purely to kill?'

'Just that. He wasn't lying a nickel's worth on that. His Nibs down there had already decided that we were surplus population and should be eliminated, and he set right out to do it. So, unless some of you have some mighty valid reasons not to, I'm going to try my damndest to eliminate him, right now.'

'We *could* run, I suppose,' Margaret suggested – but not at all enthusiastically.

'I doubt it. Not without letting him burn us down to basketball size, like the Chlorans did. He undoubtedly let us get this close on purpose so we couldn't.'

Since no one else said anything, Seaton energized everything of offense he had. He tuned it as precisely as he possibly could. He assembled it into the tightest, solidest, hardest beam he could possibly build, Then, involuntarily tensing his muscles and hunching his back, he drove the whole gigantic thing squarely at where he knew the llanzlanate was.

The Llurd's outer screen scarcely flickered as it went black in nothing flat of time. The intermediate screen held for eighty-three hundredths of a second. Then the practically irresistible force of that beam met the practically immovable object that was the Klazmon's last line of defense. And as it clawed and bit and tore and smashed in ultra-pyrotechnic ferocity, solar-like flares of raw energy erupted from the area of contact and the very ether writhed and seethed and warped under the intolerable stresses of the utterly incomprehensible forces there at grips.

This went on ... and on ... and on.

Even to Seaton, who knew only that he was up against an enemy nearly as potent as the Chlorans, the full import of the enormous struggle of energies then being waged was far from clear. We can wonder now, and ask ourselves what the fate of the universe might have been if the *Skylark*'s Norlaminian designers had skimped on a course of screens, or overlooked a detail of defense. Surely its consequences would have been cataclysmic! Not only to Seaton and his Skylarkers, watching grim-faced as their gauges revealed the enormous flow of destructive forces battling each other to annihilation for countless parsecs in every direction. Not only to the Jelmi, or the Rey-See-Nees, or the Norlaminians, or Earth itself ... but to countless generations yet unborn, on planets not yet discovered ...

But they held.

And after ten endless minutes of such terrible gouts and blasts of destruction as no planet could endure for a moment, Seaton heard a voice speak to him.

He had never heard it before, but it said in good American English: 'Good morning, my friends. Or perhaps, by your clocks, it is good afternoon? I am the Llanzlon Mergon of Jelm, and I perceive that you are under attack by our old acquaintances, the Llurdi. You, I am sure, are the Seatons and the Cranes, about whom we heard so much on Earth, but whom we were not able to find.'

Even though the Llurdi had been absolute rulers of all the planets of the Jelmi for many thousands of years, it was easy for them to accept, and to adapt themselves to, the new condition of coexistence with the Realm of the Jelmi on terms of equality. That was the way they were built.

The Llanzlan fed the new data into Computer Prime and issued its findings as a directive. Since this directive was the product of pure logic, that was all there was to it.

With the Jelmi, however, even with a much simpler and easier agenda, things were distinctly otherwise. Everyone knows how difficult it is to change the political thinking of even a part of any human world. How, then, of the two hundred forty whole planets of the Jelmi? The conservatives did not want any change at all. Not even to independence. The radicals wanted everything changed; but each faction wanted each item changed in a different fashion. And the moderates, as usual, did not agree with either extreme wing on anything.

And, also as usual, no one faction would play ball with any other. Each would have its own way in setting up the Realm or there would be no Realm – it would pick up its marbles and go home.

Fortunately, however, the eight hundred best brains of the entire Jelman race were together in one place – in the fully operative base that the *Mallidaxian*'s dome had now become. Their numbers included the most capable and most highly trained specialists in every field of Jelman endeavor and they all had been living together and working together for many months.

They knew better than to go off halfcocked. They would have to develop a master-plan upon which they could all agree. Unanimously. Nothing less would do. Having developed such a plan they would put it into effect, each person or planetary group upon his or her or their home world. The constitution thus fabricated would be put into effect by reason if possible, by force if necessary. It was not to be amended except by process contained within itself.

Thus the Constitutional Committee of Eight Hundred was still living in the base and was still hard at work when the Officer of the Day called Mergon – who, after glancing at plates and instruments, called Luloy.

The ether was showing strains of a magnitude not observed since the Battle of Independence. A Llurd ship was putting out everything she had; fighting full-out against a – *something* –whose battle-screen covered such an immensity of space that Mergon could scarcely believe his instruments.

Luloy quirked an eyebrow. 'Well, what are we waiting for?'

'Nothing,' and Mergon, who could now handle projections through the fourth dimension, launched them. 'I'll keep us invisible while we see what that thing is and how big it really is.'

They went and saw – and the more they studied the immensity that was the *Skylark of Valeron* the more they marveled.

Finally, in the *Valeron*'s control room and still invisible, they studied the worldlet's personnel; the while talking to each other in the flesh at the *Mallidaxian*'s main panel.

'Except for the green-skinned couple they *are* Tellurians,' the girl insisted. 'Everything about that – that ship, if you can call it a ship – is Tellurian. Just *look* at those clothes. You never saw anything like that anywhere except on Tellus and you never will.'

'We never heard anything about anything like that mobile fortress on Tellus, either,' he objected, 'and we certainly would have if they'd known anything about it. How could they hide it?'

'Maybe it's so new that not too many people know about it yet. Anyway, whatever the truth about that, we heard a lot about Seaton and Crane. Especially Seaton. According to the lore, he's their principal god's right-hand man. He can do *anything*.'

'Or a devil's depending on who you talked to. But we wrote that off as just that – lore. If not propaganda.'

'We'll have to write it back on again. Those two *have* to be Seaton and Crane – there, the Jelm-sized one with his head in the controller, and that other bean-pole type standing there smoking a … a cigarette, they call it. And that smoking business clinches it. *Nobody* but Tellurians burn their lungs out with smoke.'

'Okay.' Mergon thickened their projections up to full visibility and spoke:

'You must be the Seatons and the Cranes, about whom we heard so much on Earth but whom we were not able to find.'

Crane the Imperturbable was startled out of his imperturbability when Mergon and Luloy appeared in the *Valeron*'s control room and Mergon spoke to him in English. But he did not show it – very much! – and realized in a moment what the truth was.

'We are,' Crane said, stepping forward and holding out his hand. These people would understand the gesture. 'I'm M. Reynolds Crane; Dr Seaton is occupied at the moment. You are of course the people who had the spaceship on the moon. We have come all the way out here in the hope of finding you somewhere in this galaxy.'

'Oh? Oh, you want the fourth-dimensional device.'

'Exactly.' Crane then introduced the others, and finally Seaton; who, having assured himself that the Brain could handle the stalemate without him, had disengaged himself from the master controller and had joined the party.

'That's right,' Seaton said. 'Since nothing like it is known to any science with which we are familiar, we hope to learn about it from you. But that … those monsters … they aren't, by any chance, friends of yours, are they?'

Luloy laughed. 'No. Not exactly … or maybe they are, after a fashion, now. But the Llurdi were our unquestioned masters for so many thousands of years that they haven't yet decided to treat us or anyone who looks like us with the courtesy reserved for equals. You see, the Llanzlan would have communicated with you in thought after he had investigated you a little.'

'Yeah.' Seaton's smile was grim. 'With the stillest, hardest probe he could build? And I'm supposed to sit still for that kind of manhandling?'

'No.' Mergon took over. 'No one but a Llurd could have expected you to. This situation is somewhat unfortunate. Until very recently they have always had overwhelmingly superior power. They never had any effective opposition until we wore them down a little, just recently.' Mergon explained the situation in as few words as possible, concluding, 'So this battle, while not due exactly to misunderstanding, is unfortunate. What I propose is that Luloy and I visit Klazmon via projection, as we are now visiting you, and explain matters to him as we have explained them to you. I take it you will cease fire if he does?'

'Of course. We didn't come here to start a war, or to bother him in any way; just to see you. So I'll do better than that; I'll cut my offense right now.'

He thought at the Brain and the raging inferno above the llanzlanate went suddenly calm and still. 'That beam is *no* pencil of force, believe me. If it should get through it would volatilize his palace and half the city, and that would be unfortunate – hey! He's quit slugging, too!'

'Of course,' Mergon said. 'As I told you, he is – all Llurdi are – completely and perfectly logical. With their own brand of logic, of course. Insanely logical, to our way of thinking ... or perhaps *un*sanely may be the better word. On the basis of the data he then had it was logical for him to attack you. Your ceasefire was a new datum, one that he cannot as yet evaluate. He has deduced the fact that we Jelmi caused it, but he does not know why you stopped. Hence he has restored the *status quo ante*, pending our explanation. He wants additional data. If our explanation is satisfactory – data sufficient – he'll probably just let the whole matter drop. If not – if it's data insufficient – I wouldn't know. He'll do whatever he decides is the logical thing to do – which is way beyond my guess-point. He might even resume the attack exactly where he left off; although I think he'll be able to deduce a reason not to.'

Seaton whistled through his teeth. 'Holy ... cat!' he said. 'If that's pure logic I'll take vanilla. But how will you make the approach?'

'Very easily. If two of you will permit us to bring you over here we will send four working projections into the Llanzlan Klazmon's study, where I'm sure he's expecting us. You, Dr Seaton, and your Dorothy, perhaps?'

'Not I!' Dorothy declared, shaking her head vigorously. 'Uh-uh. Into battle, yes; this, no. If I never see a monster like that it'll be twenty minutes too soon. You're it, Martin.'

'One more thing,' Mergon went on, as Seaton and Crane appeared in the flesh beside him. 'Since the Llurdi refuse to learn any language except their own, I must teach you Llurdan,' and he held out two Jelman thought-caps.

'I prefer my own,' Seaton said, after a very short trial. 'So will you, I think,' and he sent back for four of the *Skylark*'s latest models.

The two Jelmi put two of them on. 'Oh, I do indeed!' Luloy exclaimed, and Mergon added, 'As was to have been expected, we have much to learn from you, friends.'

'But listen,' Seaton said. 'You gave the ape all the dope on that fourth-dimensional thing. Isn't he apt to toss a superatomic into our Brain with it?'

'There's no possibility whatever of that, either soon or later. Not soon because, since they work slowly and thoroughly, it will be months yet before they have a full-scale machine. Nor later, because the mutual destruction of four hundred eighty-two populated planets – excuse me, four hundred eighty, now – is not logical in any system of logic, however cockeyed that system may be.'

It took Seaton a fraction of a second to get it, but when he did, it rocked him. 'Oh! I hadn't figured on you coming all the way in. But does he know you will?'

'He certainly does know it!' Luloy broke in. 'Beyond a doubt; or what you call peradventure.'

'Oh,' Seaton said again. 'And that's why he isn't going to resume hostilities with ordinary weapons, either? Thanks, you two, a million. We appreciate it. Okay; we're ready, I guess.'

The four projections appeared in front of the Llanzlan's desk. He was expecting them. 'Well?' he asked.

Mergon began to explain, but Seaton cut him off. Mergon could not possibly feel equal to Klazmon in a face-to-face; Seaton could and did.

'I can explain us better than you can, friend Mergon,' he said. Then, to the Llurd, 'We came here to visit the human beings whom you call the Jelmi. We did not have, have not now, and do not expect to have any interest whatever in you Llurdi or in anything Llurdan. Our purpose is to promote intergalactic commerce and interhuman friendship. The various human races have different abilities and different artifacts and different knowledges – many of each of which are of benefit to other human races.

'You made an unprovoked attack on us. Know now, Llanzlan Klazmon, that I do not permit invasion, either mental or physical, by any entity – man, beast, god, devil or Llurd – of this or of any other galaxy. Although I can imagine few subjects upon which you and I could converse profitably, if you wish to talk to me as one intelligent and logical entity to another I will so converse. But I repeat – I will not permit invasion.

'If you wish to resume battle on that account that is your right and your privilege. You will note, however, that our attack was metered precisely to a point just below your maximum capability of resistance. Know now that if you force us to destroy your city and perhaps your world it will not have been the first city or the first world we have been forced to destroy; nor, with a probability of point nine nine nine, will it have been the last. Do you want peace with us or war?'

'Peace. Data sufficient,' Klazmon said immediately. 'I have recorded the fact that there is at least one Jelmoid race other than the Jelmi themselves of which some representatives are both able and willing to employ almost

Llurdan logic,' and he switched his attention from the projections to the tape he had been studying – cutting communications as effectively as though he had removed himself to another world.

Back in the *Mallidaxian*, while Luloy stared at Seaton almost in awe, Mergon said, 'That was a beautiful job, Dr Seaton. Perfect! Much better than I could have done. You used flawless Llurdan logic.'

'Thanks to the ace in the hole you gave me with your briefing, I could do it. I'd hate to have to run a bluff on *that* ape. What's next on the agenda, Savant Mergon?'

'Make it "Merg", please, and I'll call you "Dick". Now that this is settled, why don't you put your fortress-planetoid on automatic and let us bring you all here, so that our peoples may become friends in person and may begin work upon tasks of mutual interest?'

'That's a thought, friend; that really is a thought,' Seaton said, and it was done forthwith.

Aboard the *Mallidaxian*, Seaton cut the social amenities as short as he courteously could; then went with inseparable Mergon and Luloy to Tammon's laboratory. That fourth-dimensional gizmo was what he was interested in. With his single-mindedness that was all he was interested in, at the moment, of the entire Jelman culture. All four donned Skylark thought-helmets and Seaton set out to learn everything there was to be known about that eight million cubic feet of esoteric apparatus. And Mergon, who didn't know much of anything about recent developments, was eager to catch up.

Seaton did not learn all about the fourth-dimensional device in one day, nor in one week; but when he had it all filed away in the Brain he asked, 'Is that all you have of it?' He did not mean to be insulting; he was only greatly surprised.

The old savant bristled and Seaton apologized hastily. 'I didn't mean to belittle your achievement in any sense, sir. It's probably the greatest breakthrough ever made. But it doesn't seem to be complete.'

'Of course it isn't complete!' Tammon snapped. 'I've been working on it only—'

'Oh, I didn't mean that,' Seaton broke in. 'The *concept* is incomplete. In several ways. For instance, if fourth-dimensional translation is used as a weapon, you have no defense against it.'

'Of course there's no defense against it!' Tammon defended his brain-child like a tigress defending her young. 'By the very nature of things there *can't* be any defense against it!'

At that, politeness went by the board. 'You're wrong,' Seaton said, flatly. 'By the very nature of things there has to be. All nature is built on a system of checks and balances. Doing a job so terrifically big and so brand new, I doubt if anybody could get the whole thing at once. Let's go over the theory again, together, with a microscope, to see if we can't add something to it somewhere?'

Tammon agreed, but reluctantly. Deep down in his own mind he did not believe that any other mind could improve upon any particular of his work. As the review progressed, however, he became more and more enthusiastic. As well he might; for the mathematics section of Richard Seaton's multi-compartmented mind contained, indexed and cross-indexed, all the work done by countless grand masters of the subject during half a million years.

Luloy started to pull her helmet off, but Mergon stopped her with a direct thought. 'I'm lost, too, sweet, but keep on listening. We can get bits here and there – and we'll probably never have the chance again to watch two such minds at work.'

'Hold it!' Seaton snapped, half an hour later. 'Back up – there! This integral here. Limits zero to pi over two. You're limiting the thing to a large but definitely limited volume of your generalized N-dimensional space. I think it should be between zero and infinity – and while we're at it let's scrap half of the third determinant in that no-space-no-time complex. Let's see what happens if we substitute the gamma function here and the chi there and the xi there and the omicron down there in the corner.'

'But *why*?' the old savant protested. 'I don't see any possible reason for any of it.'

Seaton grinned. 'There isn't any – any more than there was for your original brainstorm. If there had been the Norlaminian would have worked this whole shebang out a hundred thousand years ago. It's nothing but a hunch, but it's strong enough so I want to follow it up – okay? Fine then, integrating that, we get ...'

Five hours later, Tammon took his helmet off and stared at Seaton with wonder in his eyes. 'Do you realize just what you've done, young man? You have made a breakthrough at least equal to my own. Opened up a whole vast new field – a field parallel to my own, perhaps, but in no sense the same.'

'I wouldn't say that. Merely an enlargement. All I did was follow a hunch.'

'An intuition,' Tammon corrected him. 'What else, pray, makes breakthroughs?'

And Luloy, on the way out of the laboratory hand in hand with Mergon, said, 'I had no idea that Tellus ever did or ever could produce anybody like *him*. He *is* their god's fair-haired child, for a fact. Sennlloy will have to know about this, Merg.'

'She will indeed – I was sure you'd think of that.'

And as soon as Dorothy could get Seaton alone that evening she stared at him with a variety of emotions playing over her face. As though she had never seen him before; or as though she were getting acquainted with him all over again. 'I've been talking to Sennlloy,' she announced. 'Or, rather, she's been talking to me. She didn't lose much time, did she?'

Seaton blushed to the roots of his hair. 'I'll say she didn't. Not any. She knocked me for a block-long row of ash cans.'

'Uh-huh. Me, too – *and how!*' She told me you said I'd blow my red top and I just about did, until she explained. She's *quite* a gal, isn't she? And *what* a shape! You know, I'm awfully glad I'm not too bad in that shape department myself, or I'd die of mortification looking at them. But Dick – don't you suppose there are any people in this whole cockeyed universe except us and the Rayseenians who don't run around naked all the time?'

'I wouldn't know; but what has all that got to do with the price of hasheesh c.i.f. Istanbul?'

'It ties in. She must have thought I was some kind of an idiot child, but she didn't show it. She couldn't really understand my taboos, she said, since they were not in her own heredity, but she could accept them as facts in mine and work within their limitations.' Dorothy blushed, but went on, 'I'd be the only Prime Operator – and so forth. You know about the "and so forth". Anyway, before she got done she actually made me feel ashamed of myself! They really *need* your genes, Dick. You didn't let on, did you, that DuQuesne's a Tellurian, too?'

'I'll say I didn't! The less they think that ape and I came from the same world, the better I'll like it.'

'You and me both. Well, she didn't actually *say* so, but when she found out what kind of genes *you* have she decided to pour every one of DuQuesne's right down the drain.'

'Could be.' Seaton didn't agree with that conclusion at all, but he was too smart to argue the point.

At breakfast the following morning Seaton said, 'You chirped it, birdie, about their thinking us some kind of idiot children. Besides, the First Principle and Prime Tenet of all diplomacy has always been, "When in Rome be a Roman candle." So I think we'd all better peel to the raw as of now. You and I had better, whether the rest do so or not. Check?'

'Check – but I think they will. We're horribly conspicuous, dressed. People look at us as though we were things that had escaped from a zoo. And all the Green System people have always thought we were more than somewhat loco in the coco for covering up so much. We'll get used to it easily enough – look at the nudists. So lead on, my bold and valiant – I follow thee to the bitter end of all my raiment.'

'I knew you would, ace. Let's go spread the gospel.'

When they approached the Cranes and the Japanese on the subject, Margaret threw back her black-thatched head and laughed. 'We must be psychic – we were going to spring the same thing on you. And after all, actually, how much do our bathing suits hide? Yours or mine either one? And we have it to show, too – so here goes! The last one undressed is Stinker of the Day!' She began to unzip, then paused and looked at Lotus.

The Nisei girl shrugged. 'We all should, of course. I won't like it and I positively know I'll never get used to it, but if you two do I will too if it kills me.'

''At-a-girl, Lambie!' Margaret put her arm around the beautifully formed little body and squeezed. 'But you just wait – you'll have it really made. None of them ever saw anything like *you* before, you gorgeous little doll, you. With your size and build you'll be the absolute Queen of the May!'

25

Roman Candles

Countless parsecs away, Marc C. DuQuesne was carrying out his own plans – plans which would have been a most unpleasant surprise for the Skylarkers had they known about them.

DuQuesne moved the surviving Fenachrone into his *DQ* easily enough and without incident. Housing was no problem. How could it be, with millions upon millions of cubic kilometers of space available and with automatic high-order constructors to do the work? Nor was atmosphere, nor food nor any other necessity or desideratum of Fenachronian life and/or well-being a problem.

Fenachrone engineers did it all – by operating special keyboards and by thinking into carefully limited headsets – but none of them had any idea whatever of what it was that did any given task or how it did it. None of this knowledge, of either practice or theory, was in their science; and DuQuesne took great pains to be sure that none of them got any chance to learn any iota of it. He taught them, and they learned, purely by rote.

Like high-school girls learning to drive automobiles. They can become excellent drivers; but with only that type of instruction none of them will ever become able to design a hypoid gear or to understand in detail the operation of an automatic clutch.

The Fenachrone did not like such treatment. Sleemet in particular, when he began to recover some of the normal pugnaciously prideful spirit of his race, did not like it at all and said so; but DuQuesne did not care a particle whether he liked it or not.

DuQuesne's snapping black eyes stared, contemptuously unaffected, into the furiously hypnotic, red-lighted black eyes of the Fenachrone. 'You mega-lomaniacal cretin,' he sneered. 'How can you possibly figure that it makes any difference whatever to me, what you like or don't like? If you have any frac-tion of a brain you'd better start using it. If you haven't or can't or won't, I'll build you a duplicate of your original ship and turn you all loose today.'

'You will? In that case ...' Sleemet got that far and stopped cold in mid-sentence.

'Yeah.' DuQuesne's tone cut like a knife. 'Exactly. We're still within Klaz-mon's range; we will be for quite a while yet. Do you want to be turned loose here?'

'Well, no.' If the thought occurred to him that DuQuesne was lying, he didn't show it. That was just as well for Sleemet and for the Fenachrone race. DuQuesne wasn't.

'Maybe you have a brain of sorts, at that. But if you don't forget this Master Race flapdoodle, all of it and fast, you'll last quick. Remember how easily that self-styled Overlord wiped out your navy and then volatilized your whole stinking world? And how easily Klazmon of Llurdiax smacked your whole fleet down? And what a fool I made and am still making of Klazmon? And I know of one race that is as much ahead of mine as I am ahead of you; and of another race that may be somewhat ahead of us Xylmnians in some ways. As I said, you're about eleven hundred thousand years behind. Have you got brains enough to realize that instead of being top dog you're just low man on the totem pole?'

'If you're so high and we're so low,' Sleemet snarled, 'why did you take us away from the Llurd? Of what possible use can we be to you?'

'You have certain mental and physical qualities that may perhaps be of use in a project I have in mind. You are not only able and willing to fight, you really *like* to fight. These qualities should, theoretically, make you better in some respects than automatics in operating the offensive weapons of a base as large as this one is.' DuQuesne studied the Fenachrone appraisingly. 'I do not really need you, but I am willing to make the experiment on the terms I have stated. I will allow you two Xylmnian minutes in which to decide whether or not to cooperate with me in such an experiment.'

'We will cooperate,' Sleemet said in less than one minute; whereupon DuQuesne told him in broad terms what he had in mind.

And for many days thereafter the two, so unlike physically but so similar in so many respects mentally, devoted themselves wholeheartedly to the finer and ever finer refinement of the placing and tuning of mechanisms and of the training of already hard-trained personnel.

But DuQuesne knew that, given the slightest opportunity, the Fenachrone would take high delight in killing him and taking the *DQ*. Wherefore he did not at any time trust any one of them as far as he could spit.

Moreover, DuQuesne was not quite as sure of his own victory as he had given the Fenachrone to understand.

DuQuesne was not easy in his mind about Galaxy DW-427-LU. He hadn't been, not since some superpowered enemy in that galaxy had attacked Seaton's *Skylark of Valeron* without warning and had burned her down to a core before she could get out of range. And she hadn't been able to fight back. That one blast back at them couldn't have done any damage.

It had been that uneasiness that had been responsible for the *DQ*'s terrific armament and for DuQuesne's wanting the Fenachrone for a crew. Wherefore, as soon as the Fenachrone were settled in their new quarters and before they had recovered enough of their normal combativeness to become completely unmanageable, DuQuesne got 'on the com' with Sleemet.

'… I don't give a damn what happens to Earth or to Norlamin. I'm no longer interested in either,' he said in part. 'But I don't want it to happen to me and you don't want it to happen to you. You agree with me, I'm sure, that a good strategist does not leave an enemy behind him without knowing, at very least, who that enemy is and what he can do.'

'That is one of the basics, yes.'

'All right. Somebody in this galaxy here has more muscle than I like.' DuQuesne pointed out Galaxy DW-427-LU in his tank and told Sleemet what had happened to the *Skylark of Valeron*, then went on, 'On theoretical grounds, the degree of synchronization could make all the difference.' He had reached by theory the same point that Seaton had arrived at by experience. 'Hence, the greater the number of operators – of equal skill, of course – the tighter the output. The efficiency will vary directly as the cube of the number of operators.'

'I see.' Sleemet did see, and for the first time became really interested. 'That will be to our advantage as well as yours. You will have to teach us much.'

'I'll teach you everything you have to know. Nothing else.'

'That is assumed … But I see no possibility of assurance that you will keep your bargain … or will you go mind to mind that you will release us and build us a ship after this one expedition as your crew?'

'Yes. Without reservation.'

'In that case we will cooperate fully.'

And they did – and so it was that the *DQ* became the most fantastically armed and powered and defended fortress that had ever moved its own mass through space.

As the *DQ* approached Galaxy DW-427-LU, with everything she had either wide open or on the trips, DuQuesne braked her down and swung into what he called 'the curve of fastest getaway' – and as he did so, in the instant, the mighty vessel's every defense went blinding-white.

And in that same instant two thousand nine hundred seventy-seven

Fenachrone, males and females but superlatively expert technicians all, pressed activating switches and took command, each of a tightly clustered battery of micrometrically synchronized generators.

And one black-browed, hard-eyed Tellurian sat with his head buried in the *DQ*'s master-control helmet.

While he had not expected to find any significant fraction of what he actually found, he was not too appalled to go viciously and pinpoint-accurately to work. Working through the fourth dimension, with the transfinite speed of thought, he hurled bomb after bomb after multi-billion-kiloton super-atomic bomb: and the target world of each one of those bombs became a sun.

And the *DQ* got away. She was by no means intact; but, since her skin had been very much thicker than the *Valeron*'s to start with, there was still some of it left when she got out of range.

Thereupon DuQuesne put on the headset of the *DQ*'s Brain and began to think. He had tried direct attack on the galaxy of Chlorans; it had failed. His next step, obviously, was – to decide what his next step should be.

The flesh-and-blood brain that was thinking into the energy-and-metal Brain of the DQ was no whit less logical, no iota less unsentimental in its judgments than the great computer itself. Man-brain and machine-brain together considered the evidence. *Datum*: The *DQ* was not up to handling Galaxy DW-427-LU. *Datum*: Not even the added muscle conferred by the willing cooperation of the Fenachrone was enough to make it so. *Datum*: No discoverable increase of its armaments or its crew would give it even a fighting chance against the energies that had just come so close to destroying it.

Wherefore –

Finally, an hour later, DuQuesne raised the microphone of a repeating sixth-order broadcasting transmitter to his lips and said – dispassionately, unemotionally and with no more expression than if he had been ordering up his lunch:

'DuQuesne calling Seaton reply as before stop.'

26

The Talent

Seaton had thought that the visit to the Jelmi would be a short one, just long enough to get the 'gizmo,' but his own breakthrough put an end to such thinking. It took days to reduce the theory to practice and weeks to build into the *Skylark of Valeron* the gigantic installations Seaton wanted.

The very enormity of the breakthrough changed all plans, dislocated all schedules. To the Jelmi the fourth-dimensional translator had been a phenomenon – a weapon – in itself. It had extremely valuable applications, and each of them offered a long career of study. That was enough for them. But to Seaton and Crane and the Norlaminians it was something more than that; it was an effect, a new and unexplored area of knowledge, to be fitted somehow into the known and computed structure of sixth-order – perhaps of other-order – effects; and to be used and considered in conjunction with them. It was a theorist's dream – and an engineer's nightmare.

Meanwhile, the male Skylarkers, their Jelm colleagues and the Norlaminians were busily getting done the impossible task of exploring a whole new field of knowledge and transmuting it into actual structures and gigantic machines, while the women of the party were exploring the life of an alien race … and having the time of their respective lives doing it. Sitar, of course, was in her element. Bare skin and jewelry she liked. She liked to look at and to feel her mink coat, she said, but she hated to have to wear it; and as for that horrible, scratchy underwear – augh! Hence, now that the personal gravity controls were personal heaters as well, she was really enjoying herself.

Dorothy and Margaret, of course, took to it as though to the manner born. In three days neither of them was any more conscious of nudity than was Sennlloy herself. Even Lotus got used to it. While she could never become an enthusiastic nudist, she said, she did stop blushing. In fact, she almost stopped feeling like blushing.

'Dick,' Dorothy said one evening, 'I've finally made contact with them on music.'

'*Music!*' he snorted. 'Huh! It sounds to me like a gaggle of tomcats yowling on a back fence.'

She laughed. 'It's unworldly, of course, but a lot of it is beautiful, in a weird sort of way, and they have some magnificent techniques. I've been trying everything on them, you know, and they've just been sitting on their hands. I'll give you three guesses as to what I finally hit them with.'

'Strauss waltzes? Jazz? *Don't* tell me it was rock-'n'-roll.'

She laughed. 'Old-fashioned ragtime. Not what they call rag these days, but syncopation. And polkas. Specifically, three old, old recordings – with improved sound, of course. Pee Wee Hunt's *Twelfth Street Rag*, Plehal Brothers' *Beer Barrel Polka*, and – of all things! – Glahe Musette's *Hot Pretzels*. They simply grabbed the ball and ran all over the place with it. What they came up with is neither rag nor polka – in fact, it's like nothing ever heard before on any world – but it's really toe-tingling stuff. Comes the dance tomorrow evening I'll show you some steps and leaps and bounds that will knock your eyes right out of their sockets.'

'I believe that, if what the gals have been teaching me is any criterion. You have to be a mind-reader, an adagio dancer and a ground-and-lofty tumbler, and have an eidetic memory. But I *hope* I won't smash any of the girls' arches down or kick any of their faces in.'

'Don't fish, darling. I know how good you are. Ain't I been practicing with you for lo, these many periods?'

At the dance it became clear that Seaton's statement was (as, it must be admitted, some of his statements were!) somewhat exaggerated. There was a great deal of acrobatics – Seaton and Sennlloy took advantage of every clear space to perform hand-spring-and-flip routines in unison. But everything was strictly according to what each person could do and wished to do. Thus, men and women alike danced with the Osnomians as though they were afraid of breaking them in two – which they were. And thus Lotus was, as Margaret had foretold that she would be, the belle of the ball. Hard-trained gymnast and acrobat that she was, her feet were off the floor most of the time; and before the dance was an hour old she was being tossed delightedly by her partner of the moment over the heads of half a dozen couples to some other man who was signalling for a free catch.

Three days before the *Skylark*'s departure, Mergon announced that there would be a full-formal farewell party on the evening before takeoff.

'What are you going to wear, Dick?' Crane asked.

Seaton grinned. 'Urvan of Urvania's royal regalia. All of it. You?'

'I'm going as Taman, the Karbix of Osnome; with guns, knives, bracelets and legbands complete. And a pair of forty-fives besides.'

'Nice! And I'll wear my three-fifty-sevens, then, too. If I can find a place to hang them on anywhere.'

And Dorothy and Margaret each wore about eleven quarts of gems.

As the eight guests entered the dining hall – last, as protocol dictated – and the eight hundred Jelmi rose to their feet as one, the spectacle was something that not one of the six Tellurians would ever forget. DuQuesne had seen a few Jelmi in full formal panoply; but here were eight hundred of them!

After the sumptuous meal the tables vanished; music – a spine-tingling, not-too-fast march – swelled into being; and dancing began.

Dancing, if dancing it could be called, that bore no relationship whatever to the boisterous sport of which there had been so much. Each step and motion and genuflection and posture was stately, graceful, poised and studied. The whole was very evidently the finished product of centuries of refinement and perfection of technique. And at its close each of the eight honored guests was amazed to find that their movements had been so artfully yet inconspicuously guided that each of them had grasped hands once with every Jelm on the floor.

And on the way to their quarters Dorothy, her eyes brimming with unshed tears, pressed Seaton's arm against her side. 'Oh, Dick, wasn't that simply *wonderful*? I could cry. Only once in my life before has anything ever hit me as hard as that did.'

Well on the way back to Galaxy DW-427-LU, Seaton was humming happily to himself. He had gone through everything for the umpteenth time and for the umpteenth time had found everything good.

'Mart,' he said. 'We have now got exactly what it takes to make big medicine on those Chloran apes. The only question is, do we wipe 'em completely out now or do we let 'em suffer a while longer? Suffer in durance vile?'

If he had waited a few hours longer to speak so, he would have kept his mouth shut; for that same afternoon the *Skylark*'s screens again went instantaneously into full-powered incandescent defense. The Brain took evasive action at once; but it was five long hours before they got far enough away from the source of that incredible flood of energy so that it became ineffective and was cut off. During those five hours Seaton and Crane observed and computed and analyzed and thought. When it was over, Seaton scanned the *Skylark*'s reserve supply of power uranium; and his face was grim and hard when he called the others into conference.

'I wouldn't have believed it possible,' he said flatly. 'I can hardly believe it now, after watching it happen. Either they've been building stuff twenty-four hours a day ever since we left ...' He paused.

'Or they've got myriads of myria-watts,' Dunark said into that pause, 'that they couldn't sync in then, but can now.'

'Could be,' Seaton agreed. 'Let's see if we can find anything out. We're too far away to hold anything, even a planet. But with all of us looking we should be able to see something – and the gizmo can handle eight projections as easily as one. Has anybody got any better ideas?'

Since no one had, they tried it. 'Riding the beam' is a weird sensation; a sense of duality of personality that must be experienced to be either appreciated or understood. The physical body is here; its duplicate in patterns of pure force is there: the two separate entities see and hear and smell and taste and feel two entirely different environments at the same time. It is a thing that takes some getting used to; but all the Skylarkers except Lotus were used to it. And she, as has been intimated, was a quick study.

Seaton could not hold the projections anywhere near any planet; could not hold them even inside a solar system. Even with the vernier controls locked and Seaton's hands resolutely off, the point of view jumped erratically about in fantastic leaps of hundreds of billions of miles. Not even the huge – and reinforced – mass of the *Skylark of Valeron* could hold them steady. They swept dizzily into the chromospheres of suns, out into the cold dark of interstellar vacuum, through tenuous gas clouds and past orbiting planets. In theory – if theory meant anything in this unexplored area – the fourth-dimensional 'gizmo' should have been able to lock steadily on a target. In practice, they could hardly find a target to lock onto. All eight of the Skylarkers were synced in at once to the master controls, but their best efforts could not keep them even inside a solar system, much less give them the rock-steady fix that would have permitted them to spy on enemy activity.

And the magnitude of error grew. In a minute they were swinging in huge arcs of a parsec or more. In another minute the swings had become so enormous and so random that they could not measure them. Their speed was immense; they swung dizzyingly toward a cepheid variable and it winked at them like a traffic blinker, spun past a flare star and watched its great gouts of flame leap out and fall back.

Five minutes of this insane cavorting made half the party seasick, and they pulled out of projection and returned, gasping and staggering, to the welcome stability of the *Skylark*. Seaton stuck it out for half an hour. Then he pushed the 'cancel' button.

'That's what I was afraid of,' he growled. 'Every time we wiggle a finger or a fly lights on a table it changes the shape of the whole ship. Oh, for something really *rigid* to build with!' (The eternal complaint of the precise worker in any field!) 'But we each saw *something*. We'll report in turn.'

Seaton gave a brief description of his own observations. He had seen something, no more than a flicker, but clearly big and Chloran-made. Dunark had spotted what sounded like the same planet-sized mass, but in the system of a G-3 star, as nearly as he could tell; Seaton's had been an F.

The others had seen nothing. Seaton nodded. 'Okay. There are at least two solar systems having fortified Chloran planets, with one more probable. Ideas, anybody?'

Crane broke the ensuing silence. 'I can't come up with anything constructive. Just the opposite. There's something basically wrong here, Dick. As I understand the Tammon-Seaton Theory, the operators involved here are all in the no-space-no-time field, so that distance does not enter. Hence it is possible in theory, and should be in practice, to place a bomb anywhere in all total space as accurately and as easily as you can touch the end of your nose with the tip of your finger.'

Dorothy whistled, Dunark looked shocked, and the others looked blank. Seaton scowled and said, 'Yeah ... But with all points in total space coexistent – Gunther's Universe – how are you going to pick any given one out? What kind of an operator would it take? There's a hole, Mart, in either the theory or in the reduction ...' He paused, frowning in thought.

'Or both,' Crane said.

'Or both,' Seaton agreed. 'Okay, let's skip down and find it.'

They went down and worked with the Brain all the rest of the day; but they did not find the hole. Nor did they find it the next day, or the next. Then Seaton began to pace the floor.

'So, in all probability, another breakthrough is required,' Crane said. 'And I can't help you on that; I'm not the genius type.'

'Neither am I!' Seaton snorted. 'In my book one flash-in-the-pan hunch does *not* make a genius ... But here's another angle, fella. If this thing *can* be worked out it'll be so much better than that synchronization idea that it isn't funny. Also, it might not take years to work out. Don't you think it'll be worthwhile, Mart, to spend a few days seeing if we can set it up as a problem? See if we can take it out of the pure brainstorm category before we spring it on Rovol?'

'I do indeed,' and Seaton and Crane both went down to the control room and got into their master controllers.

However, before that task was finished there was a surprise for Richard Seaton.

27

CoBelligerents

'DuQuesne calling Seaton reply ...'

Since Seaton's head was inside his master controller, no speaker sounded. Since everything pertaining to DuQuesne was on file in the Brain's memory banks, there was no delay whatever in making the proper connections: Seaton cut in before the first send of the message; short as it was, was completed.

'What the *hell*, DuQuesne!' his thought blazed out. 'I didn't think even you would have the sublime guts to call on me again!'

'Save it, Seaton. This is important. Do you know how many solar systems of Chlorans there are in that galaxy where your *Skylark of Valeron* got burned out?'

Seaton paused for one microsecond. Then, cautiously:

'No idea. Hundreds, maybe. Or, in view of this – thousands?'

'You aren't even warm. My apparatus put one hundred forty-nine million three hundred nineteen thousand two hundred ninety-seven of them into my tank before my scanners went out. And they hadn't covered a quarter of the galaxy yet.'

'Je—' Seaton began, but shut himself up. Dorothy was listening in. 'But to be able to use a sixth-order analsynth *that* long you must have had a little more ... okay, gimme the dope.'

DuQuesne told his story, including his superpowered *DQ* and his Fenachrone crew, concluding, 'We knocked out over fifteen thousand of them before

I had to run. But of course that wasn't a drop in the proverbial bucket. Worse, I doubt like the devil if any mobile base possible to build can ever get that close to them again. Apparently they sync in just enough stuff – no matter how much it takes – to cope with the maximum observed threat.'

'Could be. But how come *you* are interested? I know damn well what *you* want.'

'Not any more you don't,' snapped DuQuesne's thought. 'With every two-bit Tom, Dick, and Harry of a race in all space having atomic energy already, what's the chance of a monopoly? So what good is Earth or anything else in the First Galaxy? I've changed my plans – you and Crane can both live for-ever, as far as I'm concerned.'

Seaton absorbed and filed that statement – guardedly. He only said:

'So what? Why should you give a whoop about the Chlorans? Don't tell me you're altruistic all of a sudden.'

'You apparently don't see the point. Listen – the Fenachrone *talked* about mastering the cosmos. That race of Chlorans is quietly and unobtrusively doing it. It may be too late to stop them; and I didn't help matters a bit by making them double or quadruple their synchronized output. You and I are, as far as we know, humanity's ablest operators. Each of us has stuff the other lacks. If you and I together can't stop them it can't – as of now – be done. What do you say?'

Seaton pondered. What was DuQuesne's angle this time? Or was the ape actually on the up and up? It did make sense, though – even though he was a louse and a heel and a case-hardened egomaniac, if it came down to a choice of which was going to be wiped out, those monsters or humanity … sure he would …

'Okay, Blackie. You give your word!'

'I give my word to act as one of your party until this Chloran thing is set-tled, one way or the other.'

A few days later, the ultra-fast speedster that Seaton had left on Ray-See-Nee hailed the *Valeron*, matched velocities with her, and was drawn aboard. Three women disembarked; one of whom was Kay-Lee Barlo. She introduced her black-haired mother, Madame Barlo; who, with the added poise and maturity of her extra twenty-odd years, was even better-looking than her daughter. She in turn introduced her mother, Grand Dame Barlo, who did not have a single white hair in her thick brown thatch and who did not look more than half as old as she must in reality have been.

'But, listen,' Seaton said. 'You couldn't use any sixth-order stuff at first, so you must have been on the way for weeks. What happened? Trouble with the Chlorans?'

He had been talking to Kay-Lee, but her mother, who was very evidently the head of the party, answered him.

'Oh, no. That is, they've tripled the quotas' – Seaton shot a glance at Crane. *That* tied in! – 'but with the new machinery that did not bother us at all. No. We learned many weeks ago that you would have need of us, so we came.'

'Huh?' Seaton demanded, inelegantly. 'What need?'

'We do not surely know. All we know is that it is written upon the Scroll that a time of need will come, and soon. All Ray-See-Nee is enormously and eternally in your debt: we are here to repay a tiny portion of that debt.'

'Can't you tell me more about it than that?'

'A little; not much. We received your original message, but at that time there was nothing to connect it with you as Ky-El Mokak. In studying it we encountered something unknown upon Ray-See-Nee that increased a hundredfold our range and scope and strength: three *male* poles of power of tremendous magnitude, men who, we found out later, you already know. They are Drasnik and Fodan of the planet Norlamin and Sacner Carfon of Dasor. With three such pairs of poles of power – three is the one perfect number, you know – it was a simple matter to locate those interested in your message, to develop the powers that had been latent in such people as yourself –'

'*What?*' Seaton yelped. That was all he could get out.

'– and Dr DuQuesne and others, yes,' Madame Barlo went on smoothly. 'You were, of course, not aware you possessed them.'

'That's putting it mildly, ace,' said Seaton. 'You mean *I* am ... I hate to use the word ... well, "psychic"?'

'The word is of no importance,' said the woman impatiently. 'Use any word you like. The fact is that you do have this power; we have developed it ... and we now propose to put it to use.'

Seaton's reply to that has not been recorded for posterity. Perhaps it is well. Let it only be said that even twenty-four hours later he was no more than half-convinced ... but it was the half that was convinced that was governing his actions.

One of the data that helped convince him was the fact that Madame Barlo and her daughter had not merely located these 'poles of power' – they had summoned them to the *Skylark*! They had not waited for Seaton's concurrence; before Seaton even knew what they were up to, all the named individuals from three galaxies and a dozen planets were on the way.

A shipload of Norlaminians and Dasorians – including the three preeminent 'male poles of power' – was the contingent first to arrive. Then came Tammon and Sennlloy and Mergon and Luloy and half a hundred other Jelmi; bringing with them three Tellurians: Madlyn Mannis, the red-haired stripper; Dr Stephanie de Marigny of the Rare Metals Laboratory; and Charles K. van der Gleiss, petrochemical engineer T-8. And last, but by less than an hour, came Marc C. Duquesne in person.

'Hi, Hunkie,' he said, shaking hands cordially. 'A little out of your regular orbit? Like me?'

'More than a little, Blackie – like you.' She showed two deep dimples in a wide and friendly smile. 'And if you have any idea of what I'm here for I'd be delighted to have you tell me what it is.'

'I scarcely know what I'm here for myself,' and DuQuesne turned to the others; nodding at them as though he had left them only minutes before. He was no whit embarrassed or ill at ease; nor conscious of any resentment or ill-will directed at him. He was actually as unconcerned as, and bore himself very much like, a world-renowned specialist called into consultation on an unusually difficult case.

Before the situation could become strained, the three Rayseenian women came into the big conference room and approached the conference table – a table forty feet long and three feet wide.

Their faces were white; their eyes were wide and staring. All three were doped to the ears. 'Doctor Seaton,' Madame Barlo said, 'you will cover the top of this table with one large sheet of paper, please?'

Seaton donned his helmet and a sheet of drafting paper covered exactly the table's top, adhering to it as though glued down.

'You mean to say, doc, you're going along with this magic flummery?' one of the Jelmi asked.

'I certainly am,' Seaton said. 'You will leave the room until this test is over. So will everyone else with a mind closed to what these women are trying to do.' The scoffer and two other Jelmi walked toward the door and Seaton quirked an eyebrow at DuQuesne.

'I'm staying,' that worthy said. 'I can't say that I'm a hundred per cent sold; but I'm interested enough to give it a solid try.'

The two older women stationed themselves, one at each end of the table; Kay-Lee stood at her mother's right, holding in her hand a red-ink ballpoint at least a foot long.

Majestic Fodan, the Chief of the Five of Norlamin, stood behind Madame Barlo, but did not touch her; Drasnik and Sacner Carfon stood similarly behind Grand Dame Barlo and Kay-Lee. Each of the three women rubbed a drop of something (it was actually Seaton's citrated blood) between thumb and forefinger and Madame Barlo said:

'You will all look fixedly at any one of the six of us and think of our success with everything that in you lies. Help us with all your might to succeed; give us your total mental strength. Kay-Lee, daughter, the time is … now!'

Reaching across the end of the table, Kay-Lee began to write a column eighteen inches wide; the height of which was to be the thirty-six-inch width of the table. When she got to the middle of the fourth line, however, a man gasped in astonishment and the pen's point stopped. This Jelm, a mathematician, had let his eyes slip from the operator to the paper – and what he saw was high – *very* high! – math! Mathematics of a complexity that none of those women, by any possible stretch of the imagination, could know anything about!

'Quit peeking!' Seaton snarled. 'You're lousing up the whole deal! Concentrate! Think, dammit, THINK!'

Everyone resumed thinking and Kay-Lee resumed writing. She wrote smoothly and effortlessly, with the precision and with almost the speed of the operating point of a geometric lathe.

She wrote the first column and the second and the third and the fourth – six feet by three feet of tightly packed equations and other mathematical shorthand. Then came twelve feet of exquisitely detailed 'wiring' diagram. Then, covering all the rest of the paper, came working drawings of and meticulously detailed specifications for machines that no one there had ever heard of.

Then all three women collapsed. As well they might; they had worked without a let-up for three hours.

Men and women sprang to their aid with restoratives, and they began to recover.

'Mr Fodan,' Madlyn Mannis said then, coming up to the Chief of the Five arm-in-arm with Stephanie de Marigny. Her usually vivid face was strangely pale. 'I can understand Hunkie here having a place in a brawl like this, she's got half the letters in the alphabet after her name, but what good could I do? Possibly? I only went to school one day in my life and that day it rained and the teacher didn't come.'

'Formal education does not matter, child; it is what you intrinsically are that counts. You and your friend Charles are two perfectly matched male and female poles of tremendous power. You felt your paired power at work, I'm sure.'

'Wel-l-l, I felt *something*.' Madlyn looked up at her Charley, her eyes full of question marks. 'My whole brain was full of … well, it was all kind of sizzly like champagne tastes.' And:

'That's it exactly,' van der Gleiss agreed.

Kay-Lee, fully recovered now, looked in surprise at some of the equations she had written, then turned to Sacner Carfon. 'Did it come out all right?' she asked hopefully. 'Oh, I *hope* it did!'

'I think so,' the porpoise-man replied. 'At least, all of it I can understand makes sense.'

The T-8 engineer stared at Kay-Lee. 'But didn't you *know* what you were doing?'

'Of course she didn't.' Again Madame Barlo did the talking. 'None of us did, consciously. We are not masters of the Power, but Its servants. We are merely Its tools; the agents through which It does Its work.'

And, off to one side, Dorothy was saying, 'Dick, those women actually *are* witches! I *liked* Kay-Lee, too … but real, live, practicing *witches*! I got goose bumps as big as peas. I don't *believe* in witchcraft, darn it!'

'I don't either. That is, I never did before … but what else are you going to call it now?'

28

Project Rho

The mathematicians and physical scientists began at once to study the wealth of new data. Drasnik, the First of Psychology, after conferring with Fodan, with Sacner Carfon and with each of the three witches in turn, actually rushed over to the group of Tellurians. It was the first time Seaton had ever seen an excited Norlaminian.

'Ah, youths of Tellus, I thank you!' he enthused. 'I thank you immensely for the inestimable privilege of meeting the ladies Barlo! They possess a talent that is indubitably of the most tremendous—'

'*Talent*?' Dorothy snorted. 'Do you call *witchcraft* a talent? Why, the very idea of it makes me …' She paused.

'Uh-huh, me too,' Madlyn agreed fervently. 'If I have to believe in practicing witches I'll go not-so-slowly nuts.'

'Witchcraft, my children? Bosh and fiddle-faddle! It is a *talent*. Extremely rare and lamentably rudimentary in our part of the universe, yet these women have it in astoundingly full measure. Unfortunately, you have no name for it except "witchcraft", which term has deplorable connotations. It is the ability to … but the English has no words for that, either. But no matter, you have seen it in fine, full action. Fodan and Sacner and I each have a very little of it …'

'But those women couldn't *possibly* have known anything about that kind of stuff!' Madlyn protested.

'Of course they didn't. Richard here and Tammon and Dr DuQuesne were the principal sources of information. But all three of them together lacked a great deal of having full knowledge, and the rest of us had very little indeed. While the comparison is lamentably loose, consider a large, finely cut jigsaw puzzle. Seaton and DuQuesne and Tammon could each assemble an area. But no two of the three areas were contiguous, while none of the rest of us could fit more than a very few pieces together. But the ladies Barlo – particularly Grand Dame Barlo, who is a veritable powerhouse of strength – with some little help from the rest of us, exerted and directed the Power. The Power that, by tapping the reservoir of infinite knowledge, enabled the scribe Kay-Lee to fill in the missing parts of the puzzle.'

'But why ...' Seaton began, but changed his mind. 'I see. You didn't tell me anything about it because at that time it was both insignificant and inapplicable.'

'That is correct. As I was saying, our Fodan, who has more of it than any other entity previously known, had perhaps the thousandth of what Kay-Lee, the weakest by far of the three, has. That is why he is Chief of the Five. And they tell me that there are other women of their race who also have this talent. Remarkable!' At this thought Drasnik, who had quieted down, became excited all over again. 'When this is all over I shall go at once to Ray-See-Nee and study. Marvelous! They did not know even that it is a talent or that, when they learn, there will be no need to drug themselves into half-unconsciousness to employ it successfully. Thank you again, young friends, for this wonderful opportunity. Marvelous!' and Drasnik scurried away.

The Seatons and Madlyn and van der Gleiss started after the Norlaminian until he was out of sight. They turned and stared at each other.

'Well ... I'll ... be ... a ... dirty ... name,' Madlyn said.

Seaton was pacing the floor, talking to Dorothy, emitting a cloud of smoke from his battered and reeking briar. 'I like to do my thinking with you, ace.'

She chuckled. 'At me, you mean, don't you? That stuff is over my head like a beach umbrella.'

'Don't fish, sweetie. You not only have a body and some hair, but also a brain. One that fires on all sixteen barrels all the time.'

She laughed delightedly. 'Thank you so much. You know that isn't true, but you also know how I lap it up and purr. But to proceed, Dunark wants to smash them all with planets, the way he was going to smash Urvania. Martin and Peggy, after talking the way they did, crawfished and are now talking about enclosing the whole galaxy in a stasis of time ...'

'Huh? That's news to me. How's he figuring on doing it – did he say?'

'Uh-uh. I didn't talk to him. Peggy says he isn't going to say anything about it until he can present the package.'

'He should live so long. But 'scuse, please; go ahead.'

'Only one more. Fodan, the simple-minded old darling, wants to *work* with them. *Convert* them!'

'Yeah. Make Christians of 'em. I've got a life-sized picture in technicolor of anybody ever accomplishing *that* feat. The trouble is, everybody wants to do something different and none of their ideas are any good at all.'

'Oh? I noticed that you haven't been enthusiastic about any of them. Pretty grim, in fact. Why not?'

'Because none of 'em will come even close to getting 'em all and this has got to be a one hundred point zero zero zero per cent cleanup. You know how they operate on a cancer. They cut deep enough and wide enough to get it all. Every cell. If they don't get it all it spreads all over the body and the patient dies. This is a cancer. It's already eaten just about all of that galaxy by Chlora-typing planets wherever they go – or rather, enslaved humans are doing it for them – and it's spreading fast. And when that galaxy begins to get crowded they won't just jump to one other; they'll go for hundreds or thousands of galaxies and there goes the ball game. So that cancer has got to be operated on before it spreads any farther.'

Dorothy's face began to pale. 'By that analogy you mean destroy the whole galaxy! How can such a thing be possible? It can't *possibly* be possible!'

He told her how the operation could be performed. That apparatus that the Barlo women had dredged up out of nowhere had a lot of capabilities that did not appear on the surface. Blackie DuQuesne had perceived one set of those possibilities, and he and Blackie had been working on the hardware. They were calling it Project Rho.

Her face, already pale, turned white as he talked; and when he had finished:

'Project … Rho,' she breathed. 'How utterly horrible! And yet … I never dreamed … have you talked to Martin yet?'

'No. You first. I don't want to even think about pushing that kind of a button without being sure you're standing at my back.'

'I'll do better than that, Dick,' She looked him steadily in the eye. 'I'll take half of it. My finger will be right beside yours on that button.'

'You are an ace, ace. As maybe I've said once before.'

'Uh-huh, at least once – but we're one, remember?'

After a moment she went on, 'But we can't possibly sell the Norlaminians any such bill of goods as that.'

'I'll say we can't. They'd cry their eyes out all over the place. Or wait. When they find out that they can't stop it, they'll help save the human planets, which will be all to the good; the witches can use the help. But basically, the grand slam will be up to DuQuesne and his Fenachrone and the witches and Mart and me. Even Mart will need some persuasion, I'm afraid; and you'll have to really work on Peg. She'll simply have a litter of kittens.'

'Why, Dick; *what* a way to talk!' She smiled in spite of herself, but sobered quickly. 'She'll come around, I'm sure; she'll have to. But Dick, is it actually physically possible? It's so *huge!*'

'Definitely. You see, we'll be operating in a Gunther universe, so that mass as such won't enter and power will be no problem. All we have to do is build an apparatus to alter the properties of space around and throughout the object to be moved – altering those properties in such a way as to make its three-dimensional attributes incompatible with those of its—'

She stopped him with an upraised hand. 'Hold it! Wait up, please. We'll dispense with the high math, if you don't mind. It's the sheer *size* of the thing that scares me witless.'

Seaton did grin then. 'Well, you've always known that making things bigger and better is the fondest thing I am of. But we know exactly how to do it, and I think we can get it done before the Norlaminians finish theirs. But DuQuesne should be about ready to take off. I'll flip myself over there and see.'

He did so and said, 'How're you doing, Blackie?'

'A few minutes yet to finish final checking. I've been thinking. What kind of a celestial object will that galaxy be when we get done with it? Not a quasi-stellar, certainly; that's only a star with the energy of a hundred thousand million stars. This will be a galaxy with the energy of a hundred thousand million galaxies – the energy of an entire universe.'

'Yeah. Something new, I'd say. It'll give some astronomers a thrill, some day. But what I can't compute is, whether or not it will sterilize the interstellar space of that galaxy,' Seaton said.

'Well, if it doesn't, you might put the Osnomians and Urvanians on it. Keep 'em from thinking about fighting each other.'

'You know, Blackie, I'd thought of doing exactly that? "Great minds" and so forth. Bye now; be seein' ya,' and Seaton flipped himself back home.

En route to his destination – barren planet in a star-cluster on the opposite side of the galaxy from the *Skylark of Valeron* – DuQuesne again went into a huddle with Sleemet.

'So far, you've done a job,' he began. 'What I told you to do – what I knew how to do – and done it well. But nothing else. Now I want something more than that. Something you can do, if you will, that I can't. As you know, I've made arrangements so that in case of my death this whole planetoid goes up in an atomic blast. That was to keep you from killing me and making off with it. The same thing will happen, though, if those Chlorans kill me in the fracas that's coming. It would seem as though that fact would be enough to make you make an honest-to-God effort to be sure that they *don't* kill me by doing your damnedest to help me kill them. Mentally. Both you and the Chlorans know more about one phase of that than I do – as yet. So, as added inducement to really top effort, if you'll really tear into it on this Project Rho I'll teach you everything I know that you can take. And I'll help you build any kind of spacecraft you want before you leave; one even as big as this one. What do you say?'

Sleemet's strange eyes glowed. 'If you will go mind to mind with me on that I can now assure you of such cooperation as no member of my race has ever given to any non-Fenachrone form of life,' he declared; and DuQuesne handed him a headset.

It wasn't easy, not even for such an accomplished liar as Marc C. DuQuesne was, to make the four-dim gizmo very much more incomprehensible than it actually was; but he accomplished the feat – and he actually did give Sleemet practically everything else.

The *DQ* went into a one-day orbit above one point of an immense plain of the barren planet that was its goal. A plain some ten thousand square miles of which became forthwith an Area of Work. Enormous mechanisms sprang into being, by means of which DuQuesne and several hundred top-bracket Fenachrone engineers sent gigantic beams of force hurtling across the galaxy to the *Skylark of Valeron* and to hundreds of thousands of other micrometrically determined points.

But not Sleemet. That wight, knowing now almost everything that DuQuesne knew, was working in his own private laboratory – working with all the power of his tremendous mind on the various mental aspects of the battle of giants to come.

Hour after hour, Crane worked in his master control at the base of the Brain, with Madame Barlo and Drasnik and Margaret, each wearing an extra-complex headset, sitting close to him. They were mapping and modeling three galaxies, on such a large scale that the vast 'tank' of the *Skylark of Valeron* was millions of times too small. They were using a discus-shaped volume of open space some ten light-years in diameter and three light-years thick.

Galaxy DW-427-LU was already meticulously in place; its every celestial body represented by a characteristically colored light. 'Above' Galaxy DW-427-LU and 'below' it (the terms are used in the explanatory sense only; 'on one side of' and 'on the other side of' could be used just as well), as close to it as possible, two other galaxies were being modeled; each as nearly like DW-427-LU in size and shape as could be found in that part of the First Universe. They were so close together that in many places the three models actually interpenetrated.

Now in the space-time continuum of the strictly material – the plenum in which we ungifted human beings live and which our friends the semanticists would have us believe is the only one having any reality – the map is not the territory. That is taken as being axiomatic. In the demesne of the Talent, however, known to some scholars as psionics and to scoffers as magic or witchcraft, the map is – and *definitely* – the territory.

Thus, as Madame Barlo and Drasnik, those two matched poles of tremendous power; and Crane, the superlatively able coordinator and his matching pole Margaret; and that immense Brain – as these five labored together, the 'map' (in this case the meticulously accurate space-chart) became filled with tendrils and filaments of psionic force, connecting models of suns with models of suns and those of planets with those of planets. And as those joinings occurred in the map, the same joinings occurred in the actual galaxies out in deep space.

Those joinings were invisible, it is true, and intangible, and undetectable to any physical instrument. But they were nevertheless as real as was the almost infinite power from which they sprang.

The other pairs of psiontists were also hard at work. Fodan and Grand Dame Barlo, Sacner Carfon and Kay-Lee, Charles van der Gleiss and Madlyn Mannis, Mergon and his Luloy, Tammon and Sennlloy – all were shooting heavy charges fast and flawlessly straight. And as all those matched pairs labored, and as the automatics of pure psionic force they produced reproduced themselves in geometric ratio, the intergalactic couplings increased at a rate that was that ratio squared.

Seaton was fantastically busy, too. He was deep in his controller, with Dorothy and Stephanie de Marigny, both helmeted, one on each side of him. Dorothy, was, of course, his matched pole of power; Stephanie was his link to DuQuesne. He, too, was operating a ten-thousand-square-mile Area of Work with the speed of thought and he was not making any mistakes. It is true that the *Skylark of Valeron* was the biggest thing he had ever built before, and that the members with which he was working now were parsecs instead of inches long. Nevertheless each one fitted perfectly into place and every one that was supposed to connect with anything of DuQuesne's connected perfectly therewith.

After many hours of this furiously grinding work, a myriad of hells began to break out, at the rate of hundreds of thousands per second. Of hells, that is, infinitely hotter than anything imaginable by man. Of super-novae, no less.

In one galaxy, A, a large hot sun vanished.

It reappeared instantaneously – with no lapse of time whatever – close beside the sun of a Chloran-dominated solar system in Galaxy DW-427-LU.

And in that same no-time the Tellus-type planet in the Chloran system vanished therefrom and reappeared in a precisely similar orbit around a Type G dwarf sun in Galaxy B, the third galaxy in the psiontists' tremendous working model.

And those two suns in the Chloran solar system in Galaxy DW-427-LU, with photospheres in contact and with intrinsic velocities not only diametrically opposed but increased horribly by their mutual force of gravitation, crashed together in direct central impact and splashed with tremendous force.

Except for the heat, the collision might have lasted for a long time. But heat was the all-important factor – the starkly incomprehensible heat of hundreds of millions of Centigrade degrees.

Each of those suns was already an atomic furnace in precise equilibrium; generating and radiating the energy of some five million tons per second of matter being converted completely into energy. Thus there was no place for the added energy of billions of tons of matter to go. It could not be absorbed and it could not be radiated. Therefore the whole enormous mass of super-hot, super-dense material began to go into the long series of ultra-atomic explosions that is the formation of a super-super-nova – the most utterly, the most fantastically violent display of pure, raw energy known to or possible in the universe of man.

Flares and prominences of this insanely detonating material were hurled upward and outward for millions upon millions of miles. Shock-wave after shock-wave, so hellishly hot as to be invisible for days, raged and raved spherically outward; converting instantaneously all the flotsam in their paths into their own unknown composition or atomic and subatomic debris. Planets lasted a little longer. Oceans and mountain ranges boiled briefly; after which each world evaporated comparatively slowly, as does a drop of water riding a cushion of its own steam on a hot steel plate.

And the sphere of annihilation, ravening outward with unabated ferocity, reached and passed the outermost limits of the Chloran solar system and kept on going ...

On and on ...

And on ...

Until there came to pass an event which not even Seaton, not even Madame Barlo herself had foreseen ... and an event which nearly canceled all their efforts and their lives as well; for the Chlorans were not left without resources even in the destruction of their galaxy ...

29

DuQuesne to the Rescue

As has been said, the Chlorans of Galaxy DW-427-LU as a race were more conversant with the Talent than were any of the human or near-human races of the First Galaxy: that is, with the phases or facets of it that had to do with the remarkable hypnotic qualities of their minds. Thus their mathematicians were more or less familiar with no-space-no-time theory, and some of the Greater Great Ones had played with it a little more or less for fun, in practice. Since they had never had any real use for it as a weapon, however, it had never been fully developed.

Thus there were no detectors or feeling for that type of attack. 'It was not sixth-order, but no-space-no-time, which is no-order.' Thus millions upon millions of Chloran planets were destroyed without any intelligent entity either giving or receiving warning that an attack was being made.

And that was the way Richard Seaton wanted it. This was not a game; not a chivalric tournament. This was a matter of life and death, in which the forces of human civilization, outnumbered untold billions to one, needed all the advantage they could get.

Unfortunately for Seaton's desires and expectations, the Chlorans had a Galactic Institute for Advanced Study.

In common with all such institutions everywhere, its halls harbored at least one devotee of any nameable subject, however recondite or arcane that subject might be. So there was one old professor of advanced optical hypnosis who, as a hobby, had been delving into no-space-no-time for a couple of hundred years. He did not feel the light preliminary surveying tendrils of the human witches; but when the big Gunther beams began to come in he became interested fast and got busy fast.

He called his first assistant and his most advanced student – the latter a Greater Great One who was also interested in and a possessor of the Talent and thus familiar with the mysterious power of the number three – and, synchronizing their three minds, they traced those beams to the *Skylark of Valeron* and the *DQ*, and to Seaton and to Crane and to DuQuesne.

'First,' the professor told his two weaker fellows, 'we will attune our Union of Three to theirs and break it apart with blasts of psionic force. Then, each of us having tuned to one of the separated strands, we will kill the three murderers forthwith.'

And the Chlorans proceeded to do their best to bring this event about – and their best was very potent indeed.

If things did not quite work out the way they had planned it, it was no fault of the individual Chlorans. Their minds were fully capable of killing three 'murderers' at a distance. The first enormous surge of mental energy they thrust into the Tellurian union of minds destroyed its fabric. The coupling of 'poles of power' was wrenched asunder. The individual minds of the operators were left alone against the Chloran thrust ... and each of the three Chlorans selected one of the three mightiest intellects of their enemies and commanded it to die.

In that moment, Seaton, Crane and DuQuesne were seized and pinned. The minds that thundered destruction at them were not merely of great intrinsic power, carefully trained: they were backed up by all the million-year evolution of Chloran science, aided by the impact of total surprise.

The three helpless Tellurians were helpless before they knew what hit them.

But they did not die. What saved them was DuQuesne's bargain with the Fenachrone. Sleemet had had a few microseconds' warning by that Fenachrone ferocity, and the backing of every last member of his feral race.

His primary purpose was, of course, the defense of DuQuesne's life – not for the sake of DuQuesne, to be sure, but for the protection of the Fenachrone. He succeeded. DuQuesne's rigidity melted and he was back in control of himself, his own great intellect reinforcing Sleemet's counterblows. The two of them had enough psionic power left over to help Seaton and Crane … but not enough. The blow had been too powerful and too sudden.

Both Seaton and Crane slumped bonelessly to the floor of the control room, leaving their controllers empty and idle.

In that moment the one great pole of strength left to humankind was – Dr Marc C. DuQuesne.

To Dorothy Seaton, that moment was pure horror. It was every terrible fear she had ever thought of, all come to pass at once: Seaton disabled, perhaps dying; DuQuesne in control of all the mighty resources of the *Skylark*. Dorothy shrieked and leaped from her chair –

And was stopped in her tracks by DuQuesne's shout, crackling out of a speaker to emphasize his hard-driven thoughts:

'Dorothy! Margaret! Quit it! Pick up your loads and *carry* 'em. Pole to me!'

And Dorothy hesitated, irresolute, torn between her love for Seaton and her urgent duty to help against the Chlorans, while the whole vast net of human mental energies wavered and hung in the balance.

'*Now!*' snarled DuQuesne, the thought like a lash. 'Move! To hell with the dead' – Dorothy screamed again – '*you're* still alive! But you won't be long if you goof off!' Rapidly he scanned the quavering net. 'You Barlo women and your poles! Drop what you're doing and locate this interference for me – *fast*! All of you – find it for me so I can slug it! Hunkie? Yeah – good girl! Stay with it just as you are!'

'But DuQuesne,' Dorothy protested, 'I've *got* to—'

'Oh, *hell*!' DuQuesne wrenched out, every nuance of his tone showing the tremendous strain under which he was laboring. 'Savant Sennlloy! You can't be spared from there, but have you got a couple of girls who can tune themselves to me?'

'Yes, Dr DuQuesne.' Neither she nor any other Jelm aboard understood why Seeker Sevance of Xylmny had been masquerading as Dr Marc C. DuQuesne of Tellus when he received his Call. They knew, however, that it had to do with his Seeking; hence none of them did anything to interfere with it. 'We have many very good mentalists in our party.'

'Fine! Have two of 'em relieve these two weak sisters here – and fast!'

'Here we are, sir,' two thoughts came in, in unison. And two powerful female Jelman minds – the minds of two girls with whom he was already very well acquainted – fitted themselves snugglingly to his and picked up the loads that the two Earthwomen had been unable to carry.

It was not that either of those Earthwomen was weak. Both were tremendously strong; mentally and psychically. Both disliked DuQuesne so intensely, however, that it was psychologically impossible for either of them to work with him. Of course, he regarded that fact itself as an extreme weakness. Sentiment was as bad as sentimentality, he held, and both bored him to tears.

'Ah, that's better.' DuQuesne's thought was a sigh of relief. 'That makes it at least possible.'

And it did. DuQuesne and his two new assistants did not do much to keep the wave of destruction sweeping through Galaxy DW-427-LU, but he and they, with a lot of very high-powered Fenachrone help, did hold the Chloran attackers at bay until the three witches and the three warlocks found the planet upon which the Chloran Galactic Institute of Advanced Study was located. Then, with locked teeth and hard-set muscles and sweating face, he made the superhuman effort required to drive that three-man beam single-handed and keep those rabid Chloran attackers at bay besides.

By a miracle of coordination and timing he did it – and practically collapsed when all attack and all necessity of resistance ceased. The Chloran Institute simply ceased to be. Its members died. DuQuesne recovered so quickly that no one else except the two Jelman girls knew that he had been affected at all.

'Dorothy! Margaret! Break it up!' he snapped. Doctors had been working on Seaton and Crane for minutes. Both were beginning to recover consciousness. Neither, apparently, had been permanently damaged; and both their wives were making enthusiastically joyful noises. 'Come on, come on, take them home to do your slobbering over them. The rest of us have work to do – or do you expect us to hold this demolition job up until they organize another threesome to go to the mat with us?'

Stretchermen carried Seaton and Crane away; Dorothy and Margaret went along. The Chloran blow at the lives of the two Skylarkers had been deadly and fast, but it had not succeeded – quite.

And the 'demolition job' went on.

In the great light-years-thick 'tank' that was the psiontists' working model of the three galaxies they were manipulating, lights were winking out and reappearing as stars and planets were hurled through four-dimensional curves to new orbits and positions. Already Galaxy A – the 'raw-material' source that was being used for a supply of suns – was visibly dimmer, visibly poorer in stars. Tens of millions of them had already been stolen away and tossed through four-space into Chloran suns in Galaxy DW-427-LU. And when they reappeared, in a head-on collision course with those Chloran suns, and struck, and destroyed themselves in the titanic outflow of energies that produced super-nova blasts, the model of Galaxy DW-427-LU showed another tiny but blindingly bright flare – and another – and another –

There were more than fifty thousand million suns to move, in all. As the first targets had been the strongest and most dangerous Chloran systems, resistance soon ceased to matter; the task became monotonous, exhausting and mind-deadening.

To the Chlorans, of course, it was something else again. They died in uncounted trillions. The greeny-yellow soup that served them for air boiled away. Their halogenous flesh was charred, baked and desiccated in the split-second of the passing of the wave front from each exploding double star, moments before their planets themselves began to seethe and boil. Many died unaware. Most died fighting. Some died in terrible, frantic efforts to escape …

But they all died.

And for each sun that DuQuesne's remorseless net located and flung into the Chloran galaxy, an oxygen-bearing, human-populated planet was snatched out of the teeth of the resulting explosion and carried through four-space into the safety of Galaxy B, there to slip quietly into orbit around a pre-selected, hospitable sun. No human world was destroyed in all of Galaxy DW-427-LU.

It went on and on …

And then it was over.

Marc DuQuesne rose, stretched and yawned. 'That's all. Everybody dismissed,' he said, and at once the vast psionic net ceased to be. He was alone for the first time in many hours.

His face was lined, his eyes deeper and darker than ever. Apart from that there was no sign of the great extermination he had just conducted. He was simply Marc DuQuesne. The man who slew a galaxy looked no different after the deed than he had before.

He allowed his sense of perception to roam for a moment about the 'working model'. In Galaxy A, where billions of suns had gone through the stellar cycle of evolution for billions of years, there was scarcely a corporal's guard of primaries left. It was a strange, almost a frightening sight. For with the loss of the suns the composition of the galaxy had changed to something never before seen in all the plenum of universes. Nearly every sun had had planets; nearly every planet remained behind when its sun was stolen. Now they roamed at random – uncontrolled, barren, uninhabited – lacking not only the light and heat of their primaries, but freed from their gravitational reins as well.

Galaxy B, on the other hand, looked quite normal – in 'working model'. The planets it had acquired, both from the exploded Chloran suns and from the looted solar systems of Galaxy A, were not even visible. Galactically speaking, it was essentially unchanged; the additional mass of a few billion planets did not matter, and each of the new planets was already in orbit around a friendly sun. There would be readjustments, of course. It would be necessary to keep a watch on the developments of each affected solar system, over a period of years. But that was no problem of Marc DuQuesne's.

But the Chloran galaxy! What *was* it?

In the 'working model' it was rapidly becoming a single, light-years-thick concentration of living flame. In the reality it was even huger, even more deadly. A name would be invented for it some day – quasi-stellar? Or something greater still?

But that, too, was no longer a concern for Marc DuQuesne. He dropped from his mind, without a qualm, the memory of the trillions of lives he had taken, the billions of worlds he had dislocated. He ignored the question of Richard Ballinger Seaton, now stirring back to consciousness, to worry – and ultimately, to reassurance – somewhere on the *Valeron*. He had more pressing business to take care of. Personal business. And to DuQuesne that was the most pressing of all.

Shrugging his shoulders, he sent Stephanie de Marigny a tight-beamed thought:

'Hunkie – some time before you go back to Washington, can I flip you over to the *DQ* for a private conference that we know will be private?'

Her beautifully dimpled smile flashed on. 'I should say not! You know I'm not *that* kind of a ...' she began; then, as she perceived how much in earnest he was, she changed tone instantly and went on, 'Of course, Blackie. Any time. Just give me time to pack a toothbrush and my pajamas. Top Secret, or can you give me a hint to allay my 'satiable curiosity?'

'Hint; large economy size. Every time I think of what those damned observers are doing to you – feeding a mind like *yours* with an eye-dropper instead of a seventy-two-inch pipeline – it makes me madder and madder. I can give you everything that Seaton, I, Crane and half the Norlaminians know, and give it to you in five hours.'

'You can *what*?' The thought was a mental scream. She licked her lips, gulped twice, and said, 'In that case we needn't wait for either toothbrush or pajamas. Do it now.'

He laughed deeply. 'I wasn't sure that would be your attitude, but I'm glad it is. But I can't do it this minute. I have to help Sleemet finish building his planetoid, watch him very carefully for a while on course and do a couple of other crash-pri chores. Three or four days, probably. Say Saturday, seventeen hours?'

'That'll be fine, Blackie, and thanks. I'll be here with my ears pinned back and my teeth filed down to needle points.'

30

Emperor

The Fenachrone had taken off and DuQuesne had watched them go, taking extreme precautions – none of which, it turned out, had been necessary – that they did not eliminate either him or the rest of the party as soon as it became safe for them to do so. He had taken Stephanie de Marigny and all her belongings aboard, saying that he was going close enough to Tellus so that it would be no trouble at all to drop her off there. And lastly, when Seaton and Crane had insisted upon thanking him for what he had done:

'Save it,' he had sneered. 'Remember, that time on X-World, what I told you to do with that kind of crap! That still goes,' and he had taken off at full touring drive on course one seven five Universal. This course, which would give the First Galaxy a near miss, was the most direct route to a galaxy that was distant indeed; the galaxy lying on the extreme southern rim of the First Universe; the galaxy in which the *DQ* had been built; the galaxy that DuQuesne had surveyed so thoroughly and which he intended to rule.

DuQuesne and Stephanie were in the *DQ*'s control room, which was an exact duplicate of the *Skylark of Valeron*'s. He placed her in the seat that on the *Valeron* was Crane's, showed her how to elevate herself into his own station.

'Oh,' she said. 'You're going to give me the whole gigantic Brain?'

'That's the best and easiest way to do it. I boiled down about ten thousand lifetimes of knowledge and experience into ten half-hour sessions. The ten tapes on that player there are coded instructions for the Brain – what to give you and how. There are minds who could take the whole jolt in seconds, but yours and mine aren't that type – yet. But you'll get it all in five hours. Every detail. It'll shock you all hell's worth and it'll scare you right out of your panties, but it won't hurt you and it won't damage your brain. Yours is one of the very few human brains that *can* take it. I'll start it and in five hours I'll be back. Ready?'

'As much so as I ever will be, I guess. Go.'

He started the player; and, after waiting a few minutes to be sure that everything was going as programmed, he left the room …

He came back in just as the machine clicked off, lowered her 'chair,' and lifted her to her feet.

'Good – God – in Heaven!' she gasped. Her skin, normally so dark, was a yellowish white; so pale that her scattered freckles stood out sharply, each one in bold relief. 'I don't. I can't … I simply can't *grasp* it! I know it, but …' She paused.

He shook his head in sympathy. Which, for Marc C. DuQuesne, was a rare gesture indeed. 'I know. I couldn't tell you what it would be like – no possible warning can be enough. But that's the bare minimum you'll have to start with, and it won't take you very long to assimilate it all. Ready for some talk?'

'Not only ready, I'm eager. First, though, I want to give you a vote of full confidence. I'm sure that you'll succeed in everything you try from now on; even to becoming Emperor Marc the First of some empire.'

'Huh? Where did you get *that*?'

'By reading between the lines. Do you think I'm stupid, is that why you gave me all this?'

'Okay. You've always known, as an empirical, non-germane fact, that the Earth and all it carries isn't even a flyspeck in a galaxy, to say nothing of a universe; but now you know and really understand just how little it actually does amount to.'

She shuddered. 'Yes. It's … it's appalling.'

'Not when viewed in the proper perspective. I set out to rule Earth, yes; but after I began to learn something I lost that idea in a hurry. For a long time now I haven't wanted Earth or any part of it. Its medical science is dedicated whole-heartedly to the deterioration of the human race by devoting its every effort to the preservation of the lives of the unfit. In Earth's wars its best men – its best breeding stock – are killed. Earth simply is not worth saving even if it could be saved; which I doubt. Neither is Norlamin. Not because its conquest is at present impossible, but because the Norlaminians aren't worth anything, either. All they do – all they *can* do – is think. They haven't done anything constructive in their entire history and they never will. They're such bred-in-the-bone pacifists – look at the way the damned sissies acted in this Chloran thing – that it is psychologically impossible for any one of them to pull a trigger. No; Sleemet had the right idea. And Ravindau – you have him in mind?'

'Vividly. Preserve the race – in *his* way and on *his terms*.'

'You're a precisionist; that's my idea exactly. To pick out a few hundred people – we won't need many, as there are billions already where we're going – as much as possible like us, and build a civilization that will be what a civilization ought to be.'

The girl gasped, but her eyes began to sparkle. ' "In a distant galaxy", as Ravindau said?'

'Very distant. Clear out on the rim of this universe. The last galaxy out on the rim, in fact; five degrees east of Universal south.'

'And you'll be Emperor Marc the First after all. But you won't live long enough to rule very much.'

'You're wrong, Steff. The ordinary people are already there, and it's ridiculous for a sound and healthy body to deteriorate and die at a hundred. We'll live ten or fifteen times that long, what with what I already know and the advances our medical science will make. Especially with the elimination of the unfit.'

'Sterilization, you mean?'

'No; death. Don't go soft on me, girl. There will be no second-class citizens, at least in the upper stratum. Testing for that stratum will be by super-computer. Upper-stratum families will be fairly large.'

'Families?' she broke in. 'You've come to realize, then, that the family is the *sine qua non* of civilization?'

'I've always known that.' Forestalling another interruption with a wave of his hand, he went on, 'I know. I've never been a family man. On Earth or in our present cultures I would never become one. But skipping that for the moment, it's your turn now.'

'I like it.' She thought in silence for a couple of minutes, then went on, 'It must be an autocracy, of course, and you're the man to make it work. The only flaw I can see is that even absolute authority can not make a dictated marriage either tolerable or productive. It automatically isn't, on both counts.'

'Who said anything about dictated marriage? Free choice within the upper stratum and by test the lower. With everybody good breeding stock, what difference will it make who marries whom?'

'Oh. I see. That does it, of course. Contrary to all appearances, then, you actually do believe in love. The implication has been pellucidly clear all along that you expect—'

'"Expect" is too strong a word. Make it that I'm "exploring the possibility of".'

'I'll accept that. You are exploring the possibility of me becoming your empress. From all the given premises, the only valid conclusion is that you love me. Check?'

'The word "love" has so many and such tricky meanings that it is actually meaningless. Thus, I don't know whether I love you or not, in your interpret-ation of the term. If it means to you that I will jump off a cliff or blow my brains out if you refuse, I don't. Or that I'll pine away and not marry a second best, I don't. If, however, it means a lot of other things, I do. Whatever it means, will you marry me?'

'Of course I will, Blackie. I've loved you a long time.'

If you've enjoyed these books and would
like to read more, you'll find literally thousands
of classic Science Fiction & Fantasy titles
through the **SF Gateway**

✳

For the new home of
Science Fiction & Fantasy . . .

✳

For the most comprehensive collection
of classic SF on the internet . . .

✳

Visit the SF Gateway

www.sfgateway.com

E.E. 'Doc' Smith (1890–1965)

Edward Elmer Smith was born in Wisconsin in 1890. He attended the University of Idaho and graduated with degrees in chemical engineering; he went on to attain a PhD in the same subject, and spent his working life as a food engineer. Smith is best known for the 'Skylark' and 'Lensman' series of novels, which are arguably the earliest examples of what a modern audience would recognise as Space Opera. Early novels in both series were serialised in the dominant pulp magazines of the day: *Argosy*, *Amazing Stories*, *Wonder Stories* and a pre-Campbell *Astounding*, although his most successful works were published under Campbell's editorship. Although he won no major SF awards, Smith was Guest of Honour at the second World Science Fiction Convention in Chicago, in 1940. He died in 1965.